Lost in the Mist of Time

Karen Michelle Nutt

PublishAmerica
Baltimore

© 2005 by Karen Michelle Nutt.
All rights reserved. No part of this book may be reproduced, stored in a retrieval system or transmitted in any form or by any means without the prior written permission of the publishers, except by a reviewer who may quote brief passages in a review to be printed in a newspaper, magazine or journal.

First printing

This is a work of fiction set in a background of history. Public personages both living and dead may appear in the story under their right names. Scenes and dialogue involving them with fictitious characters are of course invented. Any other usage of real people's names is coincidental. Any resemblance of the imaginary characters to actual persons, living or dead, is entirely coincidental.

ISBN: 1-4137-9302-9
PUBLISHED BY PUBLISHAMERICA, LLLP
www.publishamerica.com
Baltimore

Printed in the United States of America

A special dedication to:

My wonderful family, my husband Greg, my children Kendra, Katrina (my most devoted reader), and Vincent.
To my father and mother, Jim and Margaret.
To my brothers, James and Thomas, my travel buddies in Ireland, and to my sisters Barbara and Margaret.
To Cathy and Stephanie who have shared in many adventures from tea parties to ghost tours…thanks for the exceptional memories!

…And last but not least, to those with an adventurous heart.

And God stands winding His lonely horn,
And time and the world are ever in flight….

—W.B. Yeats

Chapter One

Sixteenth Century Ireland

"What is it, old woman? Why have ye summoned me?" He was civil though to anyone that knew Dougray Fitzpatrick, they would have known that he was not pleased to be beckoned forth in the middle of the night.

Neala, the woman of the glen was not a fool. She was well aware that this man was strong enough to crush her with one powerful blow. Yet she was not afraid. She knew him better than perhaps he knew himself. He would grumble and threaten, but he would never raise a hand to do harm. Her high-pitched cackle was proof enough that she feared him not.

"Milord, ye speak gruffly, but I'll forgive ye. Come follow me, so only ye can hear what I have been destined to reveal."

Dougray could not help but roll his eyes wishing that he had stayed back at the castle where he was nice and warm with the fire burning hot and his goblet filled to the brim. He sighed, knowing if he didn't let the old crone speak her mind, there would be no end to this charade. Reluctantly he made his feet move to follow her.

She waved a crooked finger at him, so that he would lean ever closer.

"Well, woman?" He threw up his hands. "I lose patience."

"Then listen well, young lord, for ye will have to keep the wits about ye, when ye are cast from this place and time."

"What are ye babbling about?"

She shook her head, but continued determined to make him listen to her. "Ye will be sent to another place and time for it has been written. Learn what need be so that ye can save yer future born." He was about to give her an unpleasant retort but she silenced him. "I have more to say to ye before ye go wagging yer tongue."

He gave her a rather unpleasant snort letting her know just how annoyed he was with her prattling. When she folded her arms against her chest and narrowed her silver-gray eyes at him, he finally gave in with an irritated harrumph, nodding for her to continue. "Ye will meet a lass that will believe yer tale. She will be the *vision,* a *dream*. Do not rush what should not be.

Listen to yer heart, and ye will find yer true love. Do ye understand me Fitzpatrick?"

"Aye, aye," he said with impatience to be gone. He wasn't one to believe in fanciful tales, and most especially if they involved matters of the heart.

"Ye will do well, young lord." She placed her gnarled hand on his. "Please pray ye will not tarry long in this other world."

Tarry? Dougray couldn't help but chuckle. "How is it, old crone, that I will be thrust from this time and place?" Neala was well aware that he was just humoring her, but all the same she felt it was her duty to answer him.

"A mist like no other will appear covering ye like it were a woolen blanket. When ye finally come out of its heaviness, ye will be where yer destiny has sent ye."

Once more, Dougray's deep vibrant chuckle filled the night air. "I'll take heed, old crone. If ever I see such a mist, I'll do as ye bid. Now if that is all, I would like to get back to the warmth of my fire."

"I have spoken." With a wave of her hand, she turned away from him with her dismissal.

He shook his head wondering why he allowed her to give him orders. He straightened his mantle and strode back to his horse thinking no more of the old woman's prediction. "Magical mists!" he exclaimed. *"Dar Dia!"*

Murrough didn't miss the Lord of Dunhaven's scowl. He had known the man long enough to realize that he was not troubled but rather perturbed. Obviously the old witch had not given him bad news, only information that thoroughly irked him. "So what did she say of our meeting with the Butler?"

Dougray shrugged his shoulders. "It seems, my friend, that we were summoned out here for no reason at all. She had no news. Rather she wanted to warn me of a magical mist."

For a moment, Murrough just sat there upon his horse wondering if he were joking. Neala was known for peculiarities, but this? "Milord, surely ye jest."

"Ah, that I were. It seems the old woman has dipped into the spirits this night. She babbled about me finding my true love." He chuckled, though it was the troubled laugh that Murrough recognized all too well. Neala may have been talking nonsense, but she had hit a sore spot.

Dougray had been married once to the beautiful fair-haired Ella, the daughter of his now hated enemy, Fingham Butler the Lord of Castlehold. It had been a good match for the clans, ending the petty quarrels that had plagued the land. The marriage was even approved by the Tudor King bestowing favor once more to the inhabitants of Dunhaven. By the stars, their love had been of youth's strong devotion, but tragedy befell Ella only a few weeks after the blessed nuptials.

Dougray vowed that he would never love again. As far as Murrough knew, he was holding strong to that promise.

As for Ella's father, he blamed Dougray for her death, and was determined to avenge her. The raids and skirmishes were now a weekly occurrence to that pledge.

Tomorrow marked the anniversary of Ella's death, and Fingham summoned a meeting. He proclaimed that he just wanted to converse, but Murrough didn't trust it. He had the men well prepared in case of trickery. If only he could convince Dougray to finish the deed, but his friend wouldn't force Fingham to the death. He still insisted that they try to find peace.

"We best head home." Dougray clicked his mount into motion.

They rode in silence for a while before Murrough sparked a conversation wondering if Neala wasn't right to have spoken of a new love. "Are ye ever going to open yer heart to another?"

"Why do ye continue to ask me this? You know Ella was the only woman for me."

"Aye. Ye loved her, but she is gone but one year now. You need to think of the future. What of an heir?"

"An heir can be sought without love. When the time comes, I will choose someone that will make do this task."

Murrough shook his head. "Do ye not think that a woman would want more than to lie down and take your seed?"

"Perhaps." He chuckled at the way Murrough was so concerned over his personal life. "Maybe I will ask Fiona to do the honors. She has been more than willing to give in to my needs without promise of more."

"Aye, and she is willing with half of the keep." This won Murrough a sideways glare, which he chose to ignore as he continued, "Maybe this mist would be a godsend."

"Don't tell me ye believe the old crone?"

Murrough sighed not knowing if he believed it or not. Neala was of the old ways and was known to have a second sight. "Stranger things have happened. In ancient times, an O'Donoghue of the Glens was supposed to have gone over to the fairies. According to the legend on May Day, he glided over the Lakes of Killarney on a white horse. And the unearthly music could be heard while his troops of spirits scattered flowers."

"*Dar Dia*! I would loathed to go into battle, worried that my back was not covered because ye were looking for the wee folk, or worst this mist the old woman speaks of."

Murrough's red, bushy brows furrowed with irked displeasure. "I must tell ye that I take offence to that statement. Have I ever let ye down?"

Dougray hadn't meant for his teasing to offend him and immediately tried to make amends. "Never, my friend. Ye're the only one that I have ever trusted. I know without a doubt that I would never have to worry as long as ye're at my side."

"Apology accepted."

"Good. Now tell me Murrough, why have ye not married?"

"I am not cut out for marriage. Women are of a troublesome breed." He said this with such venom that it caused Dougray to laugh.

"Ye had another argument with Rhiannon, didn't ye?"

"Bah! The woman has a bite. I'll tell ye. She was put out because I had forgotten to take home the shirt that she had made for me. Come morning, I went straightaway to her door, and the foul woman nearly spit in my face. She said that I didn't love her, that I didn't care a wink about her feelings. Can ye believe this? Me?" He pounded his chest. "I do everything, but kiss that woman's…well ye know what I'm saying."

"Bring her some flowers and she will surely welcome ye back."

"I'm not crawling back to her. I've done so much groveling, that my knees are near worn thin."

Dougray let his friend vent, but he already knew that Murrough would be at Rhiannon's door as soon as they returned to the keep. It was Murrough's way. He didn't like any dispute to last more than a day's time, and unfortunately Rhiannon also was aware of this. She'd pout for a while then she'd forgive him. He was sure that come tomorrow's light, when they rode out to meet the Butler, Murrough would be wearing a satisfying grin.

Chapter Two

Dougray adjusted his leather jerkin as he headed outside and to his mount. Once upon his large gray, he went out to meet his men. He could tell by the morning fog that the visibility was not going to be good. This left him with an uneasy feeling.

"Good day, milord." Dermot eagerly greeted him. Dougray acknowledged him with a nod as he rode by. The man was loyal that much he knew, but he tried too hard to be liked among the men. So much so that he became more of a nuisance than anything else.

Dougray saw Murrough in the distance and he came forward to ride beside him. "There is a heavy mist this morning." Murrough spoke the obvious but there was also a bit of a hidden meaning behind it.

"Aye, Murrough. I can see it well enough." He eyed his friend with a half-cocked smile. "Tell me, ye aren't thinking that this is the mist the old crone spoke of?"

Murrough squirmed uncomfortably in his seat indicating that it had crossed his mind. "Just stay near me. I would be hard press to explain how a mist came and swept the Lord of Dunhaven away."

"Aye, that it would prove a most difficult task." He leaned near and clasped his friend's shoulder. "Do not worry. This world has proved far too troublesome for me. I have no wish to explore others that could possibly be far worse."

Murrough gave him a quick smile. "Aye, but what if it were better?"

"Then I would hope for this mist to take me posthaste."

The moment that he spoke the words a gush of cool wind caused the low clouds to thicken around him. Everything seemed to disappear behind the filmy white blanket. Even Murrough's voice seemed to fade as though he had moved far away. Then just as quickly the haze glided hence. Murrough was looking at him, seemingly waiting for him to make a reply.

"I am sorry, did ye ask something of me?"

Murrough nodded. "Only that I was wondering if we should not send some of the men ahead to scout out Fingham's position."

"Aye. We'll send Dermot and Cormac."

"Pardon me for asking, but did ye say Dermot?"

"That I did. The lad wants to prove his worth. Now is the time."

"Aye." Murrough wrapped his mantle closer as the wind blew stronger.

"Are ye cold, my friend?" Dougray asked.

"Aye, it is the devil himself that has made me leave the warmth and comfort of my bed."

Dougray gave him a wry look. "And is there someone keeping those blankets warm come your return?"

Murrough's contented smile spoke for itself. "My sweet Rhiannon. She is my only comfort."

"I see she has forgiven ye…yet again."

"A good woman she is. One day, I plan on marrying her."

"Aye and ye best do it soon before ye fill her belly with a child. Ye think that Rhiannon has a temper. If her father gets a hold of ye…well more's the pity."

"I can handle old Padrig."

"I hope that this is true, for I hate to lose a good man."

Murrough smiled. "Are ye talking about me, my friend, or the blacksmith?" They both chuckled.

Fingham Butler waited upon his steed for his nephew Tremain to return. He was impatient and chilled to the bone from being out in this damp weather. He pulled his mantle closer around him hoping to gain some warmth. Finally through the shifting haze, he saw Tremain riding toward him.

"Well?" Fingham barely let the man catch his breath.

"He comes, milord."

"Aye." He nodded his head. "I knew that he would, but how many men?"

"Could not say for sure. The blasted mist covers almost everything." He paused a moment unsure if he dared to speak so boldly, but he had to try. He cleared his throat before he began. "This mist is not a good sign to commence a fight."

Fingham's frown made his aged features more pronounced. "We will hold our ground, Tremain."

His nephew hid his apprehension and nodded. Fingham then raised his hand and with a quick swipe lowered it as he moved his mount forward, his men following behind.

As ordered Dermot and Cormac had made a quick sweep of the area and knew that the enemy was moving toward the designated spot. As far as they could see, which was not saying much, they could detect nothing out of the ordinary.

Armed men on both sides were ready to lift their swords if someone even breathed the wrong way. Dougray with Murrough at his side move forward to meet Fingham who had Tremain at his right hand. The fog swirled around them, making the approaching figures look more like something out of a dream than of flesh and blood.

"That is far enough, Butler," Dougray called out to him. To his surprise Fingham actually pulled back on his reins. "I know that ye are anxious to draw blood this day...."

"Only yers, Fitzpatrick," he interrupted.

Dougray sighed wearily. "Then take it and be done with it. Why do ye plague me with these assaults? Ye've killed innocent men that otherwise would be home with their wives, warming themselves in front of a roaring fire."

Fingham let out a laugh that was no more humorous than this meeting. "That is why I make ye watch for I know ye suffer with each throat that I sever."

"If ye believe that I care so much for my people, then why can ye not see how much that I cared for Ella?"

"Do not speak my daughter's name!" he bellowed, shaking his closed fist in the air. "Ye are not worthy to have her beautiful memory spoken from yer deceitful lips."

"I loved her." Dougray knew that it was useless to try and reason with the man, but still he had to try. He wanted peace, peace for both of them.

"Love? Surely ye jest. If ye had loved her as ye so claim, ye would have not sent her to her death."

He flinched at his words as though he had been physically assaulted. He closed his eyes for a moment, trying to block out the anguish. "I wish that it were I that had died that day."

"As do I," Fingham flung back.

They both eyed one another, their horses moving uneasily, anxious to charge. "I would like to grant ye yer wish, Fingham, but alas I must decline the offer this day. I will not endanger my men in this mist. We will meet another day of yer choosing."

Fingham's blood ran cold with the anger that surged through his body. How dare the man decide that today's fight would not commence? He had no rights here. He was at his mercy and only lived because he fancied it. Before

Tremain could stop him, Fingham let out a blood-curdling yell as he charged forth.

Murrough and Dougray at the same time pulled their swords from their scabbard. Men from both sides ran forward to guard their lord, while the fog swirled around their heads, thick and foreboding.

Murrough jabbed his sword into a man, knocking him to the ground. He looked to his right expecting to see Dougray, but the mist was like a wall, blocking his view. He was not even sure if he was still locked in a fight with Fingham.

Chapter Three

Present-Day Southern California

Beverly Johnson had arranged for the book signing months ago for Aislinn Hennessy to promote her bestseller, *To Trust Again*. She expected all her writers to show up bright eyed and cheery no matter what was happening in their hectic lives. A.J., as they called her, was there smiling, and chatting pleasantly with her fans, but Bev saw the signs, dark shadows under her gorgeous, almond-shaped eyes, and she had cut her hair almost pixie style, short and above the ears. To anyone that truly knew her, the radical change signified that once again her love life was in shambles. Such a shame too, A.J. was an intelligent and charming woman, and to top it off she had a body that men couldn't help but want to touch. Unfortunately, she picked guys that could only look that far, and had no interest in the mind that was behind that perfect combination of curves.

Bev waited until the two young women left with their autographed copies before she spoke pushing her black-rimmed glasses back on the bridge of her nose. "You look positively horrible." Leave it to Bev to speak with such honesty.

"Thanks."

"Well, I do have to call it as I see it. Hey, count yourself lucky. Even at your worst, us poor slobs don't stand a chance." How could anyone keep up? She was in a *kickboxing* class four days a week, hiking once a month with her family, and of course every year there was the cross-country race that she and her brother, Connor, trained for nine months out of the year. Was it a wonder that her six-foot frame looked like it belonged to a top model? "Roger is history, isn't he?"

"Nothing gets passed you. Are you a mind reader or something?"

"No. It has been over your usual two-month standard. That's about when you dump them."

"You mean they dump me."

"Mentally, you've already sent them packing. I've seen you in action. You fall fast and hard, then within a week you have seen through their superficial existence."

"I'm still trying to figure out what draws me to them."

"That's easy. It's your strong mother instinct. None of these men, if you could even call them that...were men. They were little boys that haven't found themselves, and have no direction in life other than being your boyfriend. No goals, no ambitions, and you soon realize that you can't change them."

"Are you a shrink now too?"

"If I need to be." They were silent for a few moments then Bev leaned forward. "If you're going to keep picking these guys with the capital *L* stamped on their forehead, then just sleep with them quickly and toss them aside."

"I couldn't."

"Why? Men do that all the time to women. They don't seem to mind."

"Well I do. I want a meaningful relationship."

"Still looking for the knight in shining armor, are you?"

"Don't forget the white horse." They both laughed, before Bev became serious.

"That's a fairytale, honey. There aren't any men out there like that. I know. I've been married three times."

"My mother found my father."

"Then he's the last of the breed." She shook her head. "My advice to you is use the bastards then move on."

"I'm selfish, Bev. I want the real thing. You know, to fall in love. Until that happens, I won't take that next step in the relationship. I'm willing to wait it out."

"What are you saying? That you never slept with any of the guys you dated?"

"Do you mind keeping it down?" Aislinn looked around to see if anyone overheard.

"How in the world do you write steamy romance novels like you do, if you never experienced the real deal?"

"I'm human, Bev. I have desires. I just never let it go that far. Jumping in bed only confuses the issue." For a moment wistfulness in her expression stole across her face. "He's out there. I just haven't found him yet."

"Here's a little hint, he ain't likely to be standing in the welfare lines."

"Ha, ha. Do you mind if we stop talking about my personal life? I have books to sign."

"Fine. I'll fetch us some coffee before the official line up begins." She left A.J. as another Hennessy follower walked up.

A couple of hours flew by with an occasional slow point where Bev pulled out her planner and was able to corner Aislinn on two more book signings, and a guest appearance on the local radio station.

"Don't forget, I'll be gone a month."

"A month!"

"Ireland with my family. We've had this planned for a year. You know, a return to the roots sort of thing. My father migrated from the Emerald Island."

"Any family left over there?"

"Not that I'm aware of, but I think that my pop was homesick. It's been over twenty years for him."

"Maybe you can use this little excursion as a research tool for your next novel. You've started on it, haven't you?"

With the breakup, she hadn't exactly felt like writing. She hedged trying to think of a plausible excuse, other than the obvious. She turned away startled to see that someone was hovering over her.

Even Bev was taken aback. "Where did she come from?" slipped out before she could stop herself.

The lady had to be the oldest person either one of them had ever seen with so many wrinkles that it was hard to tell where the lines ended, and where the next ones began.

"Do you wish to have an autographed book?" Aislinn asked feeling almost uneasy by the way the woman was just staring at her.

She finally spoke her voice raspy thin, *"Tá sé in am agat imeacht."*

"I'm sorry we don't speak..." Beverly began only to realize she wasn't sure what language the woman had used.

"Céard a deir tú?" Aislinn answered in the same gibberish making Beverly's jaw drop.

The old woman just nodded and handed Aislinn what she had been cradling against her chest. Aislinn stared at the decrepit, leather-bound book that had been placed in her hands. She glanced up again to ask the woman what she wanted her to do with it, but she had already moved away, disappearing behind a line of school kids that had just entered the store. Aislinn jumped up, weaving around them trying to wave the woman down. She rushed outside after her, but it was as if the woman had simply disappeared.

"What was that about?" Beverly asked when Aislinn had returned, "and what language were you conversing in?"

"Irish. The woman spoke Gaelic." She opened the book that was handwritten in the old script.

"That looks absolutely ancient." Beverly looked over her shoulder to have a closer look.

"I know and for the life of me I cannot think of a reason why she would have given it to me." On the front-page the initials F.O. were inked in a heavy hand. "I guess it was asking too much for there to be a name and address where I could send it back."

"Looks like a journal. Are you able to read it, A.J.?"

"I'm sure if I looked it over I could translate most of it." Aislinn turned the pages carefully so not to tear the fragile parchment.

Beverly glanced at her watch. "We're about finished here if you want to head out now. I can tell you're just itching to get started."

"Thanks, Bev. I'll let you know if there's anything interesting."

Chapter Four

She read it again. She almost felt that she could hear the anguish in the words that were written, and her heart went out to the man that had grieved so deeply.

"*Cailleadh roimhaois é*. He died before his time," the person had written. "I was too late to save him. It was my fault for not seeing the trap that was waiting for us. I have seen death, but this was like nothing that I have ever witnessed. What my dear cousin had endured in the last moments of his life could have been avoided. How I wish that I could somehow turn back time, so that I may stop the slaughter from ever taking place. I sent him to a torturous death. He fought well that much was obvious for there were many of the enemy scattered in bloody piles around him.

I could not let them take his body away to do with as they wished, for there was no doubt that they would have mutilated it without a thought. He was, after all, to them, just a man that had betrayed them. It never amazes me how they make these lies up to suit their needs. I have hidden his body well, in an unmarked grave, but of sacred ground. Forgive me, cousin, for not protecting you. Forgive me."

Aislinn closed her eyes as grief squeezed at her heart. The passages had left her drained as if she was reliving the final scene from memory rather than words that were written. An odd feeling since she didn't know these people that had lived so long ago, and yet…there was a sense of a connection. Where she could almost see the man's face that the author had spoken of with such reverence.

Aislinn glanced at the clock on the wall with a sigh. She knew that she had to put the journal down, if she was ever to get ready to go over to her parents' for dinner. It was almost five o'clock and she promised Connor that she would pick him up on the way.

At the Hennessys, dinner was skinless, grilled chicken on a bed of wild rice. Aislinn helped to throw together a tossed salad. She was grateful that so far no one brought up the fact that there was an empty seat where Roger used to sit. Thank God, Ireland had been a family vacation, and she hadn't purchased a ticket for Roger to go with them.

"We want to make a full sweep of Ireland." Conner poured himself another glass of wine. "I think I could get some pretty nifty pictures for the magazine. The place is full of castles and ruins and it's so green. How could I go wrong?" Her brother was a freelance photographer with a gifted talent where magazines sought him out, rather than the other way around.

"I think as long as we follow our plan, and utilize our time wisely, we can see about everything," Francine Hennessy added. Their mother was a well-organized person. They could pretty much depend on her to handle that aspect of the itinerary.

"Pop," Aislinn looked at her father, "where exactly do the Hennessys hail from?"

"At one time there were four Hennessy Septs spread all over Munster and Leinster. There were towns named Ballyhennessy. Our stronghold was in the north Offaly and near the hill of Croghan and Kilbeggan. We shared its lordship with the O'Holohans. This was where you would have found our family but after the Norman invasion the clan went south to Cork, Limerick and Tipperary…the Pale." He added the last with almost a sound of disgust.

"Is there anyone still there that you know?" Connor asked.

"Nay." Their father shook his head almost sadly. "Everyone is long dead and buried I suppose." Francine reached across the table gently placing her hand on his. Aislinn always wondered why her father spoke of his ancestors with that subtle melancholy of someone who was speaking of a close endearing relative that had just passed away. What she could remember, his family had all perished long before Connor or she had been born.

"Didn't you have a friend?" Connor snapped his fingers. "What's his name? Fierce Ax, wasn't he from Ireland too?"

"Aye. Knew my family well that man did." Donagh's blue eyes glimmered with the memory of him. "I miss him more times than not," his voice had taken on a husky tone, and he quickly rose from his seat hoping no one noticed how emotional he had become. "Let's clear the table and take out the maps," he added gruffly.

While Aislinn and Connor were cleaning up, Francine pulled her husband aside not fooled in the least that he had nearly broken down. "Are you sure that you want to go back?"

"To me own home? Aye, I am ready to face the ghosts. The question is, are ye all right with it? Ye are not worried?"

"I am, but I can do this as long as I am with you." She hugged the brawny man of hers, and he wrapped his arms lovingly around her slim form, making her instantly feel like she was well protected.

After the plans were set, Aislinn went out to the porch. She wrapped a large blanket around her and sat down on the lawn chair. She noticed that there was a full moon on this clear night.

She hadn't been out there long when her father had decided to join her. He handed her a mug that contained freshly brewed coffee.

"Yer mother thinks that ye will catch a chill." Aislinn took the cup, warming her hands against the ceramic.

"This was just what I was hoping for. Are you going to join me, Pop?"

Donagh pulled up another lawn chair. They just sat there, father and daughter enjoying the company without saying a word. They could always do that without it seeming uncomfortable, but after a moment Aislinn realized by the way her father was fidgeting that he wanted to discuss something with her. Finally, he spoke, "Aislinn." He only called her by her given name when he was going to speak of something of great importance. "I worry about ye finding yer way."

She chuckled. "I think that you should worry about Connor."

He shook his head. "Nay, it is ye that I worry about. Are ye all right with this parting of ways that ye and Roger have taken?"

"Yeah, Pop. He wasn't the one." She sighed deeply with regret.

"The right one is very important. We are two halves of a whole."

"And we should fit together like we were never apart. I know, Pop. Like you and Mom."

He nodded. "*Daoine d'aon mhianach,* Kindred Souls. I had prayed for a woman, the likes of yer mother. I was blessed. Be patient and ye will find that someone too. Aye?"

She looked at her father and smiled. How wonderful it would be to find a love like her parents with that inherent strength that made marriage last a lifetime. "I almost forgot. I wanted you to take a look at something. I could make out most of it, but I thought you might be interested in it, too." She put down her mug and went inside the house to grab her backpack. She retrieved the journal and handed it to her father.

"What is this?" He took the book from her.

"I had a visitor today at my book signing. She spoke Gaelic."

Donagh gave his daughter a startled look. "The old tongue?"

"How she knew that I would understand her is beyond me. Then she handed me this and disappeared."

"Disappeared?" His graying brows furrowed.

"I guess I'm being a little dramatic. I lost her in the crowd. Now look." She leaned over her father's shoulder. "See how old it is?"

Donagh had already scanned a page and he knew of what time and place it had come from. He swallowed the lump in his throat as he glanced at his daughter who was intrigued by the mystery, but all he could feel was apprehension.

"Aislinn will be the one to go, Francine." Donagh felt his wife move beside him and he slipped his arm around her small waist. They waved goodbye to their children as they pulled out of the driveway.

"What makes you so sure?"

"Because she is searching for something that she cannot find here. I believe it is the same pull that drew ye to me." He looked down at his sweet woman he had married twenty-six years ago. She was still so beautiful, and if it were possible, he loved her even more today.

"But will she be ready?"

"We trained her well, Francine. She's versed in the languages. She is strong physically and mentally as well. She is prepared."

"I still worry if we are doing the right thing. Maybe she won't find what she is looking for in Ireland. Maybe we shouldn't have insisted that she...."

"Shush now." He gently silenced her with his finger on her lips. "It has already been written. Ye will see. It is like the old woman had predicted."

Francine sighed knowing that her husband was right, but still it didn't make her feel comforted with the fact. "The past must be set straight for the future to be secure."

"Aye. She is of Hennessy blood…"

"You do know that I had something to do with her existence too."

He chuckled. "I was getting to that. She has the strength to survive and the know how to do it. We should count ourselves lucky that she was an able pupil."

"This is our daughter you are speaking of."

"Are we not her parents? We are here to teach her the way of the world so that she can enter it without stumbling on her first go. And if she should fall, we have ensured in her the strength to rise from the ground and go full force again. Strength, self worth, and determination are wonderful gifts to bless a child with, Francine. We accomplished just that." He gently hugged her close, kissing the top of her head. "We did that, *mo ghrá*."

Chapter Five

They were actually going to Ireland. The flight was uneventful, at least after Connor drank himself into oblivion. When the pilot announced that they were flying over the island, Aislinn nudged her brother awake.

"Wha…t?" He yawned. "Are we there?"

"Just look, Connor." She leaned back so that he could take a peak.

"Yeah. Looks a little flat."

"Is that all you can say?" She touched the window. "It's like home."

"What did you say?"

She hadn't realized she had spoken the words out loud. "Nothing, Connor, go back to sleep. I'll wake you when we land."

"Good by me." He punched at his pillow as if it would make it softer then settled down and shut his eyes.

After landing, they managed to obtain their rental and have a light dinner before retiring. The next day, they were ready to hit the pavement. Connor had just entered the room and tossed the travel guide to Aislinn before he threw himself down on the bed. "Mom had the book in her suitcase. What was it that you wanted to see?"

"Trinity College for one. They have the books of Kells there. It's a must." She flipped through the guidebook. "St. Patrick Cathedral and…."

Connor sat up leaning his forearms against his knees. "I happened to catch something that I wouldn't mind seeing."

Aislinn brows arched high up on her forehead. "What is it? So help me Connor if you suggest another pub, I'm going to strangle you."

He gave her a sheepish grin. "That's for later. I want to see St. Michan's Cathedral. Flip to page eleven. It'll tell you all about it."

After skimming through it, she looked up at him. "You want to see the mummified bodies? That seems a little morbid, don't you think?"

"On the contrary, my dear sister, it sounds absolutely fascinating." He sprang from the bed. "Come on, let's get Mom and Pop on the move. It looks like we have a full day ahead of us, if we plan on walking the city."

As they passed the Inns Quay and turned toward Church Street, they could see the Square tower. "That's it." Connor pointed to it. "That's St. Michan's. The church was originally built in 1095. Then sometime in the 1600s they rebuilt a larger church on the same site to accommodate the congregation." Connor stopped to adjust the lens of his camera for a picture.

"The name doesn't sound a bit Irish to me," Aislinn commented.

"Nope," Connor answered. "I read that there was a Danish church on the sight. Michan happens to be an old, Danish Saint."

"I guess that would explain it," Aislinn muttered uneasily. She didn't want to go down below where…she shook her head. She didn't understand why she was feeling so scared. She was actually afraid of going beneath the church as if she were going to be trapped. Biting her lower lip, she tore her gaze away from the foreboding architecture.

Her parents had noticed the change in their daughter. Francine almost suggested that they take a tour at St. Patrick's Cathedral first, but her husband took a firm hold on her arm, his eyes softening a little when he realized how apprehensive she seemed. "We must go, Francine." He knew the moment that she had accepted the decision for she gave him a trembling smile letting him lead her forward.

"Ye four will be the last tour for the day." The guide by the name Paddy smiled at them. He was friendly enough, and full of information of how the church was built and reconstructed. He explained that there was evidence that at one time there was another opening to the underground vaults but for some reason it had been sealed up. "Now if you will follow me outside we will see the most famous feature of St. Michan's."

When Aislinn seemed rooted in her spot, Connor pulled on her arm. "Come on."

"You know, I think I'll just wait this one out if you don't mind."

"Uh uh. You're coming." He yanked on her arm.

Paddy opened the doors and looked back to the Hennessys. "I will ask y'not to take photographs or video tape while we are down here. Now please watch your heads, when descending the steps." One by one, Aislinn watched her family disappear below. The guide looked at her with reassuring smile. "Y'are next, lass."

She knew that she was being silly. What was there to be afraid of? Right? She took a deep breath and descended the rough, ancient stones to the long passageway where burial chambers were on both sides guarded by rod iron gates.

"Each compartment belongs to a single family," he explained. "There are still a few families that possess a key to the burial chamber. Come closer." The guide motioned. "If you look into one of the chambers you will see that there are coffins that are heaped upon one another. Does anyone know why this would be like this?"

Connor shrugged. "I don't know. They wanted to save room?"

"Could be." The guide nodded.

"They were spooked to come down here in the dead of night," Aislinn spoke. "They tossed the coffins in before they ran." When she realized all eyes were on her, she awkwardly cleared her throat. "Just a thought."

"She may have a point," the guide agreed. "Most burials were done at night and this being Ireland with all its superstitions, most likely they were frightened that the spirits of the dead would greet them."

"The coffins look brand new." Francine couldn't help but notice. "Look, you can see the velvet that covers the wood and the brass nails."

"That's right." The guide was impressed that she had noticed. "You see the vaults are very dry and the only signs of life are the large cobwebs in some of the chambers. The floor is covered with a fine powdery dust and if you will notice the temperature is moderate. It remains the same all the time no matter what the weather is up above. Now, follow me. The last compartment houses what you came down here to see." He moved on ahead with her family, but Aislinn hung in the back. The whole idea of the mummified bodies sent an eerie chill down her spine. At one time, these bodies were living human beings with a passion for life. They loved, laughed, and cried, but now they were nothing more than a mere withering shell on display for all to see.

The guide came to the end of the passageway pointing as he spoke, "Y'will see in the vault the wooden coffins have fallen away exposing the mummified bodies. There are five in all that have turned brown in color. The bodies are very old and the skin is like leather, but the features can still be distinguished. Lean in." He motioned to each of them to take a closer look. Aislinn was trying not to be physically ill as she heard the guide continue.

"The fingernails are still evident, the knees and the other joints are still pliable. Under the skin y'can see the heart and the lungs.

"Unfortunately, we do not know who these people once were. The one way in the back was a very big man, even to standards nowadays. He probably was well over seven feet tall. They had to break his legs so that he would fit in the coffin. We have estimated that this man probably lived about 800 or so years ago. It was a privilege to be buried on such sacred ground. The man is believed to have been a Crusader."

"Near him, you see the remains of a woman and the theory is that she was a nun. The one next to her is thought that he may have been an executed man."

"Why do you think that?" Connor leaned in.

"If you will look closer the man is missing a hand. At one time if you were accused of a crime, let's say stealing...."

"They would cut off your hand," Connor finished for him.

Aislinn wasn't paying attention anymore. She couldn't tear her gaze away from the last body that was lying there for all to view. Fearful images began to build in her mind, flashes of ...him? "And the last body?" She tightly hugged herself.

"Those remains are also a mystery to us. We do know that he did not die of natural causes. We have reason to believe that this man either was in a battle or had been murdered. There are various indications that he suffered multiple wounds, defensive gashes on his forearms and hands. This man had struggled dearly to live."

Aislinn tried to concentrate on what the guide was saying, but the world seemed to dim and the tour guide's voice was so far away, almost dream like. Impossible as it should have been, she felt an icy cool breeze in the dry interior. She watched her family follow the guide back down the passageway, but she was paralyzed with fear, unable to call out for help. They weren't alone. Something was down here.

"I would die for ye," the baritone voice whispered near her ear as she felt a hand brush against her cheek.

Aislinn's fragile control unraveled in an instant letting loose a bloodcurdling scream.

After the fiasco at St. Michan's Cathedral, her parents had made their apologies and had brought her back to the hotel. She was still a little shaken over what had happened as well as embarrassed to have behaved like a raving lunatic. She had scared everyone including the poor tour guide. Of course no one had been there behind her, but it still didn't make her feel any better. She felt him, heard him, and what made it worse, she was positive that the ghost, apparition, or whatever you wanted to call it, was the unidentified murdered man. She was so sure of it that she would bet her life on it, well maybe not her life. She was convinced that was the reason she had felt such apprehension about going down to the crypt. The man's spirit was still lingering there.

Now that she had calmed down enough to think about this logically, she knew that the ghost hadn't meant to harm her. He was only giving her a caress. Maybe she had inadvertently reminded him of someone that he had deeply cared for, loved enough that he would die for her. Maybe he had died for her.

Connor and her parents kept staring at her, as if they were afraid she was going to go spastic on them again. "I'm fine, really. I want to go to dinner."

"Are you sure, honey?" Francine felt her forehead.

"Mom, I'm not sick."

"Frannie, let the poor girl alone." Aislinn could have kissed her father at that moment. "I'm starved for one, and if A.J. wants to go out to eat why are we stopping her?" He leaned down and gave her a kiss on top of her head. "We'll take a quick shower and meet ye downstairs."

"Thanks, Pop." She smiled her appreciation.

As soon as they left the room, Connor pounced on her for answers. "So, what was it? What did you see? You can tell your brother."

She rose from the chair and went over to her suitcase looking for something that she could change into. "I told you, it was nothing."

"Yeah. I know what you said to Mom and Pop, but you can tell me the truth. You saw something." He was at her side, his eyes boring into her.

"You'll think I'm crazy."

"Hot dog!" He slapped his knee. "I knew you saw something. A ghost? That crusader guy in the corner? I'd tell you, if I had my legs broken and curled up behind me, dead or not I would haunt the place."

Aislinn just shook her head. "It wasn't like I saw something. I felt a presence. I can't explain it, but it touched me."

"It touched you?" His hazel eyes widen. "Like bony hands encircling your throat? That kind of touching?"

"I swear, Connor, you are like a twelve-year-old boy."

"Thank you, and you didn't answer my question."

"No. The touch was gentle and he whispered...."

"He spoke to you? Boy this just gets better and better."

"Do you want to know what happened or not?"

"Go on. I'll keep quiet."

"He said, *I would die for you.*"

"That's it?" He seemed disappointed.

"Yes. What did you expect a ghost to say?" She was beginning to regret ever mentioning it to him.

"Well, I guess the dude did what he said."

"What do you mean?"

"He's dead, isn't he? Which one do you think it was? You said *he*, so I can assume we can rule out the nun."

"The murdered one."

"You seem awfully sure of that."

She looked at him. "I can't explain it, but yeah. I'm pretty sure it was him."

"Spooky. Hey, let's go back there and see if he'll speak to you again."

"Are you nuts?"

"Aren't you the least bit curious why the ghost reached out to you? The man had been murdered. Maybe he was seeking someone out to help him solve the mystery of who done it."

"Even if it were true, the culprits would be dead. There's nothing that we can do. It's not like we can bring them to justice."

"True or not, the man died violently. Everyone knows that if a person dies a violent death, they always come back to haunt."

"Who told you that?" She gave him a skeptical look.

"It's a known fact," he insisted with such conviction that Aislinn almost believed him. "Come on, you have to be curious."

"Maybe just a tad, but not enough to go back down in the vault. Besides, with the way I behaved the tour guide probably has me written down as a fruitcake, and if I ever returned, I would be committed on sight."

"Oh come now. He probably just wrote you off as another crazy American."

She laughed. "You're probably right." She took out her blue-gray sweater and black slacks and headed to the bathroom. "Right now, I would like to forget about ghosts and take a shower."

"And later? Another visit to the old cathedral?"

"Connor, I thought that you outgrew the *Ghost Busters*."

"No. I just pretended to."

Aislinn rolled her eyes. "I'm not going back." She shut the door, hopefully closing the subject. As much as she was curious, she also had no wish to have a repeat performance of what happened earlier. She turned on the shower faucet and let it run so that the water could warm. Maybe her next novel should be a ghost story. She saw her backpack leaning against the wall and she went over to it. Unzipping it, she noticed the leather-bound journal that the old woman had given her, and she took it out. No wonder she was haunted by ghosts. She had read the entries to a man's untimely death so many times that she could practically recite it from memory.

She put it on the sink and pulled out her notebook. She jotted down a few lines. *She sensed the man, knowing full well that if she turned around no one would be there.* She felt the hackles on the back of her neck rise making her turn quickly to see if anyone was behind her. She felt silly, but quite relieved that she was still very much alone.

While Connor waited for his sister to freshen up, he viewed the events of the day on the camcorder. He nearly came unglued with excitement when he realized that he hadn't turned off the camera when they went down below St. Michan's Church. It was dark but he could see Aislinn clearly for she had stayed to the back of them. Just seconds before she let out her deafening scream, he thought that he saw something. He stopped the video and rewound it. Then hit the play button again. "I'll be damned." There was no mistaking the swirl of fragmented light that whirled briefly around his sister.

He nearly jumped at her the moment she came out of the bathroom. "Come here, A.J., and take a look at this."

She couldn't ignore the excited implication of his words. She went over to him expecting to see anything but what he was showing her. The color drained from her face and she had to sit down to steady herself. "You taped while we were down in the tomb? You know that you weren't supposed to do that."

"Will you forget that for a moment, and by the way I didn't mean to." He rewound the tape to the spot he wanted her to view. "Do you see it, A.J.?"

She saw, and immediately turned off the camera. "Erase it."

"I will not. This is proof that something was there. We have to go back now."

"I won't go, Connor. So just forget it. The ghost will just have to haunt someone else."

"But…."

His sister threw him a lethal stare that shut him up immediately. "Drop it. Do you hear me?"

"Fine." He began putting the camera back in its case. He would drop it for now, but he had every intention of going back to the church with or without her.

Chapter Six

"I don't see why we had to rent a car," Donagh was still complaining. "God gave us two feet and we would do well to use them."

"Pop." Aislinn laced her arm through his. "It'll be fun. Think of it as an adventure. We'll still take the trail as soon as we reach the *Glendalough* visitor center."

He still was grumbling when he took the back seat of the rented vehicle beside Francine. Aislinn volunteered to drive while Connor rode shotgun.

It was early morning with a light mist that covered the land making it almost seem unearthly. "It's beautiful," Aislinn breathed.

Connor was slouched against the side of the door half asleep. He peek opened one eye at her. "What is?"

She glanced at him for a moment. "Out there silly. You're missing it."

"Missing what? It's fog. Just wake me when we arrive."

"Maybe we should wait until this burns off," their mother commented from the back seat.

"If we had walked…" Donagh began only to have his children interrupt.

"Pop," both Connor and Aislinn whined at the same time.

"Okay already. I'll be quiet."

As the mist thickened, Aislinn began to feel more and more uneasy. Not so much about the visibility, but that she had an eerie feeling that they shouldn't be here.

To take her mind off it, she began to hum and before long to everyone's dismay she was singing.

Connor leaned forward to turn on the radio. "Sorry, A.J., I can only take so much of your screeching."

"I thought I was getting better," she joked knowing full well that she was tone deaf.

"Take it from me, don't quit your day job. Hey, that's strange." He moved the dials on the radio again. "It's dead."

"Here, let me try." Aislinn took over. She only glanced down for a second.

"Hey watch out!" Connor warned.

She looked up in time to see something large, furry...it was a person standing directly in her path. She swerved as he jumped out of the way. They ended up spinning to a stop on the opposite side of the road. "Is everyone all right?" A quick look and she knew that they were shaken but not harmed. "God!" She jumped out of the car and ran across the street. Her brother and parents were close behind her, but the mist drifted in patches making it hard to follow.

"A.J., hold on!" Connor shouted to her, but she didn't stop. Her heart was pounding against her chest. What if she killed someone? She didn't think she hit him but...she hurried on through the thickening mist.

There was a groan and her eyes scanned the area below. She realized that the side of the road indented to what looked like a ditch. Finally her eyes made out an outline of a man sprawled out on the ground. She didn't hesitate, but ran toward him. His head rested on the rocks, as if they were soft pillows. At this moment, she was wishing that they were. She knelt down beside him to assess the damage.

He groaned again, his head lolling to the side. "He's breathing. That's a good sign." She brushed his long dark hair out of his eyes. She was startled to find that she was looking at a relatively handsome face that was bronzed by wind and sun. He had a square jaw with a generous mouth and mustache that in her opinion needed to be trimmed back, but still it did not take away the fact that his strong features held a certain sensuality. She then glanced at the man's strange attire of wool hide and thick mantle, and not far from where he had fallen she caught sight of a large broad sword. She wondered why he was dressed like this, way out here in the middle of nowhere.

She moved the thick cloak aside, her eyes widening in surprise at how his massive shoulders filled out his shirt. She took in the length of him and realized he was tall even for her standards. His legs were bare, muscular and thick, Viking legs. "He's gorgeous." She then shook her head, chastising herself for goggling at a poor defenseless man when he could be bleeding to death. She began looking to see where he was injured. That was when she caught the glitter of the amulet before her. It was a spiral of intertwining lines that formed a circle, and in the center was a large stone that looked like dark amber. For a moment, she forgot everything else and reached for the amulet, touching its fineness. She let out a gasp, when the once unconscious man grabbed a hold of her hand with a grip that made her wince.

"Are ye a thief, young waif?" His beautiful, pale blue, eyes bore into hers. Flustered beyond belief, she at first failed to realize that he had spoken to her in Gaelic.

But as fear was replaced by anger, she came to her senses. She answered him in the Irish. She was amazed that under the circumstances that she could recall the words at all. "Lig amach mé!"

He seemed stunned by her response and she wondered if she had misunderstood. Maybe he hadn't spoken in Gaelic. She repeated just as forcefully in English, "I said, unhand me."

Dougray eyed her with suspicion. He had thought that he was looking at a young boy; the hair was cut so short but that voice was definitely feminine. To make sure he reached out and grabbed at her chest. She was so swift that he didn't even see it coming. Before he knew it, she had sent a powerful blow to his jaw. He fell back, hitting his head once more on the hard rocks, blackness engulfing him.

"What are you doing?" Connor had come down the embankment to see her plow the guy.

She stood up with disgust. "He grabbed me." She pointed at the man accusingly.

"Grabbed you?" Connor moved forward to look at the unconscious man.

"Yes. He's obviously a pervert or something."

"Looks like he was headed to a party. Look how he's dressed." He bent down and picked up the sword. "Wow, this thing is heavy."

Just then their parents appeared. "There you are." Her mother threw her arms around Aislinn as though she had thought to never see her again. Aislinn looked at her father who seemed just as uneasy. Before she could say anything, Francine let go of her and went over to where the man was sprawled out on the ground. "Is he…is he…."

"No, Mom. He's quite alive." The terseness in Aislinn voice caused her mother to look at her questionably. Aislinn shrugged. "We had somewhat of a limited conversation."

"And then he passed out again?" she asked.

"Not exactly." Connor swung the sword around.

"Let me take a look at that." Donagh came forward admiring the weapon.

"Boys." Francine shook her head. "We have a man down."

"I thought A.J. said he spoke," Donagh said as he swung the sword. "Well balanced." He swung it again.

"Yeah, that is until she knocked him out cold again," Connor was good enough to inform everyone.

"What?" Both her parents looked at her.

"Well he...." It did seem awful that she punched the man when he was obviously hurt. When he spoke to her, he didn't even make any sense. "Oh forget it." She bent down again to look at the guy. "God, look at how he's dressed." He was attractive even in the ridiculous garb making her stomach do flip-flops. She leaned forward to make sure he was still breathing. She closed her eyes as she put her hand on his chest, warmth radiating up her arm. "He smells so...." She was about to say wonderfully male. Her eyes shot open to find her family looking at her as if she had lost her mind. Physically shaken by her reaction to the stranger, she cleared her throat. "I don't think he's bathed in a while." She jumped to her feet moving a safe distance away.

Her father gave Connor the sword so that he could take a look.

"I think it's his head," Aislinn offered. "He wasn't making much sense when he was conscious. He called me a waif or something of the sort, and in Gaelic if you can believe that."

Donagh and Francine exchanged a quick look. "I'm calling for help," her mother announced as she pulled out her cell phone. "Do they have 911 here?"

"Get an operator. They'll connect you." Connor stood by his mother.

Francine tried, but the phone kept blinking off. "I thought you charged this thing." She looked to Donagh.

"I did." Her husband looked up.

"Well it's dead now." She flipped the lid down. She became aware of her surroundings then and not liking it one bit. "The mist, Donagh."

He just nodded as though in agreement of whatever she had meant by *the mist*. "Let's try carrying him to the car."

"Should we move him, Pop?" Aislinn was concerned that they could end up doing more harm than good, but of course her punching him hadn't been much help.

"No broken bones that I can tell. Better to get him to a hospital, than to leave him out here in the damp air." He looked up at his son. "Think you can help me?"

"Sure." He handed the sword to his mother.

"What in the world would the man need this for?" Aislinn asked and her mother flinched at the question. She was acting quite peculiar as she nervously looked around her, like she expected someone or something to jump out at her.

"I don't know," she finally answered as her daughter took the weapon from her.

"Looks authentic, doesn't it? It's heavy."

"He must be part of the theatrical group or something." Her mother seemed too eager to explain.

"Mom, there's nothing out here."

Donagh and Connor had started the process of moving the unconscious man. "How can you be sure?" Connor spoke up with a hint of sarcasm. "I can't see more than a few feet in front of me. As far as we can tell, there could be a castle beyond the mist." They started up the incline, Aislinn and her mother right behind them.

"I read the map, Connor," Aislinn insisted. "There isn't anything around here for miles."

"Maybe we took a wrong turn." Connor was still fishing for a logical explanation.

"I know that I didn't." They made it to the road and there the fog had vanished as if a curtain had lifted and now they were center stage. "How very odd." Aislinn looked over her shoulder to where the sea of mist was so dense that she couldn't see through it. She was about to turn away but she heard something that sounded like horses, and clanging of metal. She started to go back and investigate.

"A.J., are you coming or what?" Her brother had taken the driver seat and had leaned out the window wondering what was taking her so long to get into the car.

"Coming," she called back, hesitating for a second trying to listen for the strange sounds she had heard, but she couldn't detect anything other than the purr of the car engine.

Chapter Seven

Dougray had been awake for some time now, but he was playing it safe, trying to get his bearings before he made this fact known. Was he in the custody of friend or foe?

"I know that you are awake," a rather sultry voice with an edge of sarcasm lacing it had spoken. He knew it was no use continuing with the charade, and opened his eyes to view his captor. She stood there before him with her arms folded across her chest. It was the girl or rather woman that he had gravely mistaken for a young lad. He felt quite silly over that assumption now, for if he had looked passed the garments and the short-cropped hair, there was no mistaking the feminine features. She was quite alarmingly striking with her dark hair the color of midnight and her eyes…. Never had he seen eyes so dark, and they were framed with such thick sooty lashes. They were simply beautiful even with the accusing flash of anger within their depths.

He lifted his hand and felt the side of his jaw. It felt like he had been hit with the end of a battle-ax. "Are ye going to be taking a swing at me again?"

She heard the glimmer of amusement and she lost some of her hostility. "That depends."

His brows lifted. "Depends?"

"Yes, on if you are going to manhandle me."

"Aye." He sighed but not completely with regret. He saw her eyes flash with anger again, and he was quick to rectify the slight. There was no need to antagonize this woman when he still was not sure if he was a captive. She was speaking to him in his native tongue but he recognized a slight difference in the dialect indicating it was not her first language. "I apologize. I didn't realize that ye were a lady, that was only dressed in a man's attire." *Eccentric attire at that,* he thought to himself.

Aislinn was puzzled for she was just wearing a pair of jeans and a T-shirt, nothing out of the ordinary. "Do you remember what happened to you?"

"Not really. It seems that a few things do not fit well. I do not recognize ye. Are ye with the Butler clan?" He was still wondering why he knew the name when she answered.

"I'm sorry. I don't know any Butlers."

He sat up a little. "Are you friend or foe?" Where was his sword? Furthermore where were his clothes? He was wearing some kind of thin material that barely covered him.

She realized that she was being rude. The man had every right to be suspicious of her. She immediately tried to put him at ease. "I guess, friend." She came forward then to stand beside the bed. "My father changed you so that we could have your clothing laundered."

"Ye should not have bothered."

"They needed it," she said a little too hastily. She took a deep breath before she started in again. "They were covered in mud. You know from your fall."

"The fall?" He tried to recall what had happened but everything seemed a little hazy.

"Yes. Don't you remember?"

There was something that seemed rather important or so he thought. It nagged at the edge of his memory, but then it was gone.

"What is your name?" she asked hoping to find the identity of the man she had run off the road, so that they could contact his family.

His eyebrows knitted together. Something so simple as his name was eluding him at the moment. "I'm not sure."

Just then another woman entered the room. "How's our patient…oh, he's up." As the woman approached, Dougray realized that she was older than the other one that stood watch over him. She was still very attractive. The only telltale signs of age were the slight lines around her large brown eyes. She was slim, petite really, and when she smiled he could see that she still had all her teeth. That was miraculous indeed for he had seen many older women in England that…*England.* He had been in England to study. Yes, he remembered that.

"My name is Francine Hennessy." She extended her hand to him. "And you are?"

He stared for a second at the woman's opened palm that was extended toward him. He took hold of it and turned it slightly so that he could place a light kiss on the top, befitting of what a lady should expect. She withdrew her hand and he read the surprise there before she could conceal it. What had she expected him to do with her hand? "Milady, I fear that ye have me at a disadvantage. I cannot recall my name, nor do I remember meeting ye or…." He looked at the tall dark woman that was eyeing him closely as if she feared he might attack. "How did I come to be in yer company?" He looked at the older woman again, feeling she would be the easier of the two to deal with.

"We found you on the side of the road. We would have brought you home but we didn't know where you lived." They had all agreed for now to not say anything about nearly running him down unless the man brought it up. "You didn't have any identification on your person."

"Ye do not know me then?"

Francine shook her head. "No. We were hoping that you could tell us."

He ran his hand through his dark hair, his eyes darting from one woman to the other. He didn't sense that he was in any danger, but something seemed to unsettle him. The strange clothes for one and the room, the bed, his whole surroundings seemed odd and out of place.

"Maybe seeing something that is yours will help." Francine pulled the amulet out of her pocket and handed it to him. "You were wearing this." He took the piece from her and turned it around in his hand, rubbing the smooth amber. The spiral lines looked oddly familiar, maybe even important, but he didn't know why.

"You were dressed like you were going to a costume party," the younger woman offered making him look at her.

"How so?"

"You were wearing garments that were of another century, royalty or something, and you had a sword with you. Does this help you in any way?" Aislinn waited for him to answer.

"Sword?" He closed his eyes trying to recall something, anything. His name was at the tip of his tongue. "My name…Doug…Dougray." His eyes flew open and his face eased with relief that he had remembered something.

The tall woman spoke again, "Doug. That's your name?"

He was about to correct her when the door flew opened and this time two men came bursting in. They both started talking at once and the women joined in making it impossible for him to make heads or tails of the conversation, that was obviously now conducted in some form of English. Finally the older of the men came forward to eye him closely. He was a large man with bulging muscles that were evident beneath his shirt. His unwavering gaze and his stance that bordered on defiance made Dougray take note that this man would be a dangerous opponent if he were an enemy. "So, young man, yer name is Doug Gray." His Irish was impeccable, but the way he said his name, it didn't sound quite right.

"Aye," he answered slowly. Again he wondered who these people were. He understood them, but still their speech was foreign to him. They were not from his region. This made him pause for how did he know that?

The older man rubbed his chin thoughtfully. "Ye don't know where ye live?"

"I am not sure. The blow to my head has me disoriented. Could I trouble ye to bring me back from whence ye first found me? Maybe then my memory will return."

"That would probably be a good idea, and soon as ye are up to it, we will do so." The older man agreed. "My name is Donagh Hennessy." He extended his hand to the young stranger. "Ye met my daughter, A.J." He motioned behind him toward the tall woman with the dark eyes. So that was her name. An odd name for a woman, he thought before he listened to the rest of the introductions. "My wife, Francine." The older woman came forward with a smile on her face, but there was a sympathetic expression bordering her eyes. "And my son, Connor," Donagh finished.

The younger man eyed him closely, his hand stashed in his pockets. He finally nodded his head toward him with a quick jerk. "Hey."

Dougray could only assume that this was a greeting of some sort. "I am in yer debt for coming to my rescue." He didn't miss the exchange the four gave each other. Were they hiding something?

"We'll get you something to eat," the woman they called A.J. offered hastily leaving the room before he could thank her.

"Now for clothes." Donagh pursed his lips. "Can't have ye going around in the ones we found ye in." He looked at Connor. Though his son was probably the same height as Dougray, he was of a slighter built. He decided that maybe his clothes, though he was heavier, might fit the man better. "I'll let ye borrow something of mine."

"Thank ye. I will repay yer kindness."

"That won't be necessary. We only want to help."

Connor and Donagh left the room then. As soon as the door closed behind them, Connor gave his father an anxious look. "What are we going to do, when the man remembers we are the cause of him forgetting who he is, in the first place? God, Pop, A.J. ran him off the road."

"We will worry about that when the time comes."

"Right. Besides, it's not all our fault. The fog was so thick and what in the world was he doing out in the middle of nowhere and dressed like a lord of a castle? Did you get a load of the way he talks? He doesn't sound like one of the locals. Do you think the blow to his head triggered him to think he actually is from that time period? Maybe the man's an actor or something."

Donagh just nodded his head. "Could be a possibility. We'll make some inquiries and see if we can find out anything."

Chapter Eight

They stayed an extra two days in Dublin, while Aislinn asked around, showing a picture of Dougray, but no one recognized him. They were at a loss what to do with him. He was in perfect health other than he had no memory of anything prior to waking up in their hotel room.

"I say we continue our trip," Connor announced as soon as they were all situated for the Hennessy meeting.

"That's a little insensitive, don't you think?" Aislinn moved away from the window. They had decided to meet in their parents' room while their guest used the shower to freshen up. After he had gotten the hang of it, he enjoyed taking the warm showers. He had told them that he didn't remember ever taking one before. It was just another piece of the puzzle to add to the obvious. She tried to think of every possibility of why the man was roaming around a deserted area dressed like a warrior. She even went as far as the possibility that he was a vagrant, but she had to dismiss the idea for the man was carrying gold coins that had to be worth a mint. His sword was unbelievably authentic and the clothes seemed to be just as realistic. He was well built; his biceps bulged beneath the T-shirts that their father had given him. His hands had calluses indicating that he was not afraid of hard work. He could carry on a conversation, even though he spoke as if he had just been transported from the world of the past where both English as well as the old Gaelic were spoken. "We just can't abandon him. Not that he isn't capable of getting along, but he does seem…I don't know, not aware of how the world works."

"I agree." Her mother nodded her head. "We can't just let him wander around Ireland alone. He needs our help."

"There they go again, Pop. Out to save the world." Something the Hennessy women were prone to do. They took in strays only they were men and women rather than furry cuddly animals.

Donagh just smiled. "We are somewhat responsible for his condition."

"How do you know?" Connor had their attention. "Maybe he was always like this. Maybe he never could remember his name. Maybe this is all a scam."

"A scam?" Aislinn didn't believe that for a moment. "How do you suppose that? One, he offered us the gold coins for payment. Two, we were the ones that mowed him down or have you forgotten? It was an empty road, Connor. Did you think he just stood out there all morning waiting for the first car to come by? And just his luck, it was foggy to boot."

Connor lifted his hands to ward off anymore of his sister's verbal lashing. "Okay already. I still say we continue our trip. Let's just take the guy with us. Maybe he'll see something that looks familiar to him."

"That's an idea." Donagh smiled at his son. "Sound all right with the rest of ye?"

"Fine by me, but don't you think we should ask Doug?" Aislinn wasn't at all sure if the man would agree to tag along with them. Even though he seemed hesitant to the outside world, he had squared his shoulders taking in everything he saw as he tried to make sense of it. She could tell that he was actually frightened at times, but he was able to overcome his fears and made them explain what he didn't understand.

It bothered her that he didn't recognize simple things, like the light switches, cars, or even a telephone. Of course, she was not sure how amnesia worked. It could be that what he was experiencing was normal.

"Travel along with ye?" Dougray eyed the Hennessys one by one. He didn't know if that would be a good idea. He couldn't remember where he belonged, but a part of him felt that he needed to stay here. But at the same time, he felt anxious to be on his way. He was supposed to be somewhere. He had duties, responsibilities, and it was driving him mad that he couldn't remember what they were.

These kind people had been nice enough to take him under their wing. He knew that he was in Dublin for they had told him. The name did sound oddly familiar, but a thorough walk of the city did nothing to help him jog his memory. There were landmarks that he recognized well enough, but there were added buildings that he had never seen in his life. If he were to honestly admit it, the world out there was frighteningly imposing, for he didn't understand a thing of what these people seemed to take for granted. He sensed, rather than knew, for a fact that he was not ordinarily a man who was easily frightened, but he was most uneasy at the thought of being left alone to face the unknown. "I think that it is very good of ye to offer. I would be most pleased to accompany ye." He pulled at his shirt that fit him like a second skin. The clothes were not what he was used to. At first he had thought their garments were different because they did not come from this land, but last night when they had walked the town, he realized that everyone about him wore somewhat similar attire.

He nearly fell over himself, when he took in the revealing ways that some of the women dressed. Even the boyish woman, A.J., wore clothing that hugged tight to her slim figure. He glanced at her now over his cup that held the dark, bitter liquid Connor had informed him was called coffee. Of the four, A.J. was the one that made his head spin. He couldn't quite figure her out with her contradicting motives. She seemed to like him well enough, but there was a wall that she put up that clearly spoke that she did not wish him, or anyone else for that matter, to climb over. Yet she was helpful and considerate, almost to the point of annoyance.

She was not exactly what he would have normally been attracted to. Her dark hair was cut too short, and her eyes of midnight raked over him as if suspicious of his every move. She was a tall woman, but anything but large. He would almost say that she was rather slender for her height, but he couldn't help but notice that her arms were well defined as though she wielded a sword on a daily basis. She had long shapely legs that seemed to go on forever. She almost stood eye to eye to him. He did not see much of her mother in her other than the coloring perhaps. Her mother was quite small in comparison and she always spoke softly and patiently, whereas A.J. seemed always to be in a hurry. She barely sat still and she could talk an ear off you, if you let her. Yet she could be so silent that it made him wonder, just what was going on in that pretty little head of hers.

He noticed that she always carried a notebook, and a huge travel bag upon her back. He was most curious to know what she had in there that she needed to carry it with her at all times. Indeed she seemed to be an intriguingly complicated woman.

He found that he liked that.

Chapter Nine

Donagh sat down next to the tall stranger from the mist. He may not remember who he was, but it didn't matter when it came to judging a man's integrity. Memory or not that would still be intact. "How are ye doing this fine day?"

Dougray turned to look at him. "Well, I'll thank ye." They were silent for a moment, but there were too many questions that raged through Dougray's mind. "Ye're from around these parts?" He was sure for the slight lilt in his voice was still in evidence even though he spoke the English well.

"I was, but a very long time ago."

The younger man nodded. His eyes wandered over to where Aislinn had just entered. His gaze lingered just long enough for Donagh to recognize the obvious attraction.

"I'm not sure yer daughter likes me over much," Dougray commented making Donagh bellow.

"A.J. is a complicated woman. She tends to pick out the weaker of the male species for she has this overwhelming tendency to coddle." Dougray found the older man looking him over as if he were trying to decide just what category he fit into. He seemed to find him in good favor for he smiled as he spoke, "I do not think ye would want to be coddled. Aye?"

This time Dougray chuckled. "Nay. I may not have my memory of whence I came, but I feel that I am safe to say that I am my own man and do not need a woman to lead me by the hand."

"Hmm." Donagh touched his clean-shaved chin. "I do not think me daughter dislikes ye. She does not know what to make of ye is all."

"How so?"

"Ye are a man, and she has only been surrounded by boys. Connor and I excluded."

"Of course." Dougray again turned his attention toward Aislinn. She had spotted them now and was walking toward them.

"Tread softly, young lord, for she will be worth yer trouble."

Before Dougray could ask Hennessy what he meant, Aislinn had arrived. Both men stood and waited for her to be seated. "Such gentlemen this morning," she teased but her eyes showed the appreciation of the gesture.

"As a lady, ye should always be treated so." Dougray held her gaze making her feel slightly uncomfortable. She was confused by her own feelings toward this man. It wasn't just his rugged good looks, though he was very appealing. It was more his demeanor that seemed to engulf her with its undeniable strength. Just before she dropped her gaze, she saw his lips twitch with a smile.

"I'm starving." Connor had arrived and pulled out a chair, plopping himself down. His hair was matted on one side and on the other it was sticking straight up.

Aislinn chuckled. "Good God, Connor, you look like you just rolled out of bed."

Connor glanced at his watch. "Yep, just about two minutes ago to be exact. So what's for breakfast?"

Chapter Ten

It was already past seven, when they arrived in Sligo where Connor insisted that they hit the local pub that he had heard about from one of his friends.

It was packed full, making it hard to move around, but Connor and Dougray had managed to find a couple of chairs up at the bar. Connor was fairly drunk and his tongue was wagging, exposing a great deal of the Hennessys' secrets. "Take a look at this one." He handed the camcorder over to Dougray. "That was last Christmas. Yet again A.J. has a new loser hanging on her arm."

"You do not care for her choice of men?" Even he could tell that she was not in love with the man that insisted on hanging all over her. She smiled, but she seemed rather annoyed with the open affection that he was displaying in front of her family.

"My sister is a great gal, don't get me wrong. I just worry about her, is all. She tends to find herself with men who cannot stand on their own two feet. It doesn't help that she's the nurturing type." He took another generous swallow of his Guinness. "I tell you if she ever finds herself a real man, she wouldn't know what to do with him."

Dougray watched the Christmas festivities on this wonder that Connor had called a camcorder. It was amazing, but try as he might, he couldn't understand how the item worked. He didn't think it was magic or some kind of witchery for he noticed on their travels that others possessed similar items. He looked at Connor who seemed in deep thought. "Yer sister seems to be a strong woman."

"You can say that again."

"Why would I say it again?"

Connor laughed. "Just a saying, dude. That's all."

"Oh."

"A.J. has a big heart. You remember that." He slapped Dougray on the back.

"Aye, that I will."

"She tries to hide behind a thick hide but that's only because she's never met anyone that has been worthy of her heart." He snorted. "I guess I have been reading too many of her smut books."

"Her what?"

"Oh, I didn't tell you, did I? She writes romance stories. They're not half bad either, not that these are my type of books, mind you. I have to read it if my sister wrote it, don't I?"

"It would be the polite thing to do."

"That's what I say." He took another gulp plopping his mug down. "I only wish that she could find the romantic hunks that she writes about instead of what she ends up attracting." He shrugged. "She can't help it. She's a Hennessy. We open our door to all. We're the helpers of the sick and needy, even if they are a helpless loser. My sister just forgot that she didn't have to go so far as date them. I tell you, it's like she has a bum magnet attached to her somewhere. The bigger the loser, the harder she will end up falling for him. Luckily, she wises up before she ends up doing something really stupid like marrying one of them." He finished his drink. "Hey, don't repeat anything of this to her. God, if A.J. knew that I told you this, she'd kick my patootie."

"What about your patootie?" Aislinn slapped him on the back and he nearly toppled off his chair. "Are you already drunk?"

"Heck no, just heavily tipsy. Come to join us, A.J.?"

She glanced at Dougray, who seemed to be studying her a little too closely. Just what had her brother been telling him? She tore her gaze away, long enough to smile at her brother. "Sure why not?" She motioned to the bartender.

"What will it be, miss?"

"What are you two boys drinking?"

"Guinness," Dougray answered. He was growing quite fond of the dark liquid.

She nodded. "That's what I'd like. Can't leave Ireland without tasting Guinness."

Dougray noticed that there weren't any more stools and he stood. "Why don't ye take my seat?" he offered to Aislinn.

"Are you sure?" She seemed hesitant.

"Please." He motioned with his left hand. The moment she sat down the bartender came back with her mug. She stared at the glass for a moment. "Here goes." She took a deep breath. Lifting the glass, she took her first taste of the dark liquid and nearly choked. "Yuck. That's awful."

Connor looked over her shoulder to Dougray. "She's not a drinker. She'll probably be drunk from that one sip. I'll relieve you of that." She gratefully let him take the glass from her. "I'll get you something that you'll enjoy. Let your big brother take care of you."

"That's a scary thought." She smiled letting him motion for the bartender.

"Another?" The bartender looked at her.

Connor spoke up, "Something different for the lady. Do you happen to know how to make a *Cape Cod*?" He saw the blank look the guy gave him and rushed on. "Here let me help. Do you have any cranberry juice?"

"Don't think so, but let me check." He went to the little refrigerated. He looked over his shoulder and shouted over the noise, "No cranberry juice, but there's orange juice."

"That'll do." Connor yelled back. "Put a little Vodka on the bottom of the glass and fill the rest with orange juice."

"A *screwdriver*?" Aislinn lifted a brow.

"Yep. You can handle that. Not exactly Irish but...."

The bartender handed her the new drink and Connor paid. She took a cautious sip. "Not too bad."

Someone behind them decided to start singing. At first it was hard to hear him over the yells of the others but as his rich voice continued strong and true, others began to join in.

"We have a lively crowd tonight," Aislinn commented.

Dougray nodded. Everything seemed oddly familiar and yet none of it did. Had he been in a pub like this before? Possibly even this one? He looked down at the dark liquid he had been consuming. It was good, but didn't seem to be something that he had ever had before this night.

"What are you thinking about, Doug?" Aislinn drew his attention.

"Just wondering if I had been here before." He looked around the crowded room. He didn't think he had, but possibly he had been somewhere similar to this.

She placed her hand on his. "Don't worry, we'll find where you belong."

He smiled, but he couldn't quite shake the feeling that something wasn't quite right with all this. It was frustrating that he just couldn't put his finger on it. Like his name, he had told the Hennessys that his name was Doug Gray or rather A.J. had assumed that this was his name. *Doug Gray,* he said over and over in his mind, knowing it wasn't right.

"Hey, Patrick!" A man with reddish color hair pushed his way through the crowded pub, waving to someone that was over on the other side. "Patrick!" he bellowed again as he maneuvered his way past.

Patrick? Dougray repeated the name that seemed to spark a chord of recognition. *Patrick...Aye. Fitzpatrick.* He remembered. His name wasn't Doug Gray. It was Dougray Fitzpatrick of…of…" He felt that he was on the verge of remembering something important, but at that precise moment, Connor chose to topple from his stool breaking his concentration.

"Connor!" Aislinn was already trying to pull the young man to his feet. Dougray quickly put down his glass to help.

"I'm all right." Connor laughed, trying to stand.

"Sure you are. That's why you're sitting on the floor." Aislinn looked over to Dougray. "Would you mind helping me take him back to the hotel?"

"No trouble at all, milady."

Aislinn's brows furrowed. Did the man just call her milady? She didn't have a chance to ask for Connor leaned heavily on her shoulder nearly knocking her down. Luckily, Dougray came to the rescue before they ended up wiping up the floor.

"Here, let me take hold of him."

She nodded. They were just about to head out when the older Hennessys appeared.

"Hey, where are ye young kids going?" Donagh shouted above the noise.

"Connor has had a little too much to drink," Aislinn informed her father.

"I'm fine, Pop." He stood up straighter. "See?"

His mother gave him a withering look. "You don't look fine."

"Do ye want us to take him back?" her father offered but Aislinn shook her head.

"That's okay. Doug said he help me. You stay with Mom and have a good time."

He patted his daughter on the arm and nodded his appreciation toward Dougray.

Connor steadied himself as they started their walk back to the hotel. "Hey, let's go to another pub. I know this little…"

"No!"

"Nay!"

Dougray and Aislinn spoke at the same time.

"You guys are no fun." He was silent for a moment then he looked at Dougray and then to Aislinn. "You two should go out."

"Connor, stop it." Aislinn nudged him.

"Why? You probably haven't been on a date since what's his name?"

"Roger. His name is Roger."

"Yeah, whatever. So have you?"

"Connor, just concentrate on putting one foot in front of the other."

"You need a suitable man to go out with." He stopped in his tracks making both Dougray and Aislinn turn to look at him.

"What now?" Aislinn put her hands on her hips.

"He's a man." He pointed at Dougray with a sweeping motion. "I have to say with the memory loss and all, he's a better man than any of the other dweebs you have brought home."

"Dweebs?" Dougray asked not liking being grouped into the bunch, even if Connor thought he was better than the rest.

"You know, losers. Hey, I'm in no way saying you're a loser. You know that, don't you?"

"That's enough." Aislinn grabbed a hold of her brother's arm and squeezed it just a little harder than she had meant to, making him wince.

"Hey, that hurts." But he did pick up the pace, and surprisingly he was rather quiet.

They took the elevator up the room not wanting to chance the stairs. They finally got him in the room and he fell onto the bed. Aislinn removed his shoes and covered him with a blanket. When she turned around, she came up short surprised that Dougray was still there. His eyes were regarding her with a contemplating gaze. She spoke feeling she had to. "He'll sleep it off."

"I suppose that he will."

Again, silence. She swung her arms and then stretched them over her head. "I think I'll turn in."

"It is early." He was still watching her wondering why she seemed so edgy.

"It is?" She was feeling more uncomfortable, but it had nothing to do with him saying or doing anything other than standing there with the rich outlines of his shoulders straining against the fabric of his t-shirt, while looking handsome enough to…. "Do you want to play a game?" She ran to where she had thrown her backpack. "I have…let's see…cards, chess and…."

"Ye have a chessboard in there?"

She looked at him. "Well not a full-size board. A travel kit." She pulled it out and tossed it to him. "You interested?"

He gazed at the miniature box turning it over for examination before he again looked at her. "I'm up to it." He moved to the table to set up the game. "I've never seen such small pieces. Look. They stick to the board."

"They're magnetic, so when you traveling the pieces don't fall off."

"Ingenious." He lifted the black knight off the board then let the magnet pull it back. "Amazing."

Aislinn just shook her head. "The simplest things seem to fascinate you."

His startling blue-gray eyes sparkled at her. "They're simple to ye, but it's like I'm seeing all this for the first time."

"But you do remember how to play chess, don't you?" She pulled up a chair.

"Most certainly, and as I recall, I was rather good."

"Put your money where your mouth is." She pulled out a few coins and tossed them on the table.

He smiled and pulled out a few gold coins of his own. "Should I began or should ye?"

She waved her hand in front of her. "Go ahead."

He didn't think more than a few seconds before he made his move. She was just as quick and so it went for a few moments.

"Who is Roger?" Dougray asked sending her emotions into a fluster. She made a careless move.

"Connor obviously has been free with his mouth." She was angry with her brother and had a mind to wake him up out of his drunken stupor and tell him so. "Roger is someone of my past." Dougray relieved her of one of her rooks and she realized the mistake of her last move. Luckily she could still rectify it, if she remained focused.

"Was he yer mate?"

She nearly choked. "Mate?" Who talked like that? "He was…hey are you trying to distract me?"

He chuckled and his mouth quirked into a lazy smile. He leaned back in his chair studying her while he twirled the end of his mustache. "Just trying to get acquainted."

"Let's not get so personal, okay?" She concentrated on her next move.

"Roger was the man that hung on you, but it looked as though ye wanted to flee from his touch."

"How did…?"

"Connor shared yer…what was it called?"

"Christmas video." She remembered that her father had wanted to finish the tape and had brought it on the trip.

"Aye, that was it."

She made her move nearly grinding the chess piece into the board.

"So?" he continued knowing full well that she wished the subject to be dropped.

"Yes, that was Roger. Are you satisfied?"

He moved his bishop. "Hmm?"

"What are you getting at?"

"Nothing. It's yer turn."

He watched her make a few more careless moves that would cost her dearly. Obviously she was quite distracted by having her private life exposed.

"Are you hinting at something?" she inquired.

"Nay." He just smiled completely annoying her to no end.

"Why don't I believe you?"

"I don't know." He took his turn with a determined gleam in his eyes. "Checkmate."

"What?" Her mouth dropped open in amazement that she had actually lost. "You cheated."

"I most certainly did not."

"You purposely distracted me."

"Did I now?" he teased.

"Rematch," she insisted causing him to laugh.

"Ye don't like to lose do ye?"

"No." She smiled as she pushed her coins toward him. "Is that a yes?"

He sighed with a chuckle. "Aye, but I'll have ye know that I like to win too."

"Ah, you've uncovered another memory."

Chapter Eleven

It was early morning, long before anyone else had risen. Aislinn especially liked this time for she could sit and watch the sun rise high above the horizon and drink at least two cups of coffee without any interruptions. Today however, there was a light mist and she couldn't see the sun even if she had wanted to. She had already showered and decided that she wanted to walk down to the beach. She quickly dressed in her dark blue slacks and T-shirt. After running a comb threw her short strands and throwing on her gray sweatshirt, she slipped from the room. She didn't bother with the elevator, but galloped down the four flights of stairs. She could hear people in the kitchen already preparing for the morning meal, and the aroma of sizzling sausage and warm bread reached her nostrils.

She smiled at the young woman at the front desk. "Good morning."

"Good morning, Miss. Are y' going to be heading outdoors?"

"I thought that I would."

"It's a bit damp. I must warn ye."

"I don't mind. See you when the coffee's good and hot." She was out the door before the receptionist could say another word.

She headed down the empty road to where she knew would lead her closer to the beach. The mist wasn't too thick that she couldn't see where she was going and she hurried along. Making the short hike down, she walked close to where the water was slowly receding in and out. She sat down on her haunches and just watched, feeling at peace. She loved the smell of the salt air mixed with the mist and the peat fires. She could stay out here forever and not tire of it. "Yeats, I know now why you were so inspired here in Sligo."

"Yeats?"

Aislinn came to her feet in a sudden rush. It was obvious that she had been startled and she felt a little foolish when she saw that it was only their guest. "Doug, warn someone that you're approaching."

"I apologize. I did not mean to intrude on yer solitude."

"It's all right." They stood there for a moment not saying anything. "You're up early," she commented.

"I can say the same about ye."

"I just wanted to see the ocean, you know embrace it so that I could remember everything about it."

"So that ye can share your experience with Yeats?"

She couldn't help but chuckle. "That would take some doing since the man has been dead for about sixty or more odd years. He was a poet and his family used to frequent Sligo. He's buried in a churchyard in Drumcliff." She cleared her throat. "'Cast a cold eye on life, on death. Horseman, pass by!' That's the saying he requested to be put on his gravestone." She moved away from him then picked up a seashell.

"Ye are fond of poetry?"

"I like to pick up a book now and again and try to imagine what the poet was thinking at the time that he or she had written it. I have favorites of course." She had a faraway look on her face as they walked. He assumed she was probably thinking about one of those verses she was so fond of.

"Do ye know of one ye can share with me?"

She glanced at him now. "It's not an Irish poet, but I have always enjoyed this poem. It's by Dante Gabriel Rossetti called 'Sudden Light.'" She took a moment to go over it in her mind before she began in a clear voice. "'I have been here before. But when and how, I cannot tell....'" When she finished she looked at him wanting to know what he had thought of it.

"I have been here before." He breathed as though he were in deep thought. His gaze met hers. He spoke in an odd, but gentle, tone. "The poem seems to speak to me."

"Isn't that funny that you should say that, for those were my very words the first time that I had heard it."

They walked along the beach for a while not really saying anything and realizing that it didn't matter. They seemed to share a comforting silence where no words were needed.

Aislinn glanced sideways at Dougray. She couldn't help but admire the man. What woman wouldn't? His dark hair had been trimmed and brushed back, giving his face a more chiseled look, rugged without being hard. The mustache was bit much, but that could be shaved. His eyes were beautifully shaped and framed with dark lashes and the color was a startling silver, so light and clear. His hair wasn't quite as dark as hers, for it held tinges of auburn highlights that shimmered in the light. She had the urge to run her hands through the tresses, which completely caught her by surprise. She didn't even know the man, not really, but more important the man didn't even know who he was.

"I think that I have recalled my name."

"Huh?" She heard the last few words. "I'm sorry, what did you say?"

"I remembered my family name. It came to me that night in the pub. I didn't say anything before because I wanted to make sure."

"And you're sure now?"

"Aye. Dougray Fitzpatrick is what I am called."

She stopped and looked at him. "Not Doug Gray?"

He shook his head. "Dougray, together as a first name."

"We were inquiring about someone that didn't exist. It's Fitzpatrick then? We need to start over." And she knew that they were running out of time. Their vacation was half over already. If they didn't find out where he belonged, she wasn't sure what to do. She wouldn't feel right just going back to the States and leaving the man stranded. The guy didn't even have any money, other than the old coins he carried with him. If they were even real, which the more she thought about it seemed highly unlikely, for they would be worth a fortune if they were.

He had been watching the shifting emotions that crossed her face and knew she was struggling with how she was going to take care of him. "Ye know that ye do not have an obligation to me. I am sure that now that I know my full name, someone will come forward and claim me." He tried to smile but he didn't feel quite up to it. The thought of the Hennessys going back home and leaving him to this awkward world was almost frightening. He didn't remember any of the things he encountered other than the land itself and even that was vastly changed from what his memory recalled. He didn't understand it. It was like he had lived isolated from time and the world had sped by without him.

"Dougray." She tried the name on for size. It did seem to suit him now that she said the name aloud. "I wouldn't feel right abandoning you, until I was positive that you knew where you belonged."

"Why do ye feel this obligation? I am but a stranger to ye?"

She looked away. "Because I do is all. Partially because it was I that ran you off the road in the first place, but…." She met his gaze. "Don't be angry with me, I meant to tell you. What were you doing out there in the middle of nowhere and in the fog?"

It took him a moment to take in what she had said triggering the memory of lights coming toward him before he hurled himself out of its path. He shook his head. "Ye did nothing to cause my confusion. I do not blame ye."

"Maybe you should." She threw up her hands in frustration. "If we all left, what would you do? Where would you go?"

"I'd find a place. I am strong, healthy. I would manage."

Aislinn wasn't at all sure. Yes, he was strong and obviously well educated, but socially…well somehow he missed out in what was going on around him. Conveniences that she took for granted seemed to be completely foreign to him. Strange as it may seem, she didn't think his loss of memory was the reason for it. It was like he had walked from the past into this time and was witnessing hundreds of years of advancement in one fell swoop. She shook her head at that preposterous assumption, but still she had a hard time shaking the reality of it.

"What are ye thinking about, A.J.?" He could see the indecision behind those dark eyes.

"Just that I wouldn't feel right is all. Leaving you, that is."

He gave her a sad smile before he walked away with long determined strides.

"Hey, where are you going?" She easily caught up to him. She placed her hand on his arm halting his steps. "What was that about?"

He looked at her for a long time, his silvery blue eyes caressing her soul. She shivered and took a step back not quite understanding her own reaction.

He sighed with a tinge of sadness. "I may not remember a lot of things, but I do recall from the recess of my mind that I was a man that took no charity. I stood on my own two feet and never would have expected a woman to coddle me like an infant."

"That's not…."

"Nay?" he interrupted. "I see the way ye look at me and it is not a flattering observation. Ye make me feel less of a man and I don't like it."

"Well sorry. Excuse me for giving a damn." She started to storm away but his had flew out to stop her.

"I am not finished."

She tried to yank her arm away, but he kept his hold on her, infuriating her further. "Unhand me or so help me…."

"So help ye what? I only speak the truth to ye and ye run away. Does it trouble ye so that a man could be strong enough to stand his ground? Are ye a woman that only feels alive, if she can possess the man to bend to her will? I am no such man. I appreciate what ye have done, but I do not need ye to save me. Do ye understand?"

She pulled her arm away. "I understand that you are in ingrate. I…we all just wanted to help you."

"Aye, but to what cost?"

"What is that supposed to mean?"

"I fear, lass, that ye would possess a man's soul if he were to let ye." This time, he moved on ahead, and for a moment, she stood there gaping at his broad retreating back.

They both walked into the lobby just as Connor had come downstairs. "There you two are. I thought that you might have ditched me. Have you eaten yet?"

"Not yet." Aislinn purposely walked right passed Dougray and led the way into the now buzzing dining room.

"Where did you two go?" Connor eyed the tall Irishman and then his sister, who looked a little flustered.

"I was walking down at the beach," Aislinn answered coolly.

Dougray just shrugged. "Guess we both had the same idea this morning."

"Really? How very interesting." He saw his sister give him a sharp look but he chose to ignore it and moved on ahead of her. "Coffee. Where's the coffee?"

Chapter Twelve

Now that Dougray had discovered his true name they decided to backtrack. They had arrived back in Dublin that morning and had the good fortune to check into the same hotel they had stayed at on their previous visit. Connor and Aislinn had accompanied Dougray to see if the city now would trigger a memory. He stood in front of what they had called the Dublin Castle. He knew it too for the name was familiar. It even looked vaguely familiar, and yet like so many things, it did not. He took the tour with them and all along he kept thinking that he needed his sword. Little tidbits of his past seemed to come to his mind. King Henry VIII was a name that seemed to mean something to him but not in the sense of what the tour guide betrayed. He did not know of this man's death, and they spoke of his daughter, Mary then Elizabeth, a bastard child from the woman Ann Boleyn taking the throne. This Ann Boleyn was the granddaughter to the 7th Earl of Ormond, a Butler. He placed his hand on the side of his head, rubbing his throbbing temple.

"Is something the matter?" Aislinn asked becoming concerned that he was going to be ill. He looked a little pale.

"I need fresh air." He headed for the doors and Aislinn motioned for Connor to follow. Outside in the courtyard, Dougray viewed the remaining towers wondering why he felt that there should be more to the castle than what remained.

"Are you going to be all right?" Aislinn asked.

"I'm fine. Let's walk. Do ye mind?"

"Not at all." Aislinn glanced at Connor who shrugged. Each Hennessy took a place beside Dougray just in case the tall Irishman actually did pass out. He seemed disoriented, his face drawn and tensed as they walked in silence.

They passed the Christ Cathedral where Dougray stopped, eyes lingered on the place longer than necessary for he recognized it, but not with the bustling of cars that drove passed. Places that were familiar, but had changed in some way. Without a word, he hurried on. He had a cousin, he thought, or some close friend that resided....

Realizing where they were heading, a flicker of apprehension coursed through Aislinn. She wasn't afraid of many things, but St. Michan's church with its mummified bodies sent a chill down her spine. She didn't want to hear the ghost call to her as if it knew her, or feel the touch that seemed to want to possess her.

When they arrived in front of it, she stood across the street while Connor and Dougray crossed over to the other side to have a closer look. Dougray stood there for a long time just staring up at the church trying to force a memory back into his brain. He shook his head violently, frustrated that he couldn't. He jogged around the back until he was in the graveyard looking at the worn out headstones. He came to the doors that would lead down below to the tombs and stopped cold. Sweat seemed to pour down his face, as some hidden dread was forcing its way to the surface, but his subconscious was gratefully holding it at bay.

Connor moved beside him. "Do you remember something?"

"What?" He blinked his eyes trying to focus on the man beside him, trying to recall why he was there with him. The flashing scenes from his past seemed to fade in and out until he felt lightheaded.

Connor steadied him. "Are you all right?"

Dougray nodded. He looked up to see Aislinn cautiously crossing the street to join them. He couldn't help but notice that she was gnawing on her lower lip and her eyes were darting back and forth as if she were frightened of attack. Her gaze met his as he spoke, "Someone I once knew was here and yet…." He shivered despite himself. "Someone has walked over my grave." He watched Aislinn's eyes widen as if she was in fear for her very life. He was sure that the only reason she hadn't screamed was that her voice had simply forsaken her. He swallowed the lump in his throat, trying to shake the disturbing presence of doom. "Let us leave. I do not know why I thought to come here."

Aislinn was more than happy to move on and started to jog across the street barely taking time to see if cars were coming. She could hear the voice reaching for her. *"I'd die for ye."* She whirled around expecting to see a ghostly figure chasing after her.

Dougray placed his hand upon her shoulder and she jumped stumbling over the curb. She would have fallen, but he quickly pulled her to him. Locked in his strong embrace, she looked up into his smoky eyes that gazed upon her with such compelling magnetism. His brows furrowed, as if he was battling with his own emotions.

"Hey, you two," Connor interrupted the moment. "You're starting to draw attention."

They immediately came apart both feeling a little flustered over the strange sensation that seemed to electrify between them.

"Let us go back to the hotel," Dougray said flatly as he began walking away.

Dougray had been sleeping, dreaming, actually, of a life that was quite comfortable for him. There were people that he felt dear to him who were imploring him to return. In the distance, he spotted an old woman who had seen many years approaching. Her high cackle grated on his nerves. "Ye are tarrying, milord." She shook her head. "Did I nah tell ye, nah to do this?" Dougray woke up with a start, bolting straight up in bed.

His memory came flooding back nearly knocking him over with the reality of where his old life had been. He ran his hand through his thick hair. "I remember." He wasn't particularly sure that this was a good thing. "Ah, witch, where did ye send me? And how do I return?" He threw back the covers from him. He needed to go back to where the Hennessys had first found him. That had to be the answer. "From whence ye came." *Glendalough* was not far from where they had come upon him. "I met with the Butler near there."

As much as he hated just to leave like a thief in the night, he knew that he had to. Now that he was aware that some kind of magic was at work here, he was not sure he wanted risk telling the Hennessys about it. Most likely they would think him mad. Maybe he was mad. The thought was most unsettling making him anxious to be on his way at once to prove otherwise.

He left a good portion of his gold coins with a quick note of appreciation. He glanced at the strange instrument that held ink inside of it, so that he didn't have to dip it into an inkwell. "I will miss this."

He glanced around the room and knew there was much more that he would miss than just these modern conveniences. The Hennessys were kind, decent people who didn't care where he had come from. They just took him in and treated him as their own. He was saddened that he would never be able to repay them for their kindness.

Dressed in his own clothing, mantle and all, he slipped from the room. It would be a long hike. He hoped that enough of the familiar landscape was left so that he would be able to find his way.

Connor was the one to announce that their guest had flown the coup. He handed the note to Aislinn. "He had enough of us, I guess."

She scanned the hastily written words. "We have to go after him."

"What are you talking about?" Connor couldn't believe his sister. "The man wanted to go. Why do you think he left before we awoke?"

"I can't help it. If I don't at least see that he makes it to his intended destination, I will never be able to live with myself."

He shook his head. "A.J., A.J., when are you going to learn to just let go? You did your duty. He said goodbye." He watched his sister pack personal items into her backpack.

"What are you doing?"

"I'm going after him. I'll just offer him a lift is all. Then I'll meet you back here before we have to meet Mom and Pop."

"You're crazy."

"Maybe but I'm going."

"Then I'm going with you."

"You can't. If Mom and Pop arrive and we aren't here, they'll worry that something happened to us."

"And just what do you think they'll say, when I tell them that I let you take off to chase a man we barely know?"

"They'll understand." She was finished packing and gave her brother a quick kiss on the cheek. "It won't take me long. He couldn't have gotten very far."

Connor knew that it was useless to argue with her. She would just end up going anyway. "Be careful, will you?"

"Aren't I always?"

Driving was slow, once the fog seemed to roll in to surround her car. She was rather surprised that she even spotted the lone figure wearing the long thick mantle. He was farther than she had expected him to be. She slowed down to match his stride and rolled down her window. "I'll give you a lift."

He turned toward her with a suggestion of annoyance hovering in his eyes. "I thought that I was quite clear in the letter that I would no longer need yer assistance."

"Do you even know where you're going?"

He kept up his pace and didn't answer.

"At least let me drive you there. This way I'll have a clear conscience that I did all I could to see you to safety. You won't ever have to see me again."

He glanced her way seeing the determination set in her eyes. He wasn't sure if the exact spot was needed for him to go back to his time, but maybe he shouldn't take that chance. Still he was not sure it would be wise to have her there when he reentered into his world. He shook his head, struggling to maintain an even, conciliatory tone so not to offend her. "Nay. I do thank ye, but I must do this myself."

"What are you talking about, *I must do this myself*, business? You might as well just get in the car because I'll follow you, all the way if I have to."

"*Dar Dia*! Ye are a stubborn lass."

"Yep, that's me. Now come on, get in, will you?"

He threw up his hands in defeat. "Very well. If ye must insist what choice do I have?"

"None."

With all his huffing and the dramatic slamming of the door, it was quite obvious he wasn't pleased.

"Grumbling will not make me find the place any faster you know."

"Aye, that I am aware, but it makes me feel better. Please keep yer eyes on the road. I'll not want to be a party to ye running down another hapless victim."

She drew in a deep breath stopping her from the unpleasant retort she had wanted to throw at him. She had to wonder why she was even bothering. The man obviously didn't want her help. So why was she forcing him to comply? She refused to dwell on that question and kept her eyes straight ahead.

After about five minutes of cold silence, Dougray began to feel just a tiny bit guilty for his scornful words he had spoken to her. He was about to apologize, when she suddenly slammed on the brakes. He flew forward smacking his head against the dash. He slowly lifted his head and gave her a lethal glare.

"Sorry." She shrugged her shoulders. "But we're here." She pointed and he turned his gaze. He saw nothing but the thick white haze.

"Ye are sure of this?" Doubt was evident in his voice.

"Yes. Really, must you always question me?"

His eyelids fluttered and he clenched his jaw trying desperately not to return an angry reply. What did he have to lose? "I will have to take yer word. Thank ye again for yer kindness." There was a definite finality in his voice but again she refused to hear it. When he got out of the vehicle, she followed him with her backpack in tow. "It was there." She pointed below.

His eyes tried to make out something that might indicate a door of some sort, but for the life of him he could not detect a change in the land.

"What are you looking for?"

He didn't answer her question but looked back to where she stood. "I'm fine now. Ye can go."

"Here? There's nothing out there. You just want me to leave you out here in the wilderness?"

"Aye. This is where ye found me. I was by myself then. Was I not?"

"Well, yes, but...." Something tugged at her subconscious. This felt wrong. He shouldn't go down there.

"I bid ye good day." He was about to walk away but something in her gaze made him take pause, an inkling of remembrance, a fleeing thought of holding her close and comforting her. He shook his head trying to rid his mind of such fancies, but the feeling was too strong. On impulse, he pulled her to him. He told himself that it was only to distract her from wanting to follow, make her angry enough to leave him, but he knew this wasn't entirely true.

He gave her lips a whisper of a touch but it was enough to ignite a strong vivid desire that coursed through him like fire. She must have had a similar reaction for he felt it with the way her eyes gazed longingly at him. Surrendering to the crush of feelings that drew them together, he kissed her again, pressing every inch of her body against his. His senses reeled as the blood pounded in his brain, and his heart nearly leapt from his chest. He deepened the caress as though searching for a lost passion and trying to reclaim it with the softness she was offering him.

For a moment when he raised his head to look at her, he felt an uncertainty of emotions sweep through him. Stains of scarlet appeared on her cheeks and her dark eyes made him feel this invisible warmth that he had never felt before, not even from Ella. As much as he wanted to reach out and embrace this feeling, he felt oddly disturbed by it and mentally backed away. She was not of his world and her temperament proved that well enough. He smiled almost regretfully. "Ye are indeed a worthy lass." With that final statement, he left her side to become one with the mist.

She just stood there baffled over what had transpired between them, for she had felt something touch her, an emotion that left her senses reeling as if they suffered a chance of short circuiting.

On wobbly legs, she turned to go back to her car with a heavy heart, feeling certain she would never see Dougray Fitzpatrick again. She had only taken a few steps, when a low groan reached her ears. She whirled around expecting to see someone behind her. "Are you all right, Dougray?" She called out, but no one answered. She took a step forward. "Dougray?" The hackles on the back of her neck rose. She couldn't shake the feeling that she was entering something that she would not understand, but still she went forward through the cloudy mist where no light could seep through. She had to make sure that he was all right before she just drove away. She was about to call out again when a large hand covered her mouth, stifling the scream that was stuck in her throat.

Chapter Thirteen

Connor purposely watched for his parents out the window in his room. When he finally spotted them entering the hotel, he was still trying to decide what exactly he was going to tell them. "I should have gone with her," he said to the empty room as he let the curtain fall.

He went over to the bed and grabbed his baseball cap, slamming it onto his head. He decided that he would meet his folks downstairs. He would break the news to them at dinner. His last supper so to speak since his father was going to strangle him for letting his sister go after Dougray alone. "Should have gone with her," he said again as he entered the elevator and pushed the button.

Just his luck when the doors opened Francine and Donagh were there. "Connor," Donagh greeted his son. "We were just coming up to get everyone. Where's A.J.?"

"She's with Dougray." He sounded too nervous and his parents immediately became suspicious. "Let's go to dinner. I'm starved." He grabbed hold of his mother's arm as he came out of the elevator. "Where do you want to go?"

"Why aren't we waiting for A.J. and Dougray?" His mother wanted to know.

"They said not to, that's why. They were doing a little investigating today and said that they wouldn't be back until late."

Francine and Donagh exchanged looks of concern, but they didn't speak their fears. They let their son lead them to the hotel restaurant where they were sure he would eventually break down and tell them what was really going on.

It took a few glasses of wine before he did. "Okay already. You can stop looking at me that way. She told me not to go. She said that I should wait for you guys here, so that you wouldn't worry."

"Worry about what?" Donagh pinned his son down with a gaze that penetrated him to the core. That look brought back memories of his youth, where he had learned to tell the truth from the start or suffer the consequences. He gulped.

"I'm sure there is no need to worry."

"Get to the point of this story, Connor, and let us be the judge of that." His father folded his arms against his chest and waited.

"Dougray left us a note this morning stating that he was going back to where we had first found him. He thanked us, paid us with his gold coins and was gone before we awoke, but you know how A.J. can be. She couldn't let it go. She mumbled something about obligation, that she felt responsible for him, and that she just needed to know that he made it back to wherever it was he was heading. So she left."

"And you let her go?" His mother, who had remained silent until now, spoke up with obvious fear threading her words.

"Well, yeah. She insisted. By God, you know when A.J. sets her mind to something there is no stopping her."

"We have to go after her." Francine was on her feet, but Donagh placed his hand on her arm. She looked at her husband pausing with indecision. Connor saw that there was some kind of silent message passing between them for his mother seemed to calm down almost immediately.

He looked to his father then to his mother again in confusion as to what just had happened. "Maybe Mom is right. Maybe we should go look for her."

"We have nothing to worry about. A.J. can take care of herself, and as for Dougray, he is a good man. He will not see harm come to her."

Connor didn't know if it was all the wine he had consumed or if he was simply missing something vitally important. "I don't understand. What are you trying to say, Pop?"

Donagh sighed heavily as he took Francine's hand. "We will not find them now, son. It is too late."

Chapter Fourteen

As soon as Dougray advanced, no more than twenty paces or more, the strange overhanging mist abruptly cleared as if it had never been there. He glanced back knowing only moments before he had left the dawning of a new day, but now he faced the twilight hues of evening. He had entered his century, and to confirm it, he could see in front of him three rough-looking men who were just starting to make camp. By their appearance and their talk, they were individuals that he had no wish to encounter, especially alone and far from his own territory. He was grateful that they had not spotted him and he quietly moved back into the swirling mist, hoping to find another spot farther down to re-enter into his world. It was an unsettling feeling to think that low-hanging clouds could be a doorway to another time. Ireland was well known for its mist. What if he stumbled upon another like it?

He glanced around him and realized that the whiteness was not exactly typical. It looked different, with a peculiar smell of something that seemed oddly familiar, only he couldn't quite place its origin. It was more of a combination of things that he would call welcoming, like a warm fire and the fresh baked bread with honey. "Bah, what a fanciful fool ye have become. This is yer doing, Neala. Just wait until I get back to the keep and have a word with ye."

He stopped in his tracks for he thought he heard Aislinn's voice. Why wouldn't the woman listen and just go back to her hotel where she would be safe? How many times did he have to tell her good-bye? A part of him just wanted to keep going and let her fend for herself, but that only lasted about a fraction of a second. He couldn't leave her defenseless out in his world. He chuckled to himself, recalling the punch she had given him on their first meeting. Defenseless was the last word he should use to describe her. Still, he couldn't let her stumble upon those other men. With an irritated grumble, he hurried back the way he had just come. In his rush, he missed his step and stumbled over a pile of rocks, which, he was sure moments ago, had not been there. He hit the ground hard with a curse upon his lips. He quickly scrambled to his feet and continued on. Finally he saw her, and before she gave their whereabouts away with another shout of his name, he grabbed for her placing his hand over her mouth. Of course she struggled. He had expected no less from her, and yet he was not prepared for the force she laid into him. He fell back taking her with him, where she landed hard against his chest, knocking the air out of him. His grip had lessened and she was quick to use that to her advantage and broke free. She was on her feet. With an effort that he almost could not bring forth, he forced himself to lunge at her. With pure luck he grabbed a hold of her right ankle, but she immediately twisted around and sent a kicked with her left that nearly broke his nose. She was about to kick him again, but this time he was ready and quickly moved out of the way. She was free again and on the move, but he was determined to stop her. Using his full weight he knocked her to the ground, backpack and all. Stunned for a moment, she didn't move.

He finally caught his breath, just when she was about to put up another fight. "A.J.," he hissed. At the sound of her name, she stilled. "It is I, Dougray." He moved from her and she whipped around throwing her words at him as though they were stones.

"What the hell are you doing?"

He shushed her as his eyes darted to and fro, his hand going to the hilt of his sword.

"What's wrong?" She also looked, wondering what kind of danger they were in.

After a moment of complete silence, he rose to his feet and offered his hand to her. "Ye must go back. Leave this mist at once. Do ye understand?"

"You're scaring me. Why? What's out there?"

"Ye don't want to know. It's another world that ye best not witness." He dusted off his clothes and straightened his mantle.

"Then why would you want...?" He shushed her and she lowered her voice to match his. "Why would you want to stay here? I can drive you someplace else."

"I belong there."

"I don't understand."

"I am aware. I'm not sure that I understand it. But I do know that ye have to go." He took hold of her arm and started dragging her toward where he thought the car would be located.

"What are you doing?" She tried to pull away. "And why are we whispering?"

He continued to drag her behind him. "Just keep yer voice low. Nay. It would be better if ye were not talking at all. And I'm taking ye back to yer car and waiting until ye drive safely away from here."

"You're going the wrong way." Rancor had sharpened her voice to a pitch of annoyance. "The car is the other way." He stopped and turned to look at her.

"Are ye sure?"

"Yes."

He looked around him, but he couldn't make out a thing other than the swirling fog like mist. He was positive that he had been going in the right direction, but again with everything covered in this wall of nothingness, it was hard to tell. "Let's go." He started back where they had just come from, but she pulled on his arm. "What now, lass?"

"This way." She pointed to the right of her.

"Fine." He seemed perturbed if not a little embarrassed and would not allow her to take the initiative but continued to lead the way.

They walked in silence for a time, until it became apparent to them both that they were lost. He stopped and looked at her again with one dark brow raised high on his forehead. "Sure were ye?"

"I could have sworn it was the right way, but maybe when you attacked me and threw me to the ground, I lost my sense of direction. Excuse me." The last two words were drawn out to exaggerate every syllable.

He ignored her sarcasm and looked around him to see if anything looked familiar. There had to be a way of detecting where they were. "Come on." He grabbed her hand. His only mission right now was to see her safely out of here.

Another ten minutes went by and there was no end to the mist, in any course that they took. "Face it. We're lost," Aislinn announced the obvious fact, which infuriated Dougray.

"Ye think that I don't know this?"

"Hey, I don't like this anymore than you do."

He stopped suddenly and she plowed right into his hard back. He glanced behind him, his eyes glaring with annoyance. He turned away only to study the land again. Out of the corner of his eye, he caught a movement. An animal? He wasn't quite sure. He moved forward, slower this time. Then he saw it again. It was an animal, but it was too hard to distinguish what kind. It was either as lost as they were, or maybe it knew the way out of this mess. He hoped it was the latter.

"What do you see?" Aislinn searched the dense area before her.

"I am not positive." But he moved forward, still keeping hold of Aislinn's hand.

"Do you think that it's wise to follow something that you can't identify?"

"If it is a creature out to stalk us, it would have already attacked us. It seems that it knows its way around this wall of whiteness and unless ye want to…there." He pointed to a fleeting image.

"It looks like a wolf."

"Aye." And he pressed forward. He squeezed her hand assuredly with his left, but kept his right on the hilt of his sword just in case he had been wrong about the assumption of the animal's motive. A few more paces and they saw the white wolf standing there like a ghost, looking at them, eyes gleaming in the denseness. It appeared as if it had been waiting for them. As they approached, it turned sharply and proceeded forward only to disappear once again. They followed and ended up stumbling out of the mist as though the blanket had never existed.

Both Aislinn and Dougray whirled around, trying to get their bearings. Dougray with sword poised had released Aislinn's hand from his grip. He crouched down on his haunches searching for the prints of the wolf. He rose then and followed them back to where the mist was still thick. Had they missed the animal backtracking? It was as if it had led them out and decided to return…return to what? He didn't understand any of this and he was not sure that he wanted to.

One look around and he knew that he was indeed back in his time, for the land was more congested with foliage and trees that were missing in the latter time. He glanced at Aislinn who was studying him, her large dark eyes wide with apprehension and her right brow arched in question. He sighed, trying to decide how he was going to tell her that she had just traveled to another century. "We have nothing to fear now. The beast is gone." He sheathed his sword and walked over to her. He felt the wolf had led them to safety. So to go back now would mean what? They would enter another time, one that neither would be familiar with? He didn't want to even think of the possibilities. "We best not go back in there."

"No kidding." She glanced around her, not recognizing anything. How far had they walked? How long? It was so dark. "The car is obviously back the other way. How about we wait until the fog lifts so that we can see where we're going?"

"Let us sit a spell."

"What here?" She had no interest in sitting down on the damp earth.

"I have to tell ye something that may not seem plausible in yer mind, but it is of the utmost importance that ye believe it. Sit, please."

She folded her arms against her chest. "Just tell me."

"Sit first." He was losing his patience.

"I don't…."

"Sit!" He hadn't meant for the word to come out so harshly, but the woman could be so difficult. "Please," he added hoping to soften his demand.

"Fine." She took off her pack and plopped herself down. She could tell that he wanted to inform her of something of importance, but was obviously having a difficult time trying to decide just where to begin. He paced a few steps back and forth and ran his hand through his dark hair. She rested her chin on the palm of her right hand leaning her elbow against her knee, wondering what in the world was so momentous that he wanted her to sit down before he could even tell her. "I'm waiting." She decided to push him along. He stopped then and looked at her with…what would she call that look…pity? Sadness? Regret? She was so busy trying to decipher his expression that she hadn't heard, but the last few words of his obvious speech to her. "What did you say?" She blinked into awareness.

"Were ye not listening to me at all?" He threw up his hands in frustration. "I said," he took a deep breath and let it out with a rush showing his obvious irritable mood, "we will not be able to find the vehicle because it doesn't exist."

"Have you been drinking? Of course it exists."

"Not here. Not in this time and place. Ye see, ye have traveled back in time." He had begun to pace again as he sorted out what he wanted to say, trying to make some kind of sense of what had happened to them. "I am not all sure how this mystical happening occurs but…."

"Wait one minute."

He stopped pacing to face her.

"Traveled back in time? Are you insane? That was a heavy mist…." She looked to where the fog had hung so thickly, and now it was no more than a whispering smoke of what was once there. "Look, it's clear now."

He turned to see that indeed the wall had dissipated, leaving the open space clear to view. He fixed his eyes on her again, her expression indicating just how surprised she was that it had vanished. "Magic is at work here," he said.

"Magic? Good God, you're…oh forget it." She rose to her feet and grabbed her backpack. Swinging it behind her as she started passed him.

"Where are ye off to?"

She didn't even stop. "Back to the car. You want to play games? You can do that all by yourself. I should have listened to Connor. He told me just to let you go. If you had wanted my help, you would have asked for it. But no, I had to go after you like a complete idiot." She chuckled without mirth. "What a dolt I am. Chase after losers, only this time I picked one that has a few screws loose. Mister, I highly recommend that you see a psychiatrist. Maybe there can still be some help for you."

By this time, he had caught up to her keeping pace with her hostile steps. "It won't be there."

"I will prove to you that it is, then you can stop this insane talk of yours. You can go your way and …" She looked at him with a glare. "…I can go on mine." She walked a little faster.

"Fine. Ye find the vehicle and I will gladly seek out this…what did you call it…psychiatrist?"

He saw her eyelids fluttered with disgust before she answered him. "I'll go one better. I'll have one come pick you up. I'm sure they will have a nice padded cell waiting just for you."

"Ach! Ye think that I should be locked up? What have I done that I warrant such extreme measures?"

She stopped then and glowered at him. "Time travel? Does that ring a bell?"

"Aye, but ye have not disproved me." He waved his hand in front of him. "Move on, milady."

He showed such confidence that he was right that she hesitated for a moment. But then with a huff, she resumed her hike in silence, letting him continue to converse in his one-sided dialogue. It bothered her that he seemed obviously quite sure that he was correct with his assumptions. Time travel? It was ridiculous to even consider.

"Don't ye find it peculiar that it is now dusk instead of dawn?"

She swallowed the uneasiness that formed in the back of her throat. Something wasn't right. She picked up speed until she was jogging. She had to get back. She didn't even care that he was keeping up with her.

She saw the incline ahead of her and started up. She saw their footprints in the soft earth to confirm it was indeed the place, but when she reached the top, not only was the car not there the road was gone. She stopped in her tracks and her mouth dropped open. It couldn't be. She whirled around and pointed an accusing finger at Dougray.

"Where is it?"

In spite of the seriousness of the situation, he let out a chuckle. "What? The road, the car, or both? Ye think that I hid them?" He padded his clothing then held out his hands, palms up. "Not in there. Now where could I have put them?"

Without warning, she came at him with her fist flying. "God dammit! What did you do? What kind of trick is this?" She beat at him and he had to ward off her attack, the best way that he could without hurting her.

"Calm down. I did not do this?"

"Put it back. Put the road back now." She lunged at him again; this time he was ready for her. He swung her around, so that her back was to him, as he held down her arms in a fierce hug.

"If I could do what ye ask, surely ye don't think that I would continue to be insulted by ye." Still she struggled. "Settle down or I will be force to be rash with…. Ach!" He let her go the moment her foot came in contact with his shin. She took off running and he limped after her. His leg was no doubt bruised, but he couldn't let her continue to flee or she would end up into trouble. It was his obvious misfortune that he had to feel this obligation to protect the pigheaded woman, even if it was from herself. He caught up to her and tackled her to the ground.

"Get off me." She thrashed like a fish out of water.

"Ye leave me no choice then." With his knee pressed firmly in the small of her back, he removed the rope he had tied at his waist. He yanked her hands behind her back, wrapping them tightly. He knew he was not being gentle, but she left him no options. Just as unceremoniously, he threw her around. For a second, she was stunned that this man, whom she had befriended, would treat her in this way. The hesitation gave him the leeway that he needed. Even though she was nearly his height, he lifted her off the ground with ease and just as effortlessly tossed her over his shoulder. By this time, she had come to her senses and tried to squirm out of his clutches. That cost her a smack, good and hard on her behind.

"That hurt!" she screeched at him.

"And well it should have. If ye have listened to reason, I would not have to treat ye like a child."

"Child! Put me down me now and I won't press charges."

He just chuckled and didn't slow his pace. "Ye are not in a position to make demands. Now are ye?"

"Why you…." She kicked her feet and he smacked her again. "Ouch!" That stopped her from moving but it in no way stopped the flow of words that poured from her mouth. He had not known that there were so many words that could damn him to hell and back.

"Keep it up and I'll have a mind to gag ye as well."

He heard her take a deep breath to make another what he was sure an unseemly remark, but he halted her with another warning.

"Be careful."

She remained silent, but he could tell that she was still fuming. He had gone quite a distance before he felt that they were safe from the men he had spotted earlier. He lowered Aislinn to the ground. "*Fan ort!*" Then he resorted back to English. "Stay!"

"I understand you just fine in both languages."

"Then I shall use the one that I prefer," he said in the Irish, knowing it would perturb her. He eyed her for a moment admiring her courage. She had to be frightened, but she glared at him as though she could send daggers from her eye sockets. If it were possible, he would have been thoroughly slain. He shook his head, wondering if he should leave her even for a second, but he didn't have a choice. He had to secure the area. "So help me, A.J., if I have to chase you down, I'll turn ye over my knee and give yer bottom a beating that it has never seen before. Do I make myself clear enough for ye?"

She didn't answer but settled down against the tree trunk. He nodded then and left her there to make sure they would be safe for the night. He had enough problems with this troublesome woman without having to worry about being attacked.

Aislinn watched Dougray disappear into the forest, sword in hand. What had she gotten herself into? For about two seconds, she thought about running, but she ended up dismissing the idea because her hands were still bound. She wouldn't be able to move fast and Dougray would easily catch up to her. She had no doubt that he meant it, when he said that he would give her a thrashing. Her sore backside was proof enough that it would not be pleasant if he carried out that threat. But what could she do? Even though she didn't feel that she had to fear him really hurting her, she also knew that she couldn't stay with him. The man obviously was not dealing with a full deck. He thought that he could travel back in time for goodness' sakes.

Well maybe if she acted like a damsel in distress, he would bring her back to her car and she could get away from him.

After he had made a full sweep of the area and nothing seemed out of the ordinary, Dougray felt that he could relax. Finally he came back, and was half surprise to see that she was still sitting right where he had left her. His threat of a beating had actually frightened her? Somehow he doubted it.

He approached her then. She looked at him with her eyes shielded demurely behind half-closed lids.

"Oh, you finally returned, brave knight." Her voice was syrupy, much too sweet for her. He immediately became on guard expecting the worst. But not letting her know he was on to her, he played along just to see where this little game was going to lead them.

"Aye, milady. Fear not for I have returned." He bowed ever so slightly, trying not to smile.

"Kind sir, can you remove my bounds? They have become ever so uncomfortable." She moved slightly, so that he could see the rope pressing against her delicate skin.

He sighed. "I do not know if I should."

"I promise that I will not cause you anymore trouble. I didn't understand the gravity of our situation before, but now that I do, I will make sure to stay at your side."

He pretended to consider her obvious lie. "I do not know, milady…."

"Oh please, Dougray." Her dark eyes pleaded and she even pouted her lips making him almost believe her. Almost….

"Ah. If ye promise?"

She nodded her head completely unaware of the captivating picture she made when she smiled. "I promise."

He crouched down behind her intending to loosen the bounds, but then a thoughtful smile curved his lips. "Ye know," he said as he lightly caressed her arm. "When a knight rescues a lady, she usually offers him a kiss." He felt her muscles tense beneath his hand. His smile broadened for he knew that he had her. That temper of hers was ready to show itself. "Well?" he continued to push.

She slowly turned her head and he was surprised at how well she was able to control her emotions. There was not a trace of animosity in that sweet smile of hers and yet he knew, without a doubt, that if her hands were free she would strangle him. "I will give you a kiss and more, if you untie me."

He was rather enjoying this banter of mock pretense though he tried to keep his features deceptively composed. A losing battle he realized once his eyes centered on her inviting lips. His treacherous memories recalled the passionate kiss they had shared not that long ago, and he was eager to find out if he had imagined the fervor that had sprung alive between them. "A kiss first." He caressed her face. "Then ye can please me further."

For a second, he saw the flash of anger light her eyes but she quickly dropped her gaze, hiding behind half closed lids. "All right."

He took hold of her shoulders causing her to gasp in surprise, but before she could say a word, he planted his lips against hers. The sudden movement caught her completely off guard as he had meant to do. He kissed her hard, shocked at his own eagerness to claim her. She was rigid in his arms only for a second, until his mouth devoured hers into submission. Then just as suddenly as he had demanded her compliance, he pushed her away. He was shaken by the intimacy of the kiss, but somehow still managed a mock gleam in his eyes. "Dear lady, if you wish me to untie ye, ye have to at least pretend to enjoy this. I have had better tantalizing from a fish."

Her mind was still reeling from the way his lips had so easily roused her to passion and for a moment she was confused over his statement, but as his obvious insult seeped into her consciousness, all currents of desire vanished and reality whirled at her full force. A bucket of cold water could not have been more effective. Her eyes blazed with fury and her heated words just tumbled out of her mouth before she could stop them. "Then go find that river flowing creature and brutally assault it!" The moment she saw the corner of his lips tug at a smile, she knew that he had known all along that she was only partaking in an elaborate charade. He wasn't just a lunatic; he was a clever lunatic making him even more dangerous than she had originally thought.

Dougray immediately became contrite for he could sense the mistrust she felt for him, and to be perfectly honest, he couldn't blame her. He had never before treated a woman in this manner. He shook his head wondering what had gotten into him. "A.J., I am not going to hurt ye. I am only trying to protect ye, from others that might not take too kindly to our invading their privacy." His blue eyes pinned her down. "Maybe we can stop all this nonsense. Hmm?"

"Nonsense? What am I supposed to think? You are the one who has been acting like a nutcase. You talk about time travel like it is a simple matter of opening a door to the next room. Then you attack me, tie me up, and carry me off like you're a…a…a cave man."

"Tsk, tsk." He shook his head. "And here I thought ye would at least try to be a little understanding."

"Understanding? You kidnapped me?"

His expression clouded into anger. "I did no such thing. Ye followed me. If ye stayed behind like I had told ye, ye wouldn't be here now."

"Oh, believe me, if you had mentioned that you could time travel, I would have left you faster than you could say H.G. Wells."

"H.G....forget it. The fact remains, believe it or not, yer time does not exist yet and ye do not have to take my word on it. Ye will see soon enough. Now turn around."

"Why?"

"*Dar Dia!*" He looked skyward for a moment as though he hoped for divine intervention. Then his gaze of icy annoyance glared down on her. When he spoke, his voice was frosted with his impatience, "Because against my better judgment, I am going to untie ye so that ye will see that I am not the monster ye have made me out to be."

With the task done, he moved away from her, waiting to see what she would do. He knew he was taking a great risk for she could bolt into the night endangering them both to whatever predator lurked within its depths, be it human or not.

Surprisingly she didn't jump to her feet. She just sat there eyeing his every move, while she rubbed her sore wrists obviously weighing her options.

Aislinn glanced around her, knowing that nothing looked even vaguely familiar. Her car was definitely gone, and she was miles away from anyone. Even if she fled from this man, where was she going to go?

She glanced at Dougray who at this moment had his back to her. It was odd, but she didn't fear him even with his delusional notions. It was apparent that something out of the ordinary had happened here, and it was just as obvious that it was out of this man's control. That much she was certain. Thinking rationally again, she realized it wouldn't be wise on her part to just stomp off into the wilderness. She supposed for the time being that she would be safer with him.

Dougray waited patiently for Aislinn to break the silence. He knew that once she did he would know her intentions. He hoped with this ploy that she would realize he wasn't going to harm her. His tactic seemed to work for she hadn't as yet bolted into the night. But what was he going to do with her? Back at the keep, she would stick out like a sore thumb. Her appearance for one with her short, cropped hair and her clothing she wore were enough to have his people raise questions. She was taller than any woman that he had ever known and her eyes were darker than midnight, not like the lighter shades of the people of his keep. Within seconds they would know her to be a foreigner, but this was not his main concern. What really had him apprehensive was that she possessed such a defiant stance. She was more like one of his warriors than like a woman of genteel birth. He was not sure how he should present her or how he was to protect her without having her defy him every step of the way.

"Are we just going to stand around here all night?" She had moved beside him, but not too close. She may have decided not to run away, but she still did not trust him whole heartedly.

"Hmm? Aye. We will camp here tonight and then I will take ye to my home."

"You live around here?"

"Not exactly, but it's not far. Maybe two or three days…."

"Days? You must be kidding."

"Ye can leave then. See where the road takes ye, but be that I warned ye, that ye may not like what ye find." When he saw that she wasn't going to bulk him, he nodded his head. "I'll start a small fire, then find us something to eat."

She didn't argue, but she pouted and glared at him with those prodding, dark eyes of hers. After a while, he decided that he much preferred to have her raving insults than to have her icy, cold silence.

The earth proved to be damp as though there had recently been rain and it took a little longer for him to get a good strong fire going, but when he did he noticed that she had moved closer to the warmth. Obviously she was cold, but was not going to say anything. "I'll be back."

"Great," she grumbled under her breath.

"Did ye address me?" He cocked an eyebrow and she shot him another glare. He just shook his head leaving her to her thoughts.

Aislinn finally removed her backpack. She was grateful that Dougray had started the fire before he left. She felt almost comfortable now that the flames were beginning to thaw out her chilled bones. "Where is he going to find food?" she said aloud, not caring if he was in hearing range. "There's nothing out here." Hands warm now, she opened up her pack and pulled out her notebook and pen. This experience was worth something she supposed. She flipped to a blank page and wrote: "I have been abducted by a man that thinks he is King Arthur and wants to prove he is man enough to slay a dragon for the fair princess. Delusional? Perhaps. Time will tell."

Twenty minutes later she was still sitting alone. She curled her feet closer to her body and looked out into the darkness. She was beginning to be a little spooked. Where was he? Maybe something had happened to him. She stood and moved toward where she had seen him disappear into the night, debating if she should go after him or continue to wait.

"Miss me?"

She jumped and whirled around to see Dougray's all too handsome face grinning at her. She was about to reprimand him for scaring her nearly to death, when he lifted a fury dead animal in front of her face making the words choke in her throat. "Dinner is about to be served," he announced and then walked back to the fire to begin the process of skinning the thing.

Astonishment touched her pale face taking all of her will power not to gag. "You don't expect me to eat that, do you?"

He paused and looked up at her, an amused expression spread across his rugged features. "Ye don't have to, but there's not much else to be had." He turned back to his chore completely ignoring her, or so she thought. After a moment, she made a wide curve back to her side of the fire. She picked up her pen and notebook. She wrote: "He lures animals out and slices their throats with…." She glanced up at him wondering just what he had used. Dagger? She shrugged and wrote down the weapon of choice.

As much as she hated to admit it, the meat roasting over the open flame smelt really good and her stomach rebelled with rumbling noises that seemed to penetrate the silence. Dougray was watching her, an arched brow indicating his humorous surprise. A blush like a shadow ran over her cheeks and she quickly turned her attention elsewhere.

She felt rather than saw him move beside her. "Here." She turned to see the offering of a juicy, mouthwatering piece of meat. "I don't want to hear any protests," he insisted. "If I have to hear yer stomach growling all night, I won't be able to sleep." She grabbed the dagger that held the tantalizing meat, causing him to chuckle at her. At that point, she was simply too famished to really care that he was taking great delight in her embarrassment.

One taste and she was in heaven. "This is good." He detected a thawing in her tone.

"A compliment?" He had retrieved his half of the dinner.

She shrugged and took another bite. "Thanks," she added this time with a grin.

His eyes met hers from across the flames. "Ye're welcome."

Finished with her dinner, Aislinn took out her water bottle and took a large swallow. When she lowered it from her mouth, she realized that maybe Dougray might be thirsty too. She supposed that it would only be polite to offer him a drink, since he had been so kind to share his dinner with her. "Want some?"

"Aye." He nodded.

She closed the lid and tossed it over to him. After a few swallows, he wiped his face with the back of his hand. He eyed her from where he sat. She seemed to have accepted her fate at least for now, making him feel a little guilty that she had to be dragged into it. It wasn't her fault, after all, that she was trapped in this time. Hopefully once he spoke with Neala, they would know how to send her back.

He found that she was the one studying him and surprisingly with less hostility than before. She looked rather comely with the glow of the firelight warming her cheeks to a bright pink. *A.J.*, he spun the name in his mind. It was an unusual name, obviously a nickname of some sort, though until now he had not thought to ask her about it. "What's yer name?" He broke from his native tongue to converse in hers.

"You know what it is?"

"A.J. must stand for something."

"What's it to you?"

"Nothing." He shrugged with indifference. "I just thought that ye'd like me to call ye by yer given name. I guess I can continue to call ye lass." He saw the unadulterated fire in her eyes making his mouth twitch in humor. She had a strong spirit. He found that he actually admired her spunk.

"You've been calling me A.J. for the last two weeks, and now you can't?"

"I never much cared for it. Besides if I am to introduce ye as a lady…well Lady A.J. doesn't quite have an elegant ring to it."

She couldn't believe that he still held fast to this cockamamie story of his, but what the heck. She could give him her real name. What did it matter? Once they found civilization, he would be forced to face reality. "My name is Aislinn Jacqueline, thus A.J. Aislinn is a Celtic name and Jacqueline is French. I should thank the Lord that they didn't throw in a Cheyenne name to add to the other part of my heritage."

Dougray's face drained of any color. "Aislinn is yer first name?" He sat up straighter.

"If you're going to make some wise crack, I'll kick you in the teeth."

"Do ye know what yer name means?"

"Dream or vision, something of the sort. Why?"

Dougray raised his hands in the air, looking to the heavens as though he were talking to someone. "Old woman, ye do have a sense of humor." He started laughing almost hysterically, making Aislinn again think that he was indeed a raving lunatic.

"I fail to see what is so funny."

He stopped his chortling to observe her obvious disdain. "Nay, it seems that ye wouldn't. An old woman prophesized that I would cross to yer world, claiming that I was to seek a *vision*."

"So?" She shrugged.

"Well, does it not make sense? Yer name means vision. Seek a vision."

"That's the stupidest thing I ever heard. Couldn't you come up with a better story?"

"I am only telling ye what she foretold." He was frustrated with her attitude and fell silent again.

After a while, he decided to make himself ready for slumber. He removed his sword placing it beside him. He noticed that she was getting comfortable and had removed her shoes so that she could warm her feet by the fire. He studied her beneath half-closed lids. She was such a mystery to him. She was spirited and strong, and yet he knew that she sought men that were of no match for her. This much he learned from Connor. He had viewed her actions on the camcorder, but yet he had not heard her side of the story. Without dwelling on why he had decided to do so, he again broke the silence as if he was purposely trying to goad her into an argument. "Did ye want Roger to be yer mate?"

"What?" She looked at him with utter wonderment. "Are we talking about that again?"

"As I recall, ye never really answered me."

"Well he's...." What had he been to her? She had wanted the relationship to be more, but the passion was not there for her. "He was my boyfriend for a time. I certainly never thought of him as a mate, as you so elegantly put it."

He was totally bewildered by her response. He saw in evidence for himself that this Roger had been in pursuit. So what had she been after? "Ye were not intimate then?"

She made such a fuss over his simple question with her huffing and the rolling of her eyes that it left him even more baffled. He had no idea that he had aroused old fears and uncertainties in her ability to have a deeper bond. "Really, I don't believe it is any of your concern."

He shrugged with indifference. "Just making conversation is all."

"Well you could have asked about the weather or something. You have only been around for two weeks and with a memory loss, may I remind you. I don't know anything about you, and you certainly do not know me. And if you think...."

"Well enough," he interrupted. "I get the point." What on earth had possessed him to open his mouth? They were silent again for a good length of time. Then out of the blue, she decided to answer the question.

"No." He locked his gaze with hers wondering why she had changed her mind, and revealed a part of her that she seemed determined to hide. "No, we…Roger and I were not intimate," she added at the last moment making him raise his brows ever so slightly.

"Hmm. I figured as much, or at least if ye had been, ye would have tired of him soon enough."

"You what?" There was that high-pitch tone again. It was really beginning to grate on his nerves. "You were not thinking that," she continued, "or you wouldn't have asked." She folded her arms defensively against her chest and her lips pressed together into a fine line. He was beginning to recognize this angry silent stance of hers. It spoke that he had broken all the rules and had tried to cross her protective barrier. He had thought that the conversation was terminated but again she surprised him. "Why did you think that? How could you, when you never even met the man?"

"I didn't have to. It said it all in the few minutes that yer brother had me view the video. It was quite obvious that he was no match for ye."

"My match? What the hell is that supposed to mean?"

"I can easily see the fire in yer spirit. Ye would devour that weak man or…."

"Or what?" she snapped. "And Roger is not weak," she added just a little too late.

"He is, as ye well know it. He would have ended up extinguishing that flame ye possess, as if ye were a wick being covered with a snuffer."

"Oh, don't be ridiculous. Who asked you anyway?"

"Ye did. And I gave ye my opinion."

"I was in love with him," she insisted in a matter-of-fact way, which surely spoke the opposite.

"Then ye don't know what being in love is all about. But perhaps deep down ye really do know. Ye didn't marry the weak man. Think about that, Aislinn." Her eyes blazed over him, but he didn't care. Maybe it was about time that someone told her the truth.

"I suppose since you have me all figured out that you could tell just what kind of man that I should be looking for." His lively twinkle in his eye only incensed her more. "You perhaps? Are you strong enough to match my will?" She could have bitten her tongue off. What in the world was she doing? This man had practically kidnapped her. Did she really want to provoke him when she was at his mercy?

He gave her an appraising look as though he was actually seriously considering her challenge. She couldn't help but squirm under is icy blue stare.

Dougray found that he was not completely sure what he thought of her. Her short hair was rather unflattering and boyish. She was very tall, and thin, far too thin for his liking. He loved the feel of a woman with rounded curves. Still, there was something about the boyish lass that drew him. Maybe it was her strength that he liked. She was haughty to a fault and not afraid to voice what was on her mind. The other women that he had ever cared to converse with could never hold their own more than five minutes. Even his sweet dear Ella was not one to say much, and then there was Fiona but he could not think of one conversation that he had ever held with her. It had never mattered. If conversation was needed, he sought out one of his men.

Aislinn Hennessy was different in every way. He found he was intrigued with that. She was intelligent and had already proved quite interesting, if not just downright entertaining. He would never be bored with her that much he was certain, not when she took hold of an issue and wouldn't let it go.

His eyes lingered on her full lips. Even in anger, they begged to be kissed and those few stolen caresses that they had shared made him long for more. His gaze finally met hers and he knew instantly by the contempt in her eyes that he could never let her know any of this, at least not right now. He shuddered at the thought of what she would do with the information. For surely she would sever his manhood with one fell swoop and enjoy every torturous moment of it. She obviously was under the impression that she wanted someone she could control, and he was not one that would ever allow a woman to tell him what to do.

"Nay. I'd be too much of a man for the likes of ye." It took all his will power not to smile, for she nearly threw a temper tantrum from his outright rejection.

"Too much of a man! You…you jerk!" He had no idea what that meant but it couldn't be good. "You bastard." Now she was getting personal. He came to his feet and took a step forward. She grabbed her shoe and threw it at him. "Stay away or so help me, I'll render you unable to perform any manly duties from this day forth."

That halted him, but it didn't stop him from throwing back his head with a laugh. "Maybe I was wrong. With that much energy, a quick toss could prove to be quite vigorous. I'm willing to give it a try," he teased.

She screamed and threw her other shoe, which he easily knocked away. Still chuckling, he again sat down near the fire.

After a long moment of her glaring into the flames, she raised her gaze to him. "Give me back my shoes," she demanded without even a please.

"Come over here and get them yerself. Unless," he paused as he thoughtfully twisted his mustache, "you're afraid to come near me."

"Humph! Afraid indeed."

He lifted his brows in a bemused gesture and waved his hand toward the items she wanted so badly.

"Oh, go to hell." She curled up her knees and hugged them close to her chest.

"Ye keep cursing in that fashion and most likely ye will be joining me in those fiery depths. Just think, an eternity together, now wouldn't that be grand?" Her dark eyes clawed like talons before she jumped to her feet to retrieve the shoes. He pretended to lunge toward her and she jumped back with a scream upon her lips. He just shook his head, chuckling uncontrollably.

"You think you're so funny?" She stomped back to her seat a safe distance away from him and away from the warmth of the fire.

He was still smiling as he added wood to rekindle the blaze. Then he made himself comfortable on the hard ground. Shaking out his mantle he draped it over him and closed his eyes. After a moment, he chanced a look at her still figure, and addressed her as though he had forgotten that she had been there at all. "If I were ye, I wouldn't stray too far. It gets mighty cool at night and there be animals out there too." He closed his eyes again, but only halfway. He could see her nervously looking around her. He turned to his side confident that she would move closer. "*Oiche mhaith*, Aislinn."

"Good night indeed," she mumbled under her breath. Just what she wanted to do, spend a night out in the open with a madman and animals lurking in every corner.

She sat for a long time determined to stay awake, but her body rebelled and soon her eyes started to droop. She woke with a start when she almost toppled over. She was cold and little afraid. It was so dark out there. She scooted closer to the fire, but the warmth didn't quite take the dampness away and she shivered. Her eyes wandered over to where Dougray was lying and she noticed that he was not sleeping, but watching her. "Ye are cold," he said in English without a hint of sarcasm.

"Of course, I'm cold. I'm used to sleeping in a nice warm bed. Not on the hard cold dirt."

"Come here then." He lifted the mantle indicating that she crawl in with him."

"I will do no such thing."

"Lass, I did not say that I was going to ravish ye. To get warm, that's all. Come on now. I swear that yer virtue will still be intact come the morning's light." He could tell that she was weighing the options. Warmth obviously won out.

"You swear?"

"Aye."

She stood and hurriedly walked around the fire to where he lay with his offering. She stretched out her long body next to him with her backside against his hard chest. She felt his arms brush over her as he drew the covers. In a few minutes, she actually began to feel every part of her body start to warm. Only she wasn't sure if it was because of the blanket covering her or the fact that she was so close to this man that played havoc with her emotions.

"There now, isn't that better?" His voice caressed her.

She swallowed the lump in her throat before she half turned to look at him. "Yes. Thank you."

"Sleep now." He patted her shoulder and turned around on his side so that their backs touched each other. Aislinn was surprised that she actually felt comforted by his broad back leaning against hers. Soon she began to relax and blessed sleep overtook her.

Chapter Fifteen

They started out again in early hours of the morning, shortly after dawn. Aislinn grumbled that she was hungry but it was more in protest of his grumpy attitude, and his relentless pace he was making her endure. Dougray had enough of her complaints and whirled on her, his silvery eyes clouded like thunderclouds. She clamped her jaw shut and backed up a few steps, but she was still brave enough to counter with an icy stare of her own. He opened his mouth to impale her with his fury when he took notice that everything around them had become unearthly still. Immediately, he became alert and unsheathed his sword and motioned for her to be silent. She came up very close to him. Chewing her lower lip, her dark eyes darted to and fro trying to see if she could detect anything out of the ordinary. She encircled her arm around his forearm making him glance at her in surprise.

Her touch sent him propelling where he had no place to be, for at that moment they could be in deep peril. If she only realized what a beautiful picture she betrayed…. She was anxious like a damsel in distress. Surprisingly he had this sudden urge to kiss her contemptuous lips and tell her everything would be all right, that he was here to protect her.

She must have felt his heated gaze because she finally took notice. She immediately put up the barriers, squaring back her shoulders with her usual haughty stance. "What?" Then her eyes wondered to where her own arm was resting, finally realized that in her sudden fear, she had just latched onto him like a frighten child. She immediately dropped her arm and took a step back.

"Just stay here," he demanded of her. He hadn't intended to be so gruff, but his emotions had caught him by surprise. He saw her eyes flash with anger, but he quickly left her side to investigate what had caused every bird to stop singing.

Aislinn backed up to the nearest tree wishing that she had insisted that she go with him. She heard a twig snap in the quietness of the forest and knew she wasn't alone. "Dougray? Is that you?"

Silence was her answer and she backed up a step. She caught a glimpse of movement to the side of her, but before she could scream a large grimy hand clamped firmly over her mouth. The man held her against his chest with a dagger pressing against the delicate part of her neck, indicating that he meant business. "Make a sound and we won't hesitate to slit ye throat. Do ye understand, lad?"

She didn't think this was the right time to correct him of her gender, and just nodded her head that she understood perfectly. He dragged her away where two other men of the same caliber were waiting. The man who held her fast shoved her to a kneeling position. She saw Dougray come into view and attempted to make a move to be free of her captor, but again the man pressed the knife to her throat.

Dougray looked around him, perturbed that Aislinn was not where he told her to wait. "Now where did she go? Blast the foolish lass." He started forward and Aislinn knew if she didn't do something, he would walk right into the ambush. She closed her eyes, praying she would not have her throat slit for her actions. She threw all of her weight back upon her captor toppling him over.

Dougray heard the noise and was ready for anything. "Aislinn?"

"It's a trap!" she managed to say as she jumped to her feet, facing the man with the dagger. "There are three of them."

"I have two in my sight now." He raised his sword to protect himself from the charging men.

Aislinn could hear the clanging of metal upon metal and she felt sick to her stomach. This was becoming all too real.

"So ye are a lass, are ye now?" The man grinned, his blackened teeth visible. He took a cautious step toward her. "Now, lass, no more trouble, aye?"

"Trouble is my middle name." She surprised him by making a move herself and it wasn't to flee. Before he could jump aside, one long leg swept up with a hard kick to his hand causing the dagger to fly from his grip. She swung around and with the other foot made contact with his face. The jar knocked him sideways, but somehow he managed to stay on his feet.

Aislinn knew that she was fighting for her life and every move that her father had ever taught her came flashing back full force. Her fist plowed into the attacker's nose, the other at his neck, and still another quick kick where she knew it would count. The man doubled over in agony and was unable to let out a groan for he could barely breathe through his bruised windpipe.

Seeing him fall to the ground made her finally pause in her assault, though she still bounced on the balls of her feet ready to plow into the guy, if he even looked at her funny. Finally realizing that the man was incapable of being a threat, she headed to the clearing to see how Dougray was fairing.

She nearly tripped over the bloody body of one of the men that Dougray had already killed. Luckily she was quick to sidestep before she fell. She could see Dougray battling with the remaining ruffian. Their swords clanged menacingly, each determined to draw blood. Her eyes searched for something she could use as a weapon. She grabbed for a rock and waited until Dougray moved out of harm's way. With all her strength she hurled it, but at the moment of impact that should have hit the enemy, Dougray had moved into the direct line of fire. He cried out in pain and barely jumped out of the way, when the man lunged with his sword.

Aislinn's hands went to her mouth. "Oh God!" She moaned for she nearly caused Dougray to be slain.

He glanced her way. "Don't help, lass!" He fended off another blow.

She didn't heed his words. She wouldn't sit back and watch him get cut down. She grabbed another rock to throw, but by the time she had turned, the two men had moved the battle right where she was standing. She tried to move out of the way, but ended up knocking into Dougray throwing him off balance. She fell on top of the dead man and let out a deafening scream. At least this caused a distraction, so that Dougray could move out of harm's way.

"I said to stand back!" Dougray barked at her.

She may have considered his request if the man he fought wasn't so huge. He had to weigh close to three hundred pounds, but he was agile on his feet and each powerful blow he threw nearly knocked Dougray to the ground. The giant of a man swung up and around making Dougray's sword fly out of his hands. He barely scrambled out of the way as the ruffian sliced through his shirt. It was only luck that the blade did not touch his skin. "Aislinn, weapon now!" he shouted at her.

She looked beside her and grabbed the dead man's dagger. She hurried to her feet. "I thought that you didn't want my help."

"I changed my mind." He moved around just as she tossed the weapon. With a quick throw of his arm, the dagger lodged into the man's throat. For one horrible second, Aislinn thought that the man was not going to stop. He had raised his sword above his head, but before he could give the final blow that would have ended Dougray's life, a horrible gurgling sound bubbled from his lips and his eyes glazed over. He fell hard to the ground causing the earth to shake.

Dougray's chest was heaving from the exertion, but quite grateful to still be alive. He quickly glanced at Aislinn, his eyes taking in the length of her as he searched for any life-threatening injuries. "Are ye all right then?"

She nodded, not able to speak.

"The other one, where is he?"

She had forgotten all about him. "I left him over there." She pointed to the bushes.

"Alive?" He lifted his brow wondering how she could have managed to get away from the man and without a weapon.

"He was alive when I left him, but hurting pretty badly."

Dougray picked up his sword and cautiously went to investigate. Aislinn was close behind.

The man was lying unconscious upon the ground and in his own vomit. Dougray crouched down and grabbed hold of the man's hair to lift his face. He was shocked at the bloody mess. The man's nose was definitely broken, his lips were swollen and his neck was sorely bruised.

Dougray let go of the man's hair and his head bobbed to the ground. He stood looking down at the man in awed silence. Thoughtfully rubbing his chin, he then glanced back at Aislinn. "Ye did this damage?" His eyes roved over the woman in a new light. She had height on her side, that much he would give her, but she seemed rather thin to him, barely any meat at all on her bones. How in the world did she manage to beat a seasoned warrior to a bloody pulp?

Aislinn shrugged almost embarrassed at what she had done. "I was scared."

"Aye. Remind me to not startle ye, then." He knelt down and nudged the man until his eyes opened. The guy jumped back only to lie back down in obvious pain.

"Don't hurt me." He rolled up into a ball, holding his private parts as though he feared they were going to be removed from his body.

"Ye may live to see another day, if ye answer my questions well."

The man nodded.

"Are ye one of Fingham Butler's men?"

"Nay," he croaked.

Dougray pressed the sword against the man's already bruised throat. "Are ye telling me the truth?"

"Aye. I swear that I am." It was pathetic the way he was whimpering.

"Who else was with ye?"

"No one, but me brothers, that is all."

"There was no one else?"

This time he did let out a cry. "Nay! I swear on me dear sainted mother's life."

Dougray stood then and sheathed his sword. "Well then, ye best heed my warning. Ye may send someone to collect yer brothers for they did not fair as well as ye did. Then I had better not see ye again in these parts or ye will be joining yer brothers' fate."

"Aye. Ye will never lay eyes on me from this day forward."

"Good. Now get up and move before I change my mind."

The man could barely get to his feet. He warily glanced at Aislinn as if he thought that she might attack him again. He hobbled away in one direction, and after Dougray gathered their belongings, he hurriedly led Aislinn in the other.

"We have to keep moving. I want to put as much distance from this place and us. No telling who else may be lurking near by." He glanced at her pale face. "Are ye going to be all right?" She looked at him with pain-filled eyes before she bolted from his side into the nearest bush. "Where are ye…?" He heard her retching and knew. He waited patiently for her to finish, sympathizing with how she felt. When she could somewhat compose herself she reappeared.

"Better?" He handed her a cloth to wipe her mouth.

She nodded avoiding eye contact. "I don't know what got over me. I just…I've never seen anyone killed before."

"It's a natural reaction. My first experience with battle, I was so scared that I threw up before we went, and then for the next week, every time I thought about what I had seen I'd be sick all over again."

He looked so powerful to her. It was hard to imagine that he could be frightened of anything. "Really? You're not just saying this to make me feel better?"

"Would I do that? Really, it's true. Here let me take yer pack." She handed it to him without an argument. "We had no choice in the matter, Aislinn. It was either them or us, and frankly, I think we made the better choice."

"Killing doesn't bother you?"

"Oh it bothers me enough. I just try not to think about it, once it's done. Come now. We'll get away from here and ye'll see that ye'll feel much better then."

"Are you actually trying to be civil to me?" She tried to smile and he returned the gesture.

"I know that ye won't believe this, but I have been known to on occasion to be quite charming."

She sighed as she moved past him. "Charming? Hmm. This I would have to see."

He easily matched her stride. After a few minutes, he turned to her. "Where did ye learn to…?" She looked at him without missing a step. "Ye know to defend yerself in such a fashion?"

"My father taught me the fundamentals of defending myself. And at the gym, I have been taking kickboxing lessons. The class was meant to keep me in shape, not to fight villains of the forest."

He shook his head. We speak the same language, but at times, I fear that I lose the meaning behind yer words. "Gym? Kickboxing?"

"A gym is a place where people go to work out." He still looked confused and she went on to explain. "You prepare yourself for battle, don't you?"

"Of course."

"That is what the gym is used for, only it isn't necessarily for self-preservation. It's for fun, to keep in shape for a healthier existence."

"Hmm. And the kickboxing?"

"It's a series of kicks and punches that works almost every muscle in your body."

"It keeps ye strong?" He looked her over not even hiding the fact that he was actually checking her out.

"Hey." She jumped to the side to face him. "What do you think you're looking at?"

"Just seeing if the classes were working."

"And?" She gave him a cocky grin.

"And what?"

She stepped beside him again with a nudge. "I've worked really hard to stay in shape."

He glanced at her with an unusual glint in his eyes. "You seem a bit thin to me, but…." He shrugged. "I say that it suits ye well." It sounded like a compliment, but again she wasn't sure with him.

"I can take my pack now," she offered, her hand already stretched out to take it.

"I've got it," he insisted.

"No really. I can take it."

"I said that I have it."

She stopped moving causing him to go the few spaces back to where she was standing with her hands on her hips. "The pack…please."

He shook his head and handed her the item. "They teach ye this at the gym, also?"

She slipped her arms through the straps of the backpack before she spoke, "Teach me what?"

"Not to need anyone." He didn't wait for her reply as he turned on his heel and moved on through the foliage. For a moment, she just stood there. Is this how he viewed her? As someone that didn't need anyone? It wasn't exactly a flattering attribute, when it was put that way. She wanted to be independent, but she didn't want to be alone. How did one accomplish both?

She moved forward.

Now that some of her fear had subsided, she had time to think. The reality of everything that had happened, from the moment she left her car, came at her full force. Dougray had been telling her the truth. She had somehow stepped back in time, for how else could she explain the sword fighting, the strange clothing, and the fact that the land was a little more rugged, full of trees and foliage that should not exist?

She shook her head. It wasn't possible, was it? She glanced at Dougray trying desperately to think of a plausible explanation for why he hadn't understood a thing about her present time. The blow to his head had not caused him to forget modern conveniences. It was simply that he had never experienced them. "Stop!" she bellowed, causing Dougray to draw his sword in fear that they were once again under attack. When he saw that they were not in danger, he re-sheathed the weapon and walked over to her with a question upon his lips. He was about to reprimand her for startling him so, but then he realized that she seemed on the verge of collapse.

"Ye are trembling." He instinctively pulled her to his chest and he heard her intake of breath as though she was trying desperately not to cry. "It's all right." His large hand gently rubbed her back.

"How can you say that?" She relaxed against him, her chin resting on his broad shoulder. "I have traveled back in time."

He smiled sadly. "So ye believe me now, do ye?"

She pulled away and looked at him. "I don't want to, but...." She lifted her hands in a shrug. "How? Why?"

"I do not have the answers, but I know of a woman that may."

"She can get me back to where I belong?" She glanced around her, feeling insecure, not safe.

"I do not know, but maybe."

"That mist…it wasn't normal was it?"

He shook his head. "It must be a passageway, but I do not know how it appears or when. These questions, I hope Neala will be able to answer."

"Neala?"

"Aye. The old woman I spoke of. She knows of the old ways that have been forgotten."

"She lives at your house?"

He chuckled. "Nay. She lives among the trees where she feels more at home." He put down his satchel. "Sit and I will procure us something to eat and then we will talk some more. I am sure that ye have many questions."

She nodded and removed her own pack. By the time that he had returned from hunting, she already had the fire going. "Self sufficient, too," he said under his breath.

"Did you say something?" She looked up as he approached.

"Nay." He thought it better to refrain from repeating the words for he was too tired to argue with her.

As the meat cooked, he tried to tell her a little about where they were heading and about the people that she would encounter. He needed to prepare her, so that she could adjust.

"Now who did you say was your trusted friend?" She was taking notes. One day, he would like to see all that she had written in that journal of hers. She looked up at him, waiting for the answer.

"Murrough O'Donoghue. Ye won't be able to miss him. He'll be the tall man with the red hair and a drooping mustache."

"A mustache like yours?" She shook her head and he couldn't help but chuckle at her odd expression.

"Why do ye speak of my mustache in the peculiar tone? Do ye not like it?"

"Well…" She debated about a half a second not to tell him the truth, but she knew that he would see right through a blatant lie. "…not really."

"And why not, may I ask?" Rather than being offended, his silvery eyes gleamed with amusement.

"It's too bushy and long. You have a rather handsome face and I don't know why you'd want to hide it." His brows shot up in surprise at her blunt honesty. Maybe she shouldn't have said anything, but once she was started there was no stopping her. "Frankly, I don't know how the other women you kiss can stand the ticklish feeling, when it's pressed to their lips." For a moment her whole face flushed from what she had just revealed, but she quickly brought her attention to her notebook. "Now Murrough and you have been friends for a long time?" He marveled at how quickly she could change the subject.

He was still smiling when he answered her. "Since we were boys. We schooled together commissioned by my father and grandfather. Ordered by the king. Education was best abroad, so as to learn the ways of others. We returned after I learned of my parents' death." He avoided meeting her gaze, while he busied himself by testing the meat to make sure that it was cooked through.

"How did they die? Your parents?"

His face clouded with uneasiness as he carefully removed the meat from the flame. Only then did he carefully meet her gaze. "There was a fire…they didn't make it out before the ceiling collapsed." He saw that she was about to question him further and he headed her off. "Do ye mind if we do not discuss this? It is a uncomfortable for me to do so."

"Sure," though she was disappointed that he wouldn't open up to her. He had told her about his home and of the people he knew, but he was carefully guarded when it came to anything that pertained to him. She found that she actually wanted to get to know him. When he wasn't completely annoying her with his arrogance, he was rather pleasant company, not to mention that he was extremely good looking in a rugged sort of way, but there was also a polished essence about him. He had such compelling eyes that changed to different shades of blue depending on his mood, and the man had many she came to find out. They were a pale serene color when he was smiling, but a thunderous gray when his temper flared. She noticed that when he had kissed her they changed yet again to a deep, silvery smoke color hue. His hair was dark but the strands glimmered with auburn when the sun hit them just right. His firm features that forever had a shadow of a beard gave him even more of a manly aura, and the confident set of his shoulders made her want to reach out…. She cleared her throat rather disturbed where her mind had led her.

Once again she tried to drag some information out of her host. "So, Dougray, is there a girl back home that's pining away for you…or is there possibly a wife?"

His eyes clouded to a turbulent gray and his face closed as though he was guarding a secret. "Nay, there is no one that matters. Here." He handed her a piece of the freshly prepared meat. "Ye better eat before it gets cold." He stood then and walked away.

His sudden departure made her wonder what he was hiding. Was there a wife then? He said there wasn't anyone that matters. That wasn't exactly the same thing as saying there was no wife. "How very interesting." She jotted down in her notebook. Dougray has a secret. She underlined it, determined to find out just what that secret was. Closing her notebook, she began devouring her lunch. He was secretive, but boy, he could cook up a good meal.

The day had warmed up considerably and Aislinn removed her sweatshirt. Stuffing it into her backpack, she caught sight of the things she had carelessly thrown in there when she had packed for her vacation. Thank goodness she had brought her pack with her. It held all of her toiletries, regular Tylenol, the one with codeine that her dentist had prescribed for her when she had needed a root canal, and of course the penicillin that she never got around to taking. How he had scolded her for that. She had been fortunate that her tooth hadn't bothered her. Her tongue glided over the tooth that had been recently crowned.

"What is going on in that head of yers?" Dougray had been studying her for some time now. "Ye have a hundred and one expressions. I have no doubt that it would take me a lifetime to learn what each one means."

"My mother used to tell me that I wore my heart on my sleeve and there was no doubt to the way I was feeling."

"Aye, but she was yer mother. She knew ye from birth. She would recognize what the crinkling of yer nose meant."

She couldn't help but chuckle. "That's easy. I smell something unpleasant and it might just be me. I could use a shower just about now."

"The shower," he sighed. "Aye, warm water at a touch of hand, this I will miss." He glanced at her again. "In yer world, ye tend to bathe quite frequently and ye still seem healthy." He recalled his many years in England, where he was frowned upon if he had insisted on bathing. The English tended to try and cover up their odor with expensive perfumes.

"The cleaner the better. Stops diseases from spreading, infections from starting, and it makes living with one another a little more pleasant."

He nodded as he thought this over. He would have to keep this in mind. "Same with the teeth?" He remembered the toothbrush that Connor had bought for him. He had packed the item in his bag, along with the mint paste.

"Keeps the teeth healthy as possible. We've come a long way with that. No more having false teeth by the time you're a grandparent."

"Hmm. I like that idea. I'd hate to have to give up my meat."

"That's a whole other issue, but we can cover that later. Is there any chance of taking a dip in the lake?" She pointed up ahead.

"Aye. But let's climb to the upper portion. We can better ensure that we will not be chanced upon."

"Where are we exactly? Everything looks so different that I'm not completely sure."

"Aye. There are more oak trees for one. I have always taken them for granted for they cover most of Ireland. Now I can see that cutting these massive beauties, we are slowly destroying our forests. To answer yer question...." He put a hand on her arm halting her progress. He took her shoulder and turned her towards the area he wanted to point out. "Do ye see the stone that just reach above the tree tops?" She nodded. "That's the Round Tower that was used about the 12th century for a campanile and a warning system against enemies. If we went over the ridge, not far ye would see the churches. Some burned I am afraid. It is believed that St. Kevin himself picked this place. Beautiful, aye?" He puffed out his chest rather proud as if he had proclaimed the site himself.

"Glendalough?"

"So ye know."

"I've read up on some of Ireland's history right before we made this trip. So much turmoil has been on Irish soil. Many lives will be forfeited, and a great deal will be destroyed."

He nodded recalling the many ruins he had seen in her century. Dunhaven was not even mentioned. It was disturbing to think that one day, all he held dear would simply cease to exist. "Come on. Follow me."

It took them another half an hour to reach the water, but the time was worth it. Aislinn removed her pack and took a step closer to the embankment. "Oh, it's beautiful." The ground was soggy and she was careful when she leaned forward and touched the cool water. Actually it felt good for she was hot from the long hike. She turned to look at Dougray, who had also removed his pack and mantle. "It's safe to swim in?"

He came to stand next to her. "Aye, nothing in there that can harm ye. Ye can keep afloat then?"

"I used to be a pretty good swimmer. The butterfly stroke was my specialty."

"I will have to take yer word for it then. I am not sure I know what that is."

"I'll show you. You are coming in, aren't you?"

His eyes searched her face, wondering if this was an invitation, but there was not a hint of seductiveness in her gaze. Rather she was looking at him so innocently that he felt foolish for even thinking otherwise. "I best not. I'll start a fire for it is certain that ye will want to warm yerself." He started back to where they had left their belongings.

Aislinn found that she was rather grateful for the privacy. Using the foliage for cover, she stripped down to her underclothes. She waded into the water before diving under its surface. She only swam for a short time for her body began to rebel against the icy coolness. Cold limbs and all, she would have never missed this for the world.

Dougray hadn't meant to watch, but once he caught sight of her gliding through the water like it was home to her, he couldn't pull himself away. She seemed so calm and at ease with nature, and though he could not see her face, he knew that she was smiling.

When she started her trek back to shore, he knew it was time that he made his leave. He didn't want her accusing him of spying on her. He put his mantle next to her clothes and quickly retreated.

Aislinn was pleasantly surprised to find his gift, and picked up the heavy covering that smelt of their campfire and of…. She held it close to her face. It smelt of him, not in the least distasteful. It was a manly scent that was comforting, making her feel safe. She removed her underclothes and draped the heavy blanket over her; immediately her chilled body felt warmer.

Grabbing her clothes, she made her way through the trees and over to where Dougray was waiting. He glanced up just before she reached him. His eyes smoldering with…she thought maybe desire but that was completely ridiculous. They were barely able to stay civil to each other let alone begin to feel something more. Yet, when he gazed at her like that, she felt a tingling in the pit of her stomach.

"Did ye have a good swim?" he managed to say as his eyes took in her bare feet and traveled up the length of her body that was cloaked with his mantle.

"What? Oh…yes." she stammered, impatiently pulling her drifting thoughts together before she got herself into trouble. "Thanks for the cover."

"Ye're welcome." He stirred the fire with a stick, afraid to look at her again. His mind kept wandering to images of her long, slim body bare against his cloak. It had been a long time since he had enjoyed the comforts of a woman, too long. "Are ye hungry yet?"

"No, I'm fine." She sat down and took hold of her backpack. After a moment's search, she found her lotion. She opened the travel bottle and dropped some of the sweet-smelling ointment onto the palm of her hand. She began to rub some on her arms and then she proceeded to her calves. The pleasurable smell reached Dougray, making him squirm uncomfortably. It was one thing to imagine how soft she would feel beneath his touch, but now he had to smell how she would taste. He jumped to his feet, startling her.

"What's wrong? Did you see something?"

"Lass, do ye not know what torture ye are giving me?"

He saw the blank look on her face, making him feel foolish for making such a fuss.

"What? I'm not doing anything."

"We may bicker like there is no tomorrow, but ye are…*Dar Dia*! I am a man." Like this explained everything.

"Yes," she said slowly. "And I'm a woman."

"Do not be coy with me." He threw down his stick. "Ye can't expect me to watch ye undress and then torture me further by massaging each bare limb…." He turned away trying to regain his composure.

Aislinn glanced down finally realizing what he was trying to say to her, and quickly pulled the garment down to cover her legs. She was becoming just a little too comfortable with his company. "I'm sorry…. I didn't think…."

He whirled around and stormed right passed her. She turned to view his retreating back. "Where are you going?"

"Just stay there."

She turned around, stunned over the way he was behaving. Then slowly a smile spread across her face. "So you are attracted to me." But just as quickly, a worried frown replaced her grin. With her own thoughts straying, she wasn't sure that this was at all a good thing. She had waited this long to find the right person to give herself completely to, and it wasn't going to be to a man who should have been dead for centuries. That thought startled her. "He should have long been dead and buried." She rubbed the warm covering. But he wasn't dead. She was here with him now, and he was very much alive. "What's wrong with me?" she chided herself. "So what? He's a good looking guy? I've dated others just as attractive and never lost my senses." She rose to her feet and started getting dressed, damp underclothes and all. "God, I don't even like him all that much. He has that maddening hint of arrogance about him that just about drives me nuts…Jeez." She laughed out loud. "What was I thinking?"

Satisfied that she had her emotions in check, she sat back down by the fire and waited for Dougray to return. She dozed off and woke with a start to find that darkness had all but descended upon the forest, and the fire had nearly gone out. She was a little concerned since Dougray obviously had not returned. *Where was he?* She came to her feet and added a few sticks to the fire. "What if he didn't come back? Or maybe he was hurt. Stop it! He's a grown man and one that was quite capable." She continued to have a conversation with herself as she paced and minutes passed by. She noticed his dagger on top of his bag, and decided that she'd rather have it near her.

She couldn't wait anymore. Securing the weapon to her belt, she moved away from the safety of the fire. She immediately felt the cold wind whip around her causing her to shiver. She wished that she had put on her sweatshirt, but she didn't stop to go back. She was anxious now and had to make sure that he was all right. She just hoped that she could find him before the light failed her. She didn't particularly want to be lost in the forest.

Dougray had walked a good distance, mumbling all the way that he couldn't believe his misfortune of being stranded with a woman that battled with him in every situation. "She's headstrong, opinionated, too outspoken...." He threw up his hand in frustration. If he believed all these things, then why were his feelings for her starting to intensify? "It's ridiculous," he said to the trees. "She's not even all that attractive...well maybe that is not completely true. Her hair's too short," he argued with himself. "It belongs on a young lad of twelve." Oh but tonight she didn't look anything like a lad. When she had shown up all wrapped up in his mantle, obviously completely bare underneath.... "Bah! She's far too thin for my liking," he voiced this but his mind thought otherwise. *Aye thin, but she does have firm, long legs.... Ach!* "What are ye doing to yerself?" He had finally reached the water's edge. He threw down his sword and began to undress. "Ye need a good dunking in that cold water to bring ye to yer senses." He didn't even ease his way in, but rather plunged beneath the cold surface, swimming at a fast pace. Finally the tension seemed to ebb from his body and he began to slow down until he was treading water. He noticed now that it was just beginning to get dark, and fool that he was, he had come out pretty far from the shore. It was time that he had better start swimming back.

The earth was soft and Aislinn was able to follow the footsteps easily enough. When she came upon the scattered clothes on the ground, she picked up what she thought was called a tunic. They were Dougray's. Obviously he had decided on a swim after all. She peeked her head through the trees to see if she could see him. He was there, just standing at the embankment, looking out toward the water. She pulled back a branch ready to go over to him, when she realized that he was completely naked. She drew in a sharp breath and let the branch move back into place. She knew that she should turn away, but a part of her didn't want to. He couldn't see her. What harm was it in just looking? She slowly moved the branch down. What a striking figure he portrayed. Tall, broad shoulders with a muscular back that tapered to a small waist, perfectly V shaped. "Nice buns, too." At that moment, he turned around giving her a complete frontal view. Her mouth fell open and she stumbled back, falling on her backside.

He was heading this way! She would rather die than have him find out that she had been standing there ogling him. She scrambled to her feet and practically ran all the way back to where they had made camp.

The fire was low again and she frantically stoked it until it blazed hot. She paced a few moments taking deep breaths and lifting her arms in the air, so that she would appear calm by the time he returned. When she thought that she could, she sat down and pulled her legs close to her body, resting her chin on her knees. Not long after, she saw him come into view. Nonchalantly as possible, she lifted her head and smiled. "You're back."

Dougray nodded. "Aye. Took a swim."

"I know." She saw his dark brow raise and she quickly added, pointing out the fact, "Your hair is wet."

He touched the damp strands. "So it is." He walked around the fire and to his pack. "Ye want to know something curious?"

She looked at him nervously biting her lower lip.

"I could have sworn that I left my dagger here." He pulled the item in question out and he heard her little intake of breath before she quickly fell into a series of explanations.

"You must have taken it. It can't get up and walk by itself, can it?" She chuckled nervously turning away from him. She closed her eyes expecting him at any moment to accuse her of spying on him.

"Maybe but…." He watched her tense and he had to bite the inside of his cheek just to stop himself from laughing. He knew exactly how the dagger happened to be tossed among his clothes. She had left enough evidence to convict her without a trial. Broken branches, footprints, and well, the knife had been the sure clincher. He had been quite curious to know just how long she stood there watching him. And now, he had a good idea by the way she was acting. For now, he would let her have her little secret.

He sighed heavily. "Ye are probably right. I must have taken it with me." He smiled and turned away to put the dagger in its rightful place.

They said little that night for the tension was weighed heavy between them, each aware of the slender delicate thread that had begun to form between them.

While Dougray busied himself with securing the area, Aislinn wrote in her notebook that was beginning to sound more like a personal journal. She didn't just jot down ideas for a future book, but was now putting down her innermost thoughts. She reminisced about the tranquility of the lake and the trees that lined its shores. For a moment, she even allowed her thoughts to conjure up the moment that she had stumbled upon Dougray. She couldn't resist writing about that since it had been just about the highlight of the whole evening. She wrote in bold letters, "Anticipation, intrigue, and of course, desire." She chuckled causing Dougray to glance her way.

"Ye find something amusing?" He noticed the high color that shone on her cheeks.

"It was nothing." She shrugged. "Just writing."

"What do ye find to write about? Never seen someone have so much to put to paper."

"How could I not find something to write about? I'm in an adventure that most writers will only dream about. I can write from an actual account. I'm here, seeing, feeling, and smelling everything around me. This is a setting for one heck of a novel."

"A smut book?"

She chuckled. "What?"

"Yer brother…."

"Say no more. That's Connor for you. I tend to think that my books have at least a story behind it, and maybe just a little bit of sex added to spice it up."

"Sex? This is what smut is then?"

"Connor was trying to be funny. Smut really means scandalous."

"Connor told me that yer novels would make my hair curl."

She couldn't help it. She burst out laughing. "I'm sorry," she apologized, but she was still smiling.

"Ye write about sex? This does conjure up a whole different picture. Ye write from experience then?" It seemed that this woman was an ever-changing mystery, for he would have thought by the way she blushed that she was still an innocent.

"Not exactly." She hesitated to say more.

"What do ye mean by *not exactly?*"

"It's more like how I imagine it to be."

He gave her sidelong glance, too curious not to ask. "Ye are still untouched?"

"Well don't act so surprised. I don't jump into bed with every guy I date. I've kissed…fondled a little but…" She looked away, a blush evident even in the firelight. "I haven't done…you know…it." She was suddenly anxious to escape from his disturbing gaze for she had no wish to have him ridicule her personal decision. But when he had remained silent, she chanced a look at him. He wasn't laughing or even smiling. He was looking at her as if he had made a shocked discovery.

"Ye are not young. What could ye possibly be waiting for?"

"I'm not young...." Her mouth opened and shut not believing that he thought she was old. "Love," she finally snapped at him. "I'm waiting for the man that I will love forever. Something you obviously wouldn't understand."

"Ye think that ye have me all figured out, do ye?" The bridled anger in his voice was unmistakable and he rose to his full height now. "Do ye think me incapable of knowing love?"

"I don't know." She permitted herself a withering stare. "We can't even have a decent conversation for me to figure you out. Really, I think I liked you more when you didn't have a memory at all. Now you're just grumpy all the time."

"What do ye mean grumpy?" He took a step toward her. She looked so vulnerable, so sweet that he wanted to press his lips to her and show her how agreeable he could be. Instead he halted his steps. "Grumpy indeed!" he shouted and turned on his heels tending to just walk away.

Aislinn sighed and turned her attention to her writing, deciding that once again their conversation was over, but he whirled around and came back to where she was seated.

"I'll have ye know that I have never been grumpy in my life."

"You could have fooled me," she mumbled but he heard her.

"Bah! Why do I even bother?" He waved his hand at her and stalked out into the night.

Aislinn just shook her head. The man was impossible to get along with. She wrote in her journal, "Dougray Fitzpatrick is the most irritable human being alive..." She paused for a moment. Then with a curious smile, she jotted down: "...but he does have nice buns." She closed the book then and put it away in her backpack.

She retrieved the mantle that had become their blanket at night and draped it over her. She was not going to let his foul mood ruin her rest.

Dougray hadn't strayed too far from the camp, but just far enough away so that he could become a rational human being again. How the woman could with a single word cause his temper to flare. Not even a Butler was capable of doing that.

He was still a little perturbed when he had finally decided to return, but the moment that he saw her all curled up on one side with his cloak tucked under her chin, he lost some of his ire. He knelt down beside her, studying her peaceful expression. "Ye look like an angel." He couldn't resist feeling the soft strands of her dark hair and letting them feather through his fingers. Only when she stirred did he pull his hand away with a sigh. "Ah, I take it back; ye are a temptress."

He moved beside her and pulled a bit of covering over him. Oddly, he felt comforted by her body leaning against his back.

After a somewhat uncomfortably quiet breakfast, Aislinn insisted that she have a few moments alone to ready herself. Dougray was fuming that they had wasted so much of the morning, but finally he had relented.

He decided to take a walk, and when he had returned, he saw her on the ground engaged in some sort of exercise ritual. He could see the muscles in her arms flex with each up and downward motion. She was indeed a strong woman. "What are ye doing?"

"Push ups." She did a few more before she came to her feet and proceeded to jump in the air clapping her hands above her. "Jumping Jacks," she informed him before he could ask. "I don't plan on having shin splints. You should really warm up too. Loosen up those muscles."

He just shook his head. "Ye are a strange lass." Though in actuality, he found her intriguing, but not everyone would have the same opinion as he had. Again, he was plagued with how he was going to present her to his clan.

"We will have to come up with a story of where ye are from and one that will seem plausible."

"Telling them that I'm from the future wouldn't do?"

"Ye may if ye like the notion of being burned at the stake."

"Ha, ha." She was now stretching her long legs, to one side and then to the other. "What about saying that I am a distant cousin of yours, who has come to visit, or maybe you can tell them that I was the daughter of your father's closest friend who had been abducted by…."

He shook his head.

"What? Am I getting a little too carried away?"

"Aye. We need to make this simple, so that we will remember the story. Ye will have to be visiting from another country. That should be plausible, for though ye speak the Irish, there are slight differences. And to be perfectly honest, ye are too much of yer world."

Finished with her morning stretches, she turned to face him. "Are you trying to say that I will stick out like a sore thumb?" He didn't even have to nod for her to know that this was exactly what he had been thinking. "Not to worry. I can blend in, when need be. Now where will I be staying once we arrive at your home?"

He was still trying to picture her blending in. "What?"

"Where will I be staying?"

"Ye will stay in the castle, of course. Whatever we decide, ye will have to become a lady."

She put her hands on her hips. "Are you saying that I'm not?"

This was not going well. "Do not vent, I am saying that we will present ye as noble birth, so that ye warrant the protection of the keep. Ye'll be safer there and I can watch over ye, and hopefully avoid any complications."

"You live in the castle?" She was rather impressed.

"Aye." To her disappointment, he didn't elaborate. "Come now. Let us put a few more hours behind us. I am anxious to be home."

Darkness was descending upon them faster than Dougray had anticipated, and he was becoming more and more uneasy with the fact. For some time now, he had the feeling that they were being followed. Two people out alone were easy targets to those that had nothing to lose. He glanced over his shoulder expecting to see someone jump out of the shadows. He picked up the pace, his hand on the hilt of his sword.

"Hey, what's the rush?" Aislinn matched his step. At this moment, he was glad that she was able to keep up with him. "Are you pissed off about something?" She continued to talk but not getting any answers from him. "What's wrong with you?"

He threw her a lethal glare. "Hush, lass, and keep moving." He took hold of her arm and she let out a yelp from the sudden grip.

She was about to make another retort, when Dougray suddenly stopped and drew his sword. It seemed that they had come out of nowhere, but there they were surrounding every exit. "Gypsies," Dougray breathed.

Aislinn took a step closer to him, when she saw a man with a black scruffy beard move forward and with two powerful-looking men beside him. Their muscles nearly bulged tight against the fabric they wore, and each had a weapon that gleamed menacingly in the light of their torches. The man in the center presented himself with authority, his leer sending chills down her spine. They were surrounded and she instinctively knew that if they so much as breathed wrong, that they would be killed.

Chapter Sixteen

"Just let us pass and we will forget this little misunderstanding," Dougray voiced with confidence making even Aislinn want to laugh. Didn't he realize they were ten to one here, definitely not the time for boasting?

The man that seemed to be the leader just stared at him for a long moment before he burst out with a harsh laugh that made Aislinn cringe. "Ye dare make threats to me? Me the great Merrick?" He pounded his broad chest with his fist. "I only have to raise my hand and ye will be choking on yer own blood."

"Aye, I can see that well enough, but I assure ye that I am not easily captured. I will make it my duty to take a few of ye with me on my way to hell, and I will be starting with ye first."

Aislinn heard the calm and sure tone of his voice but she knew better for she could feel the muscles tense in his back. He was a darn good actor. She just hoped that this Merrick thought so too.

He seemed to be weighing the words spoken to him as he warily eyed the heavy sword that Dougray held with confidence. Finally he spoke again, "Ye are a brave soul, and ye should count yerself lucky that I like that. I may consider releasin' ye both, but for a fair price?" Merrick smiled, but it didn't quite make him look any friendlier.

"I can assure ye, that ye will be paid handsomely." Dougray nodded hoping that this meant they would get out of this alive, but somehow he sensed it was not going to be that easy.

"Riches are indeed an added bonus, but what I wish is from the lady." He looked at Aislinn now, his eyes seductively roving over her. Instinctively Dougray moved completely in front of her, as if he could single-handedly protect her. If the situation hadn't been so serious, she would have kissed him for the sweet gesture.

"I'd advise ye to reconsider." There was no denying the threat that lay behind Dougray's words. Aislinn looked around her, as each man moved a step forward. Even with her help, there was no way that they could fend off so many.

"Very admirable of ye." The gypsy chuckled again. "Protectin' the lady's virtue to the death." His hand swept around him indicating just how many men were on his side.

"If the need be." Dougray was still insistent that he could keep her safe.

Aislinn couldn't help but lift her brows. The man barely tolerated her and yet he was risking his life for her? She again looked to where the men stood within the shadows. No matter how strong or brave Dougray thought he was, there was no way that he could stand up to so many. She felt obligated to at least make an offer to help with this situation. "Maybe you should…."

He cut her off with a hiss. "Ye say another word and I'll gladly hand ye over to them without another thought to it. Do I make myself clear?"

She wisely remained silent.

After a tense moment, the leader again grinned. "I like ye, milord." He waved his hand for his men to step back. "Rest easy. I have a woman of me own. I am nah after yer lady's favors. I only wish to be entertained with a song."

Aislinn gripped Dougray's shoulders. "Sing?" Her voice croaked out the word. She couldn't sing.

"A moment please," Dougray asked and Merrick nodded. To the side now, Dougray lowered his voice so that only Aislinn could hear him.

"All ye have to do is…."

"I can't sing, Dougray," she interrupted. "I sound like a drowned rat."

"Ye are just exaggerating. Are ye not?" He hoped to God that she was joking.

"No, I am completely serious. I can't carry a tune. It's the truth." She glanced over his shoulder to see the gypsy leader conversing with his men. She looked back to Dougray. "Maybe you could sing."

"He did not ask for me."

"Well, all I can say is that I can try, but I am telling you, after one stanza, even you will wish that he killed us."

Dougray pursed his lips together. How could the woman not know how to sing? He shook his head before he turned to face the leader, once more. "I fear the lady is shy and would ask that ye not insist."

Merrick's face turned murderous. "I am bein' generous and ye slap me face?" He lifted his hands for his men to seize them.

"Wait!" Aislinn stepped forward. "I accept."

"What are ye doing?" Dougray hissed. "Did ye not tell me, just moments before that ye could not carry a tune? Are ye deliberately trying to get us killed?"

"As I see it, we are as good as dead if I don't at least try," she whispered right back.

"Just give me a dagger now," he mumbled under his breath.

"This will buy us some time and then you can think of a plan to get us out of here."

"A plan? Lass, we will need a miracle."

"Then I suggest that you start praying for one."

He wanted to say more but a gypsy with the gold earring was coming toward them with the intent of relieving them of weapons.

They were lavishly fed and treated with upmost respect, but it was quite clear that they were not guests. Try as he might, Dougray could not think of a way that they could escape this without being seriously injured or worse. Aislinn had to sing, that was all there was to it.

Later they were led to where Merrick was seated before the great fire. They were again heavily guarded on all sides, making escape utterly impossible. Aislinn took a deep breath, knowing that it was all up to her. She bravely stood and hoped that her plan was going to work. "Great and noble Merrick." She bowed slightly before him. "I want to thank you for your open hospitality." The man nodded looking quite pleased. She continued, "This coziness around the fire reminds me of my home where I have spent many evenings with my family and friends. With your permission, great one, I would like to share with you a tradition that has been passed on for generations. It would do me a great honor, if I may entertain you with 'The Legend of Sleepy Hollow.' It is an appropriate story for a campfire such as this."

Dougray's eyes flashed with disbelief. Why was she purposely enticing the man to anger?

The leader leaned forward cocking an eyebrow. "What is this campfire story? I wanted a sweet melody."

"A song? Yes, I could do this, but you would be missing something far more entertaining. Why my father, the great Chief Hennessy had the best legend teller in the whole village."

"Yer father is a great Chief? I ha' nah heard of him."

"Oh but we come from a land far from here. Alas we have not heard of your glorious self, but yet here you are. Be it known that I will bring back tales of your bravery and prestige among your people." She heard Dougray groan but she didn't miss a beat. "Like yourself, my father is well respected among his followers."

Merrick thought about this for a few moments. Try as he might, he couldn't see that she was trying to trick him in any way. And he found that he rather liked this unusual woman. "A campfire story, hey?"

"Yes. One to spark the imagination to the fullest." She played to the crowd now. "How many of you like to hear ghost stories, unexplained happenings that will scare the wits out of you?" She heard murmurs that they did and she noticed that a few had even nodded their heads. She turned her attention back to Merrick. "This tale is only for the bravest of all. All else should be wise to leave." No one moved as their leader eyed each and every man with a warning that they better not move.

Merrick then waved his hand in front of him giving her the okay to continue.

She moved around the campfire dramatically waving her hands as she spoke. "Back in my country there is a strange little town by the name of Sleepy Hollow. It is a beautiful place with trees that bloom in the spring and leaves that turn shades of orange, yellow and gold in the fall. This place was everyone's dream, but like everything that seems so perfect there was a downside to this paradise. They had a terrible secret that they tried to keep hidden." Aislinn's dark eyes widened and she waited for just the right moment before she spoke again in a tone that sent chills down everyone's spine. "They were terrorized by the *headless horseman.*" She heard a few intakes of breath and she continued, "Every Hallows Eve, this headless horseman was in search of a new head. If you were unfortunate enough to be out when you should be tucked safe in your beds, he was liable to take yours." She deliberately pointed to the gypsy with the earring. The man's eyes widened and he took a step back like he was afraid that the horsemen indeed would come after him. Some couldn't help but chuckled.

"Ichabod Crane was a well-educated man, the school teacher of the town...." She went on with the Washington Irving story, adding a few things of her own if she couldn't remember the story exactly the way it should be, and loving every minute of it. She could tell that even Dougray started to relax. By the time she had completed the tale, he had actually enjoyed the show.

"...And the little town of Sleepy Hollow never saw the old school master again." She ended with a bow. Merrick clapped his hands, and she lifted her gaze to meet his with a smile upon her lips.

"Well done, milady. I was most pleased. Ye may go home to tell yer great chief that ye are a grand storyteller yerself."

"Thank you." She graciously bowed again.

Merrick snapped his fingers and the man with the gold earring came forward. "Ye will give them a horse and some food to take with them. They are free to be on their way." Merrick rose and so did Dougray to stand beside Aislinn. The gypsy leader came forward to speak to them. "Yer belongin's will be returned to ye."

"We are most grateful for yer kind hospitality, Merrick." Dougray nodded his head.

"Aye, but ye should be thankin' the lady." He took her hand and brushed his lips against her knuckles. "If we should meet again, I will have a campfire story for ye."

"I would be most pleased to hear it."

With that Merrick moved on into the night.

Aislinn was seated behind Dougray on the large horse, her arms wrapped around his waist. One of Merrick's men led them part of the way before he bid them a good travel. The man was quick to disappear into the shadows. They were alone now, and Aislinn couldn't help but let out a relieved chuckle.

"Something has amused ye, milady?"

"Only that I saved your butt."

"Humph!"

"Oh come on now. Admit it. Words were stronger than your sword."

"Aye, this time perhaps, but if I should find myself in the midst of a battle, I would still rather have a weapon in my hands."

"Ah yes," she sighed. "That is how men think. Draw blood to solve their problems."

"If there was another way, and if others would listen, I would gladly talk my way out of it. But alas, milady, there are those that have plugged their ears to a reasoning voice."

She was silent wondering if he was speaking of his own experiences.

As they continued on for hours, she became drowsy. She leaned forward resting her head against his back. She felt him straighten making her sit up also. "Is something the matter?"

"Nay," he lied. "Just settling myself." Her arms around him had stirred emotions that he had thought were beyond him now. He patted her hands to reassure her that all was well. She resettled her head against his back. It surprised him that he liked the feel of her long arms on his waist.

Aislinn's grip tightened. How strong he felt, firm, broad back. She had to resist letting her hands explore more. Indeed, she had to be tired if her thoughts were going there. She reminded herself that she thought him arrogant, bull headed, opinionated and these were his better qualities, but then…she couldn't deny that he was very, very brave. She smiled to herself, those thoughts filtering through her mind as she drifted off to sleep.

She was jerked half-awake by a sudden pull on her arm. "What…what is it Prince Charming?"

"What did ye say?" Dougray turned in his seat to peer at her.

Fully awake now, she realized what she had just called him. She tried to cover it up with a yawn. "I guess I fell asleep."

"I'd say. I nearly lost ye back there." He pulled back on the reins. "We will stop for the night."

Aislinn wasn't at all sure that was a good idea, at least not after the dream she just had with her being Cinderella and Dougray, being Prince Charming. Strong arms holding her tight, lips caressing her…. "What?"

"Ye will have to loosen yer grip so that I can help ye down."

"Oh. Oh, I can do it." She was off the mount before he could say another word.

She stood a safe distance away, while he made camp. She was still a little disturbed over her dream of the *Prince*…no, Dougray's lips that were kissing her.

"Aislinn." She jumped at the sound of his voice. "What is the matter with ye? Ye seem skittish."

"Nothing." Her voice croaked and she coughed seemingly trying to clear it. "Nothing's the matter. I'm just tired. It's been a rough few days, if you haven't noticed." Her voice rose with each word making it sound as though she was angry with him.

"Sorry that I asked," he mumbled as he sat down upon the ground. He pulled the hides over him and raised his eyes to meet hers. "Are ye just going to stand there?"

She swallowed the lump in her throat.

"Aislinn." At the sound of his voice she jumped again.

"Oh, stop your bellowing. I swear, you are not happy unless you are issuing orders." She plopped down beside him turning away from him. She drew her pack close using it as a pillow. She could feel his eyes on her for a long time, as though he was contemplating saying something to her, but in the end he settled down moving closer until his back was leaning against hers. She chewed on her lower lip. This was going to be a long night, but to her surprised she slowly drifted to sleep, and when the first rays of the morning sun warmed her face, she snuggled closer relishing in the feel of the strong hands that caressed her.

Strong hands?

Caressing?

Her eyes popped open with accusing words on her lips, but to her surprise Dougray was sound asleep curled around her with one bare leg draped over her hip, and his hand softly moving over her breasts. She didn't want to wake him and tried to untangle herself, but he held on tighter pulling her closer.

"Do not go, Ella."

Ella? A frown penetrated her brow. He was dreaming of holding another woman! "Wake up!" She jabbed him for good measure, not really sure if she was angry over the compromising position they were in, or that the man had called her by another woman's name.

Dougray felt warm, his body responding to the feminine softness. His eyes slowly opened ready to greet…. His smile slipped from his face the moment that he realized who he had clutched against him. But she had felt so soft, so right in his arms. With sleep still fogging his mind, he acted on his feelings leaning forward to place claim to her lips. Aislinn shoved at his chest, but it was her glowering expression that had finally sobered him. With a sigh, he reluctantly rolled away coming to his feet.

He cleared his throat and chose not to address what he had been about to do. He ran his hand through his hair. *What was he about to do?* "We better get moving." His voice was choked with emotion making his request sound more like a gruff order. He was a little surprised when she answered him without one of her haughty retorts.

"Sure." She slowly stood up. "Dougray?"

He paused, his back straightening to his full height. Slowly he turned, knowing he would have to face her wrath sometime and it might as well be now. "What just happened was a mistake," he defended himself. "I was sleeping. Ye can't hold me responsible for that, can ye?"

"Hey, I understand." She shrugged showing her relief.

He chuckled nervously. "Ye and me together." He shook his head. "Absurd. Right?"

"Oh yes, ridiculous," she agreed. "Hey, you're way too old for me anyway. I mean I won't even be born for another five centuries or so." She tried to laugh but somehow it didn't seem funny.

He stared at her, his gaze dropping from her eyes to her shoulders to her chest, then as quickly he looked away clearing his throat. "We have to start moving."

"Uh, yeah." She may not be a good judge of men with her disastrous relationships trailing behind her, but she felt in her heart that Dougray was an honorable man. He wouldn't take advantage of her just because he felt an attraction, and she wasn't blind to the fact that he was looking. Heck, she was staring right back, but starting something with him, no matter how noble he was, would surely end up being the biggest mistake of her life. They argued endlessly, and she couldn't forget the fact that she was from another century. As soon as she was able to talk to this Neala woman, she was going to go back to where she belonged. There could be no future between them.

Dougray was unsettled over what had transpired. He was not opposed to a casual coming together of a man and a woman, but Aislinn, as brazen as she may appear, was not a lass to be cast aside after they had both been pleasured. As for anything else…well that was impossible. She was too strong willed for his liking. They would be at each other's throats, more than they would ever be beneath the covers.

"Who is Ella?"

He was so startled to hear the name that he whirled around to face her, his bright dove-colored eyes clouding to a deep gray. Had that been it then? Were his desires only for Ella? Had he been dreaming about her? Even as the thought crossed his mind, he knew it was not entirely true. He had known it was not his tiny petite Ella that he held in his arms. "I do not wish to speak of her to ye."

"Why not?" Her eyes flashed with anger. "Your grimy paws groped over me with that woman's name on your lips. Oh, I think that you owe me at least an explanation."

"I owe ye nothing, lass."

"And stop calling me lass." She stomped her foot, her hands clenched as if she wished to punch him. "I have a name, damn you!" With that she stormed away from him. He thought about going after her to explain, but then in the end, he decided that maybe it was for the best that she cooled off first. He went back to the task at hand not ready to face his own feelings. Though his thoughts kept wondering back to how Aislinn's taut body had felt under his caress. He may have spoken Ella's name, but in his dreams it was not his dear departed wife's face that he had wanted to kiss.

How he angered her to the point of wanting to throttle him. "The arrogant man!" She continued stomping away not caring if he was following her or not. She had to get away or the alternative was to send her fist into his face. She swung a branch out of her way. She would have continued on, but a voice from somewhere to her right startled her into an abrupt halt.

"If ye wish to live, do not go farther." This masculine voice dared to demand his threat in the native tongue of the land. How she hated this world. Not a moment of peace before another man spoke orders that she bow to his will.

She slowly turned to face her opponent. He was tall, in his late twenties or so, with red hair that lay across his forehead and a mustache that draped near to his bare chin. He approached her, his sword drawn.

She spread her arms out, opening her palms. "As you can see, I am not armed." She used the Gaelic since it seemed to be the language of choice.

The man stopped short. "Ye are a woman?" He seemed utterly amazed and that really pissed her off.

"Why does everyone keep saying that?"

The man seemed confused over her strange outburst and didn't answer her. Instead he came forward. "Ye will need to come with me."

"I think not." Her swift kick found its mark before the man was able to take another step. He doubled over in pain, and she grabbed hold of his hair and jabbed her knee into his head. Before the man fell to the ground in agony, Aislinn turned and fled. She only managed a few yards before plowing into Dougray's hard chest.

"There ye are." He grabbed hold of her arm, ready to scold her for wandering off so far away from camp.

She struggled to be free. "Let me go, you fool. Once more, we're being attacked."

Dougray looked over her shoulder to see an angry man fighting with his mantle that had flipped over his head. Dougray moved Aislinn aside drawing his sword.

The man was cursing by the time he freed himself from the threatening cover. Dougray lost his ominous stance, and the man's hostile retort choked in his throat.

"Murrough, well are ye not a sight for sore eyes." Dougray sheathed his sword.

The man in question let out boisterous laugh and came forward. The two men embraced as only two friends would do. "We thought that Butler had captured ye, and scurried ye away to hold ye hostage at Castlehold. My friend, where have ye been these last three days?" As he waited for Dougray to fill him in with the details, he eyed Aislinn suspiciously. His hand raised to his nose that felt just as tender as the lower portion of his body felt. He was most curious to know who Dougray's traveling companion was, but was polite enough to wait for the introduction.

"These last three days?" Dougray was a little perplexed over this new information. By his calculations he had been gone almost two weeks.

Murrough became concerned. "Aye," he said carefully. "Do ye not remember this? We met with the Butler, but the man would not listen to reason and attacked without warning."

"I well remember it, Murrough. I just had thought that more time had passed that is all. How did we fair?"

"Only a few wounded, milord. The mist was so thick that the Butlers were forced to retreat. It was only when we had regrouped that we realized that ye were not among us. We searched the surrounding area, but only came across yer mount. We assumed the worst accusing the Butler of foul play, which he most profusely denied."

"And with due cause, for he did not capture me."

"As well I can see, milord." Again Murrough glanced at the woman who had nearly knocked him senseless, and this was not a small feat to be had.

Dougray finally realized that he had not made the proper introductions. He turned to her. "This is Lady Aislinn Hennessey."

Murrough gave him a rather comical look. "Lady Aislinn Hennessy?"

"Aye." He kept his voice bland of emotion. "In the skirmish, I must have hit my head. It was the lady's family that were good enough to care for me."

Murrough eyed the all too quiet woman in question. She didn't look like a lady, and a woman of noble birth would never travel alone with a man without escorts. "Where are the others, milord?"

"Others?"

"Aye. The lady's family?"

"They were detained."

"And her attendants?" Murrough persisted.

"We were attacked by highwaymen. Unfortunately, the young lady's attendant was killed." Dougray never had lied to Murrough, and he hated that he had to now, but there just wasn't any other choice. He glanced at Aislinn wishing she would say something. By the glowering expression she threw at him, he knew she was still upset. He cleared his throat. "Milady, may I present Murrough O'Donoghue."

Aislinn nodded her head. "We've met." She stepped forward then and Murrough met her halfway.

"I apologize for the way that I greeted you, milady." He bowed.

"And I apologize for my response."

Dougray could well imagine what had transpired. The woman was quick as lightning, striking without warning.

"Where do ye hail from?" Murrough questioned. "I'm afraid that I cannot place the tell of your words."

"Across the seas, a land far from here. We are only visiting, to see how the other side of the world lives." The way that Murrough was looking at her, she felt that maybe she had said too much. She never thought to ask what year this was, but by their dress she could only assume that this was possibly the sixteenth century.

"The other side of the world, milady. That is indeed far." There was skepticism in his voice.

Dougray decided to take over. "Her father is Donagh Hennessy, chieftain to her clan."

Murrough looked to Aislinn then back to his friend once more. He couldn't see why Dougray would mislead him. "Ye speak as though ye have known this clan? Are they related to the Hennessys that live beyond Dublin?"

"Uh...yes, but that was a long time ago. We live..." Aislinn realized that they hadn't come up with where she was going to pretend she was from. Obviously she couldn't say the United States since it didn't exist yet. "We live far from here," she finished lamely.

Murrough had no choice but to believe this tale, since Dougray did nothing to rebuke the claim. Truly it was not hard to imagine that she came from another land for her dress proved that well enough. And the way she fought, well it was like she was of the ancient times where the women fought beside their men, trained for battle. "A violent world ye must come from that a lass is educated in the art of warfare."

"My father believed that everyone should be able to fend for themselves. Why leave a weak link, when it could easily be avoided?"

"Maybe we should look into this, Murrough." Dougray hit the man on the back, hoping to distract him by leading the conversation away from Aislinn. "Give Rhiannon a new way to speak her mind."

"Ach! Indeed! The woman need not to use her muscle, her tongue leaves me bruised well enough."

Dougray laughed. "She is at it again, I see."

"Aye. She fails to understand my duties."

"Well when we are home again, ye can set things right between ye."

"Aye," he grumbled.

"Where are ye camped?"

"Not far from here. Do ye need help with the lady's belongings?"

"Nay, almost all of milady's belongings were taken. We will manage."

Dougray's men were grateful that he was safe and no harm had befallen him. Of course they wanted to hear where he had been, but he felt distracted wanting to be away so that he could smooth things over with Aislinn.

When he had the chance, he sought her out, spotting her sitting alone and away from the others. She had been extremely subdued after her encounter with Murrough. He should be grateful for this fact, but instead he found himself ill at ease. It was like he had entered into the eye of a storm, where it appeared calm and quiet, but he knew that the wind and rain that would drown everything in its path was just waiting to emerge. This was not a comforting thought.

She was writing furiously in her notebook, but when he had approached her, she snapped it shut and stood to face him.

"I would have a word with ye." He wasn't going to take no for an answer and had already taken hold of her arm. Of course she struggled only making him hold on all the tighter. "I warn ye do not make a scene. It wouldn't look well with Murrough watching us. She glanced over her shoulder and saw that the man was indeed following their every move.

"I'll go without you dragging me." She jerked her hand again and he released her.

When they were a safe distance away, he spoke again. "Ye are still upset with me."

She crossed her arms defensively across her chest, but didn't answer.

"I apologized for making undue advances. What more can I say?" He shrugged.

"Advances?" She let her arms drop. She was long over that episode. She was more interested in why Murrough referred to him as lord. "Who are you?"

"Ye know well enough. Dougray Fitzpatrick."

"No, that is not what I mean. That man," she pointed to where Murrough waited for them, "he calls you milord and the other men nearly bow down to you like you are someone of importance. So now tell me the truth. Who are you?"

"Ah the title. I am just a man, Aislinn, nothing more, but if it will make you happy," he bowed before her in a grand gesture, "I am Sir Dougray Fitzpatrick, Lord of Dunhaven." He looked up then with a smile for she was staring at him with her mouth open.

"You are a lord of a castle? *The* lord? Not some peon, but the actual lord?"

"Aye," he said slowly not sure where she was going with this.

"And you didn't see fit to tell me that?" she accused him.

"Ye did not ask."

"Oh, forgive me." She dragged out every syllable making it quite obvious that she was being sarcastic and not caring in the least.

"Pray tell, would ye have treated me better if I were to have informed ye of my title sooner?"

She didn't even hesitate to answer. "Not in the least."

"I thought as much. Then *Dar Dia*!" He raised his hands to the sky. "Why are ye making such a fuss?"

"I don't like surprises."

"Well now ye know, and ye can start behaving like a lady should. It will be hard enough to present ye as it is without ye being difficult on top of it all. Murrough already suspects that things are not what they seem."

"You said that he was your friend. Would he cause trouble?"

"Because he is my friend, we do not have to worry about him. Others will not be so gracious to overlook the masculine qualities that ye possess."

"Are you saying that I am less than a woman?" Her voice raised another octave sorely testing his patience.

"Let me think…ah ye curse like the devil himself, ye fight like a she-wolf, and ye dress like ye are out to do battle. But…." His eyes glimmered dangerously before he grabbed her, pulling her in a crushing embrace. He punished her with his kisses, while she clawed at him to be free. He only released her when he had heard Murrough behind him clear his throat. Aislinn's eyes glared, and without a care that one of Dougray's men was standing there, she slapped him hard against the cheek. Then she stormed away back to the heart of the camp.

Dougray touched his face feeling the definite sting. He turned to see Murrough lift one red bushy brow at him. "The lady does not seem willing, milord." The mirth in his voice only made Dougray's scowl deepen.

"She does not know what she wants."

"Seemed quite apparent that she did."

"Did ye interrupt me for a reason or were ye just interested in giving me advice?"

"Sorry. I just wanted to inform ye that all the men have returned and I have set up watch for the night."

Aislinn was fuming over the way Dougray had just treated her. Did he think he could just paw her at his whim because he was a lord of some castle? Well he had another thing coming. No one reigned over her and the sooner he realized it the better. She marched right over to where the men were seated causing the conversation to wither and die into silence.

"Please don't stop on my account. I only wish to warm myself by the fire and…." She noticed that they all had a tankard in their hands. She was a bit parched herself. "Would there be anymore of what you're all drinking?"

Dermot rose to do the honors.

The men were aware that she was the Lady Aislinn Hennessy who was in their care, but they were rather awestruck by her boldness.

"Here ye go, milady." Dermot was walking toward her with a full tankard. Unfortunately he wasn't paying attention and tripped over Cormac's sword. It sent him stumbling into Aislinn throwing her to the ground and him on top of her.

By this time, Dougray had stepped into the clearing to witness Aislinn pinned below Dermot in an unseemly manner. Aislinn was about to take care of the situation, but Dougray had charged forward kicking the unexpected man away from her. Aislinn barely moved out of the way, before Dougray had his sword drawn and the tip of the blade pressed against Dermot's throat. Blood slowly trickled from the man's flesh and his eyes bulged wide with fright.

"Ye will die for this insult," he shouted making all around back up a step.

"Don't you dare!" Aislinn screamed, pushing his arm away and stepping in front of the man and in harm's way. "What is the matter with you?"

"What's the matter with me?" His nostrils flared with fury. "Ye leave my sight for a minute, and I find one of my men on top of ye like a rutting dog. And ye ask me what is the matter? I give up. Ye are impossible."

"If ye will let me explain." Dermot crawled to his feet. "I was…."

"No words from ye." Dougray pointed his sword. "Be gone from my sight before I kill ye, just to appease my anger." Dermot did not have to be told twice.

"That was uncalled for." Aislinn placed her hands on her hips. "What you saw was only an accident. He was offering me a drink and tripped knocking me off balance."

"He was not molesting ye?"

"No," she retorted. Then as she purposely brushed by him, she added her insult for his ears only, "I guess molesting is only for the lord of the keep."

Murrough had walked over to Dougray sensing that his foul mood had increased. "I presume that the lady was not harmed?"

"Aye, she is fine. Her tongue and claws are sharpened to slash ye to death."

Murrough chuckled. "How do we find women of such nature?"

Dougray threw his friend a startled look not sharing in his mirth. "Ye may have a woman like that, but I have no wish to be lacerated day in and day out. The sooner I can send that she-wolf back home, all the better." He moved past Murrough without another word.

Chapter Seventeen

The drawbridge was already lowered when the Lord of Dunhaven arrived with Aislinn in tow. The men, woman and children of the keep were there to greet him with cheers and banners waving. Obviously he was well liked for there was no denying the adoration evident in the eyes of the people.

Aislinn found that Dunhaven was strategically set with acres of splendid oak and ash trees that surrounded it. The spacious settlement was protected within the walls. The fort consisted of a large courtyard with a towered gatehouse in the center of the east wall. There was a rectangular tower situated to the west and a southwest tower close by. Some distance from the walls there was a moat filled with water from the nearby lake. There were outer buildings, one Aislinn was sure was the chapel for she spotted a steeple. The other was probably the kitchen. She remembered her father telling her that a lot of the castle homes had their kitchens purposely built outside, merely for safety reasons. This insured that if there was an unavoidable cooking fire only the kitchen would be lost, and not the main housing area. She shielded her eyes as she studied the main structure where she would be staying, letting her eyes wander to the very top of it. It had to be at least five stories high, if not more. She noticed that most of the lower windows were mere slits. Another safety measure, she recalled. If they happened to find themselves under attack, a stray arrow would have a hard time penetrating to the interior.

Dougray easily dismounted then offered his hand to Aislinn. She was about to accept the gesture for appearance's sake when a rather beautiful woman interrupted him. Her hair was swept up above her head with lustrous gold waves of tresses cascading around her heart-shaped face. She curtsied so low that her rather large breasts were in danger of spilling over the top of her stylish gown.

Aislinn's left brow lifted wondering if this was *the* Ella, of Dougray's dreams. If not, she sure was distracting him from his purpose. Aislinn dismounted with the ease of a veteran rider. She stood beside Dougray and smiled at the woman that seemed overly friendly toward her lord. "Dia Dhuit." Aislinn drew the attention of the woman in question. "I am A.J. Hennessy and you would be?"

"Ye are a lady in men's attire?" Fiona's eyes had widened in disbelief.

Aislinn put her hands on her hips. "Now why is this so hard to believe?"

Dougray could clearly see a potential problem developing and decided to intervene. He took hold of Aislinn's arm looping it through his. "May I present, Lady Aislinn Hennessy." He corrected her first introduction with her formal name. She glanced his way smiling and actually batted her eyes. He was not amused with her mock performance. It was best that he took her inside and quickly. "Good day to ye," he bid Fiona.

"Yes, good day," Aislinn repeated in a syrupy voice. She knew immediately that *Miss big chest* and she would never become close friends. One, she didn't like the way the woman eyed Dougray like she owned him, and second…well second was something she didn't wish to think about at this moment.

With a firm hold on her arm, Dougray led her into the castle. They hadn't gone far when Cahir Dunphy, which Aislinn learned was the physician of the castle, halted them. "Milord, we were all so worried." The bald-headed man couldn't stop his surprised look as his eyes rested on Aislinn and the strange attire she donned. He cleared his throat and tried to concentrate on what he had been about to say. "I am glad to see that ye are looking fine, but if ye would like I could…."

"I am quite fit, Cahir," he interrupted, "so don't get any ideas of taking out yer instruments."

"Of course, but if…."

"I will call for ye if I need yer assistance." Again he ushered Aislinn forward.

She watched another man approach the physician who was wearing a long flowing robe of a lustrous deep color that looked like red wine. His beady eyes seemed to follow her and she leaned near Dougray. "Who is that?"

"The Abbot Kirwan."

"Oh. He doesn't look like he cares for me."

"That is just the way he looks. Do not let it bother ye." He led her up a flight of winding steps that seemed to go on forever. They finally reached the top of the fifth floor and to what she assumed would be her quarters. He opened it and bade her entry. It was actually a two-room compartment, a sitting room and the bedroom adjoining it. She was surprised to see how spacious the room actually was.

She was immediately drawn to the window that was quite a bit larger than anything she had noticed down below. She couldn't help but be pleased that she wouldn't be cooped up in a room with nothing to look at but the four walls. Directly beneath its window frame there was a seat with fluffy maroon cushions. The light would be absolutely perfect for reading or writing.

She knelt down on the bench and leaned out the opened window to take in the gorgeous view. Out in the distance she could see the enormous oak trees that seemed to blend into one another, and there were gentle rolling hills that surrounded most of the area. Farther to the right, she caught a glimpse of the sparkling lake. It was strange but Dunhaven seemed to provoke a sense of romance, a feeling of timeless beauty that caused her to give a moment of reverence.

"Impressive." She sighed and finally turned to look at him. "So how did you come to be a lord of a castle, by birth or by force? Hmm?" She was only teasing, but he seemed determined to set her straight.

"I was fostered in England, in hopes that I would keep loyalty to the crown. Dunhaven has been in my family for generations, but with the death of my father there was no one to tend to the lands. I fought for it and was finally given what was rightfully mine."

"And?"

"I happened to be in the right place at the right time. I pleased King Henry by saving his trusted friend from what would have been a sure death. It was merely one of his whims, but he knighted me for my bravery. How could I resist?"

"I sense there is more to that statement," she pushed for him to open up.

"Aye. English raised since I was twelve but my genuine love has always been for Dunhaven. The Fitzpatricks are true people of Ireland, and we can trace back our roots as far as one can decipher. I have sworn my fidelity to King Henry because it was expected of me." He shook his head sadly. "Ye've come to a troubled time, Aislinn, where the clans are torn on whom they should trust. We fight among ourselves when we should unite to keep Ireland ours."

It was rather a noble speech that he gave her. Unfortunately Aislinn was unable to comment on it, for a young woman had entered the room. She was round faced with high set brows and large, almond-shaped eyes, fringed with dark lashes to match her long, dark hair that was plated behind her. She curtsied nervously before Dougray. "Ye sent for me, milord?"

"Aye, that I did, young Moira. I ask that ye be handmaid to Lady Aislinn." The girl smiled before she could help herself.

"Oh, milord, ye will not be disappointed to be sure."

"See that I'm not." He turned to Aislinn then. "Moira will see to yer needs." He was about leave, but Aislinn halted his departure.

"Where are you going?" She had reverted back to speaking English. "You're going to just leave me?"

"Milady, I have many duties to attend to. Surely ye did not think that I would be at yer side every waking moment?" He took some satisfaction that he was able to shock her into silence. He quickly left the room before she recovered.

Moira couldn't help eyeing the tall woman that was dressed in men's attire. She had already heard the stories about her before she had been summoned. Never had she seen a lady dressed so. There was no finery in the threads that she bore, there was no elegance in her stance, and her hair was cropped in an unusual manner.

Aislinn finally took notice of the girl. "So what am I to do with you?"

"Whatever ye wish, milady." She curtsied grateful that she spoke the language. There were many that were starting to learn the English but she still hadn't grasped it.

"Hmm." She walked over to her door shutting it before she leaned against it. "Let's get one thing straight here. When this door is closed, you will remember that you and I are the same. I will not have you calling me milady every time that we have a conversation. "My friends back home call me A.J., and I would hope that you will do the same."

"We are to be friends?" Moira was confused. She never heard of a lady's maid being friends with the lady herself. She was always taught to only speak when spoken to.

"Yes, friends. I will need one. How old are you?"

"I am almost ten and six, milady…I mean A.J." It was kind of an odd name, but she tried it, so that she could please the lady that she would be assisting.

"Almost sixteen?" She was young, but she assumed it was not young by standards in this century. "Now, Moira, you are going to be great help to me."

"I am?"

"Yes. You see I am not from your country. I am not sure of your ways. I am hoping that you could coach me."

"Coach ye? I do not understand."

"Help me to be what is expected of a lady here. I may or may not follow everything, but I will give it the old college try." She saw the confused look on Moira's face and knew that she had better slow down. "How about starting with the proper attire?"

"Oh, I can see to that. We will have something made for ye. Milord has given orders to have ye fitted with the best that our dressmaker has to offer. Ye must be special. Aye?" Everyone was talking about the lady that the Lord of Dunhaven had brought home.

Aislinn would have laughed if the girl hadn't given her such a profound look. Special? The man wanted to be rid of her. This much was obvious by the way he had deposited her practically running from the room. He was probably anxious to see that buxom blonde who had greeted them down below. She didn't know why, but the thought of that woman throwing her arms around him bothered her immensely. "I am just a friend, nothing special. Though I am quite curious, Moira. We haven't been here long. So how could Dougray arrange all this?"

"Milord sent Teige ahead to prepare. We have known for hours that ye would be arriving. We were to give ye the finest hospitality."

"Really?" She was baffled over Dougray's behavior. He argued with her endlessly, managed to piss her off about every other second, but still found time to think of her comforts.

Chapter Eighteen

Dougray was already waiting at the stables when his redheaded friend made his way across the yard. "Ye wanted to see me?"

"Aye, Murrough. I need ye to promise me that ye will guard Aislinn. She is in a strange land and will not understand all our ways."

"She is different, I will grant ye that. Though I fear that it will be others that will need protecting, especially if they were to catch her ire. She throws a mighty blow. I tell ye this as a friend and hope that ye will never repeat it. The lass nearly did me in."

Dougray chuckled. "Nay, yer secret is safe with me."

"What is this lass to ye, Dougray?" Murrough had been wondering about this from the very first moment that they were introduced. The two had been traveling for a few days and apparently alone. "The father, Hennessy, ye say. Will he be seeking compensation?"

"Why would he?"

"Well, ye were not chaperoned…ye are a man and she a…woman." He hinted further. "Ye did not steal her away, did ye?"

His face split into a grin. "Ye think that the woman could be whisked away, if she did not wish it to be?" He gripped Murrough's shoulder in a friendly gesture. "Rest assured, old friend, Hennessys will not be banging down our doors. I have not taken the lass and her virtue was not compromised by me." He saw the relief spread across Murrough's face making him chuckle. "And she may forever keep that virtue for no man will want to suffer bodily harm to take it from her."

"Aye, I can see yer point." He nodded. "I don't mean to be changing the subject, but what of the matter with Dermot?"

"Dermot," he grumbled with a definite frown proving that, for some reason, he still held a grudge toward the lad. "Make sure that he stays away. He is not to ride with us from this day forward. I will not tolerate the behavior that he has bestowed to my honored guest."

"The lady explained the situation. Will ye not reconsider? Dermot is young…."

"All the more reason to teach him a lesson. He must learn now or he will forever be making mistakes. Nay, what I say stands." With this he made his leave.

Murrough crawled into bed where Rhiannon was sitting up, waiting for him. Her sweet smile could make him forget his troubles, but not tonight. He was bewildered over Dougray's odd behavior. He had known his friend long enough to be aware that he was hiding something from him, but he was not certain what it could be.

Rhiannon had run her hand down his flank making him conscious of how much he needed her touch. He turned to her now gently caressing her cheek.

"Ye still worry about, milord?" He was about to say otherwise but she placed a finger on his lips. "Nay, do not go denying it, Murrough O'Donoghue. I see it in yer eyes."

"Ye know me too well." He kissed her full lips, lovingly and long for he had missed her so. Still holding her close, he spoke again, "I worry that something more happened those days that Dougray was gone. He seemed not to know how much time had passed."

"Ye have no cause to worry. Did ye not say that he was preoccupied with the lady?"

"Aye, another piece of the puzzle, to be sure. Lady Aislinn is most unusual, and the way they came to be traveling together has me still baffled." His red brows slanted in a frown and Rhiannon brushed her lips to them, hoping to draw him out of his seriousness. It seemed to work, for in one swift move, he pulled her onto his lap. "Enough of Dougray." His finger traced the delicate skin of her neck and let it trail to the more womanly curves. "Tonight, my sweet, I only want to have thoughts of ye."

"Ye will have no complaints here."

Fiona was at first pleased that Dougray had come to her, but soon found herself regretting that he had bothered. She tried to entice him with kisses, special caresses that he had in the past enjoyed, but he had remained aloof barely noticing her at all.

"Milord, what has ye so occupied?

Dougray seemed to come out of his trance to find Fiona pouting at him. He on occasion had sought out her company to satisfy the hunger that a man felt, but he never talked to her more than a few minutes at a time. She never seemed to want words from him. Everyone knew that Fiona was free with her affections, but in the last year she had left herself solely for him. Even hinting that they should make a more permanent arrangement. They couldn't have a marriage in the church for she was not of his rank, but in Brehon law he was allowed to have a marriage of the fourth degree. He looked at her now with her flowing golden hair. She could be called beautiful, but there was something hard and unapproachable in the depths of her eyes. He would never marry her and a part of him felt dreadful that he hadn't stopped the relationship from the start. If only he hadn't been so guilt ridden about Ella's death, or so terribly lonely. Fiona had come to him offering a few moments of solace, and he had selfishly taken it. For a time, he was able to lose himself within her velvety softness, but now it seemed hollow and maybe a little unsound. "I am tired, Fiona."

"Lie back." She gently nudged him until he rested his head upon the feather mattress, a gift from him that she had treasured. "I will rub yer back and loosen those tight muscles." Again he let her guide him by rolling onto his stomach. He rested his chin on the top of his hands. As Fiona tried to work her magic, his mind kept wondering to Aislinn. Annoyingly she had preoccupied his thoughts most of the day. He could see her haughty expression and hear her sharp tongue lecturing. Even with this vision, he still found that he wished that it were her hands touching him and that he was in her bed. He closed his eyes, but still she haunted him. "She-wolf," he grumbled, sitting up and moving Fiona to the side.

"What have I done?" She sounded like she was near tears.

Dougray sat on the edge of the bed hastily dressing. "It is not ye."

"But where are ye going? I thought that ye would be staying with me tonight."

"Nay. I cannot tonight, Fiona. I have been gone too long and have much to accomplish. I cannot relax until then." Barely dressed, he was out the door as if the hounds of hell were at his heels.

Fiona just sat there, for a moment in stunned silence. She didn't know what had just happened. Never had his lordship left her bed without satisfying her, or she doing the same for him. She threw on her light spun gown that was almost transparent. She ran to the door to call him back, but he was already too far away for him to hear her.

Cormac had just left his guard duty and happened to see Dougray's quick departure. He swaggered over to Fiona to see if he could erase the pout on her beautiful face. "Looks like ye are free tonight." His eyes swept over her body approvingly.

She looked at him, maybe seeing him for the first time. He was a broad-shouldered man with thick thighs. His face was not bad to look at either. It had been a long time since she had offered herself to another but.... She looked to where Dougray was now disappearing into the keep. "It is a cold night."

"Aye, that it is." His eyes caressed her softness.

Fiona put on her prettiest smiled. "Ye are still young, Cormac. Do ye even know how to pleasure a woman?"

"Never had complaints before." He grinned.

She offered her hand to him. "Show me and I may share a few things with ye as well."

Chapter Nineteen

For two days Aislinn endured the seamstress', Rhiannon's, probing and prodding. If the conversation hadn't been comforting, she would have gone into hiding. Finally Rhiannon had what she needed, and had disappeared to make the elaborate wardrobe that would transform Aislinn into what society would deem a lady. Aislinn could have cared less. She would have liked it better if Rhiannon would just whip her up a pair of comfortable slacks.

Since she had nothing better to do, Aislinn roamed the castle only to find that it was loud and unorganized with a throng of people that warded suspicion. She was afraid to turn her back.

She didn't see Dougray among the many faces, and even though he irritated her to no end, she would have gladly welcomed his company. Upon making a few inquiries, she was informed that he had been called away on matters concerning his tenants and would not be returning until the end of the week.

Since the first day, Moira had been practically glued to her side, which most of the time Aislinn really didn't mind. They went outside for it had proven to be an unusually bright and comfortably warm day. Aislinn was surprised to see that Dunhaven was like a small town within the fortification. People bustled around conversing while they tended to their business.

A group of children drew Aislinn's attention making her wonder what game they were playing by surrounding a young boy. As she neared, she realized that this was not a friendly game for they were taunting the child with sticks. She had every intentions of breaking it up, but before she was able say anything, one of the children threw something at the defenseless boy.

"Milady!" Moira called after her, but Aislinn didn't hear her for she had already broken into a full run.

"What are you doing?" Aislinn shouted at the children. One large boy turned to look at her, with a mud ball still oozing in his hand. "You should all be ashamed of yourselves, picking on someone when there are five of you."

"It is only Hamish." A girl with freckles that covered her entire face spoke up.

"And who might you be?" Aislinn asked her.

"Lynelle," the girl answered. "Are ye the she-man from the castle?"

By this time, Moira had caught up and was quick to correct Lynelle. "This is Lady Aislinn to ye, missy."

"It's all right, Moira. I was just getting acquainted with the children and their unusual custom." She looked to the boy that still held on to his muddy clod as if his very life depended on it. "You, young man…what was your name?"

Lynelle was good enough to answer. "That there be me brother, Regan."

"Ah yes, I do see the resemblance. The same freckles and reddish hair." She rubbed her hand on her jaw and paced the group, eyeing each child, who seemed frozen in their places. "Now, Regan, what is this custom? You throw globs of mud at anyone named Hamish?" This caused all the children except the boy in question to burst out laughing. "Did I say something amusing?" They became quiet once more as her eyes swept across each of their faces ending again with Regan. "Well are you not going to answer me?

"Hamish is a cripple." Regan finally found his voice.

"And this means?"

"He's a cripple," the boy repeated as though this explained everything. When he realized that it obviously did not, he elaborated. "He is worthless to all, taking our food and doing nothing to earn it." Regan was rather a large boy who could go without one or two meals.

"I see. So the rule is that you throw clumps of dirt at anyone that is different. Now who decided this? Where did this rule come from?"

They looked at each other wondering who had the answer. Regan decided it didn't matter and spoke up, "It is just so."

"Hmm. It is just so." She paced around the group making sure she made eye contact with each person, last with the muddy boy that they called cripple. She winked at him. The boy's large eyes nearly popped out of his head. She then turned her attention to Regan. "So how about I make a new rule today?"

"What do ye mean?"

She leaned down and gathered up some of the thick gooey mud. She matted it into a firm ball as she spoke, "I say today that any boy that is a bit over weight and has a face full of freckles is the target." With that she threw the perfectly round ball straight at the surprised Regan. The mud slid down his face.

"What did ye do that for?" he wailed.

"Isn't this how it works? Someone that looks different is the target. Come on, boys and girls, join in." She waved her hands to the kids. She picked up another clump of mud.

"Hey, ye can't do that." The boy backed up, just as she threw another dirt clod at him. "Why can't I? This is rather fun." She looked at Hamish. "Care to give it a try?" The poor boy just shook his head. "Come on." She looked around her.

"I'll give it a try." Lynelle decided. "He's always picking on me."

"Lynelle, ye better not or I'll…." Smack, the mud hit him in the mouth. With a sputtered scream, he turned and ran away.

"Now who will be next?" Aislinn turned to look at the other kids. They all scattered in every which direction, all except for the boy who had been harassed. Aislinn looked at him now. "Well, Hamish, it is only you and I now, but I think you have had enough fun for one day."

"Thank ye, milady. I have to be goin'."

"Sure, but before you do, may I ask what happened to your leg?"

"It doesn't work." He patted it with his right hand. "Broke it when I was five and it never grew right. It is a bit shorter than the other one."

"I see."

"I'm good for nothin' just like Regan told ye." His eyes fell from hers, obviously embarrassed with his situation.

"Well if you believe that then you are nothing." This made him look at her again. "You can be whatever you set your mind to."

"I don't think so."

"Come on now what do you want to do?"

He swallowed hard and managed to give her a feeble answer. "I want to be a warrior."

"A warrior?" She was a bit put back at this, but once she saw the boy's crestfallen face, she nodded her head. "There are other things that you can do that could mean as much, but if a warrior is what you want to be, then you will have to train for it."

He lifted his head to see if she was making fun of him. She didn't appear to be. "Begging your pardon, but how?"

"Well first." She took hold of his skinny arms as if inspecting them. "We need to build up your muscles." She glanced down at his bony legs. "We will build up those legs too." She looked him square in the eyes. "This won't be easy. So say it now, if you aren't going to try."

"I'll do anything."

"Good. Meet me in the yard tomorrow at the crack of dawn. Mind that you're not late."

"I'll be there." He actually smiled before he limped away. He turned once and she waved to him.

Moira moved forward now giving her a rag to wipe her hands. "Should ye go promising such a grand feat?"

"I don't know what makes a warrior, but I would assume that at first he must believe he can be one. I know exercises that will strengthen the body and give him endurance, but the rest will be up to him."

"But his leg, milady?"

"This could be a problem but we will have to see. The limp seems minor enough; maybe something can be done to compensate for it."

"Compen…what did ye say?"

"We will have to make do with what we can get our hands on, Moira." She looked at the girl. "Who makes a good pair of shoes?"

"Shoes?"

Aislinn had noticed that many did not even own a pair, but for Hamish it would be a necessity. "Yes, shoes. You do know someone, don't you?"

She nodded still not understanding why she needed a cobbler. "That would be Padrig."

"Tomorrow we will have to go and see him." With that Aislinn moved on and Moira had to run to keep up with her. She liked her mistress, but sometimes she was most difficult to follow.

Chapter Twenty

Dougray wore a grim face as he surveyed the damage of his ship. He was amazed that the men were even able to maneuver their way back home. "Do ye know who attacked ye?"

"They were not flying a flag, but surely it was of the Butler's doing. It was waiting upon the water like it was a deserted craft. We closed in carefully and that was when they came upon us. Men flying from all places to put the galleon in motion."

Dougray didn't comment. He would have immediately thought that this was Fingham's doing but of late there had been too many incidents that didn't add up. "Just see to the repairs."

The man looked at him wondering if he had heard him correctly. Surely there was more. Usually they would retaliate from such an outspoken revolt.

"Is there anything else ye need to tell me?" Dougray was well aware that the man was ready to spill blood. He needed to put a stop to it now.

"Nay." He glanced at Murrough who stood stone faced and unreadable. "I guess I will see to the repairs then." He shook his head as he turned to leave.

Dougray walked with Murrough a distance away so that no one would overhear them speak. Murrough broke the silence first. "Ye think that someone else is behind these events?"

"I don't want to jump to any conclusions. The Butlers are not seafaring, but yet, I cannot fathom who else would want to attack us."

"It is someone that has taken great pains to see ye ruined, but I am with ye with yer suspicions. There is more that ye have not heard." Murrough dreaded to be the one to tell him but now there was no other choice. "The men that were to deliver the goods to yer cousin in Dublin…they never arrived. We received word only this morning from Father Fiach himself, direct from St. Michan's."

"Do we know what happened?"

"All slaughtered."

"And did you find the Butler's arrows?"

Murrough nodded.

"It's too messy and just too convenient to be Fingham's calling card. Send word to Father Fiach. I would like him to check into a few things in the Pale."

"I will see to it."

Chapter Twenty-One

Aislinn dressed then headed down the winding steps to the lower level of the keep. Her nostrils flared when she took in the smell of sweaty men, dogs and cattle all mixed into one. She could hear men snoring as they slept off the remains of the tankards of drink that they had consumed last night. She moved silently with every step, stopping once when she thought that she heard someone following her. She turned to look behind her, but saw no one lingering in the murky shadows. She continued on, but she couldn't shake the feeling that someone was behind her. As soon as she made it outside, she threw herself against the wall and waited. Just as she thought, a man emerged a few moments later traveling at a fast pace, until he realized his quarry was not ahead of him.

"Are you looking for someone?" The man jumped at the sound of her voice. He slowly turned to face her, his shoulders slumped in obvious embarrassment that he had been so easily discovered.

She moved out of the shadows to view her would-be follower. She raised a brow in amusement. The man was barely a man at all. He had long golden brown hair, blue eyes and a face as smooth as a baby's bottom. He was built though. She would have to give him that. His arms alone showed that he must know how to yield the heavy broadsword he had sheathed at his side.

The young man was well aware that she was assessing him and his face turned beat red. "Milady." He bowed. "I mean ye no harm."

"No? Then why are you following me like you are some common criminal ready to snatch a purse?"

"I would not stoop so low to commit such a contemptible act. I have been assigned to protect ye."

"Protect me? Is there reason that I should be in danger?"

"Nay…."

"No, but you are assigned to follow me."

"Aye…." He was flustered making Aislinn take pity on him. She decided that maybe she should go easy on the guy since it wasn't his fault that he was ordered to guard her.

"What's your name?"

"Teige, milady." He bowed again.

"Well, Teige, let's get one thing straight. I don't like being followed." She saw that he was about to protest and she held up her hand to halt him. "Let me finish. I also do not wish to have you in trouble for not obeying orders. You may go with me if you must, but at my side."

"If that is what ye wish, milady."

Aislinn nodded and moved forward with Teige keeping pace. "And Teige." He looked at her with his blue-lit eyes. "Call me A.J., okay? Milady makes me sound like an old woman and I am far from that." She picked up her pace. "Make sure you keep up, Teige," she called over her shoulder. The young man had to jog a few paces before he began to match her stride. He chanced a glance at the woman that carried herself with a commanding air of self-confidence. He couldn't help but be intrigued.

"I saw what ye did yesterday," Teige began and she looked at him as he continued, "Ye know, when ye took care of the bully Regan."

"I guess that you would have noticed since you were spying on me."

The young man blushed again. "I wasn't really spying. I was sent to make sure that no harm was to come to ye, but I fear I have only angered ye."

She sighed. "I'm sorry, Teige. My annoyance is not directed at you."

He was silent for a while, before he attempted a conversation again. "I have never seen Regan run with his tail between his legs before. He is usually the one making the other children cringe."

"Had it coming to him, did he? I kind of figured. A bully is a bully no matter where you find them. They all have the same traits. I can usually spot one a mile away."

He nodded in agreement. "Ye are meeting someone now? The cripple?"

That made Aislinn stop in her tracks. Teige immediately halted too, his hand on the hilt of his sword, as his eyes darted around expecting trouble.

"Oh relax," she snapped and Teige gazed at her questionably. "I want you to get something straight. The boy that you call cripple has a name, and from now on, I wish you to use it. Do we understand each other?"

Teige just nodded.

She started walking again with him at her heels. "A.J.?" He said her name timidly.

She looked at him, again thinking how very young he looked. He was an inch or so shorter than she was with long golden lustrous hair that was almost too lovely to be on a man's head. "Yes, Teige."

"What is the lad's name? I fear that I do not know. He has been called cripple, hey boy, or limpy for so long, that his real name has slipped away."

Aislinn shook her head. "Hamish. The boy's name is Hamish and don't go forgetting it again."

"Nay. I will remember it."

Hamish was already there, waiting for Aislinn, and when he saw her approach, he stood to greet her. He recognized Teige as one of the kern and looked hesitantly at him, wondering if he would tease him like all the others, but when he looked to Aislinn, she gave him a reassuring smile. He knew then that everything would be all right.

"Hamish, I would like you to meet Teige." She looked at Teige. "And Teige, let me introduce Hamish."

The two just nodded, obviously not sure how they should act toward each other. Aislinn chose to ignore their awkward greeting and immediately started in on business. "Today we will work on the upper body. I want you to follow my every move." She looked back at Teige. "Feel free to join in, if you wish." She didn't wait for her bodyguard to answer, but immediately turned and addressed her pupil. "Now let's begin."

They worked long and hard, first with simple stretches then graduating to extensions. She worked each muscle until Hamish cried for release, but still she commanded that he do more. Only when the sun had risen well over them did she call for a break. They sat down all three of them. Aislinn had filled her water bottle before she had left in the morning and offered it to the young boy. He gratefully took it from her. He turned the object in his hand, completely amazed at how light it was. He had thought that it was glass, but when he touched it, he knew that it was something else entirely.

Aislinn chuckled. "It's made of plastic." The boy looked at her, still bewildered. Even Teige was intrigued. "Where I come from, there a many things that are different. Drink." She nodded that it was all right. The boy drank thirstily and when he was finished, he wiped his mouth with the back of his hand. He sat there with his gangly legs stretched before him, and Aislinn's eyes wondered down the length of him. Hamish had noticed her open curiosity and tried to hide his shorter member behind the good one. Aislinn put a hand on his making him look at her. "Never hide who you are, Hamish." She moved in front of him sitting down on her haunches. Her hands moved over each leg. She bent the foot forward and then the other just to see how much of difference there was. "Maybe a half an inch," she said out loud. She looked at him then. "We need to make you a pair of shoes."

"Shoes? I have never owned a pair of shoes."

"It's about time that you did then."

Teige had thought that Aislinn would never return to her room, but finally she had called it a day. He was exhausted and ready to hit the sack and yet he knew that milady still possessed energy to do more.

Murrough stood when he saw Teige enter the Great Hall. Teige went straight over to him, and was offered a tankard. He gladly downed the honey wine before he began his report.

"Well?" Murrough was beginning to grow impatient.

"She's gone to her room now."

"What did she do all day? Ye looked haggard."

"Ye would too if ye were being dragged to this place and that. She awakened before the first light. I had to follow her out of the keep."

Murrough's brows furrowed. "Where would she go? She knows not a soul here."

"She has made friends and I can see why. Her openness is contagious. She is like no other woman that I have ever come across. She has a way of making ye think that ye are the only one that matters. Why she took young Hamish and…."

"Hamish?" Murrough interrupted.

"Aye. Ye know the lad. The cripple that they call limpy."

Murrough nodded. "Hamish, I remember now. Go on."

"She has Hamish doing all kinds of exercise that she claims will build up the muscles. I tried a few myself and I tell ye it was not an easy task." He rolled his shoulder. "I can still feel the ache, but it is a good ache mind ye. Like when ye yield a sword for longer than ye should have."

"Why on earth would the woman want Hamish to do these things?"

"Why she is going to make him a warrior."

Murrough just sat there for a moment thinking that he had not heard him correctly. "A warrior?"

"Aye." He emptied the rest of the liquid in his cup.

Murrough started laughing. When he saw that Teige was not sharing in his mirth, he quieted down a bit but still there was amusement in his voice. "Whoever heard of a cripple becoming a warrior? It is not done, I tell ye."

"With all do respects, A.J. does not like…."

"A.J.?"

"Aye, that is what she wants to be called. Anyway she wishes that the lad not be called cripple. She said that it gave him…now what did she call it?

Well whatever the word be, it meant that he would lack pride in himself. If ye think ye are nothing, then ye are nothing," he quoted her.

"Maybe so, but I like to call things as I see them. A dog is a dog, even if it wishes it were a cat. A man is either a warrior or he is not. And Hamish is not. She does more harm than good by telling the lad otherwise."

Teige shrugged. "I don't know. There was something more I saw in Hamish today. He walked a little taller."

"Ye must be joking."

"Nay, as I am sitting here, the lad actually carried on a conversation. Now when have ye heard Hamish say more than a handful of words, hey?"

As hard as Murrough tried, he could not think of a time that he had heard the boy speak. He was an outcast and no one took the time. "Hamish seems happy with this arrangement?"

"Aye. Come tomorrow A.J. is going to have Padrig make him a pair of shoes."

"Shoes? What for?"

Teige just shrugged. "I fear that I will have to tell ye tomorrow, but it seemed that it was important in some way."

Murrough nodded. Aislinn Hennessy was indeed becoming quite interesting. "Ye did fine, Teige. Ye may go. See that Cormac takes up the post for tonight. It looks like ye need some rest."

"Aye."

Chapter Twenty-Two

Cormac and Teige were inseparable friends, but both could not have been more different in personalities. They were as opposite as night is to day. Where Teige was quiet and reserved, Cormac was boisterous, and oh so charming that women, noble or not, swarmed to him like a bee to honey. His confidence was tenfold now that he had Fiona comforting his nights. So when he encountered Aislinn, which to him she seemed intriguingly exotic, he decided it was his duty to offer his assistance to see if she needed any personal comforting. Encountering numerous other ladies of standing and how they pretended to be coy, he was not put off by Aislinn profusely denying that she didn't want his attention.

"Come on, sweet, just a little kiss. I am a grand lover."

For the last time, Aislinn peeled the man's arm from her. She was getting to be a little annoyed. One more time and she would…he did it again and she came unglued. With a yell, she took her elbow and jabbed the man in the ribs. Then taking hold of his arm, she flipped him over her right side where he landed flat on his back. Cormac was so surprised that he remained there on the ground with his mouth wide open not sure of what exactly had happened.

"Now, my sweet," Aislinn imitated in a droll speech. "If ye so much as tap my shoulder, I am going to break yer hands. Do I make myself clear?"

"Aye." He didn't budge until after she had walked away. Of course, everyone that witnessed the scene couldn't help but pass it along. Before Aislinn had made it back to the hall, she had picked up a new name, *Scathach*, the woman warrior.

"Aye, Murrough. It is what I have been telling ye. She is strong, stronger than any woman I have ever come across." Cormac began reporting his day.

"Well trained this Hennessy woman," Murrough agreed. "May I ask how ye came to find this out?"

Cormac looked abashed, but he explained. "She seemed lonely and I…."

Murrough lifted his hand to stop him. "Say no more, Cormac. I've got the picture. Ye will get yerself in trouble, if ye continue to let the lower parts of yer body command ye. I advise ye not to try again with this she-wolf, especially if Dougray is around. Do ye want to share the same fate as Dermot?"

Cormac's gaze wandered over to where the man was sitting on the floor and fighting with the dogs for the scraps of meat that would be his dinner. "Nay, I have no wish to be cast out."

"Then ye best do what ye were assigned to do, and that is to watch and protect. I do not wish to hear that I have to send someone to protect the Hennessy woman from ye." He couldn't help but chuckle. "However the woman warrior seems to be able to handle the situation."

"Aye." Cormac rubbed his manly part like he was not sure that it was still attached. "I have no need for an unwilling woman, when I can have me pick."

"Like Fiona?" He couldn't help but mention.

Cormac's face actually glimmered with some personal remembrance. "That one, I'd liked to keep."

"Again ye tread on dangerous ground, my friend. Dougray has made claims to her."

"No marriage vows has he sought, Brehon or otherwise. Fiona told me that since his return, he has yet come to her. It is I that has been warming her hides."

Murrough raised his brows at this interesting piece of news. "Ye don't say?"

"He has not been to see Fiona." Murrough made a special visit to Rhiannon's home. She had been surprised at his visit since it was the middle of the day, when usually he was preoccupied with the business with the keep.

"Well this is a good. She was not right for him."

"Ye never told me this before." He followed her as she hung clothes out to dry.

"Ye never asked, but even if ye had, I'd probably would not have said much. Milord was a lost soul when his Ella was taken from him. He thought that he had failed her by not protecting her from death."

"A lost soul? And now what do ye see?"

"There is something that has come alive in his eyes that was not evident before. Purpose, I think."

"The *Scathach*?"

Rhiannon threw back her head and laughed. "Is this what they are calling her now?"

"A well befitting name, don't ye think?"

"I'm sure she would love to hear this."

"Ye see the way she dresses. She is more a man than a woman."

"Ye know nothing." Rhiannon shook her head.

"And ye do? Ye have a few conversations with her, while ye make her new attire and ye think ye understand her?"

"Even without speaking with her, I can see how she is. I've watched what she has done with Regan and the other bullying followers. Actions, I believe, best tells a person's true self. She has a good heart and is not afraid to show it. I like her already."

"I fail to understand ye, Rhiannon."

"I know this well enough, but I love ye all the same." She stood up on her tippy toes giving him a quick kiss on the cheek. "Now ye must be off, so that I may finish me chores, or ye will not be seeing me tonight, I think."

"I'm going. I'm going."

Chapter Twenty-Three

Aislinn had about enough of Cormac's care yesterday. She woke up with a kink in her neck from having to look over her shoulder to see if he was going to attack her again.

And he was the one sent to guard her!

He left her no room to breathe. The man was like her shadow, not letting her take a step without him being on her heels.

She wanted to meet with Hamish, but not with Cormac trying his best to be charming, when all he managed to do is be utterly annoying. How she wished that Teige would take up post again. Better yet, she wished that they would just leave her alone. If she could get a hold of Dougray, she'd give him a piece of her mind.

Just who did he think he was, depositing her at the castle then disappearing? She didn't care that he was a knight, a lord, or whatever. She had not seen nor heard from him for almost five days. She had just about enough of his hospitality.

Yesterday, she had overheard one of the men say that Dougray would be heading out this morning to tend to yet another one of his duties. Whatever they may be. Frankly she didn't care. She just wanted to make sure that he hadn't forgotten about finding a way to send her back home. She couldn't stay here, no matter how much she was beginning to like some of the inhabitants of Dunhaven. She wanted to go home. She missed her parents and Connor and she had her writing career, too. If she was stuck here, what alternatives did she have? To her, it didn't look like a promising future.

It was nearly dawn by the time that she tied the sheets together in knots, so that they formed a long rope. It would have been so much easier if she could have walked down the winding steps, but Cormac had planted himself right outside her door. He'd never let her by for he had already informed her that Dougray was very busy and was not to be disturbed. Escape was the only way.

Aislinn had written in her journal a list of items that she would have to acquire, if she was to stay here any length of time. Rope was number one on the list.

"I'm ready," she said as she tightened the last knot, yanking on it to make sure that it would not come loose.

"I wish that ye would reconsider, milady. It is a long way down." Moira gulped as she glanced out the window. She had the urge to slam the fortified shutters closed and lock them up tight so that Aislinn would not be able to partake in this life-threatening escapade.

"The homemade rope is long enough. I plan on swinging outward, using the castle walls as leverage. Then I'll let go and land on the soft dirt.

"The dirt does not look all that soft to me." She turned to see that Aislinn was already tying the one end of the sheet to the thick post of her bed. Moira marveled how at ease her mistress seemed over this little adventure that she was so determined to embark on. When she, herself, was a nervous wreck.

Aislinn took one look at Moira and almost laughed, for the girl looked like she was about to burst into tears. "Do not worry, Moira. You are not sending me to my death. I've done things like this before. Why I have gone bungee jumping and rock climbing with my brother Connor many times. Believe me, to keep up with him has kept me in very good shape. This is no harder than walking down the stone steps, but so much more fun. Maybe you will want to try it."

"Nay, I could not." Her blue eyes widened so much that they threatened to pop right out their sockets. This time Aislinn did laugh.

"Don't worry, Moira. I would never insist you try. Now help me get the rest of this to the window."

Dougray had been avoiding Aislinn because he felt in some way that he was being dishonest with Ella's memory. Aislinn haunted his dreams, and now seemed to be in his waking thoughts as well causing him to be quite irritable with everyone around. He didn't know what to do with her. He had promised her that he would try to find a way to send her home, but he had a feeling that this might not be so easily accomplished. He also was beginning to realize that maybe he didn't want her to go.

He wanted to laugh at himself for even having this foolish thought, for the woman drove him to distraction. They couldn't even have a decent conversation before they were both at each other's throats. So why was he dreaming about her? "*Dar Dia!* She is nothing like a woman should be." Again he was mumbling under his breath, trying to convince himself that he was not attracted to the unconventional female. He had thought by purposely staying away that he would get her out of his system and see her as she truly was, but the longer he did not converse with her, the more he desired to do so.

And the blasted woman had not stayed quiet in his absence. Within five days, she had already made a name for herself. He had heard men, woman, and children whisper her acquired name, *Scathach*, the eponymous goddess of the Island of Skye. She had been the martial teacher to the great Cuchulainn, among other great heroes. "Warrior woman, *Dar Dia!*" He continued at a brisk walk to the keep. He didn't care that it was early. He needed to talk to her especially about the latest matter that had been brought to his attention. He had been told that she took on the cripple as her student. He shook his head. "Aye, if she were *Scathach*, she most certainly would do such a thing." The goddess was known as the guardian of the young people, who sought to know their full potential. The only problem was how could she have encouraged Hamish to believe that he could be with the kern?

He looked up when he saw Cormac making a mad dash around the keep. Knowing that he was the one on guard to protect Aislinn, he was quick to follow.

What a sight that Dougray beheld. His nerves tensed immediately for sailing through the sky like winged bird in flight was Aislinn swinging from a long white rope. He was too afraid to yell at her for fear that she would lose her concentration, but she looked so at ease with her stunt as if she had done this a thousand times. Maybe she had. She never ceased to amaze him on her agile abilities to do the unexpected. Still he did not relax until he witnessed her final push from the side of the castle wall. She landed with a thump on her behind, nearly on top of his feet.

Aislinn hadn't realized until that moment that she had an audience. She looked up rather sheepishly to see Dougray's gray eyes glaring down at her. She gave him an irresistibly devastating grin that made him unsure if he wanted to throttle her or kiss her. "So there you are?" Her voice held just a hint of irritation. "I was beginning to think that you had abandoned me."

"I'm sorry, milord," Cormac began. "I did not know she would try to escape out the window. I swear that I never left my post. I was...." He stopped explaining once Dougray held up his hand to halt him.

"Nay, I do not blame ye. Go now. I wish to speak to Lady Aislinn, alone."

"Aye, milord." Cormac began walking back to the keep. He glanced behind him only once. He didn't see a submissive woman before his lord, but an angry one that was actually waving a finger at him, as though he deserved a scolding. Cormac smiled as he continued on. What man would ever be able to tame such a free spirit?

"You left me for days and without knowing a soul. Thank you very much." She poked at his chest.

"I left ye in good hands."

"In good hands! Are you daft? I have not had a moment's peace. First, I have one lurking in the shadows. I nearly had a coronary because I thought that I was being stalked, and then there is Cormac who is a gigantic nuisance. I can't even take two steps without him bumping into me."

"Obviously with good reasons." He pointed to the dangling rope. "What stunt was that, pray tell? Are ye deliberately trying to kill yerself? For if that is the case, please grant me the honor. I'll do it quickly and be done with it."

"I was not in any danger." Her dark eyes flashed imperiously. "I would not have done it if I thought that I would be hurt."

He threw up his hands. "*Dar Dia*! Do ye think that ye can predict when ye might make a mistake?"

"I don't make mistakes."

"I give up. I give up!" He grabbed her hand and started dragging her back to the keep.

"What are you doing? Let go of me this instant." She tried to pull away from him.

"Ye have caused enough trouble and I will take over from here on end."

"I'm warning you, Dougray Fitzpatrick, if you don't let go of me so help me God I'll…"

He stopped quick and turned on her. "Ye'll what? Huh?" He was so close to her face that she could see that his eyes were bloodshot, as though he had not been sleeping well. This infuriated her further, for obviously someone was keeping him up late, and she had a hunch that she knew just who that someone was.

Without warning, she acted out her aggressions. With one quick sweep of her leg, she landed him on his backside. His mouth opened in surprise at how quick she had been. "You bastard!" she hissed, adding insult to injury. She was about to storm away but he had about enough of her temper tantrums and he grabbed at her leg, bringing her down on top of him. She fought and rolled to get away, but he fought harder and was able to hold her down. He straddled her and pinned her arms above her head.

His mouth was just inches from hers. "Don't ever do that again," he spat at her with such venom that she stilled her movements.

"Better. Now let's set the record straight. That was the second time ye made reference to my parentage. Let me inform ye that I am legitimate and I will not hear ye say that I am not." He pushed away from her and came to his feet. "I must be mad to put up with this! First ye scare me to death. Ye try to do bodily harm to my person and then call me names. Pray tell what do ye do for an encore? To think that I actually sought to share yer company."

She sat there her legs arched so that she could rest her arms upon her knees. "Why? Did your little tart need to rest?" The sarcasm dripped from each word. "You look a sight, I'll have you know."

"What are ye talking about?" His eyes narrowed.

She came to her feet and brushed off her pants. "The woman with the big wannabagos." She used her hands to get her point across with a quick pretend squeeze of a large chest.

He almost smiled at her description. "Fiona?"

"Fiona?" She was put back. She had thought they were talking about Ella. "Who's Fiona? There are others?"

Now he was completely confused. "Others?"

She stomped her foot. "Stop answering me with a question, like you don't know what I'm talking about."

"I don't know what yer talking about."

"Oh forget it!" She threw up her arms and started back to the keep. "Just forget it. What do I care who you sleep with? Sleep with the whole damn village if you want to."

So this was what had her all rankled. She thought that he was fulfilling his basic needs and she was…upset? That rather captured him by surprise. He easily caught up to her. "Blast it, lass, stop."

She did, but reluctantly with her arms folded against her heaving chest. "Be quick."

"Why? Do ye have another window that ye need to be jumping out of?"

"That's it!" She turned to leave and this time it was final or so she thought.

"Then I guess ye are not interested in seeing the one and only person that may be able to send ye back home."

That stilled her departure. She turned around and covered the distance that separated them. "You'll take me to Neala? Now?"

"After we break fast. It is quite a walk to where she resides."

She was so happy that she threw her arms around his neck but just as quickly she pulled away to look at him. "Now why do you have to be so difficult?"

"Difficult?" He was still reeling from her sudden show of affection.

"There you go again, answering my questions with a question, and yes, difficult. You could have said this to me in the beginning and there never would have been this little misunderstanding."

He opened his mouth to tell her this was not the reason they argued, but he decided that it was better to let the matter drop. He shook his head. "Come." He took her arm, which she quickly pulled away as they walked beside each other. He still needed to bring up the matter of Hamish, but thought that he would wait to broach that subject when he had a full stomach. It was not wise to enter a battle without nourishment.

There were many in the banquet hall that broke fast with them. Aislinn was even beginning to know quite a few of them by name and they acknowledged her as well. They weren't as rough and unapproachable as she had first thought.

Dougray leaned near. "Ye seemed to have made a few friends in my absence."

"One does what one must." She drank the warm milk that was given to her. She wasn't particularly fond of it, but there wasn't much else to drink. "What I wouldn't do for a café mocha about now."

Dougray chuckled. "One of those coffee drinks?"

"Yes. I wouldn't be so grumpy in the morning, you know, if I could start my day out with a little caffeine."

"Believe me if I were able to, I would give it to you gladly. God knows that I would love to have ye agreeable. Personally, I do not know how ye were able to drink the concoction. It left my hands trembling a mite."

"That would be the caffeine and the sugar combined. If you aren't used to the combination I suppose that it could do that to you."

"Now the tea that ye had me try, that I enjoyed." He stabbed his knife into a slab of venison and took a large bite. He saw her grimace. "Do ye not like the meat?"

"Never cared much for it in the morning. A nice scone would be wonderful."

"Hmm, the sweet biscuit. Not very filling though."

"That's about all my stomach can handle."

Dougray turned to the servants standing behind them. With a snap of his fingers, a young boy came forward. "Please go to the kitchen and see if Roth has some fresh bread ready."

"Dougray, don't do that."

He turned to her. "It is not any trouble." He looked to the boy who seemed to be hesitating. "Go." The boy bowed before scurrying off to do his lord's bidding. "I can't have ye going with me on an empty stomach. Warm milk is not enough."

"Thank you," she mumbled wishing he wouldn't have bothered anyone.

"What did ye say?" He had heard her but wanted her to repeat it. She looked at him with open suspicion.

"You heard me, my lord, so don't go asking me to repeat it." Seeing the amusement in her eyes, he laughed.

"Ye don't say more than a few nice words to me; I thought I'd relish in it for a few hands of time."

She lightly slapped his arm. "I'm nice to you."

"Ye? Surely ye jest, milady, for if ye have displayed warm affections to me, I do not recall them."

She was about to make another retort, but the young boy had returned with a plate of freshly baked bread. He bowed slightly when he placed the dish before her. "That smells wonderful." She was about to indulge, when she saw the young boy lick his lips. For the first time, she noticed how very thin the child was and her heart went out to him. "Here have some." She offered the bread to him. She saw panic in the child's face, as he first glanced at her and then to Dougray.

Dougray placed his hand over hers. "That is not how it is done."

Her eyes flashed with anger. "What? I cannot share my meal with a starving child?"

"The lad will have his share later."

Aislinn again glanced at the boy who looked like he hadn't had a decent meal in a long time. "I want him to have some of my bread. I cannot possibly eat a whole loaf all by myself. It's good now while it's still warm." She met Dougray's disapproving gaze ready to cause a scene if necessary.

"Go on then. Give the lad yer food. Feed the whole keep if ye see fit. I have lost my appetite." He rose then glowering down at her, "I will meet ye outside the keep. I assume ye will be able to find the way without mishap?"

"Can you?" she shot back. He didn't answer her but stormed from her sight.

She looked back to the young boy, who seemed unsure what to do. Aislinn lowered her voice hoping to put the child at ease. "What is your name?"

"Edmond, milady."

"Well, Edmond, the bread is yours to share with others, if you wish."

"Thank ye, milady." He took the loaf from her hands. He was about to make his leave when she halted him.

"Edmond, you did hear what your lord said, that I may feed the whole keep if I saw fit to do so?"

The boy hesitated. "Aye, but I do not think...."

"It does not matter what he truly meant. The point is he gave me permission." She smiled to herself at the opportunity this represented. She looked up to see that Edmond was scurrying away, clutching his meal to his chest.

Aislinn took her time, finished her milk for she saw no reason to rush to Dougray with his temperament still unleashed. When she felt enough time had lapsed, she started for the doors, but before she left the hall, she noticed a man sitting against the wall as if he was trying to blend into its thickness. That alone made her stop, and when she leaned down to see if he was all right, astonishment washed over her face for she recognized him as the man that Dougray had nearly killed for knocking her down. "I know you."

"Aye, milady. I am Dermot." He was surprised that she would stop to converse with him.

"Yes, I remember. I never had the opportunity to thank you for trying to bring me a drink." She looked at the man who seemed not to have bathed in a while. He didn't look like he had eaten well either.

He never thought that he would smile again, but she had a way about her that put people at ease. "I practically drenched ye."

"Well...the gesture was well meant and I appreciate the effort. Tell me, Dermot, why aren't you with the other men?"

He looked at his feet, afraid to meet her gaze. "I have been disgraced, milady."

"Disgraced? For what?" Then it all started to make sense. "Dermot, are you disgraced because of the incident with me?"

He nodded.

"I will straighten this out." She stood to leave, but Dermot took hold of her arm in a desperate plea.

"Nay, milady. I beg of ye, do not do this. It will only make things worse. In time milord may forgive me and let me into his services again. Do not interfere and draw attention to me."

"But if I could help...."

"Please...." His grip tightened.

"If that is what you wish." He nodded and released her arm with a sigh of relief.

Aislinn left the hall not understanding at all why the man wanted to be punished for something that he didn't even do. Furthermore it angered her that Dougray would discipline the man so unfairly.

Lost in thought, she wasn't looking where she was going and nearly ran into Murrough. "Pardon me." She looked up to see that he was staring at her with a suspicious expression.

"Milady." He nodded. She was about to move passed him, but he addressed her again. "Ye best not speak with the likes of Dermot."

"And why is that?" She met his gaze not in the least bit intimidated.

"It is not done. He is in disfavor with the lord of this keep."

She chuckled without humor evident in her voice. "I do not care in the least who Dougray likes or dislikes. Furthermore he was wrong about Dermot. He did nothing wrong."

"Milord does not see it that way."

"Tell me, Murrough, do you not have a thought of your own?" She saw him flinch at her words.

"I do not question what milord states."

"Well maybe you should. He seems to trust you. You should be honest with what you deem is right, and tell him when he has made a poor judgment. That is what a true friend would do."

"Are ye questioning my loyalty?"

"Calm down, Murrough. I see that you are loyal to your lord. I'm just saying that you should voice your opinions a little more loudly. Come now, do you think that Dermot deserved to be cast aside in the manner that he was?" Murrough didn't answer but his stance spoke louder than any words ever could. Aislinn sighed. "Dougray is but a man and he can make mistakes too."

"Ye will do best not to question the man that houses ye."

She shook her head. "You are not getting the point here. I respect Dougray. He's a strong, decent man who seems to care about others, but he is far from perfect. It is up to his close friends to set him straight." With that she swept around Murrough, who just stood there staring at her retreating back. He failed to understand her. She talked about respect for Dougray and in the same breath she criticized him. Which was it? Did she want the best for him, or did she wish to destroy him? She was a walking contradiction and needed to be watched. He didn't care that others thought of her as the goddess *Scathach*. He knew that she wasn't at all what she appeared to be, and what made it so disturbing was the fact that Dougray obviously knew the secret. This baffled him for his friend had never kept anything from him before, but somehow this woman had managed to convince him to do so. He didn't like it.

Chapter Twenty-Four

They walked into the forest of oaks, with Aislinn taking in the tranquil surroundings. She was finally going to meet the woman who would help her find her way home. The sooner she left, the happier she would be. "How much farther?"

Dougray glanced at her. "Tired?" His voice was laced with sarcasm.

"I can out walk you any day. I just wanted to know so that I can count the minutes when I can be gone from here." She walked up ahead just to prove her point.

His nostrils flared. "Well, I cannot wait to wash my hands of ye." He caught up and passed her in one breath. "Keep up, will ye?" he shot over his shoulder. "I don't want ye dallying and prolonging my responsibility for ye."

She clenched her fists. "Oooh!"

Finally at the same time, they both broke through the clearing to where a beautiful lake seemed to materialize out of nowhere. Dougray continued forward and ducked into Neala's meager dwelling only to find it empty. He went on ahead to search for her, but Aislinn for the moment forgot her hurry to go home and stood there captivated. Large oaks lined the entire lake giving it a tranquil beauty of enchantment. The truth of what she was feeling washed over her features in a peaceful smile.

"Aah, ye are spellbound by it, as I was the very first time I set eyes on this place."

Aislinn turned surprised to see that the old woman was standing so near. Surprisingly, she was not at all frightened.

"It is breathtaking," Aislinn answered her with all honesty.

"Aye, that it is." The old woman held Aislinn's gaze.

"You must be Neala." Aislinn only asked to confirm what she already knew.

"Aye." Her smile showed a nearly toothless grin. "Ye must be the traveler."

"I suppose that I am. I'm A.J. Hennessy."

"Is it, now?" Her brows rose ever so slightly as she waited for her to say more.

"Well, A.J. is just a nickname. My given name is Aislinn, Aislinn Jacqueline."

Neala seemed satisfied with that introduction and moved passed her. "Come, Aislinn Jacqueline, and warm yerself by me fire."

She followed. "Dougray is around here, somewhere."

"I'm sure that he is."

Aislinn sat down on the large rock while Neala threw a peat log onto the fire making the flames spark to life. Then with a seemingly great effort, the old woman sat down across from her. She was covered with endless lines of age and gnarled by arthritis, making her look as ancient as the oak trees that stood around them. She hardly seemed the appropriate candidate to rescue her from her apparent dilemma.

The old woman stared at her from across the fire. It was like she wanted to read into Aislinn's mind, but instead of making her feel uneasy, she began to relax becoming aware of the brilliantly intelligent sheen behind Neala's eyes that beckoned her to trust her.

Aislinn cleared her throat and leaned forward resting her elbows and forearm on her knees. "So?"

The old woman lifted her gray brows and waited for Aislinn to speak her mind.

"I want to go home," she stated with finality.

"Ye've only just arrived. Is me hospitality so bad that ye want to run back to the keep?"

"No," she said hastily, not wanting to offend her. "I don't mean I want to go back to the castle. I'm saying that I want to go home, to my real home. Dougray said…well he led me to believe that you would be able to…you know…zap." She snapped her fingers.

"Zap?" Neala resisted the urge to laugh and carefully kept a straight face so that Aislinn would continue.

"Pardon me, but are you not the witch?"

This was too much and she let out a chortle, which indeed sounded like an old crone's cackle. "Witch to some I suppose, but I wouldn't go claiming it as fact or the Christian priests would surely have me burned at the stake."

Aislinn sat there for a full minute before the dreaded truth seemed to wash over her, drowning any hope. "You can't send me back, can you?"

"Powers beyond me brought ye here. I have no control over such things. I can only see what will happen, and even then, it does nah mean they will come to pass. The power is sometimes unpredictable."

Aislinn stood, rubbing her forehead as her disappointment started developing into a horrendous headache. "I don't want to stay."

"Then why did ye come?"

"I didn't come willingly." She threw up her hands.

"Nay?" The old woman questioned her like she suspected that this was not entirely true.

Aislinn couldn't meet her scrutinizing gaze as she stumbled over her words. "Well, I might have…I did follow, but God! If I had known what I was getting into, I would have run back in the other direction."

"We seldom listen to reason." Neala's eyes became gentle with compassion for her obvious plight.

Trying to appear calm when in all reality she was ready to scream. She managed to take a deep breath and smoothed her brow with both hands. "Why am I here? Do you know that at least?"

"Only ye can know for sure."

Aislinn in her frustration began pacing, her hands bunched at her sides. "I don't know why I'm here. You were supposed to tell me."

Neala shook her head in dismay. "Young lass, ye must learn to be patient. Ye will see the truth unfold before ye, and then ye will be able to go back to whence ye've came, but unfortunately not until then. Ye're one of the travelers and the power that brought ye here is very strong. It'll most likely see it through, now that it has begun."

Aislinn stopped before the fire to face her with her dark accusing eyes. "You talk in riddles. What power?"

"Don't look so hard for the answers. They're there waiting to be understood; ye make yer own puzzles."

"What do you mean? I don't' understand."

Dougray had thought that he would have to inform Aislinn that he could not find Neala. All the way back, he was preparing himself for what he was sure would be a tirade of accusing disappointment. So he was quite surprised to find that the old witch somehow had been able to sneak past him, and had forgone the formalities of introducing herself. "I see that ye two are already well acquainted."

"What game are you playing?" Aislinn shot the words at him causing him to immediately become on guard.

"What now, lass? You said that ye wished to speak with Neala and I have brought ye to her."

"You told me that she would be able to send me back to my time."

He looked questionably at Neala, who was sitting so peacefully next to the peat fire as though this was a family gathering and nothing more. "Well, old woman, ye heard her. She wishes to go back. Do us all a favor and quickly do as she bids."

She sighed long and hard knowing that they blamed her for something she had no control over. She shook her head in dismay. "Ye young fools understand nothing of the power of the universe. I did none of this. Ye must play this to the end and see what lies before ye."

"See." Aislinn lifted her hands palms up in a jerking manner letting him know just how much she was fed up with this whole situation. "This is ridiculous. If you didn't know how this procedure worked, why in the world did you involve someone else? I was vacationing with my family, and you had to come along and ruin my perfectly organized life."

He looked at her with a sardonic expression. "As far as I could see, yer life was not so perfect."

"What is that supposed to mean?" She glared at him with her hands on her hips. All that was missing from her angry stance was an impatient tapping foot.

"Oh forget it." He decided that it wasn't worth getting into, but she wouldn't let it go.

"I won't forget it. You started this and I want to know what you meant by that loudmouth remark."

He knew that he should just bite his tongue, but she had pushed him one too many times. "Well if ye insist."

"Oooh, I do."

"Fine. Sit down and I'll tell ye." She refused to move. "I said sit!" The bellowing demand surprised her into at least somewhat complying. She sat down, but she made such a production out of it that there was no room for doubt that she obeyed his command under absolute protest.

He circled her before he began his open assessment of her. "I think that ye are running away."

"I am not running away. I was…." She tried to stand only to have his hand come down on her shoulder, forcing her to remain seated.

"Uh uh…I wasn't finished yet." She folded her arms across her chest and waited. He began again, "I see a woman that's courageous beyond belief, but I also see a frightened child beneath that hard exterior ye've created for yerself. Yer parents made ye strong and independent, but so much so that ye have fortified an unapproachable wall around ye. Ye simply do not know how to rely on anyone else and not because ye don't want to. Ye're just afraid to take a chance with a real man that would treat ye the way ye should be treated.

"Yer brother played that family gathering on the contraption ye own and I saw the type of man that ye seemed to take under your wing, trying to shape him into whatever you're looking for and knowing all along that you will fail. Ye pick mere lads that have no idea how to even begin to be a man. How I loathe whatever made ye retreat behind that insufferable wall of yers."

She just sat there stunned and uncomfortable with the fact that he knew her so well. She did choose men that would never stand up to her, so that she could domineer the relationship, and when she wanted to, she would encourage its end without ever allowing herself to get too close. She was well aware that it was a definite quandary, but she had no idea how to rectify it, so that she could have something substantial and fulfilling, things she so desperately craved.

All of it was true, but she wasn't ready to admit her faults publicly and especially not to him. She tried desperately to defend herself. "I sabotaged the relationships on purpose because they weren't…I was waiting for…." Her eyes locked with his gray turbulent ones causing her to lose her train of thought.

"Ye are waiting for what, Aislinn?" He moved toward her with a look upon his face that showed such tenderness that she should have felt comfortable enough to open up to him, but instead it invoked a multitude of emotions that petrified her. She fought the panic that rose to suffocate her by lashing out with heated words. "It's none of your business! Just forget it and write me off as a lost cause."

Instead of returning a retort of his own, he withdrew for he had heard the faint thread of frightened hysteria in her voice. Whatever it was she was waiting for had put her in a frozen limbo, where all decisions and actions were impossible, but yet he knew that she still could be reached if someone was persistent enough to try. "Ye are not a lost cause, Aislinn. There is always hope, and I envy the man that will unlock yer passion." His gaze was as soft as a caress and it sent a dim flush racing like a fever across her face. Her mind reeled with confusion, making her feel like she had somehow lost direction.

She jumped to her feet again covering up her self-consciousness with anger. "Are you finished now?"

He eyed her unblinkingly for a few seconds before he nodded. "Aye."

She looked him over from head to toe in the most condescending way. "You think that you have me all figured out. Well what about you? Hmm?"

"What about me?" He squared his shoulder not at all sure that he wanted her to give a rendition of what she thought of him. They circled each other like caged animals ready to lunge at each other's throats. Neala just sat there rather amused over this little turn of events and said not a word to calm the heated passions.

"You, my lord, are so closed minded when the mood suits you that you have no idea what is really going on. Oh you are indeed heroic almost to a fault, but you fail to realize that not everyone needs or wants your saving."

"I think that is…."

"Oh no, my lord. It is only fair that you hear me out." He clamped his mouth shut and she continued. "I also see a man who would never stop himself from enjoying the pleasures that only a woman could grant him, if…" She let the "if" hang in the air just long enough to make sure she had his full attention. "…there was not a commitment involved."

"And where would ye get a ridiculous idea like that?"

"Let me refresh your memory. While you groped me, you called out another woman's name. She's probably of the past since when we arrived, it was only *Miss well endowed* that was there to greet you. What was her name? Fiona." She could see that he was going to deny that claim but she put up her hand to halt his words. "Uh uh. I am not blind, Dougray. There is something between you and Fiona, and it wasn't the friendliness of a sister." The clenching of his jaw muscles at work, along with his silence, was all she needed to know that she was right.

She had wanted to hurt him, but instead she thought that she sounded more like a jealous lover, a claim she had no right to. To try and stifle these unwarranted feelings, again heated words flew from her mouth, as if they had life all their own. "If I were to analyze your aloofness, I would say that you've been hurt in the past. Possibly it was the woman Ella? Maybe you thought that you were in love with her, and she left you without warning. Now you are too afraid to expose your heart to another. You want to keep it simple, have a relationship that you know will go nowhere."

"Enough!" How close to the truth she had come. Somehow she was aware of his fears, but what she didn't realize was that when he was with her, she made that emptiness go away. She made him want again only she wasn't willing to go there.

"What? Oh I see how it is: I was supposed to just sit there and listen to you tear me down, but when it comes to hearing the truth, you can't take it. Tsk, tsk, my lord." As she paused to catch her breath, her own personal fears seemed to crash down on her. He stood there tall and straight like a towering black oak. Despite all her brave words, she was trembling for his ruggedness and vital power attracted her, drew her like a moth to a flame. He thought that she was only attracted to a man that she could control, but he was wrong. She wanted…. She shook her head trying to deny what she felt for him, but the endless silence that they shared only seemed to electrify the tangible bond between them. If he took a step toward her, kissed her as he had before, it would be her undoing.

She wanted him to make the move, but at the same time her mind screamed to resist. He was not a man to toy with. Like a frightened animal that has only retreat on its side to survive, she somehow made her feet move. She had to get away to sort out her emotions. She purposely turned and walked away, praying he would not stop her.

"Where are ye going?" His voice was barely edged with control. Something had passed between them, but before he could come to terms with it, she was fleeing.

She just continued to walk throwing him the answer, confusing him further, "Oh take a load off, will you? I'm just walking down to the water's edge." Her obvious sarcasm rang through the air, making Neala chuckle.

Dougray threw her a lethal glare. It was almost like he had forgotten that she was there and was offended that she had not made her presence known sooner. "This is most interesting, do ye nah think?" she questioned him.

"The woman is impossible." He waved his hand in dismissal. "I have followed yer orders, Neala. Unbelievable as it may still seem, I brought her back with me and against my will, I might add. And just look where it has gotten me? Nowhere," he answered himself. "She has done nothing but give me a headache and ye think that she is important to the future. How? Is she to drive me mad? I have enough problems with the Butlers without having a troublesome female to contend to."

"There are multitudes of happenings that are important to the future. The power is surrounding ye and that lass." She nodded to Aislinn's retreating figure. "I see fire in yer eyes, Fitzpatrick, that I had long thought was gone. She has already done well."

"Ye see fire, old woman, because she has pushed me to the brink of distraction. I can only thank God that I was not stranded in her time and place. I could not stand to be with a lass who does not know her place."

"And where is a woman's place, milord?"

He hesitated, surprised by her question. "Well ye know where…in…well in her place is all." He was beginning to be perturbed with the old crone.

"I see. Ye favor simpleminded women so that ye can tell her how she should be thinking."

"That's absurd. I do not fancy a simpleminded woman. I welcome one that can challenge a man's mind."

"Aislinn is very capable, aye?"

He felt like he had just been led into a trap, and his eyes narrowed knowingly. "Aye, but too capable."

"Aah, maybe, but…" She studied him through her half-closed eyes. "…I think, ye like her."

"Like her? Haven't ye been listening, old woman?"

"Aye. I have heard clearly." She nodded her head.

Dougray found her sitting near the water's edge, her arms securely hugging her knees close to her body, while her chin rested on the top of them. She didn't give any indication that she had heard him come up behind her, until he sat down. She tilted her head to look at him. Those brown eyes looked so sad and maybe even a little lost, so much so that he had the urge to pull her close to comfort her, but he felt that she would balk against such a gesture. He did not want to have another argument.

"When I was small," she broke the silence and he took pause to listen. "I used to sit in our backyard that had a pool with trees and plants that surrounded it. I used to pretend all kinds of adventures. My favorite was that the pool was actually a large lake in the woods, and that I was the lady of the glen waiting for my knight. This was a magical place I created in my mind. If I closed my eyes, I could see that man oh so clearly."

"What did he look like?" He didn't want her to stop talking, for this was the first time that she had offered a glimpse to her thoughts.

She wore faraway smile on her face as she recalled those long ago memories. "Oh, he was tall, dark and handsome. You know the typical fantasy any young, healthy girl of pre-teen years would have."

"And would this knight love ye?"

There was a pensive shimmer in the shadow of her eyes. "With all his heart. He would do anything for me, save me if deemed necessary."

"And ye would care for him in the same manner?" His voice was oddly gentle.

For a moment, she regarded him with a speculative gaze, for she was beginning to wonder what they were truly talking about. In the end, she answered him with all honesty. "I would love him right back." She turned away then, fearing that she had revealed too much. "Why can't life be like our dreams?"

He let out a long tired breath. "I do not have the answer."

She was beginning to feel stiff from sitting so long and she rolled her shoulders back and forth. Her gaze found his once more. "What now? It doesn't look like my knight in shining armor is going to whisk me home anytime soon."

He placed a reassuringly strong hand on her forearm. "I will not abandon ye. We will think of something, aye?" Their eyes locked and he could see the frightened little girl beneath the tough exterior. At that moment, he wanted to lean forward and kiss away all her uncertainties. She seemed to sense his purpose and turned away. He sighed regretting that he hadn't acted on his impulse.

"Besides..." he purposely let the word hang, forcing her to look at him again.

"Besides what?"

"...if a knight in shining armor actually did come to rescue ye," his voice was laced with humor, "ye would end up knocking him on his arse and taking his horse away from him."

Try as she might, she couldn't help but smile at the picture he had conjured up.

"See, things are not so bad." He easily rose to his feet and offered her his hand. "Come. Neala has welcomed us to share a meal with her. Then we must be on our way before nightfall catches us too far from home."

Home? But home was not supposed to be a lonely room in an old drafty keep.

She looked at his offering and sighed. It was odd, but as soon as her reaching fingers touched the warmth of his hand, she felt a sense of security.

Chapter Twenty-Five

Dougray sat at the long table in the Great Hall and listened to each and every tenant's grievances. They were usually nothing of grave importance, just petty arguments that were easily settled. He noticed that Fiona had entered the room and his eyes roved over her gown that clung to curves he knew all too well. She smiled. Once he would not have been able to resist her charm, but now he had no desire for her.

Fiona saw him look away causing her smile to falter, but she refused to be daunted. She patiently waited her turn so that she might speak. She walked up to the table and curtsied with a slow meaningful bow, exposing the tops of her creamy white breasts. Dougray heard Murrough cough behind his hand, but he ignored it. "*Dia dhuit*, milord."

"*Dia dhuit*," he said anxious for her to finish her flamboyant greeting. "Ye have something ye wish to present?"

Fiona was not sure how to take his somewhat removed tone. She had dressed in her most revealing gown, and had brushed her hair until it shone to perfection with wisps of golden tresses shaping her face. She even added a bit of color to her face knowing that it would heighten her cheekbones, but yet Dougray sat there completely unaffected. She cleared her throat. "Milord, I need to draw yer attention to what has transpired, for surely ye must not know of what is going on."

"Please get to the point, Fiona. I have others whom I must tend to as well." He nodded toward the line of people that still waited to have an audience with him.

"Very well. I will not sugar coat it. It seems that Rhiannon has been instructed to make garments for the Lady Aislinn."

"Aye, that is what she is supposed to do."

"But garments befitting a man? She is sewing together fabrics to make trews and some other trousers that somewhat resembled the outfit she arrived in. Surely this is not what ye had intended."

On Dougray's right hand side Murrough shifted uncomfortably. Surely, Rhiannon would not go against her lord's requests.

Dougray knew that Fiona was fishing for trouble and he was in no way going to give her the satisfaction. "Rhiannon is very capable and I have no doubt that the garments will be of good standing."

Fiona's mouth dropped not believing she had heard him correctly. "But…."

"Is that all?"

What more could she say? He obviously was going to let Aislinn do whatever she pleased. Was there no fault that he would ever find with his guest? She refused to believe that and was determined to find something that would shower disfavor on her. "That is all. I was not aware that ye already knew of this. Good day." This time she did not curtsey but turned on her heels with her hair flying behind her as she stomped out of the room, shoving people aside as she went. Dougray saw Cormac look hesitantly at him before he hurried after her.

Murrough leaned forward. "Do ye wish for me to have a word with Cormac?"

"Nay. If the lad wishes to be with Fiona, I have no difficulty with it. I actually welcome the idea."

"Ye have parted with her then?"

"I guess that I have." Until that moment, he had not been sure.

"And what of Rhiannon? Ye wish for her to continue to make the garments for milady?"

"Murrough, I want Aislinn to feel at home here. If the comforts of trews makes this so, then I have no uncertainties with it, but…" He paused for a moment and rubbed his chin that was in a need of a good shave. "…make sure that Rhiannon is aware that I wish the gowns I requested to be made also."

"Aye, milord, consider it done."

Dougray waved the next person forward, who happened to be the cook and he was dragging young Edmond behind him. "What seems to be yer complaint, Roth?" Dougray asked, as he glanced at the young lad curiously.

"It is milady." Roth's bug-like eyes widened making him look like a toad. "She has entered the kitchen in a whirl of activity."

He had expected a complaint against the child not of Aislinn. "Milady?"

"Aye, she is shouting orders to my assistants and to me." He tapped his chest. "Me, the head cook!"

"What is this about?"

"Milord, I expected ye to explain it. She says that ye gave her permission to have a feast put together. She is ordering meat, fish and vegetables to be prepared. Right now she has my assistants cleaning every pot and pan for she said that they were an utter disgrace. Disgrace!" he shouted not at all hiding the fact that he had been offended.

Dougray was at a loss to what she had planned. He sat back in his chair and looked to the boy who was purposely avoiding his gaze. "What of ye, Edmond? Do ye know why milady is doing this?"

Roth jerked the boy in front of him. "Tell him. Tell him what ye told me."

Edmond was trembling from head to toe and was afraid to meet the piercing silvery gray of Dougray's gaze. "She is planning a feast for all that tend to the needs of the keep."

The silence that radiated from Dougray made Edmond glance up, wondering if he was about to be thrashed for being so bold.

"Tell him the rest." Roth pushed at him.

He cleared his throat. "Ye gave her permission, milord."

"I what?"

"Ye said that she could do as she wished. Ye remember the morning that ye broke fast and she handed me the loaf of warm bread?"

Dougray remembered the morning and the heated words he threw at her. He shook his head at her ingenious display. She had heard the granted reign he bestowed to her, though she knew perfectly well that he had said it in anger, not as something he intended for her to follow through with. He looked to Roth. "How are our storerooms stocked?"

"Well prepared, milord."

"Then I see no reason not to have a feast granted to those that tend to my needs. Ye will follow Lady Aislinn's instructions."

"But milord, she is so demanding. And begging your pardon, but interfering as well."

"I will explain to her that she is to come to ye with the orders to be carried out. Will this be agreeable?"

"Aye," he grumbled knowing that there was going to be no other way around it.

"Good." Then he addressed Edmond. "Go fetch milady for I wish to have a word with her." The boy was about to leave, but he called him back with his words. "And Edmond?"

"Aye, milord."

"Do not let her convince ye that she has no need to seek me out. If I do not see her here, then I will be coming to see ye personally. Tell her this if ye must."

The boy nodded with a gulp and tore out of the hall, like it was ablazed with fire. Dougray chuckled.

"Ye are amused?" Murrough failed to see the humor here.

"Oh, I would love to see the look on her face when she is told that she must come to me."

"What makes ye so sure that she will comply?"

"Oh, she will because she likes Edmond. She will fear that I will take her disobedience out on the lad."

"I see the cleverness of yer actions, but are ye sure that she cares that much?"

Dougray looked at his redheaded friend wondering where he had been hiding these past weeks that he did not notice the woman's caring notions. "Did she not take on Hamish?" he pointed out. "Regan and the other children? Her motherly instincts are working full force."

"If she is so motherly as ye say, why is she not wed with babes suckling from her breast?" He shook his head, wondering why Dougray wished to defend the unmanageable woman.

"That is a good question, Murrough. I believe there has not been a man able to capture her long enough to tempt her with marriage." His chuckle was full of admiration that irked Murrough to no end. It was like he condoned Aislinn's unseemly behavior.

"She is a woman!" He tried to make him see reason. "She should have been wed long before now with a man to put her in her place. She has to be at least ten years passed the marrying age. Her insides will be dry and not be able to carry a man's seed."

Before Dougray could make a comment, Aislinn made her entry like a white squall ready to crush every living thing that dared to get in her way. She marched right past the awestruck tenants who had been waiting hours to speak to him, her dark eyes accusing him of the injustice she thought him to have done. Reaching the table, she leaned forward with her hands bracing her. "You dare threaten a child?" He was rather impressed that she was able to control her voice, so that her grievance with him was not made public. But even so, there was no mistaking the anger in each and every word that passed her lips. "What is wrong with you?"

Murrough was surprised at Dougray's calm acceptance of this hellion's temper. No one spoke to the Fitzpatrick in such a manner and expected to walk out of the hall on his own two feet. But there he sat, with a smile threatening to spread across his face. "*Dia dhuit* to ye, also," he greeted her, completely throwing her aback. She eyed him suspiciously, her dark eyes narrowing.

"What are you up to?"

"Me? And I thought we were to discuss yer actions. I hear it on good word that ye have decided to take over the ways of what have originally been for the lady of the keep." He leaned forward. His face just inches from hers. He had the urge to rile her further and kiss those oh so tempting lips that were forever determined to frown at him. He managed to restrain himself, and only because he feared that he might be clawed to death for the effort. "But as far as I can remember, ye are not wed to me."

"And thank my lucky stars for that. And for your information, you gave me permission to do as I wished and that is what I am doing. Instead of scaring little children to death, you should be showering me with praises that I decided to step in. The kitchen was a disaster. Definitely not a five-star establishment, with all its bacteria and infectious possibilities lurking within the partially cleaned pots and tables that have not been wiped off since they were put in the place. I just want to gag knowing that I have been eating meals served under those conditions."

"Ye never complained before now."

"I didn't know. And I will tell you, now that I do, it is going to change whether I am the lady of this keep or not." She stood and crossed her arms across her chest and straightened to her full height, quite bravely daring him to tell her otherwise.

Dougray purposely sat there for a long moment, as though he was mulling over her ultimatum, when in fact, he had already made up his mind long before she came to see him. "I agree," he finally spoke.

"What?" Her arms came uncrossed as her eyes narrowed with suspicion. She was so utterly thrown off track that he couldn't help but chuckle.

"I agree. Ye will make sure that the keep is in order. A job perhaps ye will take pride in?"

She couldn't detect any trickery in his offer. "I will not relent until it is up to snuff."

"Good. Now that this matter is settled, there is one more thing that we must lay down on the table." He ignored the roll of her eyes and continued. "Roth is the head cook in the kitchen, and a fine one, I might add. Ye may not wish to make an enemy of him."

"That was not my intention." Realizing she may have been rash, she added, "I will speak to him directly and smooth matters over."

"And about this feast…" He paused waiting to see if she would blast him with more retaliations but she kept her mouth firmly closed. "…I would like to be in attendance at this gathering. I am most anxious to see your expertise."

Again he surprised her. "You will not be disappointed." She nodded her head before she left the hall, in nearly the same fashion that she had arrived, large long strides befitting a man, but Dougray did not miss the ever so slight sway of her slender hips. He smiled.

"Why do ye give her so much reign?" Murrough for the life of him couldn't understand.

"I give her something to occupy her time, so that she will not get into any trouble." He looked at him. "The lass has energy, not at all like someone passed their prime, aye?" He couldn't help but tease him for his earlier observation of Aislinn being a dried-up old spinster.

"Nay, that much is true, but the fact remains that she will not attract a mate with that tongue about her. Do ye not agree?"

Dougray just looked away not giving him an answer.

Aislinn marched back to the kitchen to be greeted by Roth, a knife in his hand and a scowl upon his face.

"Well Roth, it seems we got off to a bad start. I would like to rectify that now."

The older man with the round thick middle eyed her suspiciously as he watched her roll up her sleeves. "What do ye think ye are doing?"

"Direct me to the buckets and a good rag and I'll start another part of the kitchen, while you ready the others to prepare the feast."

Roth nervously glanced at his assistants. It was one thing to have a lady try to take over his domain, but to have her on her hands and knees, scrubbing like she was the scullery maid, well that simply was not done.

Edmond came forward. "Milady, ye cannot dirty yer hands."

Aislinn chuckled. "Of course I can and I intend to. I don't expect any of you to do something that I would not. Now please we are wasting time."

Edmond looked to Roth for permission and the older man nodded. In his eyes, Aislinn had gone up a few notches. "Ye heard her, lad. She intends to help."

"Thank you, Roth. I cannot wait to taste the wonderful dishes you are so well known for."

The old cook nearly beamed with pride from the compliment.

For two days, they prepared. Roth began to admire Aislinn and was sorely pressed that he had misjudged her. Once he had thought her an interfering female, but now he found that he actually looked forward to her opinions.

Not only had she supervised the cleansing of the kitchen, she also saw to the castle. Every corner was swept, scrubbed and cleaned to perfection and the dogs that once ruled the bottom floor were relocated to the stables. No one had seen the castle look so grand. It was nearly fit for a king.

Aislinn wanted everything set in a special way for this banquet, allowing for all its elegance to shine through. Roth shook his head, thinking she was going to too much trouble, for they were only entertaining the servants, but he became so wrapped up in her enthusiasm that he did not discourage her. She was bubbling over with excitement and everyone who was invited to attend could barely stop talking about it.

"Is she not as I told ye?" Edmond had cleaned his hands and wiped them on the towel. He then started placing the freshly baked bread in the baskets.

"She is that and more," Roth agreed. "A cunning lass that one is and not a bit too high and mighty that she won't dirty her hands with the likes of us lowly kitchen help."

"Would she not make a splendid lady for milord?"

Roth's knife paused in midair over the vegetable that he was about to slice and looked at Edmond with definite concern. "Now don't ye go spreading a thing like that. Ye have no right deciding whom milord should take to wed." His attention was drawn away when he noticed that the sun that usually shone through the door had diminished. His gaze took in the tall, broad-shouldered man and the unmistakable blue-gray eyes that were gazing at them questionably.

"Milord," Roth's voice barely rasped out his greeting. He feared that he might have overheard what Edmond had suggested.

"I came to see for myself how things fared." Dougray was rather impressed how clean and orderly the kitchen appeared.

"We are just finishing up the final touches."

"Good, for I am famished." He was about to make his leave, but at the door, he turned back with a smile. "If I were in search of a new wife, it would be an honor to have Lady Aislinn at my side. *Slán leat*, Roth, Edmond." He was gone before the two of them could recover from their lord's admission.

"He heard us," Edmond choked.

"Aye, and be glad that it wasn't an insult he was hearing. Now stop yer daydreaming and give me a hand."

Abbot Kirwan waited for Dougray to leave the kitchen and fell into step beside him. "Ye are really going to let this woman, who is barely civilized, prepare an elaborate banquet and for all the servants?"

"I did grant her permission. I see no harm giving to those that have served our needs well. I for one am most interested in knowing how the lady handles the duties of a home."

His beady eyes looked even smaller for he had narrowed them to slits. "To what curiosity do ye have for this? Ye are not entertaining a thought of marriage to this chit?"

"Nay, marriage is the last thing on my mind."

With Moira and Rhiannon's help, Aislinn was able to decorate the banquet hall in a festive mood with the tables adorned with garland of fresh greens and ribbons intertwined. The goblets were readied upon the tables for the honeyed wine to be served, and Hamish saw to the lighting of every torch on its sconce to make the room feel warm with its welcome.

While the women were busy with the decorations, Roth saw to each and every preparation of the meal. He checked on the progress of the venison that had been roasting on the sharpened spits. Using a large spoon, he personally poured rich meat juices to ensure it would become a tender morsel. He removed the oak cakes from the open hearth only when they were browned to a golden hue, and he placed the honeyed pears in bowls for the final course. He had been pleased that Aislinn had decided on the sweet. It was a personal favorite of his.

Everything was going as planned until Aislinn informed Roth that she would help with the serving. He was fuming muttering beneath his breath of how stubborn the Lady Aislinn was, but he could see no other way around it without upsetting the evening. She had smartly arranged for the servants to take shifts, so that everyone could enjoy the feast that was being laid out before them.

Dougray had scowled when Aislinn had told him that she would not sit at his side, but he ended up accepting her explanation for she nearly shone with a sense of pride for what had been accomplished. He had to admit that he was impressed how every course was elegantly served in a smooth, effortless way. It was like watching a dance in motion, as every wooden trencher that was filled with the mouth-watering meat was delivered to each and every hungry man, woman and child.

Aislinn lifted her head to find him watching her. The reflected light from the torches glimmered over his handsome face, like beams of icy radiance, and his Celtic grayish-blue eyes seemed to hold an invitation in their smoldering depths. His lips broadened in approval and he raised his goblet to her in a salute.

Chapter Twenty-Six

It was the second week and Hamish was already a changed boy, his whole demeanor, not only his attitude, but his physical strength as well. Aislinn had been relentless with him and she would have never accepted anything less.

"Come on, Hamish. You can do one more push up." She actually got down on the damp earth and looked him in the eyes. "One more."

"I cannot." He squeezed his eyes shut, his limbs already shaking.

"Yes, you can. Now do it!" The command seemed to push him, and he lowered himself to the ground and somehow he found the strength to push himself up again.

"I did it." His face lit up with his accomplishment and he relaxed letting his body fall. "That's how many now?" He moved to a sitting position.

"Twenty-five, Hamish." She threw her arms around him. "I'm so proud of you."

He beamed with pride. "Thank ye."

"Now we don't want to be late. Padrig is supposed to have that surprise ready for you."

"Did someone say me name?"

Hamish and Aislinn both turned at the same time to see the gray-haired man was walking toward them. "I decided to see for meself what was going on. He pulled the shoes out of the leather bag that he had slung over his shoulders. "I did as ye said." He handed them to Aislinn, who was now inspecting them. The left shoe was thicker in the sole, just as she had requested. She looked up at the old man with a generous smile of appreciation. "Perfect, Padrig. It's perfect." She turned to Hamish then and handed him his new pair of shoes.

"They're for me?" He looked at the items in awe.

"Of course. You have proved to me that you are serious about your decided career in life, and I would say that a man who will one day wield a sword had better have a pair of shoes. Now try them on."

The boy sat down on the ground and quickly secured them to his feet. He glanced up, unsure if he should move, but once he saw Aislinn nod, he slowly stood. "I'm standing on both me feet at the same time." He looked up at

Padrig then to Aislinn. "I cannot remember a time that I could do that." Joy bubbled in his laugh. Aislinn was caught up in his excitement and took his hands in an affectionate grip.

"Are you ready to take your first steps?" The words were meant to encourage him, but he looked startled, almost panicked. "Well you didn't think that you were just going to look at them, did you?"

Aislinn's gentle teasing reassured him. He decided that if she felt he could manage to walk like everyone else that he would do all that was in his power not to disappoint her. He took a few steps and realized that he was walking without awkwardly throwing his hip. "I'm not limping." He took a few more steps, faster and faster. He was laughing for he was so wonderfully happy that for once in his life, he actually felt normal.

"It is truly amazing," Padrig agreed. "I would have never thought that it would be possible." He gazed at the remarkable woman that had taken the time to look upon a boy and see that there was more to him than just his imperfection. His face beamed with pride. "Ye did well, milady."

Aislinn put her arm around the older man. "No, Padrig, we did well."

She then cupped her hand over her mouth and yelled, "Run, Hamish." He lifted his feet, but it was still quite awkward for him. He ended up stumbling over his own feet falling to the ground. Aislinn let go of Padrig and tore off in a full gallop.

"Hamish!" Panic was in her voice that he might be injured. But when she reached him, she could see that he was perfectly fine. Even though he was lying there flat on his back, there was a large smile spread across his face.

"I ran. I never thought…I ran, milady."

"Yes, you did, Hamish."

"Is the lad goin' to live to see another day?" Padrig was out of breath by the time he finally caught up to them.

"He's all right, Padrig," Aislinn assured him. She offered Hamish a hand and brought him once again to his feet. "I think you should start out at a brisk walk, just until you break those shoes in."

"Then I can run?"

"You may do whatever you wish. I'll give you a few days to get used to balancing your body weight, then we'll go to work strengthening your leg muscles."

"When will I be able to wield a sword?"

Padrig looked at Aislinn wondering what the woman was planning.

"One thing at a time, Hamish." She ruffled his fawn-colored hair. "One thing at a time."

Chapter Twenty-Seven

Dougray was pacing back and forth in the library waiting for Teige to report back to him with Aislinn's whereabouts. He had important matters to tend to. Like the raiders who were becoming bolder in their insults, and the tenet disputes he had to settle, but he couldn't concentrate until he knew that Aislinn was safe. Why did she always refuse to obey his orders?

Finally Teige returned escorting Aislinn into the room. Relief washed over him giving him the inclination to grab her and kiss her soundly before he took great pleasure in throttling her. She didn't even have the decency to look chastised for making him fret.

Dougray dismissed Teige and he closed the door behind him. Aislinn sauntered in like there was not a concern in the world. "We need to talk," she had the nerve to say to him.

"Aye, and I intend to go first."

She plopped herself down on the velvet cushion that was a little more comfortable than the hard wooden seats. "What happened to ladies first?"

He ignored her sarcasm. "Where were ye?"

She was studying her fingernails, obviously bored with the whole conversation. "I told you that I was meeting with Hamish." She saw his blank look. "The boy. Don't you remember?"

"Aye, Hamish." He waved his hand with impatience. He had forgotten about her teaching the lad, but he wasn't concerned with that. "Ye went without an escort. Teige had no inclination to where ye had run off to."

Something in his voice made her take pause to look at him. His brow was creased in a frown and he was running his hand through his long strands of hair. Her eyebrow winged up. "You were worried?"

"Worried? *Dar Dia*, ye infernal lass! There has been trouble in these parts." He pointed toward the window slit, like she could see what he was talking about. "It's just not safe for ye to be running around by yerself."

"I was with Hamish and Padrig."

"Ach!" He threw up his hands. "I feel so much better now. Ye were with an old man and a cripple."

She came to her feet in one swift move wagging her finger at him. "The cripple, as you so elegantly put it, has a name."

"Fine, Hamish. Is that better?"

"Yes, for a start. The boy is doing well by the way. That's why I wanted to speak to you." He just stared at her in utter disbelief. She had dismissed him and his worries as if they were passing comments about the weather. "You'd hardly recognize him now," she had continued not even taking a breath.

"We are not finished discussing the reason that ye should not be without Teige or Cormac at your side."

"Oh? I thought that we were."

"*Dar Dia*, lass, are ye trying to age me? I have taken care of tenets, livestock and made trades without as much trouble as ye have caused me."

She sat back in her seat and looked at him intently. "I don't know why you're getting your hoses all tangled up in a knot." She glanced at his attire of an Irish lord, bare legs and all. She chuckled. "Oops, you aren't wearing any today." It seemed to be the wrong thing to say for his face turned red with fury. He raised his finger in a lecturing position and just shook it at her without uttering a single word. "Okay, already. Settle down." She shook her head at him. "You look like you're ready to have a coronary. I promise you, I'll make sure Teige…or Cormac tag along." She raised her right hand and actually saluted him.

"Why do ye do this?"

"What already? I promised you, didn't I? What else do you want? Blood? Here." She offered him both her hands. "Just slice my wrists now and be done with it."

"Ye sorely tempt me, Aislinn Hennessy. Ye have no idea." He stood over her, hands on his hips. Slowly his anger seemed to evaporate. She looked at him so innocently that it was hard to stay angry with her. She was safe after all. She smiled then successfully disarming him completely. "Put your hands down. Ye look ridiculous."

"Am I forgiven then?"

"Aye."

"Good. Then there is something else that I would like to speak to you about."

"I'm afraid to ask."

"I would like to have Dermot show the boy how to wield a sword." She held her breath as she waited for the answer. She had to do something to change the man's status. She refused to have him groveling in the corners and all because of a misunderstanding.

"Dermot!" He recalled how the man had been sprawled on top of her, his hands sliding down her body and not a move did she make to stop him. Was it a mere accident? Most likely, but his stubborn pride saw it as a deliberate slight, when only moments before that incident, she had seen fit to claw him for trying to give her a kiss. And now she adds insult to injury by coming to the man's defense. "I would sooner have him tied and quartered. Ye are not to speak of this man in my presence. Not ever!"

"What in the world is wrong with you? Dermot did nothing improper, but yet you have ostracized him. I thought I had explained the situation."

"Do not question me, Aislinn," his temper rising again. "What I say stands, and furthermore, ye are not to leave the grounds. Ye will stay put so that I can keep an eye on ye. I don't have time to be searching the area to see if the Butlers have put a knife to yer throat."

"I just told you that I'd take someone with me."

"I changed my mind."

"You can't do that."

"I can and I am. If ye so leave without my permission, I will lock ye in the dungeon." With that he turned on his heel and left her fuming in the now empty room.

"Oooh!" She screamed her frustration stomping her feet in the process. "The man is impossible!"

"Most are, milady." Rhiannon had just passed the fuming Dougray in the hall.

Aislinn was glad to see her. She had grown quite fond of Padrig's daughter. "He's the worst. He says that I am a guest here, but he treats me like a prisoner."

"He worries about ye, is all. There are situations that ye may not be aware of. He does not wish ye to be in danger."

"The Butlers?"

"Aye, for one."

"And what about the way he is treating poor Dermot?"

Rhiannon sighed. "I am not to question milord, but the punishment seems a bit harsh."

"I'd say. It doesn't make any sense to me at all, but I plan on fixing it."

"I am not sure if there is anything we can do. Murrough has told me that it would take something short of an heroic deed to set Dermot back into milord's good graces."

"A heroic deed?"

"Aye," Rhiannon said slowly as she watched Aislinn tap her fingers on her leg. "What are ye plannin'?"

"What? Oh nothing. Just thinking out loud is all."

"Methinks that it is dangerous when ye do that, aye?"

Aislinn just chuckled. "Don't worry, Rhiannon. I may just have a plan that will set things straight."

"Hmm. It will have to wait. Ye have a private dinner tonight with honored guests, and ye need to look yer best. One of the gowns that I made for ye would be appropriate."

"Are you suggesting that my unconventional trews are not the highlight of feminine attire?" She looked down at her comfortable garment. How she hated to put on one of those dresses that had so much material that she feared she would end up getting all tangled up in it. "Who's going to be here tonight? Do you know?"

"The Chieftain Owen Dubhdara, and one of the Burkes will be in attendance also. Because of the raids, milord is in need of more men to help guard Dunhaven. If he can insure their support, it will also take care of his other dilemma. Clans that have not given their oath to serve the the Tudor King are suspicious of one another. The Chieftain Dubhdara is well respected. He controls the region on the two Umhalls. He is wise in many ways. He knows the waters and ways to bring in needed products. He is fair with matters of conflict. He is not hot tempered like the O'Flahertys that fight at the drop of a hat. An alliance with him would ensure others that milord will not so readily relinquish his lands to the English though he has sworn fidelity to the king there."

"I'm little confused. Dougray was fostered in England, and it is no secret that he has secured his lands from King Henry. So why all the fuss that he will just hand them back again?"

"It is a long story," she sighed, and then decided that Aislinn maybe needed to hear it so that she could possibly better understand the man that housed her. "Shane Fitzpatrick and Mary Halstead had two children, milord Dougray and his sister Lady Miriam. Henry Tudor was against Mary Halstead's marriage to an Irish chieftain, especially one who refused to consider him his king. But the two were in love and were not going to be apart. Shane literally stole Lady Mary from her home and hid her away until she was with child. This infuriated both her father and the Tudor King, but the damage had been done and Mary's father would not have his daughter harmed. A deal was struck. Shane's first-born son would be fostered in England, and if daughters were all to be had, Sir Halstead would see to the marriages himself.

"Not exactly what Lord Shane would have liked to agree to but he relented, for he had not only a wife to worry about, but also a child.

"For many years, Lord Shane thought of one way and then another to stall sending his children into the hands of the English, but it had to come to an end. Sir Halstead convinced him that it was the only way to keep the family safe, for Henry Tudor was after blood. Sir Halstead assured Lord Shane that he would see to young Dougray's care in England.

"Arrangements were made and milord was taken hostage insuring his father's loyalty to the crown. Lord Dougray was but a small boy when he was fostered out, but he was lucky enough to bring a friend with him so not to be lonely."

"Let me guess, Murrough?"

She nodded. "But his poor sister was not so fortunate. She was given to marriage to a man that was more than twice her age. But he was a man who would die whispering his fidelity to Henry Tudor and that seemed all that her grandfather cared about."

"What happened to Dougray's parents?"

"Two years ago, Lord Shane and Lady Mary met an untimely death. They were visiting in Dublin, staying at an inn, and a fire swept through the quarters where they slept. There was not a thing that anyone could do about it. Some feared it had something to do with the FitzGeralds for Lord Shane was fond of Oliver FitzGerald and tried to intervene with the sentencing that the Tudor King put forth, but nothing could be done. All FitzGeralds, Gerald Og, and his four brothers James, Oliver, John and Garrett and his son Silken Thomas were put to death at Tyburn, but one male child of the FitzGerald's was still left and the Tudor King wanted his head as well. Shane would not let a mere child be slaughtered and helped with whisking the lad away to safety.

The FitzGeralds, the name had sounded familiar to Aislinn and now she knew why.

"Do ye know of what deeds the Tudor King does?"

"I believe so." Aislinn shuttered at the thought.

"So ye see," Rhiannon continued. "Milord was only given back what had been taken away when his father died. Rest assured, milord had to suffer his tender years bowing to the Tudor King, but he bided his time. He endured, so that he could once again return to his home. He had not bargained to be knighted and given back his lands, but fate sometimes is ironic."

"But isn't his loyalties dangerous, knowing how the king is fond of eliminating anyone that he considers a threat?"

"It is dangerous even if ye do bow down to the man. Gerald Og is proof enough for that." Rhiannon realized that the room had become shades darker indicating that she had talked long enough. "Moira asked me to make sure that ye wouldn't linger, and just look what I've done. We must hurry now for Moira had wanted to have time to arrange yer hair."

Aislinn couldn't help but laugh, as her hand went to her short tresses. "Tell me, how could this take long to arrange?"

Rhiannon just gave her a knowing smile. "Moira has something quite special in mind. She thinks even milord will find it appealing and perhaps his temper may be appeased."

"Humph! What do I care if he finds it appealing or not?"

Rhiannon watched Aislinn as she nervously ran her hand over the back of the fine wood of the sofa. She looked up then with uncertainty in her words. "Do you really think that she could do something with it? My hair, I mean. It would be nice if something would please the old grump. Nothing I do ever makes him smile. He's always yelling and complaining about one thing or another."

"He cares for ye. Is it not obvious to ye then?"

Aislinn's eyebrows furrowed. "He feels an obligation. There's a difference."

"Nay, not always. I see the way that he looks at ye."

"What? With disgust?"

Rhiannon chuckled. "Nay. He looks at ye with warmth; his soul reaches for ye."

"Most likely you are seeing the part that's trying to reach out and strangle me." Even though she said those words, Aislinn wanted to believe that it could be possible that he at least liked her. Dougray was strong, determined and opinionated, nothing like any of the men whom she had ever dated.

"Methinks that ye underestimate yerself. Admit it: ye are drawn to him also."

"I might like him, if he would not be so ill tempered. Occasionally I see a redeeming quality or two, but not enough to make me imagine that anything could ever come of it. We'd kill each other if we were ever left alone in a room long enough."

"Maybe we should put this to the test, aye? Could prove most interesting who would come out the victor."

"Don't get any ideas." They continued to talk as they headed up the winding stairs.

After a long soaking in the tub with fresh roses floating around her, Aislinn felt revived. She was ready to face anything, even if it was one of Dougray's sour moods. Moira had laid out a beautiful red velvet dress that was cut tight to the hips and fell in folds to the ground. With Aislinn's long, slender physique, it was a stunning effect, molding perfectly to each and every curve. "I've never worn anything like this before." Aislinn looked down at herself wondering if she should dare to wear it. "Are you sure it looks all right?" Her gaze found both Rhiannon and Moira smiling.

"Ye are beautiful. Trust me, A.J. Now come sit." Moira pointed to the velvet-lined chair. "I will do yer hair and then ye can make yer grand entrance." She did seem to work magic, curling a few ends of her dark hair and pinning to her head a tightly woven net that was made out of gold strands. It gave the appearance that her hair was long and was tucked beneath the headdress. "No one will know that ye have cut off all yer hair."

"Not that I care," Aislinn informed them.

"Of course not," both women answered in return.

They handed her the mirror. The glass was not as clear like the mirrors in her century, but she could make out her image. She was amazed. She actually looked like a picture-book lady.

"Are ye pleased?" Moira hoped.

Aislinn looked at her, warmth evident in her eyes. "Now where were you when I went to the senior prom?" She saw the confused look and she waved her hand. "Forget I said that. I love what you did, Moira. I feel like a princess." She stood and took a deep breath before she headed toward the door. "I just hope that I don't trip or something."

"Ye will do fine," Rhiannon encouraged.

After she headed down to meet Dougray and his guests, Rhiannon looked to Moira. "Ye think that she never owned anything so fine."

"I don't think that she has. She did not come with anything, but the attire that is only befitting of a man."

"She must have come from a strange world with women dressing like men. Do ye suppose the men dress like women?" Rhiannon asked and they both burst out laughing. "I suppose not. If the women are as tough as Aislinn, then the men must be even more so."

"I do not think that I would want to come across one of her clansmen." Moira shook her head. "I would be frightened."

"Oh, Moira, men are all the same and after one thing from us. We fit together."

"Ye wouldn't think so by the way the Abbot Kirwan preaches every week. I had to do penance for just a thought. Ye'd think that I committed a mortal sin."

"Yer religion is a strange one. The old ways are much simpler." Rhiannon mulled over the differences.

"Are ye not afraid that yer soul will burn in hell for yer heathen ways?"

Rhiannon laughed. "Nay. A soul lives on forever and not in this one place called heaven that yer priest has told ye. Unlike ye Christians, I do not fear what lies beyond death. It will only be the next step in my life."

"If ye do not mind, I will pray for yer soul anyway, Rhiannon," she half-heartedly joked.

"And I will ask the gods to be kind to yers." She smiled joining in her mirth.

Aislinn could hear Dougray's voice above the other guests. They were conversing in Gaelic and she readied herself to do the same. She found that it was becoming easier and easier to do so since most of the inhabitants of Dunhaven still clung to the old language.

She would have felt more comfortable if she could have made her entrance in her sweatshirt and homemade slacks. "Oh well, here goes." She squared her shoulders and took a deep breath.

Everyone fell silent, making her feel incredibly uncomfortable. Her eyes met Dougray's and she was not sure that she felt any better. He stared at her, like he didn't even recognize her. His gaze clung to her every movement and his eyes flashed with azure fire. What she didn't realize was the red velvet of her dress had heightened her smooth skin making it glow with pale gold undertones. Dougary had known that she was a striking woman, but tonight she seemed to outshine his expectations.

"Dougray, are ye not going to introduce us to this lovely creature?" This came from the older man with broad shoulders who was now standing next to him. Wind and sun bronzed the man's face. There was an inherent strength in his features that made him remarkably handsome with his dark hair and light eyes.

Finally Dougray came to his senses and moved forward to greet her. He leaned close so that only she would hear his words. "Ye look enchanting." She gave him a startled look and his deep chuckle met her ears. "Don't look so stunned. I am known to give a compliment when one is due." He took hold of her arm and led her forward to meet the honored guests. He started with the dark-haired gentleman first. "May I introduce Lady Aislinn Hennessy. She is of a land far from here, and in my care until I am able to return her safely to her father." It was amazing how this fabricated story could flow from his lips, as if it were the gospel truth.

"I cannot believe that a father would leave this beautiful lass in yer care. What could he have been thinking?" The older man's eyes twinkled with mischief. Aislinn was sure that he had quite a way with the women.

"Milady, this brass gent is Chieftain Owen Dubhdara," Dougray introduced him and the chieftain bowed ever so slightly.

"And…" Dougray pointed to the other gentleman who had moved forward now to be introduced. He was a thin man with a rather pointed nose. His hair was light brown with streaks of gray. His mouth was small causing his smile to appear like an unnatural curve. "…this is Sir Robert Burke," Dougray finished, as the man took her hand brushing his lips over her knuckles.

"It is always a pleasure to meet a beautiful young woman." He released his grip. "If I had known that ye would be greeting my ship, I would have taken to the seas myself. I thought only savages resided in distant lands." It seemed as though he was giving her a compliment, but Aislinn recognized a slight undertone that spoke differently.

"Oh, trust me, kind sir, we are savages." Her brows arched and her eyes glowed mischievously. She felt Dougray's slight, warning pressure on her arm, but still she did not stop. "Where I come from, we dance around naked most of the time and only wear clothes when forced." She smiled completely, putting Robert Burke off guard, but she could tell that Dubhdara was fighting a smile that tugged dangerously at the corners of his mouth. She then laughed a loud boisterous laugh. "I am only joking." Again she felt Dougray's grip tighten, but she heard his light chuckle and knew he wasn't too upset with her.

Even Dubhdara's chortle was rich and sincere making Aislinn like him immediately. Burke, on the other hand, laughed behind his open palm, a courtesy laugh, as though he had not understood the joke. He made her feel uneasy with the way he stared at her.

At dinner, Aislinn was seated beside Dubhdara and Dougray at the high table. She was pleasant and answered many of the questions that were put to her. She was free to say whatever she pleased, within limits, of course. She didn't want her story to sound so far fetched that they would question her.

The company was pleasant enough but she was anxious to have it move along a little faster. She had something up her sleeve for this evening, as long as everything went according to plan. The day had proven to be warm and the night was pleasant enough without a hint of rain. She knew that the entertainment would be moved to the court area outdoors. An Irish clear night was something to behold and it allowed her the freedom that she needed.

Aislinn waited for she knew that soon the men would retire to a more private setting, so that they may discuss the real issue of this visit. The name Dubhdara O'Malley seemed vaguely familiar to her, but she was not at all sure why. She knew some of the Irish history that her father had told her, but she had listened with a child's interest. Now she wished that she had paid closer attention. She might have been able to help with decisions that had cost Ireland its freedom. Maybe this was the reason she was here. Could history really be changed, and if so, to what cost? These questions plagued her mind.

Her eyes caught just the person she had been searching for. "Edmond," she called to the boy. He came to her side immediately, anxious to be of any service.

"Milady." He bowed.

"Edmond, I was wondering if you could do me a favor."

"Aye, milady."

"Do you know Dermot...I'm sorry I do not know his last name. He is about so high." She held her hand to where her shoulders were indicating how tall the man was to her. "He was one of the kern."

"Aye, milady. I know whom ye speak of."

She put her hands on the boy's shoulders giving them a quick squeeze. "Good. I need you to find him and tell him to meet me over at the far corner near that alcove." She turned the boy around and indicated the area that she meant. "Do you understand?"

Edmond nodded. "I will not fail ye." He took off in search of Dermot, as if his life depended on it.

Aislinn slowly made her way to the area that would shield her from prying eyes, but would also enable her to draw attention of a certain lord when the time was appropriate. Now all she had to do was wait for Edmond to bring Dermot to her.

She had felt simply awful that she had been the cause of the man losing face in the eyes of his peers. Here she had thought by insisting that his life be spared everything would have been all right. Now it looked like death would have been less torturous for the man. She had witnessed the ridicule that

Dermot had to endure, and all because of Dougray's stubborn pride. It was beyond cruel, and if she didn't do something quick, next she'd have Dermot's suicide on her head.

Finally Dermot came into view, but he did not see her and was about to turn away. She stepped away from the shadows. "Dermot," she hissed drawing his attention. He turned toward her with obvious dread making her heart go out to him. She waved to him wanting him to come closer.

"Please, milady, I cannot be seen with ye. Do ye want me banished as well?"

She ignored his plea for if her planned worked everything would be back to the way it should be. "Listen, we don't have much time." She glanced over his shoulder to make sure that no one was watching. "I want to correct what has happened to you. I have a plan." She pulled him farther away from view of anyone who might happen by, and closer to the edge of the alcove. She peeked over the side. It was a long way down and if she slipped it would be her death, but she was confident that this would never happen. She was strong and able to do sixty or so pull-ups. This should be a cinch.

"What are ye plannin'?" Dermot was beginning to become skittish. The woman was trouble, and for him, just being near her could prove disastrous. "Because I see it in yer eyes, and it is something I've no wish to be a part of." He started to back away, but she grabbed hold of his hand.

"You will thank me later for this. All I'm going to do is dangle over this ledge."

"What?" He knew now that she must be mad, and she was going to get him killed along with her. He might as well just jump, when she did.

"I'll be fine. Trust me. All you have to do is pull me to safety and you'll be deemed a hero. Ta da, you will be back in his lord's good graces." She waved her hand like she was the fairy of good fortune, granting him his wish.

"I'll be strung up," his voice squeaked. "Do not do this. I implore ye. I am in so much trouble as it is. I will be near a hundred before I can prove that I am once more a worthy man."

Aislinn was not listening and had already climbed onto the ledge, which was not an easy feat with the long dress that she had been forced to wear. It was a good thing that the castle stone was not damp from rain. Her grip was secure.

"Stop, please," he hissed and glanced over his shoulder to see if anyone had noticed. Without warning, she let out a blood-curdling scream. He nearly bolted from fear. Cormac was the first to reach them.

Aislinn drew Dermot's attention with her whispering plea. "You fool. Pull me up now before someone does it for you." Her urgent demand moved him into action. He grabbed a hold of her forearms, though he was sure she was pulling herself over more than he was managing the deed. One last tug and she fell forward sending them both to the ground. At that moment, Dougray and his honored guests made an appearance. Dermot closed his eyes in dismay. This compromising scene didn't bode well.

"What is going on here!" Dougray bellowed his outrage causing the others to part to one side, so that their lord could move forward. He glared down at Aislinn who was sprawled across Dermot in a most unladylike fashion. "Dermot, this is the last straw. You will die by this sword." Aislinn heard the metal scrape, as it was unsheathed. She was upon her feet in a flash.

"Don't be utterly ridiculous. You should be praising Dermot for his courage."

Dougray hesitated as he looked at Dermot who still had not risen. "Explain."

"He saved my life. I was leaning over the ledge." She pointed just to make her point. "And I guess that I leaned too far and ended up falling over. If it weren't for Dermot, I would have fallen to my death. He's a hero." She motioned for Dermot to stand. He couldn't claim the title on his derrière.

"Aye, milord." Cormac came forward. "I saw it all for myself. Dermot indeed saved the lady." Thank God for Cormac because Dermot was still sputtering like a fool, but at least he was on his feet now.

"A man who needs to be congratulated." The O'Malley's voice bellowed as he pounded Dougray on the back.

Aislinn could tell that Dougray was not entirely buying this whole scene, but knowing he had no other choice right now but to accept it. "Aye. Dermot, we will speak later on the reward, for now come join us in a drink."

Sir Robert Burke looked to Aislinn, his brows lifted questionably. She quickly looked away, not wanting to meet his scrutinizing gaze.

The crowd started to withdraw, ready to hear Dermot's version of his quick thinking that led to saving Lady Aislinn.

Aislinn would have followed but Dougray put a restraining hand on her arm. "A word with ye, milady." He had lowered his voice so that only she could hear him. He smiled and nodded as each person went on their way, but when they were alone his gaze was anything but pleasant. He let go of her arm and walked over to the ledge that she had been dangling from. He closed his eyes, as the image of her falling to her death nearly choked him. When he composed himself once more, he looked at her. "Why?" was all he said, as he folded his arms against his chest and leaned against the stoned wall.

"I'm not sure that I understand the question."

"Oh ye understand it well enough. Ye risked yer life for a man who was not worthy for ye to bother with."

His flippant remark angered her. "Not worthy? And who gave you the right to decide that?"

He straightened to his full height, his brows drawing together in an angry frown. "The man has never held his own. Even the trivial of tasks, he has botched up. That is why I know this. I only gave him a chance as a favor I owed to his family."

"You call sleeping and eating with the dogs a favor? He is barely a man, Dougray, in case you hadn't noticed. Haven't you ever made mistakes?"

"Ye do not have a right to criticize me. I was doing Dermot a favor by toughening him up, for there is no room for mistakes. Ye make an error and yer dead."

She hadn't thought that he was only issuing a lesson to the man. She had forgotten that she was from a different world. "But you were going to kill him." She couldn't forget the rage in his eyes.

"If any man ever tried to molest ye…." He paused for a moment, surprised at his own admission with his sense of protecting her as if she were his. He cleared his throat before continuing. "I would do the same for any woman."

"Oh." She turned away wondering why she was disappointed that she was lumped into a group worthy of his protection. She looked to where a crowd had circled around Dermot as he told his tale.

"Ye never answered me why ye did it." She didn't have to turn around to know that he was standing very close to her.

She sighed, wondering if she could ever make him understand. "To give the man back his life."

Dougray's eyes wandered over to where Dermot was standing. He was nearly beaming with pride. He then gazed at the woman responsible for it all. She was such a mystery to him. She did things that he didn't understand. She took cripples under her wing, befriended the servants, and now she risked harm to herself for a stranger. "Ye could have fallen to yer death."

She turned toward him with a beguiling smile. "I was never at any risk. What I did was child's play. I've done more daring escapades at home."

"Hmm. I am just beginning to understand this. But we can have no more." He took another step closer to her. He reached out and she flinched, causing him to look at her curiously. "Yer hair piece is loose." This time when he lifted his hand toward her she stood still, letting him refasten the shimmering piece. "There. Not as perfect as Moira could do, but it will suffice." His eyes met her dark ones, wishing he could read her thoughts, for there was so much emotion in those depths. "Now, I implore ye to listen to reason. No more climbing out windows, and…" He motioned over his shoulder. "…no more dangling from ledges, and in return, I will not be so hard on Dermot. Do we have a deal?"

"Yes, my lord." She even curtsied causing him to chuckle.

"Why is it when ye say 'aye, milord' I think ye mean something entirely of a different sort?"

"I don't know what you mean." She batted her eyes.

"Tell me, Aislinn." He took a hold of her arm, as he led her out to join the others. "Were ye this much trouble for yer parents?"

"Oh much, much more. I had to keep up with all of Connor's antics."

"I was afraid of that."

Aislinn excused herself when the time seemed appropriate and Dougray made it a point to escort her personally back to her room. She leaned against the door, feeling the effects of all the wine that she had consumed.

Dougray touched her flush cheek as his eyes caressed hers. "Aislinn…." He seemed lost for the right words that he wanted to use.

She thought that maybe he was going to kiss her. Surprisingly, she was almost hoping that he would. When she heard him sigh, she knew that for some reason, he had changed his mind. "Well, I'll bid ye good night." He took her hand and raised it to his lips.

"Good night?" She couldn't help but sound a little disappointed. "Jeez, my lord." She lightly touched his forearm. "I got all dressed up and everything. Don't I qualify for a good-night kiss?"

He slightly lifted his brows trying not to show his surprise at her request. She took his silence as a rejection. Her smile dropped. "Well don't let me force you." She turned to open her door, but his hand shot out to stop her. She stood frozen in time, her back to his hard chest. Gently he turned her around to face him.

"I did not mean to offend ye. Ye merely took me by surprise." He gently brushed his hand against her cheek and his eyes lingered on her parted lips. "I have wanted to kiss ye all evening…" He was very close now, his breath lightly touching hers. "…among other things." He claimed her lips before she could ask him what he meant. Hot, moist, so demanding was his ardor that it sent a tingling feeling down to the pit of her stomach. She closed her eyes and gave into the warmth that was washing over her. His tongue gently teased until she let him taste her fully. She felt herself weakening to the forceful domination of his lips and he pressed against her, leaving no doubt how much he wanted her. Warning bells went off in her brain. She couldn't let it go that far, for there could never be a future for them. Reluctantly she managed to turn her head breaking the caress.

"I think we'd better stop." Her words came out in a ragged breath.

For a moment, he considered not releasing her from his grip, but he knew if he kissed her again he would want more than she was willing to give. "Aye," he cleared his throat, agreeing with her. "Ye sleep well, Aislinn." His hand lingered on her shoulder. Feeling her tremble, he lifted his gaze to meet hers, but she quickly turned away and opened the door. Safely inside the arch now, she felt that she could breathe easier and she turned to him with a smile.

"You're a pretty good kisser, my lord, almost as good as you quarrel."

The smile that spread across his handsome face caused her heart to beat a little faster. Thank goodness she was halfway behind the thick, wood door or she might have thrown her arms around him begging him to stay.

"What a pleasant surprise it was to me," she could hear the teasing note in his voice, "that ye're mouth could be used for something other than yelling insults."

"I'll take that as a compliment, and on that note, again good night." She shut the door before she wouldn't be able to.

Dougray leaned his head against the barrier. Closing his eyes he willed himself not to throw caution to the wind and take the woman. What a surprise it was to him that she could intoxicate his senses so that he could barely see reason.

Dougray led Robert Burke and the O'Malley to the Great Hall, while the others continued the festivities above. Murrough was also present and shut the door behind them.

"Ye do yerself well." O'Malley patted his stomach. "I have not had such a feast in a long time."

"I am honored to have ye here as my guest." He walked over to the table where a decanter and goblets were set. "Whiskey?" he offered.

"Don't mind that I do." O'Malley settled himself on one of the chairs near the fireplace, so that he could warm his hands.

"And ye, Robert?" Dougray was not sure how to take this man. His reputation as a fine warrior and leader preceded him, but he was too quiet for Dougray's liking, making him believe that the man had much to hide.

"Why not?" Robert answered him after a long moment. He then moved closer to the fire.

Murrough came forward to relieve Dougray of two of the small goblets filled with the strong-grained whiskey and handed one to each of the guests.

"Can I speak frankly?" Dubhdara O'Malley looked at his host.

"Aye." Dougray nodded.

"I like ye, lad." The older man leaned forward resting his forearms on the top of his knees. "I know that ye want to guarantee loyalties to me in exchange that I give ye support from the Butler attacks, and as well if others decide to question yer loyalties here with the clans. I may have a mind to do so on the mere sentiment that ye are related by blood, no matter how far and in between it is now, but there is more that I seek. Being that ye are near to the other side of the country, it may be an advantage to have eyes and ears where I have not had them before…for a price that is."

"What is it ye have in mind?"

"A portion of the profits ye make from yer sea ventures. I have heard that ye have done quite well."

"Well enough, though I have heard the same thing about ye. What could I possibly have that ye could not already attain for yerself?"

"It is always wise to have an alternate plan. Ye never know when hard luck might strike."

"What of the trouble we have in the Northeast?" Robert spoke up not liking that Dubhdara would so readily lend a hand. "Do we dare pull out men from our garrison for Fitzpatrick's needs? It rankles me, O'Malley, that ye would give yer word to the Fitzpatrick, when ye know full well that he has been granted back the lands from his association with the Tudor King."

"We could question yer worth also." Murrough stepped forward hand on the hilt of his sword as he eyed Robert. "Ye are of Anglo-Norman descent. Ye are not of Gaelic blood though ye claim the ways."

"Nay, he has the right to speak." Dougray put down his drink, resting a hand on his friend's arm. "I do not deny that I have been living in England, being schooled and approved by the English society. And when the time arose to take back what was rightfully mine, I did it wisely without spitting on the man that granted it. Ye may not want to hear it, but hear it ye must. King Henry's reach is far. He is dangerous in his ambition and should not be brushed aside. That is why we should band together here before it is too late."

"Loyal as yer father was?" Burke spat not even hiding his sarcasm.

Dougray's anger chilled his eyes with reserve and his voice was just as cold and exact. "My father was forced to comply or see his family slain. He did what a man could under such circumstances. Never did he grant fidelity to the Tudor King."

"Nay, he left that to his son."

O'Malley, not wanting the evening to end in a full-out battle before negotiations could even begin, decided to calm the heated conversation. "We have much to discuss before we come to an agreement that fits well on all sides." He looked to Robert and then to his host hoping for signs that the tension would ease between them. "For tonight, I wish to call this meeting to an end. I thank ye again for your hospitality, Fitzpatrick, but my weary bones cry for rest."

"As ye wish." Dougray bowed before his eyes landed on Robert Burke's expression of clouded anger. The man may prove to be a problem.

O'Malley had already left the hall with his men but still Robert stayed until he had finished his drink. Finally he came forward to announce his leave.

"Rest well." Dougray tried to remain detached. "Hopefully ye will come to understand that I only wish to enhance what is already yers."

Burke refused to be pacified. "Maybe ye can fool the Dubhdara, but ye can not pull the lamb's wool over my eyes."

He looked at him with a sardonic expression. "Are ye saying that the O'Malley does not know what is presented to him?"

Burke's face turned red, his nostrils flaring in his anger and his hand went to his sword. Murrough moved forward his intent just as evident. For a tense moment, Dougray actually thought that Burke would draw his weapon on him, but then an uncertainty crept into his expression as he eyed both of his opponents. He was not a careless man and knew the odds of killing Fitzpatrick and surviving the act were next to none. He forced himself to remain calm and he carefully lowered his hand to his side. "I think that it is best that we discuss this in the morning."

"Aye," Dougray agreed. With a quick nod, Burke turned on his heels and left the hall.

"I'll have him watched." Murrough didn't bother to hide his dislike of the man.

"He wasn't very friendly, was he?" Dougray went over to the table to pour himself another drink. It wasn't every day that his life was threatened in such a manner.

"And what do ye make of the O'Malley?"

"He is a good man; honest is what I have heard. If he says that he will side with us, we need not fear that he won't do as he says." Dougray looked at Murrough. "Any news on the latest attack?"

"As always, the signs point to Fingham Butler."

Dougray thought about this as he swirled the liquid in his cup, watching it as it spun around, threatening to spill over the rim. He sighed and raised his head to look at Murrough. "Fingham has made attacks, but not ones like these. Someone knew that the shipment of supplies had come in. They could have easily taken it at the port without killing anyone. Why would they wait?"

"Fingham is tired of the cat and mouse game. Maybe he is ready to end this."

"Ye think that? He has claimed more than once that he wants to see me dead."

"He wants to see ye suffer first."

"Aye, that too, but never has he killed so maliciously. It has always been in a fair fight. Do ye not see the difference?"

Murrough nodded his head in agreement. "But if it is not him, then with whom do we deal?"

"That, my friend, is a very good question. Obviously someone who has taken great pains to make me believe the Butlers were responsible, someone who wants me to flat out retaliate to avenge the deaths, but the question is why?"

Chapter Twenty-Eight

Aislinn had dressed in her homemade slacks that Rhiannon had sewn for her. The material was somewhat different than she was used to, but they were comfortable and that was what really mattered. She threw on her sweatshirt and was ready to go. She had plans to spend the morning with Neala before she was to meet with Hamish for another lesson.

At first she had made the visits with Neala because she thought that she could learn something about the mist that had carried her through time, but now she found that she actually enjoyed their conversations.

She had been walking for some time before she noticed that she was being followed. She was a little concerned since Dougray had made such a fuss about security, but did she listen? No, here she was out again by herself, and Teige probably searching for her.

She quickly hurried on ahead until she reached a curve in the path, and then slowly backtracked. Careful not to make a sound, she crouched down on her haunches and waited.

She was rather surprised when she saw that her *would-be attacker* was only a young girl. She didn't recognize the child as one from the keep. She could only assume that she had arrived with one of the guests that she had met last night. She moved from her hiding place, purposely startling the girl to awareness.

"Ye scared me!" she shouted as her hand flew to her chest.

Aislinn realized the girl was much younger than she had originally thought. She still had the rounded childish look about her, but she was tall with strong Gaelic features, dark long hair. She was quite tanned making the color of her eyes a startling pale blue. "Is there a reason that you are following me?" She was curious to know.

The girl had recovered somewhat from her fright and stepped forward. "I'm Gráinne Ni Mhálle." She said her name with an almost smug look upon her face.

Aislinn couldn't help but laugh a loud contagious laugh that took the young girl completely by surprise.

"Why are ye laughing at me?"

"I'm sorry but you announced your name as if I should bow down and give you a certain amount of reverence."

Gráinne seemed to lose some of her haughtiness for she had no wish to offend the Lady Aislinn. "I'm the daughter of Owen Dubhdara."

"Oh. I didn't realize that he had a daughter."

"He sometimes let's me sail with him, but my mother does not approve." She tilted her head to one side. "Why are ye dressed in men's…what exactly are those. They do not look like trews?"

"No, they aren't. They're pants that are quite popular in my country, and I prefer them to the confining dresses that are either too tight, or too long. I like my freedom to move with ease."

The girl nodded her head. "I see yer point. I have often thought that too. May I walk with ye?"

"I suppose Neala will not mind one more visitor. Come on." She waved her hand for her to follow and they started back on the trail.

"What should I call ye?" the little girl asked.

"A.J. would be fine."

"Ye may call me Grania…if ye want to."

"All right, Grania it shall be."

The girl was not familiar with all the words that Aislinn spoke even though she used Gaelic. Some of her speech seemed foreign, but she caught on quick enough. "Do ye always go as ye please without an escort?"

"Only when I can sneak out."

The little girl chuckled; the echoing seemed to shock her and she covered her mouth embarrassed that she had been so loud.

Aislinn stopped in her tracks with her hands on her hips. "Now what kind of laugh was that?"

Grania just shrugged.

"If you are going to bother to laugh at all, then you should let loose, letting the laughs come from the gut. Like this." She let out a bellow causing the birds to fly from their nests. "Now you try."

Grania tried but it was anything but boisterous. She looked at Aislinn for approval.

"Tsk, tsk Grania. You are the daughter of a great Chieftain. Is that all you can do?"

Grania gave her a defiant look. With hands on her hip, legs spread slightly apart she leaned back her head and let out a guffaw that was worthy of someone that was much older than she.

"Now that was better."

They continued on, but after a long moment the girl spoke again in a most serious manner. "A.J., I think that my mother will not like me laughing so. She will think that I sound like a man."

"Maybe so, but men do not have the cornerstone on laughter. If you find something is humorous, then by all means let loose."

"I will remember that."

Neala was waiting for them. She had hot water boiling and three cups set out with herbs ready to make her concoction that nearly resembled tea. Aislinn often longed to have the real thing, but in this century, coffee and tea had not become a popular drink yet.

"How did she know we were coming?" Grania had noticed the place settings.

Aislinn shrugged. "I've stopped questioning. She just seems to know." She dropped her backpack and gave the old woman a hug. "Can I help?"

"No, child. Just sit. I see ye brought a friend. I knew that ye were, but had no idea it would be such a young lass." Neala walked over to Grania giving her a scrutinizing appraisal. "Ye are of the old Gaelic blood. I see it in yer features. A strong lass." She cackled making the lines around her eyes crease with humor. "No wonder ye attached yerself to Aislinn."

"Ye mean A.J.," Grania corrected.

"Aye." Neala smiled showing her nearly toothless mouth. "Sit, child. Sit." She went over to the pit and, with her apron, removed the dark kettle from the fire. She then did the honors of pouring the hot water into each cup. When she was finished, she glanced at her guests. "We'll have to wait a spell fer the leaves to settle to the bottom."

"Ye live out here?" Grania had not taken a seat but was walking around the rather meager surroundings that were this old woman's dwelling.

"Aye, as anyone may. All this is yers too." Neala followed the fine-boned child, who then looked at her with those blue eyes wide with wonder.

"Mine?"

"Nature is for everyone if they so choose. The trees the water, they all speak to ye, if ye only listen."

Grania nodded and sat down near the cozy fire. "I often have thought that I could hear the sea call my name. Is that possible?"

"All things are possible. The sea is in yer blood. An O'Malley methinks ye are."

The girl's eyes widened. "Aye. How did ye know?"

"I see a strong resemblance to The Black Oak. He is yer father?"

The girl nodded. "He is. I am Grania."

"A proud man yer father. He gives ye a gift of allowin' ye to spread yer wings like an eagle does in flight. Ye will go far, Gráinne Ni Mhálle."

It just dawned on Aislinn why the name O'Malley rang a bell. She had read a piece on the *Pirate Queen of the Irish Sea*, the English translation of her name being Grace O'Malley. Her father raised her to be a match for any man. Was it really possible that this little girl would one day become that woman?

"What is it?" Neala saw the awed expression on Aislinn's face. "Ye look like ye have seen a ghost."

She tried to smile, but she was still in wonderment that she had met someone that would one day make a name in history for herself. "Perhaps I have." She knew that she was staring and quickly turned away. "Do you think the tea is done?"

It was early afternoon when Aislinn decided it was time to take Grania back to the keep, but not before she promised Neala that they would come back tomorrow if they could manage to sneak away again.

"I like her," Grania stated as they started down the path.

"I'm glad. I like her too. She makes me feel at peace."

"Aye, it is what I was thinking."

They moved on, the little girl talking about the day and of her home near Clew Bay, but Aislinn was only half listening to what the child was saying, for she had the feeling that they were being watched. Her eyes darted back and forth between the tall oaks, but she could not distinguish a movement. Instead of this putting her at ease, the apprehension of dread seemed to increase. Grania must have sensed it too, for she had become unusually quiet. Aislinn pulled the child closer to her, and at that moment, a man came out of the clearing. His menacing stance was enough to let Aislinn know that he was not there to ask directions. She turned the child around thinking that they could go back toward the lake, but as she moved another man came into view. Aislinn instinctively put Grania behind her.

"Well, gentlemen, what's it going to be?" she asked of them.

The taller of the two highwaymen looked to his partner with a shrug before he returned his glare. He didn't say a word but started toward her. Aislinn squeezed Grania's arm whispering, "On the count of three, you run, Grania. Ye run back to the keep and for help. Can ye do that?"

"But what of ye?"

"Just do as I say. One, two, three." Aislinn let go of the girl and charged toward the man who had his dagger already drawn. Her yelling and sudden movement threw him off guard causing him to hesitate.

He had been told to apprehend this woman. He didn't expect her to be a raving lunatic. Aislinn went for the groin with a swift kick. As he doubled over, she took her full strength and hit the man on the back of his neck. He fell to the ground in an unconscious heap. She turned to send another swift kick to the other man's chest. He went down but so did Aislinn. Grania was still standing there with a stunned expression on her face.

"Run, Grania! Now!" Aislinn snapped the girl out of her trance. She took off, her long legs carrying her swiftly. Aislinn was on her feet again while her assailant had only managed to crawl to his knees. She didn't hesitate in yelling another, "Hi ah!" before she sent another kick to the man's face followed by another one to the stomach. As soon as the man went down, she grabbed the dagger that the first assailant had dropped, and took off in the direction that Grania had taken. She bought them some time, but how much she didn't know.

She was just about out of the clearing when a hand flew out to grab her. She turned and blindly swung with the dagger intent on doing as much damage as she could. The man barely ducked in time. She would have jabbed at him again, but he called her name.

"Aislinn!"

She paused arm still raised ready to strike. "Oh God! Dougray," her irrational fear already ebbing away. She lowered her hand and flew into his arms, hugging him close. Then she remembered Grania and pushed away. "There was a young girl with me. Did she...."

"She's safe. We were out looking for ye two when she came tearing out of the woods. She said that ye were attacked."

"Back there." She pointed.

Dougray waved for his men to move in that direction. "Are ye all right?" He pried the weapon from her hand.

She nodded giving him a half smile. "I am now."

"A.J., A.J.!" Aislinn turned to see Grania running toward her. Aislinn opened her arms receiving the child's embrace. "Ye are all right."

"I'm fine." Aislinn noticed that the girl's father was close behind.

Grania looked up at Aislinn with wide adoring eyes. "Never have I seen a woman as brave as ye."

The O'Malley put his hand on his daughter's shoulder, but looked at Aislinn. "Ye saved my daughter's life. I will not soon be forgetting such a deed." The emotion in his voice was evident enough of how much he cared for his child. He turned to Dougray. "When ye find those men, I would like to have a word with them myself."

"As ye wish."

O'Malley was about to leave, but on second thought turned to Dougray once more. "Ye will have my support, Dougray Fitzpatrick." With that he strode away with his daughter still looking over her shoulder at Aislinn.

"Support?" Aislinn asked him.

"Aye. There have been numerous raids and I am not sure who is to blame for them. Butler was whom I had suspected, but now I fear there is more than what meets the eye. This attack on yer person proves it well enough." He looked at the dagger that he had taken from her. "Where did ye get this?"

"One of the men tried to use it on me."

"English steel." He looked out toward the woods. Who did he know in England that would want to destroy him? The list, he had no doubt, was long. It was just deciding on which one would be willing to take the chance.

They found the men; one was dead, his throat slashed, and the other made an attempt to get away but was slain before they could apprehend him. Dougray was pacing the hall, not pleased by this outcome. He still did not know who had taken an interest in his life and of those that were close to him.

"Why would the man cut his own partner's throat?" Dougray voiced his puzzlement to Murrough. "It doesn't make any sense to me."

"Maybe he was being hushed up."

"Aye. The highwayman knew we were about, yet he took the time to commit murder before running." Dougray turned to Murrough. "We must double our security and have shifts to watch the forest. I do not want a repeat of what happened this day."

Murrough left the hall and Dougray took the steps to Aislinn's room. He knocked on the door. It was Moira that bade him entry.

She was staring out the window, her arms wrapped around her. She had seemed to be handling the attack well, calmly, but there had been a wary look in her eye that gave him poof enough that she was still rattled. It surprised him that he was beginning to know her subtle behaviors indicating her moods.

Complicating matters, in the last month she had become so much a part of his life that he failed to remember a time when she had not been in it, making him uncertain how he felt about that.

She turned noticing him for the first time and came to meet him halfway. "Did you find them? Was Neala all right?"

He removed his mantle and sword placing them on the table. He looked at Moira. "That will be all."

Moira hesitated as she looked at her mistress for the dismissal.

"It's all right, Moira."

The young woman nodded and quickly left the room. Dougray realized that Moira had bonded easily with Aislinn. She didn't even want to take his dismissal, but waited for her lady to give it. Maybe Aislinn was finally starting to conform to castle life. "Neala fares well. The men did not come her way. As for the culprits, they're dead."

"Dead? But I thought…."

"One was slain before we came upon him, the blood still wet on the other man's dagger."

"He killed his own partner?" Aislinn needed to sit down. "I don't understand."

"Neither do we." He had his hands behind his back, pacing as he spoke. "I would have dearly loved to interrogate the man to why, but he was shot with an arrow and died before we could get a word out of him." He looked at her now. "Murrough questioned everyone and no one laid claim to the killing. The arrow didn't match ours."

"What of O'Malley's or Burke's."

"They maintain it did not come from them either."

"You believe them?"

"I don't have a reason not to."

"But?"

He didn't want to reveal too much but the blasted woman would be set to defy him if he didn't give her a little. "This act was deliberate, but for what purpose only time will tell." He paused for a moment as his mind raced over the past events. The tragedy with the shipments, the raids and now the attack on Aislinn's life, but he could not dismiss the possibility that someone was after Dubhdara's daughter. Did Aislinn simply get in the way? "Aislinn, ye will not be allowed outside the walls."

"What about my walks to Neala's?"

"Ye continue to leave without a proper escort."

"But I promise…."

"Don't question me on this, Aislinn. It is for yer safety that I put these restrictions. Stay within the grounds and do not, and I repeat do not, go anywhere without Teige or Cormac." He was about to leave, when he remembered something further. "And I'll take the ropes that ye have acquired." He held out his hand palm up.

"I don't know what you're talking about." She folded her arms against her chest.

"Ye know perfectly well what I'm speaking of. Ye might as well give it up. I know Dermot gave ye the ropes. The man does not have the sense God gave him to do anything discretely. Hand it over or I'll search it out."

"Fine." She dropped her stance and marched over to the trunk. So what if she had to give up the rope. She could always resort to what she had done before.

"And don't get any ideas about asking the servants to bring ye sheets. They are under strict orders that if ye so much as ask for another covering, I am to be informed. Do I make myself clear?"

"Yes, oh high and mighty." She bowed before him with a wave of her right hand.

He chose to ignore her antics. "Good." He picked up his mantle and sword. "I would like ye to dress accordingly for the evening meal."

She gave him a defiant glare before she smiled, throwing him completely off guard. "But of course. I'll dress in my finest."

"I like blue if ye would please me with that color."

"Anything for you, my lord."

How he hated that she pretended like she was complying when he was well aware that she was doing exactly the opposite. "I will see ye this evening then." The moment that he left, Moira came charging in shutting the door behind her. She could see that her mistress was in a dour mood, obviously Lord Dougray's doing.

Aislinn turned to her to vent. "Can you believe that he had the nerve to come in here and demand that I stay within the grounds? He won't even allow me to see Neala with a guard. And he took my ropes." She threw up her hands showing her displeasure. "Confined! How I hate that. It makes me want to do just the opposite."

"Oh ye wouldn't, milady." Moira was worried. She didn't want anything to happen to her.

"I know how to take care of myself. Didn't I prove that already? He may be used to wailing women that swoon every time something remotely goes wrong, but hasn't he learned by now that I am made out of a sturdier stock? My father taught me how to take care of myself for heaven's sakes."

"But milady, the men had daggers. What they would have done…I shiver at the thought."

"I disarmed them."

"Are ye not afraid of anything?"

"Why should I be afraid? Never mind. I can't dwell on this right now. I'm running late. Hamish is probably already waiting for me, and I need to see Dermot. Do you know where I could find him?"

"Teige may know."

Chapter Twenty-Nine

Dermot was always a little nervous when it came to meeting with the Lady Aislinn. She was not like any woman he had ever known, so sure of herself and so very tall. Her height nearly matched that of each and every man of the area, if not some inches taller. She was strong too. He would never want to anger her, for he wasn't at all sure if she wouldn't actually cause some bodily harm to him.

The truth of the matter was she really scared him. When she walked into a room, just her presence alone seemed to take command. The only other soul he knew capable of accomplishing such a feat was Sir Dougray Fitzpatrick, the Lord of Dunhaven.

"She's but a woman," he said under his breath trying to convince himself that he had nothing to worry about. "Nay, I have me life to worry about." He saw her coming toward him with Teige and the cripple lad also, though the boy didn't seem to be limping. He straightened and looked again. As Hamish neared, he saw the reason for the change. The leather shoes that bound his feet were of two different sizes evening out the boy's awkward stance. "And she's clever," he added to the many admiring qualities of this woman.

"Dermot, did you remember to bring the other sword?" Aislinn asked.

"I did as ye requested, but what is this about, milady?"

"You are going to teach Hamish and I to handle a sword." Aislinn hadn't thought about it for herself until this afternoon, but now she knew that it was a necessity if she were to survive in this century.

"Ye want to wield a sword?" Teige came forward now, looking like she had asked something incredibly outrageous.

She put her hands on her hips. "Yes. It seems everyone in your land has one. I think it's time that I learn how to handle one myself."

Hamish looked uneasy. "A.J., womenfolk do not carry swords. Warriors do."

"Yes, yes, and so do knights and lords as well as thieves and murderers. I have no wish to go unprotected again." She sensed that Dermot wanted to protest further, but she held up her hand. "Not another word. Time is a wasting. Come now, hand it over."

Dermot looked imploringly at Teige for help, but the man just shrugged purposely taking a step back. Dermot was left with no other choice. With a resigned groan, he handed the weapon over to her.

Aislinn not being accustom to holding the hard steel, the weight of it made her almost drop it. She recovered quickly, lifting the weapon in a swing. Dermot and Hamish both jumped out of the way.

"Hey, watch it!" Dermot raised his voice. "Ye will kill someone handling the sword in that manner."

"Sorry, got a little carried away. I'll sit back and watch first." She handed the sword to Hamish. The boy took the weapon, a grin forming on his face. "A sword. A real sword." His hands glided over the cool steel.

"Well are ye goin' to stroke it or use it?" Dermot chuckled.

Hamish smiled too. "Use it."

"Then let's begin."

Aislinn went to stand by Teige as she watched with fascination how Hamish's clumsy movements began to transform into fluent jabs and lunges. She started to imitate the movements, pretending to be holding the weapon in her own hand. Teige just shook his head, but said nothing. He watched her parry, lunge with such grace it was almost like watching a dance.

"What do you think, Teige?" She looked back at the golden haired man.

"Not bad. But if ye don't mind me telling ye…" He cleared his throat. "…ye are a bit too graceful. If a man was coming at ye, ye would not have time to swing yer hips so."

"I'm swinging my hips?" She looked down at herself not believing it was possible. "Are you sure?"

Again Teige cleared his throat. "Aye, I am sure."

"Hmm." She tapped her chin as she thought about this for a moment. "Okay. Show me."

"Milady?"

"Come on, Teige. You know how to use a sword, so show me."

"I'm guarding ye."

"So guard me, but show me how to use the sword. I'd ask Dermot but he's busy with Hamish, and I don't want to take away any of the boy's time. Come on. You're just standing there."

"If I must." He took out his sword and demonstrated how it should be done. "See, like that."

After a few moments of watching, she wanted to feel the weapon in her hand. "Let me try it."

"With my sword?" He lowered it bringing it close to his chest.

"Yes. Why not?"

"Well for one, it's my sword. No one uses it. It was made just for my own hands and no one else's."

"Is everyone so protective?"

"Of course. A sword is yer best friend in time of battle. Ye know its weight and every contour better than ye know a woma...ye just know it better than anything." He turned crimson making Aislinn smile.

"I need a sword made for me then. Who should I see?"

"Padrig of course."

"But isn't he the cobbler?"

"He is the blacksmith, but he likes to make shoes." He shrugged. "The cobbler died last spring and we have not found someone to take his place. Ye may have noticed not many desire their feet covered."

She nodded.

"Padrig volunteered until we find someone to take over."

"Rhiannon's father seems to be quite talented. Let's pay him a visit."

"How long will it take?" Aislinn asked Padrig. She was anxious to have the weapon as soon as possible.

"I do not like to rush such things. It must fit in yer hand..."

"...like a glove," Aislinn finished for him.

Padrig shook his head. "Nay. It should be as an extension to yer hand as if they are one." He could tell that this was not a good enough answer for her. He sighed. "Come see me by the end of the week. I will have it done by then." That won him a dazzling smile.

"Thank you, Padrig." She gave the old man a quick hug before she started back to the castle.

"What was that about?" Fiona had taken hold of Teige's arm before he could get by.

"Hello, Fiona." He removed the woman's hand from him. "Why does milady's business concern ye?"

"Just making conversation."

"Ye best make it elsewhere."

"Teige, are ye still angry with me for turning ye away?" She ran her hand down his arm.

"Have ye been with so many, Fiona, that ye have mistaken me for someone else?" He left her then, her laugh grating on his nerves.

"Oh, Teige dear, ye are such a lad." Fiona went back into her one bedroom dwelling that Dougray had furnished for her. He may not come to her now because of that woman they dare call a lady, but at least he did not take his gifts back.

Cormac was the one who was good to her now, but he was far from what she wanted. She wanted a life in the castle. Her mother had told her she was reaching too high, but she didn't want to believe it. Dougray had come to her in the past. She had thought it just a passing fancy and had not thought of trying to give him a son. She had taken the precautions of her trade, the potion that rid any possibility of having a child, but now she wished that she had let nature take its course. She would have been married by now, maybe not in *his* church for she was below Dougray's station, but he could have married her by Brehon law. Dougray would have seen to all her needs then. She only would have to put up with the brat until it was old enough to be fostered out. She could have stood it that long.

Then that Hennessy woman shows up and ruins everything. For the life of her, she could not see why Dougray was interested in her, but obviously he was since he had not taken up with any other female. Fiona knew men and they needed certain things, a full belly and the comforts that only a woman could give. She'd known that since she was fourteen years old. Some things just never changed.

"What thoughts go through yer head?" Fiona looked toward the door to see Cormac's broad shoulders filling the space.

"Yer late," she stated turning away from him, angry that he had interrupted her thoughts.

"I come with an apology, and a gift."

She spun around her gray-blue eyes coming alive. "Gifts?"

He swaggered forward, a grin on his face. He was dangling a brightly colored, silk scarf. "For ye, my sweet."

She grabbed the item from his hands letting the soft fabric slide against her skin. "So beautiful. Where did ye come by this?" She had already tied it around her shoulders with a quick knot in the center.

"Ye are pleased?"

She nodded. "Oh, it is so beautiful. I never owned such finery."

He pulled her to him and she did not resist. "I think I love ye, Fiona."

She looked up, startled that he would confess this to her. She didn't know what to say. She enjoyed Cormac's company among other things, but she did not love him. She did not have time for such foolish matters of the heart. She had to keep a level head and pick only someone who could care for her in a fashion that she wished to achieve. Cormac would never be able to do that, but.... She looked at the beautiful scarf. If only he could give her gifts like this all the time. *Nay,* she silently scolded herself. The fool probably wasted his entire wages for this. She looked up into his loving eyes and smiled, hiding any of her true feelings.

The sound of someone weeping made Cormac move away. "What is that?"

"Only the wee brat that milord asked me to tend to."

"Whom do ye speak of?"

"Declan MacKenna of course." She encircled her arms around him. "Do not worry of the lad. He whimpers like that all day."

"And well it is to be expected. The lad saw his family slaughtered." He removed her hands from around his neck and went over to where the child was huddled within the folds of the shadows. He knelt down, so not to frighten the boy further. "Come here, Declan. Ye have nothing to fear from me."

The child hid his face to the wall. Cormac had a hard time swallowing the despair that threatened to choke him. It had been less than a week since they had come upon the murders of Declan's entire family. The child had hidden away and it was the only reason he was still alive. It had been a mere accident that they had even found the boy, for he had not called out for them to help him.

"Oh, leave him be." Fiona was getting impatient. "He is not all there."

"How can ye be so cold?" He stood to face her. "He is but a small babe."

She saw her mistake immediately and quickly tried to remedy it. "Ye do me a disservice. I simply do not know what I can do to help the boy. I have no children of my own, and yet I took him in. I didn't have to."

She really did look chastised over the way she had behaved, and of course he wanted to only think the best of her. "I am sorry, Fiona. It was a sad day that we found the MacKenna's." He looked to the child again and wondered if he would ever come back from where his fears held him immobilized.

"Maybe ye know of someone that could help tend to the wee one?" How she prayed that he did, for she realized all too late what a fool she had been to volunteer in the first place. It was just that she had hoped that in doing this small favor, she would make Dougray want to seek her company once more. The ploy had not worked.

"I might have a place for him. Will ye keep him until I make the arrangements?"

"Aye."

Moira watched Aislinn as she wrote in her journal with the odd-looking ink quill of hers. She had taken Aislinn's dress from the press and had already aired it out. "But I do not understand. Did ye not say that milord wanted ye to wear something blue?"

She looked up from her writing to answer her. "Oh yes, that is what he said. I intend to wear my blue sweatshirt." She pulled it out of her backpack. It was a little wrinkled so she shook it out.

"Why do ye wish to anger him?"

"That is not my wish, Moira, but I cannot let him dominate me like he owns me. I have a mind of my own."

"Does this have to do with milord taking the ropes?"

"Among other things. Like ordering me around and insisting that I have a puppy dog at my heels."

"Puppy dog?"

"A bodyguard."

"Oh, ye mean Teige."

"Yes. Nothing against the kid, but really he's just a child. I would probably end up protecting him."

"Teige is a fine warrior," Moira defended him.

Aislinn realized she was insulting someone that Moira thought very highly of. "I'm sorry. I'm sure that he is. It's just the point."

Moira was thoroughly confused. "What is the point?"

Aislinn shut her book finished with her writing, which consisted mostly of complaints of how unfair Dougray had been to her. She stood and slipped on the sweatshirt. She saw the stricken look that Moira was giving her and couldn't help but laugh at the poor girl. "What? Don't I look beautiful?" She twirled around as if she were wearing a beautiful gown.

"I wish that ye would reconsider."

"Nothing doing." She walked over to the door and threw it open. "Teige!" she called then realized that he was standing only inches away. "Oh, there you are. Are you ready to go?"

The young man's eyes widened as he took in Aislinn's appearance. She hadn't changed. He looked at Moira, who was wringing her hands. She just shook her head at Teige that there was nothing that she could do. The man kept his expression bland when he looked back to Aislinn. "Whenever ye are ready, milady."

"A.J., Teige, remember?" Aislinn said as she went on ahead nearly skipping down the winding stairs. When she entered the hall she received the same reception as she had the night before, only this time it was for obviously different reasons.

She walked over to Dougray first. "Well, my lord, what do you think?" She turned around so that he could see her entire outfit. When she was facing him again, she smiled. "I wore blue, just for you." She could tell that he was absolutely fuming and she was grateful that the long table separated them. "I will just sit down over there." She pointed to where Cormac and Dermot were already eating. "Come on, Teige. I don't want you to lose me." She took hold of Teige's arm and nearly dragged him away.

Robert Burke was simply appalled of the lack of grace the woman possessed. "What happen to her hair?"

Dubhdara just let out a bellow and hit Dougray on the back. "My man, what a strong will that lass of yers has. If I were ye, I'd see if the father of hers would grant ye permission to marry her off, and soon I would wager would be for the best." He watched her laughing with the men and taking a seat right with them. "She is still a handsome woman, but she is not as young as most would wish."

"Aye, but she is spirited to a fault," Dougray mumbled. "That is most likely why she is still without a husband."

Both O'Malley and Burke laughed agreeing that this could be the reason. "Still," Dubhdara continued, "there could be an advantage, if ye could convince her father to let ye find a husband for her, one perhaps who would secure support for all of us concerned."

Dougray had not thought of having her marry. He frowned not at all sure that he liked the idea of her belonging to another. O'Malley saw the expression and couldn't help but comment. "Or do ye have designs on the spitfire? The Hennessys beyond Dublin could be an asset in knowing what is going on in the Pale. We want to avoid conflict with these foreigners, but I have no wish to relinquish my holdings to them. If ye were to marry the lass, I would not object to the union."

"What?" He looked at the older man who was looking quite amused at his suggestion. He was quick to set him straight. "Nay. She is more than a handful that I wish not to have thrust at me for a lifetime of commitment."

"But what of my other suggestion? May it be of interest to the Hennessy?"

"Maybe. I will have to see."

"He named ye guardian, did he not?"

"Aye, of course."

"Then think of what I suggest."

Dougray nodded. As the night wore on, he found that he had trouble whole-heartedly listening to the conversation. Every so often he was drawn to where Aislinn was seated. Her laughter would reach him, irritating him that she seemed to fit in so well with his men. They actually looked to be enjoying her company.

"Dougray," Murrough leaned near enough so that he could only hear him, "ye might want to consider what the O'Malley suggested. Aislinn married to another clan could be good for us. Especially for ye."

Dougray threw him a heated look. "What do ye mean by that?"

"Only that ye have been preoccupied ever since that woman has been in yer care. What of this Hennessy? Are ye able to send word?"

"What?"

Again Dougray was not paying attention. Murrough decided that he would inquire about the woman's family by sending word directly to the Hennessy sept that was situated here in Ireland. Surely if they were related, the clan would see fit to lend a hand with one of their own.

For the last half-hour, Aislinn had been listening to the men share stories of their battles of great feats. She marveled that they could laugh at themselves even when they talked about how they faced death.

"And here was Cormac," Teige chuckled, "waltzing in after the battle had commenced, with not a stick of clothing on wondering what was going on. I never saw someone look so dumbfounded."

"Well if ye hadn't given me the rest of the strong grain whiskey, I would have been just fine."

"If ye just slept through all the yelling and clamoring ye would have been fine also."

"And what happened next?" Aislinn wished she had her notebook with her. The story was worth writing down.

"Well, the clan we were fighting saw him standing there in all his natural glory, and they stopped their assault staring at him as if he was an apparition. We took the advantage and were able to turn the tide. Murrough threw Cormac a sword and he fought like I have never seen him fight before."

"I had no choice," Cormac voiced. "I had me family jewels out in the open and I had to protect me future children, aye?" He slammed down his tankard with a thud and burst out with laughter that set everyone rolling.

"What of yer clan, Aislinn? Ye must have tales that ye can share with us," Dermot encouraged.

"Oh, there is fighting, but things are really different than here. One, I don't have to have a bodyguard." She put her hand on Teige's for brief moment. "No offense."

He nodded. "None taken."

She addressed the others that were listening. "My world is different is all I can say. You'd have to see it to believe it." She thought that she better put an end to it there. She couldn't reveal too much of what they would never understand.

"Hey, ye want to see me war scar?" A young man that obviously had too much to drink pushed his way through.

"She don't want to see yer ugly hide." Cormac pushed him away.

"Sure she does." He pulled up his shirt to reveal a long scar that went from one end of his chest to the other. "Got that fighting an Anglo-Norman. Nearly died, ye know."

"You must have been very brave."

"I have one, too." Cormac didn't want to be outdone.

Aislinn's rich laughter filled the room. "Please, Cormac, before you go any further, you aren't going to show me your family jewels are you?" That caused the others to join in on the laughter.

"Nay, I wouldn't do that." There was that mischievous glint in his eyes. "Unless ye wanted me to."

Aislinn held up her hands. "That's quite all right. I will have to decline. So let me see this impressive scar of yours."

"He lifted his shirt and showed her his back. "Take a look there. A chunk of my back was hacked away."

There was indeed an indentation. She could only imagine what these men had gone through. Such violence and they talked about it as though it were nothing other than another day's work.

"Show her yers, Teige." Cormac nudged him. "He's a little shy, if ye haven't noticed."

"Oh come on, Teige," Aislinn encouraged. "If you show me yours, I'll show you mine." That caused a few catcalls.

"Pipe down." Teige gave them a chilling look before turning his attention to Aislinn. "I'll show ye." He pulled up his shirt revealing a nasty scar on his shoulder, then he turned to show her how the sword had cut through to his back."

"Physician Cahir gave him up for dead," Dermot remembered. "Sent for the priest, ye know."

"I wasn't about to give up." Teige took over. "I had only had ten and six summers behind me."

"And still had not had a woman." Cormac nudged him again.

"Well that too." He smiled, his face turning scarlet. "All I knew is that I didn't want to die." He met Aislinn's gaze and she squeezed his hand.

"I'm glad that you recovered."

"Now, A.J., it is your turn." Teige was through being the center of attention.

"Well mine is not as impressive as all of yours." She took off her right shoe to show them the scar on the side of her foot. "This was from a dare that my brother issued, daring me to jump from the roof of our house. Of course, I was never able to resist a challenge, especially from him. So I jumped and ended up landing on some shears that my mother had been using to trim back the rose bushes. The shears went right through my shoe, slicing the side of my foot. I guess I was lucky that my injury only required twenty-five stitches, but that was the least of my pain. I received a lecture from my parents that you wouldn't believe." She noticed that everyone had become unusually quiet, and she turned to see that Dougray was glowering down at her.

"Are ye through?" His voice sounded like distant thunder. His men immediately dispersed.

"Jeez, you sure know how to ruin a party." She donned her sock and shoe once more.

"A word with ye please."

"Are you going to reprimand me, because if you are, I don't want to speak to you?"

Cormac snickered, causing him to receive a lethal look that melted the grin right off his face.

Dougray took hold of her arm. "I was not asking ye, I was commanding it."

"All right, already." She barely got to her feet before he was dragging her across the crowded hall. When they were a safe distance away from the others, he released her.

"What exactly do ye think ye are doing?"

"I was having a conversation, until you so rudely interrupted me."

"It's not what it looked like from where I was sitting and where our guests were sitting as well."

"Really, *Dougy*, you shouldn't be so worried what other's think."

"Well I do, and ye would be wise to stop calling me *Dougy*. That is not my name."

"Just what is your problem? Do you want me to be miserable in your God forsaken time? Is that it? I never wanted to be here in the first place. I'm trying desperately to survive here, but all you ever do is yell at me. Nothing I ever do pleases you. Do you hate me so much? Is that it?" All at once the events that had occurred in the last month came washing upon her like a tidal wave. She was at her breaking point and couldn't take anymore. She turned away from him, not wanting him to see that she had become so emotional. When a sobbed escaped her, Dougray hesitated. He was equally put back as she was. He was by now used to her angry tirades and knew how to respond to them. But to see her cry, he didn't know what to do.

"I don't hate ye, lass." He put his hand on her shoulder but she shrugged it away. He moved in front of her forcing her to look at him. "I don't hate ye. I am worried about ye. I am responsible for yer safety, but ye make it very hard for me to protect ye. I know that ye want to go back to yer time, but I don't know if it will ever be possible. Ye need to adjust to here…now. It's the only way ye will survive."

She didn't respond like he had hoped. "I wish to retire now," her voice void of any emotion. "If you will excuse me…."

He let her go, but he motioned to Teige asking him to make sure that she arrived safely back to her room.

She was awfully quiet, making Teige wonder what Dougray had said to her. At her bedroom door, she turned to him with a half smile. "Thank you for a lovely evening."

"Ye are welcome at our table anytime." He bowed.

"Thank you." She entered her chambers bolting the door behind her. The fire was still burning bright, illuminating the room with dancing shadows that almost looked like people. "Am I destined to live my life here in this castle?" The fiery shadows did not answer.

Dougray was just about ready to be seated again, when Abbot Kirwan intercepted him. "I happened to hear the suggestion that O'Malley made to ye."

"Which suggestion is that, Kirwan?" Dougray of late had lost patience with the abbot. The man seemed too interested in his business.

"The Hennessy woman, of course. I must speak for I fear for yer soul."

Now Dougray couldn't help but chuckle. "My soul is not in any danger from Aislinn."

"Forgive me, milord, but ye have been away too long in England. I fear that ye have been influenced by the Protestants and their ways."

Dougray's brows creased and his eyes narrowed. "Are ye questioning my judgment?"

"Nay," Kirwan was quick to answer. "I only suggest that ye feel responsible for the woman since Hennessy has given ye guardianship, but she is different in her thinking. She may be influenced by these foreigners."

Dougray again laughed. "She is not from England. So therefore, she is not influenced by them." He tried to move passed the abbot, but he prolonged him further.

"I have heard of lands that have savages. How the woman behaves is proof abundance."

"Enough, Kirwan, ye tread on dangerous grounds. The lady is from a family of good standing with me and with the O'Malley. To say anything to discredit her is to cause undue problems for ye."

"Is this a threat?"

"Kirwan, ye are thought highly of in the sept. Ye have served the clan of Fitzpatrick well, but ye must keep to the teachings of the church, and let me handle the affairs of the clans and what is best for all of us."

"The church must have a say in the matter...."

"Enough, Kirwan. I have guests." This time he was successful in moving on. Kirwan was not at all pleased at being brushed aside. He straightened his robe and removed a piece of lent that was on his sleeve.

"The man speaks rashly."

The abbot turned to see Robert Burke. He was not pleased to have to converse with the Anglo-Norman. It didn't matter to Kirwan that the Burkes were so much a part of Ireland now that they were every bit like the Irish. "He has much on his mind."

"He does," Burke agreed. "But the question is, where does the man's loyalties fall?" He left the question open as he moved back to the long table.

Chapter Thirty

Regan was teasing his sister again, chasing her around the marketplace. Finally, Lynelle found sanctuary under one of the tables that lined the wall. Aislinn happened to see her fly beneath it, only seconds before Regan came to a screeching halt. The freckle-faced youth looked one way then the other, trying to figure out where his sister could have hidden herself. Aislinn purposely walked over to the particular table looking at the baskets. Regan sidestepped. He didn't want to have another episode with the warrior woman, but it seemed that he wasn't going to have a choice. "How are you doing, Regan?"

"Grand," he answered carefully wondering if she was going to trick him in some way.

"And how is that wonderful sister of yours? Lynelle, isn't it?"

He nodded. "Lynelle is well."

Aislinn picked up an item like she was interested in purchasing it. "I sure hope that she remains that way. You wouldn't be chasing her or anything, would you?"

"Nay." He gulped sure that she knew that he was lying to her.

"Are you sure? Because I thought I saw you running. It looked like you were playing another game and I wanted to join in."

"Nay, no game." He backed up another step.

"I think it's time to chase you." She made a lunge toward him. He immediately bolted in the other direction.

Moira laughed. "I never thought I'd see it: Regan running away."

"It never hurts to let him know that there is always someone bigger than him and that no one's invincible." She bent down and lifted the covering to take a look at the girl. "It's safe to come out now, Lynelle."

She still didn't seem too sure and cautiously peek out to see for herself. "He's always picking on me." She brushed her red strands out of her eyes.

"That's what brothers do." Aislinn could recall many a time that Connor sent her crying to her parents.

Lynelle tilted her head to one side. "How do ye know?"

"I have a brother of my own. Used to pick on me until I stood up to him."

"Regan is bigger than me."

"Size does not matter. If you have the courage, yer suddenly ten feet tall." Aislinn urged the child to follow her. "Let's walk for a while."

Moira stayed close and Lynelle took hold of Aislinn's hand. "Where are we going?"

"Do you remember Hamish?"

"Of course. I've seen what ye have done with him." The girl looked up at her with awe.

"All I did is give the boy respect. The rest was all his doing."

"But he is so strong now. He's not at all like before."

"Did you ever think that it was because you never allowed yourself to know him?"

Lynelle looked almost ashamed. Of course, they didn't bother with Hamish. They didn't think he was worthy of their company, but now…well now she was beginning to see how wrong she had been. "We never gave him a chance, did we?"

"No, you didn't and what a shame that has been, but you can change all that now. Want to see if you can find some of the other children? We'll play a game. Would you like that?"

"It's not like the game ye played on Regan, is it?"

Aislinn chuckled. "That kind of playing is for someone that doesn't always abide by the rules. I have a hunch though that Regan will soon come around."

"I don't know about that. Regan has a pretty thick skull."

"Time will tell. Now scoot and round up a few friends. We're going to play soccer."

"What is soccer?" The girl was intrigued.

"It's a game that you use a ball. You do know where we could obtain one?"

"Aye, 'tis not a problem." She ran off to find some of the children. In the meantime, Aislinn rounded up Grania and Hamish. In about a half an hour's time there were enough players to start a real game. Of course, Aislinn was the only one that knew how to play. So for the next twenty minutes, she explained the rules. The children gathered around, eyes wide with interest. Teige stood guard while Dermot and Cormac set up a kind of field with fishing net for the goal and penalty area. With Aislinn's direction, they attached the net to poles and firmly put them in the ground. Once the field was set up, she led the children around to indicate everything she had been telling them.

"The line is the center." She pointed to a long rope that was placed on the ground. "One team on each side. Now, Lynelle, you will be fullback, which is the left and back. Hamish, you will be halfback and Grania you can be forward left, which is right up there close to the line. Edmond you'll be forward right." She recruited Moira to be halfback, though she had to practically drag her onto the field.

"I just couldn't," she kept on insisting.

"Oh, Moira, you have to learn to loosen up a little. You'll have fun. I guarantee it." Moira still didn't seem sure, but she decided it was easier not to argue the point.

Aislinn was about to pick someone to be fullback right when Regan came to see what everyone was doing. Aislinn decided to make the effort and walked over to him. "Would you like to join us? We still need another player."

"Ye would let me play too?" Regan looked at the other children who were already in position. He glanced back at Aislinn. "I would like to give it a try."

"Good. Run out to the field and I'll join you.

After a few trial runs, the kids were ready for a real game. Aislinn would referee, for she volunteered Dermot to play on one of the teams. Teige, who took his guarding seriously, came to stand by Aislinn and Cormac joined them.

"Ye have a way with children," Cormac spoke the obvious and with admiration.

"Children are easy to please. You show them some attention and they come alive. You'll be amazed how much they can show you. Look at Lynelle for instance. Do you see how her eyes light up, when she has the ball? Then you take a look at Edmond and you see the determination on his small face. He wants to win and would do about anything to see it happen. Even Regan seems to be enjoying himself. Children can open up a whole new world." Aislinn put her fingers in her mouth and whistled. "All right, Moira. You scored."

Cormac looked at Teige who was eyeing him suspiciously. He had already mentioned to his friend that he needed to find a place for the young MacKenna boy. He hadn't thought of asking Aislinn, but now maybe it would be the best for the child. Maybe she could even help him. She had already done wonders with Hamish and even Dermot, who had been such a clod, but now showed a sense of confidence.

"Milady?"

"A.J., Cormac, remember?"

"Aye. A. J., I would ask a wee favor of ye."

Her curiosity was piqued and she turned her attention toward him. "What might that be?"

"Seeing how ye are taken with children, I was wondering if ye might help a small lad. He lost his ma and da, ye see. He does not speak and stares without seeing. Do ye know what I mean?"

"He's in shock? Did his parent's die suddenly?"

"Aye. They were murdered in front of the boy, we be thinking."

Her hand flew to her chest. "That's horrible. No wonder the poor child can't speak."

"Will ye see if ye can help?"

"Cormac, I am not a professional in these matters and...."

"I'm sorry that I bothered you, but Fiona..."

"Fiona?"

"Aye. Fiona is taking care of the child and she is beside herself what to do."

Aislinn had no doubt and did not hide her disgust that the woman was given the chance to try. Fiona didn't strike her as the nurturing type. "I'd like to see the boy. I can't promise you that I can do anything, but I will try."

"Thank ye." He felt a sense of relief.

Dougray was with Murrough and Robert Burke, when he came across the game that Aislinn had instigated. He stopped his horse for a moment and leaned forward to watch. Aislinn was running from one end of the field to the other yelling directions. At one point the game came to a halt and Aislinn seemed to be explaining something to the children before she took the ball and showed them obviously what she meant them to do.

"That is the Hennessy woman down there?" Burke commented with obvious distaste.

Murrough nodded. "She seems to have a following, does she not?"

Dougray smiled. "For the moment, she is out of trouble and that is more than I could ever hope for. Let her indulge with the children." He pointed. "Just look at them smiling and laughing. They are having a good time of it."

"What is this game that she has them engaged in?" Burke, despite his distaste for Aislinn, was intrigued by it.

"I am not sure, but it reminds me of a game outlawed in England, Futball or some sort of name of that origin. After studies we engaged in a bit of this archaic game to pass the time away. It was rather brutal at times, but all so invigorating. " With that Dougray led his horse on.

Aislinn was acutely aware of Dougray and the other men approaching, but she didn't turn to acknowledge them. She was having fun and she wasn't going to let anyone ruin that.

"Regan, keep the ball close to you." At that point the ball was taken away from him and was now heading down the opposite way.

Dougray dismounted and walked over to stand beside her. "Interesting play ye have the children engaged in."

She didn't have time to answer him. She ran down toward the center of the field. "Moira, take the ball. Take it! Yes!" she shouted when Moira somehow maneuvered her way around one of the boys to kick the ball away and started heading it down to the goal net. Aislinn headed back to Dougray. "It is called soccer. I just love the game. Connor and I both played." Again she shouted for one of the kids to move into position. "The children caught on so quickly."

"Even Hamish has joined in, I see."

"He's a changed boy."

"I am well aware of the changes." He watched Aislinn race away, down the field. What an amazing woman she was, and it seemed he was only beginning to realize all of her remarkable qualities.

"Ye are going to allow this display?" Robert Burke had approached him and it took all of his will power not to look at the man with annoyance.

"I do not see the harm in it. Looks rather fun, if I do say so myself."

At that moment, Abbot Kirwan came upon them, his displeasure showing without reproach. "Here, here, what evil is this?" Kirwan saw Dougray and halted his condemning. It was obvious that he had been unaware that his lord was viewing what he had called an evil event. "Begging yer pardon, but do ye think it wise to let this…this…." He waved his hand before him.

"Futball, or rather soccer, game continue?" Dougray was quite amused by the old man's fear of child's play.

The abbot made the sign of the cross. "This can only lead to violence."

At that moment, Regan let out a yell as he attacked the ball.

"See what I mean?" The abbot was quite serious. "Why do ye let this woman run loose here?"

"I am glad, Abbot Kirwan, that ye see what I do." Burke was nice enough to speak his displeasure, now that he had an ally. "It's not an appropriate display for a young woman to participate in."

"These are children, Burke." Dougray took a defensive pose.

"I am speaking of Lady Aislinn. Look how she is running around and in trews or whatever the blasted attire is called. Ye are her guardian; I would have thought that ye would have insisted that she dress according to her station."

"A woman should not be dressed so." Kirwan nodded his head in agreement.

Dougray was losing his patience. "I see no harm in her wearing what is comfortable. She is not from here and it is not her way to wear the flowing gowns that we insist our women to wear."

"Then perhaps ye should inform her of our customs. The way the children look up to this woman...well look, even Dubhdara's daughter is among the young girls out there. Would ye have all our young woman getting ideas?" Burke looked to the abbot who in turn was nodding his head.

"Oh heaven forbid!" Dougray spat. "It is just cloth formed to a new design. It does not make what the person is inside." He walked away before he was tempted to say something that would cause more tension.

Robert Burke was indeed upset. How dare Dougray Fitzpatrick speak to him in that manner? Murrough had not been far behind and had heard the exchange. He did not trust Robert Burke. There was something that bothered him about the man. It seemed that there was more to him than met the eye, and it didn't bode well. At that moment, Robert turned to meet Murrough's steady gaze, but the Burke was the first to look away.

Abbot Kirwan decided to try another approach to see if Aislinn could be better controlled. "Murrough, ye are his friend. He will listen to ye."

Aislinn noticed the angry glances in her direction. Obviously yet again, it was over something that she had done. She made her way over to Murrough and the abbot. "I don't think that we have been properly introduced," she said in her finest Gaelic throwing the impeccable abbot completely off guard. The man even stopped brushing the dirt from his sleeve. She came to the conclusion that the man never had a hair out of place and expected as much from everyone else. She wondered what he would say if she offered her sweaty palm to him. She was almost tempted.

Of course, Kirwan had heard all kinds of rumors about this woman. Everyone knew of her and her strange ways. What concerned him was that in the month's time she had been with them, not once had she attended Mass. He looked to Dougray with an accusing eye. He felt he needed to personally rectify this slight. He again turned his attention to Aislinn who towered over him with her Celtic structure. He couldn't help but take a step back. "I am

Abbot Kirwan obviously sent to save yer soul."

Aislinn didn't mean to, but a chuckle escaped her lips. "I didn't know it was in need of saving."

"No Christian woman would dress the way ye do nor would she defile young children. Ye woman will be damned, if ye continue yer evil ways."

Aislinn's temper rose. How dare this man accuse her in such a way? "I believe you are out of line, dear Abbot. I do nothing to threaten these children and never would. They are playing a game and having fun. That is all. If you see something more to it, then maybe it is you that should search your soul for the evil that is obviously residing there."

The Abbot Kirwan's mouth dropped opened, so stunned that she would dare say such things to him. "Are ye a heathen that ye speak to me in such a manner?"

She took a step forward, but Dougray took hold of her arm and pulled her slightly behind him. "She is of the Christian faith, as ye and I are."

Aislinn would have rather fought her own battles, but seeing the situation was out of hand, she was wise enough to remain silent.

Kirwan looked to the woman that had her hair cut more like a man's and who spoke with strong words. "I would like to hear it from her. Do ye practice the Catholic faith?"

She was about to make another retort that would have definitely gotten her in deeper trouble, but she wisely decided against it. She took a deep breath to calm herself. "I do. So you can rest assured that my soul is not in danger."

"Ye have been here near a month and yet ye have not been to confess yer sins."

"Maybe I have none to confess," Aislinn nearly shouted.

"That will be enough." Again Dougray intervened. "Abbot Kirwan, I will take care of the matters here. We will see ye at Mass tomorrow."

He didn't want to be dismissed, but when Dougray spoke a demand, even he would not question it. He nodded, but his gaze found Aislinn's. His beady eyes bore into hers, but she did not flinch, causing him to be even more perturbed. He moved on and Robert Burke was quick to follow him.

Murrough approached Dougray. "Abbot Kirwan and Robert Burke locking heads together will not amount to any good. Do ye want me to go with them?"

"Aye, but let them do all the conversing."

"Understood." Murrough hurried off to catch up with them.

Dougray then turned his attention to Aislinn. "Just appease me here. Why do ye insist on causing problems?" Just when she was about to give him a reply, he held up his hand to halt her words. "Nay, do not go denying it. I want ye to listen to me on this, if not anything else. Abbot Kirwan, though I do not believe in his ethics, will make yer life miserable, especially if he believes ye to be the worst kind of sinner."

"Then why do you allow him to be here?"

"Dunhaven has been his home for many years now. He is to stay. The people come to confess their sins to him."

"And you? Do you confess your sins to that man?"

"That man is from a holy order as was many of his family before him. Ye will speak of him with respect."

"I respect people who deserve it, and as far as I could see, that man didn't qualify."

"I refuse to argue with ye further. Ye will bite yer tongue where Abbot Kirwan is concerned, or I'll have ye gagged and bound."

"Fine." She turned away from him to watch the children, who were oblivious to what had just happened.

Dougray had not wanted to fight with her, but yet again it seemed that they were at each other's throat. "Aislinn?" She wouldn't look at him and by the set of her jaw he could tell that she was upset. "We have both been under a lot of tension of late." The apologetic tone he took drew her back to him. "Maybe ye would like to have some privacy tonight, without the clamoring of hungry men ringing in yer ears. May I interest ye in a quiet dinner with me and maybe a game of chess?"

"Is this a date?"

"Date?" He wasn't sure what she meant.

"Never mind. I would love to." She was called away when Regan decided to attack Edmond for not making a goal. By the time she had settled the two down, she noticed that Dougray had already mounted his horse and was heading in the direction of the keep.

After dinner, Dougray began to set up the chess pieces. It wasn't for the game itself, but to enable him to have some time alone with Aislinn. He found himself thinking of her far too often during his hectic days, bringing a smile to his face as he recalled something she had told him. He found that when she wasn't trying so thoroughly hard to annoy him, he actually looked forward to her company.

And now after their long, leisurely dinner they were ready for a game of chess. She insisted that he start it. After a few moments, he decided on his strategy and his topic of conversation. "What other pastimes did ye enjoy back home?"

"Oh just about everything. Basketball, baseball, absolutely loved swimming and track. I never felt so free when I was running for long distances. I did a lot of my thinking and sorting out on those occasions."

His brows lifted in a quirky arch. "Running long distances?"

"Yeah, Connor and I run cross country."

"Hmm." He studied the board before he made his next move. "Ye like to keep busy."

"Doesn't everyone?" She was quick with her turn, making him think that she wasn't paying much attention to what she was doing. She lifted her bold dark eyes to meet his.

He reluctantly let his gaze drop, if only to study the board again. "Not everyone has the energy that ye possess, Aislinn."

"Never was one to sit for very long, unless I'm writing."

"Aah aye, your smut books," he teased her. "Ye do like the written words."

"As much as I like to keep physically active, my mind is going a hundred miles an hour in the imaginary phase. Stories flit across my mind, and I just can't wait to get them onto paper. I remember as a kid that I used to love to tell stories. You know not just the little tiny short ones, but the elaborate detailed kind. Once I was started, I could go on forever without taking a breath."

"As well I can imagine." His smile remained on his extremely handsome face, warming her from across the table.

"Now you must answer a few questions of my own."

His smiled slipped, and for a moment, she thought that he was going to refuse, but then he nodded.

"You are Catholic?"

"Aye."

"Not quite a practicing one, are you? I mean I haven't seen you running to the chapel for mass."

"It is difficult to explain. The old ways are present here at Dunhaven, what the priests call the pagan teachings. Neala was my teacher long before I was obligated to endure the teachings of the church. Then when I was forced to go to England, my grandfather immersed me in the protestant ways. I have had enough of religion to last me a lifetime." He turned the questioning to her. "Ye stated to Abbot Kirwan that ye were of the faith, or was this simply a way to appease him?"

"It was the truth." She nodded. "Baptized and raised Catholic from the day I was born. I will admit that since I moved out of my parent's house I have been more than a little relaxed. I am now of the guilt-ridden club that only attend twice a year, once for Christmas and then Easter to fulfill my moral obligations." She leaned her elbows on the table and folded her hands under her chin. "Why is the Butler so determined to have your head?"

"He dislikes me." He was avoiding her gaze with a pretense of studying the game at hand, but she knew better.

She made an annoying buzzer like sound causing him to look at her. "Not good enough. Try another one."

He hesitated for a moment. "It is of a personal nature, that much I will tell ye. He blames me for something that I had no control over."

"You explained to him that it wasn't your fault?"

"Aye, many times, but he listens with a deaf ear."

"That does make it difficult. Okay, if you aren't going to elaborate on your feud, how about telling me a little about your time in England."

"Ye are a nosey one, aren't ye?"

"Yep." The even whiteness of her smile was dazzling making him feel relaxed. He was enjoying their time together, getting to know each other.

"They were long years that made me wish for home more times than not. My grandfather was forever on my back to learn the ways of the court, but I had no desires to be paraded around like some beast in a cage. It was my great pleasure to accept being knighted, especially since it enabled me to return to Dunhaven." He took his turn before looking at her again. "Now it is my turn to ask ye a question."

"Shoot." She leaned back in her chair and waited for him to ask away.

"Ye speak the language well enough, as though it were a second skin to ye. How did ye come by this knowledge?"

"Spoken in the home by both my parents, along with French, Italian, Spanish and Cheyenne for good measure."

"What is this Cheyenne?"

"Native American Indian." She grinned. "It's where I get my dark eyes."

"Beautiful eyes, I might add."

"Thank you." She accepted the compliment graciously. "My mother is a quarter Cheyenne and her grandmother was adamant that she not forget her heritage. Languages were so much a part of our lives that I thought everyone spoke a multitude of them. What a shock it was to find out I was wrong. I have to admit that finally one of the languages I know has come in handy."

"Very well, I would think. Ye know our language better than the Irish know it themselves. And I'm referring to your century. I could not help but notice that they mainly speak the English tongue. There has been much change for that to occur."

He saw the sorrow cross her face before she spoke and it pained him to know that his home would surely suffer. "A country should be allowed to speak their own language, but I am afraid that there will be events that will drastically change the way the people of Ireland live. English rule in the end will dominate."

"I don't understand. We have great Chieftains, seasoned warriors. How could we be defeated?"

"I'm afraid a lot of the loss was because Ireland would not unite and fight as one. Something I do know though that might put a smile on your face. Believe it or not Grania O'Malley will grow up to be a great chieftain, but unfortunately no one will grant her the title."

"That little gangly lass, Dubhdara's daughter?"

"Yes. She grows up and causes quite a bit of havoc on the sea, for nearly forty years."

"Well if miracles never cease to exist. It is good that ye saved her from those men."

Instantly their eyes locked. "Could this be the reason why I was brought here?"

"Could be, and if what ye say is the truth, then I am grateful for it. Female or not, I will take anyone causing mayhem for the English."

Aislinn chuckled causing him to join her. "Rather good of you to say so. Hey, why are you being so nice to me?"

"Puts ye off guard, does it?" His mustache twitched and he winked at her.

Her grin turned almost mischievous. "Well maybe just a little, but…" She looked at the board game and made her last move. "…but not enough to let you win. Check mate."

His smile left his face as he gazed down at the board, not believing that he had lost. His blue-gray eyes lifted to her beaming face of triumph, causing him to grin also. "It seems that it was I who has been distracted, milady."

"Care to go for another round?" She was already setting up the board.

"I'll have to warn ye, I will be keeping my mind on the game this time."

Chapter Thirty-One

Aislinn had waited for Dougray in the library until it became apparent that he was not going to show. She was disappointed for he had promised her that they were to tour the countryside this morning. Teige finally found out from Dermot that he had left before dawn, but he wasn't sure on what business or when he would be returning.

She didn't want to be cooped up in the castle so she made her way out to the courtyard, where people were already set up for the day, selling and buying their goods. Teige walked at her side, which she found she didn't mind so much. She rather liked the young man's company.

She browsed around the tables not seriously shopping, but enjoying the conversations. She was about to move on when she happened to spot Dougray conversing with the over-voluptuous Fiona. Her feet failed to move and her eyes narrowed dangerously, as it slowly dawned on her why Dougray had stood her up. Obviously the woman had been the one to detain him. A surge of jealousy coursed through her veins, and it nearly took all her restraint not to stalk right over there and pull out every golden strand of hair from Fiona's head.

Teige seeing her arrested expression followed her line of vision. "Damnation," was whispered under his breath but Aislinn had heard him.

She pinned him down for some answers. "Okay, you know something, don't you?"

"Know what, milady?"

"Don't milady me, Teige. I see it in your eyes. Who is that woman to Dougray? She has him simply entranced."

"Trapped is more like it."

This did not make her feel better. "Come clean, Teige."

"Fiona…. She is…."

"Yes?" Her intense gaze was making him squirm.

"She is just Fiona." He couldn't meet her gaze.

"Since you're not going to tell me straight out, how about if I guess." When he didn't say anything, she continued. "I think that Fiona has designs on yer lord, does she?"

"She likes many men I am afraid, but seems to love none of them."

The dawning of his words seeped in. "Oh, and what does Dougray feel for her? Don't spare me."

"I don't want to make things difficult for milord and ye."

"Difficult?" She laughed. "Do not worry. Dougray can be with whomever he wishes." She shrugged trying to show him she really didn't care. "I was only curious."

"Ye mean ye don't mind? I thought that…."

"What did you think?"

"Nothing, milady."

"Please stop with the milady. A.J., remember?" She gave him a nudge and smile, but once they began walking again, that grin slipped from her face. She didn't know much about Fiona, but she did know that she didn't like the woman's hands on Dougray. She strode up to the two, not caring in the least that she just might be barging in on a private conversation.

"So we meet again…Fiona, isn't it?" Aislinn smiled pleasantly enough, but Fiona was not fooled.

"Aye, milady." She gave a slight nod. "If ye will excuse me, I have business to attend to." She strode away with an air of dismissal.

"Was it something I said?" Aislinn asked innocently.

"Fiona has an errand to run," Dougray stated simply, forcing Aislinn to bite her tongue with the retort, *"I bet she does."*

"You stood me up, you know?"

"Stood you up?"

"We were to go riding, Dougray."

"I did not forget." He had been looking forward to spending time alone with her, but he received pressing news that he couldn't ignore. "I fear that I have to postpone our riding excursion. There has been another incident with the Butlers. I must tend to this matter personally."

"Oh, I understand." She couldn't quite keep the disappointment out of her voice.

"Another time perhaps?" His eyes had wavered over to where Fiona was standing watching them.

Aislinn noticed the exchange, pissing her off all over again. "Don't bother." She started to move away, but his hand shot out to stop her. She whirled around; her anger blazed tightly in those dark eyes. Confused, he let her go watching her stalk off in a fit of underlined fury.

When he saw Teige glance at him with a small shake of his head, he was even more puzzled. He scratched his head trying to make sense of what had just happened.

Dougray silently rode alongside Murrough out to the small piece of land that had been taken care of by the MacKennas. Declan MacKenna, the youngest son, had made it out alive and was the only link to what had happened. The only problem was he was four years old and was unable to tell them a blasted thing. What could he expect? By the time they had found the lad, he was shivering in the cold and in shock.

Dougray wanted to go back to the homestead and see if they had missed any clues, anything that might help them to uncover who had murdered the whole family and slaughtered the livestock.

While Dougray was preoccupied with other more pressing matters, Aislinn busied herself with the children. Another game of soccer was put together and this time she didn't hesitate to join in.

Cormac walked over to Teige who was still on guard. "Looks like fun," he commented.

"Aye, that it does. Wouldn't mind if I had a go at it too."

"A.J. would probably slaughter us." Cormac chuckled and Teige's mouth twitched with amusement.

"She is strong woman, Cormac, if ever I knew one. I sometimes wonder who is guarding whom."

"I have had the same thought myself."

They watched the process of the game for a moment. Cormac became quite involved and let out a yell for Lynelle to watch out for her brother, for he was close on her heels. "Moira I see has joined in on the fun." He couldn't help but notice how her slim hips moved to and fro as she tried to block Regan from passing her. Cormac let out a low whistle. "The lass has grown to a woman right before me eyes. Now why have I not seen this before?"

"Aye," Teige answered. "She has beautiful dark hair, don't ye think? And her eyes…her eyes are like the blue of a clear lake."

Cormac let out a chortle and he slapped Teige on the back, nearly knocking him forward. "Ye are smitten, are ye not?"

"Me?"

"Aye. Ye going on the way ye are describing the lass, as if she were a goddess."

Teige took a deep breath that was more of a sigh. "She's grand."

"Have ye let her know how ye feel?" Cormac asked making Teige feel a little foolish. His sheepish look was answer enough. "Ye haven't. What are ye waiting for? Ye think she'll wait forever for ye to say something? If ye don't speak yer mind, I'll be forced to ask her myself."

He looked sharply at Cormac. "Ye wouldn't dare."

"Ye don't think so? I have a mind to go right now…." He moved forward and Teige's hand shot out to stop him.

"I will talk to the lass."

Cormac smiled, satisfied that he had given his friend a nudge toward starting a well-needed love life.

Aislinn spotted Cormac, and as soon as she could break away from the game, she went over to him. "Were you able to arrange for me to meet with Declan?"

"Aye. I will bring him by later this afternoon, if that is all right by ye."

"Bring him to my quarters." She left him then to rejoin the game.

By the afternoon, it had begun to rain. It was a good downpour, sending everyone scattering to find cover. Aislinn raced up to her room so that she could remove her wet clothing and dry her hair before Cormac arrived with the MacKenna boy. She had donned a robe, while Moira was still trying to get a fire started in the fireplace. "Here, let me do it," Aislinn offered. "You better change yourself before you catch cold."

"But, milady…."

"Don't argue with me, Moira. Go grab one of my robes."

"Ye are so kind." She started to untie the laces of her dress, when she noticed that Aislinn had pulled something from her pack. She watched curiously as the item sprouted flame. Her gasp caused Aislinn to turn to look at her. "I am sorry…" Moira stammered, "but what was that ye did? Flames flying from yer finger tips."

"This?" She held up the lighter for her to see. "It's something we use back home. It's called a lighter. See?" With that, she flicked it and it came to life. The wonderment on the girl's face was almost comical. "Nothing to it."

"Yer land has many oddities that I do not understand, but I think that I like them."

No sooner were they dry and warm, Cormac arrived with the little boy. Aislinn took one look at the blond-haired child who had big blue eyes, fringed with the darkest of lashes, and she immediately wanted to cradle him close to her and erase the hurt that was bottle up inside of him.

"May I?" She offered her arms to take the child from Cormac. The boy did not protest, but he did not cling to her either. "Declan, I am A.J., and I would love it if we could be friends." The child just stared straight ahead, without so much as a fluttering of an eyelid to indicate if he heard her at all, but Aislinn continued to speak as though he were intently listening to every word. "And this is Moira."

"Hello, Declan," she greeted him, but she was a little wary of the way the lad was behaving. She looked at Cormac and he answered her silent question.

"He is *fairy-taken*."

Moira nodded understanding immediately, but Aislinn was a bit put back. She knew from her father's many stories that people of this time were superstitious to a fault. They blamed unexplained ailments on the fairy folk and there was no use trying to explain that it was otherwise.

"Are you cold?" Aislinn carried the child closer to the fire. "I bet that you are. We'll just sit here, you and I," she told the child as she sat down on the chair cradling him against her. "I believe that it is a perfect day to tell you a story." She gently rubbed his head and spoke to him in a smooth clear voice. Slowly Declan seemed to relax against her, and though he did not utter a word, his small hand moved over hers.

When he had fallen asleep, she rose from her seat. She saw that Cormac was ready to take him, but she shook her head. "Let him stay here."

"Ye don't mind, milady?"

"No, not at all."

Moira had moved back the covers on the bed and she placed the sleeping child down. "He looks so exhausted."

"Fiona told me," Cormac felt he should warn Aislinn, "that Declan has not slept through a night. He is still having nightmares."

Aislinn's heart went out to the child. "Have you caught the person or persons responsible for his family's murders?"

"Nay, not as yet."

Aislinn tucked the covers under Declan's chin before she looked at Cormac. "I hope when you do that you pay them as much kindness that they have bestowed upon this child."

"Ye can rest assured they will be dealt with accordingly."

Dougray was quite worried when he had learned that Aislinn had taken her evening meal in her room. He wanted to check in on her before he retired, just to make sure that she was all right.

Moira must have gone to bed for Aislinn was the one who greeted him at the door. "Are ye ill?" His gaze took in her appearance. She was dressed for bed, barefoot and a robe hanging loosely around her. She didn't look sleepy, but her hair was messed in a way that led him to believe that she had been in bed. He could not find fault in the way she looked with all the wisps of dark hair that framed her face. He had the urge to brush his hand against her soft skin.

"I'm fine," she said slowly and in a whisper bringing him back to the reason he had bothered her in the first place. He noticed that she made no move to let him enter. Matter of fact, she seemed to be purposely blocking his way. "What made you think otherwise?" she said nervously and even looked over her shoulder, as if she thought that someone would hear her.

"Ye did not," he found himself whispering too, "take your meal in the hall."

"Not because I was ill," her voice was still just as quiet, but with a definite edge to it.

"If ye are not ill…and why are we whispering?" he questioned her as he again took in her disheveled appearance. She apparently was not sick, so why had she decided to stay in her room? Over her shoulder, his eyes found the evidence. There were two plates not one. His mood veered sharply to anger. "Ye are hiding someone?" He didn't wait for her to answer, but forced his way in. "Where is he?"

"In bed." Aislinn had known that she couldn't keep the boy a secret for long. She had just hoped that she could have explained everything to him in the morning. "Please lower your voice. You'll wake him and he is exhausted."

The glower he gave her made her cringe. "Ye don't even try to deny ye have someone in yer bed and ye gloat on how ye exhausted him?"

"What are you talking about?" Her temper rose at his accusation. "You must know what the boy has been through. I did nothing to excite him."

"Lad?" Now he seemed confused, which totally baffled her.

"Declan MacKenna." She saw his expression change to what could only be relief, then embarrassment before he looked away. "Just whom did you think I had in my bed?"

He ran his hand through his dark hair feeling rather foolish for the assumption. "I thought that ye were…." He let the sentence trail off to silence hoping that she would just leave it alone. No such luck.

It took a moment, but it finally dawned on her what he had meant. "You thought that I was entertaining someone, didn't you?" His answer was a shrug. "And if I did have a man in my bed? What did you think you were going to do?"

"I was…" What exactly had he planned? He was not so sure. He just knew that he hadn't liked the idea of it. "Ye are my responsibility and…."

"And you will decide if and when I may have a relationship?"

His eyes narrowed. "Do ye want to take a man to yer bed, Aislinn? What happened to ye waiting for yer true love?"

"I'm not getting any younger, you know, so I might as well just find out what I'm missing." Why in the world had she baited him? It seemed that this man was forever capable of provoking her to say things that she really didn't mean.

"Well, darling, I could be a service to ye then." He made a move toward her and she backed up, bumping into the small table she had used for the evening meal. Without taking her eyes off him, she grabbed the first thing her hand came in contact with and she waved it at him. It so happened to be a chicken bone. It wasn't too threatening, but she didn't care. She pointed it at him as though it were a weapon. "Stay away or so help me."

"So help ye what? Ye going to beat me with chicken scraps?" He just shook his head. "If ye are going to make an offer, Aislinn, ye should be willing to see it through. The next man ye say this to may not know ye do not mean it." That remark cost him a lethal glare. He didn't move fast enough when she decided to let the bone fly from her fingertips. It hit him in the head. "Ach! What was that for?"

"For making me want to kill you."

She stood there so tall and angry beyond belief, but she couldn't have looked more tantalizing to him. Before she could say anything more, he held up his hands. "Truce?"

"Fine."

They stood there for a few moments, before Dougray spoke in a controlled voice. "May I ask ye why the lad is here? Fiona was to care for him, until I could find a home for him. I spoke to her only today about Declan. She did not mention that she would be bringing him here."

Aislinn nearly smiled when she realized that this was why Dougray was talking to Fiona this morning. "Cormac was worried about Declan and thought that I might be of help."

"He should not have imposed."

"I don't mind." She moved toward him and gently touched his arm. "Come and see for yourself." He followed into the adjoining room and his gaze found the small form lying upon the bed within the comforts of the blankets. The child appeared to be in a deep sleep, his thumb securely locked inside his mouth. He did look comfortable, peaceful. He glanced at her then.

"Ye are a good lass, Aislinn Hennessy, for taking in this poor soul."

The tenderness in his compliment touched her like a caress, confusing her. She lowered her gaze, before she spoke again. "You will let him stay with me, won't you?"

"Aye. He looks content, and I thought I would never to see him that way again."

It was still early when Aislinn arose and dressed, letting the exhausted Declan sleep. She did her early morning stretches before she sat down on the rug to do her sit-ups. This was a ritual she did at home for good practice, but here it was a necessity to get warm. The room even with the fire going could be somewhat drafty, at least to what she was used to in sunny California.

Sit-ups were what she was doing when the blond-haired child peeked over the edge of the bed to view her. His thumb was in his mouth and his blue eyes were wide with wonder. Finally she realized that she was being watched. Ending her exercise for the moment, she looked at the child with a welcoming smile. "Good morning, Declan, I hope you slept well. Are you hungry? I think I have just about worked up an appetite and Moira should be arriving soon. As if on cue, the girl entered with a tray full of wonderful food that smelled delicious.

"Good morning, A.J., young Declan. I brought some vittles."

Declan looked at the plates full of food and his thumb dropped from his mouth.

Aislinn was on her feet and she offered the boy her hand. "Let's see what Moira brought us. Shall we?"

He didn't object and his appetite was ravenous. If she didn't know better, she would have thought the poor child hadn't had a meal in days.

"Slow down, Declan. You don't have to be in a rush." That seemed to work and he took smaller bites of his warm bread. "That's better."

Cormac arrived soon after to take the boy for a while. Aislinn was already growing attached to him and she made Cormac promise to bring him back by the afternoon.

With the rain of the early morning all but gone, a rainbow appeared overhead and the weather cleared bringing out the sun. Aislinn was quick to change into her trews and sling her backpack behind her. She nearly ran to meet with Rhiannon, whom she knew would already be hard at work by the curtain wall, where she tended the gardens. Aislinn spotted the fair-haired woman and waved to her.

Rhiannon's green eyes sparkled with delight and waved back. She was glad to have the company.

"I'm ready to get my hands dirty." Aislinn smiled as she threw down her pack.

"And ye will. Trust me." She handed her some gloves that she just happened to bring along with her.

They worked side by side, conversing and laughing until their sides hurt. Rhiannon had been telling her about her childhood and growing up at Dunhaven.

"The Celtic festivals are still held even though the Catholic priests want to condemn them as the work of the devil. It will be a shame if they are eliminated, for they are fond memories to me. I first gave myself to Murrough at Beltane."

"I don't mean to sound like a prude, but this is permitted?"

"Encouraged actually." When she saw that Aislinn had stopped what she was doing and was now studying her, she wondered if she shouldn't have been so blunt. "I do not offend ye, do I?"

"No, not at all. You've piqued my curiosity; please tell me more about this festival."

"It is the season where trees are in full leaves and flowers are a plenty. It is the season of life where we will engage in projects and plans, which we have waited a long winter to fulfill. On Beltane eve, a fire is kindled, and there is dancing and singing. Unmarried couples and sweethearts pair off and go to the woods." Rhiannon was well aware of the teachings of the church, but she did not understand how something so beautiful as the coming together of a man and woman could be considered wicked. Aislinn was, no doubt, of the Christian faith. She was rather curious to know how a Christian woman thought. "Have ye not wanted to be with a man?"

"Well of course, but I can't see myself just sleeping with any man just for curiosity sake. I would have to love him before I would give myself so completely."

"As it was with me."

She was helpless to stop the embarrassment that rose inside of her. "I'm sorry, Rhiannon. I didn't mean to imply…."

Rhiannon just laughed with a shake of her head. "I know ye didn't. I was just saying that I have found the man who makes my heart sing."

"Murrough?" She still had a hard time picturing the two of them together. Murrough was so big and always seemed to have a frown set into his granite-stone features, his dark red mustache drooping down his face exaggerating the effect. As for Rhiannon, she was determined that much was certain, but she was also very kind hearted, much too sweet and petite for the abominable giant. They seemed the most two unlikely people to be thought of as a couple, but then she saw how Rhiannon's face beamed with pride when she spoke his name. She had to wonder what it was that she was missing.

"He may not look it, but he is a gentle man."

"I'm sorry, but I just have a hard time imagining this. With the withering looks he gives me, I think he wishes me gone from this place, as soon as possible."

"Murrough does not understand yer ways is all. He sees how ye occupy milord's mind and it worries him."

"Occupy...who? You mean Dougray?"

"Milord speaks of no other woman than ye."

"What about...well I thought that he was with...you know, Fiona."

"Dougray is no monk." She smiled at her almost sympathetically. "He was a pained soul seeking comfort and Fiona was willing, but she was never someone that would give him a lifetime commitment. They are at odds with the goals they have mapped out in this life."

Aislinn became silent then, making Rhiannon wonder what she was thinking. Maybe she had revealed too much.

"Rhiannon?" She paused, as she thought of how she should word her question. She decided it was best just to be direct. "You speak as though Fiona is of the past." She tried not to look hopeful, but had failed miserably.

"I believe that milord's eyes are elsewhere. Are ye not curious about the man intimately?" Rhiannon's eyes clung to hers analyzing her reaction to what she had asked.

Aislinn was thoughtful for a moment as she weighed each word. Curious was putting it mildly. She thought about him the moment she awoke and couldn't wait to see him, even if they ended up arguing. Her last thoughts before she fell asleep at night were of this man and even then he seemed to creep into her dreams, filling them with wanting. "I would be lying if I didn't say that I was, but I am not from here and I have all intentions of returning to my home, if the time presents itself. I can't allow myself to have fanciful thoughts when there could be no future for them."

"Would ye not stay if he asked ye to?"

"I can't...I couldn't...Rhiannon, he would never ask me anyway." She made herself busy trying not to dwell on what Rhiannon had said, but how could she not? The mere suggestion intrigued her.

"If ye are still here at Beltane, maybe ye could persuade him to join ye."

"It would never happen. He is Catholic and the church forbids such activities."

Rhiannon couldn't help but notice that she didn't say that she wouldn't *want to ask* only that she felt that she would be *refused*. "Aye, ye are right about the Christian church, but it is still allowed in the Brehon laws and they still govern Ireland." She studied the woman who had strength befitting a man, but seemed to shake with fear at her own desires. "And if he decides to ask ye, Aislinn? Would ye go with him?"

She never had the chance to answer for just then she spotted Murrough and Dougray approaching. As they neared she could see that Dougray wore a scowl that made his eyes look gray as the turbulent sea.

"A word with ye now!" Dougray demanded without waiting for Aislinn to refuse. He grabbed her backpack and took hold of her arm, nearly dragging her away. Rhiannon looked to Murrough for an explanation to the rude behavior.

"Do not look at me that way, woman. I do not know of her deed that warranted Dougray's wrath, but I am sure that it is well justified. The woman is always causing mischief."

"Why do ye say this? She is a good, decent woman, and ye would do well if ye would open yer eyes and see it as so."

"Now, Rhiannon..."

"Do not patronize me, Murrough O'Donoghue."

"Blast it! Will ye not let me speak?"

"When ye learn to say something that I wish to hear, then ye may." She turned away from him then, but he would not let her go.

"Nay. Ye are not going to take this out on me." He pulled her into an embrace covering her lips with his. "Now." He released her only to caress her face. Her expression had softened, as did her temper. "This is more of the greeting I had expected."

"It is not a bad way to greet."

Her smile could always set his blood afire.

"Let go." Aislinn tried to pull away from his steel-like grip, but he seemed not to be listening to her at all, as he continued to pull her behind him. She had no choice but to keep up, for she had no doubt that he would just drag her all the way back to the castle.

He did not say a word the whole way. He made her climb the spiral stairs and proceeded to drag her to the library, practically throwing her down on the hard wood bench, backpack and all. He turned away from her only long enough to slam the doors shut, so that they would not be disturbed.

"Have ye lost yer senses?"

Anger singed the corners of her control and she didn't hold back her retort, "I was going to ask you the same question."

He ignored her sarcasm and continued his ranting. "I have obviously given ye too much credit. Ye are an educated woman, and yet ye refuse to use yer brain."

"Do you mind letting me know what in the hell you're talking about?" Her voice had risen to match his bellowing.

"Yesterday, when ye helped to start up a fire, what did ye use?"

She had forgotten about that. "Moira is the only one that saw me," she defended herself.

"And be glad that it was only Moira, for the lass likes ye. She only told me about it because she was in awe over the magical contraption that ye possessed. Now let me have it." He held out his hand expecting her to just relinquish it.

"I will not." She tried to stand, but he firmly pushed her back down.

"Uh uh. Ye will hand it over now. Is it in that backpack?" He knew that it probably was and tried to take it from her. She kicked him in the shins for the effort, quickly moving out of his way. His bellow rang through the room. "Ye little...." He went after her, and even though he was limping, he managed to catch her. "So help me, Aislinn, if ye kick me again, ye will rue the day. Now are ye going to hand over the backpack or do I have to tie ye up to take it from ye?"

"It's mine. You have no right to my private property." She struggled to hold onto it and he being the stronger finally tore it from her hands. Never had he had someone so unafraid of his authority. The woman was unbelievable.

"Now sit!" He was so thunderously commanding that she did as she was told though she was definitely not happy about it. She folded her arms defensively against her chest, as she saw all of her possessions that she had left in the world being dumped onto the table for his inspection.

He paused for a moment when he saw the many items that were completely foreign to him. "Why would ye need all this?"

"I need them. That's all you have to know about it. I don't go through your personal items deciding what you may have."

"My possessions will not have me burned at the stake."

She made a very unladylike snort.

Hairbrush, toothbrush he threw back into the pack. He held up the bottle of Penicillin reading its contents.

"Hey, we might need that. It's medication that can fight off infections." She was relieved that after a moment's consideration, he decided not to discard it. His next item under inspection was the notebook. He desperately tried to think of a good reason why she couldn't have it.

"Don't you even think you're going to take that away from me." She jumped to her feet.

"Sit!"

She did, but if looks could kill, he'd be deader than doornail. Reluctantly, he put the notebook back in the pack. "The inkless pen will have to be relinquished."

"You can't do that. What am I going to use to write with?"

He ignored her and continued to go through her items. He came across the lighter, but he wasn't quite sure if that was what it was, until she so ungraciously confirmed it.

"That's what you were looking for." Her voice held a definite edge.

He scrutinized over the strange looking item. Curiosity got the better of him and he decided to try it out. After about the third attempt, he happened to get lucky. The sudden flame had him leaping back with a quick breath of astonishment. He heard her suppressed chuckle and he flashed her a thunderous glare, quickly silencing her.

"I didn't say anything." She shrugged innocently, but her eyes still flickered with amusement.

He picked up something that he couldn't even begin to guess what it was, but she seemed to have quite a few items like that.

"I need those." She jumped toward him, trying to grab for it but he was quicker and held the item out of reach.

"Tell me what it is, and I'll decide if ye can keep it or not."

"It's a…" She suddenly felt timid about sharing the fact that he was holding a tampon.

"Go on. It's a…" He waved his hand for her to continue the explanation.

"It's personal," she finished knowing he would not be satisfied with that answer.

"If ye won't tell me, it goes in the fireplace."

"Damn it, Dougray." She stomped her foot. "Don't you understand the word private?"

"Into the flames it goes then."

"No." She sounded positively desperate even to her own ears, but she couldn't help it. She had very few of those blessed modern conveniences. "What a curse it is to be a woman here," she declared under her breath.

"What?"

"It's a tampon, all right!" She threw up her hands like this explained everything to him.

"What is a tampon?" He looked at it a little more closely. "What do you do with it?"

"It's made for a woman. You know, a woman has…you know…." He looked at her wondering why she just couldn't say what she meant. "You do know about a woman having monthly cycles?"

He was getting just a little perturbed. "Aye. And?"

"That's used…so…God, do I have to spell it out? It would be quite an inconvenience without it."

"I still don't…." Then all at once he realized what she was trying to tell him. "But where do ye…."

"Damn it, Dougray, use yer imagination."

He just stared at her with a puzzled frown. She knew the moment it finally dawned on him how it could be used. "*Dar Dia!*" He threw the item into the pack, glad to have it out of his hands.

"I tried to tell you." She shook her head and sat back down to wait for him to finish. He was quicker now, not dwelling on how the item might work. If it looked suspicious, he took it. It was as simple as that. Finally, he was finished. He walked over to her and handed her the now considerably lighter bundle. She nearly tore it out of his hands.

"Now that wasn't so bad."

She shot him a cold look. "If you call being violated not so bad."

He sighed heavily. "I do this for yer own good. I am…."

"…responsible," she finished for him. "Yes, yes, yes. I know. God, you've been saying that over and over again. I can't take it anymore." She jumped to her feet ready to make her exit, but his hand touched her arm halting her.

"Don't be angry with me, Aislinn."

She moved away. "And why the hell not or do you have the corner on my emotions too?" She made it to the door without him stopping her.

Dougray ran his hand through his thick hair. He didn't know what else he could have done. Surely she would come to see this and later thank him for it.

"I hate him!" Aislinn was still fuming. She was pacing her room while Moira just stood by not knowing what she could do to make things better.

"I'm sorry, milady. I didn't know that he would be angry that ye had the magical item."

Aislinn stopped her ranting for a moment to look at the young girl. "It is not your fault, Moira. I'm not angry with you. It's that infernal man that has me pissed off. Who does he think he is anyway?"

"Lord of the keep," came the answer from the door. Both women turned to see Dougray filling its frame.

"I never have any peace from you!" Aislinn threw up her hands and Moira just looked horrified that her mistress had spoken so rashly.

"Ye may leave us," Dougray addressed the girl, who quickly ran from the room.

"You frighten her," Aislinn accused.

"And ye don't think ye do? I could hear yer complaints clear as a bell being rung at the chapel." He went over to the drapes to let some light in. With his back turned Aislinn made a face at him, sticking out her tongue. He happened to choose that precise moment to turn and witness it.

"Quite childish." Dougray chuckled.

"Well what do you expect when that's the way you treat me?" Again she took her defensive stance folding her arms against her chest, her lower lip sticking out in a pout.

"I come with a peace offering."

This threw her off. "A what?"

He showed her the wooden box that he had brought with him. "It's for ye."

She slowly walked over to him. "What is it?"

"So suspicious, Aislinn. Take it and see for yerself. I think ye will be pleased with it."

He watched her open it seeing her face light up with delight.

"Oh, Dougray! I can still write." She held up the ink and quill. "What is this for?"

He stepped closer to see. "That is the sand." She looked at him blankly and he explained further. "Sprinkle a little on the ink to help it dry. Ye are pleased then?"

"Oh, yes!" She turned nearly leaping into his arms, startling him with her show of affection.

"I just wanted ye to have it," his voice was a low husky whisper, his breath hot against her ear. Automatically his hands went around her waist. Her soft curves molding perfectly to him.

She stilled as she realized the intimacy of their embrace. She took a deep unsteady breath, pulling back to meet his gaze. There was a faintly eager look that flashed in his eyes sending a shiver of wanting down her spine.

"Aislinn?" It was a hopeful question, but she shook her head backing away breaking that invisible web before it fully spun around them. When she turned away, she thought that she heard him heave a sigh. "I should be going." When she didn't answer, he started for the door.

"Dougray?"

He turned to look at her, his eyes somehow touching her even from that distance. Her heart pounded against her chest, causing her voice to change, becoming drenched with emotion. "Thank you. It was so very thoughtful. Thank you." She held the box close to her.

He smiled, and with a nod, he made his leave.

She immediately sat down at the desk and took out her journal. It took a few attempts for her to get used to the quill, but she managed. "So the rugged, handsome lord of the keep has a heart after all...."

Chapter Thirty-Two

Padrig had finally finished the sword for Aislinn. He felt proud that he had been chosen to make such a prized item for the lady whom so many called the *Scathach*. He was a blacksmith, after all, and dedicated to the goddess. He ran his large hand over the fine steel, as he whispered the final blessing that would protect the owner of the sword. He called on the four elements, Earth, Air, Fire and Water, as he had always done in the past when making a weapon that he was about to present to its owner.

Aislinn watched as he preformed the ritual. Then Padrig handed the sword over to her with reverence, bowing slightly as he did so. Aislinn was in awe. Tears sprung to her eyes and her throat constricted with the overwhelming emotion that surged through her.

"It's beautiful." She turned the weapon over in her hands, the metal catching the light.

"Try it," Padrig encouraged.

She gripped it in her right hand and swung it with fluent ease. A smile spread across her face as she met Padrig's gaze. "A perfect fit."

"Aye. Is it not what I told ye? With a little patience, I can create a lasting piece that will serve ye well."

Teige walked over to Padrig. "The sword ye crafted for me has never let me down." He clasped his hand in a friendly gesture on the older man's shoulder before he addressed Aislinn. "Are ye ready for a real lesson, A.J.?" He already knew that she would be a quick learner.

"I'm ready. En garde." She pointed the sword at Teige in a grand gesture. He unsheathed his own weapon.

"As ye wish, milady."

Aislinn had needled Dougray until he finally relented, agreeing to let her visit Neala if she took Teige and Dermot with her as her escorts. She wasn't thrilled about the arrangement, but refrained from saying so, not wanting to press her luck and have him change his mind.

"Ye brought friends I see." Neala lifted her ancient eyes toward the two men, making them both stumble backwards trying to put as much distance as possible between them. Neala laughed. "Scared they are." She jerked her head in their direction.

"They just don't know you." Aislinn sat down ready to hear more about the Druidic lore. She opened her backpack pulling out her journal. Neala had encouraged her to keep a record so the stories would not all be forgotten.

"*Tháinig an scéal ó bhéal go béal aniar ón tseanaimsir.*" She always started her stories this way. "The story has been handed down from olden times." Today, though, she was interested in seeing the sword that Padrig had designed. "Fine work, *Nuada's* sword from *Findias*." She saw Aislinn's blank look and she went on to explain. "The *Tuatha De Danann* were the children of the Goddess *Danu*. Some legends say they came from the sky. They were skilled in poetry and magic. With them they brought us great treasures." She handed Aislinn her new weapon. "*Nuada* brought the sword, *Lugh* the terrible spear from *Gorias*, *Dagda* a cauldron from *Murias,* and the Stone of *Fal* from *Falias*. They landed on Beltane, hidden by magic used by the *Morrigu, Badb* and *Macha.*"

"Beltane, Rhiannon mentioned the event."

"Aye, Rhiannon will be present this year as well. It is on the first of May, the first full moon of Taurus. It is the time of the Horned God and the Lady of the Greenwood. It is a time to give honor to the house guardian…" Then she smiled. "…a good time to find a love."

Aislinn had to smile. "Rhiannon told me it was for coupling."

"Aye, that too. But some wed, and in a year's time decides if it will work."

"And if it doesn't?"

Neala shrugged. "They part company."

"That's not very promising." Aislinn wondered why they would bother with such a ritual, but who was she to judge? In her time, people made similar arrangements that were not permanent.

"I see yer face. Ye are thinking of the failures and nah of the ones that last."

They talked for a while longer before Aislinn decided that she would like to bathe before she went back to the keep. Teige and Dermot stayed out of view, but not so far away that they couldn't hear her if she cried for help. She didn't feel uncomfortable with their presence, trusting them to respect her privacy. She undressed quickly and entered the cool water.

Neala looked up when the young lord came through the trees. She had expected him earlier and wondered what had kept him. "How goes the day, old woman?" He handed her a bag full of what she was sure were treats.

"Ye spoil me of late, milord."

"It is nothing." He looked around disappointed that he did not find Aislinn with her.

"Are ye looking for something milord?"

He glanced back at her, feeling a little foolish. "Nay." He sat down then. "It is a little warm today, is it not?"

"Aye. Maybe ye would want to take a swim to cool down."

"Not a bad idea. Do ye mind?" He stood.

"Ye go ahead, young lad. I'll be here waiting on yer return."

Dougray started to walk down to the left, but Neala halted him. "Milord, why nah go toward this bank." She pointed to the right. "I find that the moss is nah so thick, so ye won't lose yer footing."

"Thank ye." He headed in the direction that she indicated. He went as far as the first indentation before he paused to remove his clothing. He entered the cool water letting the wetness soothe every part of his body. He leisurely waded farther out, and as he did so, he happened to notice that someone else was in the lake with him. He was about to swim the other way wanting his privacy, but as he turned, he realized that it was Aislinn's lone figure gliding gracefully through the water. He could not tear his gaze from her. She looked somehow freer, more at peace. He found that he was drawn to her, as if she was a water sprite beckoning him forward. *Ye knew, old woman, that she was here,* Dougray thought. *What are ye up to, Neala?*

He knew that he should make his presence known, but he wasn't quite ready to do so. He swam closer dunking under the surface before she would notice him. He resurfaced inches from her side startling her so much that her instincts were to lash out first, ask questions later. He fended off her attack the only way that he knew how by grabbing hold of her and drawing her against him. "Aislinn, it is only I." She stilled, her eyes widening as she realized who held her captive. Then for propriety, she hit him again.

"What was that for?"

"For scaring me half out of my wits."

He chuckled. "I didn't mean to, lass. I remember well what happened to those that frighten ye." He reached out and lightly fingered the loose tendril of hair on her cheek. He felt her tense as she realized he had not let her go. She nervously ran her tongue over her generously curved lips, fingers subconsciously tightening on his arms.

The coolness of the water was oblivious to them for their blood coursed hot within their veins warming them instantly, and the only sound to be heard was of the ripples of the water lapping against their shoulders…and the thudding of their own hearts.

His hands were around her holding her closer making it painfully obvious to Aislinn that every inch of his powerful well-muscled body was pressed against her bare skin. His hand gently caressed the small of her back sending a multitude of emotions coursing through her veins. His handsome face was kindled with a sort of passionate beauty that made her long for more. She knew the moment that he had decided to kiss her, for she saw sheen purpose lying within the silvery blue of his eyes. So conscious of where his warm flesh touched hers that she could barely breathe, he dipped forward ready to claim her lips.

"Milady? Is all…well?" Teige's strong voice rang through the air, slapping them back to reality.

Dougray swore under is breath, wishing at that moment that he hadn't insisted she be guarded at all times. Aislinn pushed against his chest, struggling to get away. Reluctantly he let her go. "I am fine, Teige," she shouted back, praying that he would not break through the clearing and see that she wasn't alone.

"I thought that I heard ye call out." Teige sounded unconvinced and Aislinn knew she had to reassure him before he decided to investigate.

"I slipped is all, but I am all right now."

"I am not far, if ye need me."

"Thank you, Teige." She looked back to Dougray. "What are you doing here?" She had lowered her voice to almost a whisper, but her eyes narrowed dangerously with her accusation.

"Isn't it obvious?" He was amused at how quickly her ardor had changed to mounting contempt. With a shrug, he looked around him, indicating that he was bathing as she had been doing.

"Well, yes…." She knew that he could not clearly see her state of undress for the water hid her well, but the fact remained they were both naked and his hands had held her! That was enough to make her feel extremely uncomfortable.

"Ye are blushing, Aislinn." He waded forward, hoping that possibly he could bring her back into his embrace. He wanted her, and he knew by way she had clung to him that she had wanted him too.

"That's far enough." Panic was laced with that demand.

"I only want to speak with ye, Aislinn." A smile spread across his handsome face, not making her feel any better. She felt like she was being hunted and he was the hunter. "I have not seen ye fer days. Ye are either with Hamish or with Grania, and I fear Teige and Dermot converse with ye more than I do."

His strange mood, along with the huskiness of his voice, was confusing her. She wanted to feel his strong arms around her, but at the same time she wanted him as far away from her as possible. She didn't trust him. That wasn't entirely true. She didn't trust herself. "Since when do you want to talk to me? You usually scold."

"Do I?" He seemed almost surprised at this. "I don't wish to." He moved forward again and she had nowhere else to go without coming out of the water and completely exposing herself.

"I..." Her eyes darted back and forth for a way out. There was none. She looked back finding him just a breath a way.

"Don't be afraid," he muttered as he let his mouth lightly touch hers.

"I'm not afraid." She pushed him away before she dived under the water.

Dougray waited until she resurfaced. "Not afraid, huh?" He shook his head with a chuckle.

"Just because I don't wish for you to fondle me does not mean I am afraid, Dougray Fitzpatrick. I know that you must be used to women falling for your charms, but I am not like them."

"For yer information, I do not have droves of women falling at my feet."

"What about big booby?"

"Big...oh, Fiona? Ye are worried about her? It makes me wonder why." He swam toward her, only to have her swim back the other way. He stopped and waded in one place. "Is this a game we play?"

"I for one am not interested in your game. You leave me be. I have no wish to be one of your dalliances."

He sighed dramatically. "Mores the pity. I had hoped that with yer fiery temper there might just lie a passionate soul."

He sounded like he was teasing, but she wasn't at all sure and was definitely not going to wait any longer to find out. "Just turn around." She waved her hand at him. "I want to get out of the water."

"Come, come. It is only fair that ye let me view ye, as ye did me that time at the lake." Her mouth dropped opened and a sound that was very close to a yelp escaped her lips. "Come now, Aislinn. Ye left a long trail of yer hurried departure. How could I not know?"

"I can explain...." She let the sentence drop. There was nothing she could say to explain her spying, and the grin Dougray wore was proof enough that he darn well knew that. "Oh you! Just turn around."

"Seems completely unfair to me, but as ye wish." He turned around to give her ample time to make her escape. She was behind the trees hurriedly dressing by the time he looked back. This was quite amusing, to find that the great warrior woman was so timid about intimacies.

Aislinn threw her clothes on without worrying that they clung to her wet skin. She came out of her hiding place with a glare. "Thanks so much for ruining my time alone."

"I didn't chase ye away, did I?" He lifted his brows as though he was shocked that she was upset with him. "Aislinn, there is plenty of water for both of us."

"Not when you're hogging it all. I could barely breathe you were swimming so close."

"I take yer breath away, do I?"

"Ooh!" She stomped her foot. Without another word she practically ran away, calling for Dermot and Teige. Dougray shook his head still smiling. It wasn't until the quietness of the lake took over that he became sober. What game had he been playing here? His mind easily recalled the touch of her bare skin sending desire coursing through him once again. It had felt so right, didn't it?

"Bah!" He hit the water with his fist over his stupidity. Of course it had felt right. He had not been with a woman for months, and Aislinn had been there, like a vision, wet…naked. "*Dar Dia!*" With this line of thinking, he was going to drive himself mad with want.

Dermot and Teige, worried, exchanged glances as they tried to keep up with Aislinn. She hadn't said a word, but seemed to be in a great hurry to get back to where the old woman was waiting. When she arrived she threw down her pack and stood before the fire trying to warm up. Her clothes were drenched, her hair dripping down her face.

"Ye look out of sorts," Neala commented innocently.

"He was there," she whispered.

"He?" she whispered back.

"Dougray."

"Why are we whispering?" Neala asked.

Aislinn covered her face with her hands, trying to stop herself from trembling. She nervously glanced at the old woman who was eyeing her curiously. "You knew." It just dawned on her that he would have passed by here first.

"Aye. He wanted to swim. Said he was hot."

"But…." The old woman looked at her so innocently that she didn't know what else to say. "Never mind."

Teige nudged Dermot when he saw Dougray walking toward them. "His hair is wet." Dermot spoke the obvious.

"He was there at the lake?" Teige's eyes sought out Aislinn's. She looked away seeming ill at ease at seeing their lord's approach.

Dougray nodded toward her before he took a seat by the fire, too.

"Ye had a nice swim, milord?" Neala leaned forward.

"Aye. Most refreshing." Again he looked at Aislinn. She just wanted to die. She could feel Teige and Dermot's gaze upon her as they wondered what exactly had gone on down there.

"Ye look a bit damp, Aislinn. Were ye there too?"

She knitted her brows wondering why Dougray was putting up this farce when it was obvious to everyone concerned that she had been there with him. She just nodded her head.

He rose from his seat. Removing his mantle, he draped it around her shoulders. "There ye go now. Ye'll be warm soon enough."

"Thank you."

He knelt down on his haunches beside her. He had noticed the sword earlier that she had attached to her girdle and now he took a closer look at it, since she had placed it next her. "May I?" He pointed to the weapon. She nodded and he inspected the quality of the piece. "Where did ye come by this?"

"I asked Padrig to make it for me."

He chuckled as he spoke, "What on earth for?"

She frowned and nearly tore the weapon from his grip. "I am learning how to use it. Protection, I thought it would be quite obvious. Why do you carry one?"

"I have offended ye yet again, I see." He sat down next to her. "And who is training ye?"

Teige stepped forward. "I am, milord."

Dougray stared at the man for a moment then nodded his approval. "Teige can handle the steel well enough."

"Milady learns quickly," he offered his praise.

"It does not surprise me." His eyes gleamed over her completely confusing her.

"You aren't upset then?"

"Why would I be?" he said as he came easily to his feet. "I need to be heading back." Aislinn started to remove the mantle, but he laid a hand on her shoulder. "Nay. Ye keep it. Ye may return it to me later." He bowed slightly toward her, as his silvery gray eyes seemed to caress her. When her color rose to a near crimson, a smile touched his lips. He turned then and nodded his farewell to the others.

"I just don't get him." Aislinn watched Dougray mount his horse in one graceful move.

"What do ye nah understand?" Neala's wrinkled brow rose.

"He was actually civil."

Neala shook her head. "So much conflict ye two have that ye can nah see that ye are the balance for each other's life."

"You do jest. Ever since I have met the man, nothing has ever been right. He adds pandemonium to my life that I once thought was in order."

"Hmm, strange that ye say this. For ye are alone with no mate."

"Neala, I see no mate for you here," she accused. "And who says that I want one or need one?"

"I am one with nature now. I have no need of a person fulfilling what nature has already done for me. Ye are made differently. Ye seek exactly what is in front of ye, but refuse to take hold of it." She shook her head sadly. "*Cailte le cuimhne na seacht sinsear*. Lost in the mist of time. That is what is wrong with ye, wrong with both of ye. Stubbornness will be yer undoing."

"I don't want to be lost. Tell me how to get back home and I'll go."

"Ye hear, but ye do nah listen."

"But ye said I was lost in the mist of time."

"Aye, but ye only have to see and ye will not be lost. It's there, but nah as yer thinking."

"I don't understand. Explain it to me. Show me what you mean."

"*Ni thig liomsa dada a dhéanamh faoin scéal*." She walked away leaving Aislinn wondering why she had said that to her. She turned to Dermot and Teige.

"She is helpless in the matter?" Dermot repeated with a shrug not understanding why the old woman would say that.

Aislinn had about enough of this visit and rose to her feet to gather her belongings.

Chapter Thirty-Three

Grania O'Malley had become Aislinn's shadow of late. The little girl had a quick wit and could carry on a conversation far beyond her years giving Aislinn an inkling of how she would one day become a leader commanding her own fleet.

When Grania was elected to be team captain, she was able to quickly assemble an order that would allow them the best advantage to win. If there was a quarrel, she was able to hear out the problem and solve it without a fight. She was fair in her judgment and did not show favoritism. She was proud of the would-be pirate queen.

Grania also became close friends with Hamish, which did the boy's confidence wonders. She enjoyed helping him with his training, hunting for the largest rocks that she could find. He then would do his track running, using the rocks as weights to strengthen his upper body. She even joined in on occasion running alongside him.

"I can well imagine what my mother would say if she saw me running with ye both." Grania would then throw back her head and laugh.

"Yer mother is a fine lady," Hamish told her as he kept pace with her. "She is not used to such things."

"I'm never going to be like her. She doesn't know how to live, always locked up inside worrying and praying all the time. Look about ye, Hamish." He followed her gaze skyward. "We're free!"

Aislinn chuckled at that too. "I'd look where you're going before you end up sprawled on the ground." Grania turned her head toward her with an impish grin.

"Do ye know, A.J., what I have decided?"

"And what is that, Grania?"

"I am going to be just like ye. I will answer to no man."

"That's silly." Hamish shook his head. "Ye're a lass."

"And what is that supposed to mean?" Her blue eyes snapped with fury.

"Just that. Ye'll marry and have children. That's what women are destined to do. Ye best get those fanciful ideas out of yer head."

"I will not. Look at A.J. and how old she is."

"Hey, watch it," Aislinn shouted back.

"I don't mean it as an insult. Ye are strong and no man has forced ye into a marriage ye do not want."

Aislinn knew that Grania would not have that choice while she was young and relying on her father. But one day she would call the shots. She was a woman before her time. Who knows, maybe it was because of her influence here at Dunhaven that enabled Grania to grasp for her independence while giving her strength to stand up to men who would have otherwise dominated her.

They had come to a stop, making the final lap. Aislinn shook her arms to loosen up the muscles, as did the two children imitating her movements. "Grania, I am going to tell you something that is going to sound really strange, but in the future you will recall my words and understand." She stopped moving around and put her hands on her hips. "Remember that things will not always be the same. You will probably one day marry...."

"I will not," the stubborn little girl interrupted.

She smiled patiently. "Just listen. You might marry. It may not be all you would have imagined it to be, but it will work out. You are a strong-willed person. That is what you must remember first and foremost. Not that you are a woman, but you are a person, a human being who deserves to have dreams come true. Don't ever be afraid to reach for them. You have the ability to lead. Men will listen to you and respect you, as long as you return that respect."

Hamish and Grania exchanged glances, wondering why Aislinn had said these things, but they were still young and didn't dwell long on the matter. Grania still had grand ideas of what her life would be like, but when Queen Elizabeth ruled, reality would set in. It will be then that she may recall the *Scathach*, the warrior woman's strange words.

Teige ushered Dermot forward so that they could start the next lesson. Aislinn's sword fit in her hand well. As her strength increased from running with the weights, it began to feel as light as a feather.

Teige gave her pointers, while Dermot became primarily Hamish's teacher. Grania wanted to get in there and try it herself. Why not? She one day would be the Pirate Queen. She might as well start now.

"Ye're improving." Teige complimented Aislinn as he barely defended himself with a blow that she sent him.

"I have a good teacher." She barely blocked his attempt. "Are you trying to distract me, Teige?"

"Only making it as it would be if an opponent was actually after yer blood." He jabbed and she jumped out of the way. "Good, A.J." And so it went on every day.

Teige liked the idea of being her teacher, as well as her friend. He took over most of the duty of guarding her, relieving Cormac of the task. Cormac didn't mind. It freed him so that he could actively court Fiona. Teige tried to warn him that the woman was a waste of time, but he wouldn't listen. He was head over heels for her, and there wasn't a thing anyone could do about it. Teige just hoped that when Fiona found herself another man to warm her robes, that his friend would not be crushed.

Fiona waited until she was sure that she could approach Dougray without having anyone send her away. She knew that on occasion the man liked his solitude and would go to the gravesite of his beloved Ella. She saw him standing there, entranced as if he could see Ella's ghost. Fiona shivered at the thought. She took a deep breath and moved forward. Her movement caused him to turn around, hand on the hilt of his sword. He relaxed his stance when he realized who it was. "Fiona, what brings ye here?"

"Why ye, milord," she purred in her sweetest voice and purposely rubbed her breast over his arm. "I missed ye," she told him in all honesty. "Why have ye not been to see me?"

"I was under the impression that Cormac shared yer bed." The rumors had reached his ears, but instead of being angered by them, he was almost grateful that she had moved on.

"A lass gets lonely and ye have neglected me."

"I have been busy."

"I have not been blinded, milord. The foreigner ye have brought back with ye seems not to know how to conduct herself."

There seemed to be a tinge of malice behind those words, causing him to frown. "It does not become ye to act as though ye are jealous."

She didn't like the idea that he did not even bother to deny the fact that he was with Aislinn. "Well, I am jealous. I cannot help it. I thought ye and I had something special." She hugged him close, resting her cheek against his hard chest.

"Did we?" He had never thought of what they had as anything but two people enjoying each other's bodies. They never spoke but slept together, giving release to the more animalistic qualities that every human being possessed.

"I thought that we did. Ye are the only one that has ever made me feel…" She growled low and seductively. "…like a woman should." Her hand boldly caressed him, but when she roamed to a more private area, he halted her attentions. She looked up at him with almost a stunned expression.

In all fairness, he felt that he owed her at least something for she had seen him through times when he thought that he would die without Ella, but it had all been physical and nothing to do with healing of the mind. In all truth, he would have never sought Fiona out if she had not been the one who was persistent. It was a weak excuse at best, but it was the truth.

It had never been a secret that Fiona was free with her affections, but he was just now beginning to realize that maybe she had grander plans in mind. "Do not do this, Fiona," he warned gently.

"What? Don't love ye?" Her blue eyes filled with tears.

"Ye don't love me." He turned away from her.

"But I do," she insisted making him look at her again. Her golden blond hair fell over her left shoulder in a cascade of curls. The woman was beautiful, if nothing else.

"Ye loved me so much that ye took Cormac to yer bed?"

"Oh that," she said like it was nothing but a mere friendship he was referring to. "I will tell him I cannot see him anymore." It was amazing how fast the woman could dry her tears. Oh yes, she was heartbroken all right, as heartbroken as a dog in heat.

"Do not bother, Fiona. Ye will do well to keep Cormac. He cares about ye."

"What are ye saying?" she snapped.

"We have nothing together. We never had."

She came at him, her fists flying. "Ye used me!" She pounded her closed hands against his chest and he quickly took hold of her arms.

"That was never my intention. I fear that I owe ye an apology, if ye thought that I wanted more from ye."

"An apology! Oh ye owe me much more." She didn't wait for him to respond, but turned on her heels and stomped away. Dougray was glad that she was gone and hopefully for good.

Pacing back and forth, Cormac wondered where Fiona had gone. She had told him to be at the cottage before the noon meal. He had already been waiting close to an hour and was furious with himself for doing so. He was about to leave, when she unlatched the door.

She halted in her tracks and for a fleeting moment was caught off guard. But before Cormac could grow suspicious, she smiled her sweet seductive smile, moving forward to greet him, slim hips swinging in a hypnotizing motion.

"Where have ye...?" Cormac began only to be cut off by her mouth pressing against his. He relaxed, his anger ebbing away to something else. Without a word she pushed him toward the bed and ripped at his clothes, anxious to have them removed. She had always been aggressive, but this was something more. It seemed she was desperate. Cormac threw her down on the bed, not having any trouble complying.

Fiona wanted Cormac fast, hard, furious. She closed her eyes imagining that it was Dougray, not Cormac, who was pounding against her, but when it was all over reality set in. It was Cormac's blond hair that she saw not the dark strands of Dougray's.

"Ach." Cormac chuckled. "Yer grip is tearing at me skin, love."

She released her hold. "Sorry." She was gentle then, as she thought of what she could do to win Dougray back. "Ye care for me, Cormac?"

"Ye know that I do."

"Enough that ye would do anything for me?"

"I'd move heaven and earth for ye," he answered sleepily, as he cuddled close to her. A smile spread across Fiona's face.

Chapter Thirty-Four

Aislinn was anxious to be on her way and didn't have the patience to wait any longer for Teige. She grabbed her backpack swinging it behind her back then picked up her sword. "Come on, Declan." She took his hand.

She knew that Dougray would be angry if she just took off without an official guard so she nabbed Hamish on her way out of the keep. She refused to miss her walk with Declan just because she couldn't find someone to go with her.

Along the way, Grania caught sight of them and ran over to join them. Her father, the great Dubhdara, seemed to give her the freedom to do just about anything that she wished, so long as she stayed inside the castle's grounds. Of course Grania failed to inform anyone else of her father's stipulations.

Aislinn had been stranded in time for almost two months, and she was yet to figure out her purpose here. Neala was not much help with her unclear statements and riddles that spoke of nothing at all. And she had so many questions. Why her? What could she possibly do here to help? She didn't even know if she would ever return home to her family. She missed being able to call her parents at the drop of a hat, and longed to go on one of her father's famous hikes. She missed Connor's carefree attitude and companionship. He would have been the one thrilled to travel back in time. This adventure was more his style. He would have relished every minute of it. But he wasn't here; she was and she didn't know her purpose.

Before all this happened, she had thought that she was in control of herself, her life. At least, this is how she perceived herself. "Self-assured" could have been her middle name.

She felt anything but confident now. Her life was in constant turmoil. Her emotions were a mess. For though she longed for home, she would miss Dougray, his arrogance and all.

"Ye look kind of sad today," Grania stated not afraid to speak whatever thought came to her mind.

"You know, Grania, I am a little bit. I miss my family. They have been on my mind of late." They finally had arrived at the lake where Aislinn took the small wrap from her backpack so they could sit down. She glanced at Grania realizing she knew more about her future than her own. She would one day be the Pirate Queen. "A noble profession for this time." She sighed.

"What is?" Grania asked.

"Pirating."

"Seems dangerous to me. My da is always telling me about his battles, and I have seen his scars. Yuck!" Grania waded into the water.

"You'll change your mind." Aislinn knelt down on her haunches and started to take off Declan's shoes.

Grania studied Aislinn for a moment, thinking how different she was to any other woman whom she had ever met. She sensed that she had a special sight into the future. It was almost frightening, but not enough that she wasn't intrigued. "Why do ye say things like that to me?"

Aislinn looked at her. "Like what?"

"I don't know. It is like ye see the future."

Aislinn knew that she had to be careful here. It wouldn't be wise to reveal too much. "I see you is all. I am anticipating what kind of woman you will grow up to be."

"Is it good? My mother is not so sure. She blames my da for my unruly ways."

"Then you should hug your father and thank him, for he is making you strong enough to survive the changes of Ireland."

"See there ye go again." She looked back at Hamish. "Don't ye hear it?"

Hamish nodded. He wasn't too talkative today for he felt that he had to be on guard since Teige was not with them. It was a great responsibility for a twelve-year-old boy to protect a lady, a young lad, and the daughter of the great O'Malley.

"Come sit with us." Grania tried to persuade him.

"I feel better if I stand back here. I need to keep me eyes open."

"Let him guard," Aislinn said quietly to Grania. She could see that this job was important to Hamish and she was not going to take it away from him. "Confidence builds a person's character, Grania. It makes a man...or woman."

"I feel like ye are teaching me in some subtle way. Am I right?"

Aislinn just smiled. No one could ever say that Grania was not intuitive.

Roth had been good enough to pack them a parcel full of bite-size morsels, so there was no hurry to head home, and they had ended up staying later than they had planned.

The howling of a wolf brought them back to reality, making them realize just how late it had actually become. Hamish's eyes widened in fear, but he tried very hard not to let his voice tremble. "Milady, we must head back."

Aislinn was in full agreement and was already donning her shoes. She grabbed her sword and took hold of Declan's hand. "Come on, let's go."

They were on the path that led to the castle when they saw the lone wolf, its eyes glowing dangerously in the dark. "What do we do now?" Grania drew closer and Aislinn felt Declan grip her hand tighter.

She wished that she had an answer, but she didn't. They were alone out here and too far away to run back to the keep. All they had were two swords between them and she didn't quite fancy the idea of having to ward off a hungry wolf with a blade. Why hadn't she thought to take the bow and arrows too? Hamish was thinking along the same lines. Withdrawing his sword, he stood in front of them. Aislinn felt a sense of pride. It was hard to believe that just over a month ago the boy would have cowered in fear.

"Milady, I'll distract the beast, if ye will take the wee ones and head through the trees there. Keep going straight and ye will end up in front of the castle gates.

"We're not going without you, Hamish."

"The wolf though."

Aislinn wondered about that. It seemed to be eyeing them, but not making so much as a move toward them. The thought entered her mind that maybe it was the same wolf that had led Dougray and her out of the mist. It might be far fetched, but again so was traveling through time.

Her mother's stories of the North American Indians came to mind. She had often mentioned how the Celtic beliefs were very similar. If she remembered correctly, her mother had done her thesis on the subject. "A spirit guide."

"What?" Hamish questioned her over his shoulder.

"Nothing." But she couldn't shake the feeling. The Cheyenne believed in them and she was sure that her mother had mentioned that the Celts…. Oh, she was being completely ridiculous now. Why was she even considering spirit guides? "Come on through the trees." She pointed.

Aislinn glanced behind her. She couldn't see the wolf, but this did not ease her fear. She knew it was following them "Hurry." She picked up Declan hoping to go faster. They came out of the clearing, nearly running into Teige and Cormac. Teige looked frantic with worry until he laid eyes on Aislinn.

"Milady, I have been looking all over for ye." If the others were not around, he might have hugged her so relieved he was that she was all right.

"I'm sorry, Teige. I didn't mean to worry you. We went down to the water's edge and lost track of the time."

Cormac was staring back toward the woods, his torch held high. He handed the torch to Hamish and slowly reached back behind him to remove an arrow. Teige became alert.

"What do ye see?"

"There was a wolf out there," Hamish offered. "That's why we had to cross through the trees."

"Wolf?" Teige questioned. "Just one?"

Aislinn nodded. "Is that odd to see one?"

"Usually they run in packs, and I have not seen one so close to the keep before. Teige also removed an arrow.

"Go that way." Cormac motioned to Teige pointing to the right as he moved toward the left.

Aislinn shivered. A part of her did not believe that the wolf meant them any harm. "I don't see anything." She raised her voice causing both men to look at her with displeasure. She didn't care. She hoped that the wolf would hear and escape.

"I should help," Hamish voiced.

"And how will ye help?" Grania's blue eyes glared at him. "Ye only have a sword. It will tear ye apart before ye can get to it."

"Thanks for the confidence, Grania."

Aislinn could only listen and wait. She couldn't believe that she was actually praying that the wolf escaped unharmed. After an agonizing five or so minutes the men returned. "Nothing." Teige shook his head and Cormac nodded in agreement.

"It got away," Aislinn said with relief. Luckily no one noticed.

"Aye, it did," Cormac answered. "It was a big one by the size of the paws. It was strange though. I followed the tracks for a bit, but then they simply disappeared."

"How?" Teige questioned. "Wolves cannot fly."

The tracks were there; then they were not." He looked out toward the forest not at all liking that a lone wolf was stalking them now that the fog was starting to roll in. "Looks like we will have a thick mist tonight."

Aislinn eyes darted to him. Could it be possible that it was the mist that would bring her back to her time? She would have to wait and see.

"Come on." Teige took the torch from Hamish. "Let's head back. Milord was not pleased that we did not know where ye had gone." He looked at Aislinn with a pained expression. "I wish ye did not leave without me."

"I was not alone as you can see. Hamish was here to protect us."

"Aye," Teige answered and he nervously glanced at Cormac.

Chapter Thirty-Five

Aislinn was taking a bath trying to soak away the tension and her loneliness for home, when Dougray came storming in with not so much as a knock. His mouth opened to vent his displeasure, but viewing her long, curved body beneath the water made him nearly choke on his words.

"Yes, my lord," she said in a mocking tone unaware that though he was standing across the room, he was tall enough to see a good deal of her bare skin over the rim of the bathtub.

He dragged his eyes reluctantly to her face so that he could concentrate on why he had sought her out in the first place. "Ye were told to stay near the grounds, but ye continue to disobey me! Not only that ye went without an escort."

"I did not. I took Hamish with me and Grania and Declan went too. Did you forget that I also have a sword of my own?"

"Oh, I feel so much better now." He threw up his hands. "Ye have a sword and ye had a mere child to protect ye. Are ye daft, woman? I have Butler's men lurking about, an unknown assailant, and yet ye want to play games. If ye have no care for yerself, at least think of the children. Declan has seen enough grief and still has not recovered enough to speak. Grania is the daughter of the O'Malley, King of Connaught. If something were to happen to her, it is I who would be held accountable. Do ye want to be in the midst of a clan war?"

"Why are you in such a huff. No harm came from our walk. The kids were in no danger, and for your information, Hamish is very capable. As you can see, I'm here safe and sound."

His eyes roved over her naked form making him think to himself that she was not going to be safe for long if he had to continue the discussion in here.

"Now if you don't mind," she broke through his reverie, "I'd like to continue my bath in peace, or is having my solitude also a bother to you?"

He could tell by the spark in her dark eyes that she was quite perturbed with him. Perturbed at him, the lord of the keep! Why did she always seem to get the upper hand? "Nay, but your attitude does offend me."

"You're so sensitive. Do I need to bow to you every time that you enter a room? Will that make you feel better?" Her tone was condescending, but she just waited for him to answer her as though she were completely serious.

"That would be a start." He decided to play her game.

"Really and what would you do if I did not yield?"

"Are ye challenging me, milady?"

"Let's get something straight. I am not your lady, and yes, someone needs to challenge your pompous ass."

He was about to open his mouth with another retort, but arguing with her when she was in such a state of undress was making it difficult for him to concentrate. He took a deep breath, and between clenched teeth, he spoke once more. "When ye're finished with yer bath, I want ye to meet me in my chambers...I mean the library!" he quickly corrected himself.

Aislinn couldn't help but smile. Obviously the rugged lord of the keep was human after all, and she could well imagine where his mind had wondered just then. "As you wish, my lord."

He bowed ever so slightly and left the room.

"Ye really shouldn't entice him to a fight, milady." Moira came closer now that Dougray had left. "He does have a temper on him at times."

"Moira please don't fret. Your lord is as tame as a lamb."

Moira just shook her head wondering what kind of lambs that her lady was accustomed to in her homeland, for Lord Dougray's roar was mighty fierce.

How Dougray wanted her compliance to sound like she really meant it, but he supposed that this was expecting too much. He may be attracted to her, but he would not excuse her actions. It was obvious this brazen woman had her own ideas and thought that she could do as she pleased. Well she was here now and there was no telling how long she would remain. He refused to stand by and let her dominate him a moment longer. The O'Malley's suggestion came to mind. He should find someone to take her off his hands, and at the same time forge an alliance that would help his position.

Aislinn was very beautiful, but he had to face the fact that she was beyond bold. She was almost uncontrollable, but maybe he could convince a man of his choosing to overlook this. She was older than most preferred in their brides, but she was strong and would most likely produce healthy children.

He went over to the desk and sat down. Yes, he would have to choose someone and quickly before he was forced to have her in his care forever. Frankly he wasn't sure he had the energy to continue their exhausting banters.

She was wearing him down. God, the woman had spirit, and surprisingly a tremendous mothering nature. If she were to have a child of her own to tend to, maybe she would settle down.

Aislinn **purposely** took her time finishing her bath. She wasn't going to rush just because Dougray commanded it. "Ye should hurry." Moira couldn't hide her uneasiness.

"I am not going anywhere until my hair is dry."

"Please, A.J., stand near the fire." She nearly dragged her over to it. "Are ye going to wear yer trews?" She crossed her fingers hoping that she wasn't. Milord was already upset with her.

"No. Tonight I will wear one of the gowns."

"The blue one?" Moira eyes lit up."

"Sure. Why not?" Aislinn knew that he would still be angry, but maybe she could throw him off a tad if she wore the dress he favored.

Once her hair was good and dry she let Moira brush it back with ribbons making her look very feminine. She then slowly made her way to the library.

By now, Dougray was fuming. Aislinn had entered the room to see him pacing, his hands clenched behind his back.

"My lord," Aislinn announced her presence. He whirled around with a lashing response on his lips, only to fall silent. Aislinn had curtsied before him in full sweep, giving him ample view of her smooth skin right above the revealing neckline.

Dougray's anger seemed to melt away. Aislinn was dressed in a blue velvet gown that made her skin glow to perfection. Her shiny black hair was adorned with flowers and ribbons. She looked so very much the lady that he forgot for a moment that she possessed an obstinate nature.

"You wanted to see me?" She tilted her head to one side, as she patiently waited for him to speak.

Desire pulsed hot within Dougray's veins. He was barely able to drag his eyes away from the vision she portrayed. What was wrong with him anyway? One would think that he was a lovesick fool by the way he had been gawking at her. He cleared his throat and looked at her once more. This time, shielding his emotions. He had to if he was going to go through with his plan. "I have made up my mind that by the end of this week I will have ye wed."

"What the hell?" Her voice raised two octaves while her eyes spoke of murder. Any other person would have backed away, but Dougray held his ground. She would not intimidate him. "Think again, buster," she continued.

"I will never marry you. Not even if you were the last person on earth would I even consider it." She folded her hands defensively across her chest.

Dougray had been thinking how he wanted to devour every portion of her body with his kisses, but her words were like a bucket of cold water thrown in his face reminding him why he was not marrying her himself. Still, it angered him to think that she held such an aversion toward him when he could barely keep his emotions in check. He chuckled over the irony of it, but it was his anger that controlled his voice. "I never said that ye would be marrying me. I would no sooner wish to share yer bed than ye would mine. I am responsible for ye and I will find ye a suitable mate."

Aislinn almost didn't hear the rest of what he said for she had stopped listening after he had claimed he would not want to share her bed. Why wouldn't he? Didn't he find her attractive? She could have sworn that he....

"That is all. Ye may be excused."

Aislinn blinked twice shaking her head. "I'm excused!" There was no way that he was going to get away with this. "I think not. We haven't even begun to discuss this matter. What makes you think that I would want to be married? Remember, I'm going home."

"But ye see, there lies the problem. We do not know when that will be."

"I'm going back," she said more to convince herself. "I am not staying in this stinking century."

"I don't know how to send ye back to yer world. If I had the power, I would do it this instant." He lifted his arms in a shrug. "You may be with us indefinitely. Do ye want to be alone, Aislinn?"

She hadn't thought of that possibility until now. She may actually be stuck here. Did she want to live out her life without ever being married? The answer was no, but she didn't want to rush into something. "I thank you, kindly but I will choose my own husband."

Dougray laughed. "Really? I have seen yer choice in men; I think that ye better leave the matching to me."

"Maybe I don't want to marry," she threw at him hoping to get him to change his mind for she knew that if she didn't, she would have no choice in the matter. There wasn't anyone who would come to her rescue. "Did you ever think about that? Maybe I like being single."

"I may give ye that." He leaned against his desk deciding that he had to persuade her in another way. "Ye don't expect me to take care of ye forever, do ye?" He wished that he had never said that to her. Her expression was so full of pain, he felt as if he had just slapped her.

"Aislinn I didn't...."

She squared her shoulders and glared at him with those ever so dark eyes. "Do you think that I can't take care of myself?"

"Nay...." What was he saying? "Fine. I do not wish to argue about this all evening. So be it. I will allow ye to choose yer husband."

"Thank you, for understand...."

"By the end of this week, or I'll do it for ye."

"I can't choose someone that fast. I would have to get to know him, and he would have to know me and of course there is the fact, hello..." She tapped her head. "...I would have to be in love with the man."

"Ach!" Now he had her. "Love has nothing to do with marriage."

"It sure in the heck helps."

"Then fall in love with someone by the end of the week, and we'll all be happy." He turned away thinking that he had decided the matter and the subject was now closed to discussion. How wrong he was.

"Don't you dare turn your back on me."

He looked at her with his piercing gray eyes that boarded on being black with his fury. "Are ye addressing me? For surely ye wouldn't be, with that tone that ye are using."

"I most certainly am." She approached him now and stood no more than a few inches away.

Dougray's nostrils filled with the sweet smell of her intoxicating him.

"You," she continued her onslaught of words, "you may be lord of this damn castle, but you are not lord over me. You can't make me do anything that I do not wish to do." She took her index finger and poked it into his chest several times. "Is that clear?"

Coming to his senses, he grabbed her hand. "I can hear ye, woman. Everyone in the keep can hear ye. Say as ye may, but listen to this: If ye defy me, I will throw ye in the dungeon and think of ye not again. Do I make myself perfectly clear?"

Aislinn yanked her arm away. She didn't speak, but he could tell by her eyes that she had not yielded. What spirit this woman had. He could imagine a better way for her to use that energy.

Aislinn racked her brain for a good excuse out of this situation before she found herself married off to some guy whom she didn't know, but it seemed there was no way out, unless.... Dougray saw the gleam in her eye and he wondered what possible mischief she was about to suggest. "Fine, I'll marry at the end of the week, but...."

Here it comes, he thought. The woman had so many stipulations that it was maddening.

"...on one condition," she ended.

"And what is that?" He folded his arms waiting for her demand.

"Go ahead and pick the man whom you had in mind for me, but I will only marry him if he can best me in a formal combat."

Dougray stared at her for a moment sure that she must be joking, but then he realized that she was being completely serious. He couldn't help it. He threw back his head and laughed. He laughed so long and hard that his sides hurt. When he could somewhat contain himself he saw that she was still standing there with not so much as a smile upon her lips.

"I fail to see what is so funny." She put her hands on her hips and her brows seemed to have knitted together with her frown.

"Oh, milady, I am sorry if ye do not see the humor in yer request." He sighed then. "The men that I would consider are all trained in battle. Do ye really think that this kickboxing thing that ye do will save ye from a marriage bed?"

"You accept my challenge then?" Aislinn held her ground. She wouldn't let on that she was also a black belt in karate. He wouldn't even know what that was anyway. Her father made sure she was well trained to protect herself, and had not been lenient because she was a girl. If anything, he had been even harder on her. She had never thought that she would thank him for that, but boy, if he was here right now, she'd have given him a great big kiss.

Dougray was still smiling quite amused that she would even consider such a travesty. There was nothing to lose by accepting her challenge. In the end, she would have to surrender, and he would have her married with an alliance. Why not have the entertainment? "Ye may have yer fight, but ye will have to accept the challenge from whomever steps forward to accept it."

"Bring them on." She was about to make her leave when his chuckle stopped her. She turned her annoyed gaze on him.

"I'm sorry. I was just thinking...may the best man win."

"You mean woman, because I intend to win, Dougray Fitzpatrick."

Moira was worried about Aislinn. She came back from her meeting with Dougray and had immediately changed back into her more unconventional clothing. Without a word, she dropped to the floor and started doing pushups. Aislinn did so many that Moira didn't think that she would be able to move her arms come tomorrow.

"What happened, A.J.? Why are ye so driven to punish yerself?"

Aislinn came to her feet. "Oh, I am not punishing myself. I'm preparing for battle, the most important battle that I will ever have to face."

"Battle?" Moira was scared now. "What battle?"

"The avoidance of being dominated by a man."

"Begging yer pardon, milady, but what are ye talking about?"

"Your jerk of a lord has decided to sell me off to the highest bidder." Aislinn began stretching out.

"Oh, he wouldn't do that. It is a most grave charge."

"I'd say it's grave. I'll end up being nothing but a slave. I might as well just throw myself in the dungeon this instant for all the freedom that I will have."

Moira wrung her apron nervously. "Surely there is something that we can do."

"Oh there is. I plan on beating anyone who tries to take me. I will not go willingly."

"Oh, mistress." Moira was in tears. She ran over to her and threw her arms around her neck.

"Hey, hey, you're choking me." Moira let go, but the tears had not stopped. "Come on, girl, get a hold of yourself. Even if the worst happens, I will survive."

"But to be sold into slavery."

Aislinn realized then that Moira misunderstood. She couldn't help but laugh. She gave the confused woman a hug. "I'm sorry, Moira. I wasn't being clear, was I? Dougray isn't selling me into slavery." Though in her opinion, it wasn't much better. "He wants me to marry."

Moira hiccupped. "Ye are to wed?"

"Yes."

Moira felt completely embarrassed. "What a fool I am. Carrying on so, but..." But she was still confused. "...why are ye so unhappy about this? Do ye have no wish to wed?"

"Well not to just any Tom, Dick or Harry."

"Tom, Dick.... Who?"

Aislinn waved her hand. "It's not important. I want to marry someone that I love."

"But milord will make ye a good match. Do ye not want to be taken care of in yer old age?"

"I don't want to get married." How could she make the girl understand when all she knew was arranged marriages? Aislinn walked over to the window and looked outside. She couldn't see very far for the mist had rolled in. "Mist!" How could she have forgotten? She threw on her sweatshirt and dashed for the door. She didn't even stop when she saw Teige rise from his seat.

"Where's she going?" He looked at Moira for the explanation.

"I don't know. She just said, 'mist,' then bolted out of the room."

"I best follow then." He was down the hall, when he ran into Dougray.

"Where are ye off to in such a hurry?" Dougray questioned.

"Lady Aislinn just took off running. I'm not sure, but I think that she may be heading outdoors."

"Go then. Go," Dougray said as he started for the stairs. Where could she be heading and why? All kinds of thoughts came to his mind and he didn't like any of them. He took the stairs two at a time. As he came to the last step, he caught a glimpse of her as she headed out the doors. He was right behind.

"Aislinn!" he called to her, but she didn't stop.

She had to reach the thickness of the mist. She just had to get there.

Dougray grabbed hold of her sweatshirt, but still she did not slow down. He was force to pull her against him in a tight embrace.

"Let me go. The mist, it's here. I can go home."

There was indeed a thick fog, but it was not the same that had transported him from one time to the other. "It's just a regular mist, Aislinn. It is just fog."

She stopped struggling and looked around her. She could make out the keep's gate, the same gate that was always there. Nothing had vanished indicating that another time awaited her. She slumped against him, her chest heaving. She wanted to cry, but no tears came. She was trapped and she was terrified that it would be forever.

Dougray caressed her hair, loving the feel of her leaning against him. He was afraid to say anything for the spell would be broken, and she would again become the unreachable *Scathach*. His eyes caught a movement in the distance, and as the mist shifted, he saw the lone wolf sitting there, watching. He was sure that it was the one that had led them out of the mist. Was it here to take Aislinn back? As if in answer, the wolf raised its head and howled to the sky. He instinctively hugged Aislinn closer to him, wrapping his mantle like a shield around her.

She finally let him lead her back inside, but she wouldn't speak to him. She immediately broke away, running to her room before he could catch up. She had slammed the door in his face. Feeling helpless with this new development, he took out his frustrations by hitting his closed fist on the doorframe. How he wanted to console her, to tell her that everything would be all right, but he didn't know how he could possibly do that now. He knew if he approached her that she'd only push him away. He had only himself to blame. The moment that he had made the decision to have her married off he had made it impossible for her to confide in him about her fears. His insufferable pride had forged an even larger gap between them. "What did ye expect?"

"Milord?"

Dougray turned in bewilderment for he had not realized that Teige had followed behind. "Nothing, Teige." He walked by. "Nothing at all."

Teige sat beside Dermot and Cormac and they offered him a tankard of ale. He had such a faraway look about him that the other two exchanged quick glances. Cormac wasn't too far in his drink not to find out what was ailing him. "Ye look like ye saw yer best friend put to the sword."

"What?" He glanced at Cormac with a grim smile. "I was just thinking, is all."

"Thinking? Well that is a new one." Leave it to Cormac to always make light of the situation.

"This is serious, I fear."

"Serious?" Dermot was only a drink more sober than Cormac, but managed to give his full attention. "Is something amiss? Is it the Butler?" He felt under his vest for his dagger.

"Nay." He held up his hand. "It is about A.J and Lord Dougray."

"Are they a fighting again?" Dermot just shook his head. This was nothing new. The two were forever at each other's throats.

"Not fighting per se. I saw something pass between them this night."

"Are ye sure it wasn't Aislinn's sword?" Cormac chuckled causing Dermot to have a fit of laughter himself.

"Do ye want to hear me out or not?" Teige was ready to take his tankard and join some of the other men that would care to hear what he had to say.

"Oh come on. What is it, man?" Cormac knew when it was time to put the drink aside and lend an ear. He made sure Dermot did the same.

"This evening, A.J. came bolting out of her room like the devil himself was after her." Teige crossed himself as he said this. "Of course I followed and so did milord. She was muttering something about the mist, like she needed to reach it before it was no more."

"Was it as if the fairies were calling her then?" Dermot was a little spooked glancing over his shoulder.

"I am not sure, but again I cannot disregard it. Actually it was what milord whispered to her that left me wanting to walk backwards, all the way to the keep, so that I could keep my eyes on the very mist that hung before us. He told her it was not *the mist,* just like he was trying to let her know that he knew of others that she most likely sought. A.J. collapsed against him then, as though all her strength had gone out of her."

"What did milord do?" Dermot asked.

"He held her close. It was like he thought that she would slip through his embrace. Then when she was able to walk again, he brought her back to her chambers. Silent she was and pale as death. Milord seemed almost…I don't know…beside himself."

"Most peculiar." Cormac sat back and rubbed his chin, as if he was going over every detail that Teige had given him. Finally he looked at the two expectant faces waiting for his opinion. He laughed outrageously loud, slapping his knee while tears coursed down his cheeks.

Both Dermot and Teige just stared at him, as if he had lost his mind.

"Oh come now." Cormac wiped his eyes and tried to gain control. "Mists and strange behaviors? Everyone is just a little tired is all. It's been a long and trying day. Didn't ye say that Lord Dougray has decided to make a match for A.J.? And that she is quite determined to have her way? Don't ye think she would be in a somber mood to have that privilege taken away from her?"

"Nay, that was not it, I tell ye. She clung to him like a woman does to a man when they share a bond, and he held her as though he wanted to shield her from any pain."

"Then why would milord arrange for her to marry another?" Dermot couldn't help but voice.

"My point exactly."

Cormac put down his tankard. "It is simple, lads. How could ye not realize it yerselves? Alliances have always come first. The ways of the heart are not considered."

The hooded figure stood in the shadows, as Robert Burke read the message in hand. His eyes glared at the person who had delivered this information. "I will comply."

The dark-hooded figure was silent.

Robert Burke was not at all pleased dealing with someone who would not show his face and uttered not a word. It was unsettling, but he had been left with little choice in the matter.

"Be gone then. I will soon deliver my answer." Burke crumpled the note he held in his hand.

Again the hooded messenger nodded and backed up into the shadows, until Burke could no longer see him.

Chapter Thirty-Six

Dougray paced while Neala watched. She shook her head. "Why don't ye sit, milord?"

"Bah! I cannot. That woman is driving me mad." He threw up his hands and paced the other way. "She doesn't heed a word that I say. She leaves the keep unattended and she refuses to wear the dresses that I have made for her, unless the mood strikes her to do so."

"Well soon, milord, ye will nah have to worry, aye?" She chuckled, thoroughly enjoying Dougray's discomfort. The words spread like wildfire that Aislinn was going to fight the man who would take her hand in marriage. There was not a person for miles around who wouldn't be attending this event. "Ye will have her married, and she will be some other man's responsibility." He shot her a cold look, causing her to lift her brows. "Perhaps ye have reconsidered?"

"Reconsidered?"

"Aye. Mayhap ye want the lass for yerself."

"Ach!" He openly showed his disgust and he sat down on the moss-laced rock, his mantle draping around him. "I have no time nor need of a woman who does not know her place."

"She is nah of this time or have ye forgotten so soon?"

"Nay, it is always on my mind. It troubles me that I do not know the reason why she is here. I have been at a loss what to do with her. She is miserable." He rested his head in his hands, rubbing his tired eyes.

"Ye could change that."

He looked up. "Pray tell."

"Ye could marry her."

His laugh was thunderous. "Surely ye jest, old woman. Aislinn would sooner run me through with a sword than wed me."

"She may surprise ye, aye?"

He stood now. "It doesn't matter."

"Why is this?"

"I married once and look how wonderful that turned out. Ella was my life, and I couldn't...."

She made a disgusting sound causing him to look at her. "Ella was nah yer life, ye young fool." He was about to say something, but she raised her gnarled hand to him. "Ye will listen first. Ella was a special lass, no one is denying this, but ye are wrong when ye say that she was yer life. She only shared a moment in the circle of all and now she is gone. And here ye stand; ye still have nah let her go. She is a restless spirit wandering around this glen."

"A restless spirit?"

"Aye. Ye heard me. Ye need to say yer good-byes and get on with yer life, or ye might as well crawl in next to Ella ending it now. There I have spoken." She turned away from him and threw another peat onto the fire. It blazed hot, casting shadows, making them look like angry phantoms.

"It was my fault Ella died."

Neala looked up at him. "Ye?"

"I was the one who tightened the saddle. I led her to her death."

She saw the pain etched in his features. He was indeed an honorable man and would grieve to despair, if she couldn't help him move forward. "Do nah continue to punish yerself. It was an accident, milord. All ye do is prevent yerself from having the happiness ye deserve."

"Aislinn wants love, and I cannot give her that." He felt tormented by his confusing emotions. He wanted her at his side, and at the same time, he couldn't see him pledging a lifetime commitment to her. She expected too much. Truth be known, he was afraid of failing her, as he had failed Ella.

"Ye say she wants love and yet ye force her to marry someone she does not know. How do ye manage to accomplish love for her then?"

He looked away hastily, his movements restless as he struggled with his conscience. He had made the decree. He could not go back on it now. He had tried to convince himself that it was for the best, but in fact he had acted hastily and out of anger. Her defiance had taken its toll, and for once he had thought to show her who had the upper hand. Well he had, hadn't he? It was unavoidable fact: Aislinn would lose, and she would have to marry. Only now he wasn't sure that he was going to be pleased with the victory.

"Milord? I am waiting. How will ye ensure love for Aislinn?"

He turned to her with his answer. "Love will have to come later. Surely it can happen. Ye can grow to love a person. Why I loved Ella. I did not know her but a week before we said our vows before God."

"Bah! Ye were in lust of her fine features."

"How dare ye!" His eyes blazed with fury that she would speak to him in such a manner.

"I speak the truth as well ye know it. Now sit and stop throwing daggers at me with those looks of yers. It's quite annoying, and childish I might add."

Dougray continued to stare her down, but she would not look away. Finally he took a deep cleansing breath, lest he forget that she was just an old woman. He again came to sit by the fire.

"Now…" She came closer. "…ye claim love for Ella and it might have been so, but I ask yerself to be honest with yer heart. What made ye think that it was love that drew ye to her?"

"I do not have to answer such a question." He was definitely uneasy with this and he knew that the old crone was well aware of it.

"Do ye nah wish to answer me, or is it that ye do nah know?"

"That's absurd. Of course I know." He clasped his hands to his knees as he tried to think of the answer. "She was beautiful and fair. Her voice was sweet as a melody, and she had eyes the color of…." He paused for a horribly long moment, as he tried to recall Ella's features to mind. A stab of guilt lay buried in his breast for didn't know. He didn't know the color of Ella's eyes.

"They were green as moss with a tinge of brown thrown in, milord."

His anguished, gray eyes lifted to hers. "I did not know." It was a simple thing, but yet it troubled him. If he didn't perceive something that should have been so obvious to him, how much more did he not appreciate of his wife?

"She liked to ride." He felt almost relieved that he was conscious of this, but then it saddened him for it was all that he knew about her. How ironic that it had been her passion that had ended up killing her.

He ran his hand through his hair. He had wanted to marry Ella. She was so fair haired and lovely, but he was faced with the fact that he had not known her. "I loved her," but his conviction seemed hollow.

Neala sighed. "Aye, then ye did and there is no one that can say otherwise. But remember, young lord, there are many different kinds of love that we share with others. We love our parents for they care for our needs, and in return, we love our children unconditionally. It is an endless giving love we bestow upon our offspring.

"When we care for whom we take to wed, it is to stand by their side, protect and provide. It may not start out as much, but as years go by, time is laced with joy, as well as sorrow. This is how the bond is formed. This is also love.

"Then there are those who are fortunate to experience love that runs deep down to the very core of their hearts, to their souls, and that is indeed a special love to know. Wouldn't it be a shame to let a special love like that pass? Yer parent's shared such a love." He looked at her then. "Now, young lord, ye say that it is love that ye felt for Ella, and ye are the only one that would know this. But I ask ye to consider yer feelings for Aislinn in the same manner. I have a hunch that ye will find that not only do ye know the color of her eyes, but ye know what each of her expressions mean."

Dougray didn't reply, but he knew the answer as certainly as if Aislinn were standing in front of him. Her eyes were always full of emotion, letting him know how she felt, and they were a dark alluring color of brown.

Chapter Thirty-Seven

"You seem distracted." Murrough raised his glass to his lips, as he watched Dougray move around the table.

"Aye, that I am. Do ye think that I am doing the right thing by forcing Aislinn to wed?" He looked at his friend.

Murrough leaned forward, resting his arms on his knees. "She is a most troublesome woman. This stipulation she has set, I am most surprised that you agreed to it, but then I can see yer reasoning for it. She needs to be taught a lesson. A woman should know her place. Aye?" He sat back in his seat again. "Ye are wise to have someone take her off your hands."

"Then why does it not set well with me?"

"Doesn't set well?" He didn't understand, but before he could make a comment on it, Aislinn came charging into the room.

"How dare you!" She pointed her finger at Dougray, who in turned quirked a brow in question.

"What have I done now, milady?"

"Are you going to just stand there and pretend that you don't know?"

"I assure ye that I don't. Pretend or not, I cannot say if ye don't explain it."

"Abbot Kirwan has banned me from the library, locking the doors." Fire nearly sprouted from her roar.

"Ye want to read? This is all?" Dougray came forward. "I thought that you would be training for your big day."

"Do not worry yourself. I will be prepared. Maybe you should see to the men. Frankly I was not impressed with my competition."

Dougray's eyes narrowed. How she could make his blood boil and not for the reasons that he wished she would. "Ye should be thanking me lass that I have not thrown ye to the wolves. Though it is hard to believe, ye will be presented as a noble woman and only those befitting of that station will be able to participate."

"There is not one reason for me to thank you. It's barbaric to be forced to marry a man that I don't even know."

He sighed. "It is for yer best interest."

"My best interest or yours? You dragged me here against my wishes, I might add, and now you want to find a way to get rid of me. The solution would be simple if you could just conjure up that mist so I can go back to my time."

Murrough stood now causing Aislinn to take a step back. She hadn't noticed him there in the shadows. "Yer time, milady?" he questioned.

Dougray moved forward hand on the hilt of his sword causing Murrough to hesitate. Never had his friend threatened him, but there was no denying the intent in Dougray's stance.

"I will show ye to the library," Dougray said to Aislinn, but he did not take his eyes off of Murrough.

"Uh...thank you." How could she have been so careless?

"Please wait for me, Murrough."

"Aye."

Dougray grabbed a hold of Aislinn's arm and nearly dragged her from the room. "Not a wise move, milady." She glanced at his hard features and shivered. Even though his voice was controlled, she knew by the darkening of his smoke-colored eyes that his anger was ready to explode. "Ye are lucky that it is Murrough that has heard ye speak of this. He is my trusted friend and will not repeat what he has heard. If anyone else had heard, ye wouldn't have to worry about a marriage, for ye would have been accused as a witch. Do I need to tell ye what that would mean?" His grip tightened making her wince.

"No. I think that I can imagine."

"Good. Vent yer anger at me, but make sure that there are no other ears around to hear." They had reached the library doors and she shrugged her arm away.

"And pray tell, how will I do that once I am married? Do you think that my husband will allow me to seek out your audience?"

He closed his eyes for a moment. The woman exhausted him. With a deep breath, he looked at her now, noticing that her lower lip trembled. It was slight, but he knew that it was so. She was brave, but was she actually frightened? He was aware that some people showed fear through anger. Could this possibly be the case with her? "Aislinn," he said so softly that she was taken aback from the gentleness of his tone, "my only wish, is to make ye comfortable. Do ye not think that I feel guilty about taking ye away from yer home? Yer family?"

She almost believed that he was sincere, but her defenses were up and she dismissed the honesty of his voice. "If this is so, my lord, then try harder to send me back. Now are you going to open the door or not?"

Dougray bit back his heated retort. Whatever had he been thinking? Frightened? The woman was made out of steel, unbendable and definitely unyielding. He took out the key, and unlocked the door. "There ye go, milady." She walked right past him, but turned to glance his way when he spoke again. "Ye might try to find a book on how to hold yer tongue. Yer husband may not be as lenient as I have been." He didn't wait for her to answer but shut the door in her face.

With a scowl still penetrating his features, he stormed all the way back to where Murrough was waiting for him. "I need a drink."

"It is poured." Murrough pointed to the goblet that was set upon the table.

"Thank ye." Dougray felt guilty that he had not explained everything sooner to his best friend. He easily read the mistrust in the man's eyes and he couldn't blame him in the least. He downed the drink, letting the liquid warm his blood. "Remember when ye could not find me after the battle with Fingham?"

"Aye, it was like ye had disappeared." Murrough nodded.

"It was the mist that Neala spoke of. I stepped into another time and place." He held up his hand. "I know that ye think this is mad and so did I, but truly it happened. I somehow was able to cross the line into the future and that is where I met Aislinn." He shook his head. "It was an unbelievable place. The future…so much change." He could see that Murrough was not at all convinced. "I know that this is unbelievable, but can ye at least try to understand, for I swear to ye, as I am standing here, that it is all true."

"How do you know that the woman is not a witch, and has cast some spell on ye to make ye think that this tale is so?"

"Aislinn is many things, that I will grant ye, but witch is not one of them. She is human like ye and me. She is trapped where she doesn't belong. Remember Neala had told me that I would meet a woman, and that I would bring her back with me?"

"Aye. I remember that tale well."

"I brought her back. It is just that Neala does not know why she needed to be here. Only that she must."

"I thought that this woman she spoke of was supposed to be yer true love, or have ye forgotten that part of Neala's prediction?"

"Obviously she was mistaken on that part or I have taken the wrong woman." He sat down. "Maybe I was to take her mother," he said with a chuckle.

"Her mother, milord?"

"Aye. I spent time with Aislinn's family. It was all so confusing that all I could think about was finding my way home. Aislinn followed me, leaving me no choice but to take her here."

"Then it was meant to be."

"Maybe."

"Then why do ye wish to have her married off?"

"She will be wed to someone that is loyal to me. If I uncover the reason that she is here, I will be able to request an audience with her."

Murrough considered all that Dougray had revealed. He did not believe that it was possible to travel to the future, but again there have been stranger things that have happened in his lifetime. The point was that Dougray believe it was so. Therefore he was forced to at least consider the possibility. Only there was something that had him baffled. As much as Dougray called Aislinn a nuisance, he also sensed that there was more than just duty that tied the man to the unusual lady. He'd protect her, even if it meant that he would have to test their friendship. He feared that Dougray had fallen in love with the woman, only he refused to see it. "Are ye sure that ye will not be bothered by another man bedding Lady Aislinn?"

He chuckled uncomfortably. "What do I care?" He poured himself another drink and nearly downed it in one gulp. He hadn't thought about another man taking her to bed, which was ridiculous since what else would a husband be doing? He closed his eyes, trying to will the disturbing image from his mind.

"I'm glad to hear this."

Dougray gritted his teeth. "Why do ye say that?"

"Just that we have enough problems with Fingham Butler. It will be good to have yer distraction elsewhere."

"Aislinn does not distract me." His voice held a note of impatience and Murrough noticed that his hands were shaking as he poured himself yet another drink.

"Of course not. I was just saying that ye'll have more time to concentrate on other matters. Milady can be most demanding. Is that not what ye have said?"

"Aye, of course." He slammed down his goblet. "Now about what I have confided in ye."

"Ye need to ask?" Murrough sighed miserably that it had come to this. "Ye have my word that no one will hear about what was voiced in this room."

"Thank ye, Murrough." He suddenly felt exhausted, the effects of the wine starting to cloud his thoughts. "Murrough?"

"Aye."

"Do ye know the color of Rhiannon's eyes?" He raised his gaze to find his friend's curious expression. "Well, Murrough, do ye know?"

There was something disturbing in the way that Dougray looked at him, as though this answer weighed heavily on a decision that was most complicated. Slowly he nodded. "Aye. Her eyes are the color of the hills of Ireland."

Dougray leaned back in his chair. He couldn't stop the dull ache of foreboding.

"Do ye wish to talk about it?"

Dougray looked at him, being careful to guard his feelings. "There is nothing to say. I am bone weary, is all."

"Once this event is over, ye will no doubt feel better."

"Perhaps."

Murrough heard the doubt in that response but was unsure why. "Do ye really believe that milady will be able to hold her own? She seemed overly confident of herself."

"That will be her downfall."

"With all due respect, I have seen the list. The men that will ask for her hand are not… well how should I put it? They are not seasoned. They have had many months of sedentary behavior. I don't mean to put too much in the woman's abilities but I have seen her move. She is quite impressive."

"Aye, that she is." He took on a faraway look as he remembered seeing her in action. She was remarkable.

Murrough cleared his throat. "She is being referred to as the 'woman warrior.'"

"Aye. I have heard. Is there a point to all this, Murrough?"

He nodded. "Only that we should add another name to the list, just in case, milord."

Again Dougray felt uncomfortable with this whole sequence of events. "Whom did ye have in mind?"

"Keefe…Milord."

Chapter Thirty-Eight

Dougray agreed to let Keefe participate. The man was of his sept a cousin to the Fitzpatricks with lands of his own. It would be a good match, but…. He eyed the man in question; he was boisterous with flaming red hair, limbs that were strong and firm.

Keefe was now making his acquaintance with Aislinn. "*Dar Dia!*" Dougray mumbled under his breath. Aislinn was actually smiling.

Aislinn noticed Dougray the moment that he had entered the room, but she was careful not to let him know that she had spotted him. She wondered what he would do if she actually pretended to like her opponents. She had every intention of finding out. "You must be…."

"Keefe will do. Never cared for formalities." The redheaded giant nodded. "Ye are the *Scathach*?" His eyes boldly roved over her taking in every aspect that he could see, tall, thin with womanly curves where it mattered.

"Hardly a warrior," she answered him with a smile threatening her lips.

He met her eyes, a grin spreading wider on his face. "Ye want to fight for a husband?"

"See you have it wrong. I wish to fight to be free of matrimony."

"Hmm. Then we do have a problem." He leaned very close. "Ye now have given me a reason to want to win."

Aislinn couldn't help but chuckle. He was rather charming in a rugged sort of way. "You look strong enough."

"As do ye." He took her arm and felt the firmness. "Ye are well trained."

"This does not bother you? A woman that can handle herself if the need arose?"

"I honor it. My mother was a descendent of Gaul; the women there fought beside their men." He let her hand go. "I will meet ye tomorrow?"

"Agreed." She nodded.

Keefe was most impressed with the woman who had been granted the name *Scathach*. Her hair was a bit short, but her face was to his liking with her strong Celtic features and those dark eyes were his undoing. The contrast was most bewitching. And the fact that she was strong was a plus to him. He was a big man towering well above most of the women. He feared that he would crush them beneath his weight, but Lady Aislinn Hennessy would not crumble beneath his touch. He had every intention of winning the dark-eyed beauty.

Dougray made his way over to him, hoping to find out what his cousin felt about Aislinn. "What say ye, Keefe?"

"I am pleased with what I saw. I will fight." Keefe smiled, knowing that he had finally found a woman who would be worthy to be his bride.

The confident grin made Dougray want to punch him in the mouth. "Ye have time to share a tankard with me, cousin?" he said between clenched teeth.

Keefe thought that he should refuse, but then he could never refuse a drink. "One should not hurt."

"Nay, one will not hurt at all." Dougray hit him on his broad back and led the man to a table.

The night wore on. Tankard after tankard was put before Keefe while Dougray pretended to indulge. They drank to their health, to their family, and to the sight of another tankard full to the brim. Dougray thought the man would never succumb to the alcohol, but finally on the tenth round, he fell face first onto the hard wood table.

Dougray motioned for Cormac and Teige to help him with his burden. "Keefe was drinking?" Teige looked up surprised that the man would indulge on the night before he would enter the ring.

"It appears so. Take him away to a quiet place and let him sleep it off."

"What of tomorrow?" Cormac wanted to know. "He was to fight Lady Aislinn."

"If he is awake by then, he will." With that Dougray left the hall a slight smile curving his lips.

Teige grinned making Cormac look at him suspiciously. "What are ye smiling about?"

"Ye don't see that the Fitzpatrick wants A.J. for himself?"

"Ye cannot be serious. He is the one who put forth this battle for her hand. If he wanted her, why didn't he just take her?"

"Conquest."

Cormac shook his head. "Ye are becoming too much the romantic."

Keefe moaned drawing their attention.

Cormac half lifted him. "Let's just get him to bed."

Throngs of people were arriving since the first light of day to witness the tournament for Lady Aislinn's hand. Roth was beside himself trying to run the kitchen making sure that he had enough food to serve, and enough drink so that no tankard went empty. No one had expected such a turnout.

Aislinn had stayed in her room until the last minute too nervous to do otherwise. She tried to ignore the fact that she was being made a spectacle and concentrate on what she needed to do to ensure her freedom.

The first man who stepped into the ring had the height, but he didn't have the agile moves that Aislinn possessed. Before he knew what had happened, he was flat on his back with Aislinn's boot at his neck. After this display, two of the men whom Dougray had chosen quickly declined the offer. They had no intentions of possibly losing face if they were unfortunate to become victims to this woman with unspeakable strength.

The next man to take his place was young and overconfident. Again Aislinn was able to best one of her suitors. The crowd was actually cheering Aislinn and Dougray found that this infuriated him. What kind of men did he have that they couldn't take down the lass? Yes, she had height for an advantage but by God these were trained men.

"Milord?" Murrough leaned near so that only he would hear him. "It seems that Keefe has not made an appearance."

"Oh?" Dougray tried to sound surprised. What was wrong with him anyway? He didn't want Aislinn to win, but he didn't want the one man who would probably best her to have a chance. Keefe was a strong, good-looking man who would treat Aislinn well, but he had not wanted her to be attracted to him. With the little display he witnessed yesterday, it looked like she had been at least interested. He had told himself that he wanted her to be happy but with…. He wouldn't finish that thought. It would mean he would have to search his true feelings about the woman. "Maybe Keefe had a change of heart?"

Murrough cleared his throat. "Nay, the man was stinking drunk the last I saw him."

O'Malley was quite amused with the events and made his pleasure known. "The woman is indeed the *Scathach* or surely the descendent. See how she defends herself? I have not seen such moves before, and the lass does not even seem to be tiring."

"I can see that for myself," Dougray grumbled wishing now that he hadn't allowed this unseemly display to take place. He should have just married her off and been done with it. But if that was what he truly had wanted, why did he make sure Keefe was unable to participate?

"Are these your best men?" Robert Burke was quite amused.

"I do believe the one now lying on his back is from your clan." Dougray could not resist throwing in a jibe of his own. Burke's face turned beet red with anger, but he held his tongue on any further comments.

"It is not that they could not best the lass." O'Malley looked to Burke. "It is that they think she is only a woman, and did not need to put forth an effort. See how she plays with them. She lures them to her, as if she is a weak little mouse, and then she pounces like the ferocious lioness that she is. The men are too pompous for their own good, and she is smart enough to take advantage of that."

O'Malley had been studying Dougray too, since the event started. It surprised him that the young lord did not just admit his attraction and be done with it. He decided to play devil's advocate, and leaned close to Dougray trying to hide the mirth from his voice. "Lady Aislinn is a tall one, aye? Made of the old stock where a lass stands by her man, even if it is to fight. She is a fine bony lass too with lush hips and wiles that will make a man weep with joy." He nodded with a sigh. "I envy the man who wins her hand."

Dougray bit the inside of his cheek, so not to tell the King of Connaught to shut his mouth before he shut it for him.

When the last suitor was carried away because he could not stand on his own two feet, Aislinn sauntered over to Dougray and curtsied before him, which looked completely ridiculous in the masculine outfit that she wore. "My lord, it looks as though there are no more men that wish to seek my hand. I guess that…."

Dougray was not listening anymore. He was still stinging from O'Malley's words and he was furious that she could have out smarted him with this ploy. Murrough saw Dougray make his move, and he would have stopped him if the O'Malley had not put a hand on his arm. Dougray leaned forward in his seat and did the unthinkable. "I take the challenge." The hall full of people from miles around had crowded together, making it difficult to hear someone who was standing right next to them, except when those four words were uttered by their lord. The entire room fell completely silent, as if they were holding their breaths. Even Aislinn seemed to hesitate.

"What?" Her dark eyes widened as she stared at him in stunned belief.

He was seated above her at the high table and now he stood, making him appear taller and horribly formidable. She had to look up at him to meet his eyes. "I said that I challenge ye. Defeat me and ye will be free to do as ye wish. But, milady, lose, and ye will agree to marry me."

Aislinn swallowed the lump that was in her throat and she wiped her palms on her leggings. Why was she so timid all of a sudden? Dougray was just a man, after all, no different than any of the other men whom she bested today, but yet, she was unsure that she wanted him to lose. She hadn't realized until that moment that she thought of him as a pillar of strength. He was a man who walked into the room and demanded instant obedience. She could feel the power that coiled within him. If she bested him, then she would lose what little sense of security she still held onto.

Dougray tried to read the many emotions that seemed to flit across her face. Did the thought of marrying him offend her so much that it had rendered her speechless? Angered by what he thought was her way of rejecting him, he baited her for a response. "Or ye can marry me now and we can forget all this nonsense. With energy like ye have, ye'll make a lively bed partner." The snickering around the room woke her up and he saw the fire in her eyes once more.

"I'll take your challenge. Have no fear, it will be you that will be on your back and not I." Again the crowd roared, making Dougray more than determined to show everyone just who was in control here. He gave her a curt nod and removed his cloak. "Wait," she demanded. Again the room fell quiet. "I have fought four men while you, my lord, have sat there resting. I request a short break; then I will meet you on the floor."

Dougray couldn't very well reject her offer for a reprieve. "I agree."

Murrough followed Dougray back to the main hall, anxious to find out what he was up to, but it was Dougray who spoke first. "I know what ye are thinking, but I could not let the infuriating woman win. How would it look that she come out the victor?"

"But why ye, Dougray? Ye were resolved to send her away from here, so not to be troubled by her. Now ye will take her challenge and make her yer wife. I do not understand this ploy."

He didn't understand it either, but what could he say that would make any sense? "When I am her husband, she will be forced to obey." He said this without conviction for he couldn't imagine Aislinn ever bending to his will.

Murrough just stood there staring at his friend as though the man had lost his senses. He knew Aislinn as well as Dougray did. The woman followed no rules but her own. Marriage or not she would continue on in the same fashion of an ill-mannered chit. "Just tell me what ye have accomplished this day?" He did not wait for an answer but continued, "Are ye in love with the lass? Is that what this is all about?"

Dougray laughed but Murrough noticed that he did not deny the claim. "She needs to be taught a lesson."

"And if ye lose?"

"Do ye doubt my capabilities?" His voice was thunderous making Murrough regret that he had spoken the words.

"Of course not…it is just that…."

"I do not plan on losing, Murrough, especially to Aislinn. She will bend to my will, and if that means I have to take her challenge to do it, so be it." With that he stormed out of the hall.

Aislinn was in her room stretching and limbering up, so that she could meet her opponent. She was so nervous that she feared she was going to be ill.

Moira came forward. "Milady, the Fitzpatrick is a good man. Ye should think about what ye are doing."

"Oh, I have thought plenty. I have to win him. If I don't he will think that he owns me. I will not be controlled by any man, especially him."

"Milord is not that way. He is very fair in all matters."

Aislinn stopped what she was doing and looked at the young girl. "I'm sorry. I did not mean to offend you or belittle Dougray. He is a good man. I do believe that. It's just I have no wish to have him or any man for a husband. Can you at least understand my point?"

"I am trying, milady, but I am having a difficult time of it. Ye see, I feel ye should be honored. Lord Dougray is a fine-looking man, decent and strong. He would take care of ye and give ye strong children to care for."

"Children?" She nearly choked. "We're getting ahead of ourselves here."

She went over to Moira and put her arm around her. "What you say about Dougray is probably all true and I should be flattered, but the fact remains I would be forced to marry when I am not ready for it."

"Pardon me for saying so, but ye are past the age that most women do marry."

"Not where I am from."

Moira shook her head. "What a strange land ye come from."

Aislinn didn't answer her. She just gave her a quick squeeze and tried not to think of her upcoming battle for freedom.

Murrough went to see Rhiannon. She was the only one these days whom he felt he could truly confide in. She met him openly, her beautiful hair falling over his forearm. He held her close for a moment, just savoring the warmth of her body. "Come sit by the fire," she insisted. "I have made some warm bread and there's milk to be had if that is to yer liking." She hurried to serve him. Murrough stared into the fireplace, his thoughts seemingly elsewhere.

She placed the warm bread in front of him. "Something is wrong?" she said as she touched his arm. He looked up at her, his large hand covering her small one.

"Dougray I fear is not using his better judgment." It was hard for him to say this, but he was confident that his fears would go no further than these four walls.

"Ye do not agree with his choice of mate?"

"Peugh!" He rose from his seat. "The woman is uncouth."

"She is strong in her convictions."

"She fights like...well, like a man."

"She defends her rights," Rhiannon countered.

"She cares for no one but herself."

"She's caring of all. She defends the weak and helps them to become strong. When she sees someone fall, where others would step on them, she picks them up and carries them along."

Murrough stared at Rhiannon, letting her words sink in. "Ye always see good in people."

"I see what is true," she answered with serene calmness.

Murrough ran his hand through his red hair, perturbed at himself for not seeing Aislinn in the same light. She was all that Rhiannon had claimed. He could not refute it. "It's just that she's so...."

"Different?"

"Aye."

"We all are in some degree or other."

"But for her to marry Dougray...."

"He could do no worse. She is a fine match for him."

"Ye think so?"

"Aye, that I do. Both fierce, both caring, but most of all, both needing a partner to fill the emptiness in their hearts."

"Ye see all this, do ye?"

"Is it not obvious?"

"Nay." Murrough went over to her and pulled her into his arms. "Nay, lass, it is not, but now that ye mention it, I am forced to see it all too clearly."

"Ye will not worry now?"

He shook his head.

"Then sit and have some nourishment."

The contest was to begin. Dougray and Aislinn walked to the center of the floor taking their positions. Aislinn raised her gaze to him and her spirits seemed to leap out of tempo with the tense drawn face that greeted her. Her mind was a crazy mixture with fear of losing, but also with the frightening aspect that she would win.

She had gnawed away so much of her confidence that her first few moves were reckless and Dougray nearly brought her down. The arrogant set of his jaw gave her the determination she needed. She wasn't so careless after that and fought with speed and agility.

All afternoon Dougray had carefully watched her techniques, as she bested each and every opponent. He was sure that he could mimic those same moves with little difficulty, but he became just a little too sure of himself and she brought him to one knee. He quickly backed away to regain his composure. If she had matched him in weight, she may have taken him that time.

Aislinn's blood was flowing now and she was sure that she could win. She moved in for the kill, but she was distracted when Dougray spoke to her. It was no more than a whisper for it was meant for her ears only. "When I make love to ye, you'll know the meaning of yielding." Before she could give her lethal retort, he took the advantage of her distraction, swiftly throwing his leg behind her knees. She went down with a crash and he was upon her before she could catch her breath.

She looked up at him in stunned disbelief. He had straddled her and pinned her arms immobilizing them to the ground.

She had lost!

This should have been disturbing enough, but she found that what unsettled her more was the expression in Dougray's steel-gray eyes. Slowly and seductively, his gaze boldly assessed her, sending her heart thudding against her chest.

"Ye are mine, Aislinn." He bowed down and claimed her lips before all of his people.

Chapter Thirty-Nine

"Ye can't hide in there forever." Dougray pounded on the door to Aislinn's room furious with himself that he was there waiting in the hall, like a besotted fool.

"I can and I will," she yelled back to him. "I won't marry you. Do you hear me? I won't."

"Before everyone ye made this wager and ye lost, Aislinn. Ye lost to me and will abide by the rules. Abbot Kirwan will marry us."

"Married in the church?" Her voice had now become a shrill of panic. "I take that seriously."

"As do I," he shot back.

"But I'm leaving. I can't." She paced back and forth in her room trying desperately to think of a way out of this horrible mess she had gotten herself into. She wasn't supposed to have lost the event.

She glanced at Moira who was looking like she wanted to cry. "I'm sorry, Moira. I should have let you go." She glanced then at little Declan. His large eyes were bright with fear. Poor thing, he didn't understand any of this. She went over to him and gave him a warm hug to reassure him that everything was all right.

"Nay, mistress." Moira came to stand by her. "Me place is with ye." She glanced at the door as though she thought that Dougray might break it down. Maybe he would. "A.J.?" Moira pulled at her apron. "Maybe ye should reconsider. Why do ye not wish to marry, and where will ye be getting yerself off to, if ye don't?"

"I can't stay here forever, Moira. I have other obligations and I will be leaving when the time is right." To herself, she had more to say. *I refuse to enter my century as a married woman!*

On the other side of the door, Dougray looked to Murrough and Cormac. "I want the door knocked down. Now!" He pounded on it again drawing Aislinn's attention. "I'm giving ye one more chance to open that door or I am having it torn off the hinges. I am warning ye, Aislinn. Ye will not like it, if I must come in by force."

She was about to yell back her retort when a rather forceful and definitely unfamiliar male voice interrupted her. "Ye will do nothing of the sort."

Dougray whirled around to face an older gentleman with graying hair and a long drooping mustache that nearly touched his chin. "Who are ye to command me in my own castle?" Dougray noticed that Teige and Dermot had escorted the man in and he turned his anger on them. "As for ye two, I will have a word with ye later."

Teige gave a grave nod. "As ye wish, milord, but we were acting on yer orders. Ye swore us to protect Lady Aislinn."

"And what in God's name does that have to do with ye letting this man into the castle?"

The older gentleman frowned, his eyes leveled under drawn brows. "If I am not mistaken, that is Lady Aislinn Hennessy, daughter of Lord Donagh Hennessy, ye have trapped behind that door. I am here to see that she is treated as a daughter of a chieftain should be treated."

"Ye still have not answered me. Who are ye, man?"

"I am to believe that I am the uncle of that woman ye are holding hostage."

Dougray fell silent though his lips thinned in irritation.

Aislinn had heard the complete exchange and found she was rather baffled why the man would make a journey here to claim her as a relative. Dougray as well as she knew that it was impossible, and yet the man knew her father's name.

Chapter Forty

Dougray was furious and was not quiet about his displeasure. He snapped out orders and slammed things about. The servants were afraid to even draw near. He called Murrough to him, but even his friend was hesitant. He had never seen him so livid.

"I want to know who sent word to Lord Aengus and I want to know now!" He slammed his fist into the hard wood table, oblivious to the pain that shot up his arm.

Murrough opened his mouth to speak but closed it again. He was suddenly anxious to escape his disturbing presence.

"What is it?" Dougray bellowed.

He took a deep breath. "Milord, it was I who sent word to the Hennessy clan."

"Ye?" His friend whom he had always laid trust with? He was the one who betrayed him? "Ye sent word without informing me of doing so?" He let out a yell and jumped over the table with his sword drawn. Murrough was forced to defend himself and had also drawn his own weapon. "I will kill ye for this!" Dougray recklessly charged and Murrough deflected the blow.

"Listen." Murrough tried to defend his actions. "I thought that I was doing the right thing. Ye said that the woman was a tiresome thorn in yer side. I was trying to locate her father to take her off yer hands." Dougray threw another blow that he barely blocked.

"Since when do ye see fit to do as ye please?" The metal upon metal clanged against each other as they parried around the room.

"Dougray, I am yer friend."

"Then ye would not have gone behind my back." He threw a blow sending Murrough's sword flying from his grip. He came forward stalking the now defenseless man. Murrough stood still and spread his arms out beside him.

"I am at yer mercy, Dougray. If ye think that I have betrayed ye, then I give ye my life."

He hesitated as the realization of what he was doing finally sunk in. This was his friend, a man he cherished above all others and he had raised his weapon to him, but then the anger rose again when he thought how this very friend had gone behind his back. He ran forward with a bellow his eyes glazed with his fury.

Murrough eyes widened as he stood to meet the deathblow, but at the last possible moment, when he thought that the sword would surely pierce him, Dougray had dropped the weapon and threw his right fist into Murrough's jaw. He fell to the ground holding his bruised face, as he stared up at Dougray's furious expression. "Ye at least deserved that." Dougray spat, but after a moment, he offered his hand to help him to his feet.

"Maybe so, but I tell ye, I thought I was doing what was right. I sent the letter before ye told me of how ye came by Aislinn, but once I knew, I assumed that the Hennessys would not respond since she couldn't possibly be their responsibility."

"Well now, they have, haven't they? A fine mess I find myself in. The old man claims he is the uncle and how am I to say otherwise?"

"Surely Lady Aislinn will set him straight on the matter."

Dougray was not so sure. Aislinn had no wish to be married and most likely would try any means to make sure a wedding didn't take place. "Damn it all to hell!"

Aislinn was seated across from her would-be uncle. She took in his rugged features and was rather surprised that he actually did resemble her father in many ways. So much so that it was almost uncanny. If the man shaved the mustache, trimmed his hair…."

"Why do ye look at me so?"

"You look a bit like my father?"

"Ye seem surprised. He is my brother."

Aislinn was a little confused for Aengus Hennessy seemed to accept the idea that she was indeed his brother's daughter. "Now it is you that is staring my lord."

He smiled. "Aye, so I am. Ye look a bit like Donagh, but yer eyes are dark like hers."

"Hers?" What did he mean?

"Yer mother of course. She was quite beautiful, as I recall."

Aislinn was beginning to feel a little uncomfortable. It was like this man really knew her parents, but that was impossible, wasn't it? "You met my mother?"

"Again ye seem surprised."

"Well…yes. My father has been away for a long time. I assumed my mother had not met him until much later."

"Nay, they met on the eve of St. Brigid. My brother made the pilgrimage and had drunk from the water. He claimed that he had wished for a woman who would make him whole. That evening at our fire celebration, she wandered into our camp. It had been a thick fog that rolled in that night."

"She came out of the fog?"

Aengus chuckled. "Aye, it seemed as she did."

She couldn't believe it was possible that her own mother traveled back in time. Her mind was whirling at the possibility.

"Yer parents left with no word or reason. Just one day they were no longer here. That was over twenty-eight years ago. We had thought that some horrible fate had befallen them." He looked Aislinn over, knowing now that this was not so. "They are well, Aislinn?"

She nodded. "Last I saw of them, they were." This just couldn't be happening. "Are you sure that we are speaking about the same couple? Could it be possible that I am not your niece?"

"I suppose that it could be so. The woman whom my brother married, yer mother, her name is Francine. She is not more than this high." He lifted his hand to indicate where she would stand next to his large frame. My brother is taller than I, blue eyes and laughs like there is no tomorrow. A fierce warrior he once was, the most feared of our clan. Only yer mother was able to tame him."

She didn't say anything. She couldn't. If her parents knew of time traveling, and had actually experienced it first hand, then why had they not mentioned it? Why hadn't they suspected that Dougray was from the past? God, if this was all true, her own father was from this time. "They should have warned me."

"Warned ye?" Aengus didn't know what she was talking about.

"I apologize. I am just overwhelmed by all this. My parents never told me that I had an uncle."

"Aah so he still holds the grudge." He shook his head. "We fought over differences of how we should keep the peace between the clans. I made the decision against his will. Many were slaughtered and he blamed me. I blamed myself, and before I could beg for forgiveness, my brother had taken his wife and had left our home, our lands."

"No uncle it is not why they left. They had no choice in the matter. I do recall that he spoke of a man that he fought with in many battles. I had always assumed it was someone he had served with in the military…anyway he called him Fierce Ax."

The old man smiled in forgotten remembrance. "I have not heard that name in ages. He spoke kindly of this man?"

"Yes, always. I could tell by the sound in his voice that he loved him. He said that he owed him his life."

Aengus' eyes watered and his Adam's apple bobbed up and down as he tried to swallow back the tears.

"My father was talking about you, wasn't he?"

"Aye. Fierce Ax was a name he called me." Aengus Hennessy had to sit down.

"Then it's true. You are my uncle."

He nodded. "And as yer a living relative I can protect ye, but I need to ask ye a question. I have heard many stories on my travels to Dunhaven. Many spoke of a woman whom they believed was the spirit of *Scathach*. Are ye the woman whom they speak of?"

"I have heard them call me that."

"A reverend compliment they give ye. She is the dark goddess of *Skye*. The warrior of martial arts, who was known to have trained the great warrior *Cu Chulainn*." He looked thoughtfully at his niece before he broached his next troublesome question. "Did ye make an arrangement to fight, the winner being the one who would take yer hand in marriage?"

She nodded completely embarrassed on how that sounded. "But I only did that because Dougray was giving me no other choice. I was trying to find a way out of being married."

"Nay? What else would ye do? Do not be offended but it rather surprises me that a woman of yer age is not already married with children to show for the years."

"Thank God I come from a place where a woman is not just a baby factory. We have other choices."

"And Donagh accepts this?"

"I owe both my parents for whom I am today. My father made me physically strong by insisting I learn the different ways to defend myself."

"And your mother gave ye compassion," Aengus added and he watched her raise a dark brow. That trait was her father's. He couldn't help but smile. "I have heard ye trained a cripple to be a warrior, and a clumsy man to be looked upon with respect."

"They are only what they are. I did nothing."

"Modesty would be yer mother's influence also." He sighed. "This arrangement ye agreed to, how is it that the Lord of Dunhaven himself participated?"

"That is a mystery to me." She shrugged. "I was under the impression that he was tired of me, and wanted me out of his life."

She sounded put out by this making him wonder why. "Taking yer challenge does not sound like a behavior of a man who wanted ye out of his life."

"It was his pride then that made him challenge me. You see, I was about to be granted my freedom and he couldn't stand being bested by me. He hates to lose, you know."

"Aah, pride can make ye do many things that ye may not do otherwise." He leaned his forearms on his knees as he studied Aislinn from his seat. "Are ye that opposed to this union then?"

"Marrying Dougray?" She chuckled nervously and waved her hand like she thought the whole idea was an outrageous prank.

"It would not be an unfavorable match. He is known for his bravery."

Her dark eyes snapped to him. "I don't want to marry. Doesn't anyone understand this? I want to go home, only I don't know if I ever can."

"Nay?"

"It's is a long story, Uncle. Right now I'm stuck here and maybe it will be forever…I don't know."

"Then why not make a life with a man who fought to have ye?"

He fought to have her? If only she could believe he had done that because of love, and not because he wanted to teach her a lesson. She miserably looked away, but not before Aengus saw the pained expression in her eyes.

"There is a way that ye can keep yer promise and have a way out if the match does not suit ye." He saw that this intrigued her and he continued, "It is the old way, the Brehon way. Ye marry for one-year time. At the end of that year, if ye do not think the marriage will work, ye can part company. Not approved by the priests, but it can be done this way."

"Would Dougray agree to such a union?"

"He would have no choice. Ye would be keeping yer end of the bargain. There could be no argument."

"There's not another choice?" He shook his head and she sighed miserably. "Fine."

"Good, then I will present it."

Aengus Hennessy was careful to watch Dougray's features to see if he would betray his true feeling toward his niece. "I would know yer intentions, Lord Dougray."

"I will provide and protect as I have done all along." His response held a note of annoyance that he was even being questioned.

"And why is it ye feel responsible to do this? The Fitzpatricks have never been responsible for the Hennessys."

He hesitated for a moment, for he couldn't very well tell him the complete truth, so he settled on part of it. "Her family was kind to me. I am obligated to protect their daughter."

Aengus was silent for a moment. He sat down moving his sword to the side. "Obligated enough to marry her. Seems a little extreme." For the moment, Dougray was at a loss for words. He wanted her and not out of obligation and definitely not by force, but how could he convince Aislinn to give them a chance? With every hour that Aengus Hennessy stayed under his roof, he felt that he came that much closer to losing her.

Aengus noticed that Dougray's once carefully hooded eyes were visible to him and what he saw in their depths made his decision. "If ye are in love with her, lad, why have ye not told her?"

"Who says that I am? She is pigheaded, opinionated and has no idea of how a woman should behave."

"And that is why ye want to marry her in front of God and the whole country?" Aengus was enjoying this. Two people who claimed that they did not care for each other but yet it was quite obvious that they did. "Well? No answer?"

"I…we had a fair fight and she lost to me." Even as he said this, he knew that it did not sound like a concrete reason for anything.

Hennessy would not let him off so easily. "Is this to teach her a lesson then?"

"Of course not!" He did not hide the fact that he was offended by the accusation. "I am responsible…."

"Ye not be now. I can see that she is properly cared for."

A flicker of apprehension coursed through him. This man could lay claim to Aislinn and he would have no say. He grasped at straws. "If ye haven't noticed, she is no longer a child. She made a contract. Does a Hennessy's word mean nothing then?"

"No one doubts a Hennessy's word. If she made a contract, she will honor it…. She knew of the consequences of all this?" He already knew the answer, but he would make Dougray say it.

"Of course she did."

Aengus took a deep breath, as though he was having difficulty accepting the poor woman's fate, when in reality, he had to bite the inside of his cheeks to keep himself from smiling over the joy of it. "Then she will have to comply." He saw Dougray's shoulders relax and he could almost hear a sigh of relief form his lips. "But as her blood relative," he continued, "I feel that I have to insist that the union be done the old way."

"Ye do not want to see yer niece married in the church?"

"That I do, but only if she so chooses. She is obligated to marry ye since she's made this unwise pact, but obligation doesn't have to be for a lifetime. I will agree to this marriage by Brehon law. If in one year, ye cannot make her see that ye want her for other reasons than a prize that ye won, then she can leave ye and come to live at my home until she can find a more suitable husband."

"That's ridiculous."

"Ye think so? Thus far everything that I have witnessed has been ridiculous. From ye having a woman battle against seasoned men for a husband, and more for ye taking the challenge yerself. Ye will have no choice but to do it the way I see fit." He stood now. "I advise ye, Fitzpatrick, that ye stop being stubborn or ye may lose what ye fought so hard to obtain." With those stinging words, he parted from the room.

Chapter Forty-One

A scowl penetrated Dougray's features, while Aislinn sat there so calm and collected not at all appearing disturbed over the new developments.

"Dougray Fitzpatrick, ye do understand this contract?" The Brehon Darius MacEgan asked again.

"Am I of Celtic blood?" Dougray's voice thundered through the room. "I know the Brehon laws as well as ye do."

"Then ye will agree to the terms?"

"Aye, for one year and a day certain." Dougray stared at Aislinn, his steel-gray eyes boring into hers. "Ye do understand all this, Aislinn? If I am unhappy with ye in a year's time, I can also ask for the marriage to be dissolved."

"I understand perfectly," she answered with more confidence than she felt. It was all happening so fast. This Hennessy that took her under his wing was overwhelming her with his decisions to do right by her. The more she thought about it now, the more she wished that she hadn't agreed to this kind of marriage. She was simply shacking up with the guy and that didn't sit well with her. She cared for Dougray more than she wished she did. She didn't want him to cast her aside after a year. What if he decided that this was what he wanted to do? If she married him in the church, he would at least be obligated to try and make the marriage work.

She let her gaze wander to where he was standing. His features were hard and unyielding. His jaw clenched so tight that she could see the pulsing sensation in his cheek. He would never insist now that they should be married in the presence of a priest.

Dougray stormed from the room. Aislinn had half the mind to run after him and tell him it had all been a mistake.

"My dear, ye need not worry if this does not work out. Ye are welcomed to stay with me, unless ye wish to go back to yer father. Surely by a year's time he will have returned."

Highly unlikely since he's happily living in the twenty-first century. She just nodded her head feeling miserable.

"The Hennessy woman could prove to be a problem." Abbot Kirwan gave his opinion to the dark-cloaked person before him. The abbot did not care for Aislinn and would feel no remorse if she were eliminated. The hooded figure nodded, but Abbot Kirwan was not sure that was an agreement or not. Can ye believe that the woman insisted that the marriage be done the ancient way? Sacrilege is what it is. God will surely see fit to send her to the fiery depths of hell."

The hooded figure placed a hand on the abbot to silence him. He then handed him a note that was sealed with a crest.

"Are these the instructions?" Again the hooded figure nodded. The abbot was not particularly fond of meeting with a faceless individual, but yet he had to make sure that the lands that Dougray Fitzpatrick was granted stayed in the Irish hands. The English had already taken too much of what was not theirs. Yet these idiots seemed not to notice. If they didn't put a stop to it now, there would be more English than Irish in Ireland. It was bad enough that they shared the land with other foreigners. But at least they had the decency to adopt the Irish ways, not like the English who insisted that they were the ones to change. Kirwan looked at the messenger. "I will carry out the instructions to the letter."

Again the hooded figure nodded, this time as a dismissal.

Chapter Forty-Two

Dougray was in a dour mood and wanted to be left alone. As a matter of fact it was what he had ordered, but Rhiannon was determined to speak with him anyway.

He sat slumped in the chair near the hearth a drink in his hand. It was days before his wedding and he was not in the least bit happy about the event that was to take place. She approached him making her presence known by clearing her throat.

He looked in her direction, but made no attempt to bid her enter. Rhiannon took another step forward, and since he didn't demand that she leave his presence at once, she took it as a good sign. "Milord, I wanted to wish ye good for yer wedding day." His glare sent a chill down her spine but she did not waver from her intent. "An old Brehon wedding will be nice and it will be done in the old tradition on the Calends of May. I know that ye think that Lady Aislinn is not perceptive to the idea of marriage, but she will be once she is with child. Nothing would make a woman endear herself more to a man than when she is carrying his babe close to her heart." Still he did not respond. "Well then, I wish ye well, milord."

Rhiannon was nearly out the door before Dougray realized what she was trying to tell him. He turned in his seat. "Wait."

She suppressed the smile that threatened to spread across her face and walked back to him. "Aye, milord?"

"If Aislinn were with child, I could insist that the marriage not be dissolved…for the child's sake."

Rhiannon smiled. "Aye, milord, that would be the right thing to do."

He was just beginning to see why Murrough loved this woman. "I am grateful for yer blessing, Rhiannon."

As soon as she stepped into the hall, Murrough nabbed her, drawing her away so that no one could hear them. "What do ye have planned here?"

"The way it should be. Aislinn belongs here with the Fitzpatricks and not with the Hennessy Clan."

"She belongs to the Hennessys," which was true even if it wasn't from this time and place.

"Aye, but Dougray Fitzpatrick is the other half of her soul."
"Ye talk of the old ways."
"Old ways are sometimes the best. Why do ye think I stay with ye?"
Murrough grumbled, "I have often wondered this myself."

Dougray entered the room where Aislinn had set up a corner for her exercise rituals. He watched her for a moment as she slammed her fists into the burlap bag that was stuffed full of turf. It swung back and forth as she continued to pummel the object, as if her survival depended on if she could beat it to death. He saw Teige and he nodded toward the man indicating that he wanted to be alone with her. It irritated him when he saw that Teige hesitated before he moved away, but not so far that he couldn't come to his lady's aid.

Aislinn punched the bundle one more time before she faced him. Her face was flushed from the exertion making her all so…desirable. "May I speak freely?"

She nodded curious to know why he was here. She had thought they had said all that could be said days ago, leaving this endless void that was between them. She watched him pace. Every so often he looked at her as though he was about to say something; then he would resume his relentless pacing. She folded her arms across her chest and waited for him to speak.

He had stopped once more and looked at her again, his dark brows furrowing together to form his displeasure. Finally, he seemed to find his voice, "Why do ye go with this pretense that Aengus Hennessy is your uncle?"

"Because he is." Her simple answer threw him aback, for he hadn't expected her to blatantly lie about it.

"We both know that this is an impossibility."

"Is it? You traveled to my time and with only a few steps through a strange fog, and how easily I managed to wonder into yours. Not only that, I find that my own parents did the very same thing. Aengus Hennessy was, no is, my father's brother. Of course, Lord Aengus does not know what became of his brother nor does he understand how I have come to be here. I don't even want to try and explain it to him, but I can assure you, Dougray, Aengus is my uncle, first generation uncle to be exact."

He sat down.

Aislinn was quite patient while he digested this knew bit of information. "Yer parents never told ye?" He found this unbelievable. "They never even hinted?"

"Not a word. And believe me, I have been going over all this in my mind. You'd think that they would have warned me about the strange mist that could swallow you up and send you to where you don't belong. Why would they let me wander right into it, knowing that I could be trapped?"

He looked at her with a steady gaze but inside it shattered him to know she felt nothing but trapped in his world. A stab of guilt lay buried in his chest for he had been the cause of her misfortune. He should have somehow stopped her. If he had, she would be safe and sound in her own world. He sighed regretfully. He couldn't change what had happened, but he could help her adjust. He owed her that much. "Maybe…." He shrugged. There really wasn't a plausible explanation why her parents would keep this incredible secret from her, but there was something that Donagh had said to him that made him wonder if this wasn't entirely true. "Ye were well trained in the Irish language. Ye were acquainted in the traditions of this time, as well as ways to ensure ye could protect yerself."

"What are you trying to say?"

"That maybe ye were not told, but ye were being prepared in case that it would happen."

She thought about it for a moment and it did make sense. She had never questioned her parents' ways, but she had known from the beginning that they were different from all her friends' parents.

"They always took in strangers." She thought of the many faces that shared meals with them.

"What do ye mean?"

"I always wondered why they would take people in and feed them and help them if they could. They were people who had no homes or seemingly any families."

"Time travelers?" He was beginning to understand.

"Maybe not all of them…but some I knew were, you know…different."

"You think they time traveled?"

She shook her head. "I don't know, maybe…." She punched the bag again. "Still they should have warned me."

"Would ye have believed them?"

"I would…I could have…." Again she slammed her fist into the bag. "Probably not," she finally answered.

"So now where does this leave us?" How he wanted her to accept her fate and let him take care of her, but he knew that she would never concede to it. She would always fight to obtain a way back to her time and place.

As much as they bickered and fought, he could not imagine her not at his side. Maybe he could convince her that they belonged together. Who knows? Maybe it was destiny that brought the mist, so that they could cross the bridge that separated them. "Aislinn…."

"Dougray…." They spoke at the same time.

"Go on." He urged her to speak first.

She had been thinking about the upcoming marriage, or trial one, if that is what they wanted to call it, and she didn't want to go through with it. It just didn't seem right. It was like they were going to play house with no commitments. There had to be a way out. There just had to be. "Dougray, about us…you know…getting married?" She chuckled nervously, while her hand moved up and down the burlap bag almost like a caress. "What I'm trying to say is, don't you think that there is some way we could just…I don't know…forget the whole thing?" She met his gaze now, hoping that he would agree. His gray eyes held hers for a long time, almost to the point that it was beginning to make her feel uncomfortable.

"Ye detest me that much, do ye?" He sighed heavily his voice filled with a hint of anguish that she had not expected.

"I don't hate you. I…." She didn't finish for she wasn't quite sure what she felt.

"I see."

He stood now, his feelings obviously hurt, but she didn't know why. Hadn't she said that she didn't hate him? What more did he want?

"We will marry under the Brehon law," he spoke evenly. "At this point, we do not have a choice."

"But I thought…."

"Nay." He cut her off. "Now that yer uncle is involved, we have no other option but go through with it. If I called it off, it would cause a riff between the clans and I can ill afford another sept wanting to destroy Dunhaven."

"What if I talk to my uncle and explain…."

"Explain what? That ye are from another place and time? He would not believe ye, and it would only make things worse for ye."

"I can refuse the marriage."

A swift shadow of anger swept across his face. Why was she so dead set against becoming his wife? He was the only one who would ever understand her for he knew where she had come from. She could confide in him, and he in return would do his best to make her happy. He would have thought that she would consider all this. "Yer uncle will not allow it. The word of a Hennessy would be in question. Nay, he will insist ye marry."

"Just to save face? That's ridiculous!"

"Is it? To have allies ye have to be able to trust. Without it ye are dead."

"And when I find a way back home and suddenly disappear, what then of my word?"

"Then it will be only of a disobedient wife and nothing more. Being married under the Brehon law entitles me to cast ye aside, which I will do immediately upon yer departure."

"How wonderful this must all seem to you." Her glare nearly cut him down, but he would not let her get the upper hand and he met her stance straight on.

"Explain yerself, lass."

"You get to have your fill of me and no one will say a word to stop this barbaric marriage. Then when I finally can go home, you are free to marry once more, as though I never existed! God, I find that insulting!"

He listened to her tirade with bewilderment. She didn't want to marry him. He wasn't even sure that she even liked him, but yet she was furious that he would move on once she was gone. "Ye have the audacity to judge me? What of ye? Maybe it is ye that is the one being insulting to my person. Ye will go back to yer time and pretend that I was no more than a figment of yer imagination. How do ye think that makes me feel?"

"I really don't care," she threw at him, immediately regretting the words. She did care; that was the problem. She was torn between what she truly wished for here and what she had in her time. She longed to be with her family again, but the strong feelings that she had for Dougray could not be denied no matter how confusing and frightening they were to her. But instead of sharing her fears with him, she let anger rule. "When I see the mist, I will gladly rush toward it and never look back."

He refused to let her see how those words wounded him and lashed back without a care. "Once ye are out of my life, I will celebrate that I no longer have a thorn in my side." With that, he turned on his heel and strode away.

Aislinn whirled around and took out her aggressions on the bag. She pounded and pounded, until she was out of breath and even then the fight was not out of her.

Once Dougray had left the room, Teige had come forward. He was wise enough not to say a word until she seemed more in control of her emotions. She looked at him now. With the back of her hand, she wiped the sweat from her brow. "What are you looking at?" she snapped at him.

"I was only wondering why ye fight so much to be apart from milord when ye are in love with him."

"In love? Isn't that a laugh. The man is impossible. I couldn't love him in a million years. I wouldn't want to. Why I'd rather love the devil himself before ever allowing myself to love Dougray Fitzpatrick." She turned away then not wanting to meet Teige's raised brows or to see him shake his head at her.

Chapter Forty-Three

Neala handed Aislinn the warm herb liquid as soon as she had finished arranging the blanket around Declan. The young boy was exhausted from playing and had fallen asleep next to the fire.

Neala would miss Aislinn's warm heart when she was gone. She knew that it was all predestined, but when it would happen she had no idea. Aislinn could be here ten years or she could leave come the next full moon. The gods were always so unpredictable in these matters. Time meant nothing to them, not as it did to the mere mortal. Secretly, she hoped that Aislinn would be with them for a long time. "Ye looked troubled, lass."

Aislinn tried to smile and was about to deny the fact, but she knew the older woman would see right through her façade. "Neala, I don't know what to do."

"Do, lass?" The older woman sat down on the rock leaning heavily on her walking stick.

"I can't marry him."

"Him? Oh, ye mean the Fitzpatrick."

"Yes. Who else?"

"Why can ye nah wed the man? Has he mistreated ye in any way?"

"No," she said quickly, "of course not."

"Then why?"

"You know."

"Enlighten me." Her wise eyes seemed to see right through Aislinn, but still she had to defend her reasons even if they were flimsy ones.

"Well, one, I am from another time."

"Ah, this is a problem with ye. Time. What exactly is time to ye?"

"Well it's a set of motion of hours, minutes that add up to years of events."

Neala smiled. "A fine definition ye gave. Ye are right too. Time is events that add up to years. Years are what man has made to keep track of where they have been or what they have done. Who is to say what order of time ye must follow? Ye did nah follow it the conventional way, and neither did the Fitzpatrick."

"What you're suggesting is crazy. What we did was a fluke of nature. Time is supposed to follow an order. But let's just say, for argument's sake, that I am wrong, that stepping through the mist was not a fluke. Then why haven't time travelers from every era bombarded us? Why then can't we just walk from one century to the next and then back again?"

"That would lead to chaos, do ye not think?"

"You were the one that suggested the possibility."

"Nay. I was only saying that time is running along, always, everywhere."

"Simultaneously, is that what you mean?"

"Aye, at the same time. If one knew the way, they could step from one river of life to the other without mishap."

"Well I didn't know the way and somehow I stumbled right into the time warp and ended up right here. It seemed easy enough to do, but for some reason I have this distinct feeling that it was not all that simple. I feel like I am missing something vitally important, maybe even something that could help me to find my way back."

"Do ye dream, Aislinn?"

"Of course."

"When ye dream are ye nah in another place and time, different from when ye are awake?"

"Well yes, but it's not real."

"Ye do nah believe it so, but perhaps it is what ye call awake that is not real."

"That doesn't make any sense."

"Sometimes what makes sense is not always the right path. Sometimes the most unreasonable deduction is what is the correct course." Neala could tell that she was still uncertain. "I believe that there are people sensitive to the subtle doors to space and time. Maybe even drawn to them."

"But why? For what purpose?"

"That ye'll need to search yer soul for. Ye are nah the only one who has found the way. Others have come and gone before ye."

"My parents," she said making Neala raise a gray brow.

"It runs in yer blood then?"

"I only recently realized this. It would have been nice to have been enlightened before I took this little side trip."

"Ah, but ye were nah ready to hear the truth. This much I am certain."

Aislinn was silent for a moment, contemplating. Neala had a point. If her parents had suggested time travel, she would have thought that they had lost their minds.

She thought back, slowly piecing together all that her parents had taught Connor and her, the long tedious lessons on speaking the Irish language among other dialects until it came natural to carry on a conversation. Then there were the self-defense classes she was forced to endure when she would have rather gone to the beach and worked on a tan. It was true. From the moment she could speak, they had been training her for now, but it still didn't explain why they hadn't told her. She rubbed her fingertips at her temples. Never had she thought her trip to Ireland would end up so complicated. But if she was to be honest with herself, she had sensed that it would be different before she had even landed. It seems her experience at St. Michan's was the starting proof of that, but then she recalled the incident at the bookstore before.... A soft gasp escaped her lips.

"What is it, child?"

"Before I took this trip, an old woman came to see me. She called me the traveler." She took a quick breath. "How could I have forgotten? She gave me a book, a journal actually."

"And did ye read it?"

"I did. It was tragic, Neala, and it all happened here. The person wrote about a man; his cousin that had been murdered." Her eyes clung to Neala's. "Do you think it is possible that she wanted me to have the journal because she knew that I would be traveling back in time?" She brushed her hand briefly over her lips. "Maybe I am to stop the murder." She stood now. Her nerves a jumble, she began to pace.

"Where is this book?" Neala was curious to know for it could possibly be an important clue to the reasons that she was brought here.

Aislinn turned toward her with a look of defeat. "Back in my time. I packed it in my suitcase." She sat down again. "What good is that now? It was probably a clue and I left it behind."

"It may be nothing. It is hard to say. Were any names mentioned?"

She shook her head as she remembered how odd that had seemed. "Not a one. It was as though the person needed to confess his sins, but didn't trust a priest for it."

"May nah be all that odd, since ye say he spoke of a man's murder. He may have also feared for his life as well."

She felt defeated once more. "It couldn't be my purpose if I don't have the book, a name or a location. I only know it happened here."

"Ye need to be patient. Maybe nah all has been revealed to ye. Be aware, Aislinn: there may be more to come." She handed Aislinn her cup once more, knowing that she needed to relax. "Thank you." She looked at Neala while she sipped the smooth-tasting liquid, already feeling better. "I believe we strayed from my original question."

Neala smiled her toothless smile. "Marrying the Fitzpatrick? I have nah forgotten. I see a good match between ye two."

"Surely you jest."

"Ye need a resourceful man, Aislinn, and the Fitzpatrick needs a capable woman. Ye are evenly matched. Life is all about keeping balance with the universe."

"I don't need a man, resourceful or otherwise, and what does me marrying Dougray have to do with balancing the universe?"

The old woman shook her head. "Things are patterned just so. This is what keeps the spiral of life. As for ye not needing anyone, ye are wrong, lass. We are all in need of someone. It is our human nature."

"What of you? Nature can't be all you need."

"I am but years older than ye. I had a man, but he has gone on ahead of me in our life's journey."

Aislinn was ashamed that she had been so rash. It had never occurred to her that Neala might have had a husband. "I'm sorry…I…."

"Ye have no need to be sorry. I have not lost the man whom I loved. He has only moved to a different infinite distance. I will soon join him and we will continue as we once did."

"You mean time travel?"

Neala chuckled. "Nay, nah quite the same. Death is another level of traveling, but we can discuss that on another day. Now, we need to solve yer dilemma. There is more to the reason ye do not want to marry."

Aislinn was amazed how the woman always seemed be so perceptive. She came all this way to speak to her. She might as well let her know all of her fears. Maybe saying them out loud will help in some way. "There is another thing that has me worried…actually petrified. The idea of possibly having a child."

"Why would this frighten ye? Children are our legacy, the proof that we have existed."

"But I don't exist here. I haven't even been thought of yet. How can I have a child when I know that I will go back to my time?"

"Ye assume that ye will be blessed with children. I say that ye should let fate take the lead. If ye were meant to have a wee babe grow in yer womb then all will work out."

"Fate? Work out? Please, I don't have that much faith. I believe you have to make your way in life with decisions, wise decisions, and not leave your life to destiny. That's ridiculous." She put her cup down. "Don't you see, Neala? I can't do it. Truly I wouldn't be good at it. I can't have a baby. It is too much commitment. You didn't know me before I came here, but I was never one to commit to any relationship for very long. Three months max. How can I marry and raise children with that track record? I'm not one for the long haul. It's not in my nature."

"Ye were helpful with Hamish. I hear the boy has changed because of ye."

"Sure, I'm great with fix-you-up kind of people. I have no problem with that. I help, I guide them, and then I send them on their way. Not exactly a mother's way of looking at things."

"Ye have young Declan. Know it or not, the boy has latched onto ye like a babe does to a mother."

Aislinn glanced at the sleeping child. She didn't mind in the least to take care of him. Yet again he was a person in need. The child seemed to be healing for he did not have as many nightmares, but the boy still had not uttered a single word. "Don't you see, Neala? Declan needs me still, but once he has regained his confidence...." She let her statement trail off to silence. She loved the little boy. It would pain her to let him go.

"I see it in yer eyes, Aislinn. Ye care for Declan in a way that only a mother could. Ye guide a child to know right from wrong. Ye help as much as ye can to steer them down the right path and to know who they are and what they can be. Ye give confidence that will help them through life. In the short time that ye were with Hamish, ye already accomplished this. It is only a matter of time that ye will do the same for Declan. Ye underestimate yerself, Aislinn. Ye have all the qualities of being a good parent." She rose from her seat to stir what was simmering over the open fire. "Tell me honestly, Aislinn. If ye had the chance this moment to go forward to yer time, would ye go?" Just as Aislinn was about to answer her, she raised her hand to halt her response. "I want ye to think on this. Ye would have to go this moment without uttering a word to a soul. Ye would just have to turn ye back on everyone ye have met here. Would ye do it?"

She hesitated then. Sure she wanted to go back to her life, to her family, but she had met people here whom she cared for too. She would want to at least say good-bye to them. She would want to thank Dougray.... Then it dawned on her, the whole reality of it all. She would never see any of them again. They would all be ghosts of her past and nothing more. She swallowed the lump in her throat.

"Nah so easy to answer, is it now?"

"I don't have to worry about it. Obviously, it would never happen that way."

"Because of yer caring nature, ye may find leaving us will nah be so easy as ye thought. Tell me this now: if ye knew that ye could never go back home, would marrying milord be so terrible?"

"We don't get along."

"That wasn't my question."

"He doesn't even like me."

"This is why he chose to wed ye then?"

"He just couldn't stand losing a bet. That's what prompted all this. I'm just a prize for his trouble."

"Ye know better than this. The man does not have trophies. If he did nah want to marry ye, he would nah have stood to take yer challenge. I see the problem here. Ye are both so blind to what is there for the taking."

"All I see for our future is bickering and knocking of heads. I see being trapped in a loveless marriage."

Again Neala shook her head. "Ye make yer own prison then."

Long after Aislinn had left the glen, Neala waited for the other visitor to make his presence known. She was not surprised when it was the Fitzpatrick himself who made his way to her. She marveled at how these two spirits refused to be united, especially when it would end all their anguish.

"Ye honor my presence, young lord." She offered the bowl for him so that he may wash his hands. When the formalities were done, he sat down beside the fire. He didn't speak at once and Neala did not push him to make his reasons known for this little visit. She was a patient woman.

"She is not happy here." Dougray looked into the fire almost seeming mesmerized by it. "All she speaks of is returning to her own time. Why can she not learn to accept things as they are?" Now he looked at Neala hoping that the old woman might enlighten him with the answers.

"This is all new to her, many changes for her to handle at one time. She is unsure also."

"Unsure?"

"Aye. The woman knows not what lies ahead of her. She is a compassionate woman, do ye nah agree?"

"Aye. More so than any woman I have ever known. She cares for everyone around her. It's like she has this magical cloak that she opens up to embrace every soul that she meets. She looks at people differently than most. She sees more to them than first impressions may give ye. She tends to see good where I saw nothing redeeming. Where I saw a forsaken soul, she sees one worth rescuing."

"Ye admire the lass?"

Dougray sighed. "Aye. That I do, but also she angers me to no end."

"And yet ye seek her company, nay?"

"As a moth seeks the flame and I seem to not mind that I get burned each and every time." He ran his hand through his hair. He was tired and confused over his emotions toward this woman. She drained him of his strength and yet he gladly sought her out for such a purpose. "Am I doing the right thing by marrying her?"

"Only ye can answer that question, milord."

Dougray looked into the old woman's eyes hoping to find some kind of answer that would inspire him. "I dread that I may send a wedge deeper between us."

"May I speak boldly?"

Dougray gave her a small smile. "That is the only reason I take heed to what ye say."

"Then think upon this, milord. Do ye marry the lass out of spite because she challenges yer authority or do ye marry her because ye love her?"

Dougray didn't answer at once. Yes, the woman did challenge him on everything she possibly could, but he did not think he was marrying her out of spite. Yet he was not sure that he was marrying her for love either. "I am not a vindictive man."

"I have always thought that ye were fair with all."

"But love? We are at each other's throats most of the day."

"Aah, it is built up tension between ye. Would it not be grand to unite yer souls, as well as yer bodies with those passionate emotions?"

Dougray just raised his dark brows at her. The old woman spoke boldly all right, but maybe she had a point. His nights of late were often filled with him imagining how it would be to touch Aislinn in a way that only a man could do. Then his brows furrowed as he thought of the words that she had told him more than once. She wanted true love before she gave her body and soul away.

"What has ye troubled, milord?"

"Lady Aislinn will not be so pleased to have our union completed."

"Ye do nah look close enough. Ye only see the anger she shows. Look deeper and ye will see that fear of the unknown lies beneath that hostility. She is unsure of her own desires for she has never felt like this before. Be patient, milord, and the rewards will be grand."

Chapter Forty-Four

The weather was glorious permitting the wedding to take place as planned, outdoors beside the lake. Even though Neala could not be seen, Aislinn knew that she was there and would be wishing her well.

Her wedding dress was of bright colors of red and warm blues and the petticoat lined with green ribbon. This wasn't exactly how she pictured what she would wear for a wedding, but she found she rather liked the lovely homemade dress that Rhiannon had made for her. Moira brushed her hair until it shone and left it loose and flowing where her once short strands now nearly reached her shoulders. A crown of beautiful spring flowers was then placed upon her head.

There was not a wedding march but there was music. The sweet melody of the harp filled her ears, as did the strong clear voice of the bard. Nothing was how she'd imagined this sacred ceremony to be, but yet she felt a warm glow flow through her. She didn't understand how she could feel this way when it was all a sham. She was being bound to a man who won her at her own game. It was a vicious and horrible way to enter a marriage. And yet, when she raised her eyes to see Dougray waiting for her in his finery of dark blue and gold and his family amulet hanging around his neck with the amber stone shining brightly, she had to swallow the lump in her throat. He was so handsome, this future husband of hers. His dark hair shimmered with auburn hues, and his bright silvery eyes of gray touched her. For a moment, she actually believed that he looked upon her as a man in love.

Dougray inhaled a deep breath when he beheld the vision before him. Aislinn was stunning, her glorious ebony hair shining with sleekness, her gown hugging her trim figure to perfection, and she was walking toward him to join hands. He knew that she was unhappy with this union, but still he could not help that his heart sang with delight for she would soon be his. Somehow he would prove to her that they belonged together.

She reached him then, standing so very tall and bravely meeting his gaze. Only when he covered her hands with his own did he realize that she was trembling.

The ceremony was brief with words spoken from the Brehon, Darius MacEgan. He again emphasized the contract terms that the marriage would be for one year certain. Aislinn closed her eyes trying to block out the words that made the marriage such a mockery. She said a silent prayer that before the year was up that she would find a way back to where she belonged and would never have to know if Dougray planned to cast her aside once he was tired of her.

They had a grand procession back to the castle where the main hall was decorated with garland swags with beautiful foxgloves, roses and rhododendrons. There were so many faces she didn't recognize and there would be more arriving. Dougray had family and close friends that had been detained, but they had sent word that they would arrive within the week.

There would be days of feasting. Roth had seen that goose and venison had been prepared, as well as whole deer roasted in a pit, with the meat wrapped in wet sedge to keep the flesh from burning. Dougray ordered the tankards never to be empty. From mead to Noble port, or whatever one wanted to quench their thirst.

Much later into the night, Dougray was whisked away, while women gathered around Aislinn, offering their well wishes.

For Dougray, the day passed as if in slow motion. He was a married man, once again. Not exactly how he would have liked to plan this union, but the infernal woman left him no other options. He happened a glance at her where she stood surrounded by women. She nodded her head and greeted everyone with politeness that was befitting of a lady, but he was aware that she was not happy. He recognized her subtle expressions, her jaw slightly jutted forward, the crinkling lines on the forehead, and last but not least, the forced smile. He knew that she wished to be anywhere but here. This was not a very good sign for the wedding night to come.

Moira arrived and Aislinn was all too willing to leave the hall, though she was not thrilled with the idea that Dougray would soon be joining her. The thought terrified her. All her convictions would be put aside. She married a man who did not love her.

She dreamed about a wedding night being special. She wanted to look into her husband's eyes and see that he would cherish her as much as she would cherish him, but all she managed to do is marry a man who wished to possess her. Everything was wrong, and the more she thought about it, the angrier she became. This had all been but a game to Dougray and now he was going to reap the rewards and throw her away in a year's time.

Well forget it!

"Ye look beautiful." Moira smiled for she knew that Dougray would be most pleased. Aislinn looked down at the white-laced nightgown not really seeing it. She didn't even remember changing out of her wedding dress and into this delicate garment. "I'll let him know that ye are ready." Moira turned to leave.

"Wait! I need to see Declan. I didn't even say goodnight to him." Aislinn didn't care that her voice sounded panicked. She was panicked!

Moira's eyebrows slanted in a frown for she didn't understand her lady's hesitation. "A.J., Declan is fast asleep by now. Do not worry so. Rhiannon will take care of him." She walked over to her then and took Aislinn's hands in hers. "Ye will please milord if that is what is worrying ye." She patted her hand.

Aislinn closed her eyes. She wanted to bar the door as soon as Moira left, but then Dougray would probably demand that it be knocked down. It would be better to face him head on. She opened her eyes to see Moira still waiting for her to give the order. "Tell him I'm ready."

Dougray was trying to be patient. He was not insensitive to the fact that Aislinn would be nervous, maybe even a little fearful, since this would be her first time. He would be gentle with her and hopefully she would come to trust him enough to know that he wanted their marriage to last as long as she was willing to be with him.

He had already heard an earful from Abbot Kirwan of his evil ways. He was relieved when Dubhdara came to his rescue and whisked the man away. But still, the sooner he could convince Aislinn to marry him in the eyes of the Lord and have it sanctioned by the church, the better it would be for everyone concerned.

He made his way to what would be their room and where Aislinn would now be waiting. A delightful shiver of wanting ran through him, as he thought of how she would feel beneath his touch.

He took a deep breath and opened the door to his future.

He was promptly greeted with a flying object that crashed against the hard stone right above his right ear. Another object came flying at him and he ducked just in time for it to shatter just inches from his head. His anger flared. It was their wedding night! He would not put up with this unwarranted temper tantrum.

Aislinn started in on the insults. "You filthy scum!" The vase flew from her hand hitting him on the shoulder before it fell to the floor in a million pieces. The impact stunned him more than it actually hurt, but his hesitation made her pause in her brutal attack. That's when Dougray made his move. He nearly leaped through the air and tackled her to the floor. As soon as she was able to catch her breath, she started struggling to be free. "Let go of me."

"I will if you promise me that ye will be civilized."

"Civilized!" she screeched. "You want civilized when you act like a cave man?" She saw by his blank look that he was trying to decipher her meaning, but she didn't stop. "You man; me woman. Well, buster, that's right. I'm woman with substance and I will not be dominated!"

"The whole keep can hear ye." He tried to calm her.

"I'm not your property."

"Nay, but I'm your husband."

"Ooh! Don't remind me. It wasn't my choice. You forced me."

"Ye made the rules," he gently reminded her. "Ye said that ye would marry the man who could best ye."

"You didn't say you were going to join in."

"I didn't say that I wasn't either."

"You tricked me."

"Outsmarted ye," he corrected.

She was silent as her eyes smoldered him with her burnt anger. She knew full well that he was right and she was acting like a sore loser, but she couldn't help it. She had thought that she could get out of marrying anyone. She was going back where she belonged and she wanted to be single when she managed the feat. "Get off me. You're breaking my back."

Dougray released her and she scrambled away. They glared at each other from across the room.

Dougray's eyes had wandered down the length of her, and for the first time, he realized the nightgown that she wore was nearly transparent.

"What are you looking at?" Aislinn snapped noticing the lazy seductive look in his eyes. She glanced down at her attire and almost died of embarrassment. She might as well have just stood there completely naked for him, for all the material seemed to hide. She hurried over to the bed and pulled the robe around her. Dougray couldn't help but chuckle at the absurdity of her sudden shyness.

"Dear lady, ye are not hiding anything that I have not seen on a woman before."

She sliced him with her glare. "Well, you may have seen it on others, but you haven't seen me and that's the way it's going to be."

He lifted one dark brow thinking it probably wasn't the best time to remind her that he had held her in his arms at the lake, and with less on. "And what if I decide to exercise my rights?"

"You'd force a woman to your will?" She knew she was mocking him, but couldn't seem to stop herself.

"Don't tempt me to teach ye a lesson, Aislinn." There was a silken thread of warning in his voice as he took a step toward her.

"I don't want to be here." She threw up her hands and backed away from him. "I don't want to be married. I want to go home, Dougray. You promised me that you would send me home." The last of her words were spoken in desperation as she sat down on the edge of the bed, folding her arms protectively against her.

There was a heavy feeling in the pit of his stomach for he had not realized how deep her despair had run. "Do ye find it that terrible here then?"

"Yes," she answered at first until she noticed the tired sadness that passed over his features. "I mean no. Oh, Dougray, don't you understand?"

"Ye could make Dunhaven yer home, if ye only try."

"How? I'm either stuck within these walls like a prisoner or followed around with no privacy."

"I have explained all that to ye. It is not...."

"Not safe. Yes, yes. So you've told me. Well that's not all that's wrong. I had a job. I'm a writer and I like that people want to read what I've written. Who is going to read a romance novel here?"

"I know ye miss your writing, but ye could still tell stories to the children. They enjoy them so well and ye have the campfire stories. I could set aside...."

She interrupted him with a groan. "Oh never mind. You simply don't get it." She threw herself face down upon the bed. "Just leave me alone," came her muffled voice.

Dougray was at a loss what to do to comfort her. Neala had prophesied that she was to come to this time, but to what purpose? Surely it wasn't just to make her miserable. He wanted to go to her, but he knew that she would not welcome him. She had made it perfectly clear that she didn't even want him as a husband. His face was bleak with sorrow that he could not reach her heart. Without another word, he quietly left the room. At least he could grant her one of her wishes.

Dougray left the festivities behind and wandered through the glen, his purpose to speak to Neala. He knew that her fire was always lit far into the night.

The old woman looked up and he could tell by her face that she had been expecting him.

"Trouble with yer lass so soon?" The old woman handed Dougray a cup of spirits.

"Sometimes I want to strangle her until there is no life left in her, and in the same breath, I want to hold her near my heart and keep her safe. Bah!" He moved away from the old woman thoroughly disgusted.

"Ye know what yer problem is?"

He looked at Neala, his eyes flashing impatience. "*Dar Dia*! Enlighten me please."

"Ye've fallen fer her, ye did. Ye love her."

"I do not."

The old woman laughed. "Sure ye don't. If that were true, ye wouldn't be so vexed."

"Woman, ye irritate me almost as much as she does. Why do I bother to come to ye for advice?"

"Because, ye know I will nah lie to ye."

Dougray opened his mouth to make another retort but what could he say? She was right. He trusted her to tell him the truth. "What am I to do with her? She has refused my bed." Saying the words out loud sent a disturbing chord through him. She had denied him his right. "I should go to her and just take her and be done with it."

"And what would that accomplish, eh?"

A sudden icy contempt was evident in his eyes. "I would satisfied my hunger for her, and damn it, she would know what it was to be touched by a man."

Her eyes narrowed and her lips pinched together in disgust. "Then be gone from my sight and do yer deed if that is what ye wish to accomplish."

He clenched his jaw shut. How he hated the way that she could make him feel like a child who needed to be reprimanded.

Neala nodded her head as a smile touched her worn lips. "I see that ye still stand here."

"*Dar Dia*!" He ran his hand through his hair. "Is it asking so much that she give us a chance?"

"She is frightened of the commitment ye have forced upon her, but ye can surely convince her otherwise. Ye are young, strong and…" She cackled. "…ye still could turn a young lass' head, aye?"

His eyes flashed a familiar display of impatience. "Is there a point to all this?"

Her sigh was long. "Do I need to spell it out fer ye then? Very well. Romance her, let her see that ye want her to share a life with ye at Dunhaven and all else will fall into place."

His perturbed expression was replaced with a determination. "I will think on yer words, old woman, but now…" He handed her his cup. "…I think that I'm going to retire. Thank ye for yer words and yer frankness."

The old woman nodded her head. "If ye want to be knowing, she be in love with ye too."

His mouth twisted wryly in disbelief. "That is to be seen."

The next day, Dougray decided to make amends with Aislinn. If a little courting needed to be done, then so be it. He would romance his wife until she was willing to give herself freely to him.

He had been up all night trying to think of something that would please her, and he had finally come up with the perfect plan that would also ensure that they had time alone.

He entered the chambers expecting to find her fast asleep, for the sun had not fully risen in the sky. What greeted him was an empty bed, the fire all but embers and Aislinn missing. Fear struck him first, letting his imagination take over. He went as far as to believe that she had been so frightened of him that she ran away into the night. Then as he began to think logically, he realized that she was not a witless fool, and if she planned to leave him, that she would most likely seek sanctuary with her uncle. Well he wouldn't have it. He would find Aengus Hennessy and demand that he see his niece sent back to him. He was her husband now, and by God, he would not let her go that easily. He turned on his heels so quickly that he had not seen the silent figure standing behind him.

He ended up plowing right into the very woman he sought. She would have fallen to the ground but Dougray's strong hand quickly came to the rescue and steadied her. "Ye're up and about rather early." His voice sounded terse, more than he intended it too.

She ignored his comment and quickly moved away. "Where were you heading in such hurry? You nearly killed me."

"I apologize. I didn't see ye behind me."

"I'll give you warning next time."

"You were in the library, I see." He nodded toward the book she was holding.

"I couldn't sleep." She lifted the book that she held, confirming her whereabouts and eliminating any suspicions he might have harbored.

"Ye really do like to read."

"Why do you seem so surprised? You'd think by now you would have realized this."

"Hmm." This was not how he had planned to confront her this morning. He took a deep breath and started over. "Am I able to persuade ye to read yer book later?"

"Why?" She was on guard for she was unsure of what he might suggest. He was after all her husband now. *Her husband,* it seemed so strange to say, but it was true and she had to face the reality of it.

After her long night alone, where she had time to contemplate over her options, she realized that she had only two choices here: She could either beg her uncle to take her away, or she could try and make this marriage work.

Frankly the idea of living with her uncle, as kind as she found him, was not an appealing prospect simply because she would not have as much freedom, which was almost laughable, since she was guarded at all times.

If she chose to stay with Dougray, she could continue on the way she had been. The only drawback would be that she would be expected to share the man's bed and…. Well now that she saw him this morning, looking so incredibly handsome, maybe that wouldn't be so awful. She was attracted to him. She could do no worse for a husband, she supposed. He was a decent man after all.

"I want to show you something." He saw her eyes nervously glance over his shoulder and he followed her gaze to the bed. A smile tugged at his lips. "That's not what I had in mind, though I could be easily persuaded." His right brow lifted slightly, waiting for her response.

Her cheeks flushed making her look so sweet, innocent and at the same time captivating. "It's a tempting offer, but I will have to decline." She bit her lower lip waiting, actually hoping that he might insist. She didn't want to have to make the decision. She wanted him to just take her in his arms and make love to her, get it over and be done with it. She knew she wasn't making any sense, but none of this did. She wasn't supposed to be here in this century. She wasn't supposed to be married to a man who drove her to a point of where she wanted to beat the living daylights out of him, and at the same time wanted to lose her self-control and let passion be her guide.

"Then perhaps ye might let me tempt ye with another activity?" he offered with a sensual smile upon his lips. "Would you like to go riding?"

If only he could have known what she was thinking, he would have been more than happy to oblige. He wanted nothing more than to touch her smooth skin and feel her warm body beneath his. Unfortunately, possessing the ability of the sixth sense was not one of his strong qualities and he interpreted her expression as purely apprehension of being alone with him. "Ye are not opposed to my company as well?" he inquired.

She cleared her throat. "No."

"Where are yer thoughts, Aislinn? Ye seem to be elsewhere."

She had to calm her nerves and force herself to smile not wanting to take any chances that he might change his mind. Dougray's heart nearly stopped for she was even more beautiful when a smile softened her lips. "To escape these four walls for a day? Why I could…well I could kiss you, Dougray."

"I would not be opposed to such an idea," he teased thinking she would never act upon it. But she fooled him, taking a quick step forward and brushing her lips across his cheek.

"When do we leave?"

A smile ruffled his mouth. He had hopes that this outing might bring her around to his thinking. "Now, if ye'd like."

It was wonderful to be so free and without a worry. She admired the beautiful wildflowers and the forest of oak trees that still covered the land making everything look so different from what she had viewed in her century. Dougray walked up beside her. "What are ye thinking?"

She turned and smiled at him, an actual genuine smile for she was enjoying the afternoon and the company. "Just admiring everything. It is such a shame that all these beautiful ancient trees will one day be gone."

"I will stop it from happening."

"How? You are just one person, Dougray. How do you plan on stopping the inevitable?"

"We could try?"

"We?" She couldn't help but sound skeptical.

"I then." He had a blanket set out and they both sat down.

"Are you going to fight the English all by yourself?"

"I could unite the clans and we could…." He saw her forlorn expression and knew that she knew more. "It will never happen, will it?"

"No."

They were silent while Dougray unwrapped the bundle he had brought with him. He didn't want to talk about Ireland's trouble for now. He wanted to concentrate on them. That was the whole purpose of taking her away from the keep. They would have a nice lunch and long ride back.

He noticed that her lovely dark eyes watched him with open interest. She was at least somewhat curious. "Aislinn, what do ye expect from me?"

Her brows furrowed together and her voice held a tinge of caution. "What do you mean?"

"We are married and I would want ye to be comfortable. I ask ye again, what do ye want from me?"

Want? She looked at him. He was so incredibly arrogant, strong, determined, but he was also good, decent and handsome as well. His silvery gray eyes mesmerized her, and his lips, how she remembered those lips. They were firm and oh so sensual. She would swear that he had the monopoly on virility. She frowned. He was dangerous in that aspect, very dangerous, and he would end up breaking her heart. "I want friendship," she blurted out immediately looking away before he would read the desire in her eyes.

He knew that he had made her nervous for she was wringing her hands, but still he would not let the subject drop. They had to talk this out. "Don't ye want more?" His fingers lightly touched hers causing panic to riot within her. "Aislinn, I would be gentle…."

"No!" she nearly shouted at him, as she pulled her hand away. The awkward silence that followed seemed to be more deafening. She cleared her throat, trying to maintain the fragile control on her senses. "I only want your friendship, Dougray. Please understand and not demand more."

"Friendship is what ye be wanting then?" There was a slight edge to his reply and she couldn't blame him. "Aislinn?" Her dark eyes touched him and it took all his will power not to pull her to him and end the torture for both of them. "Friendship is grand to be sure." He gave an exaggerated sigh, like he was remembering something in particular, something so wonderful that his smile seemed to light up his whole face. "But tenderness behind closed doors can be heavenly."

She remained silent for she could not refute his statement, seeing that she had never experienced it. She again turned away, her face clouding with uneasiness. She needed to think of a way to distract his thoughts to a safer ground.

While she was preoccupied, he decided to take advantage of the moment. After all she had responded to his kisses before. As a matter of fact, if memory served him right, she had even asked him to kiss her. That was a start to intimacy and he didn't see a reason not to try and recapture that moment again.

His sudden movement caught her off guard, and she fell backwards to the ground with him on top of her. She opened her mouth to reprimand him but his lips had covered hers, making speech impossible. She hit at him and struggled to be free, but he continued to be insistent with his caress. Hot, moist and all so tantalizing that she nearly gave in to the moment…almost, until sanity sunk in. She was not going to have her first time with a man be out in an open field for anyone to come along and see them. She gave him another powerful shove and finally he seemed to realize that she was not going to respond in the fashion that he had hoped for.

He let her go.

She was red with fury and her eyes darkened as black as a starless night. "What was that display?"

He shrugged. "I had to try."

"Try what? Ye just attacked me like an animal."

He chuckled and shook his head. "Don't ye know when a man wants ye, Aislinn? We took vows, and we have yet to make it official."

"You asked me what I wanted," as though this made all the difference in the world.

"Aye, that I did." He nodded. "And I heard ye well enough, but dear wife, ye forgot to ask me what I wished."

"But…."

She began only to have him silence her. "I will not take ye by force, Aislinn, but do not expect me not to try and persuade ye to see reason."

Chapter Forty-Five

The more Aislinn had thought about what Dougray had declared, the more determined she was to discourage him. He was going to try and persuade her to jump in bed with him without the benefit of love. Well he could give it his best shot, but she was not going to be all that easy. She wanted love, and if he could not give her that, then he was not going to get anything from her. He claimed that he would not force her. Well she would definitely use that to her advantage.

Moira helped her quickly to dress in her deep blue, wool gown for the evening's festivities. More guests had been arriving all day to offer special honor for the newly married couple.

Married! Hah!

What a laugh that was. They had joined hands and said they would play house for a year, then go their separate ways.

When Aislinn stepped into the room, Dougray rose from his seat where he had been waiting for her. His eyes swept over her approvingly. The gown was of a rich, deep blue with the bodice fitted with a V-shaped neckline and intricate lace front attached. At her slim waist, she wore a decorative belt of pearls with a sapphire pendant clasp. The headdress was simple cauls of silver and tiny wisps of hair escaped from beneath its confines to frame her lovely face. Granted she was scowling at him, but that made her cheeks flush, heightening her beauty.

He approached her then and took her left hand. She tried to pull it away but he held fast. "I have a gift, milady." With that he slipped a beautiful Celtic knot ring onto her finger. The stone was an exquisite Amber stone with flecks of dark colors in the center of it. She was momentarily stunned, and her mouth slightly dropped open. "Are we speechless, my sweet lass of abundant words?"

She clamped her mouth shut and her eyes flew to his face. "I can't accept this." Again she tried to pull her hand away, but he would not let her go.

His changeable, gray eyes sharpened. "Nay, ye will accept it. I have taken ye as a wife and all shall know it."

"But…." He silenced her with his mouth. He had moved so swiftly that she didn't have a chance to sidestep. One hand went to the small of her back, while the other held her head so that she could not escape his caress. After a moment, she didn't care to. His lips were more persuasive than she would have liked to admit, drugging her senses, sending her heart pounding. His tongue moved with hers and shivers of desire raced through her veins. When he raised his mouth from hers, her head moved forward as if the sudden release left her seeking more. He gazed into her eyes and knew she had been greatly affected. He hid his pleased smile by giving her a quick kiss on her forehead. "Now that is what I prefer when I bestow a gift upon ye."

She blinked back to reality. "You beast!" She pushed away, her words stinging as if she had slapped him. "I will not be bought."

"That was not my intentions and it seems I do not need to buy ye. Yer mouth was most willing."

"It most certainly was not!" she lied miserably. "You had me trapped in your grip and I had no choice but to suffer your painful attack."

His eyes narrowed. "Painful? What do ye mean?"

"That…that…" She searched her brain to come up with something, anything that might discourage him. "…that infernal mustache of yours. It rubs my skin raw. I detest the horrible, hairy thing!"

She knew that she had pushed too far for she saw muscles in his jaw contract, as he clenched his teeth. He held back another angry retort with a deep, cleansing breath, for quarrelsome words would not endear her to him. "Deny it as ye will, but ye felt it as well as I did. Ye want to be with me, Aislinn, and the sooner ye admit it, we can put an end to this torment."

Her mouth fell open to protest but no sound came out. He was right and he knew it. She had been affected. She did want him. She closed her mouth and just glared at him, angry that he could read her so readily.

"We will have time to discuss this later, but now guests await." He took hold of her arm and escorted her to the Banqueting Hall.

Once again everything was decorated to perfection. Aislinn smiled until her cheeks hurt and was very gracious to all, but all she could think about was that *damn* kiss. She could still feel the intimacy of it. And she didn't want to!

To top it off, she had to endure the closeness of the very man whom she wanted to forget. Just his presence was overwhelming her to distraction. She wanted to run, get away before she suffocated, and the confounded dress she wore wasn't helping. She could barely breathe.

"Sit still, Aislinn, and try to act like a lady," Dougray whispered to her.

She pulled at her bodice of her gown. "Damn. This garment itches and it's so tight over my breasts that I think I'm going to pass out."

"At least it would be quieter then," he said under his breath, while all the time he was smiling to the people that were gathering around to witness their happy union.

Happy? Wasn't that a joke.

She detests my mustache! Dougray could think of nothing else. It was the height of fashion and she had ridiculed him. He knew he was being completely vain to think that way, but with that statement, she had added insult to injury. The woman refused his bed; if that didn't just destroy a man's ego, he didn't know what would. "Aislinn, smile; everyone is watching." He plastered a strained grin on his own face. "Don't make me do something drastic, like cover yer mouth with my detestable mustache."

"You are a lowlife beast. I hope you know that."

"I didn't know it until this afternoon, and I forgot to thank you for the compliment."

"It wasn't a compliment."

"Nay? I thought ye were commenting on my animal magnetism. We both know that ye're attracted to me."

"I most certainly am not!"

He looked at her then with his hypnotic, clear, gray eyes. He inclined his head causing his dark, thick hair to move over his shoulder. She could just imagine running her fingers through its richness. God, he was so gorgeous, and by the arrogant smile he gave her, he very well knew it. "Should I prove it to ye?" He leaned toward her and she shoved him away.

"Oh you...."

"Ye are at loss for words…again, I see."

"No, I was going to tell you to go to hell, but then I realized that the devil himself would probably throw you out, you detestable fiend."

Dougray couldn't help it. He threw back his head and laughed. Even when she was being insulting, he found her stimulating to be around.

"I scorn you and you laugh. What is it with you?"

"I'm truly sorry."

"You are not."

"Aye, of course ye are right, but still…." He put his hand firmly on her leg. "I laugh only because I now know that yer insults are yer little endearments, and I look forward to each and every one of them."

She shoved his hand away from her leg. "You are a conceited baboon. And don't touch me."

"Why? Do I tempt ye when I do?" He purposely put his hand on her leg once more.

She smiled sweetly right before she pinched his flesh between his thumb and forefinger.

"Ouch!" He quickly pulled his hand away, like he was really hurt, but in actuality he was trying desperately not to laugh.

"Oh, you're such a baby."

Just then Aislinn noticed a beautiful blonde had swept into the room, her eyes resting on Dougray in a bold, maybe even seductive, manner. She might have dismissed the woman as just being flirtatious if she hadn't felt Dougray straighten in his seat. She turned to look at him and he seemed not to be able to take his eyes off her. So that's how it was. The jealousy surged through her veins. Her dark eyes snapped at him, her voice sounding like a hiss. "You slime ball. You want her, don't you? Well go to her." She waved her hand as if dismissing him from her sight. "See if I care."

His quick gray eyes were humorously resting on her and a smile of pleased satisfaction spread across his face. "Do I detect some jealousy? Maybe you care for me after all." He tried to put his hand on her leg again, but she quickly slapped it away.

"Oh, stop it. It's not jealousy you see. It's disgust. This is our night and you sit there and make eyes with that brazen hussy."

She was jealous even if she wouldn't admit it, and maybe he could use this to his advantage. "I'll give ye all ye want." He waived his hand in the air. "I'll even give up that woman ye think I'm attracted to." He leaned really close to her now. "If ye will grant me a...."

"I won't sleep with you." She crossed her arms across her chest.

"Tsk, tsk. Is that all that is on yer mind?" She shot him a withering look. He loved it when he cut through her protective reserve. "I was merely going to ask ye to dance with me."

She felt utterly foolish that she had presumed, and she had no doubt that this was exactly what he had intended to do. "What do I care? Go to the woman and take out your sexual aggressions out on her."

He chuckled. "Oh, ye care, Aislinn."

"Fine," she spit out behind clenched teeth. She did care and she didn't want him making a fool out of her, by chasing after the blond hussy. "I'll agree to one dance with you, if you put the little tart in her place, agreed?"

He shrugged. "Sure. Why not?"

"Well here's your chance, my lord, for she's weaving her way toward you." She couldn't wait to see him squirm.

The beautiful blond had reached them and showed absolutely no qualms at all that she was addressing a married man. Dougray gave the woman the most heartwarming of smiles. Aislinn wanted to gag at the syrupy sweetness he was exhibiting. "Miriam, it is so good to see you again…my love." He added at the last moment and that caused him to receive a swift kick from beneath the table. He nearly bit his lip but recovered quickly. He took Aislinn's hand in his and she tried to pry it loose, but he would not let her go.

Miriam noticed the strange behavior but said nothing. Actually she had to keep herself from smiling at the obvious trouble Dougray's woman was causing him.

"Miriam, I would like ye to meet my wife, Aislinn."

Aislinn glared at Miriam not even bothering to hide her open contempt. The woman arched her golden brows with surprise, for she couldn't fathom why the woman would hold ill feelings toward her.

Dougray found this meeting to be rather amusing and hated to put an end to it, but he knew that he must. "Aislinn, may I introduce…."

"Miriam. I caught the name." Aislinn ripped out the words and was further irked when he gazed at her with an amused smile. "Frankly, Dougray, I am rather amazed that you were able to break away from your activities to join me tonight. You seem well acquainted with this woman, so I can only assume that you have had relations with her." Aislinn's cold frankness shocked Miriam further and there were not many who could do that.

Miriam looked at Dougray to explain what exactly was going on here for obviously she was missing something, but he was no help at all, for he was too busy laughing. "Dougray, I don't find this at all amusing." Miriam's eyes narrowed with annoyance.

"I'm…sorry." He managed between guffaws. "It's just that it's so very funny, if ye would just allow yerself to see it." When neither woman seemed to share in his mirth, he brought himself under control. "Very well then." He glanced at Aislinn who looked like she wanted to murder him. His smile widened loving that she was actually jealous. "Aislinn, may I present my sister, Miriam."

He wouldn't have wanted to miss this for the world. The color in Aislinn's face completely drained and he was sure if she could have crawled under the table and disappeared, she would have done just that.

Out of the corner of her eye, Aislinn slowly glanced at the woman Dougray had called sister. She didn't look at all pleased with her and she couldn't blame her.

"I…" She stammered not sure what she should say to make amends. "…I'm sorry that I offended you. I thought…well the way you looked at each other…I misread the look as more…." She lowered her head and closed her eyes. She was beyond embarrassed. What on earth could have made her behave so inappropriately?

"I accept yer apology." Miriam's voice was musical to the ear and very sincere. "I know my brother. Being the cad that he is, I am sure he is responsible for this seemingly awkward situation."

Aislinn showed her gratitude with a genuine smile. She was going to like Dougray's sister.

"Really, Dougray…" Miriam gave her brother a withering look. "…how could ye make yer bride think that I was yer lover?"

"Me?" His hand touched his chest right above his heart in feign innocence. "I've been wounded surely."

"I'll wound you all right." Aislinn kicked him again.

Miriam smiled. "Ye've met yer match, dear brother. We'll talk later." She lovingly kissed him on his cheek before she departed to speak to a man who was standing over to the side. He had obviously heard the whole exchange for his mouth was quirked in a smile as he gave Dougray a salute.

After the meal, the music began and Dougray looked at Aislinn with a fierce sparkling that lit his eyes. "A dance, milady."

"Uh uh. You tricked me and you didn't…." He didn't wait for her to finish her complaint. Instead he grabbed her hand and nearly dragged her from the table.

"I was not asking ye for permission. I was telling ye my plans." They had reached the dance floor and he pulled her close. "Dance," he demanded of her.

Aislinn had no idea what to do. Dance how? She didn't know the steps. Dougray didn't seem to notice and he twirled her around the floor. She began to relax, and for once, she let him lead.

Miriam sat down next to her cousin, Fiach Ó'Colmáin. The priest turned and offered her a sudden, arresting smile. "Ye make it difficult for a man of the cloth to keep to his vow of celibacy." He took her hand and graciously bestowed a welcoming kiss. The response was Miriam's rich chuckle.

"Fiach dear cousin, ye have not changed. I am still baffled how ye maintain yer oath when ye have always had a roving eye."

"Age, me love, has mellowed me. Besides the women run too fast for me to catch them now." Despite his claim at being old, there was nothing antiquated about the man. He still looked strong and attractive, as he did in his prime.

"I find that hard to believe. Ye loved to love and I still find it hard to accept that ye have put it all behind ye."

He smiled almost mischievously. "Sacrilege," he teased. "Tsk, tsk. I may have taken the vows that the church requires of me, but I am still a man, Miriam. A beautiful woman still may turn my head, but that is all. I have found peace with God's work that is more fulfilling than a woman's touch."

Miriam arched her brows. "Ye are serious?"

"Most assuredly."

"Well then I stand corrected." They sat side by side and watched the dancing couples. Dougray and Aislinn stood out among them, both so tall. Miriam took notice that Aislinn nearly matched her brother in height, making them elegantly suited as their bodies mingled closely. They indeed made an attractive couple. "Fiach, what do ye say of this woman whom my brother has taken as wife?"

He glanced at the lady in question. "She is not Ella if that is what ye are hinting."

Miriam couldn't help but laugh. "Nay, she is not. Ella was not a woman whom I would have chosen for my brother. The lady had not a brain in her pretty little head."

"Oh, but what a pretty little head she did have. I never laid eyes on a fairer woman since."

"Be careful, priest."

"Posh. Ye forget that I am not dead. I still have eyes in my head, ye know."

She ignored his little outburst. "Ella may have been a lovely face, but that was all there was to her. My brother would have tired of her soon enough." She again drew her attention to Dougray and his bride. "This wife has fire behind those dark eyes."

"Aye, that she does. Never seen such dark eyes as she possesses."

"Ye talk of her attributes, but I am referring to the intelligence and spirit of the woman."

"It is all the same in my book."

Miriam rolled her eyes revealing her annoyance. "Really, Fiach, talking to ye is like talking to a child that has yet learned tact."

The priest chuckled. "And ye, my dear, are too serious for words. Loosen up a bit and enjoy the evening. Look there...." He motioned to where Aislinn and Dougray had moved from the dance floor. "Looks as though your brother intends to retire early."

"Don't ye find their relationship odd?"

"If ye mean that he fought her and won, which I have heard was not an easy task, then aye."

"*Scathach*, the warrior woman, I have heard them call her."

"A well deserved title, I have been led to believe. Now, I for one feel a woman with that kind of energy would best be used in the...."

"Fiach, do not say another word or I will be forced to teach ye a lesson."

"Don't tell me ye still wrestle people to the ground?" he teased her, remembering how she had been as a child. When she didn't like what someone said she knocked them flat.

"Only those who are begging for it," she answered good-heartedly.

He sighed as if he had surrendered. "Then I best behave." Then on a somewhat serious note he addressed his cousin once more. "Yer brother has done well with the Hennessy match. Ye have no reason to worry. What I witnessed earlier with ye, as the brunt of the joke, was enough to convince me that she will keep him in line."

"And the Butlers? Do they still cause problems?"

"That I fear will never be resolved. Ella had been our only hope for our clans to reunite, but her death put an end to that ever happening."

"It is as I feared," she sighed. Then after a moment, she hesitantly asked what she truly wanted to know. "Does Tremain still command the Butler's men?"

"Aye."

"So the man still lives." She smiled slightly as she remembered him when he had been barely a man at all. He was strong, handsome, and his beautiful long-fingered hands that knew how to make her feel so very special.

Fiach couldn't help but notice the whimsical expression on her face. "He is not the same, Miriam."

"I don't know what ye mean." She pretended to straighten her attire, but she knew that she couldn't fool him. No one knew her feelings for Tremain better than Fiach. She had gone to him, begged him to interfere with her father's decision and then later cried on his shoulder when nothing could be done.

"Ye were not to marry him, lass."

"Maybe if it had been allowed none of this mess with the Butlers would have transpired."

"He had no lands and yer were the daughter of…"

"…a Chieftain's daughter. Ye think that I do not know this?"

"With Tremain, ye tended to forget that fact."

"So this is why I was sold to the highest bidder."

"Yer husband cared for ye."

"Aye, but the man was near seeing his sixty-fifth year and older in body. My only salvation was that he was too old to care to share my bed more than a few times, and God forgive me, his death was my salvation."

"Is this a confession, my dear?"

"How come it is convenient now that ye remember ye are a priest?" She tried to make light of her feelings.

"It wouldn't do well for ye to lose yer immortal soul," he teased her.

"Do not worry about my soul."

He placed a hand on her arm. "Ye have a fine lad," he gently reminded her.

Her face was serene, as she thought of her son Oren who was now almost fourteen years old. The only child she would ever have, and she loved him so much. "Aye, Oren has made my sacrifices tolerable."

"Is that why ye keep the boy at yer side? It is most unusual, ye know this."

"He has been fostered out for a year at a time, but he comes home every three months for schooling by the best tutors. It is the way I want it."

"I was only inquiring, my dear."

"Well, try not to be so nosey with my doings and concentrate on my brother's transgressions. He is the one who is not married in the eyes of the church."

"I intend to remedy that. Of course, Abbot Kirwan has it in his mind that it is his responsibility."

"Kirwan." Her definite frown showed her displeasure. "When I was a little girl, the man could make my hackles rise and now…" Her eyes wandered to where the abbot was seated. At that moment, the man had turned his head and caught her gaze. He smiled, or at least she thought he had before he turned away to carry on his conversation with the physician, Cahir. "…he still makes me uneasy."

"Granted, Kirwan can go overboard with his beliefs, but he is harmless."

"Do not trust the man just because he wears the same cloth. I sense a snake."

He chuckled. "I never ignore a woman's intuition. Warning heeded, cousin. Warning heeded."

The dance ended far too soon to Aislinn's liking for she was just getting the hang of it, but Dougray had other things on his mind. He had led her away from the crowd and into the corridor. "Where are we going?"

"Nowhere, Aislinn." He pressed his lips to hers as he held her close. She fought him like the devil, finally biting his lip. He released her. "What was that for?" He wiped the blood with the back of his hand.

"You have to ask? Every time I turn around, you are jumping on me."

He took a step forward and she backed up against the wall. "Did ye ever think that ye are driving me to distraction."

"That's not my intent." She swallowed the lump in her throat. He was so dangerously attractive with the scowl that penetrated his rugged features. She was about tempted to let him finish what he had started.

"Oh, I think it is yer intent and ye are bound and determined to deny yerself as well."

"You don't know what you're talking about." She looked away but his hand shot out holding her chin in the palm of his hand, forcing her to look at him. He studied her for a long time making her feel uncomfortable under his scrutinizing gaze. She wanted him to let her go, and at the same time, she wanted him to kiss her again.

"I ask ye before and I ask ye now: What do ye want from me, Aislinn?"

Didn't he realize she wanted everything? She wanted him to take her, for her body craved his touch, but the price was too great, for without love it would be meaningless. Her emotions were running high and her voice sounded choked. "I want nothing from you, but my freedom." Before he could say anything, she broke free and she fled from his sight.

Fiach finally spotted Dougray alone and he took advantage of the moment. Many of the guests had retired for the evening, but still there were others who would continue on throughout the night. Dougray had seen to the preparations, so that no one left Dunhaven without having his fill. No one would ever say that a Fitzpatrick was not generous.

"I am quite surprised, dear cousin, that ye are still up and about. Have ye tired so soon of yer wife that ye have already left her bed?" Fiach saw Dougray frown before he could conceal it behind a chuckle.

"I have guests to tend to or have ye forgotten that?" He moved over so that Fiach could take a seat. The priest handed him a tankard seeing immediately that the man was in dire need of a drink.

"I trust ye have had all that ye need, Fiach?"

"Aye, rest assured I have not been neglected."

They sat together enjoying their drink and company. No words were needed. It had always been that way with them, and though years had separated them, nothing had changed.

"Pardon me for saying," Fiach waited for Dougray to look at him before he continued, "the lass ye have taken to wed, she is most unusual. Is it correct to say that ye won her in a fight of wills?"

"A fair fight, I assure ye."

"She is a woman. How fair could it have been?" Fiach was still at a loss how this could have taken place. It was true that Aislinn was large in stature, but surely she could not have been strong enough to battle a seasoned man.

"Aislinn is very talented in techniques that are new to us. She may not have the bulk of a warrior, but she makes up with her ability to spot weakness, and she is quick. I have never seen someone move the way that she can. She is able to toss a man that weighs twice the amount that she does, and with such ease that ye would think they weighed no more than a feather."

"And yet ye were able to best her?"

Dougray chuckled remembering her face when he had pinned her to the ground. "That, Fiach, was luck. Let me just say that I distracted her from her purpose."

The priest raised a brow. "Ye did now? Why would ye do such an act when it was said ye wanted her married and gone from yer keep? This does have me baffled. What exactly changed yer mind?"

"Simply that I decided that I did not want her to leave."

"Ye changed yer mind, did ye? So Dubhdara O'Malley did not have a say in the matter?"

"He was not opposed to the union."

"And the Hennessy?"

"I found Aislinn's uncle quite cooperative, especially when I explained that it was Aislinn who had set up the stipulations. She knew the consequences and she took the challenge willingly."

"And the marriage was done the ancient way?"

Dougray took a long sip from his cup before he answered, "Is this a lecture, Fiach? Will ye say that my soul will be damned?"

Fiach just laughed at the seriousness of his cousin's question. "Yer soul was in danger long before ye wed the young lass. I was only curious."

Dougray sighed. "It was not my wish to have it done this way, but it was the only way that the Hennessy would agree to the union. Ye see, he had not been informed of the arrangements before hand and he felt a certain obligation toward his niece, since her father could not be present."

"I understand everything up to this point, but still I am not sure I understand why ye are down here drinking when ye should be upstairs with yer wife."

Dougray thought about not explaining, but then it would do him well to confide in someone. Who better than a priest? "She is not in agreement with this union. She feels that I tricked her in some way and will not see it otherwise."

"This was not so then?"

"Of course not." He seemed a little defensive to Fiach, but years of being a priest had taught him patience. He waited until Dougray decided to continue. "I played her game and I won. It is her pride that has been sorely tested. Ye see she had been confident that she would be the victor."

"She had no wish to marry ye?"

"She had no wish to marry anyone."

"Really? She had a wish to enter the convent?"

This caused Dougray to laugh. "*Dar Dia*! The woman would be kicked out the moment she arrived. Nay, it is more complicated than that. She has the notion that marriage should be one of love."

Fiach seemed to be considering this for a moment before he chose just the right words. "It is not always a top priority, but it has been known to happen on occasion."

"Ye surprise me, cousin. Are ye now the romantic?"

"Hardly. I only tell ye that it has been something I have witnessed. Yer parents for one. Ye must remember this."

"Aye. My father would have a way of looking at my mother and I swear she would blush as though he had caressed her. It was a silent communication that only they understood. An envious relationship, but not one that can be easily duplicated."

"Nay? So it was not that way with ye and Ella?"

"I loved her, but...."

"Ye have comparison now to know the difference?" Fiach questioned.

Dougray brows arched. "What are ye saying?"

"Have ye found love with the *Scathach*?"

"Love is a complicated emotion and obviously I have yet to figure it out. I will tell ye this: I care for the lass and cannot fathom the idea of not having her at my side."

"Ye no doubt told her this?" When Dougray chose to study his drink and not answer him, Fiach was good enough to repeat the question for him. "Ye have spoke of yer devotion?"

"She must know it. I do not see the need to voice it to her."

Fiach chuckled. "Oh, dear lad, do ye not know the ways of a lass? Women love to hear that they are wanted."

"And how is it, priest, that ye are worldly of these matters?"

"Aah, again the assumption that because I wear the robes that I have ceased to be a man. For shame, Dougray, ye need to find yer way up those stairs and speak openly, as ye have done to me just now."

"I would if it would make a difference, but as I told ye before she wants to be in love before she gives herself willingly. My cold bed is proof enough that she does not feel these affections toward me."

Chapter Forty-Six

As soon as Aislinn was dressed, she located Teige so that he could escort her to Rhiannon and Padrig's home. She was anxious to pick up Declan and bring him back to the castle.

The boy still had not spoken a single word, but he was starting to show signs of healing. He may not verbally answer her, but he was aware of what she was saying. At times, he would even nod his head in response. She had told him that she would pick him up a few days after the wedding, and she did not want to break that promise for fear he might worry that she had abandoned him.

Declan must have been watching for her arrival for he ran out of the house to greet her, his blond hair flying back away from his forehead. Aislinn scooped up the little boy with open arms and swung him around. "Oh, Declan, how I missed you."

The boy's embrace became tighter indicating he returned the same sentiment. Aislinn raised her gaze to see Rhiannon smiling in the doorway.

Dougray already had a hunch where Aislinn had gone, and as soon as he had the opportunity, he headed over to the old thatched home. She was so busy with the child and talking to Rhiannon that, for a moment, he had the pleasure of just watching her. She was so patient with the lad, even when for no apparent reason, Declan decided to jump on her back. She just laughed and pulled the naughty little boy onto her lap tickling him until he was giggling.

Dougray moved forward. It was his shadow falling across her that brought her attention to him.

"Good day, milord." Rhiannon had risen. "I must check on the bread." She already knew by what Aislinn had revealed to her that the two of them needed to talk. "Come with me, Declan." The boy hesitated, but once Aislinn gave him a quick hug and a tender push, he followed Rhiannon into the house. Aislinn stood up.

"Will ye walk with me?" he asked her and she nodded. They started forward and Dougray motioned to Teige that he need not follow. "Ye are a natural with children, Aislinn."

"A compliment?"

He looked at her. "Aislinn…" Why of late was talking to her so difficult? He gently took her arm and stopped her from going further. "Ye would make a good mother."

"I am not so sure about that. Mothering requires a lot of patience and commitment. Not my better qualities I'm afraid."

"I see differently. The children adore ye. Young Declan would not have come so far if ye had not shown such compassion toward the lad." Aislinn just shrugged wondering where all this was leading. Her eyes took in Dougray's appearance. His dark hair curled at the ends and she could see that it was still wet, indicating he must have bathed before he set out to find her. His mustache was trimmed back leaving his mouth visible to her eyes. She was mesmerized over those full lips that had kissed her so lovingly. As she remembered his touch, she felt a tingling all the way to the pit of her stomach. She couldn't deny that she felt this draw toward him, more so than she wished it to be, but it would be dangerous for her to lose sight of the situation. He was a sixteenth century lord and she was….

"What did you say?" She only caught the last few words and they were enough to startle her back to reality. He was good enough to repeat the statement.

"I could give ye children of yer own."

"That is what I thought you said." She tried to walk away, but he took a hold of her shoulders making her look at him.

"Ye told me that ye want to be in love. I ask ye now if ye would even recognize it?" Her hesitation pushed him forward. "Ye do not detest my company, do ye?"

"No," she said slowly.

"I will try my best to make ye happy, Aislinn."

"By giving me children?"

"If that is yer desire?"

He just did not get it. Giving herself to him was frightening enough, but the idea of being a mother on top of that scared her to death. She was about to tell him exactly that. But when she lifted her gaze to meet his, she found herself lost within the clear silvery depths of his eyes, pleading eyes, hopeful eyes. The only thing that held her back from throwing herself at him was her own stubborn convictions and she wouldn't compromise them, not now, and no matter how compelling her attraction was to him. "I cannot be a mother. I don't want to be one." She pulled away from him and walked back to Rhiannon's leaving him confused.

He saw the way she had looked at him, and he was sure that she wanted to give in to the obvious passions that they both shared, but for some reason she always chose to shy away. "Love," he muttered under his breath. He watched Aislinn pick up Declan as though he was her own child. She declared she did not want to be a mother, and yet she gladly took on the roll for the young lad. The woman was a walking contradiction.

Lady Miriam had run into Moira, who was taking Declan up for his nap. She was good enough to inform her that she could find Aislinn in the library. Aislinn looked so comfortable there, wearing her unusual clothing and preoccupied with her writing, that she almost didn't want to interrupt. Curiosity won out for she wished to know a little about the woman whom her brother had challenged.

Aislinn looked up from her writing as Miriam pulled up a chair next to the desk. She smiled warmly. "I do hope that I am not intruding."

"No, not at all." She put down the quill. Leaning back in her chair, she smiled back at Miriam. Dougray's sister was a beautiful woman with classic features with her hair, a luminous buttercup yellow, fair skin and baby-blue eyes framed with long, dark lashes. The only resemblance she held to her brother was her quick easy smile and the way she raised her beautifully shaped brows. "Did you manage to find something to eat?" Aislinn opened the conversation.

"Aye. The food was wonderful. I should really have yer cook give mine some helpful hints."

"Roth does have a special touch. I don't believe that he has made anything that didn't taste absolutely mouth watering."

Miriam leaned forward and rested her chin on her hand. She wore a bemused smile on her lips, for she found that she liked that Aislinn was on first name basis with the help. "Is it really true that ye fought my brother in a tournament of sorts?"

Aislinn's face flushed pink with embarrassment for here before her was a woman with such refined grace and elegance making her seem nothing more than a street urchin in comparison. She wished now that she had at least donned a gown this morning, instead of throwing on her homemade pants and her reliable blue sweatshirt. She lifted her hand to smooth down her hair, hoping it wasn't sticking up in places. "I'm afraid that it is true."

"Ye are a tall lass, but my brother is taller still. Were ye much of a match for him?"

"I believe I gave him some competition." There was a slight edge in her voice causing Miriam's eyes to crinkle with amusement. Aislinn relaxed then for she realized the woman wasn't trying to find fault with her. She was only interested in hearing the story. Aislinn leaned forward on the desk. "Dougray actually distracted me and that was how he won."

"And is the rumor true that ye fought others before him?"

"Guilty as charged."

"But why would ye go to all this trouble?"

"I had no wish to marry and your brother insisted that I must." A frown set into her features, causing Miriam to suppress a giggle.

"Dougray can be so stubborn when he wants his way. Obviously, my dear, he wanted ye direly to have fought for ye."

"I think he wanted to teach me a lesson."

"Maybe so, but he married ye and I thought that he would never attempt marriage again." As soon as she saw the flash of surprised confusion penetrate Aislinn's features, she knew that she had said too much. "I am sorry. Didn't ye know that Dougray was married once before?"

"No. He failed to mention that little tidbit."

"Oh, please do not be angry. It is difficult for Dougray to speak of Ella."

"Ella!" She nearly flew out of her seat. "That scum. Do you know he still thinks about her?"

Miriam was baffled why Aislinn was so upset, but she tried to calm her. "I am sure that he would think of her now and again, but ye need not be so upset."

"And why not?" Her dark eyes blazed at Miriam as if she were dense.

"It would be a waste of your time to be jealous of the dead."

Aislinn's mouth dropped open and the color drained from her face. "Ella is dead?"

"Ye didn't know?"

"No. He never told me. He spoke out her name when he was sleeping. I asked him about her but he told me to mind my own business."

"Well I never." Miriam was perturbed with her brother's lack of grace. "He should have told ye. Ella was a Butler and her death has caused the petty clan war to rage across the land again."

"So that was what Dougray meant when he said that Fingham Butler would not forgive him for something that was beyond his control." It all made sense now.

"It is a sorry situation, I fear." She studied Aislinn as her features changed from one emotion to another. There was compassion now that she understood the circumstances. "Ye will not hold this against Dougray?"

"No." She took her seat again. "I just wish that he would have told me."

"Be patient with my brother; he will come around." She paused for a moment trying to think of how she was going to word her next question, but decided on being blunt and to the point. She didn't want to waste time on formalities and she sensed that Aislinn was one who appreciated frankness. "Are ye in love with my brother?"

Her eyes widened in surprise and she again came to her feet. She was silent for so long that Miriam didn't think that she was going to answer her, but then she faced her with a timid smile. "I care for Dougray and maybe even would call him a good friend, that is when he's not trying to piss me off. Love though?" She took a deep breath and let it out again. "I am still trying to work that one out."

"I think, then, not all is lost. Friendship is a good place to start. I knew right away I detested my husband, and till the day he died, I held fast to that conviction."

"Wow."

"Do I shock ye?"

"Maybe a little but I admire your honesty. So you are a widow?"

"Aye, and glad for it. My heart belongs to another whom I cannot be with."

"You're in love with someone else?"

"Forever."

"Doesn't he return your love?"

Miriam's face clouded with uncertainty. "He did a long time ago. He was hurt terribly when I was forced into my marriage with Sir Reynolds."

"But it wasn't your fault."

"It doesn't matter." She sighed.

"It should. Maybe now you could contact him. Let him know…." Seeing Miriam's stricken expression made her stop. "I'm sorry. I shouldn't have…."

"Nay, ye may have a point, but many would not like it and it could be dangerous."

"Dangerous? Why?"

She held Aislinn's gaze debating if she could trust her. In the end, she did. "My heart belongs to Tremain Butler."

"He's not related to the enemy, is he?" already knowing the answer.

"Fingham Butler is an enemy because he makes it so. Tremain is his nephew, and if he is as I remember him, he would never harm me."

"But you don't know that for sure now."

She shook her head, her plaited hair falling over her right shoulder. "Nay, I do not know, and I cannot risk it for I have a son that depends on me still."

"Is he here at Dunhaven?"

"He was not back from his training. He is being fostered by the O'Flahertys. It is agreed that he comes home every three months to continue with his studies and this enables us to spend time together."

"What's his name?"

"Oren and he has seen ten and four summers now. He's nearly as tall as Dougray and fine boned. Quite handsome, if I should say so myself."

"You must have been very young when you had Oren."

Her smile showed how very pleased she was with that compliment. "I was young and reckless when I became pregnant with Oren, but I don't regret it in the least. Tremain would have been proud."

"Tremain's son?"

She nodded. "He doesn't know. My father and grandfather forbade me to tell him by threat of death."

"They would kill you?"

She chuckled. "Nay not I, Tremain."

"Oh…oh how horrible."

"It had to be done. After so many years, I have come to terms with it." She smiled. "Now how did we come speak of such matters that I have not spoken of in fifteen years? Ye are indeed easy to converse with. I feel that I have known ye forever."

"I think that is the best compliment anyone has ever given me."

They smiled, each pleased that they had found a new friend. "Would ye care to continue our conversation outdoors? It looks like the weather will hold."

"I would love to." Aislinn put her journal away in her backpack. She looked up to see Miriam was waiting for her at the door. When she walked over to her, Miriam placed a delicate hand on her forearm.

"I hope that ye will find love with Dougray. He's a good man, Aislinn, and I am gladdened to know he has ye." She put her arms around her in a sisterly hug and Aislinn returned the gesture.

"Well I see the two of ye are becoming well acquainted." They parted to see Dougray standing there watching them. He wore a rust-colored tunic with beige and a blue tinge shirt that made his gray eyes look like silvery smoke. He looked quite impressive with his more adopted English style, not that the more rugged look didn't suit him.

Aislinn glanced down at her attire feeling particularly underdressed. "Before we go for our walk, I think I will change if you don't mind."

"Not at all." Miriam smiled. "I would like to fetch my wrap just in case the weather should decide to turn on us." She then turned her attention to her brother. She placed a hand on his arm. "Ye have a rare gem. Be sure ye treasure her." She ignored her brother's raised brow and gave him a quick peck on the cheek before she moved down the hall.

Dougray turned his attention to Aislinn. "What have ye two been talking about?"

"Oh this and that." Her grin told him that he wasn't going to pry any information out of her.

"I see. Well, my rare gem, let me escort ye back to yer room." How he hated to say her room when she should be in *his*. He bit his tongue though as he linked his arm around her. "I do have to say that I am a bit jealous."

"Jealous?"

"My sister converses with ye for a small space of time and ye hug each other like ye are family. While I, who have taken to handfast with ye, have yet to make…."

"Don't say it, Dougray."

He sighed heavily. "What may I do to have ye throw yer arms around me?"

"If you wouldn't ask for more than I am willing to give you, I would not hesitate to hug."

He opened the door to her room and followed her in closing it behind him. "All right then."

"All right what?"

"I accept. I would like a good morning hug. No expectations." He saw her wary look and he chuckled. "I promise."

It was a harmless request, after all. Hugging was for family and friends. Dougray surely qualified for both. "All right. One hug, then you have to leave." She walked over to him and nonchalantly placed her arms around his neck, pressing her body against his hard chest for what she thought would be a platonic embrace.

Dougray closed his eyes and hesitantly placed his hands on the small of her back. When she didn't protest, his hold on her tightened. He had made a grave error in suggesting a hug, for having her body pressed against his was beyond torturous. "*Dar Dia!*"

"What's wrong?" She leaned her head back to look at him, their lips so close that their breath mingled as one.

"I should let ye go before I forget my promise so soon." But he didn't release her and she found that she had no desire to back away. "Aislinn?" He said her name as though he was suffering. She felt his subtle movement and she closed her eyes as his lips pressed against hers gently covering her mouth, bestowing a slow drugging kiss that sang through her veins from the top of her head to the tip of her toes. She felt herself falling and unable to stop herself.

Trying to temper his passion, he raised his mouth from hers, only to be drawn to kiss the pulsing hollow at the base of her throat. He then returned to brush her lips like a whisper.

"Dougray, I…" He didn't let her finish for his mouth had descended once more showering her with a series of slow, shivery caresses. He raised his hand to gently outline the circle of her breast. She moaned against his mouth sending his senses reeling. He wanted her. He could feel that she wanted him too.

"Aislinn, I don't want to stop."

"I…don't…I…."

"Do ye want me to stop?" His lips came coaxingly down on hers, kissing her again and again.

"No…" she said against his mouth. "I mean yes."

"Which is it, Aislinn?" He pressed against her.

"Aislinn, are ye ready?" Hearing Miriam's voice brought her hurdling back to reality in one breathless sweep.

"Nay." Dougray tried to hold on to her, but she broke free, still gazing at him, her breathing labored. She lifted her trembling hand to smooth back her hair.

"Aislinn?" Miriam knocked on the door.

"I'll be but a moment. I'll meet you downstairs, okay?"

"All right."

Dougray let out a groan, his eyes pleading for her not to go. "Why do ye do this?

"You promised," her voice choked.

He cursed under his breath, and ran his hand through his hair. Slowly he nodded his head. "So I did."

"You're not angry are you?"

"Nay." He was sexually frustrated, but he kept that to himself. "Go."

She made her feet move toward the door. "Aislinn?" She turned to him. "What do ye feel when we kiss?"

"I feel like I'm losing myself." She smiled meekly, surprised at her own honesty.

"That is a good thing. Have ye never experience passion before?"

"You know I have never had...."

"I don't mean coupling. I'm talking about passion, like what we felt a moment ago?"

"No, not like that. Never like that."

His mouth spread slowly into a grin.

"Good Lord, Dougray, don't look at me like that. It makes me think ye are going to devour me."

"I just might. Come here before ye go."

"No."

"Scared?"

"Don't be ridiculous."

"Then come here...please."

She walked over to him, careful about keeping a safe distance. He chuckled and his hand snaked out causing her to gasp as he pulled her to him. He cupped his hand below her chin before he lowered his mouth to hers. She drank in the sweetness of his kiss. It was like a drug and she wanted more, so much more, but he raised his mouth from hers. "I like the way ye kiss, lass. Ye make me lose myself too." He then kissed the tip of her nose. "Ye better go now."

She blinked trying to remember where she was supposed to be.

"Miriam's waiting?"

"Yeah...oh yeah." She reluctantly moved away from his arms.

"Aislinn?"

"Hmm?" She looked at him.

"Will ye be willing to kiss again? No more I promise." His eyes held a mischievous glint and it made her laugh.

"Maybe." Then she was out the door.

Miriam was down below waiting. She was beginning to think that Aislinn wasn't going to show, but then she came galloping down the stairs. She was a bit baffled to see that she was wearing exactly what she had been wearing earlier. "I thought ye were going to change?"

Aislinn dropped her gaze to her sweatshirt, as though she couldn't believe it. From her neck to her hairline she flushed pink with embarrassment. "I guess I changed my mind," she lied miserably.

Miriam smiled and linked her arm with hers. "Did my brother distract ye again?" She nudged her and Aislinn burst out with a laugh.

"It was something like that."

Chapter Forty-Seven

It was time to say farewell to the many guests who had stayed at Dunhaven. It was a teary good-bye for Aislinn and Miriam, but they promised to write often. Dougray pledged that in a few months, when he made his visit to Dublin to speak business with Aislinn's uncle, that he would take her with him. On the way back home, they would make it a point to stop by Miriam's for a long visit.

Miriam had left with her escort along with Aengus Hennessy and his garrison hours ago and now Dubhdara O'Malley and Robert Burke were packed and readied for their journey home.

"For now Robert and I can only spare the men we have left behind and I will send others in a few months' time."

"I am grateful for yer generosity, Dubhdara."

"Good then. We will meet again soon and…" Dubhdara's gaze wandered over to where Aislinn was conversing with his daughter. "I wish ye the best of luck with yer new bride." He chuckled and shook his head. "She will be a handful, I wager."

"Already has proven to be that. And I wouldn't chuckle too loudly. Aislinn seems to be giving yer daughter some advice."

"Ach! And me wife will have an earful for me on that account. She already feels Grania possesses too free a spirit."

"I will miss ye." Grania did not care that others were watching and she threw her arms around Aislinn.

"I will miss you too, Grania. You'll remember my words?"

She pulled away and looked up at her with admiration. "Aye. I will stand tall and keep my wits about me. The sea will be my making, as long as I respect it and respect all who will follow me." Some of this seemed strange to the little girl, but she would heed the words.

"You will do well for Ireland, Grania. Do not despair when you think you are alone. You are strong and you will endure."

"I will find happiness then?"

Aislinn hesitated to answer her for there had not been very much recorded about her personal life. She finally left her with words that would be wise for anyone to follow. "Grania, we make our own happiness. Remember that and you will do fine. Not everything may work out to your expectations and there will be times that you'll make mistakes, but you must learn from them. If you do, then you will have the chance to relish in your triumphs."

Grania's thoughts weighed heavily, but she nodded and she again hugged Aislinn. "I will remember."

Aislinn stayed until she could no longer see the tall, brave girl standing at the bow of her father's ship.

Chapter Forty-Eight

Dougray was seated with Fiach and Murrough in the hall. The discussion was once again on how they would better their defenses against the Butler attacks in the south. With the extra garrison at their disposal, they should be able to cover a considerable amount of territory.

Dougray swirled the honey wine around in his goblet before he lifted it to his lips, quenching his thirst. Over the rim, he spotted Moira hurrying toward him with obvious intent. He placed the goblet down on the table. It wasn't often that Moira sought out his audience, since he was well aware that he intimidated her.

She reached him and smiled broadly before she curtsied before him. "Milord, forgive me." She curtsied again. "Milady A.J. wishes ye to see the miracle."

"Miracle?" Abbot Kirwan craned his neck. "What miracle and why was I not informed?"

Moira had not seen the abbot approaching. If she had, she would have waited for him to make his leave. She was apprehensive with her lord, but the abbot had a way of making her feel like she had committed a grave sin for just being alive. "Aye, it is a miracle," she answered him timidly. "Declan is no longer fairy taken. The lad speaks."

"I must be witness to this," Abbot Kirwan insisted indicating he would not take no for an answer.

Murrough glanced at Dougray as the abbot nearly jogged his way to the stairs. "Maybe Declan will be able to shed some light on his attacker."

"Perhaps, but I do not wish to push the matter. The lad's health comes first."

Fiach nodded. "Come, I for one do not want to be left out on a miracle, and if Kirwan is so interested, I venture that I should at least be there to make comment."

By the time the three reached the room, the boy was screaming hysterically, and was huddled against Aislinn clutching his arms around her neck.

"What has happened?" Dougray frowned as he witnessed Declan's heaving shoulders. He was holding onto Aislinn so tightly that his small hands had turned white.

"I don't know." She looked up at him while trying to calm the frightened child. "He was talking to me, telling me things about his home when, all of a sudden, he began to scream in terror." Declan was indeed loud in his protests.

"All out!" Dougray ordered.

"I think that I should stay. The lad may be possessed," Kirwan insisted only to have Dougray glower at him.

"Possessed? The child was a victim to the worst kind of injustice. Be gone, Kirwan, before I forget that ye are of the holy realm."

The abbot was lost for words. Never had he expected to be dismissed so abruptly. He sent a lethal glare at Aislinn before he turned on his heels, bumping his shoulder into Fiach without so much as a "pardon me," as he retreated.

Murrough was the last to leave and he closed the doors behind him.

After about fifteen minutes of wailing, the child's sobs finally turned to silence. "What has happened?" Dougray stopped his pacing. "Should I call for Cahir?"

"There's no need for the physician. Declan has simply exhausted himself." She rose to lay the child down upon the bed, but Dougray stepped forward to relieve her of her small burden. He looked down at the sleeping child, whose face was streaked with tears. Aislinn placed a gentle kiss on the boy's forehead. She looked up to see Dougray gazing at her curiously.

Once he put Declan to bed, he went back to speak with her.

"I don't know what happen." She rubbed her forehead trying to piece together why Declan had become so distressed. "Maybe I pushed him too hard." She was the one pacing now and he walked over to her and took her in his arms.

"It is not yer fault. Declan may never be...."

"Don't say it!" She pulled away from him. "I won't believe it. He was fine. He was."

He just nodded his head. "I'm sure he will fine tomorrow. He will most likely rest now. Will ye join me tonight for dinner?"

"I should stay. I don't want Declan to be frightened if he wakes up and finds that I am not here."

Dougray pursed his lips together and studied her for a long moment. It bothered him that she had become so preoccupied with the lad. "Ye know that ye cannot keep him." He should have never allowed her to care for the boy. She was becoming too attached.

"You could foster him. I know you do those kinds of things." The pleading in her voice was hard to ignore. She wanted Declan for her own.

"I am not in the habit of...."

"He needs special care." She grabbed hold of his arm. "I have never asked you for anything, but I am now. Please don't send him away."

"And if I grant ye this request, what will ye do for me, Aislinn?" His voice was calm, his gaze steady. She let go of his arm and moved away, before she allowed herself to speak.

"What do ye want?"

"I think that ye know." His left brow lifted as he waited for her to reply.

"But that is...."

"Unfair?" he finished for her. "Perhaps, but so is it wrongful when a wife denies her husband?" He waited for her to acknowledge his request, but her silence seemed to say it all.

She had given him glimpses of her passion, a stolen kisses here, a hug there, but he was tired of the dance they were partaking in. He wanted more. He needed more. "I see that ye must think on it." Disappointed, he turned away and left the room.

Aislinn awoke to a cold, lonely room and her heart was weighed heavily. Last night Declan had stirred from his exhausted slumber. He spoke again and did not seem to remember that he had gone into hysterics. She had no explanation for the sudden change and she feared that there might be other episodes. She couldn't let Declan be sent away, but Dougray would not let him stay unless she gave herself to him.

She sat up in bed and noticed that the fire had nearly died out in the fireplace. Reluctant to move from what little warmth that she felt to revive the fire, she pulled the covers under her chin, but still, she could not get completely comfortable. With exasperation, she threw her covers off and made a mad dash over to the hearth. She threw another peat to the smoldering remains, poking it with the long fire iron. In a few seconds the wood caught hold of the embers and the fire began to blaze. Slowly the coldness melted away from her limbs as again thoughts of last night crept into her consciousness. What was she to do with Dougray Fitzpatrick? It wouldn't be that difficult to give into the passion. She wasn't sure if she was in love with him, but she did care for him. It didn't look like she was going home anytime soon, so she just might as well make a life here with him. "He is my husband."

"Aye, that I am…" Aislinn whirled around to see Dougray standing there. For such a large man, he could move with such reticence. "…even if it's only in name," he finished.

"Dougray."

"Do ye have another husband that I am not aware of?"

She couldn't miss the terseness of his response. "No, of course not."

"I've come to bid ye farewell."

She turned sharply. "Farewell?"

"Do not fret, my sweet. I will return to ye, and I expect ye to give me a better welcoming than ye have given me thus far."

His meaning was evident and she did not care to be threatened. "Do not worry, you will receive the welcoming that you deserve and no more."

He sighed. "I have been patient with ye, Aislinn, more so than I need be." With that he turned away leaving her to think upon his words.

Chapter Forty-Nine

Tremain headed the raid, blond hair flying behind him as he reared his mount into motion. They had rounded up thirty heads of cattle by the time Dougray and his men came upon them. The fight broke out immediately sending the herd swarming in confusion, desperate to be free of the battling men.

Fitzpatrick's men couldn't help but notice that their lord fought almost recklessly, purposely putting himself in direct danger when it could have been easily avoided.

Murrough was close enough to Cormac to issue an order. "Tell Dermot to head around to the left flank. If Dougray keeps this up, Tremain will have his men surround him and take him prisoner."

"He fights as if he is trying to get himself killed."

"Ye don't think I know this? Move before he succeeds in this matter." Murrough raised his sword and charged forward. He was seething with anger, for he knew that the dark-haired woman whom his friend had married was somehow responsible for this hell-bent behavior.

The day was a blur to Dougray, as he fought to forget his troubled marriage. He didn't know why he wanted Aislinn so badly. He wanted every bit of her, her heart, and her soul. He was obsessed with the need of her and she shunned him without a thought. Her heart was made of ice, at least when it came to him.

He could have easily bedded her and been done with it, but she would have hated him for it and he would have been unable to forgive himself.

Again he defended himself with a blow that sent a sword from his attacker's hand. He turned around deflecting another attack, but before he could recover, another was upon him. He let out a loud cry as he felt the blade pierce his skin.

Aislinn held Declan as she paced the hall. She had tried to remain calm, but the word had already reached them that Dougray had fallen. When questioned no one was sure how bad his wounds were, only that he was alive.

"He is a strong man." Rhiannon walked over to her, offering to take the child from her arms.

She looked at the fair-haired beauty that was Murrough's woman and wondered how she could stand there so calm when the man whom she loved was out there too. "I know that he's capable, but still he is not invincible."

"Nay, but he does have good men to back him up."

"Murrough?" Aislinn knew that Dougray trusted him, but she had found no reason to actually like the man. He had a way of looking at her that made her feel unwelcome.

"Among others," Rhiannon added.

"I know." A tremendous amount of guilt lay heavy on her shoulders. Dougray had left the keep disappointed, maybe even a little angry with her. He needed to be alert when he went into battle and without distractions.

She didn't want to fight anymore but she didn't know how to take the steps to repair the damage. If truth be known, he scared her. He demanded of her something that no other man had ever done before. He wanted her to need him and she was afraid to let herself feel that vulnerable. It spoke of weakness and she saw it as a defect, a failing in some way.

"Sometimes it helps to talk." Rhiannon hoped to be of some comfort. She could tell that the woman was hurting and she knew that it was more than just the worry of how Dougray fared.

"We argued before he left…" She reached out and caressed Declan's face.

"If ye are thinking that ye are at fault somehow, ye can forget it this moment. Milord has seen fighting before ye ever came to live here. He is a seasoned warrior."

"What if he…." She couldn't finish it. "I need to speak to him to tell him…."

At that moment, she heard the announcement that they had arrived. She saw the physician Cahir Dunphy hurrying by. When she saw that Abbot Kirwan and Father Fiach followed, she became panicked. "I must go to him." But she hesitated for she had Declan with her.

"Do not worry." Rhiannon knew her concern. "I will care for the lad. Now go."

"Thank you, Rhiannon."

"Where is he?" Aislinn pushed her way past the guards that barred the door. Finally her eyes rested on him. A flood of relief rushed over her when she saw that he was sitting up on his own accord. Surely the wound couldn't be all that bad.

The physician Cahir chose that moment to move to the side revealing the horribly gaping slash that ran the length of his right side. She couldn't help but gasp, making both the physician and Dougray turn to look at her. Dougray's eyes narrowed and she faltered for just a moment. She had come this far and had no intentions of leaving until she knew he was going to be all right.

"They said you were injured." She caught herself glancing uneasily over the exposed raw flesh.

Dougray was in pain and he failed to hear Aislinn's concern. He growled out his response causing everyone present to flinch. "Did ye come here to see if the wound was fatal? Mark my words, I have no intention of leaving this world without a fight. So don't think ye'll get out of our marriage all too soon."

Aislinn was on the verge of snapping out a retort, but fell silent when her eyes once more fell to the gaping wound. She cringed thinking how very close he came to losing his life. She covered the distanced that separated them, not caring that he was glaring at her with distrust. She would humble herself if she had to. She was not going to let him chase her away. "You hurt my feelings. I simply was concerned."

"Concerned?" His brows rose slightly.

She took a closer look at the wound and she had to take a deep breath to steady herself. This slice by no means was anywhere near a flesh wound. It looked like his skin had been flayed away to expose bone. She looked at Cahir hoping to God that he was a competent physician. "Have you disinfected the area?"

A look passed between Cahir and Dougray that clearly indicated that they had no idea what she was asking. She realized immediately that she needed to take control. She was not going to lose Dougray over an infection that could have easily been avoided. She looked at the wound once more. She swallowed the lump in her throat. At least, she hoped it could be avoided. "I'll need some hot water, clean cloth and…" It probably needed to be stitched but it looked like dirt and who knows what else was embedded in the flesh; it would be better if it were left open. "…bring some wine, too."

The physician looked at Dougray and he nodded. "Do as she says; I could use a drink."

Cahir ordered one of the men to fetch what was needed. When the wine was handed to Aislinn, Dougray held out his hand to accept it from her, but instead she promptly doused the raw flesh. Dougray nearly hit the ceiling as he came to his feet with a death-curdling bellow. Fiach stood thinking he might have to intervene on Aislinn's behalf for his cousin had murder in his eyes.

"What the bloody hell are ye doing? Are ye tryin' to finish me off then?"

Aislinn knew she couldn't back down now, even if he was like a wounded bear ready to kill. "The wine will help fight the infection. It had to be done. So stop your roaring and sit down." He pointed his finger at her and opened his mouth to say something but she had moved forward, looking him square in the eye. "I said sit down!" Her voice rose, demanding her request. Everyone in the room seemed to be holding their breath, waiting for Dougray to vent his wrath, but to their surprise, he quietly and simply took his seat. Aislinn sighed in relief. "Really, Dougray." She shook her head, gaining some confidence now that he hadn't strangled her to death. "I can't believe you would wince over a little spilt wine."

"That hurt," he growled.

"And the sword slicing through your flesh did not?" She took the rag that Cahir handed her and dipped into the warm water.

"It was a battle ax," he corrected.

Aislinn eyes darted sharply to his face. "Dear God." She put her hand over his. "They meant to kill you."

He was astonished to realize she was genuinely concerned. He put his large hand over hers. "That is why I worry so when ye wander far from the grounds."

No one missed the tender exchange that seemed to pass between the two. When Dougray realized his men were staring, he quickly pulled his hand away. "Aislinn, ye best leave now so Cahir can tend to me."

"I can bandage you just as well." She refused to be sent away and Dougray noted the determined look in her eyes.

"Milord, if I may…" Abbot Kirwan began only to be interrupted.

"Ye heard my wife. She will tend to me. He waved his hand to dismiss the men around him, but Cahir couldn't believe that he meant for him to go too.

Aislinn eyes challenged the physician. "All of you." She swept her hand around the room. "Leave your lord so that he may rest."

Kirwan's beady eyes narrowed almost disappearing into his pudgy face. Fiach took hold of his arm. "Come now, it is for the best." Fiach thought that he might have to drag the abbot from the room, but finally he turned and left on his own accord.

Dougray watched Aislinn closely as she took care to clean his other wounds. She was biting her lower lip and her hands were trembling. "Aislinn?"

Glimmering with unshed tears, her dark eyes met his.

"It takes more than this to do a Fitzpatrick in. I'll be all right, lass."

She gave him a nervous chuckle and a weak smile. "Shouldn't I be telling you that?"

He laughed only to regret it. He closed his eyes, grimacing in pain. She immediately put her arm around him fearing he might topple over.

"Ye best help me to the bed." He had tried to remain unfaltering, but his strength was quickly ebbing away and he refused to pass out at her feet.

Carrying most of his weight, she helped him into bed pulling the covers up under his chin.

"Ye will stay?" He reached for her and she took hold of his hand in a fierce grip.

"You couldn't force me away."

"Aye, *Scathach*, I was hoping ye would say that."

Within minutes, he had fallen into a restless sleep. She watched over him, constantly checking his pulse. She wasn't sure why she was doing it, but it seemed like something she should monitor. It gave her great comfort that she could feel his strong heartbeat beneath her touch.

The first day he awoke to drink and to eat some broth, but by the second day he was feverish and racked with chills.

Hours would pass without him opening his eyes. Aislinn watched helplessly as he tossed and turned, sweat pouring down his face. She would sleep only when Rhiannon would come to relieve her and force her to go back to her own room, but she would never sleep for very long and would hurry back to his side. Again and again, she'd dampened his brow with cool water, but still his skin burned with fever. Dread filled her. She was losing him and there was nothing that she could do about it.

In his agitated state, Dougray grabbed hold of her arm and his eyes opened, pinning her with a fierce look. "Who are ye? Why have ye come?"

"It is I, Dougray, Aislinn." One minute he would know her and the next he would demand to know why she was there. He would change back and forth from English to Gaelic and sometimes in mid-sentence making it hard to follow what he wanted. "Just rest. You need to rest."

"Aislinn?" his voice softened and his hand caressed her cheek.

"Yes. I'm here." Her eyes filled with tears. "You have to rest."

"Aye. I'm so very tired." His arm dropped to the bed and she again dabbed his forehead. "Aislinn, my life was not whole without ye. Did I ever tell ye this?"

She paused for a moment before she answered him, "No. You never did."

His feverish eyes watched her. "Please don't leave me. Please promise that ye'll stay."

She sniffled back a cry and nodded her head. "First you have to get well, Dougray."

"I care so much for ye, lass." His eyes closed then as in sleep, only his body was shivering as though he was packed in ice. She pulled the covers up higher on his chest. "Nay, Ella! Ella!" Terror was in his voice and she tried to calm him. "Aislinn! Aislinn! Stay, please stay."

"I'm right here." She grabbed his hand and squeezed it. "I'm here, Dougray." She had thought of him as solid, strong, and now he was lying there, his vibrant energy ebbing away. She clenched her jaw forcing herself to rid her mind of those thoughts. He would pull through this. He just had to. What he needed was a good dose of…. She jumped to her feet, drawing in a deep breath. How could she have been so stupid? He needed antibiotics.

She ran over to her backpack frantically looking for the bottle that her dentist had prescribed for her a few months back. With it in her hand, she opened the container and nearly dumped the contents to the floor before she stilled her hands and was able to take one of the precious tablets out. She tossed the bottle back inside her backpack.

She sat down next to Dougray and lifted his head. "Come on, you have to take this." She tried to shove the pill into his mouth, but he kept fighting her. She put his head back down. She was desperate and decided to use drastic measures. She pinched his nose with her forefinger and thumb until he was forced to open his mouth for a breath. She then dropped the pill down his throat making him choke in the process.

"What witchery is this?" Cahir had entered the room to witness her act. He practically ran to her yanking her from her seat. "I saw ye put something in his mouth. What was it?"

Aislinn wondered how she had not heard him come in. Obviously, the spineless little man had been spying on her. "Unhand me at once."

"Nay. Ye've poisoned him. I saw ye. Guards! Guards!"

"I did no such thing." She managed to yank her hand free as two of Burke's men arrived. "I'm trying to save him."

"We can all see what ye've done so far. Look at him." He pointed to Dougray who was burning with fever. "He was fine a few days ago and now he is at death's door. Guards, seize her."

The two men grabbed her before she could even react. "This is nonsense. I would do nothing to harm him." She struggled to be free, but their hold was like steel.

"If Dougray lives, then we will set ye free, but if he dies, we will deal with ye accordingly. I am sure Abbot Kirwan will want to hear of this."

Dear God, this man was insane, and with Kirwan's help, she would be sentenced and tied to a stake before the night was over.

She only wanted to help Dougray, but her medical expertise was limited and she had no way of knowing if the penicillin would even help. "You would blame me for his wound becoming infected?"

"No, milady, I would blame ye for poisoning him. Now take her away." He waved his hand for the guards to move along.

"You can't do this." She struggled, panic gripping her. She had no one to call to help her. She had told Teige that she would not be leaving the castle so he had gone with the hunting party. Dermot and Hamish were out practicing their sword fighting. Cormac disappeared early this morning probably to seek out Fiona.

"Lock her in the dungeon," Cahir ordered.

She yanked one of her hands free and, with all her might, swung at the guard to her right, hitting him in the groin. With that guard on the ground she went after the other one. She lifted the folds of her dress and gave the man a swift kick to the knee. She would have kicked him again, but she got tangled up in the gown and ended up tripping herself. The guard scrambled to his feet, his sword drawn. Before she could rise, he had the point of the blade at her throat.

"Do not move again, milady. I'd hate to put a hole in that pretty little neck of yers."

The physician was standing above her now. "Take her away, and if she gives you any more trouble…" He paused and looked at her menacingly. "…kill her." He walked away then and the guards lifted her up off the ground. This time, she didn't struggle.

They had nearly dragged her down below throwing her into the cell, where she stumbled to the floor. She turned to see them slamming the door shut, taking pleasure in her unwarranted confinement.

"You'll end up rotting in here, milady," the one she had kicked in the groin was good enough to inform her.

She tried not to let fear rule her thoughts. "Tell Murrough that I wish to speak to him."

They just laughed as they walked away. She leaned her face through the bars. "Tell him!" she yelled again as they headed out of sight.

Hours passed, her cell turning into dark shadows with rats scurrying by. She sat with her feet curled up close to her body wondering how long she had been down there.

She heard the door above open and she quickly rose to her feet. She never in her life thought that she would be so relieved to see Murrough O'Donoghue. He may not trust her, but he was a fair and honest man who cared for Dougray. He would at least hear her out before he passed judgment.

The redheaded man eyed her for a moment, a little surprised that she had not lost her spirit. He had seen men crumble within hours of being locked behind these doors. He waited expecting her to plead for her life, but she remained silent obviously waiting for him to address her. "Ye wished to speak to me, milady."

"Murrough, I need your help."

He chuckled. "Me? I would have thought that I would be the last person ye would have asked for assistance."

"It is not for me actually. It's for Dougray."

His bushy brows lifted. "I would think you have done enough. Cahir told me of yer doings."

"The man's a fool and you know it. I was trying to help Dougray."

"I can't fathom how. He's worse than last I saw him."

"That was nothing that I did. He was hacked with a weapon. Did you expect him to walk away without consequences?"

Murrough knew that she spoke the truth. It was not surprising that he would be feverish. Many men died from such wounds, but the physician was sure that he saw her shove something in Dougray's mouth and then refused to tell him what it was. "Why should I believe anything ye say?"

"Because I…." She paused for a moment, but Murrough saw the raw emotion smoldering in her eyes. "Like you, Murrough, I care very much for him."

Try as he might, he could see no deception there. "What did ye give him?" he asked.

"Penicillin. It's a drug that will help fight the infection. I had the prescription filled when I had my root canal."

"Yer root…what?" He waved his hand. He didn't want to know. "Forget it. If it is supposed to help him, why is he not better then?"

"He has to have more of it. I have the bottle in my backpack. Please, I don't care what happens to me. Just give him the pills. I swear it will help. I swear on my life." Her eyes implored him to believe her.

Murrough stared at her for a long time, trying to make the right decision. Dougray was not better, but he was no worse either. "Guards!" One came immediately down the steep steps. "Take her to her room and see that she does not leave it." He heard the guard chuckle and he gave him a withering look that sobered him up quickly. "Ye may be here on order from the Burke, but ye are under my command now. Aislinn Fitzpatrick is the lady of this keep and ye will treat her accordingly. No harm better come to her. Do ye understand me?"

"Aye, sir." The man quickly took the keys from the peg.

"Thank you, Murrough." Aislinn could not hide her gratitude.

"Do not thank me just yet. For if ye have lied to me, ye will wish that ye were never born." He turned on his heel and strode back up the stairs.

"Come ye." The guard nudged her.

"I will take her up to her room," a commanding voice demanded.

Aislinn looked up to see Teige standing there. The guard appeared as though he was going to refuse but the withering gaze that Teige threw was a sure indication that he planned, if need be, on issuing this order by force.

"Fine, take her then."

Teige moved her ahead of him, still wary that the Burke's man might retaliate. "Were ye harmed, A.J.?"

She looked over her shoulder and smiled. "No. It is so good to see you, Teige. Thank you for coming."

"I will guard ye with my life, milady. Do ye not worry."

"What say ye, Fiach?" Murrough asked. "Do we trust the pills she gives us?"

Fiach took the small white tablet that had writing scrawled on it. He then glanced at his cousin who was restless in his feverish slumber. "Why do ye not ask the physician, Cahir?"

"Because Cahir does not trust Lady Aislinn. He would condemn this medication just because it comes from her hand."

"Even if it were to save Dougray?"

"Aye. Cahir, these days, seems to be bent on proving Aislinn has an ill wish for milord."

"Ye do not believe it is so?"

"Nay," Murrough was forced to admit. "She may aggravate him with her stubbornness, but I have witnessed the way she gazes at him when she thinks no one is looking. I do not think that she holds any malice."

"Then ye have yer answer." He handed the penicillin back to Murrough.

"Speak to no one of what we do," Murrough requested of the priest.

"Ye have my word."

He moved forward but turned again to address Fiach. "Do not confess to Kirwan either."

"I'd sooner burn in hell than confess my sins to Abbot Kirwan."

Murrough smiled grimly. "That may be what we will do, if this does more harm than good."

For three days, Aislinn was kept locked up in her room and away from Dougray's side. She did a lot of praying and worrying, even though Teige tried to give her an account of how he was doing.

Finally the door opened with Murrough's red hair gleaming bright from the sun's rays that slipped through the half-open window. Aislinn ran over to him, trying to read the news in his eyes. She couldn't take the man's silence and shook his arm. "Well? Please tell me. Is he all right, or are you here to have my head on a platter?"

"I see yer confinement has done nothing to tame that disposition of yers." He gave her half a smile. "He lives and he has been bellowing orders."

She closed her eyes for a moment, relief flooding over her features. "Thank God." Her eyes snapped open then. "May I see him?" Then she hesitated. What if he didn't want to see her?

Murrough sensed her hesitation and immediately put her at ease. "His first words were to demand ye come forth."

She put her hands on her hips and raised her chin defiantly. "Oh, really now. He has demanded?" A smile spread across her face, erasing the stress lines and transforming her features to one of beauty. "Then you best let me by."

Murrough bowed slightly before he moved aside. He followed behind her, barely keeping up with her large strides. They could hear Dougray barking an order for someone to find his sword. Aislinn rushed in. She could see him sitting on the bed trying to put on his tunic. He looked up and she didn't wait for him to beckon her. She ran right over to him throwing her arms around him in a big bear hug, nearly suffocating him in the process.

"You're all right." She held his head tightly against her chest.

His hands moved to her waist and a low chuckle escaped his lips. "Not that I don't like where my head is resting," came his muffled voice, "but I am having a bit of trouble breathing."

She immediately released him, cupping his face in her hands. "Don't ever scare me like that again."

"I'll try not to." He wore a large grin on his hair-stubbled face.

They were silent for a moment, as they gazed at each other with many questions whirling around in their heads. Dougray had heard how she had stayed by his side morning and night, until Cahir took her away. He also knew it was her doing that he still lived. "It seems I owe ye my life, milady. There was a pensive shimmer in the shadow of his eyes.

She gently caressed his cheek, too choked with emotion to trust her voice to speak.

Murrough cleared his throat behind a closed fist. Dougray reluctantly dropped his hands from Aislinn's trim waist and she took an involuntary step back.

"Milord, will ye still be needing my services?" Murrough could barely keep from smiling.

"Nay. I am well now. Thank ye, Murrough." Once they were alone, he reached for her again and she did not resist. When he finally spoke, it was with profound tenderness. "What am I to do with ye, *Scathach*?"

Her embrace tightened. "I am not a warrior, just a woman." Her voice swelled with emotion and he thought that he heard her sniffle. "Are ye crying?" He pushed her away only so he could see her face. "Ye are crying." He realized that he had been insensitive to what she must have endured these past few days. He lightly touched her face. "I am sorry for what ye must have been put through. Rest assured, I will tend to Cahir and those involved."

She shook her head. "That's not why I'm crying."

"Nay? Why then?"

I'm just so relieved that you're all right. I thought I might never see you again. They wouldn't let me near you, and I was afraid that I would never be able to tell you…" She stopped just realizing how much this man had come to mean to her.

"What did ye want to tell me?"

"That…well…I care for you." Slowly her eyes met his.

"Ye care for me then?" She only nodded because she couldn't trust her voice. "Well that is a start, Aislinn. I care for ye too." His eyes held hers.

"About what we last spoke of before I went off to battle, ye wanted me to foster Declan, and I agreed with stipulations." He felt her stiffen and hurried on to explain. "I will not force ye, Aislinn, to do anything ye do not deem right." He gave her a half smile. "And I'll willingly take the lad and train him well."

"Thank you." She gave him a quick peck on the cheek before looking at him, eyes swelling with gratitude. Then she surprised him thoroughly by cupping his face with her delicate hands and leaning forward to truly kiss him.

Chapter Fifty

As Cahir walked up, he saw the two guards that had taken Aislinn down to the dungeon being led out by Dermot and Cormac. He had been summoned by Dougray to answer for the actions he had taken against the Lady Aislinn. He had felt that he was justified and had been confident that he could make Dougray see his side of the story too, but now seeing the guards who had been under his instructions being led out of the keep by sword point made him not so sure.

"We do not have all day." Cahir jumped at the sound of Murrough's voice. He had stepped aside so that Cahir could enter.

Dougray had paced the library, his anger still not sated for the way Aislinn had been treated. He shuddered to think what would have become of her if he had succumbed to his injuries.

"I can explain, milord, about…" Cahir word's died in his throat.

Dougray had turned toward him, eyes clouding to black. His lips had thinned to white and his nostrils flared with fury. Cahir had the distinct impression that he was a thread away from being run through with a sword. "Ye made a grave mistake, Cahir, the moment ye sent the guards to apprehend Lady Aislinn." His voice was cold and exact, matching his dark expression. "By all rights I should send ye from Dunhaven." He paused only because he was struggling to contain his anger.

Cahir glanced uneasily at Murrough, who was guarding the door as if he suspected that he might try to make a run for it. Cahir shifted his weight and warily returned his gaze back to the man who would decide his fate. "Milord, I was only looking out for yer best interest. I thought that milady was poisoning ye."

"Obviously, ye do not know her or ye would have realized what a ridiculous statement ye have just made. She has nothing but a caring nature."

"But her temper, milord?"

"Perhaps she is a bit quarrelsome, but she is far from a murderess where ye had categorized her."

He swallowed hard, struggling to say something in his defense. "I now see my folly, milord."

"I am gladdened to hear it. From now on, if ye so wish to continue being physician here at Dunhaven, ye will treat Lady Aislinn with the same respect that ye show me. If ye so ever think that ye can take matters into yer own hands again, ye will not be dealt with so kindly. Do I make myself clear enough for ye?"

"Aye, milord." His mind was weary, but with hope now that his life would be spared.

"Then ye are dismissed." With a wave of his hand, he had finished. He was already turning his back on him.

Cahir hurried, his footsteps thundering down the hall.

"What do ye think, Murrough?"

"Ye will have no more trouble from the man."

Dougray turned to face his friend. "And of ye?"

"I have had my reservations about Lady Aislinn, but not anymore. Even locked down below in the dungeon, she did not worry of herself. Her concerns were for ye. I cannot deny such devotion."

"Aye, she cares for me." He sighed.

Murrough placed a hand on his shoulder. "What troubles ye, Dougray?"

He shrugged disparagingly. "Nothing that cannot be worked out, I suppose." He gave his friend a weak smile.

With Aislinn's help, Dougray's strength improved. She had him on an exercise regimen that tried his patience at times, but he stuck to it for the results could not be refuted. Best of all it enabled him to spend more time with her. He felt that his patience with her was paying off, for he could feel their relationship strengthening each and every day.

When they were not exercising, they would talk for hours, sometimes long into the night. With great restraint he did not take advantage of the kisses she would allow him to steal from her. He caressed her, teased her until he himself could take no more. He was well aware of the disappointment on her fine-boned features, but he was determined to have her come to him. He could tell by the way she would tremble in his hands that she was close to giving in to her passions.

Aislinn was actually put back by his restraint. She knew that he was seducing her. He kissed her until her mouth burned with desire. His lips would brush against her neck exalting her to distraction. All this from his kisses and not once had he taken his hands to her, other than in an embrace.

The man held her thoughts and she dreamt of him at night, making her wish that he was there beside her. Instead when she reached out her hand to feel for him, she only touched the cold linen and nothing more. She had moved her quarters staying in the adjoining room to his, a door that wasn't even locked. She could go to him.

She took the steps that separated them and knocked on the door. "Ye may enter," his voiced boomed through the wood. She took a deep breath and opened the door.

Dougray eyebrows rose involuntarily. "What do I owe the pleasure?"

"I knew you were back from working out, and wanted to know if you needed any help changing your dressing?"

"That would be wonderful. It is most difficult to bind my ribs securely." He just stood there and she nervously cleared her throat.

"You do realize that you'll need to remove your shirt." He noticed her face flushed with color but her gaze never wavered from his.

"Of course." She watched him remove his leather jerkin and then his linen shirt. First, exposing his broad shoulders, then his firm muscular chest, flat stomach.

She swallowed.

"Do ye want me to sit down?" he asked her.

"What? Uh…yeah…sure." She turned around and closed her eyes for a moment to compose herself.

"The linen strips are on the small table there."

"I see them." She made her feet move to bring the supplies back to where he was seated. She cut away the strips to reveal the wound that looked considerably better after a week and a half of healing. The bruised skin was starting to fade to browns and yellows. "It's healing well." She cleaned the area with tender touches that sent his pulse racing.

"Aye, I feel stronger too."

"I'm glad. You're color has improved. You were looking peaked for a while. Lift your arms and I'll wrap you up." She was inches from him as her long arms encircled him over and over again. "That's not too tight is it?"

"Nay. It feels just right." His voice had changed, deeper, huskier. Her eyes lingered on his lips and she saw his mustache twitch. She cleared her throat again, and continued to wrap. She pulled a little harder than she meant to and she heard him grunt.

"Sorry." One more once around and she tied it off nicely. "How did you do with the exercise routine today?"

"Finished everything ye mapped out for me."

"You did? You don't even look tired." She remembered the first day that he had tried to do just a few stretches. He had to sit down only after a few minutes, sweat already rolling down his face, and his breathing had become labored from the simple exertion.

"Not tired in the least, but I have come to realize that I have muscles I didn't even know I possessed because they are aching like there is no tomorrow."

"Well 'no pain, no gain' is what my father would say." She gave him an adorable smile that he couldn't resist.

"Really now." He pulled her toward him so fast that she fell against his chest. He cradled her to his lap and her hands automatically went around his neck. "Then I am beyond suffering. When do I reap the rewards?" He didn't wait for a response, but covered her lips, tongue touching, teasing her to open up to him. She deepened the embrace. *So close,* he thought. She was so close to being his.

Dougray was studying the chessboard, strategizing his next move. Every night he met Murrough or Fiach in the library for a game. It helped to keep his mind off Aislinn, to relax him so that he could sleep and not have thoughts of banging down the door that separated him from her. He had come this far and was determined to see it through. He was aware that they knew of his situation and maybe took pity on him, but tonight Murrough couldn't keep quiet a moment longer. Not caring that a priest was in the room, he spoke his mind. "Forgive me for poking my nose into yer business, but why have ye not bedded the infernal woman?"

Fiach lowered his quill for this.

Dougray just raised his brows. "I did not know this was a problem for ye."

"Pheugh! What do I care who ye have warming yer nights? I am only curious to why ye torture yerself when it is so obvious that ye two should have consummated the marriage vows long before now. I have never witness a union like this one. It is driving me mad."

Dougray chuckled. "Dear friend, I am sorry that my personal life has ye in torment." He leaned back in his chair and thoughtfully rubbed his chin. "Let me assure ye, Murrough, I have every intention of bedding her. I am only waiting for her to realize that she wants it as much as I do."

"Ye have less than a year to do that, ye know." Fiach couldn't help but tease him. "Do ye think that ye will succeed?"

"Ye doubt me, cousin? I want Aislinn and I will have her, but I want her willingly. I have no wish to slumber, the rest of my days with one eye open for she would surely want to slit my throat, if I took her without her consent. Nay, I will be patient for it will be worth the wait." He chuckled again. "And ye, my friend," he looked to Murrough now, "will have to be patient also."

Chapter Fifty-One

It was still fairly early when Aislinn walked over to where she could watch Dougray practice. He liked to come out to the field before the others would arrive to brush up on his archery skills, not that he carried arrows in a quiver upon his back. This exercise was simply therapeutic, for he had told her it relaxed him, gave him time to think and mull over what needed to be done for the day.

She watched him pull another arrow out, aim and fire. She shaded her eyes and squinted watching the butt land about 140 yards away. She could make out a quite a few shafts sticking out of the mound of earth. He had been out here awhile. She started toward him. When he noticed her approach, he acknowledged her with a small nod of his head before he let another spear fly.

"One day, I would like the opportunity to try a hand at this," Aislinn commented. "We had something like this in school, but my bow was a lightweight thing. These look like they're heavy."

"Archery is still popular in yer time then?"

"Only recreational and we set up our target with the intention of hitting a bull's eye."

"Ye put eyes of bull on the target?"

"No." She chuckled. "Not a real bull's eye. It's a round paper with circular rings, the center being a round circle. That's the bulls eye. The point of the game is to hit your arrows as close to the center as possible, so that you accumulate more points. The higher the score, the winner."

"Sounds interesting. Maybe I should start something of the sort here. Could prove entertaining." He pulled another arrow out and looked at her. "Care to give it a try?"

She smiled eagerly and accepted the longbow from him. It was heavy, just as she had expected it to be, but she held fast. "Ye hold it like so." He lifted her elbows just slightly. "Now place the arrow here. Ye need to keep it steady, pulling back until you feel the tension, then let it go." She followed his instruction, but she couldn't hold on to it and her arrow went wide landing yards away from the target. "Don't pull back as far. Loosen yer grip a bit." He had another arrow ready and stepped behind her, pressing his body close as he placed his hands over hers so that he could show her what he meant. "Now release." It was still wide but closer to the intended target. "Not bad." The sweet scent of her hair was intoxicating. He breathed deeply. She turned her head toward him, her eyes drifting to his mouth. She licked her lips, inviting him to kiss her. "Do ye want to try again?" He purposely made her wait intensifying the desire for both of them.

"What? Yeah, sure." Her heart was pounding in her ears. He handed her yet another butt shaft and again he placed his strong arms around her, showing her exactly what to do, leading her through each step. She only half listened to what he was saying for she was enjoying the closeness of him. The arrow flew.

"Did ye not see it? The arrow moved straight and true."

Like cupid's arrow toward an impending victim, she thought to herself and leaned against him, relishing in the warmth of his body.

This time when she turned her head toward him, his arms moved to encircle her waist. She felt her knees weaken as his mouth descended upon hers. She let the longbow slip from her grip and she raised her right hand to cradle the back of his head.

Fiona could not accept the fact that Dougray would want the woman that held no feminine qualities. She was more like a man than a woman.

She frowned staring at Aislinn running around with the children. The woman was getting all sweaty and dirty. It was simply disgusting. She was supposed to be married to the lord and she was out there acting as if she were a common tenant. She obviously had no proper training in a way a lady should behave. Even she, who did not have a bit of noble blood in her, knew what was expected. Surely Dougray would soon tire of her, and she would be there to step in.

Fiona's eyes wandered over to where Dougray practiced to regain his strength. He was such a fine-looking specimen of a man, his muscles rippling beneath his tunic. She missed Dougray's gentle touch. Her eyes locked onto Cormac then. He was wielding a sword with complete ease and evident force. He was not bad either. He was an ample lover too, but…well, he simply could not give her the comforts that Dougray would be able to.

"Do ye watch Cormac or Lord Dougray?"

Fiona turned to see Teige studying her with open disgust. "Both. Is there a crime against that now?"

"Only if there is a hidden agenda behind it."

"What are ye babbling about?"

"Cormac is my friend and I have no wish to see his heart broken. Frankly, I do not know what he sees in ye, but I will respect his choice, so long as his choice will be careful of his heart."

"Ye fear too much. Cormac and I are enjoying each other's company and nothing more."

"Ye know that he cares more. I warn ye, Fiona, do not prove false for I will not take lightly to the slight." With that promise, he moved forward to meet the others.

Fiona would have liked to kick the man's arse. Who did he think he was anyway? "Indeed. Break Cormac's heart?" She looked his way again and he happened to glance up giving her a salute. Did he actually love her? She found that she was almost pleased with the idea. As a matter of fact, she thought that maybe one day she might be able to use this to her advantage.

Aislinn had her horse saddled and she was taking Declan with her, so Fiona knew that she would be gone for a while. The troublesome Teige was her escort, which made it all the more perfect. Fiona smiled to herself, as she quickly entered the castle, and without anyone noticing, she ascended the spiral steps like the spider ready to snare her prey.

It was not a secret that Dougray and Aislinn did not share the same room. She planned to seek out her lord and offer the comfort that his body must be craving by now. He was a man, after all, and one who had been chaste far too long. He would make an easy conquest.

She found him lounging comfortably in the library, and with her luck holding out, he was completely alone.

He had been reading a letter from his grandfather and glanced up when he had heard her enter.

She lowered her thick, dark lashes and sauntered into the room as though she belonged there.

"Are ye lost, Fiona?"

"Nay, milord. I apologize for intruding, but I wish to speak to ye."

He rose to his feet. His gray eyes narrowed knowing that the woman was up to something. "What is it ye need?"

The smile that penetrated her features was beguiling. Fiona was a beautiful woman and she obviously wanted him to take notice. His eyes caught and held hers demanding that she get to the point, but she took his warning as encouragement. She came forward, stopping inches from their bodies touching each other, close enough that he could smell the rose fragrance that she had splashed in her hair and on her clothing. Her fingers slid sensuously over the dark fabric of his sleeve.

"What is this about, Fiona?"

She tilted her head so that her eyes met his. "I would think that ye would know."

Aislinn stepped down from her mount and handed the reigns to Teige, so that he could keep an eye on Declan. "I will be but a moment. I left my backpack in the library."

She ran back to the castle and up the steps two at a time. She had left Dougray in the library not that long ago. She smiled in remembrance of the kiss he had given her just before she had left. His lips were warm and sweet making her whole being flood with desire.

He had been patient with her, wooing her with gentle innocent caresses and stopping when things became too heated.

Maybe he would still be there sitting on the bench, reading his letter. Maybe she would surprise him and approach him on her own.

The doors of the library were ajar and she entered without a thought. The scene that unfolded before her eyes erased the smile from her face, and a sickening feeling of betrayal wrapped around her heart threatening to stop it.

Dougray was standing there with Fiona's arms wrapped around him. If it hadn't been so seriously damaging to her senses, the situation would have been quite comical. The two looked at her at the same time. Guilt radiating from Dougray's face, his gray eyes pleading for her to understand, while Fiona held a satisfying grin like a cat that had been given her favorite dish. She even had the nerve to lean her head on Dougray's chest as if it belonged there.

All this happened in a matter of a few, horrible, unforgivable seconds, just enough time to allow Aislinn to make her assumptions before she turned and bolted from the room.

Dougray pushed Fiona away, his features hard as stone. "Get out of here, woman, before I have the guards take ye away."

Fiona's mouth dropped open. Surely she could not have heard him correctly. "Dougray, we...."

"What part of get out did ye not understand?"

Crestfallen and not knowing what else to do, she picked up her cloak and walked out of the room. It was only when she had descended the last step of the stone stairs that she became furious. "The raven-haired woman has bewitched the entire castle!"

Dougray found Aislinn with Neala, just as he had expected that he would. He had purposely given her time to calm down, so that he would have a better chance of her actually hearing his explanation.

He was wrong on that notion.

The moment he entered the glen and she caught sight of him, she was on her feet. Her eyes blazed with fury, and to his amazement, she had actually drawn her sword. He lifted one dark brow as he watched the fire's light dance upon the hard steel.

"What is this, Aislinn?" He lifted his arms, palms up.

She parried around the fire careful to stay out of his reach, less he would try to disarm her. "I think it is plain enough."

"Ye want to fight me?" He couldn't help but chuckle at the lunacy of the whole situation.

Aislinn hadn't really thought of doing physical combat with the man, but now that he mentioned it, she couldn't think of a better way to act out her aggressions. "Are you afraid that I might best you?"

"Nay. Have ye forgotten, Aislinn, that I have bested ye before at yer own game? I see no reason why I would not be able to do so now." His cockiness riled her further.

"Then put your money where your mouth is." She came around the fire to stand in front of him. Her dark eyes glittered with lethal intent.

Dougray hesitated for he had no wish to draw his sword on her. He glanced at Neala for help. The old woman just shrugged her shoulders and sat down on the rock. Even young Declan with his thumb in his mouth seemed to be looking on with amusement. Teige merely turned his gaze elsewhere.

He was on his own.

He glanced back to Aislinn's unrelenting features. She by no means was going to back down. He sighed heavily. "Is this yer wish then, milady?"

"Stop stalling with your idle words and raise your sword." She swung her weapon, slicing through the air, seemingly eager to draw blood…his blood!

Dougray removed his mantle and placed it out of the way. He barely had time to remove his sword from his sheath before she was upon him. He was taken by surprise from her brutal attack and had to step back. He was forced to block her reckless jabs and meet her inexperienced lunges. He played her game for a while, but soon he grew tired of her temper tantrum. He decided to put a stop to it, and the very next time that she lunged at him, he purposely swung his sword in a circular motion. The speed along with the hard impact sent Aislinn's weapon flying from her grip.

He caught her sword in his left hand. He met her startled gaze, just has she clamped her gaping mouth shut. "Are we finished now?" he asked.

She sauntered over to him, her expression unreadable as she glared at him with those dark penetrating eyes. Then without a warning, she took her fist and swung it right smack into his jaw. He had not expected the assault and lost his balance, hitting the ground hard. She leaned over him, as he rubbed his sore chin. "Now we're finished!" She grabbed her sword, which had fallen from his grip. "Come on, Declan." She took him up in her arms as she stormed away through the trees, Teige following close behind.

Dougray slowly sat up and leaned his forearms against his knees. He looked at Neala, who was just shaking her head. "What was I supposed to do, old woman? She started this."

"Aye, and finished it."

He made a snorting sound that he wasn't at all pleased that she pointed this out to him. He came to his feet. "I am not sure what she has told ye, but I can explain."

Neala held up her hand to stop him. "Ye need not explain to me. Ye need to speak with yer wife."

Aislinn practically ran back to the keep, not stopping even to speak to Rhiannon, who saw her in passing. Teige had taken Declan from her saying that he would watch him while he played with the other children knowing she needed some time alone.

Grateful for the reprieve, she stumbled into her room and threw down her sword before she lunged for the bed. The tears came then and she was powerless to stop them. Moira had seen her mistress and had followed her back to the room. When she heard Aislinn's sobs, she didn't know what she should do. "Milady, are ye hurt? Should I find milord Dougray?" This made Aislinn cry even louder. Moira backed up a pace wringing her apron. "Milady, please tell me what I must do."

Rhiannon came up the stairs. Hearing the commotion, she didn't wait for someone to bid her entry. She silently motioned to Moira that she would take over. The young girl was more than happy to oblige. She made her exit, shutting the door as she went.

Rhiannon sat down on the bed and gently rubbed Aislinn's back. "It is good to shed tears. Let them all come forth."

"I don't want to cry," came her muffled wail. She then slammed her fist on the bed, causing her to wince.

Rhiannon took hold of Aislinn's hand, noticing that her knuckles were slightly discolored. "What happened?"

Aislinn turned toward Rhiannon glancing at her damaged knuckles. "I threw a punch at someone that was in dire need of a lesson."

"Someone has assaulted ye?"

"No, Rhiannon. I hit Dougray…the stinking rat!" She turned around and sat next to Rhiannon, hugging her knees close to her body.

"Milord had this coming to him…the punch I mean?"

"You better believe it."

Rhiannon just nodded her head. "Men tend to do foolish things that set our tempers afire."

She looked at the fair-haired woman. "Murrough pisses you off at times too?"

"Pisses me…aye, angers me," she concluded on her own. "The man can be most infuriating, but he can also be everything that I could ever hope for in a man."

"Dougray confuses me, until I can't seem to reason through my own thoughts. I thought that I knew what I wanted in life, but now…. He has my emotions in a constant turmoil. I never know if I want to kick him or just…" she let the sentence trail off to silence.

"I am not sure what has happened but maybe it is not all that bad."

"Oh, it's bad all right. I caught him."

"Sometimes we see things that are not what they appear to be. It is best that ye hear the explanation then ascertain if it is the truth."

At that moment, Dougray burst into the room. Of course he didn't even bother to ask permission. "Ye will leave us, Rhiannon."

"No, stay." Aislinn quickly rose to her feet.

"She will go!" his voice thundered.

Rhiannon gave Aislinn an encouraging smile and whispered, "Remember there is always a chance ye did not witness what ye think." She tried to hurry pass Dougray, but he stopped her before she could leave. "Make it known that we are not to be disturbed. And I would appreciate it also if ye will take Declan for the night."

"Aye, milord." Rhiannon nodded and closed the doors behind her.

The two stared at each other, leery to make a move. Aislinn let Rhiannon's words linger in the back of her mind. Could she have been wrong? Was he not guilty, for he certainly didn't act like a man that was seeking forgiveness?

He made an attempt to approach her and she moved in the other direction. She feared that being near him would be her undoing. She had to think this through without him distracting her. Her obvious retreat did not go unnoticed.

Dougray had never seen a more courageous woman. She stood up not only for herself, but also for anyone that needed assistance. She could stand her ground with the best of his men and they respected her for it, but this? She seemed to shy away from any intimacy. Frankly he was quite puzzled over it. A man and woman together was something so natural, but she seemed to be almost frightened of it.

"Why do ye do this, Aislinn?"

"Do what?" She had to stall him, anything to divert him from what she saw mirrored in his eyes. She couldn't let down her guard for it would be so easy to allow him into her heart. She refused to be hurt, used. Let him have his dalliances as long as he left her alone.

"Ye know full well what I speak of. I am yer husband now. Yet ye run away from me like a frightened rabbit."

"I do not," she said firmly as her hands went to her narrow hips. "I'm not running. I simply did not choose to be married. Remember I was forced into this union."

"Ah we are back to that again. Ye made the rules. I should remind ye."

"Whatever! Still the fact remains that I never wanted to be married, and obviously after what I witnessed with you this afternoon, it isn't what you want either."

He had moved closer and she took a step back. "What do ye want?" he asked of her.

"What?" She was confused by his questioned. She retreated another step, feeling like she was being stalked.

"What do ye want?" He repeated the question as he continued his pursuit. She finally ran out of space for she was backed into a corner. He was so very near now that she could feel the heat of his body, sweetly intoxicating her senses. She gulped as she looked up at him, meeting his clear silvery eyes.

"I'm waiting."

"I…I want to go home," which wasn't exactly the truth anymore.

Dougray sighed. "Alas, if I could, I would grant ye yer wish."

"But you can't."

"I fear not. Nor do I desire to let ye go." He studied her features that he had come to know so well. She haunted his dreams until he thought he would go mad from the want of her. "Can we not try to make this marriage work? Do ye not find me in the least bit appealing?" Though he did not touch her, he rested his hands on either side of her on the cold stone she had backed herself into.

Appealing? God if he only knew. She was having a difficult time not throwing all caution to the wind and demand he take her, but wouldn't that be the height of stupidity when only hours before she found him in the arms of Fiona? Damn, did he have to smell so good? She had to put him off guard and away from her. "I suppose you're handsome enough," she answered in a tiresome tone causing him to feel rejected.

"Oh, ye don't have to say it if ye don't mean it." He seemed so disappointed that she blurted out the truth before she could stop herself.

"I mean it. You are handsome, so much so it scares me."

A slow smile spread across his rugged features, his gaze focusing on her lips. She could feel her willpower slipping away, but then the image of Fiona in his embrace forced her to face reality. Fiona was beautiful, womanly. She was… "Do you…you know…" Why was she having such a difficult time articulating? She was a writer for Christ's sake. She closed her eyes for a moment to regain her composure. "…do you find me attractive?"

His deep chuckle filled the air. "Have I not been saying as much?"

"No," she stated flatly.

"Nay?" He seemed surprised for he thought that he had been making himself quite clear. "Well then I am saying it now. Ye more than please me, Aislinn. Ye make me long to be with ye, even when I am away."

She swallowed hard. "But you said that you hated my hair." She touched her short tresses that were only now starting to grow longer.

"The way yer hair halo's yer winsome face, it has bewitched me." His voice was smooth, low, caressing.

"I'm too tall." She would make him see her shortcomings but he knew just the right thing to say as if he had rehearsed this banter.

"Nay, ye fit well to me." He pressed against her body. "See," as if this proved his point.

"I'm too thin." Her voice was a mere whisper for she could barely breathe since she was sure that her rapidly beating heart had moved to her throat.

Putting his large hands to her waist, he drew her form against his hard body. "Ye feel perfect to me."

Her lower lip trembled. "I'm…."

"No more excuses, Aislinn." He lowered his mouth to hers. He knew she was trying to resist, but he remained persistent. Slowly, she began to respond. He made love to her only with his sweet caress, never once letting his hands roam over her body. He would proceed slowly, but he would have her this night. Finally he released her lips, but did not step away. They were so very close that he could feel her heart beating against his chest. "See. That was not so bad, eh?"

She wanted to run, hide, anything to be away from this torturous wonderful moment. He leaned forward to claim her lips, but this time she was prepared. She quickly ducked and slipped from his grasps. "No!" She put as much distance between them as she could. "Please don't."

The plea tore at his heart. "What are ye afraid of? Has a man hurt ye?"

She shook her head. "It's not what you are thinking. There are other ways to hurt someone. The body can heal, but a heart that is broken is sometimes beyond repair."

"I will not hurt ye, Aislinn. I care for ye like no other. I will provide for ye that ye shall know no fear."

"You don't get it, do you? Men just can't be trusted. I've learned that the hard way."

"What are ye saying? Do ye think me dishonest? Do ye think my word is not so?"

"I think that you are just a man and men have difficulties being faithful to one woman. How can you even ask me that, when I saw you with Fiona just hours before?"

"I would have explained, but ye refused. Now ye will listen. The woman came to me. I did not ask her to be there, nor do I wish her company. I was trying as nicely as possible to tell her this, but she is most difficult. I do not want Fiona, and she has been fair warned that I will not tolerate her making such unwarranted advances again."

"You told her that?"

"Aye. That I did." He waited for her to say more, but when she didn't, he spoke again. "Is that all ye fear? The lack of faithfulness?" He walked over to her. "I have been nothing but faithful to ye, and believe me, it was not easy when the wife is not willing."

"See what I mean?" she threw back at him.

"What?" He lifted his hands. "What did I say?"

"That it was not easy. You wanted to sleep with someone else."

"I did not say that. Do not go putting words in my mouth. I simply meant that…." He took a deep breath before he said anything more to incriminate him. "This may come to a surprise to ye, but I took our vows most seriously. I do not take lightly to dalliances. I am insulted that ye think so lowly of me."

"You don't have any inclinations to have a mistress?"

"Nay," he said firmly. "If I must be chaste because ye cannot give yerself freely then so be it, but I will not break our vows."

"You would do that? You would be chaste?" She couldn't believe that he would do such a thing. No man was capable of that, at least none that she knew of.

"Lass, trust that it is not my wish to be without the comforts of a feminine touch, but I will make ye this promise that I will do all that is in my power to make this union work."

"I don't know what to say." She had looked away. She was so confused. Never had she expected him to make such a grand offer.

He had moved beside her and took her hand. "Trust me, Aislinn. Give us a chance."

She looked into his beautiful eyes that beseeched her to believe in him. "But what if the time comes where I am able to go home?"

He sighed deeply. "I have no wish for ye to go, but if that is what ye want, I will grant yer leave."

"And if there were children?" Did she just ask that question? By his expression, it was clearly obvious that he had not thought that far ahead.

"What would ye want?"

"Personally, I would not want to make that choice, but seeing how you don't have birth control pills available and there isn't a drug store for you to obtain rubbers, then I am forced to think of the consequences of anything that may happen. That is if we decide to make this a conventional marriage." She said this all in one breath.

Dougray was lost after birth control. "*Dar Dia*! What are ye talking about?"

"I was rambling?"

"I'd say."

"Dougray, I don't know if I could leave a child behind."

"Then ye won't."

"But is it right to take our child away from you?"

"Then stay," he said simply. "Stay."

"I thought I was only here to fulfill a destiny."

"Maybe that destiny is to be here at my side. I want ye, Aislinn. I need ye so much so that I feel humbled before ye."

The honesty in his words moved her. Could she give up all that she had in her time? She might be able to if he loved her, but he never said the words. Yes, he wanted her but it wasn't the same. Yes, he could be loyal because his honor was everything to him.

She felt herself weakening beneath his gaze for she knew that she was in love with him. Maybe it would be enough. "You promise me that you will be faithful? I mean always or so help me...." He didn't let her finish for he had crushed her to him sealing her lips to his.

"I'll promise ye anything ye want, if ye will not deny me."

For one torturous moment, he waited for her response. It came with small, tentative nod. "I want you too," her voice had drifted to a hushed whisper against his neck.

He closed his eyes, his heart constricting with emotion. He swept her, weightless into his arms, and brought her to the bed. She looked up at him her dark eyes opened, speaking to him of her innocence, but trusting him all the same.

His large hand took her face and held it gently, as he placed a kiss upon her warm parted lips. Her arms encircled him encouraging him to deepen his caress. His hands roamed the length of her body setting her senses on fire, making his touch almost unbearable in its tenderness.

He felt her breath warm against his face. She kissed him, lingering, savoring, making his heart race.

His hand slipped beneath the fabric of her sweatshirt and even though he was unfamiliar with the contraption that bonded her breasts, he quickly figured it out releasing her soft roundness to his gentle touch. She moved closer to him, her hands moving underneath his tunic until she touched his flesh making it difficult for him to keep his own desires in check. Raising his mouth from hers, he gazed into her eyes. A familiar shiver of awareness rippled through him. She wanted this as much as he did.

He removed her sweatshirt and continued to explore her soft flesh with intimacy of his kisses.

She reveled from the heady sensation of his lips against her neck, the gentle nibbling of her earlobe. She never could have imagined that such sweet feathery touches could tantalize her to persuasion of giving herself to him. It shocked maybe even frightened her a little, but mostly it made her crave to have him fulfill the desire that throbbed inside of her. She felt his hand slide down her taut stomach to the swell of her hips. She let him remove the rest of her clothing until she lay there before him in an offering. "Ye're beautiful, Aislinn." She reached out and touched his cheek. He kissed her small hallow of her palm.

He removed his hindering clothes encouraging her to explore as he had done with her. She was eager to touch his skin. Her hands felt the scars that had long healed on his otherwise perfect body. He concentrated on the rosy peaks of her breasts making her quiver. His mouth tasted her flesh with featherlike kisses, while his hands blazed a trail of liquid fire across the length of her, his fingers parting the soft curling hair. Instinctively, her hips lifted in a sensuous invitation. Passion inched through her veins as her whole body flooded with desire.

She brushed her hand against his hardness causing him to let out a tormented groan. He buried his head in the hollow between her shoulder and neck, allowing his mouth to linger there. He knew that he could not wait much longer, but somehow he managed to hold back the twisting desire in his loins until he knew that she was ready for him. In that moment, his hard body was atop of hers. Slowly he entered pausing as her body stiffened allowing time for her to grow accustomed to the intrusion before gently moving. Her long legs wrapped tightly around him sending him deeper. Together they found the tempo that bound their souls together, soaring higher and higher until the hot tide of passion threatened to consume them. He never thought that he could feel this close to any woman, this woman who had held him at bay for so long. It wasn't just two bodies coming together to fulfill a primitive need. It was the surrendering of their souls, touching with open abandonment. After tonight, after this precious moment, if the time arrived where she could go back to her century, he didn't know how he would ever let her go.

Aislinn was struggling with her own awareness of what had passed between them. She saw the glowing image of fire, passion and love. She never dreamed his hands could feel so warm, so gentle, leaving her entranced by his mere touch. She soared so high that she felt she could reach the stars.

He had awakened a response in her that had been dormant for so long. It all made sense now why she had waited. Long ago, she could have quenched the thirst her body craved, but without this joining of the spiritual being, it would have been meaningless. She gave herself freely, letting herself go in the whirl of sensation, knowing that their joining had been predestined long before this night, long before the mist swept her to this place and time.

Chapter Fifty-Two

Aislinn left the warmth of the castle and ran past the early risers of Dunhaven with barely a hello. Fiona narrowed her eyes as she watched her head for the gates and without an escort. She was too curious not to follow.

Aislinn was oblivious that someone was at a distance, keeping pace with her. Her only concern was to reach the glen and to the safety of Neala's fire.

The old woman, like always, was ready for her company. She offered her a cup of one of her herb concoctions. She took it gladly for she found that most of her smooth drinks left her feeling relaxed, and that was exactly what she needed right now.

"Ye seemed troubled, milady." Neala decided to end the silence.

She sipped the hot liquid from the cup. "I have made peace with Dougray."

Neala's brows lifted. "Ye are now husband and wife, aye?"

She nodded. "Yes. It was wonderful. He was...." She smiled then in remembrance. "He was so tender. I expected many things from a man like Dougray, but such patience and gentleness.... Well it surprised me."

"I am most pleased that ye are happy with this union, but I sense that something must have brought ye to me, when ye could still be beneath a warm blanket."

"Neala, I come to you hoping that you will be able to help me."

"Help ye, lass? How so?"

"I'm assuming that you will be able to give me something so that I do not become pregnant."

Neala stared at her for a long time, letting that silence take its course. Then she rose. "Walk with me." Aislinn easily came to her feet and followed Neala down to the water's edge. The old woman leaned heavily on her walking stick so that she could kneel down. She beckoned Aislinn to do the same. "Look into the water. What do ye see?"

Aislinn's gaze followed to where she pointed at the murky darkness of blues, greens and browns. "Water of course."

"Nay, ye need to look past all that. Seek what is already there."

Aislinn looked again, and this time, she saw the water shift, until it was like she was viewing a screen of moving pictures. She knew that this was impossible, but yet she could not deny what her eyes saw. A small child running to another one in the distance, then a toddler teetering back and forth on his feet to keep up. Then she saw herself with a man. She shifted in her weight, but did not look away. The man turned around and she saw that it was Dougray. "What is this? What am I seeing?"

"What *could be,* Aislinn. The water does not lie."

As much as she wanted what she saw to come true, she couldn't allow it to happen. She didn't belong here. She had to somehow find her way back home. "I can't..." she shook her head and tore her gaze from the still pool. She nearly ran back to the fire pit. She stood there for a long time, hugging her arms close to her body, trying to stop the trembling within her. She heard Neala walk up behind her and she turned to look at her with questions on her lips, only to have them silenced when the old woman held out her gnarled hand.

"Here it is." Neala revealed a single vial, resting in her palm. "Ye drink a little of this and ye will stop milord's seed from taking hold."

Aislinn hesitated and chewed on her lower lip, trying to decide if this was what she really wanted to do.

"Are ye unsure now?"

Aislinn shook her head no. "I have to do this." She took the vial from her hand feeling almost sick inside for doing so.

"Think long and hard, Aislinn, before ye let that liquid pass yer lips. I pray ye will see that this is not the way."

Aislinn had almost reached the keep, when she caught sight of a woman chasing a toddler who seemed to be doing a good job of evading capture. Aislinn decided to help and headed the little girl off catching her with one full sweep. The mother caught up and was quite happy that she didn't have to continue the chase. "Thank ye, milady." The woman smiled. Aislinn remembered that she had bought a few blankets from her last week. Linna was her name.

Aislinn looked at the small child, who timidly smiled up at her with her light brown eyes. A tender longing seemed to flow through her, as she held the little chubby hand.

"Ye wish for a wee one of yer own?" Linna asked.

Aislinn was startled by the question making her look back at Linna. "May I ask you something?"

"Anything, milady." She bowed slightly.

"How did you know that you wanted to be a mother? How did you know that you would be able to guide her?"

"I don't know. I just always wanted to have children at me feet. I thought that it would never happen. Each child born to me perished before they drew their first breath. Six children I buried before the good Lord granted us me little darling." She gently touched her daughter's cheek and the little girl reached for her. Aislinn reluctantly gave up the warmth of having the child in her arms. "Sometimes I just watch her sleep, amazed that she is actually here. Children are a blessing, milady. They're a part of what we are and of our dreams we wish for them." Linna suddenly became embarrassed. "I'm sorry, milady. I have the tendency to run away with me mouth."

"No not at all." She touched the older woman's arm. "I thank you for your candor."

After she had moved on, Aislinn pulled out the vial that Neala had given her. She clasped it tight within her fist before shoving it back in her pocket.

"There ye are."

Aislinn jumped at the sound of his voice, but she managed to turn and face him with a smile.

If Dougray suspected anything, his face did not show it. He came forward, not caring if anyone was watching and gave her an endearing kiss upon her cheek. "I missed ye this morning." He prayed that she would not hear the uncertainty in his voice.

Aislinn placed her hand on his arm, giving it a gentle squeeze. "I was heading back to break fast with you." She lowered her gaze, but he lifted her chin, forcing her to look at him. There was such longing and hope in those silvery, smoked-filled eyes making her feel guilty that she was going to deceive him.

"Do ye have regrets, Aislinn?"

She managed to shake her head. "None."

He kissed her then full on the lips, as if he was sealing their fate. He then took hold of her hand. "Come then. I have much I must share with ye."

"I need to check on Declan."

"I have already done so. He was eating a full meal when I left him with Moira. Ye do not have to worry about him."

Without further explanation, he led her to the stable and helped her onto her large black mare. Once he was mounted, he looked at her for a long time, as though he yearned to tell her something, but didn't quite know how to broach the subject.

He turned away then and clicked his tongue, putting his horse into motion. Her mare was quick to follow.

They traveled a small distance coming to a halt at the edge of the graveyard. Dougray dismounted first and helped her down. She looked to him for an explanation, but he would not give her any indication why they were here. Instead he again took her hand and led her through the endless headstones and Celtic crosses, until he was standing in front of the one that he had purposely sought. Aislinn glanced at him before she read the words that were engraved on the heavy stone. "Ella…" Her eyes darted back to him.

"Ella was my wife, Aislinn." His eyes caught and held hers. "We had only been married less than two weeks time when she…" Even now he had a hard time thinking of her as dead. He swallowed the lump in his throat before he could continue. "The marriage was arranged to better the ties between the Fitzpatricks and the Butlers. I was not opposed to the idea, once I laid eyes on Ella. Small she was with hair a shimmering pale gold. She was so sweet, timid actually, and so very young."

"What happened to her, Dougray?" Aislinn gripped his hand tighter, encouraging him to speak. She knew from Miriam some of the story, but she felt that she needed to hear it from him.

"She went riding on my horse that I had personally saddled. I remember how she smiled down at me before she left with her escorts. It was just to be a quick ride before the noon meal. That was all it was supposed to be…." He covered his eyes with his hand, trying to still the guilty tears. "The horse, my mount, became skittish, and without warning, it bolted. Ella might have held on but the strap to the saddle snapped throwing her from her seat. The men brought her broken body to me and laid her at my feet. She looked like she was sleeping…just sleeping except for the light, bluish color of her lips. There was no chance to say good-bye to her. Her spirit was already gone."

"I'm so sorry, Dougray." She really didn't know what to say to him and maybe he didn't expect her to say anything at all. She leaned close and he wrapped his strong arm around her. He then led her away to stand before their mounts.

"I wanted ye to know that Ella was not someone ye had to worry about." She shook her head ready to deny it, but he held up his hand. "I know ye had questions and I should have told ye from the start. I will not deny that I had feelings for her, for there had been something…sweet, tender. I had wished to protect her from the world."

"You loved her?" She spoke softly without accusations, but with a thread of sadness.

"We had such a short time together. Maybe it could have been more." He gently brushed the hair away from her neck. "Ye have made me question what love is." His eyes clung to her. "I feel something deeper for ye, Aislinn, and it frightens me." She reached for the solid strength of his arm only to have him clutch her hand with both of his. His steady gaze bore into her in silent expectation wanting her to feel the same, to bond to him fully.

"You have unlocked my heart and soul, Dougray." There was a small tremor in her voice. "Please be careful with them."

His intense gaze traveled over her face like a welcoming caress. "Look into my eyes, Aislinn, and see the truth buried there. Ye are all that I want. It is I who fear being trampled." His gaze never wavered, and with a pulse-pounding certainty, she knew that he was telling her the truth.

Chapter Fifty-Three

Aislinn was telling Declan one of her own stories about the evil wizard Gerg, who was forever after the rainbow fairy that made all the colors of the lands. "And the evil wizard Gerg held poor Rainbow in the tower and every day that she was unable to see the light of day a color would fade from the land."

Dougray watched her from the doorway of their chambers, just taking in the sight that had unfolded before him. He cherished such moments, for it confirmed again that he finally had a family to call his own. Aislinn would never admit it, but she had gladly taken on the role of Declan's mother and the boy obviously thought of her also in the same respect. He did not regret that he had agreed to foster the child. Even his own heart was growing found of the boy.

Just then Declan's head turned toward him and his face beamed with happiness. He jumped from Aislinn's lap and ran over to him.

"Milord." The boy had reached him and was frantically searching the pockets of Dougray's garments. Dougray's low chuckle filled the room. "Dear lad, what is it ye think that I am hiding?"

Declan stopped and craned his head back, looking wide-eyed up at Dougray. "Ye did not bring me a sweet?"

He lowered himself so that he was eye level with the child. Aislinn noticed that a smile tugged at his lips. "Declan, I fear I have come to spoil ye." Seeing the crestfallen look spread across the child's face he hurried on, "But I love to do so." With that he pulled from the folds of his mantle a container of honey pears.

Declan's small hands clapped in delight. "Oh thank ye so. It is my favorite." He took the treat and ran over to the table.

Dougray rose then to his full height and strode over to Aislinn, who was grinning at him. "Ye look lovely, my fair story teller." He pulled her close. "Good enough to eat, I might add."

She couldn't help but giggle. "Stop. Declan will see you."

He sighed heavily and released her. "Later perhaps?" He loved it when she blushed and she was doing so now.

"A.J., do ye want some of my honey pears?" Declan offered.

"No, you go right ahead, but thank you for offering." She glanced back at Dougray who was watching her so intently. "What?"

"Nothing in particular. I was just thinking how natural mothering comes to ye, and I can't help but wish to see our own children at yer feet."

Aislinn turned away from him but not before he saw the wary expression in her eyes. He regarded her quizzically for a moment, trying to make sense of why she always avoided the discussion of having children. Surely she was aware that each time they came together there was a possibility of that happening. She could already be…. "Aislinn?"

"Do you want to go with Declan and me to see Neala? We were going to do that, as soon as I finished the story."

How quickly she had changed the subject. Against his better judgment, he let it go. "I cannot for I have business to attend to. I will join ye later."

She nodded. Only when he finally left the room did she feel that she could relax. He wanted children, but she didn't want to think about it.

They had a full day at Neala's, for the old woman had tales she wished to share, more myths and legends that Aislinn was eager to write down in her journal. She was beginning to have quite a collection now.

They had headed back at a leisurely pace. Declan skipped up ahead when he caught sight of the gates, giving Teige the opportunity to voice his worries.

"Fiona is using Cormac, I am sure. The man is besotted and a fool as well if he thinks that he should offer marriage to her."

"I am probably the wrong person to ask advice on this matter. Fiona isn't exactly at the top of my list."

"I know. That is why I hoped that ye would speak with Cormac. He respects yer opinion." He shook his head. " I've never seen him act this way with any woman."

"As much as you refuse to believe it, Cormac is most likely in love with Fiona. I'm not sure that he will listen to me, but if you want I will…. Watch Declan!" She didn't bother to explain. In a flash, she had taken off at a full run, leaving Teige wondering what in the world had just happened.

She had been drawn to the commotion over by the bargaining table where a burley man had raised his hand to hit a petite woman who was standing right in front of him. It was the scream of terror that propelled her into action.

"Stop it!" She tried to raise her voice above the man's ranting and the woman's wailing from each slap that she endured. The man either did not hear, or refused to, and continued his abuse. Aislinn saw onlookers but no one bothered to interfere. She was outraged by the time she reached them. Without thinking of her own safety, she grabbed a hold of the man's arm, just as he was about to send his fist into the now hysterical woman. The man was beyond reason at this point. He turned at his would-be attacker and landed his free hand into Aislinn's face. She never saw it coming and the punch hit her full force sending her flying back, hitting hard sprawled on the ground like an unwanted bundle.

From there, everything seemed to happen so fast. The bully, who, she would find out later, was Haggerty, wore a horrified expression, for he realized all too late what he had done. He turned to flee but Dermot and Cormac had seen what had happened and had their swords drawn ready to use if the man so much as took another step.

"Ye dare strike a lady?" Cormac jabbed the sword menacingly close to the man's throat.

"Ye will be lucky if ye live out this day," Dermot added causing the woman who had been unmercifully beaten to scream at the top of her lungs.

Teige arrived on the scene with Declan beside him. He offered his hand to Aislinn. "Are ye all right, milady?"

"I am fine." She gripped his hand thankful for his assistance, since she felt a little unsteady. "I was rash." She felt the side of her face and knew that it was probably already starting to become black and blue.

The woman, who had a bloody lip to show for the ill treatment bestowed on her, grabbed hold of Aislinn's arm. "Please, milady. That is me husband. Spare his life, I beg of ye."

Spare his life? Aislinn would like nothing more then to end it, though not literally. The miserable swine had no business walking around, pounding his fist into people. He needed to be taught a lesson. But one look at the woman's compelling eyes that were begging her to save her husband's life made her wonder if the woman's fears were warranted.

She didn't have time to respond for Cormac took matters into his own hands.

"We will see what milord thinks of ye striking Lady Aislinn, aye?" He grabbed the sobbing bully by the collar dragging him away.

Dermot cleared the crowd that had gathered, and Teige led Aislinn away from the woman, who was still pleading with her.

Dougray didn't waste a moment after he heard what had transpired. He went straight to their chambers, where Cahir was trying to apply a leach to

Aislinn's bruised face. "It will ease the swelling, milady. Do ye always have to be so difficult?"

"I'm fine," she answered him and moved away. The man had not exactly made an effort to make amends with her after he nearly had her burnt at the stake for thinking she had poisoned Dougray, and this was not making it any better with him wanting to put a bloodsucking thing on her face.

"Are ye all right?" Dougray's voice drew Aislinn to him. One look at her swollen face and he was enraged all over again. "I wanted to hear from yer lips what has happened, before I deliver a just punishment to Joseph Haggerty." Her gaze alone indicated that she wished to speak to him alone. Once everyone was ushered out, and doors closed, he again looked at her. He gingerly touched the side of her face, causing her to wince. He clenched his teeth thinking how he wanted to slam his fist into Haggerty's face for what he had done to her.

"Joseph is his name?"

"Aye."

"The man was beating on his wife. She is in worse shape than I am."

"And how did he happen to land his fists into ye?"

"I tried to stop him. I guess I should have anticipated him retaliating against whoever tried to stop him from completing his mission."

"Ye should not have interfered, Aislinn."

"How could I not? He was beating a poor woman to death."

"It was his wife. The quarrel was between them."

She just stood there for a moment not believing she had heard him correctly. When she finally found her voice, she did not hide the fact that she was thoroughly disgusted. "The quarrel was between them? You don't care that the man could have beaten her to death, and in front of witnesses, I might add. Not one person tried to stop the appalling brute from finishing his task. I can't believe you think that it was all right."

"I never said that I agreed with the behavior. I would never condone a man abusing someone who could not defend themselves, man, woman or child."

"No? Well you just did. You said that it was none of my business and shouldn't have interfered. Maybe you should just lock his wife in with him so that he could finish the job." She turned away in a huff.

"Ye must understand...."

"Understand what?" She whirled on him. "I will not understand a man beating on a defenseless woman. I don't care if he is the husband or not. It is wrong, and you, the Lord of Dunhaven, should see to it that the women are protected from such treatment. You lay down the law for other things. You could enforce this as well."

"Do not proceed to tell me how I should deal with my people. As for Joseph Haggerty, he will pay for the crime he has committed, and that was to dare lay a hand on ye."

"What are you going to do? Chop off his hand? Kill him? Boil him with hot oil? God, I am trapped in an uncivilized world."

"I'll have ye know that I do not, at a whim, torture the people whom I am responsible for. Do ye think that I am that cruel?"

She knew that he wasn't and she felt terrible that she had even suggested it. "No, I don't. But I don't see you helping the situation. You're upset of the mistreatment to me. I do appreciate it, but I don't accept the way ye can close yer eyes to the rest."

"What would ye have me do?"

"I don't know." She went over to the window seat and plopped down. She couldn't get the image of the woman out of her mind, her pleading for mercy for a husband who had abused her. "I don't want the man's death on my conscience but," she looked up at him, "I don't want the woman to be mistreated."

"An obvious dilemma then."

After careful consideration of what Aislinn had revealed to him, Dougray decided that he had the appropriate punishment for Joseph Haggerty. He waited in the Great Hall, while Cormac went down to retrieve the prisoner.

He let Haggerty stand there long after everyone had left them alone. He busied himself purposely letting the man sweat, wondering if his days were numbered. Finally he looked up, meeting the terrified man's gaze. "Come forward, Joseph."

The man was leery, but he made his feet move.

"Sit down." Dougray indicated the seat in front of him.

While Joseph pulled out the chair, Dougray poured two tankards full of mead and offered one to Joseph. Again the man hesitated, but his thirst won out. He drank heartily before he returned the tankard to the table. "Thank ye, milord."

Dougray leaned back in his chair. "I am struck with a rather difficult decision here." He paused before he continued. "Grave charges have been brought against ye."

"I did not mean to strike milady. I didn't see her."

"The bruise on her face proves ye saw her well enough." The terseness in his voice made Joseph's Adam's apple bob up and down nervously. "Lady Aislinn wishes yer miserable life spared, only she does not want ye to harm another soul." He again paused purposely letting the man's imagination run wild.

"Please I beg of ye. I will do anything ye want. I'll…."

"Silence." Dougray rose from the table and Joseph winced as if he had been struck. "Yer wife also wishes ye to be spared."

"She's a good…." His words died in his throat when he saw Dougray's lethal glare. He was wise enough to lower his gaze.

"I have decided to concede, but with strict stipulations." This drew the man's attention to Dougray once more. "I will let ye draw breath as long as ye treat yer wife with respect. If she even has a fingernail broken, I will have yer head separated from yer body. Do we have an understanding?"

The man's eyes bulged, but he managed to bob his head up and down.

"Good." Dougray went to the doors and opened them. "Murrough?" He rounded the corner. "Will ye escort Joseph back to his home?"

"Aye, milord."

Joseph had already risen, grateful to still be alive. He was almost out the door, when Dougray halted him. "Haggerty?" The man cringed, but he turned to face him. Maybe he was going to die after all.

Dougray took a swing at the man sending him flying against Murrough. Dougray towered over him his fist still clenched. "That was for Lady Aislinn." He then left the room.

"I think he broke me nose." Joseph touched his throbbing face.

"Stop yer whining, Haggerty. Ye should be thanking your lucky stars that is all he did to ye."

Dougray never explained to Aislinn what had transpired with his decision with Joseph Haggerty, and she had not asked. It was Mrs. Haggerty who informed her that her husband's life had been spared, and that he was treating her with such reverence that she was sure another man had been sent back to her.

"He is like when we first wed." The woman indeed looked radiant.

"I'm glad that everything worked out for you, but I cannot take the credit. Lord Dougray must have had a word with your husband."

"Maybe so, but again I thank ye, milady." She curtsied quickly before she left.

Hamish was with her and came to his feet. He had just finished his push-ups and heard the whole exchange. "I know Joseph Haggerty. He is changed man. I heard him even volunteer to help his wife wash the clothes."

"Hmm." She couldn't help herself from pondering over the reason why Joseph Haggerty would have changed so drastically. And she planned on thanking *him* personally.

She found Dougray in the library hard at work, but he stopped what he was doing the moment she entered. His brows arched when she closed the doors and locked them. Without a word she sat down on his lap and wrapped her arms around his neck. He opened his mouth to say something, but she silenced him with her forefinger pressing down on his lips. She then kissed the tip of his nose, then his eyes and finally she gratifyingly kissed his warm welcoming mouth. Her dark eyes met his questioning ones and she ran her finger over his mustache.

"Not that I am complaining, but how did I come to warrant such affection?"

A beguiling smile spread across her lips. "Because I think you are the most wonderful man alive."

A chuckle rumbled deep in his chest. "I am, am I?"

She nodded. "And I plan to show you just how much I appreciate the fact." Her hand slid beneath his tunic and his brows arched quite high on his forehead.

"Ye know that I have to head out, to take care of another dispute. Cattle has been taken again. It may require a few hours or more of my time."

"You can't leave yet. You're going to be busy."

"Are ye planning on seducing me in the library, lass?"

"Uh huh." She nodded.

His smile proved that he rather liked the idea. "The dispute can wait."

Chapter Fifty-Four

Cormac hadn't been with another woman since Fiona was warming his nights, and surprisingly he found that he didn't want to be with anyone else. He was to meet her now. She had been rather secretive but he knew that was how she was at times, wanting to sneak away to make love where most women would never want to go. It was exciting as if they were doing something that they shouldn't be doing.

He spotted her waiting at the designated spot, though she had not seen him as of yet. He quietly dismounted and moved swiftly behind her grabbing her in a fierce embrace. She let out a yelp of surprise. He nuzzled sweet kisses down her neck only to have her hands on his chest to stop his ardor from getting too carried away. "Follow me." She led him even farther away from the keep. Not that it mattered since he didn't have to be back until later. There was plenty of time to play this little game of hers.

Dougray still had not returned, making Aislinn feel extremely uneasy. He had told her that he was only going to be gone a few hours and that was two days ago. What could have become of him?

"Be still, milady," Moira gently scolded. She was sewing the lovely beads within her tresses. A most difficult task since though her hair had grown to nearly her shoulders, it was still quite short in comparison to what she was used to.

"Sorry, Moira. It is hard for me to sit like this when I am so worried."

"Do not fret, milady. Lord Dougray has often tarried longer than he had anticipated. These petty raids can sometimes be complicated. *Erics* have to be paid to the victim, and if a term cannot be agreed upon, there will be more discussing."

"Knowing that does not make waiting any easier."

Moira smiled. "Ye miss him."

Aislinn half turned to look up at the young girl "Yes, I do." She smiled warmly.

"He will be back soon."

There was a knock on the door and Aislinn bid the visitor to enter. It was Teige with a sealed letter. "This just arrived, milady, brought forth by a rider who did not wait to be shown in." He handed it to her. While she was busy reading its contents, Teige couldn't help but bring his attention to Moira.

She blushed prettily making her cheeks a rosy pink. Teige had known Moira since they were children, but she wasn't a little girl anymore. She was of marrying age now, and if the shy gazes she gave him were any indication of how she felt for him, he just might have a chance.

Aislinn stood so suddenly that both Teige and Moira forgot their preoccupation with each other. "Dougray has been taken. Hurry, Teige, gather Dermot and Cormac. We must leave now." Desperation rang in those words.

"Who has taken him?" Teige took the letter that she handed him.

"They will kill him if I don't go." She ran to the trunk to pull out her riding clothes. "He's being held for ransom and it says if I don't go personally...."

"A.J., this could be a trap. We need to check...."

"We can't wait!" She let go of the trunk lid letting it slam shut with a bang. "It states if I am not there by sundown, they will execute him. I refuse to take a chance with his life. Stay and check out the authenticity of it if you wish, but I am going, alone if I have to."

Teige was at a loss what to do. Instinct told him that he should see if he could find the messenger and extract the answers from him. But how could he do that and protect Aislinn at the same time? He knew she would never stay put while he did this and would end up going alone. "Just promise me ye will wait until I find Cormac and Dermot."

"Go then. Hurry." She was still rushing around the room gathering her sword and other items she felt that she might need. "I'll meet you down at the stables."

Teige had rushed down the steps nearly knocking over Hamish.

"Where are ye going in such a hurry?"

"There is trouble afoot I fear. I need to find Cormac and Dermot."

"Dermot is in the hall." Teige would have gone on but Hamish stopped him. "Can I be of assistance?"

He hesitated bringing the boy into this, but he seemed eager. He had shown great skill with the sword and Teige knew most of the men were either hunting or were needed to guard the gates. "Aye. Come with me then."

Aislinn was ready before all of them and was pacing when Teige finally arrived with Dermot and Hamish. "Where's Cormac?"

"I was unable to locate him." Teige didn't want to tell her that he had a hunch Cormac was somewhere with Fiona.

"We can't wait. We've already wasted enough time." With her order, they left the safety of the keep and headed in the direction that the ransom note indicated, toward the Butler stronghold.

Teige was more than a little uneasy with this venture. He ordered Dermot in front with Hamish, and he took up the rear hoping that they could protect Aislinn, if the need arose.

After hours of lovemaking, Cormac reluctantly left Fiona's side. She was overly vivacious, even for her. Every time he suggested that they head back to the castle, she thought of ways to make him forget that he had other duties that he needed to tend to.

He was still wearing a satisfied grin when he entered the courtyard and nodded toward one of the guards, who immediately came forward to halt him.

"Where have ye been? Teige has been looking all over for ye."

"What was so urgent?"

"Milady received notice that milord was being held for ransom."

"What say ye?" Panic spread through his veins. He was the one in charge when Murrough was away. He should have been here. "Milord left the keep with men that would guard him. How could this happen?"

"The Butlers must have done something underhanded."

Cormac's frown deepened. "Where is Lady Aislinn now?"

"Gone to meet the kidnappers."

"What? Alone?" he shouted. "And Teige let her go?"

"Teige is with her."

Cormac ran his hand through his hair, angry with himself for not being here to make sense of this. "It was obviously a trap. Who brought this letter?"

"Don't know. Teige did suggest this to milady. She would not see reason and was determined to go by herself, if she had to."

"I have no doubt that she would too," Cormac agreed unhappily. "How much of a head start do they have on us?"

"Two hours at most."

"Gather a few men and meet me back here in ten minutes. We will go after them and pray to God that we are not too late."

Chapter Fifty-Five

The attack came with such a sudden surprise that Dermot and Teige barely had time to draw their swords. Aislinn had dismounted and was not far behind with her own weapon. She immediately attacked with force.

Midst the fighting, she caught a glimpse of Hamish. At the moment, he seemed to be holding his own, though she was not sure how long his strength would hold up to the full grown men who kept coming at him.

She threw another swing at her would-be attacker knocking him flat. She then whirled about, catching her sword around the enemy's with such force that his weapon flew from him. The man looked in awe at the tall woman who had taken his sword from him, and with little or no effort at all. She was indeed every bit what had been rumored about her and more. She took a step forward, her intent obvious. "Where's Dougray?" she demanded, only he was too scared to hear the question.

"*Scathach!*" The man turned and ran. He was not going to be killed by the warrior who seemed more goddess than woman. Aislinn turned planning on going to Hamish's aid, but before she could move, she witnessed the ruthless warrior's attack on the boy, his sword lunging toward him. She let out a scream and charged the man who had slain Hamish, not caring in the least that she was being reckless in her attempt.

Her foolishness nearly cost her her life. The man twisted around to protect himself and nearly ran her through before she corrected her mistake. She wasn't fast enough. The enemy's sword managed to slice through her shirt, grazing her tender flesh. With a cry, she stumbled back falling over a victim whom Teige had finished off only moments before. Teige saw her go down, but was unable to help for he was occupied with deflecting the blows that were coming dearly close to severing his head.

Aislinn scrambled to her feet, but it was too late. Her assailant was upon her, the point of his sword pressing against her chest.

His bluish green eyes bore into hers more with amazement than with triumph. "Do not move, milady," he ordered then shouted for all the others to hear, "I have yer lady, and if ye value her life, ye will surrender now."

The fighting came to a stop. Teige and Dermot looked to where Aislinn was being held by a Butler's sword knowing the fight was over. Teige was the first who recognized him. "So, Tremain, ye still live."

Aislinn's eyes widened. This was Tremain Butler? The very man that Dougray's sister had given her heart to, but he was also the man who had killed Hamish.

"Aye." The man's eyes glared with venom. "And if I did not have me orders to deliver ye to the Butler, I would finish the job that I started long ago on ye."

Teige took a step forward but Dermot held him back. "Ye'll be dead quick enough," he hissed at him. "We have to think of A.J. There will be time later for revenge."

Tremain didn't like that Dermot was whispering and made his point known. "No need to discuss escape, unless ye plan on seeing yer lady's head removed from her shoulders."

"We will go with ye," Teige said through clenched teeth, knowing that he didn't have any other options. The other men under Tremain's orders relieved Teige and Dermot of their weapons. Dermot's gaze found Hamish's body among others that had fallen lying so still with blood seeping from the wounds. He choked back the tears as his heart clenched in his chest.

Teige couldn't allow himself to think about the boy. For right now, he needed a clear head so that he could think of an escape.

A guard pushed him forward.

Aislinn was thrown in one of the cells where darkness would soon be her company, the heavy door shutting behind her. At the moment she wasn't scared for what was in store for her, for she had a hunch that she was not in immediate danger, but she worried what they would do to Teige and Dermot.

Teige had been right and she had been a fool not to see that the letter was an elaborate trap. The Butlers didn't have Dougray, but were going to use her as bait to draw him here.

"Milady?" When she did not answer, he spoke a little louder, "A.J.?"

Aislinn heard Teige and moved closer to the door. "I'm here, Teige. And Dermot?"

"Here, milady." The man answered for himself.

"A.J., how bad is your wound?" Teige had noticed on their way here that her shirt was torn and blood had soaked through the fabric.

Aislinn had been so worried about where Tremain was taking them that she had forgotten about her injury. She looked down to see the tear in her shirt and lifted the fabric to take a look at the damage. It was bruised and tender to the touch, but at least the bleeding had stopped. "A flesh wound is all," she was relieved to report. "And the two of you?"

"We fare well," Teige answered yet again.

"We will get out of this." Dermot sounded more confident than he actually felt.

They were all silent for a moment, just enough time for helplessness to seep into their consciousness.

"I left a message at the gate for Cormac. He will come for us," Teige offered, but in his heart, he didn't think it was possible. Cormac was not one to fall back from a fight, but they were deep in Butler territory.

Aislinn moved away from the door and leaned against the wall before she let herself sink to the floor. She felt weary and couldn't help the tears that slid down her cheek. This was her fault. If she had listened to Teige, they wouldn't be in this mess and Hamish.... She sniffled and the sound echoed, reaching both Dermot and Teige. They looked at each other both worried that her hope was diminishing.

"A.J., do not dismay," Dermot tried to reach out with words.

She wiped the tears away with the back of her hand. "I killed Hamish, as surely as if I took my sword to him. It's my fault."

"It is not yer fault." Teige leaned against the door, pounding his fist against the hard wood.

"No? Hamish was but a boy and I convinced him that he could be a warrior. He should have been at home, where he would have been safe. I sentenced him to death the moment I placed that weapon in his hand."

"Ye saved him, milady. I had never seen him more alive," Dermot spoke. "Ye saved me as well. I shall be forever in yer debt."

Before Aislinn could comment, she heard footsteps approaching. She quickly dried her tears and stood to bravely meet her captor.

Chapter Fifty-Six

"What do ye mean they are missing?" Dougray stormed. Murrough had already gathered men for a search party and they were scouting the areas. "Dermot, Teige, Cormac, even Hamish, are gone?"

"It would seem so," Murrough confirmed even though Dougray already knew the answer.

"Where was Aislinn going?"

"We don't know, but we are looking into it. There is a definite trail leading from the gate. They seemed to be in a hurry by the tracks."

Dougray was beyond worried. She disobeyed often but this was out of character even for her. She usually wandered near the glen or down by the water. There was no reason for her to venture toward Butler territory. It didn't make any sense. "Send for Moira." He whirled around to face Murrough. He didn't know why he hadn't thought of it earlier.

Murrough motioned to the guard to do Dougray's bidding.

Dougray paced the room.

Abbot Kirwan decided to come forward offering his opinion. "She has always fought against yer authority, milord. She may have decided that she would take no more. Mayhap she is on her way back to the Hennessy stronghold."

Dougray turned on the man, his eyes narrowing to slits. "When I wish to hear yer opinions, dear Abbot, I will ask for them."

Kirwan turned his attention to Cahir, his beady eyes fastening onto his. Cahir was not comfortable with the abbot, but some of what he relayed to him could not be denied. He had seen firsthand what witchery the woman could perform.

At that moment, Moira was ushered in. Dougray quickly advanced upon her, nearly frightening the girl to death. He took a deep breath to calm his frantic heartbeat, so that he could better address the young woman. "Moira, did yer mistress say where she was heading this afternoon?"

Moira's eyes nervously looked between Murrough and Dougray. "Something must have happened."

"Where did she go, Moira?"

"She received a letter, milord."

"Did she mention what was in this letter?"

"I am not sure, but milady said that she was going after ye."

"Me? Ye are sure?"

Moira nodded. "She took her sword. She thought ye were in some kind of peril."

Dougray turned to Murrough. "We ride to Butler's stronghold."

"But milord…."

"Don't argue with me, Murrough. If Butler has Aislinn, he will die this night."

Dougray stormed from the hall leaving Murrough to tend to the frightened maid.

"Has harm come to milady?" Moira searched Murrough's face.

"We do not know what has become of her. But we believe that she was with Cormac and Teige."

"Aye. Teige is a strong man." Moira blushed and looked down at her folded hands.

Murrough realized that the lass must care deeply for Teige. He wondered if the man was aware of her budding attraction. He gently laid a hand on her shoulder. "Aye, lass, Teige is very capable. Do not worry so."

She brushed away a tear, trying very hard to believe him.

Sir Fingham Butler eyed the securely bound Lady Aislinn Fitzpatrick of Dunhaven with a look that would have brought forth fear in the bravest of men, yet she stood there dry eyed, shoulders back and throwing a few glaring looks of her own.

Still, she didn't look all that threatening. She was tall, as he had heard men say of her characteristics, standing nearly a full three inches above his own height. She was dressed in a riding habit, and her hair, though quite short, was decorated with beads painstakingly sewn into the strands. That seemed a little fancy for going out on a raid, but again she was an unusual woman.

She was not an overly attractive in his opinion but there was something about her eyes that seemed to captivate him. They were like pools of shimmering midnight with long dark lashes to frame them. Those bold eyes spoke of courage and he was not one to think lightly of such an attribute.

Even now at her obvious disadvantage she was blatantly eyeing him. If she was frightened in any way, he could not tell for she did not even flinch beneath his gaze. He stood in front of her now, feet apart, hands behind his back. "So, ye are the feared warrior whom they call *Scathach*." He spoke in refined English and in return she answered him readily in the same language.

"My lord, I am not aware what you might have heard about me, but I assure you that they are most likely exaggerated, as most tales usually are."

He smiled. "Most assuredly. Still, I have seen the fear in these men's eyes." He pulled out his dirk in a dramatic display hoping to unnerve her just a little. He was to be disappointed; not a single muscle did she move. Rather than being perturbed over the fact, he found himself rather impressed.

He approached her then, circling her before he took the sharp edge of his dirk and lightly ran it against the delicate portion of her neck. "Do I not frighten ye in the least?"

"No. I have decided that you must be a fair lord or you wouldn't have so many loyal men. You won't murder me in your home, especially with my hands tied behind my back because it wouldn't be honorable." She held her breath hoping that she had called his bluff. When she heard his low chuckle, she knew that she had been right.

He cut her loose and she immediately rubbed her sore members, trying to restore some circulation. "Come. Sit." Butler indicated the bench.

Once seated, she looked at him again with questions of her own. "Since I was not invited on my own accord, I can only presume that you have some alternative motive?"

He smiled. "Aye. Ye don't mince words, do ye?"

"I believe in being direct."

"Aye and so do I. We might get along yet. As ye know, the Lord of Dunhaven and I have not seen eye to eye."

"Enemies, is what I have heard."

"Ye have been informed, but do ye know how this came to be?"

"Why don't you tell me? From experience, I have learned that it is a good idea to hear both sides of the story."

"It is simple: Dougray Fitzpatrick is a murderer." This time he read unease in those dark penetrating eyes. She was human after all. "Ah, he did not tell ye this." She didn't say anything so he filled in the answers. "He murdered his wife...my only daughter."

"You have proof of this?"

"Proof! Aye, there is proof. My daughter is dead. That is all the proof that one needs." He was up and pacing then, furious that she had even questioned him.

"You witnessed the act?"

He stopped and glared at her. "If I had, Fitzpatrick would be dead now. No, he was very clever indeed. He made her death look like an accident."

"And he did this because…." She held out her hands, wanting him to back up his accusation.

"Because he wanted her holdings and nothing more."

"Dougray is a very wealthy man, why would he…."

"He has nothing but his land; his money is gone, taken with his father's death. He needed my daughter's dowry to sustain his holdings. He would have lost everything if it hadn't been for his marriage to Ella."

"Why did you agree to the marriage then?"

"I was fooled into thinking that he might actually love her. They were not married more than a few weeks before my Ella met her untimely death. She was the most beautiful woman. She could have had anyone, someone who would have cherished her. Instead, she married a man who had no means other than a title."

"It doesn't seem to be the way that Dougray saw it. He told me he loved her. He weeps at her grave for the injustice of a life that was taken too soon. You say that Dougray is responsible? Well he feels the same and blames himself. He has told me what happened. Do you wish to hear his side of the story or do you prefer to continue your hatred without really knowing?"

Fingham hesitated. He hadn't expected this woman to defend Fitzpatrick. He had heard that she had been forced into this marriage. Finally, he nodded for her to continue.

"Dougray was supposed to have gone riding that day Ella died, but he was called away to settle a petty conflict, with two men who did not have the decency to put aside their differences for one more day. Ella didn't want to wait for Dougray, feeling it could be hours before they would be able to head out. She wanted to ride in the beautiful afternoon sun and not take the chance that the weather would change."

"Why was she on Fitzpatrick's horse?"

"Dougray's mount was the only one saddled. Ella was the one who insisted that she could handle the horse."

"I don't believe ye!" he shouted, his eyes bulging. He walked over to her as though he would strike her, but Aislinn again held her ground. Still looking at her, he yelled for his man. "Tremain!" He turned toward the door as the warrior filled the doorway. Obviously, he had not been far away. "Get her out of my sight!" he ordered as he stormed out of the room.

Tremain glanced at the retreating back of his lord before he turned raised brows to Aislinn. "Follow me." He wasn't overly cordial.

She started to head toward the stairs that would lead down to the dungeon, but Tremain halted her. "Nay. Milord wishes ye to have a room."

Fingham went to his private chambers asking not to be disturbed. What if what the woman said was true? Could Fitzpatrick actually be innocent of his daughter's death? It would have been like Ella to take Dougray's mount. She never feared riding any horse. He collapsed in his chair, suddenly feeling very old and tired.

Cormac led the men in silence following the tracks readily enough. The more he dwelled on the day's events, the more troubled he became by them.

The summons that was sent to Aislinn could not be from Fingham Butler. It simply was not his way, which meant that Aislinn was heading into a sure trap. This was not the only thing that was bothering him. He had a nagging feeling that Fiona's behavior this afternoon was a well thought out plan to keep him away from the keep. Fiona had mentioned that she needed for him to do her a favor, something that would ensure all their safety. He should have questioned her, but he had been lost within her sweet embrace, but now, her words came back to haunt him.

"Ye will need to go to Dougray's aid in the Butler's territory," she cooed into his ear, as she hurried upon him. He had nodded his head, too close to rapture to comment on her strange request, and then he had fallen asleep exhausted from the hours of their lovemaking. He would have forgotten all about what she had mentioned, if he hadn't been informed of the letter that Aislinn had received. Before he left the keep, he had tried to find Fiona and question her further, but she was conveniently nowhere to be found.

They had ridden hard and fast before they came upon a small party of Butler's men. A fight immediately broke out but they had the advantage, and it ended before there was any bloodshed. From the ones captured Cormac was able to learn what had happened to Aislinn and the others.

Tremain had taken them prisoner. He swore under his breath wondering what course he should take now.

He solemnly walked over to where the bodies were thrown knowing from his captives that one of his men had fallen trying to defend Lady Aislinn. He came through the foliage spotting him only a few feet away lying there in a pool of blood. Grief washed over him like a wave. The boy had been under his command and he had failed him. He clutched the hilt of his sword, wishing that he could seek his revenge for the injustice done.

He knelt down on his haunches resting his head in his hands as the full weight of his bereavement fell upon him. He had failed everyone whom he held dear and for what? Never should he have listened to his heart.

A low moan drew his attention. He stood, his hand still on his sword for he was not sure who stirred or if there was a threat. His eyes widened in disbelief. "Hamish?"

The boy slowly turned and looked to where he saw Cormac. "What happened?" Hamish was still disoriented. He looked down at himself and saw the sticky substance that was splattered against his clothing. "I've been slaughtered!"

Cormac was beside him now searching for the wound that had caused the unsightly spillage. "Ye are speaking with a strong mind; I do not think the blood is pouring from yer body. He motioned for Hamish to look behind him. The boy turned his head to see a slain man with only part of his head still attached. Hamish quickly looked away feeling the bile rise in the back of his throat.

"Ye were lucky this day, Hamish. An amazing thing that the blood of a Butler is what has saved yer sorry arse."

Hamish nodded but his worries were not of himself. "Where is A.J.?"

"Tremain has taken her. We came upon ye after the fighting was over. We have learned already that Dermot and Teige were taken hostage as well. Tremain obviously left ye for dead." He helped the boy to his feet.

"We need to go after them." Hamish was already looking for his sword.

"We need more men. Tremain is bringing milady back to the Butler's stronghold. We will not be able to reach them in time."

"We can try."

"That would be suicide, Hamish. As it is, we endanger ourselves by staying here. They will be back to investigate what became of their men. Thinking the worst, they will bring plenty. It would not be wise for them to find us chatting about our options. Retrieve yer sword, Hamish, we must go back for help."

Dougray's men came across Hamish and Cormac almost immediately. Dougray himself rode ahead to meet them, hoping that they would tell him that Aislinn was already on her way back to the keep, but one look at Hamish was enough to send him into a panic. "What has happened here? Where are ye injuries, lad?"

"'Tis not my blood, milord, but the blood of a Butler," Hamish answered.

Dougray looked to Cormac. "And Aislinn?" His heart pounded in his ears waiting to hear his answer.

"She is alive, but Tremain has taken her to Lord Fingham. Teige and Dermot are prisoners also." Cormac could not meet Dougray's gaze for he was guilty of leaving the keep unattended.

"How much lead do they have on us?"

"No more than an hour," Cormac again answered.

Dougray looked at Hamish whose eyes were downcast. He moved his mount over to him. "Ye may go back to the keep if ye like."

The boy met Dougray's eyes and sat up a little taller. "Nay, milord. I will fight till we have A.J....I mean milady, home safe and sound."

He nodded. "Ye are a man now, Hamish. Forgive me for not seeing that sooner. He turned to Murrough. "We must be alert."

A rider approached and the men parted to let him by. Dougray's eyes widened in surprise. "Fiach Ó Colmaín what are ye doing here?" He couldn't help but notice the broadsword he carried; he looked up seeing his cousin smiling at him. "But ye are a priest."

"So ye and the others keep reminding me, but I am a man first with duties to his family. Yer wife has been taken to the enemy's keep; I am here to lend a hand."

"Ye still know how to use that rusty old thing?"

"I took vows. I did not hack off me arms. Now what do we know?"

Chapter Fifty-Seven

Aislinn still was not sure what was going to happen to her, but for now she seemed to be safe since Tremain deposited her in a private chamber with food and drink. She was treated with upmost respect, but still there was no denying that she indeed was a prisoner. She had barely touched her meal when the servant came back for the tray. She was an elderly woman with gray hair and with eyes that looked upon her with kindness. "Please tell me, my friends that were brought in with me, are they all right?"

The older woman glanced nervously behind her. "Do not ask such things." She went over to the tray, noticing that the tall dark woman had not eaten very much. She took pity on her. "They are still alive." With that she took the tray and hurried out of the room.

Aislinn couldn't help but try the door to see if it was unlocked. Of course it was not. She went back to the bed and sat down. She didn't know what she was going to do. A quick survey of her prison, she found nothing that would aid her in an escape. The windows were mere slits and she wouldn't be able to fit through them and the only weapon she could find was the heavy candlestick holder. She wasn't sure what good it was going to be against swords and daggers, but still she kept it close at hand.

There seemed nothing more she could do, but wait.

Dougray's men swiftly surrounded the outermost region of the castle, relieving some of Butler's men from their posts and securing the area.

Fiach came to stand by his cousin. "I do not mean to draw this to yer attention, but I feel it would be of some interest to ye." Dougray looked at him and nodded for him to continue. "Ye might find it a bit curious that though Hamish is covered with the enemy's blood, yer man Cormac has not a drop, not even on his sword. Ye might want to question where he was when the fight broke out." Fiach moved back to his position, but Dougray's eyes sought out Cormac. He had never in the past had reason to doubt the man, but he couldn't dismiss the obvious clues. Cormac had been acting peculiar, almost guilty…but from what?

Teige stood and walked over to the bars that held him prisoner.

"It's of no use ye know," Dermot told him.

"What's not?"

"Ye trying to see if ye can bend the bars to yer will. They're still as sturdy as they were when they first brought us in here."

Teige sighed. "I can't stand not knowing what is going on up there."

"Butler has definite plans, but I would wager that he has no intentions of hurting A.J."

"Nay. I've come to suspect that milady is bait."

"Bait?"

"Aye, Dermot. Butler wants the Fitzpatrick well enough and what better way to have him come straight to him."

"A trap sure enough."

"Aye, and us stuck below like a couple of rats." He pounded his fist against the door.

"What do ye think he has planned for us?" Dermot had been thinking about it for a while now.

Teige looked at his friend not wanting to panic him, but he was pretty sure they were not going to just be released on their own recognizance. This was Fingham Butler they were talking about and the man had not been the same since his daughter Ella had passed on to the other world. Then there was Tremain who had his own reasons to detest the Fitzpatricks and all that serve him. There would be no mercy from him either.

"Teige?" Dermot felt uneasy now.

"Do not worry, Dermot. We will think of a way out of this."

Murrough hurried over to Dougray with his news. "Ye were right. There is a hidden entrance within the stone."

"Ella was not exaggerating then." Dougray had often wondered about her tale of a secret path. "It is not guarded?"

Murrough's mustache twitched with amusement. "Not anymore. It looks like the cave travels beneath the castle. We did not walk the length of it. Did Lady Ella happen to tell ye where this secret passage leads to?"

Dougray nodded. "To one of the storage rooms located in the dungeon."

"This is yer plan?" Murrough nearly choked. "Ye are taking us into the dungeon? Forgive me for saying this, but do ye not think it would be wise to avoid the very place that Butler wants to put us?"

"Nay, Murrough. It's exactly where we want to be. He'd never suspect it." Even Fiach had to smile. "Ye are a genius, cousin."

"Genius?" Murrough shook his head. "Ye better say a few prayers, priest, that we again see the light of day."

Dougray moved toward where Hamish and Cormac were located, leaving orders for Murrough to explain to the other men about the plan.

"Cormac, a word with ye please." Dougray couldn't help but let his eyes wander to the man's sword. It was as Fiach had said. The weapon was clean. He met Cormac's eyes now. "Do ye wish to share what has ye turned inside out? I stress that now would be a good time."

Cormac had been dreading this moment but found there was no other way around it. "I swear I didn't smell the deceit until it was too late."

Dougray had no wish for this to be drawn out. "Get to the point."

"I was with Fiona when the messenger arrived to give the notice to milady. They could not find me so readily. I should have been there but I was not." His anguish evident as he continued, "I read the summons, milord. It said that if milady didn't come alone, they would withdraw and yer death would be secured.

"She was with Teige, Dermot and young Hamish. I never left her unguarded at the castle," he defended himself. "When I arrived back and was informed about what had happened, I hurried the men, but still we were too late. Tremain had already taken them prisoners. This ye know, but there is more."

"More?"

"It is just a hunch but I cannot shake it. I fear that Fiona knew that I would be needed back at the keep, but purposely kept me…busy." He cleared his throat feeling extremely uncomfortable discussing this but knowing that he must. "She said things, milord, that did not make sense at the time, but now seem only too clear. She knew. She knew that there would be a message and I was too preoccupied to…." He lowered his head not able to continue his shameful telling. Slowly he removed his sword offering it to Dougray. When he did not take it, Cormac looked up questionably.

He had listen to all that Cormac had relayed to him. He was not pleased, but he knew that he could trust this man. "I do not see what good it would do me to take yer weapon, when we are about to enter the Butler's hold."

"But I thought…."

"Aye. I know what ye thought. We have a serious situation here. If you are right about Fiona, then I want to know whom she has been talking to."

"Aye, milord. I will speak to her straight away."

"Cormac, I must warn ye that ye may not like what ye find out. Can ye handle that with the way ye feel about the lass?"

He swallowed hard nodding his head. "Aye. I have been thinking that myself. If she has been deceitful…. If she deliberately in any way…." He couldn't finish what he was about to say for the pain of her betrayal ran too deep.

Dougray patted him on the back. "We shall see. Now go back to yer position and await my word."

"Aye, milord." He moved back beside Hamish.

Murrough had waited until the discussion was complete before he walked over to Dougray. "Ye were questioning Cormac?"

He nodded. "We have another problem it seems. Fiona may have known all about this."

Murrough shook his head. "What of Cormac? Matters of the heart are a tricky business."

"Aye, but I believe that Cormac can be dependable. I wager from now on that he will not let his lower extremities interfere with his logic." Dougray saw Fiach's skeptical expression, but he chose not to acknowledge it.

Dougray knew Fiona. She was one to work things to her advantage. She wanted Aislinn's place in his heart. That was no secret. She may have assisted with the kidnapping, but she didn't orchestrate it. Someone else with means was behind this.

Tremain knocked before he entered her room with his request from Lord Fingham. She took a good look at the man, now that she was no longer seething with anger over him murdering Hamish. She hadn't forgiven him for that slight, but because Miriam had spoken so highly of him, she was rather curious to find out why.

Tremain was probably no more than ten years older than she was. She had to admit that he was handsome with thick blond hair and strikingly light greenish-blue eyes. But she could not erase the image of poor Hamish lying in a pool of blood.

Tremain had walked over to her and slightly bowed showing his respect. "Milord wishes to speak with ye."

"Really now. And do I have a choice in this matter or are you simply being polite?"

He would have smiled at her bravery, but he did not want to give the woman any encouragement. He had heard all about her of course, but now he had firsthand experience with the likes of the *Scathach*. She fought well, and had courage far beyond some of the bravest. His gaze took in her appearance. He would have thought that she would look more like a man, but she didn't look anything of the sort. She was formidably tall in structure, but elegantly sculpted creating a rare and powerful-looking woman, definitely a striking figure, beautiful even. If circumstances had permitted them to meet without malice, he may have found that he would actually like her. "Nay, it is neither. I am simply doing what is expected of me."

"So you are expected to lead a woman to a man who despises her as an enemy? Doesn't seem quite gentlemanly does it?"

Tremain's back stiffened at her remark and his eyes narrowed. "The Butler is an honorable man and that is why I chose to follow his orders. As for yer husband…well the man does not even know the meaning of the word. Be glad that I have rescued ye from a fate that would surely end in yer demise."

"You feared for my life then? This is why your men tried to cut me in half, while you were busy slaying a mere boy."

He knew she spoke of the young lad that had been killed. He felt regretful about it, but it had been unavoidable. The boy would not lay down his weapon. He supposed it was to be expected that she would have preferred it was he that had been run through. "I did what had to be done," he stated but not quickly enough, for Aislinn saw the anguish there before he could mask it. With his guard down, maybe she could risk asking about the others.

"What of Teige and Dermot? Will you let them go?"

Again Tremain was impressed. The woman did not weep for her release, but asked for her men's safety. She was indeed worthy to have Fingham Butler's favor. "It is not up to me to decide." He saw worry crease her brow and chose to tell her of his lord's plan. "They will be judged fairly, maybe even have a chance to declare their loyalty to the Butlers."

Aislinn closed her eyes to hide the anguish she felt in her heart. She knew without a doubt that Teige and Dermot would never denounce their loyalty to Dougray. So where did that leave them? When she opened her eyes, Tremain had moved and was now standing directly in front of her. She would have taken a step back, but his hand came to rest upon her shoulder. His touch was somehow comforting and the look in his eyes was not of a man who wished to do her harm. This sent a rush of confusing thoughts her way. She wanted to hate him, but yet there was something in him that spoke of honesty. "Ye must come with me now. Milord awaits."

"Before I go, will you answer a question?"

"Depends on what it is?"

"I know how you feel about Dougray, but do you hold any animosity toward his sister?"

She saw him flinch and he took his hand away. "Why would ye ask this?"

"She told me about you, Tremain, and her relationship with you. I'll have to say she painted a better picture than I have seen so far."

"She spoke of me to ye? Why?"

"You didn't answer my question."

His eyes raked over her trying to discern what point she would have in mentioning Miriam. He had not seen her since the day they took her away to be Sir Reynolds' wife. He knew the man was dead and Miriam had refused to marry another. He had often wondered if she thought of him, as he thought so often of her. Even with the Fitzpatricks being the enemy, he could not deny what his heart felt for Miriam, but all of this didn't matter. He was a man with no title and had no lands. There was no point in pursuing her and opening old wounds. "What was between Miriam and myself ended long ago and has no bearing on my life now."

"What a shame." She walked right passed him leaving him to wonder what she meant by that statement.

He led her down the long hall to where Fingham's private chambers were located. Cold fear seeped through her resolve. Was this how it was going to be? She was going to be forced to bed down with the man?

She glanced warily at Tremain for any inclination to what was in store for her, but his expression was unreadable.

He opened the doors. When she didn't make a move to enter, he gently but forcefully took hold of her elbow and led her inside.

No words were spoken. Tremain gave a slight bow before he turned and left them alone, closing the large wooden doors behind him.

She just stood there not wanting to move forward, her eyes casually searching for what she could use as a weapon for she had no intention of letting this man touch her. She heard his low chuckle and her gaze darted to where he was comfortably seated near the fire.

"You find something amusing?"

"Aye, that I do. Ye are full of spunk. It is no wonder ye were named after the fearless *Scathach*." He shook his head. "I find it most intriguing that ye were looking for a weapon. Did ye believe ye needed something to ward off any unwanted affections?" He rose and she took a step back. "Come here," he demanded.

"I will not go to you willingly. I have news for you, buster, that you will not force me to do something I don't want any part of." She took her stance, her fists raised to her sides, ready to give him a run for his money.

He quirked a brow, shocked that she was actually ready to do battle with him. Then he couldn't help himself. He had not been this amused in ages and to think that the wife of his detested enemy was the one to accomplish this. He threw back his head with a roar of a laugh.

Aislinn just stood there thinking that he must be insane.

When he finally composed himself once more, he addressed her again. "Ye would make an old man chase ye around the room? I assure ye, at one time I would have fancied that challenge, but tonight…" He sighed deeply. "…I fear I am not up to it. I only wish to talk." When she still did not come forward, he tried again to put her at ease. "I would no sooner harm ye than I would me own daughter."

Knowing how Fingham had felt about his daughter, Aislinn knew he had made a sincere promise. She lowered her hands, but she remained cautious. She slowly walked over to him. He offered her a chair near the fire and he took the other. A small table separated them and she felt a little better for it. "So what did you wish to speak to me about?"

Fingham smiled, pulling on his long gray mustache. He then leaned forward and poured wine into the goblets. He offered one of the cups to Aislinn, before he himself took a long welcomed drink. He studied her, realizing she made no move to touch her wine. "Ye can relax. I do not ravish my prisoners until after I have had my dinner." He meant it as a joke, but this remark set Aislinn to her feet. "Oh, sit, sit. I was only jesting with ye. Ye had a look about ye that made me think ye feared I would devour ye."

"You have given me no reason to think otherwise."

"Forgive me then. I was most rude. Please sit down." He then cut a piece of apple offering her a slice.

"No, thank you."

With a shrug, he ate the slice himself.

Again Aislinn took a seat though her stance told Butler that she was ready to flee the moment he gave her any reason that she should.

"Ye have given me great cause to doubt some of what I have been led to believe about Dougray Fitzpatrick. I do not like to be wrong in my convictions. Ye said that the man confided in ye his feelings about my daughter?"

"Yes. According to everyone he was a bereaved man, not the cold calculating one that you seem to think him to be."

"Why should I believe ye?"

"You don't have to. I am only stating what I know and what I've seen. I was not here when the tragedy took place, but with all that has happened of late, it makes me wonder if there is something else afoot. Maybe we could compare notes. Let me brief you on what has been going on at Dunhaven. A family was brutally murdered, leaving a small boy orphaned, ships have been attacked, and cargo has disappeared just to name a few. There was enough evidence left behind to incriminate your clan."

"Whatever Fitzpatrick may have told ye, I am not in the habit of killing innocents. It is not my style to cut a man down when he has no weapon nor do I hide behind sneak attacks. My quarrel is with Dougray Fitzpatrick and no one else. And if what ye say be true, well I would want to personally deal with the culprit who is responsible. I have also lost livestock in the plenty. So much so that I fear my people will suffer come this winter."

"Dougray did not issue the slaughter of your cattle."

He leaned forward. "Could it be that ye are so enamored by the man that ye refuse to see what he might be capable of?"

"I am only telling you what I know. I have another question for you."

"And what, pray tell, might that be?"

"Did you or did you not send me a summons stating that you would kill Dougray if I did not come directly to hear the terms?"

"A summons? I do not know of which ye speak."

"I thought not. Didn't you wonder why I was with a small escort in the heart of your territory?"

"It was either ye sought to raid us, or ye simply became lost. I voted on the latter."

"And you were lucky to come upon us? We are being played as fools and we walked right into it. It was no coincidence that your men were right where we would be heading. Someone planned it. Do you know the reason why someone would go to so much trouble?"

"Nay, I had not thought that it was anyone but Dougray causing me such grief."

"Here's something more that you might ponder. Dougray was supposed to ride the mount that your daughter took instead. I believe it was his death that was sought, but Ella simply got in the way. And since you were so bent on revenge, this someone thought that you would carry out the deed they had intended. It would mean less trouble for them. Lord Fingham, I am convinced that you are being used. Even if you don't believe me, wouldn't you wish to at least find out if that were true?"

Aislinn was not sure what Fingham Butler thought of her suspicions, for he had ordered Tremain to escort her back to her chambers. Of course, the door was once again securely locked making escape impossible. She wished that she had her journal with her so she could write about her ordeal of being captured by the infamous Butler. She had come to the conclusion that he was merely a grief-stricken man, not a murderer.

Even though she was beginning to think that she was in no immediate danger, she wasn't going to take any chances. Earlier she had palmed the knife that Fingham had been using. She placed the weapon under her pillow before she stretched out to rest. She would just close her eyes for a moment, but the toll of the last few days had taken hold and she fell into an exhausted sleep.

She most likely would have slept through the night, if she hadn't been jolted awake by the sound of a creaking door, *her door*. She reached under her pillow clutching the hilt of her knife. She could see the intruder only as a shadow, but she knew by the span of the shoulder width that it was a man. Well he would be quite surprised when he found out how unpleasant she could be when awakened from her slumber.

She waited for him to draw near for she knew if she were to strike, she would have only one chance. Her heart was beating so loud against her chest that she was afraid the culprit would know that she was awake. It was dark, the light from the fireplace was nearly out, but still she lowered her eyelids a fraction of an inch, so that he wouldn't know she was watching him. His hand reached out to touch her and that was when she sprang forth, her weapon hand raised to strike. She would have done great damage, if the man hadn't possessed quick reflexes. He clutched her hand in an iron-firm grip making her wince out in pain. She dropped the knife, but her other hand was still free and she swung with all her might.

"*Dar Dia!*" he swore beneath his breath. "Aislinn?"

She paused in her assault. "Dougray, is that you?" she whispered back.

"Aye, that it is. And I'll be telling ye that it is a fine way ye be greeting yer husband."

"Oh, Dougray." She leapt at him throwing her arms around his neck in a fierce embrace. "It's really you."

He couldn't help but chuckle. "Did ye miss me all that much?"

"More. How did you get in here?"

"I have my ways." She could not make out his features clearly, but she knew that he was grinning.

"Well, master magician, how do you plan on getting us out of here?"

"I've brought friends. Now hurry, put yer shoes on." She was about to move away from him, but she didn't get very far. He pulled her to him and his mouth covered hers hungrily. It was amazing that even though at any moment they could be discovered, even killed, his thoughts lingered where they shouldn't be. He released her then with a low grumble. "I sorely missed ye, lass." He would have told her more but Cormac had entered.

"Sorry to disturb ye, milord, but we have heard stirring. They may have realized that we have entered the grounds."

"We will be but a moment."

Aislinn shoved her foot into her shoes barely lacing them tight. "Teige and Dermot, did you find them?"

"Aye, lass. They were most anxious to be freed."

"Thank goodness. They wouldn't let me see them."

"Hurry, Aislinn. We'll discuss this later."

Ready, he ushered her out of the room and down the hall where Teige and Fiach were waiting. Dougray had them whisk Aislinn away, of course protesting every step she took saying she should be at his side in case he needed her.

Aislinn knew there would be a fight and Dougray in the midst of it. She wasn't at all pleased and was making every effort to let everyone know about it. "I'm going back." She started to march past Teige, but he held her fast.

"Nay, milady. Ye cannot. I have orders to hold ye at sword point if necessary."

"Dougray's back there." She pointed out the obvious.

"We know and milord is very capable. He is not alone."

Father Fiach couldn't help but smile. "Indeed, ye are the hellion. Tell me, young woman, what would ye do if ye were to march back in there?"

She stood straight showing her full height of nearly six feet and looked directly at the priest with her unwavering dark eyes. "I'd fight beside him."

Fiach's gaze went to Teige, who just shrugged. "She would, ye know. She can handle a weapon like the rest of us."

"So all that I have heard is true then." Fiach rubbed his chin thoughtfully before he spoke again. "If it were up to me, I'd say give ye a sword and let's finish this, but me cousin seems to fancy yer pretty little head. Ye will have to stand down."

"But…." She began only to have Fiach shake his head.

Dougray had thought that the coast was clear when he nearly ran into Tremain who was rushing to secure the area. Both men stood eyeing each other, waiting. Tremain was the first to make the move locking them into battle, their broadswords clashing against each other in equal skill, both knowing that only one could win.

Dougray had been young but he had been aware of Tremain wanting to marry his sister and the turmoil that took place when Miriam tried to run away with him. They nearly had a clan war over it. Luckily they were able to stop them before they had gone too far. Tremain had been humiliated for his rash act and had never forgiven Shane Fitzpatrick for taking his only love away. Shane may not be here, but obviously his son was good enough at the moment to take out his aggressions.

"Butler would not have harmed the Lady Aislinn. She would have been far better to live here than with ye."

"Ye forget, Tremain, she is my wife."

"Binding for a year only."

Dougray brought down his sword nearly making Tremain lose his, but he quickly moved out of the way.

"A sore spot I see." Tremain smiled. "Tell me, are ye going to murder her like ye did to Ella? Is that yer sick side of ye?"

"Ye know that I did not have anything to do with Ella's death."

Tremain lunged only to have Dougray sidestep just in time not to have his arm severed. "I know nothing of the sort. I don't trust the word of a Fitzpatrick. As far as I am concerned, ye are capable of anything."

"Ella was a good woman. I would have done anything to make her happy."

He let out a low chuckle. "Really now. Being thrown from a horse does not constitute as a good time."

Again Dougray came after him metal against metal pounding against each other. "Ye forget I married Ella of my own free will, regardless that the clans advised that I should, but what of ye, Tremain? Ye coming in the middle of the night, like a thief to take my sister hostage."

"That was not how it was. Miriam and I were in love. We were handfast, but the English do not accept that."

"She was promised to Sir Reynolds. Ye were stealing her away from her betrothed."

"Ye were just a lad of ten and two. Ye knew nothing of what the heart desired. Miriam didn't want Sir Reynolds." Again he attacked.

"Well I am a man now and I realize ye knew nothing of honor." Dougray's words were like a blade slicing Tremain in two.

"I'll give ye honor." Tremain lunged forward but Dougray was ready with a block that left Tremain weaponless. Dougray put the point of his sword against the man's throat. Tremain just met his gaze head on.

"I die at yer hands then, brother of Miriam. Ye will have yer revenge." Tremain stood tall waiting for his life to be ended. Dougray shook his head. He didn't pretend to understand this man's reasoning, but Miriam at one time had seen a redeeming quality in him. He slowly backed away.

"Nay, ye live this night. Remember it well." He took off leaving Tremain standing there completely baffled to why he was still breathing. He walked over to where his sword lay and picked up the weapon.

At that moment, two of his men burst into view. "Did ye see anyone?"

Tremain for a moment was going to send them after Fitzpatrick, but his conscience wouldn't let him. "Nay, they got away."

Aislinn was hugging Hamish not believing the miracle. He had quickly relayed the story of how he had survived, falling over a Butler and hitting his head leaving him out cold in the other man's blood. Teige and Dermot were mussing his hair and teasing him that he had the luck of the little people about him.

When Aislinn saw Dougray walking towards them, she forgot all else. She ran to him to greet him though he looked less than pleased. "Why are ye still here?" he growled at her, as he dragged her near. Over her shoulder, he sent his scowl toward Teige and Fiach.

"Don't go blaming them. I am the one who wouldn't leave, not until I knew you were going with me."

He couldn't help but grin. "Aislinn Fitzpatrick, ye never fail to amaze me." He took hold of her arm. "But come, we must not further press our luck."

Chapter Fifty-Eight

All the way back to Dunhaven, Cormac dwelled on his relationship with Fiona placing doubt to all their time they had spent together. Had she ever been honest with him? He had never before given his heart to anyone, but he had opened up to her and she had gladly taken. His hands tightened on his reins.

"It is not yer fault, Cormac." Teige had been watching his friend for some time now, as he struggled with his emotions.

"How could I have been such a fool? Me of all people should have known better." He chuckled without mirth. "Isn't it befitting that I be duped at me own game? How many women have I left weeping without a care, so that I could move on to the next conquest?"

"Ye were never cruel, Cormac."

"Nay?" His eyes darkened with anguish. "I am not so sure. It was all but a game to me, Teige. I only worried about my desires and not a thing more." He swallowed hard. "I loved her, Teige."

"I know."

Arriving, Cormac dismounted and headed toward Fiona's knowing that tonight he would not leave unscathed.

She seemed to have been waiting for him and dragged him into her home anxious to hear the news. "Is it true? Was milady taken?"

God, she was beautiful with her golden hair falling free around her heart-shaped face. How could someone who had the look of an angel be so deceitful? "Aye, and not a thing that we could do about it."

"Does she still live?"

It was slight, but Cormac could hear the thread of hope in her voice that she hoped Aislinn was dead. He had to look away before he answered her, "Not for long, we fear."

"Not to lessen the gravity of the situation, but maybe this all happened for a reason."

He whirled on her forcing himself to deny that he loved this uncaring wench. "And what reason may that be?"

"She never did fit in. Ye have to admit she was odd in her ways. She should have never been given the chance to be the Lady of Dunhaven. I am not the only one who thought this."

"Nay?" He lifted his brows in question. "Who else thought this, Fiona?" His eyes had narrowed, hardened. She suddenly felt that she was treading on dangerous ground.

She had to change tactics. She slowly sauntered over to him hoping to distract him from his questioning. Seductively she pressed her body against his, rubbing just the right places.

It almost worked.

"Ach!" Cormac pushed her away. "What do ye know, Fiona? I am involved here and I would like to be informed of what I was party to."

She thought for a moment to deny his accusation, but she knew it was too late for that. He knew that she had some doing in Aislinn's kidnapping. She shook her head. "Poor, poor Cormac, ye did nothing wrong. Actually ye should be congratulated, and once I am in the castle, I will see to it that ye are rewarded handsomely."

So that had been her ploy all along. She wanted Dougray still and had only used him as a stepping-stone. "Are ye delusional, Fiona? Ye will never have a place in the castle." He grabbed a hold of her shoulders and shook her. "What have ye done, Fiona? Whom are ye working with?"

"Let go of me. Ye're hurting me."

"I'll do more than that if ye do not tell me."

"Ye can't stop what has been started. It is above us all and they didn't want the Hennessy woman to corrupt our young with her oddities. So I helped them get rid of her. I am not sorry."

"Ye fool. Did ye ever look past what ye saw as yer opportunity? This was not a plan to take Lady Aislinn from here. It was to get milord to attack the Butlers. They wanted war, in hopes that he would be rash and his life ended."

She shook her head not wanting to believe that. "Dougray would not bother. He doesn't love her. He would never risk his own life for her."

"That is yer mistake then. Ye were so preoccupied with ye that ye did not see the truth. And here I was a fool too." He released her then and Fiona sensed it was for the last time. She reached for him, but he walked past her and threw open the door.

Her eyes widened in fear when she saw Teige and Dermot followed up by Dougray.

"What is going on here?" Again her hand reached out beseechingly toward Cormac.

"Do not expect me to help ye. Ye made yer choice long ago and it was not to be with me." He turned his back on her and Teige and Dermot came forward to take her into custody.

"I did nothing wrong," she spat as she backed up a space. "I was trying to save ye, milord. I love ye. I'd do anything for ye. Don't ye see?"

"Ye don't love me, Fiona. Ye couldn't. Especially if ye thought by sending Aislinn to her death would please me. Be glad that she is safe or ye would hang this very night for yer treachery. Take her," he ordered.

They held her, but she tried to squirm free. "Wait! Wait I say."

Dougray held up his hand to hear her. "Ye want to confess who was behind this?"

"Even if I had a name, I would not tell ye, but I will leave ye something else that might make ye wish ye left the woman ye call wife with the Butlers. Do ye not wonder why she is not with child?" She saw his jaw clench and a smile crawled to her lips curving itself like a snake. "I know firsthand how ardent a lover ye are, and without something to aid in the stopping of yer seed from taking hold, ye would already have had an heir with me. Mayhap ye need to ask yer wife about the herbs Neala can give for such things."

The anger that sparked from his eyes was enough to make her flinch. "Take her away now!"

He stormed into the room like a raging wind slamming the door behind him, which was a great feat in itself since the doors were made of solid six-inch wood. Aislinn rose from her seat not at all sure why he was so angry.

"What's wrong, Dougray?"

"Ye have to ask?" He searched around the room throwing things, desperate to find what he sought.

"What are you looking for? Maybe I can help." She took a step back when she saw his penetrated glare that bordered on hatred.

He continued his search. Then it dawned on him where she may have hid it. He looked at the bed that was turned down for the night and then he glanced at her. Her eyes widened as she realized what he was so frantically looking for. How did he know? Her hand trembled slightly as she raised it to her lips. He went over to the bed and lifted the mattress. "Dougray, wait." But it was too late. He lifted the vial from her hiding place and turned to face her. "Let me explain...."

"Explain!" he bellowed. "Explain what is all too clear to me."

"I was afraid. I didn't want to...."

"Have my child," he finished. "Do you loathe me so much that you would purposely kill what would be created between us?"

"I had to think of the future. I don't belong here. You know it. I have to go back to my time sooner or later."

"And I made a promise to ye, if there were a child, the babe would go with ye if that was yer choosing."

"You say it but I know differently. You would want your own flesh and blood beside you. You would never let a child go."

He lifted the vial with its bluish colored liquid. "So it is this ye would use. Ye would deceive me instead. Did ye think it would not come back to me that ye had seen the old woman like a common whore?"

She flinched as if he had physically slapped her. She straightened her shoulders then and lifted her chin to him. "Tell me, my lord," she said sarcastically, "are you more upset with the fact that I didn't want to become pregnant or that your people might know it as well?"

He lowered his hand, clenching the vial tightly in his fist. "Both. Ye fail to understand what is expected of me. I am the lord over Dunhaven and I must have the knowledge of all that is going on. If it were known that I could not even control my own wife, what do ye think would happen? Do ye think that I could gain their respect? I lose face with this deceit."

"That's your problem. I don't want to be controlled. I want to be your partner. I want to have my own opinions, and I want you to listen to me when I have something to say."

"I always listen, Aislinn."

"Really? Then why didn't you hear me? I never told you that I didn't wish to have children, just that it wasn't wise to."

For a moment, he didn't trust himself to speak. Why did their relationship have to be so complicated? Why did he have to fall in love with a woman that didn't belong here? The whole marriage was a sham. He knew it from the start, but he had hoped against all hope that he could make her love him. Now he saw that all his attempts were for naught. She didn't care for him in the least. All she wanted was to go home.

Could he find fault with her for such a wish? To stay here, she would be giving up so much. He had seen the wonders of her time first hand. How could he have ever thought to compete with what she could accomplish in her century?

She was looking at him with something fragile in her eyes, but he was too furious to see it. He turned to leave.

"Where are you going?" She hadn't expected him to walk away so easily.

"Ye damn our souls by taking this." He shook his fist in the air. "Milady, if ye wish not to have my child, then ye wish to not have me at all." His hand was on the latch when her next words halted him.

"When you found out about the vial, did you happen to also find out how long that I had had it in my possession?"

"What does that have to do with anything?"

"Everything, Dougray. Everything." She waved her hand at him in dismissal. "Oh, just forget it. Leave, run away from our first fight with it unresolved."

He raised his eyes to hers, thinking she had lost her mind. "Our first fight! Be Damned! We have done nothing but fight since I dragged ye to my world." He pulled opened the door then and left, slamming it once more behind him. He leaned against the frame staring down at the container, haunted by her words. He didn't care to know how long she had it in her possession. The fact remained that she had brought it to their chambers in the first place.

He went to see the old woman. The slow-paced ride there had not erased the scowl that still penetrated his features. He glared at her and raised the damning vial for her to see.

"Ye came to show me what I know already?"

"You gave this to my wife!" It was not a question but an accusation.

"Aye. She asked for it."

"She asked...." He threw up his arms. "She asked for it. Old crone, do ye know what ye have done?"

"I gave her a choice. She'd never know if I hadn't."

"Never know? Never know what? Stop speaking in riddles."

"She came to me, but once. And ye see for yerself that what I gave her is still untouched."

Dougray was silent then as he thought of Aislinn's parting words.

The old woman cackled. "See ye are thinkin' now."

"I don't understand."

"Of course ye don't. Ye can't understand her if ye are so busy tryin' to dominate her very spirit. She is different and ye were aware of this. That is the very reason ye are drawn to her, but yet ye try to possess her. Continue on this track and ye will suffocate what she would give to ye freely. Learn to listen to what she has to say. Ye may find that she has something worthy fer ye to hear. Give yer heart to her, and ye might find that she will return the gesture."

Dougray would hear none of what Neala had told him for he couldn't get past the betrayal. An uncontrollable fury raged through him every time he thought of it until he couldn't function if he stayed one more moment in her presence.

Aislinn was aware that he packed up his gear, knowing by what he took that he would be gone for some time. He wouldn't listen to her and she refused to keep defending herself when her words continued to fall on deaf ears. She watched him ride away with a small garrison, Murrough at his side. Father Fiach also traveled with them, for it was time that he returned to his duties at St. Michan's.

"He'll be back." Moira tried to convince her, but even she was not so sure. "Maybe ye should have told him about the baby."

Aislinn shook her head. "I would not have him stay because of the heir I can give him." She was well aware that she was being stubborn, but she was deeply hurt that he hadn't given her a chance to explain. "You can't have a marriage if only one wishes to try at it."

Chapter Fifty-Nine

As time passed, Aislinn pretended to continue on as though nothing had changed when, in truth, everything had. She sat down at her desk and produced her journal. She had relied on her writing more and more for pouring out her fears. "Again I was not well. It seems that the more I try to eat, the worse I feel. Just the sight of food makes my stomach churn. I know that it is only the pregnancy. I am nearing my fourth month and I pray that I will begin to feel better. Cahir, the physician, has given me some suggestions that might help, but so far not a one has done the trick. I am trying to be civil to Cahir in hopes that he will not see me as a threat to his position. This is not an easy task. I would rather have Neala at my side, but she has no wish to come to the castle. Anyway Cahir would surely not make her welcomed. I have not been to see her this week for I spent a lot of my day in bed.

"I feel so drained and so…so alone. Dougray has not returned and I find that I miss him so very much."

"Milady?" Moira had been calling Aislinn for some time now and she still had not acknowledged her. "Are ye all right?" She walked over to where Aislinn was resting her head on her writing table, the quill still poised in her hand. "Milady? A.J.?"

Her head popped up and she looked at Moira with a baffled expression on her face. For a moment, she didn't know where she was. She glanced at the journal she had been writing in. Had she fallen asleep? She looked up at Moira again.

"It's nearly time for the evening meal." Moira answered the unasked question.

"But I came in here after breakfast."

Moira nodded. "I know, milady, that is why I became so worried. Ye didn't answer when I knocked. Teige knew that ye didn't leave the keep and made me come in to check on ye. I hope ye are not angry. We were just worried."

Aislinn put down the quill. "No, I am not angry. I am a little amazed that I slept so soundly and for so long. It's strange." She rubbed her face trying to wake up. "I've slept the day away and yet I still feel exhausted."

"Ye should eat something. Maybe it will help."

"I can't. I don't feel very well. I think I will go to bed, and hopefully I will feel better in the morning." She stood. Seeing how worried Moira looked, she added, "I promise I will eat a big breakfast."

"As ye wish, milady. I will turn down the bed for ye. Ye do look tired. This wee one ye carry is draining ye."

Once Aislinn had undressed, she climbed beneath the warm blankets. "Will ye send Declan to me? I feel that I have been neglecting him."

"For a small lad, he seems to understand but I will bring him to ye straight away. Then ye must rest."

Teige was waiting for Moira and stopped her before she could go down the stairs. "And?"

"She is not well, Teige. It is like the babe she carries is poisoning her. She cannot keep what she eats down and she is weakening. This cannot be the way it should be, can it?" She looked to Teige with her wide blue eyes and hoped that he would give her an answer that would put her at ease.

"I have heard that some women have the sickness during their full confinement."

"She is so thin. She cannot possibly endure such a duration." She placed her small hand on Teige's arm, again looking up at him with her trusting eyes. "Will ye not go to Neala and ask her for some herbs? She may know of something that will help."

Moira's touch had distracted him and he could only trust himself to nod his head in response.

"Thank ye, Teige."

Dermot and Cormac stared at Teige like he was daft. "Ye are going to see the old woman…by yerself?" Dermot was not at all sure if Teige was being serious. "She's liable to turn ye into something dreadful."

"A.J. goes to see her all the time. Neala seems harmless enough and she has taken a liking to milady. She's just an old woman that knows the Druid ways."

Cormac shook his head. "Harmless ye may call it now, but if ye anger her, she may act first and ask questions later. I will go with ye, my friend. Dermot can stand by to watch over milady."

"Aye. I will stay here." Dermot was all too glad to stay behind.

Neala looked to where the two men were cautiously making their way. She fought the urge not to laugh out loud, only because she feared her mirth might end up costing her dearly. The two men were skittish enough to draw their broadswords at the slightest noise.

"Old woman…Neala." Teige cleared his throat. "We come to…."

She gave them a knowing eye. "I have no problem discerning the reason. The spirals have been interrupted and now all is nah well. Something has altered the way it should have been. It may be too late for some, but not for others." She handed Teige the small pouch. "These herbs will settle her stomach, but I do not think it will last." She looked away but not before Cormac and Teige saw the deep sadness that was evident there.

"Do ye fear that milady will perish?" Teige would not leave without knowing what the old woman thought.

"That I do not know. It is unclear to where her destiny lies. Be gone now. Pray to yer God and hope he has pity on her." She waved her hand at them in dismissal. "Be watchful of milady."

Cormac pulled at his friend's sleeve, making him come with him. "Ye heard her. She is finished talking to us. Do ye wish to anger her?"

"Nay, but what did she mean that someone has altered the way it should be? Is milady in danger?"

"I do not know, Teige, but we will be extra careful with this warning she gives us."

Chapter Sixty

Fiona paced her room that was situated in the north tower. She was heavily guarded with no chance of freedom. She had no contact with the outside world except for when someone would bring her a meal. She longed to feel the breeze blowing through her hair, feel the sun warm on her face, or just to be able to walk through the glen among the flowers. It was mid-October now and soon the weather would be turning cooler. She feared that she wouldn't have the chance to see another season change.

With only time on her hands, she was able to reflect on what she had done. She had made a terrible mistake by letting herself be governed by her jealousy. She had not realized until now what she could have had with Cormac, but it was all gone with no chance to make amends.

Dougray had not been to see her, and now that she had time to go over every detail that had led her to this end, she realized she could not blame him. She had been so very foolish to think that she could hold on to something that wasn't hers, and even a bigger fool for not seeing what she had already possessed.

"Cormac." She closed her eyes trying to block out the tormented expression she had seen on his face, when he knew for certain she had betrayed him. If only she could take it back, take it all back….

She heard the door open and she turned with hope in her eyes, only to have it extinguished. "What do ye want?"

"Now, dear lass, is this anyway to greet me?" Abbot Kirwan waved for the guard to leave them. "I have come here to see if ye want to repent yer ways."

She chuckled, but her cold stare was enough to let him know she was not amused. "I am not and will never be of yer faith, old man, so stop wasting yer breath."

"Ye would think that ye would be humbling yerself now that ye know yer fate has been sealed."

"I bow to no one, especially not to a man who believes the clothes he wears makes him more divine than the god he believes in."

Kirwan's features hardened and his eyes bore into hers. "Yer soul will be cast to the fiery depths of hell for yer blasphemous ways."

"Ye should be rejoicing for ye will not be alone in yer confinement then."

The abbot raised his hand as if to strike her, but with great resolve he managed to back away. "Ye are a fool of a woman, Fiona. Ye strove too high and now look where ye landed: alone in a lonely room to live out yer days." He smiled when she saw her flinch. Perhaps she had been too dense to realize how dire her situation had become. "Ye would be wise to accept the one God into yer heart, and milord may be lenient in his sentencing."

"Be it the old ways or yers, milord had never cared one way or the other what religion I practiced. So Kirwan, ye may take yer preaching elsewhere. I would sooner die in this room than to convert to yer way of thinking."

Again he smiled, a slow smile that seemed to say so much more. "Be very careful what ye wish for, Fiona. Ye may be granted the privilege ye seek."

Since Fiona did not have information on who was ultimately responsible for Aislinn's kidnapping and for the other deceptions, Dougray was forced to look elsewhere for the knowledge. It was like the culprits were invisible, causing havoc wherever they wished. There had to be backing from someone higher up.

A visit to his grandfather, who was presently at his estate in the Pale, seemed the best place to start. Though it irritated him to no end to have to ask the man for help, he had seen no other choice. His grandfather had ears in places that he did not.

After six weeks with no further clues, Dougray headed home. All the time away, his thoughts kept returning to the dark-eyed woman he had left behind. Despite the fact that he had felt betrayed, he couldn't put her from his mind. He missed her laughter, their conversation and, as ridiculous as it might seem, he even missed their arguing.

He wanted to forgive her for the deceit, but his pride was there to choke the response from his lips. He knew that he had no right to expect her to live a life of a woman used to this time and place, for he did not enter this marriage without the knowledge of where she had come from. He could have easily refused the union, but he hadn't. No, he had taken the steps to ensure it. He had only himself to blame for his disappointments.

He had arrived home and she was not there to greet him. Of course he had not sent word ahead that he would be arriving home. He looked toward the keep wondering where he would find Aislinn. The library? Their room?

He let the lad Regan take his mount for he was too anxious to speak with her.

"Where is she?" he asked Dermot when he entered the keep.

"Milord, we did not expect ye…."

"Where is she?" he asked again.

"In the library," Dermot answered a little too nervously.

Everyone he passed greeted him. They were pleasant enough, but there was whispering when they thought that he was not listening. It was like they were hiding something and they feared he would now discover the deception. He took the stairs two at a time and entered the library, but instead of going directly over to her, he stopped in the entryway.

She was playing chess with Teige. He heard her gregarious laugh and he felt the warmth of it flood through him. He wanted to remain a shadow among the walls, but Teige happened to look up.

"Milord," Teige murmured and Aislinn had now turned around to see him standing there. Her mouth dropped open in surprise, but she quickly recovered her composure and stood. He noticed that there was something different about her, but he couldn't quite put his finger on it. There were dark smudges beneath her eyes making her skin look pale.

"Leave us," Dougray said to Teige but he did not take his eyes off Aislinn.

Teige glanced at her to make sure that this was what she wished. She nodded her head and he turned toward Dougray once more. "As ye wish, milord."

He duly noted the loyalty that Teige bestowed toward Aislinn, but he did not say a word on the matter.

Once they were alone, he moved toward her only to have her move around the table, as if to avoid him. He was tired and anxious making his voice sound harsher than he had wished. "Stop moving." When she jumped, he regretted his outburst.

"You have been gone for six weeks. I haven't heard a word from you. Now you think you can waltz in here and just order me around? Would you like me to sit too? Roll over?"

"Still the sharp tongue ye have." He ran his hand through his hair.

"And you're still the arrogant bastard."

They were silent again as they glared at each other. It wasn't exactly how either one of them had envisioned this reunion.

Dougray tried to start over. "Aislinn…." The words were lost to him and he sighed as he looked away.

"Where were you?"

"The Pale." He glanced at her again. Something was definitely different, and it was troubling him that he couldn't quite put his finger on it.

His appreciative eye traveled the length of her, his eyes lingering on the soft skin that was visible to his eyes, due to her gown fitting snugly against her chest.

Anger, disappointment, love were the feelings that fluttered back and forth when he thought about her, but right now he desired her. He wanted her.

He again made an attempt to approach her. This time, she didn't run. He was there then, kissing her, pulling her closer against him his hands falling to her waist. She seemed fuller to the touch and yet her cheeks looked thinner. He pulled away to look at her and in that instant he knew. "Ye are with child?"

She slowly nodded her head. He didn't say another word, but just stared at her. There was a chill black silence that surrounded them, like an overpowering swell. She wanted to know what he was thinking. Wasn't this what he had wanted, or had he now changed his mind? "Say something," she demanded of him.

"Whose is it?" The thin chill hung on the edge of his accusing words.

So hurt, so insulted by his response, she lashed out at him, hitting him full force drawing blood from his lip. He knew he deserved it. He had just accused her of being unfaithful and yet he could not bring himself to apologize. She had lied when she had come to his bed, taking a liquid that would kill his seed and now she stood there saying… "That child ye carry could not be mine." His voice held a finality that could not be broken and his eyes condemned her. "Is it Fingham's? Ye were at his mercy and ye did not have yer precious poison." He didn't even give her the decency to answer him. He turned and strode to the door, obviously deciding that the discussion was over.

"Oh sure. Go. Just pretend, if you must. It would make it so easy to hate me then, if the child I carried was your enemy's. But you'll have to find another reason to despise me for this child that grows inside of me is yours!" He didn't stop and she ran after him. He was at the stairs by the time she caught up. "You coward! You dirty filthy coward!" He whirled around, and for a brief moment, she thought that he would strike her.

"Don't ever say that to me again." His voice was low, meaningful and with a thread of warning.

Her pulse began to beat erratically and she knew that she should remain silent. She knew she should let him go so he would have a chance to calm down, so they both could calm down and think logically again. But instead of listening to her own warning, she once again goaded him, poking her finger into his chest. He grabbed her wrist, instantly stilling her jabs. "We have nothing further to discuss." He pushed her away with such decisiveness that this time she let him go, but not without adding her own parting words.

"If you leave now, don't ever come back." For a second, she thought that he was going to return up the steps, for he had paused in his descent. But after a mere beat of a heart, he resumed his pace never looking back. Miserably crestfallen, she ran all the way to her room throwing herself on the bed. She couldn't stop the flow of tears from coming. She had longed for Dougray to return so that she could tell him about the baby. Well now he knew, but he didn't even believe it was his.

"Milady, are ye all right?" Moira went to her.

"No. Please, Moira, I need to be alone."

"I could…."

"No, please," she sobbed against her pillow. Moira didn't know what else she could do. She left the room, closing the door behind her.

Teige was there and he looked questionably at her. "She wishes to be alone," she told him.

"And I just heard milord yelling for a fresh mount."

"Teige?" Dermot had come up the stairs. "I am looking for Cormac. Do ye know where he might be?"

"Is there something wrong?"

"Aye, he needs to go straight away to see Fiona."

"Fiona? If the wench…."

"It isn't like that," Dermot interrupted. "He must know. Come with me and I will explain."

Chapter Sixty-One

Murrough was glad to be home, and hoped that Dougray would make amends with his wife so that life with him would be once more bearable. He walked past Padrig, who was busy hammering against the metal piece that would eventually be molded to a tool of some sort. The older man looked up with a nod toward the tall warrior.

"Good day, Padrig."

Even though Murrough appeared to be gruff with his fiery red hair and stern brow, there was no mistaking the gentleness he possessed when he took Rhiannon in his arms. Padrig approved of the man's strong affections toward his daughter and would like to see them handfast. He would have to work on it.

Murrough stooped so he could enter the house without bumping his head on the doorframe. His eyes adjusted quickly spotting Rhiannon sitting with her fabric, mending a gown. He really didn't care. He was too intent in reaching her and gathering her into his arms. "I have missed ye sorely."

"As I have ye, Murrough. So much so that at first I thought I was dreaming ye were here."

He kissed her thoroughly, lovingly, not missing a portion of her beautiful face. "Do ye still think me an illusion?"

"I am not sure. Maybe ye could show me some more proof." Her impish grin was all the encouragement he needed. He lifted her into his arms.

"My blood is on fire for ye, and rest assured, lass, by the time I am through showing ye my affections, ye will know I am truly here in the flesh.

"What's wrong with ye two? Ye look as if ye lost yer best friend." Cormac was busily cleaning his sword, and had missed the uneasy look that passed between Dermot and Teige. He only glanced up again because they were hovering over him. "What is it? Are ye in trouble again, Dermot?"

"Cormac, there is no other way to say it." Again Teige paused and glanced in Dermot's direction.

"Out with it, Teige," Cormac insisted now.

"Fiona wishes a word with ye."

"Pheugh! Enough has been said already." He returned to his cleaning. "She is lucky that milord has not seen fit to have her exiled."

"She's dyin'," Teige blurted out.

That drew his attention. "What?" His voice faltered. "What has happened?"

Dermot spoke up. "She has been ill this past week and has now taken on a fever. Her guard informed me that she has called for ye. I would not have told ye if I had not seen her for myself. She is a mere reflection of herself."

Raw emotion was evident in Cormac's eyes. Despite all that Fiona had done, he still loved her. He felt like the ground had crumbled to dust, and he was free falling with nothing to stop his descent. Fiona, his beautiful Fiona, was dying? It couldn't be possible. His gaze found both Dermot and Teige's. "I will see her."

The guard let Cormac pass leaving him with the afflicted woman. He was momentarily taken aback by the fever-wracked body that lay shivering on the cot making him not want to approach, but somehow he made his feet move. He knelt down next to her taking her hand in his. "Fiona. I am here."

Her sunken eyes opened and at first she seemed to see right through him, as if he were not even there. Finally she focused and, with the little strength she still possessed, squeezed his hand. "Do I dream or are ye really there before me?"

"It is I, Fiona."

She sobbed then. "Oh, Cormac, I have been so wrong. Please forgive me," her voice was weary and her breathing labored with a horrible rattling sound. He lifted her head and sat down on the cot so as to cradle her.

"Shush now. Do not worry yerself."

"But I must." She looked up at him with her feverish eyes and squeezed his hand against her chest. "I must know ye forgive me."

He nodded, his eyes filling with tears. "I forgive ye, Fiona. I forgive ye."

She closed her eyes then. "Kirwan," she whispered.

"Ye wish for the abbot?"

Her eyes flew open and her reply was a desperate plea. "Do no trust anyone. Do ye hear me? They are after us. The Tudor King, the man in the robe, they threaten milord. Ye will warn him, aye?"

He knew that it was only the fever talking, but he nodded. "I will tell him of yer fears."

"Ye promise? Ye promise me, Cormac?"

"I promise ye."

She nodded her head. "Ye will hold me for a while? Like ye used to."

"Aye." He gently rocked her. "I will not leave ye."

The tears fell freely from her eyes. "Ye came, Cormac, when I thought that ye would not. How could I have not seen before that ye were the one? Ye were always the one. Did ye love me a little Cormac? Ye don't have to say so, if ye don't...."

He placed a finger on her lips. "I love ye still." He held her close, willing her to be strong and not leave him.

She gazed up at him with a peaceful expression, like she was trying to memorize every detail of his face. "I will know ye again in our next life and I will do right by ye. I promise ye this." She drew one last rugged breath that seemed desperate to reach her lungs, but after that no other sound did she make.

"Fiona?" She was gone. He lifted his hand and closed her sightless eyes, letting his grief spill forth. "Oh, Fiona." Her face was so serene, without the lines of worry and the pain of her illness. Perhaps she finally found the peace that she had been unable to grasp in this world.

"Why was I not informed sooner of the woman's condition?" Dougray ran his hand through his hair.

Cahir made an attempt to explain the slight. "Fiona was known for her theatrics, milord. We did not believe she was truly ill, until Abbot Kirwan made his visit yesterday."

"Why did Kirwan see it his duty to tend to Fiona? She was not of the faith."

Cahir sighed. "To him any soul is worth saving."

"Hmm." He was silent for a moment. There wasn't any use being upset with what could have been done to save the woman. She was dead and for that he was deeply dismayed that it couldn't have been avoided. "Ye may go, Cahir."

"As ye wish, milord."

Dougray quirked a brow when the man had not made a move to leave the room. "Ye have more to say?"

"Aye. I fear I must draw to yer attention that milady has not been well either."

At first, he had been troubled by the way Aislinn had looked, but had dismissed it once he knew she was expecting. He understood perfectly what the physician's fears were and decided to put the man at ease before he started a panic. "Do not fret that a fever threatens to overrun the keep. Lady Aislinn does not suffer from what ailed Fiona. Aislinn is with child."

"I know, but…." He did not finish for Dougray seemed to have dismissed him. "Perhaps I should consider something that might bring her some comfort."

"I am sure she would a appreciate it."

Cahir nodded and this time left the room.

Dougray had Cormac summoned to the library for he wanted to speak to him privately. He was busy putting a few books away when the young man hurried in. "I came as soon as I could, milord."

"I ask ye here not because of a dire need, but to see how ye fared."

He hesitated for only a moment before he answered. "I am well."

He turned to look at Cormac to make that judgment himself. Other than the tired circles around his eyes, he seemed to be holding up. "Do ye wish time away? To grieve?"

"Nay, milord. I need to keep busy."

"I am truly sorry for yer loss, Cormac."

He could only nod for he couldn't trust his voice to speak without falling apart.

Chapter Sixty-Two

For days Dougray brooded wanting to be left alone. He should be rejoicing in that fact that Aislinn was with child, but he could not forget the potion she had purposely sought to use against him. It didn't matter that she hadn't taken it. It was the point that she had it in her possession.

He made excuses to stay away from the castle making sure he was not available for Aislinn to happen upon him. Of what he once accused her of doing, he had now built a similar wall around himself until he felt like he was imprisoned within the fortress.

He had made the appropriate preparations to visit his sister. She had asked him on numerous occasions to visit and now seemed as good a time as any. He had decided to take Declan with him too. He told himself that he was taking the boy just to have him at his side, but a part of him knew he was doing it to hurt Aislinn. She would miss Declan, yearn for him just as he himself longed for her love. That had been all he wanted from her, but she had denied him.

When Aislinn had heard that Declan's belongings were being packed, she had tried to see him, but he had refused her. He knew she was only worried about where he was taking the lad. Let her worry. Let her think the worst of him.

Dougray had Declan in front of him and was riding beside Murrough. They had nearly left the courtyard, when Teige rode up beside them. "Milord?"

"Be quick, man. I have a long ride ahead of me." He glanced at Teige, irritated that he was being delayed.

"I only ask that ye wait a few more days before ye make this journey."

"As I see it there is no need for me to be here."

"But milady is not well and...."

"Aislinn needs no one but herself. As far as I'm concerned she may have it that way. I'm through with her and this mock marriage. The sooner we part company the better."

"Surely ye do not mean that, milord."

Dougray glared down at the young man who obviously had no idea what it meant to be married to a woman who chose to be so much her own person that she shut everyone out. "We do not live well together, Teige. I do her a great service by setting her free." He was about to put his mount into motion but pulled back on his reins. He may not be back for a while, and though he did not see himself staying married to Aislinn, he did not want any harm to come to her. "Ye will protect her until I make other arrangement. I am still responsible for her welfare and the lass can get into mischief easily enough."

"Ye need not ask, milord. I would guard her with my life."

With that Dougray gave a nod of farewell and clicked his tongue. His mount immediately moved forward. They were a distance away before Murrough questioned his friend's hurried departure. Rhiannon had informed him that Dougray had not made amends with Aislinn and it bothered him that he would not open up to what was eating away at him. "Ye did not stay long."

"I saw to what needed immediate care," he answered but he remained preoccupied with his concerns. He was trying to distance himself from Aislinn, but his thoughts seemed to always drift to her. She possessed such a sharp tongue and was always so strong willed in mind, as well as in body, but now even Teige had made reference to her health. She had not appeared fit. She had dark shadows under her eyes and looked as if she had lost weight rather than gain it. If she had not had the slight roundness of her midsection, he would have never known that she was going to have a baby. She had to be about four, maybe five months along. Meaning Fingham could not possibly be the father, and she could not have taken the liquid Neala had given her. Of course, he knew the liquid was not always foolproof. She could have simply been caught.

"We could go back," Murrough suggested knowing his stubborn friend really didn't want to leave, and he wasn't in favor of going either. It had been too short of a visit with his Rhiannon and right now he was thinking about her warm embrace.

"I need time," Dougray stated. "I will see my sister then I'll decide what I must do next."

Declan let out a sob. "I want A.J. to come with us."

"Ye will be fine, Declan. Now hush. We have a long ride."

Chapter Sixty-Three

The longer that Dougray stayed away, the more despondent Aislinn began to feel. She would burst out crying for no reason and found herself not wanting to leave her bed, for she dreaded starting another day. She tried to convince herself that the emotional outbursts and the fact that she couldn't keep a meal down were due to her hormones being amuck. She had heard of morning sickness, but this didn't seem to apply to her. She was ill most of the day and the nausea hadn't begun until her second trimester. She worried that there was something wrong.

She was normally a healthy person. This experience was a rude awakening. She was beyond exhausted fighting a battle to stay well and failing miserably.

Cahir seemed concerned and had ordered special meals brought to her. He feared that she was not getting enough nourishment and frankly she had to agree with him. She kept trying for the baby's sake.

Every day was like the one before until all of them began to become a blur of idle talk and chores. Again this day would have been like all the others, but she awoke with horrific abdominal pains that seemed to rip right through her, but just as quickly as they had started they were gone again. For a long time, she didn't dare move. She may have never experienced pregnancy before, but she knew enough that she shouldn't be having contractions this soon.

She sat near the fire to keep warm and picked up the book that she had started. But after about fifteen minutes of re-reading the same page over and over again, she put the book down. She needed to feel reassured that she was all right, that the baby was okay. She needed to see Neala.

She patted her stomach already loving the idea that there would be a child. How she wished Dougray would come to realize that she had never been dishonest with him in any way. She missed him so much and she knew the longer that he stayed away, the more time he would have to harden his heart against her, while hers was breaking a little more each day. She donned her cloak. Swallowing hard and straightening her shoulders, she tried to bring herself out of the cobweb of dismay.

Subconsciously she fingered the ring Dougray had placed on her finger. She needed him. Never had she admitted needing anyone before and it frightened her to feel that vulnerable. She needed him, and he had abandoned her.

Neala listened silently to Aislinn, letting the poor girl cleanse her soul. She was worried for she could still see that all was not well with the spiral of life. Chaos and confusion clouded Aislinn and Dougray's life and she was powerless to stop its impending darkness. "Ye need to stay calm, lass."

"I'm trying, truly I am, but I'm so worried. I'm worried that Dougray will never come back. He was so angry, Neala. The way he looked at me, it was like he wished me gone from his life." She slowly raised the cup and sipped the hot liquid that Neala had given to her. "I should have listened to you, Neala. He will never forgive me for asking you for those herbs. He thinks that I have betrayed him. He even insinuated that the child I carry wasn't his. It has all turned out so horribly." Her eyes searched the older wiser woman's. "You showed me before what could be, when I gazed into the pond. Is that still possible for I don't feel that it is? Everything is slipping away."

"Anything is possible." Neala sighed.

"I sense that you know something that you aren't telling me."

"Ye took paths that ye both should not have done. There is a rift between ye two. I am not talking about the distances ye both created. It is the life force surrounding ye that is in an upheaval. Sacrifices will be asked from ye both."

Aislinn's brows furrowed. "Sacrifices?" She placed a hand over her midsection without realizing she had even done so.

Neala pursed her lips together. "There is more at work here than meets the eye and I am not sure where it will lead."

Instead of her visit with Neala putting her at ease, it only served to frighten her more with all her talk of the spirals not being defined.

Lynelle caught up with Aislinn just before she had entered the castle. "Milady, milady, will ye come play a game with us?" the freckle-faced girl pleaded making Aislinn feel that she couldn't refuse her. She let the young girl take her hand and nearly drag her to where Regan and some of the other children were already waiting.

Edward was there too and he came forward with a shy smile penetrating his small features. "It is good to see ye, milady. Ye are feeling better?"

"I am doing fine, Edward." She smiled and her spirits lifted. "What game shall we play?"

Regan put his arm around the small boy. She smiled marveling over how this child had changed. Before he would have tormented poor Edward and would have wanted to see him cry, but now he showed compassion, friendship. "I say we should play hopscotch," Regan suggested.

"I will watch then," Aislinn offered.

She was about to sit down on the ground when Regan halted her. "Wait, milady." He laid out his cloak for her.

"Why thank you, Regan."

He smiled broadly and bowed, proud of the fact that he had pleased her. She sat down and wrapped her mantle closer around her. She watched as the children hopped to and fro. It was a simple game that she had enjoyed as a child too, never thinking about the significance of it for it had somehow lost its meaning through time. Lynelle had explained to her that a visiting monk had been the one to show them the game. It was meant as a religious teaching of how the soul perils through life on its way to its final destination of paradise. If only life could be that simple. Just a hop, skip and jump away from where you wanted to be.

"It is good to see that ye have given the children a better sense of play."

Aislinn shielded her eyes against the sun to see Abbot Kirwan standing over her. How she wished the man would leave her alone. Now all she needed was to have Cahir at his side to complete the misery. At that moment the man came into view and was heading right toward her. She had to stop herself from swearing for the abbot was already convinced that she was destined for hell, and there was no use in confirming it right now. Instead she forced a smile. "I am glad that you approve, Abbot Kirwan. Do you wish to join us?"

She smiled up at him but the abbot was well aware that she had no wish for his company. He must remember to pray again for this woman's soul for now she carried the Lord of Dunhaven's child, bastard child he reminded himself. They were not married in God's eyes.

"Nay, I have things to attend to." He knelt down on his haunches so that he could meet her eyes. "Ye must repent before it is too late. I beg ye to do this." Without waiting for a comment from her, he stood then and moved on his way. Any other time, she would have ignored his words but today it chilled her. She pulled at her cloak.

"Are ye cold, milady?" Cahir asked her.

"I am fine, thank you."

"I have brought ye some nourishment. I did not see ye in the banquet hall this morning. Are ye again not feeling well?" He handed her some fruit and nuts.

She wasn't hungry, but if it would make the physician leave her in peace, she would eat just about anything. "Thank you for your concern. I was up early and had a quick bite to eat," which was a complete lie, but she wasn't in the mood to hear another lecture from him.

"I see."

She nibbled on the fresh fruit, hoping that he wouldn't stay long. The man seemed to sense this and, after a moment, bid her farewell. She was not surprised to see that he caught up with the abbot.

Edward noticed that Aislinn's face had paled and he walked over to her. "Are ye all right, milady?"

For some reason, she felt a cold uneasy knot form in her stomach. She shivered and wrapped her mantle closer around her. She nodded. "I'm fine, Edward. I'm just a little tired."

The next morning, Aislinn awakened to agony, the same as before only this time it was more intense. Desperate to reach someone to help her, she managed to drag herself to the door before she couldn't take the pain. She felt the warm liquid between her legs as she collapsed to the floor, her heart squeezing in anguish for she realized that she was losing the baby. A low, tortured sob nearly choked her as she tried to will it not to happen.

Moira was carrying a breakfast tray for Aislinn, when she came upon her lying on her side curled up like a ball. With a gasp, she let the tray fall from her grasps. "Milady!" She ran to her side to see the pool of blood. Aislinn was still breathing, but her tear-streaked face and lips were almost white in color. A shiver of panic coursed through her as she ran for help.

"Moira, where do ye go in such a hurry?" Teige questioned as he was coming out of the Great Hall with Dermot.

She immediately grabbed his arm. "Ye must hurry. It's milady. Her life's blood is slipping out of her."

Teige didn't waste a moment's time and ran ahead of Moira to the top of the stairs. "What's happened?" he yelled behind him.

"I think it's the baby," Moira offered her dreaded opinion as she fought to keep up with him.

"A.J?" Aislinn looked up when she heard Teige call her name. He didn't even know where to begin to help her. God, there was so much blood.

"It's too soon." Aislinn moaned clutching her stomach as the contractions began again.

Dermot had arrived and knelt down beside her. "Milady?" His trembling hand touched her shoulder.

"Find Cahir now," Teige ordered.

"No!" Aislinn forced the words from her lips. "No. Neala. Send for Neala."

Dermot looked questionably to Teige. "Do as she asks." He looked back to Aislinn, fearing for her life and feeling helpless to do anything about it. He gently scooped her up in his arms. Her moan made his insides churn. "A.J., ye are going to be all right."

Neala finally came out of Aislinn's room to find Teige, Dermot and Moira standing there with wide-eyed, frightened expressions. She wasn't sure if she could give them much encouragement. Aislinn was weak, body and soul, but now this added burden.... She sighed before she spoke. "She still lives." Teige could see that there was more and moved forward when she motioned him to follow. They walked a distance away before she spoke again. "The child did not make it."

Teige leaned against the cold stone. "And A.J.? Will she recover?"

"I do nah know what the gods have in store, but she is here now." She studied the young man and noted his genuine concern for Aislinn. She could trust him. "Do ye know where the fool has gone?"

"Ye mustn't say such things."

Neala chuckled. "Ah, but ye knew whom I spoke of, did ye not?"

He didn't comment and she continued, "If ye can get word to him, ye must do so now." She didn't wait for him to answer but started on her way.

"Where are ye going? Are ye not going to stay with her then?"

"Nay. There is nah more I can do."

Just then Cahir came up the stairs in a huff. "I demand to know why I was not summoned."

Dermot's and Teige's gazes met, knowing that there was going to be trouble. Moira shrank away wishing she could dissolve into the walls.

"Well?" Cahir again asked. "I am the physician here."

"No one said that ye were not," Neala spoke up. "Ye were nah where we could find ye. There was nothing ye could have done anyway."

"I should be the judge of that." He strode to the bedroom door, but Teige stepped in front of it. "What is this, Teige?"

"Milady is resting now. Neala told ye already there is nothing more that any of us can do." At that moment, Dermot came forward too and it was quite clear that the two would use force if he tried to enter the room. "Very well. If the fool woman dies, then it will be yer heads." He turned on his heels and strode down the stairs.

Neala glanced to Teige. "She does not need that man's company. I will be here tomorrow to check on her." She moved on her way.

"Cahir could cause trouble." Moira was sure of it.

"Nothing we cannot handle." Teige put a hand on her shoulder. She looked up at him with such trusting eyes and nodded. He prayed that what he claimed was true. Cahir was a powerful man and there would be others that would side with him.

"I will check on milady," Teige told the two. "Dermot, let me know immediately if Cahir returns."

"Aye."

Aislinn was awake, but she did not look at him when he came to sit by her. Silent tears poured down her face and he gently brushed them away. She flinched from his touch. "A.J.?"

"Please go away," she sobbed. "Just go away."

"I will send word to milord of what has happened."

"No!"

"But milady...."

"No." She looked at him, pleading with him not to go against her wishes. "I don't want him here. Please promise me you will not send for him. Promise me, Teige."

"Aye, milady. I will do as ye wish."

Aislinn curled to one side helpless to stop the tears. She felt her stomach where life had just begun to grow and now there was only emptiness. A new rush of tears sprung to her eyes.

Neala brought potions to Aislinn and they had begun to heal her body, but the heart and mind were another matter. Aislinn had withdrawn from everyone. Not even Lynelle or Regan's antics could bring her out of her melancholy. Moira wished that Declan could have been here, for she was sure that the little boy would have been able to draw her out of her deep depression.

Days moved to weeks. Aislinn almost never left her room, taking her meals there and returning most of the portions untouched, or when she did manage to eat something, her stomach rebelled making her ill. Moira was beside herself with worry for she feared Aislinn didn't want to get better. She had witnessed more than once how she still grieved with her trembling hands covering her face, giving vent to the agony of her loss with tears. She knew Lord Dougray needed to be brought back and soon, before it was too late. He was Aislinn's husband. Surely he could make her want to get better.

Moira set out to find Teige.

Cormac had spotted her first and nudged him. She didn't waste time and spoke at once for fear that she would lose courage to ask him. "It's milady."

"Is she worse?" Teige flew to his feet but Moira stopped him with her next flow of words.

"Nay, not exactly. Ye know that she is not taking care of herself. She is frightfully thin, Teige, and will not take nourishment. We must convince her that she should not give up on living."

Had it gone that far? he thought to himself. "I don't know what else we could do."

"She needs her husband," Moira stated simply.

Cormac, who had been silent, now spoke up. "He did not wish to be disturbed unless there was an emergency."

"And ye don't constitute the life of his wife important?" Moira shocked herself with her rash words, but she would not take them back. She was desperate. She looked at Teige again begging him to do the right thing.

Finally he sighed, knowing his promise to Aislinn would have to be broken. "I will bring him back."

When Moira smiled with such adoration, he couldn't help but think he was doing what was right.

Chapter Sixty-Four

Miriam had just about enough of her brother's moping around. He had arrived over three and half weeks ago, with the little boy Declan MacKenna, without so much as an explanation why Aislinn had not accompanied them. "Are ye going to tell me, or must I beat it out of ye?" She saw Murrough's startled look but it didn't deter her from her interrogations.

"I just wanted to visit with ye, dear sister."

She scornfully laughed at him. "Ye think that I am a dolt? Do not offend me with this mock pretense. Something dire has happened to give ye such a long face. Either ye confide in me, or I will have ye thrown out on yer ear." Murrough came to his feet and she turned to glare at him. "I know that ye are a loyal friend, but this is my brother. I will ask ye not to interfere."

"As ye wish, milady," Murrough chuckled. He was all for Miriam forcing Dougray to speak about what was troubling him. "I was only going to let the two of ye have some privacy." He bowed slightly and left the room.

"Well?" She tapped her foot with impatience.

"Oh, Miriam, ye can be so dramatic." He rose to his full height. "I just wanted to…." He met her gaze and he knew he was not going to get away with another flippant response. "Very well if ye are going to be…*Dar Dia*!" He ran his hand through his hair and just spat it out. "Aislinn is with child."

Miriam raised her brows wondering why this didn't seem to please him.

"She didn't want children," he said flatly. "At least that is what she told me."

"She will warm up to the idea surely. I saw for myself how wonderful she was with the children and Declan sings nothing but praise. That boy loves Aislinn if ye didn't know this already."

"Aye. I know. I don't understand her, Miriam." He sat down again. "I thought that perhaps she would grow to love me…I even thought that maybe she did."

"What has changed yer mind?"

"She went to see Neala."

"The old woman of the woods?"

His expression was grim as he nodded. "She asked for the herbs…. Miriam, she didn't want to have my baby."

She was stunned by his words and by the torment she heard in his voice, but she refused to condemn Aislinn. Surely there had to be more to all this. "But ye stated that she is with child now?"

"She is. Aye."

"Then does it not make sense that she didn't take the herbs?"

This question was something he had been mulling over and over again in his mind. Neala had told him she had only visited her once and the container still appeared full.

He looked at his sister. "I think she tried to tell me that, but I refused to listen to her explanation. I have begun to believe that I may have been rash in my decision to denounce her." He said these words tentatively as if testing the idea.

"Men often don't listen to their women. It is not yer fault that ye were born inferior." She tried to tease him out of his melancholy. He managed to give her a quick smile.

"I guess I've been acting the fool."

She walked over to him and gave his handsome face a kiss. "Ah, but what a wise man ye have become to realize yer mistake."

"I am sorry, milord, milady," Murrough interrupted. "Teige is here with a message from Dunhaven."

Dougray rose to his feet anxious to know why Teige himself would make the long journey when he had been left in charge to guard Aislinn. "Show him in."

The young man's usually clean hair was matted against his scalp and his legs and tunic were muddy. Obviously he had ridden hard and long to get here. "Milord, ye must make haste back to Dunhaven."

"Has there been another raid?"

"No, milord…it's Lady Aislinn"

Dougray grabbed a hold of Teige's arms, an uneasiness spreading through him. "What has happened?"

"She is very ill, milord."

He released him then thinking this was not a concern. "She is with child. Women are often…."

"Nay," he interrupted. "Soon after ye left…" He gave a worried look to the others before he gave the dreaded news. "…there was so much blood and milady would have surely died if Neala hadn't seen to her. I am sorry, milord, the child did not make it…too small to hold on to life."

A stabbing pain burrowed deep in his chest and he closed his eyes for a moment before he pinned Teige down with an accusing stare. "Why did ye not send word immediately?"

"I apologize, milord, but milady insisted that ye would not want to be bothered. I only agreed for I thought that she would recover. Neala was able to stop the hemorrhaging, but her spirit, milord. She stays too much to herself. It is like she has no more life in her. Moira and I have heard her sobs when she thinks that no one is listening. It's a woeful sound, milord." He shook his head obviously at wit's end.

Dougray was not prepared for this news. How could anyone be? He felt guilty, no… selfish, for he had known that Aislinn didn't look well when he rode away from Dunhaven, but he left her anyway. "What have I done?" he said more to himself. He had run away not wanting to hear her words. He had wanted her to suffer as she had tortured him, but not like this. Never like this.

He was silent for so long that the other three in the room wondered what he was going to do. Miriam went over to him making him look at her. "Ye must go to her, Dougray. Whatever yer differences are, ye must put them aside now and tend to her needs."

He nodded. "Ready my horse, Teige."

"Aye, milord."

"Are ye all right?" Murrough could see that his friend was raging a war within himself about the uncertainties he would have to face at Dunhaven.

"What if she will not see me?" Dougray had thought of the possibility. He wouldn't blame her, for he had forsaken her when she had needed him most. "On last we spoke, she told me if I left to never come back."

Murrough lifted a brow. "Ye have to see her."

"Don't give me that accusing look, Murrough. I am just saying she may refuse me."

"Then ye do not listen. Ye are her husband and can make that demand."

"And a fine one I have turned out to be too. My friend, I think that I should have remained single. I have buried one wife, and now have nearly killed the second."

"Ye are not responsible for the miscarriage, Dougray."

"I most likely did not help. I could see that she was having difficulties, and yet I did nothing to ease her mind. I argued with her, insulted her, and abandoned her all in one full sweep. I said things that she may never forgive me for." He sat down again and Miriam moved beside him, wishing to comfort him in some way. "I left her," he said simply. "I just left her."

Murrough and Miriam exchanged troubled looks, but neither one said a word. They could only imagine what turmoil Dougray was going through.

Chapter Sixty-Five

Long after Dougray and his men had left, Miriam received another visitor, one she feared would eventually leave her in despair, but still it did not stop her from seeing him again.

Their bodies and souls were connected in a way that no matter how many years had separated them the ties were not severed.

He had come to her out of curiosity, this much he had told her. He had thought to only view her from afar, but he couldn't leave without speaking to her about the words Aislinn had left with him. Blessed Aislinn, she had sent him to her.

He dined with her that night, met her son, but they both knew that their time together must always be kept a secret from those who would never understand. He could only be hers for a little while and she would cherish every moment.

She felt him before she heard his voice rumble against her ear. "I have missed ye, ye beautiful lass of gold."

She smiled and half-turned to receive his kiss. "And I ye, Tremain." She looked again out the window toward where her son was jousting. "What do ye think of Oren? If ye were his father, would ye be proud?"

His gazed lingered to where the lad was making quite a showing. He indeed showed great potential. He had a presence about him that spoke of authority, without being overbearing and he was strong with grace and agility far beyond his years. "Ye should be proud of him, Miriam. I have a difficult time seeing how Sir Reynolds ever gave ye such a lad to be reckoned with."

She again smiled. "I have a difficult time with that myself. But ye did not answer my question. If the child were yers, would ye be proud of him?"

"Aye, that I would. Ye have done well raising him."

"Thank ye." She turned to him then and her heart seemed to beat a little faster. He stood so tall and straight, like a towering oak. His eyes roved over her knowingly. He reached for her and she came willingly into his embrace. "God forgive me, Miriam. Ye should by all rights be my enemy, but I cannot help loving ye."

"Please never stop, Tremain," her voice broke. "Please never stop."

His lips pressed against hers before he gently covered her mouth knowing that it was forbidden but not having the strength to stop.

Chapter Sixty-Six

As they rode, Teige had given Dougray a detailed account of Aislinn's condition, making him all the more desperate to get back to the hold. He had known others who were strong in body and had still succumbed to grief. If he could help it, he was not going to allow Aislinn to go without a fight.

He rode his mount like the tempestuous wind despite the rain- and mud-soaked ground that threatened to stop his advances. He arrived back at Dunhaven well ahead of the others. He was off his horse before the beast even came to a full stop.

"Tend to my mount; it was ridden hard," he yelled over his shoulder to Hamish before he ran up the steps. "Where is Moira?" he bellowed.

Men and women alike scattered wondering what Moira had done to cause their lord to come back home with such a vengeance. He ignored the questionable looks and ran up the stairs. By this time, Moira was aware that Dougray was looking for her and met him in the hall.

He looked wild with his dark hair wind blown against his face and his blue-gray eyes blazing with anxious worry. He was intimidating before to the young woman, but now he looked like a wild man ready to slay his next victim. She took a step back nearly shaking with fear, but Dougray was oblivious to the terror he was invoking. "Answer. Is Aislinn within?"

Moira opened her mouth to say something but nothing came out.

"Speak, woman!" He didn't wait for a response but charged into the chambers. It took him a moment for his eyes to adjust to the darkness and a second longer to see the huddled form of Aislinn sitting upon the windowsill with her chin leaning on her knees and her eyes staring at something that possibly only she could see.

Nothing that Teige had told him could have prepared him for this. He had only been gone for a few weeks and in that time she had become a shadow of her former self.

She had been what he would have called thin, but healthy. Now the bones in her face were more pronounced. Her dark eyes that had been full of life were now hollow orbs, sunken deep within her skull. Her skin that had been a healthy shade of sun bronze, but now it appeared a pasty white. She lived yes, but barely.

She finally looked up. It must have taken her a moment to realize who he was, for he could see the confusion there before recognition set in. Then she turned away from him.

For a moment, he closed his lids, trying to block out the nauseating despair that he might be too late to help her. "Aislinn?" He covered the space that separated them and tried to reach out to her, but she flinched at his touch and scooted away to the far edge of the seat.

"Don't touch me." Her voice was raw and ominous. It devastated him that she sounded so tormented.

"Why don't ye want me to touch ye, Aislinn? Share with me yer grief. Let me help ye."

She began to rock as she hugged her knees closer to her body. She closed her eyes willing him away with her mind, fighting the tears that were ready to spill forth. "Just go. Just let me...." She choked back a sob.

"What, Aislinn? Let ye what? Die? Is that what ye were going to say?" At least that stopped her rocking long enough for her eyes to claw him like talons. Maybe he wasn't too late after all, if he could still spark a response like that out of her. "That's it, isn't it? Ye are giving up."

"I want to die," she cried with such conviction that he felt his heart clench with fear.

He came to her then not letting her push him away. He pulled her hard against his chest. After a moment she ceased to struggle, though she didn't return the embrace. "I wish we could...." He didn't finish the thought. "I'm sorry about the baby." He truly was too for it was just as much his loss as hers, but right now he was sure she didn't want to hear him confess it as so. He felt her whole body stiffen before she pushed him away. She jumped to her feet, nearly toppling over because of her weakened state, but somehow she managed to steady herself.

"You mean my baby." She pounded her chest. Hot tears pouring down her face. "You denied the possibility, didn't you?" She was suddenly assailed with a terrible sense of bitterness and she didn't spare him. "You didn't believe the child was yours. Why aren't you celebrating, Dougray? It's gone. The tiny little soul is gone. Sure makes it easier now, doesn't it? No worries about raising a bastard." Her sarcasm wasn't lost in the sob. Her shoulders began to heave as she breathed. "I can't believe you would think so lowly of me that you would even suggest...." She paused in her tirade meeting his gaze. "It's amazing how little you know me, Dougray."

"It goes both ways, doesn't it?"

"I hate you!" The moment she said the words, she wished that she could have taken them back, for the look he gave her was so wounded that it was like a sword had cut him in two.

He sat there for a long time, his face bleak with sorrow for the pain he had caused her. "Well," he sighed wearily as he came to his feet, "if hate is the emotion that will keep ye alive then use it, Aislinn. Feed on it. Hate me all ye want." He started toward the door, but instead of leaving, he yelled for Moira, who was there in a matter of seconds. "Have Roth make a broth for milady."

"Aye, milord."

"I won't eat it!" she screamed at him and he turned to face her. His eyes told her he was determined to see this through.

"Ye will even if I have to pour it down yer throat."

"I'll kill ye first."

He chuckled without mirth. "I'd like to see ye try. Have ye not looked at yerself lately?" She hesitantly glanced down at the clothes she wore. They hung on her like they were meant for a much larger person. "Aah, I see that ye have not," he continued. "Ye would blow away in the wind." He approached her, baiting her to fight, for if she would, then all was not lost. "Ye're pathetic." She lashed out at him but her strength was gone and she nearly fell. He held onto her steadying her. "Ye will have to do better than that if ye plan on ending my life as ye so threatened."

Her anger became a scalding fury of heated words. "I hate you! I'll hate you until I die!" She pounded on his chest, but he refused to show any compassion to her pathetic jabs.

"I thought that we had already established yer affections toward me." He pushed her onto the bed and she remained there for a moment trying to catch her breath.

"Why are you doing this?" The loathing was quite evident in her voice. "Why can't you just leave me be?"

"Nay. Ye will not die here. If ye choose to end yer life, ye will have to do it elsewhere. Ye will get well, Aislinn. I have every intention of making it so, and if ye still have the inclination to want to kill me then, at least it will be a challenge."

He turned and left the room to find out what was taking so long for the broth to be brought up.

There was so much that Dougray wanted to tell her, but where could he begin when she said that she despised him? How could he ask her to forgive him when she had no compassion left in her heart?

Dougray was true to his word. He himself brought the warm soup to Aislinn's room. He gave strict instructions that no one was to disturb them. He then shut the door securing it behind him. Aislinn's mouth dropped open when she saw his intent. He was really going to force her to eat.

"Come sit down."

"I'll eat later." She decided maybe if she would agree he would leave her alone.

"Uh uh. I don't believe ye." He pulled out the chair and motioned with his hand for her to take a seat. She backed away shaking her head. "I have all day, Aislinn. We can do this the easy way or the hard way. It is yer choice."

"You go to hell, Dougray Fitzpatrick."

"After ye, my dear." And he went after her.

Moira heard Aislinn's scream and it took all her will power not to throw open the door to see if she needed saving. Teige was just coming up the stairs when another scream penetrated the stillness. "What is going on?"

"I don't know, but milord said that no one was to disturb them. Ye don't think he would hurt her?" Just then they heard Dougray bellow.

"Nay." Teige shook his head. "I think we might have to fear for milord's safety."

After about an hour, Dougray emerged from the room. He was an utter mess. The soup stained his tunic and some was evident in his hair. "She is not to leave this room. I will be back in a few hours and I want another large bowl of broth ready. Is that understood?" Teige noticed that he was rubbing his arm.

"Are ye all right, milord?"

"Fine." He looked to Moira. "Tend to yer mistress. She could use a friendly face right about now."

"Aye, milord." She went directly in.

"She is not harmed? Is she?" Teige was embarrassed that he had voiced the question. "I am sorry, milord. I...."

"Nay, Teige, I am not angry. Ye care for Aislinn and I am most grateful that ye do. She would have died if ye had not come for me. I am in yer debt." He placed a hand on the young man's shoulder, giving it a quick squeeze before he bounded down the steps.

Neala was waiting for him when he walked through the glen. After all these years it still unsettled him that she was aware when company would arrive. She came out of her one-room shanty with a cup of welcoming liquid. "Lord of Dunhaven, what took ye so long?"

Dougray raised a brow. He wasn't sure if she was referring to their meeting now, or the fact that he had been away for weeks. He took the cup of the hot liquid from her and she led him to the fire, knowing that he would wish to speak. "She is so angry," he said as he sat upon the rock.

"And well she should be. Ye accused her of unfaithfulness and denounce the child she carried. Would ye nah be angry?" Her old eyes held his like a lecturing mother.

"She took the herbs from ye," he shot back in defense.

She sighed with disappointment. "Ye are back to that again? Have ye learned nothing from the mistakes ye have made?"

He drew in a deep breath not wanting to argue. He needed the old woman's advice to ensure Aislinn's recovery and so far he was wasting time. "Nay, I have learned. She never took the potion, but I had refused to see it. I have realized all too late what wrong I have done. She had wanted to explain, but I refused to let her have her say and now our child is lost to us."

"Think yerself lucky. Ye could have lost her as well, and ye would have never had the chance to set things right. Ye're a young fool and she is nah innocent in that matter either, bickering and fighting over naught. Ye are only here on this earth for just a breath of time, a moment, I tell ye, but ye continue to waste what could be yers."

"I hadn't intended to." He rose from his seat, not liking being scolded. "I don't want to."

"Bah!" She waved her hand at him, obviously not believing him.

"Damn it, old woman, I love her!" He didn't realize he had raised his voice until he heard the birds in the trees flutter away. "I love her," he said again but a little more quietly.

She eyed him for a long time as though she was deciding for herself if he was telling her the truth. She sighed with a nod of her head. "So ye do." She went back to her house leaving him there staring at the empty doorway. He knew not what else to do and followed the old woman inside to find her intently looking for something. "Now where is it?"

He cleared his throat drawing her attention. He needed her advice before he went back. "What can I do? She says that she loathes my presence. She even threatened my life."

Neala chuckled. "Aye, I would nah doubt that she would say this and believe it so, but I have found that love and hate run very close together." She took the cup from him and handed him two containers.

"What are these for?"

"One is for milady. Now that she is eating again, this will help settle her stomach and keep the food down." He didn't even ask how she knew.

"And the other?"

"It is for the bite on yer arm."

Now this he didn't let go. She couldn't see the wound for it was covered. "How…?"

"It is nah difficult to know. Ye favored the arm. Now go back to the castle and be persistent with her. And milord, it is important that ye bring her the food that will nourish her body. It must be from yer hands to hers. Do ye understand? Yer hands only."

All the way back to the castle, he kept wondering about the strange request Neala made of him. Why would it matter who brought the food up to the room? But Aislinn's life was at stake here and he was not going to take any chances. He went directly to the kitchen where he ran into the physician.

"Cahir?"

"Milord? Begging yer pardon." He moved away and would have continued on but Dougray stopped him.

"What business do ye have here?"

He hesitated for a moment. "I was asking Roth to try another meal for milady. Ye have seen for yerself…well she needs meat on her bones."

"Yer concern is well noted. I appreciate that ye would trouble yerself."

"I am the physician here. I felt it my duty to see if I could help. She had refused to see me, milord, or I would have intervened sooner."

"It is all right. I am here now and she will do no more refusing. Again thank ye."

Cahir nodded and hurried on his way.

Roth looked up when Dougray entered. "Milord, what brings ye here?"

"Just checking to see if the soup was ready."

"Aye, that it is, nice and hot. Hopefully milady will be able to keep it down." He shook his head sadly as he poured the hot liquid into a bowl. "She's just about dwindled down to bones."

"We'll turn it around."

"Are ye going to let Abbot Kirwan bless it?"

"Kirwan?"

"He comes by and blesses milady's food."

Dougray for a moment didn't say anything.

"Milord?"

"What?…Nay, Roth. I don't wish to wait." He took the bowl and headed for the door then on second thought he turned again to address him. "From now on, Roth, no one but ye and I will touch milady's meals. Do ye understand?"

"Whatever ye say, milord," he answered slowly wondering why he was issuing such an odd request.

"Good." Then he was gone without further explanation.

Aislinn fought him again on the next meal, calling him names he did not know the meanings to, and he was sure that he would not wish to. "Be persistent," he kept saying to himself for his resolve was weakening. He wanted to hold her and comfort her, not cause her more pain, but to let up now would mean her death. She had to keep some nourishment down.

When he arrived for the evening meal, she was lying on the bed and only lifted her head to see who had entered. He immediately became concerned. Putting the tray down, he went over to her.

"Please, I am too tired. I just can't eat another bite. I can't. I just can't." A tear slid down her face and he gently brushed it away, his heart breaking to see her so defeated.

"If ye promise to be good tomorrow…."

Her large eyes widened as she nodded her head. "I promise." She sounded so much like a child that he couldn't resist leaning down and giving her a quick kiss on the top of her head.

"Then sleep, Aislinn."

She sniffled. "Dougray?"

"Hmm?"

"Will you tell me where Declan is?" He could see that she was holding her breath, dreading his answer.

"He is here, lass. I will bring him to ye tomorrow."

Tears glistened on her pale face. "Thank you."

"Now close yer eyes." She didn't even argue for she was beyond exhausted. He stayed, gently holding her hand until she fell asleep. "I'll make this all up to ye. I promise." He kissed her hand above the amber ring that he had given her when they handfasted, making his pledge to her. "I will make amends with ye, Aislinn, if it takes me all my days to do so."

Chapter Sixty-Seven

The next day, she was good to her word and didn't fight him when it came time for a meal, but by no means was she cordial either. She had some of her spunk back and her intense glare was enough to convince him that she resented him being there. He folded his arms against his chest, refusing to leave until she had left her bowl dry. Then he had her drink the mixture that Neala had given him so that she would not have a queasy stomach.

"Now wait here." His demand seemed ludicrous since she hadn't been able to leave the room for days. A few minutes later Declan came running in to greet her.

"A.J.!" His face beamed with happiness and he ran into her welcoming arms. "I missed ye so much."

"I've missed you too." She held him tight not wanting to let him go. Tears of pleasure found their way to her eyes.

Declan pulled away to look at her, confused by her outburst. "What is the matter? Are ye not happy to see me?"

She chuckled and sniffled at the same time. "Of course, I'm happy to see you. These are tears of joy."

"They are?" He wasn't at all convinced.

"Don't try to figure it out, Declan." Dougray had been watching them from the doorway. The boy turned to look at him. "Women are a mystery to me also. Just accept what she says."

"You'll let him stay for a while, Dougray?"

She made him feel like an ogre and a part of him could not blame her. He had taken the boy away from her, obviously convincing her that he had the notion to deposit him any old place other than here. "Aye, if ye are up to a visitor."

"I feel better already. Come here, Declan, and give me a hug again. I missed you so much." The boy was all too eager to comply.

She looked over Declan's shoulder at him with the faintest of smiles. He nodded his head toward her before he left them alone.

The first few days the herbs that Neala had sent back with Dougray were a godsend. Slowly but surely her stomach did not rebel and she was able to keep the food down. Within the week she was eating solid foods and her strength was slowly returning. She even dressed in a simple gown and let Moira fix her hair with ribbons. She still needed to put on some weight, but her cheeks had begun to fill out and the dark shadows beneath her eyes were not so pronounced. She even had the energy to tell Declan stories and to play a few games with him.

Dougray knocked once but did not wait to be admitted. Both Moira and Aislinn turned to stare at him. They had not been expecting him so soon. "I finished my breakfast," she said defensively.

His lips tugged at a smile. "I am not here to question ye. I am here to take ye out for a ride."

For a moment, she was actually thrilled at the idea of an outing, but she was still not ready to let herself enjoy the luxury. She was harboring too much guilt that she had been the cause of the miscarriage. It wasn't right for her to partake in some frivolous pleasure. She turned away from him. "I don't want to go."

He was well aware she was punishing herself and he was not going to let her continue. "I was not asking, Aislinn. I was telling ye. Her cloak, Moira."

"Aye, milord." She quickly went to the chest and took out the rich-colored red cloak that was thick enough to keep her warm should the weather turn cold. Dougray took it from Moira. Facing her, he reached over her wrapping it around her shoulders, clasping it below her chin.

"I can't go."

"Ye can't hide in here forever."

"I'm not hiding."

"Nay?" He lifted his brows. "Ye know that ye are. Do ye want the whole keep to think ye are a coward?"

"I am no coward," her voice snapped with defiance.

"I thought not." And he took her hand firmly in his, pulling her behind him. She knew by his attitude that it would be useless to resist.

"Good day, milady." Teige smiled at her as Dougray hurried her along.

"Good day, Teige," she said as she passed by. "Will you slow down?" she hissed at Dougray. "You're pulling my arm out of the socket." He slowed his pace but refused to let go of her hand. She could have easily kept up with him, but she purposely lagged behind. She didn't see the point in making this easier for him.

"Milady." Dermot fell in step beside her. "Ye are looking well."

"I feel better. Thank you."

Once they were outside, Dermot went on his way and Hamish came forward with just Dougray's mount. She looked at him wondering what was going on. He didn't acknowledge her questioning gaze, but instead took hold of her waist and before she could object lifted her onto the horse's back. What else could she do? She sat sidesaddle and he was upon the mount behind her. He wrapped his right arm securely around her waist and took the reins from Hamish.

"Have a good ride, milady…and milord," he added at the end.

Dougray clicked his tongue and his mount immediately set into motion. "I could have ridden my own horse." She made the obvious known.

"Aye, that ye could have, but I much prefer it this way."

She opened her mouth to give him an unladylike retort, but seeing him grin down at her as though he expected it, she decided not to give him the satisfaction. She immediately snapped her mouth shut and looked away.

They rode only a small distance from the castle, and Aislinn began to relax. They didn't say much, but surprisingly the silence didn't seem to bother either one of them. It was a cool day that still threatened to give them rain, but it felt wonderful to Aislinn to feel the fresh breeze against her face.

Dougray didn't want to keep her out too long for he feared that she might have a relapse if he overexerted her. He made a wide sweep and headed back. Before going back to the keep though, he stopped his mount in front of Padrig's home. Murrough was visiting Rhiannon and was the one to open the door to let them enter. Aislinn realized then they had been expecting them. Obviously this was a well-planned out excursion.

Rhiannon made a wonderful sweet bread and warm herb drink that Neala had shown her how to make. It was relaxing and comforting and she was beginning to actually enjoy the day.

"Would ye like some more?" Rhiannon was already there with her kettle to refill Aislinn's cup.

"Thank you. I don't mind if I do."

"Anyone else?" She started filling her father's empty mug.

Dougray moved his closer. "What did ye call this warm liquid ye made?"

"I do not have a name for it, but Neala showed me where to pick the herbs. It takes away the cool wind that seeps into yer bones, does it not?"

"Aye, that it does." Dougray reached for another piece of bread. "The bread goes well with the drink."

"The woman is a wonderful cook." Murrough helped himself to a healthy portion.

"The other day Keefe was saying the same thing," Padrig spoke up. Murrough stop chewing, his eyes bore into the old man's.

"Who did ye say?"

Padrig was good enough to repeat the name. "Keefe. Handsome devil that Keefe, sharp too."

"Keefe?" Murrough still could not believe he was hearing this. "Keefe has been here?"

Everyone else had remained silent sensing how close the man was to losing his temper, but this did not stop Padrig in the least. "Aye. Haven't I been saying as much? He seemed very interested in a woman that could cook."

Murrough threw a thunderous glare toward Rhiannon before he again addressed her father. "Keefe thinks he can take my woman?"

Rhiannon had her hands on her hips. She had about enough of Murrough's attitude and she was going to set him straight once and for all. "I belong to no man, Murrough O'Donoghue, and ye'd do best to remember it."

He slammed his hand on the table causing everyone's cup to rattle in its place. "Ye deny that ye are with me? Ye deny this to all present?"

"With the attitude ye hold, I will be sure to deny it." Even though Rhiannon's voice was defiant, Aislinn couldn't help but notice her hands were trembling. "Please excuse me." She nodded to her guests before she left the warmth of the house.

Everyone was silent until Padrig decided to speak again, addressing Murrough, "Are ye not going after her then?"

That was all the red-haired giant needed for encouragement; he was out the door within a few strides behind Rhiannon.

The old man just smiled and took another large helping of the sweet bread.

Aislinn glanced at Dougray from across the table and he too couldn't help but grin. "I think ye are trying to get rid of a daughter, Padrig."

"Only giving it a push. I am not a young man now. I would like to know me grandchildren have a ma and a da to contend to." The moment Padrig said the words he wished he could have bitten his tongue. "I apologize, milady." He looked worriedly at Aislinn. "I should not have...."

"There is no need to apologize. Please do not treat me like I'll fall apart. I assure you that I will not crumble." Padrig still didn't look convinced. "Really, Padrig, I'm okay. I also hope to have children of my own one day."

"Neala says there is no reason that ye can't." Dougray reached across the table to take her hand, but she pulled away. Padrig witnessed this, but was good enough not to make a comment.

Just when the silence was becoming unbearable, Rhiannon and Murrough burst through the door. Their beaming faces were enough to know they had already made up. "Padrig, a word with ye please." Murrough's voice boomed through the air.

The old man turned in his seat. "What is this, Murrough? Have we not been conversing all afternoon?"

"I want to ask ye for Rhiannon's hand. We want to be wed no later than Beltane. We have waited long enough."

Beltane, Aislinn thought to herself as her dark eyes met Dougray's. In just little over three months it would be their first-year anniversary. She looked up and found that Dougray was studying her. The time had finally come to decide if their marriage would continue or if they would simply go their separate ways. She dropped her gaze. When she did, Dougray couldn't help but feel a sense of defeat. She was retreating from him. What could he hope to accomplish in a few months that he had not been able to accomplish in all the others? He would be wise to just give it up and let Aislinn move in with her uncle. Aengus had already made it perfectly clear that she would have a place with him if the marriage failed. Failed? What a horrible unforgettable word that seemed to him. He turned his attention to the happy couple. "Congratulations." He tried to smile even though he knew his own marriage was falling apart. He rose from his seat and gave Rhiannon a hug and then to Murrough a slap on the back, which the man gratefully returned before they decided to embrace. "I am truly happy for ye, my friend."

Murrough looked over Dougray's shoulder to where Aislinn was still seated. Even though Dougray was wishing him well, he could hear the anguish in those words, and by the pained expression that Aislinn wore, she was just as miserable. He knew it was not because they didn't care for each other, but rather it was just the opposite.

Long after Dougray and Aislinn had left, Murrough and Rhiannon went for a walk to have a moment alone. "Could ye not feel their pain?" Rhiannon began. "They care so much for each other and yet they seem to not recognize it."

"They have always been at each other's throats. Maybe it will be for the best that they part company."

Rhiannon stopped in her tracks. "Ye do not mean it surely. They have been through so much. It is not time to give up. Is this how ye see a marriage?"

"I wasn't referring to how it will be with us."

"Really now. Do ye think that it is easy to share yer life with someone? Ye have to work at it, take the bad times with the good. It will not be all games and laughter. It will be the hardest thing ye will ever do. Only if ye have the courage to see it through will the rewards be granted. If ye do not know this, Murrough, then I have no wish to...." In one full sweep he brought her to him and covered her lips with his, immediately silencing her words.

After a moment, her tirade had slipped away to be replaced with something more meaningful. She melted against him. He ended the caress, only to look at her.

"I gladly accept the challenge," he told her. "I do not run away from anything, Rhiannon. I love ye and I don't take the declaration lightly. Ye will be wise to do the same."

"Murrough...." She seemed stunned by his outburst of devotion but most certainly pleased.

They were nearly to the stables when Dougray decided that he could no longer remain silent. He needed some answers from Aislinn and knew he could not wait for her to be settled in her chambers. He pulled back on the reins bringing their mount to a halt.

"Why have we stopped?" She turned to look at him.

"Why do ye push away from me?"

Her eyes widened for a moment and he thought she was going to deny it, but instead she danced around the question. "What do you mean?"

"Back there, at the house, I reached for yer hand and ye pulled it away as if ye felt my touch diseased."

"I didn't mean to...I didn't realize I had." She looked away. She was tired and didn't want to discuss this. So much had happened and nothing seemed to make sense, nothing felt secure. And now in a few months of time, she would have to tell him if she still wanted to remain married to him. What frightened her more was the fact that he could also decide the fate as well.

She knew he was there now trying to make her well, but she was also not foolish enough to think it was anything more than an obligation, his responsibility to her. His sense of honor went beyond the call, but he didn't understand that she didn't want his handouts or his pity. She wanted his love. She realized that Dougray was speaking again but she hadn't registered the words. "What?" She looked at him again.

"Ye are unhappy and I am at a loss how to change that. When the Brehon comes to ask if ye want the marriage dissolved, I will not fight it. Ye are free to go to yer uncle's whenever ye wish." She just stared unblinkingly at him with those dark penetrating eyes and all he could see in their depths was a lost soul. She had retreated from him as surely as if she had returned through the mist to her own time.

She dropped her gaze before she answered him, "As you wish, my lord."

They rode the rest of the way back in silence.

Moira had hoped the outing would have done Aislinn some good, but the woman looked simply exhausted beyond words. She helped her undress and tucked her into bed. "Is there anything ye need, A.J.?"

"No," she sniffled back her sob. "No, thank you," she repeated.

"A.J., what happened today?"

"He's going to send me away." She turned her head into her pillow and let the tears flow. Moira rubbed her mistress' head trying to give her some comfort. She couldn't believe it was true. Why would milord send her away?

"That is what she told me." Moira repeated what Aislinn had confided in her.

Teige and Cormac stared at each other not accepting that this was true. "Surely ye are mistaken," Cormac decided.

"Nay. She wept last night over the fact."

"It doesn't make sense." Teige ran his hand through his hair. Moira had stepped forward and placed her hand on his arm. He felt his body responding to her innocent touch forcing him to swallow the lump in his throat.

"Ye will speak to him, will ye not?"

Cormac was completely aware of the effect the young woman was having on his friend. He could barely keep from laughing.

Teige stood a little taller. No matter what Moira asked of him, she had a way of making him feel like he could accomplish the impossible. "I will try." When she smiled her blue eyes lit up with pure unadulterated devotion. He patted her arm.

As soon as Moira had left them alone, Cormac couldn't help but tease. "Ye will speak to him, won't ye?" he mimicked Moira's plea with a high-pitched voice. Teige nudged him quite annoyed with his behavior. "Teige my lad, ye must admit it."

"What?"

"Ye are in love with the lass and still have done nothing about it. Why do ye wait?"

"Moira is still young."

"Nay. Are we still at that again? She is of age. Me own sister was married by then expecting her first child. And let me tell ye, my friend, ye do not look at Moira as if she were a young lass."

Teige had the decency to blush. "I am that obvious then?"

"Anymore obvious and I would have to protect the woman's honor."

"Get on with ye." He nudged him again.

"My question is are ye going to ask milord for Moira's hand before or after ye scold him about A.J.?"

Teige forgot for a moment about his promise. It would not do well to make the man angry. "I don't even know if Moira would want to marry me."

Cormac burst out laughing. "Surely ye jest? She only has eyes for ye. I felt near invisible, I did, when she came to make her plea."

Dougray looked up from his work. "Do ye remember the invitation my grandfather sent to me a while back to attend his small gathering at his place he holds in the Pale?"

"Ye told me ye did not wish to attend." Murrough sat forward in his seat.

"I have changed my mind."

"But is it wise to be so close to where nearly all of England resides? It could be dangerous now that ye have made yer suspicions known. Even yer grandfather heard whispers and not in yer favor. Ye could be walking right into a trap."

"Possibly, but what better way to find out what the English are up to than to be right among them?"

"But what of the threats? Do ye not fear it is from those that fancy yer loyalty lie beyond our shores? Spending time with those they do not trust will only strengthen their convictions."

"Maybe this will prompt our conspirator to come out into the open."

Teige entered the room in such a rush that Dougray came to his feet. "Has something happened?"

"No, milord. Begging yer pardon but might I have a word with ye in private?" Teige glanced at Murrough. This was going to be difficult enough without another intimidating figure eyeing him.

Dougray and Murrough's gaze met with a shrug. "I was on my way out actually." Murrough was polite enough to offer an excuse. He was already heading to the door when Dougray called after him.

"I trust that ye will make all of the arrangements for my departure and also see to the coach for Aislinn."

Murrough was rather surprised. "Ye plan on taking her with ye then?"

"Aye. It is time she come out of hiding and join the living."

Murrough bowed slightly and left the room, leaving Teige to face the man who could decide the outcome of his future.

"Well, Teige, why must ye speak to me in private?"

"It is about A.J…I mean Lady Aislinn."

"Has she become ill again?"

"Nay, but she is under the impression that ye wish to be rid of her."

Dougray was silent for a moment wondering where she would have gotten such a ridiculous idea. He sat back down with a sigh. "I have no wish for Aislinn to leave Dunhaven, but my wife seems most unhappy here. I fear for her well being. If letting her go would make her well again, then I will grant her leave. She may not wait until the year is up to end the marriage. I will not bind her to the contract."

"I don't understand why ye would let her go."

"We have been united for so long and nothing has changed. If anything, I have helped destroy the spirit that I had learned to love. Do not worry, Teige. I know ye care for her and I would never see her without someone to look after her welfare. If she so chooses, her uncle has already made the offer to take her."

"Pardon me for saying so, milord, but did ye not inform Murrough that ye were taking milady with ye when ye leave for the Pale?"

"Aye, Lord Aengus will be there and I can make all the necessary arrangements. It will do her good to be with family. Now if ye will excuse me…."

Teige knew he was being dismissed but still he couldn't believe what he had just heard. "Milord?"

Dougray looked up. "Ye had something more to discuss with me?"

"A.J. is with family." He shrugged his shoulders not willing to back down on this matter. Dougray knew it was taking great courage for the young man to speak his mind and he admired him for it.

"I will ask ye to let me worry about Lady Aislinn's welfare. Now if that is all ye wished to speak to me about I…."

"There is one more thing."

"Go on." He was beginning to become impatient with all this talk.

"I wish to ask permission to join hands with Moira."

"Moira?"

"Aye, milord. She has no one that I can speak to on this matter."

"She wishes this union also?"

Teige blushed and he tugged his tunic feeling that it was beginning to choke him. "I have not asked her as of yet."

"I see. How old is Moira now?"

"She is six and ten. Cormac's sister was already married and with child by that age," he quickly added.

"Hmm. And ye are?"

"Ten and nine, milord."

"Old enough to know if ye would want to take a wife. If the lass is willing, then I see no reason why the union should not take place."

He nearly beamed. "Thank ye, milord."

Teige went straight away to find Moira. He spotted her leaving Aislinn's room. Hurrying to catch up to her, he grabbed her arm bringing her to an immediate halt. She turned a startled look at him, and he instantly dropped his hand to his side. "Sorry, Moira…I just wanted to have a moment with ye."

She looked over her shoulder at the closed door where Aislinn was resting. She supposed that a few moments would not matter. "Aye, but ye must make it quick." She looked at him then and noticed for the first time he seemed to be gazing at her in a strange manner. "Is something amiss? Ye look distressed."

He didn't answer but leaned down and gave Moira a kiss on her cheek. She dropped her eyes, startled by his bold act. "I hope I did not offend ye," he said hurriedly, praying he had not misinterpreted the way she felt about him. Maybe he had misread the meaning in her eyes.

"Nay," she finally answered. "Ye surprised me is all." She managed to look at him again. "Why did ye…ye know?"

"I was hoping that ye would join hands with me." He was so nervous. "I mean, I would ask ye to be my wife."

"Ye want me to be yer wife?" She was aware that Teige had glanced her way now and again, but she had only dreamed that he would care for her in that way.

"Aye. I would be most honored. I would be good to ye, Moira. I would do…."

"I will marry ye," she rushed to say before he might change his mind.

"Ye will?" His eyes widened in pleasant surprise.

"I can think of nothing that would please me more."

"Agreed then." They stared at each other not really sure what they were supposed to do now, but it seemed some sort of gesture should be made.

Finally Teige took hold of her shoulders and drew her near. The tilting of her head and the slight parting of her lips was all the encouragement that he needed. His lips slowly descended to meet hers and he felt her quiver at the sweet tenderness of his kiss. It ended all too soon for Moira broke the embrace and took a nervous step back.

"Ye shouldn't do that, ye know." Moira looked over his shoulder to see if anyone had entered the hall.

Teige wasn't listening and took hold of her arm pulling her against him once more. "I don't want to stop. I have tasted yer sweet lips. How can I not kiss ye again?"

She put her hand in his chest. "As much as I like yer caresses, sir, we must not indulge."

"Ye like my kisses, do ye?" He tried to take her in his arms but she slipped from his grip.

"Very much so but now I must finish my work. Be off with ye."

As she walked down the hall, Teige smiled as he watched her hips sway back and forth. Just as she reached the stairs, she turned. She gave him a beguiling smile, making him fear his heart would leap from his chest.

Chapter Sixty-Eight

Dougray entered Aislinn's chambers to inform her of their plans. She was perched on the window seat, a forlorn expression penetrating her features. She didn't even acknowledge his presence, but continued to stare out the window.

Where had her spirit gone? She had always been bubbling over with life and now she looked to have no energy at all. How had he let this happen to his beautiful *Scathach*?

He walked over to her dinner tray and saw that the food had been moved around the plate, but nothing had been eaten. Obviously her stomach was giving her trouble again. He swallowed the lump in his throat putting aside the sympathy he was feeling for her. She needed someone to push her back to her strong determined self before it was too late.

"We will be leaving for Dublin." He thought that maybe she had not heard him for not a muscle did she move. He was about to repeat his announcement when she finally spoke.

"I don't want to go."

"Well as I see it, ye are not doing anything of importance here and ye are going." He called for Moira and waited until the young woman made her appearance. "Have milady's things packed and ready. We will leave tomorrow." He looked at Aislinn again. "Ye will be ready or I will personally drag ye down to the carriage myself."

She finally turned toward him, her dark eyes were wild, haunted. "I will not go with you. I'll…" For a moment he thought that he heard a little of her old self in that threat, but she again retreated. "I can't."

"Just have her trunk packed," he stated gruffly to Moira before he strode out of the room.

By mid morning the next day, everything was prepared and readied for their trip.

Moira had gone on ahead to inform Dougray that Aislinn would be down soon. That was over twenty minutes ago. Dougray had his hands behind his back, pacing to and fro, and with each step his temper rising.

"Blast it!" He slapped his gloves on his legs and started toward the castle with all intent of carrying out his threat of bodily dragging Aislinn out of her room, but then he spotted her.

She was elegantly dressed in a dark, green velvet gown and with black lace sleeves, her hair pulled back in a twisted braid and skewered with an emerald-jeweled bodkin. He thought she was still far too thin, but even so she was breathtakingly beautiful.

She held her head high as she started toward him and he noticed that she had Declan with her as well. He shrugged. The boy would be welcomed. He had no qualms in taking him with them. The lad seemed to make Aislinn happy, where he had failed.

She had reached him, her dark eyes challenging him to insist that Declan would have to be left behind. Instead he knelt down beside the boy. "Ye are quite dressed for the occasion. Turn around and let me have a look at ye now."

Declan did as he was told and faced Dougray with a grin. "A.J. had Rhiannon fix me up. Do I look fine?"

"Ye do indeed. Are ye ready to take another long trip to Dublin?"

"Aye, milord. Ye don't mind then?"

"Of course not." He ruffled the boy's blond hair and rose to his full height to face Aislinn. "Milady." He swept his hand toward the coach. He had to bite the inside of his cheeks to keep from smiling for she nearly glared daggers at him when he tried to help her into the carriage. "I'm not an invalid. I can manage myself."

"As ye wish." After he helped Declan and Moira in, he shut the door and he leaned in through the window. "I know ye don't want to go on this trip, but ye'll feel better for it, Aislinn."

Again the glare that most definitely told him to drop dead. "I will never feel all right. Do not proceed to tell me that I will." She looked straight ahead then, obviously dismissing him.

Miriam rested her head on Tremain, her hand idly caressing his chest. She had to tell him, but how she hated to ruin this moment. She had only begun to enjoy the union and now she would have to send him away. How she detested the clan difficulties. Men could be such children about their beliefs and convictions.

"Ye know that my grandfather has arranged for a gathering for a festive evening."

"Aye, I have heard. I don't believe I was invited." He kissed the top of her head, not really interested in conversation. His hand began to roam down her body, touching every place that he had recently kissed.

Miriam tried not to be distracted but his touch was like magic, hypnotizing her. "Ye must know that my brother will be attending."

That stilled him and his eyes raised to regard her. "Why do ye tell me this?"

"Because he will be staying here with me."

If anything could ruin his mood, this was it. He pulled away. "Here? Why here?"

"He is my brother. How could I not offer him my hospitality?"

"And how do ye expect me to just accept my enemy?" He rose from the bed and started donning his clothes.

Miriam sat up not believing that he would just leave her when every moment they spent together was precious. "Where are ye going?"

"The mood is ruined."

Miriam wasn't going to take that for an answer. She moved to the edge of the bed and reached for him. In doing so the blanket had fallen to expose her nakedness. He paused with his conviction.

"Tremain, we have so few hours together. Do not leave, especially like this."

He growled obviously upset with his own self-control. "Ach! Ye undo me with yer comeliness." He moved closer; his resolve to leave was weakening. She took advantage and brought her lips to his, leaning her taut breasts against him. The little intake of his breath was all she needed to know that he would stay. Already she could feel his body's response to her touch. "And when do ye expect yer brother?" he grumbled against her ear as he nibbled it with tender kisses.

"By the end of the week." She kissed his neck then paused to look at him, her eyes large and hesitant. "Ye will do nothing to harm him?"

Tremain remained silent.

"I told ye this only so ye would not come here and be harmed by my brother's men. So help me, Tremain, if ye so much as lay a hand on my brother...."

"Stop." He moved away. "Ye compromise me, Miriam, by telling me this. I owe my loyalty to Lord Fingham and yet..." He looked at her. "...I owe my heart to ye."

"Then follow yer heart."

"Dougray Fitzpatrick must pay for what he has done."

"Done? Surely ye do not still believe that he was responsible for Ella's death? I understand loyalty to yer lord, but for ye to actually believe a grieving father's unfounded accusations is simply ludicrous."

"He's yer brother, Miriam. Of course ye would be blinded to the truth."

"Pheugh!" Her blue eyes sparked with anger. "I assure ye that I have all my faculties intact, thank ye very much. If my brother murdered Ella, I would not pretend that it was otherwise just to protect his hide. Dougray would have never harmed Ella. He adored her. It nearly devastated him when he lost her."

"It didn't hurt his books. Rather he inherited a good sum from her dowry."

"How dare ye even suggest such a notion? Dougray did not care of the money. He would have never agreed to the meeting in the first place if it hadn't been insisted that he marry the moment he stepped foot in Ireland again.... Clans and their suspicions.... When they were the ones who had him fostered in England. Then to prove his loyalties lie with Ireland they force him to marry a woman he had not seen since she was but a child. He was obedient though, wasn't he? He did it and found that he was actually happy for it. Money be damned. Loyalty be damned. He married Ella because he loved her."

Tremain was not immune to what others had said about Dougray being grief stricken, but because of his own personal grudge against the Fitzpatricks, it was easier to believe the worse. "And of this new woman that he has taken to wed? Does he love her also?"

"Oh if ye ask me, I would say he does."

"That is an odd answer."

"Well it is a unusual marriage to be sure. They are both pigheaded and determined not to let the other know of their true feeling for each other. They are equally matched in all respects."

He thought about what she said and there was some truth to it. Aislinn Fitzpatrick was indeed a strong brave woman. Her looks were a bit dark for his taste, but there was something that drew a man's attention to her. She spoke fondly of Dougray, and she had given him the reason to seek out Miriam.

As for Dougray, obviously he cared for Aislinn. He came to her rescue without a care to how he was endangering himself. He was brave, that much he had to give him, but there was more. He had also shown a sense of honor. Dougray could have run him through when he was left defenseless, but blast it, if he hadn't just saluted him as he went on his way.

"What are ye thinking, Tremain? I'm warning ye if anything happens to my brother while he's visiting, we are through." He grabbed her then tumbling her to the bed in one long and endearing kiss. She was surely swept away but not so much that she wouldn't have an answer from him. "Give me yer word, Tremain."

He sighed deeply. "All right then. Ye have my word that I will not raise a sword to him."

"Or yer men."

"Aye, aye, already. It will be as if yer brother was not about. Is that good enough?"

She threw her arms around him in answer.

Chapter Sixty-Nine

Miriam was a gracious host and had a lavish welcome awaiting her brother and his wife. Miriam knew that Aislinn had suffered physically, barely managing to survive a miscarriage, but she was still shocked over the woman's appearance. It wasn't that she had lost weight for that was quite obvious in the way her clothing hung on her. The shock was more in her behavior. She had marveled how Aislinn had held her own, even with the men. She had been strong in every way that a human being could possibly be, but this creature her brother had brought with him did not remotely resemble that person.

Once she had her brother alone she could not stop herself from voicing her concern. "Dougray, what has happened to her? This is more than a normal case of melancholy. It is as if she is withering away."

He sat down wearily, a pained look on his face. "Ye don't think I know this? I have tried but she refuses to let me in. That is why I have sent word for her uncle to meet with me."

"Ye hope that he will be of some help?"

"I want Lord Aengus to reinstate his offer that she could return with him to the Hennessy keep."

Miriam's mouth dropped. "I cannot believe what I am hearing. Ye are giving up?"

"It would be for the best."

Miriam swatted her hand against his arm. Of course it didn't hurt him but it most certainly did get his attention.

"I do hope ye plan on explaining yerself." His eyes glared at her for her daring to address him in such a manner.

"I'd hit ye on the side of the head if that would give ye some sense. Did ye pack her bags as well?"

"It is for the best, Miriam."

"Ye will be miserable if she is out of yer life. Remember, I have seen ye two together."

"Then ye know that we were at each other's throats."

"Ye love her," she insisted.

He looked at his sister with misery so acute in the silver blue of his eyes that anguish tore at her own heart. "That is why I am letting her go."

"She wants this? She has told ye with her own words that she wishes the marriage to be annulled?"

"She does not have to. It is obvious by her actions. She will not let me near her. She recoils from my touch. What else could I possibly think?"

"She is hurting, Dougray. She lost a baby. Have ye forgotten? Ye had left her when she needed ye the most."

"*Dar Dia*, Miriam. Are ye going to be pointing out anymore of my faults? I already feel wretched enough."

"I am not trying to make ye feel worse. I was only trying to make ye see. Ye need to give her some time. Give ye both some time."

"Don't ye understand? It's over. When the Brehon asks if we will remain wed...."

"That's it, isn't it?" she interrupted. "Ye are afraid that she will leave ye, so ye are doing the leaving first."

"That's ridiculous. I just don't see the point of prolonging the obvious."

"Ye have made up yer mind then?"

"Aye. It is set." The words fell easily from his mouth, but in his heart, he knew it would never be over. He would always care for Aislinn. His heart was hers, and wherever she went, she would be taking it with her.

Aislinn moved around her room, familiarizing herself with what would be hers for the next few weeks. She immediately found herself in front of a wood-carved desk. She smiled knowing that Miriam had made sure it was well stocked with writing material. She had remembered her passion.

The wood fire was already burning and there were warm fur blankets on the bed. She felt comfortable and even felt like she had renewed energy, something she had not had for quite a while. It was rather strange, but it was like a cloud had been lifted and even her thoughts were not so muddled.

Her stomach growled and she smiled. She was actually hungry.

Dougray walked into the room wearing one of his grim faces that immediately left her with an inexplicable feeling of emptiness. How she wished she could change the way he looked at her blaming her for all the pain they had endured, but she wasn't the only one at fault.

They had never truly discussed why she had gone to Neala for the herbs; therefore he didn't know the reasons why she had never taken them. She was well aware that he felt she had betrayed him. But she hadn't, not really, but he had refused to hear her out. All he knew was that she had brought into their home what could have prevented her from conceiving and he resented her for it. Their trust had been broken as surely as if she had taken the liquid.

If their baby had lived, he might have softened his heart and possibly even learned to forgive her. Now she wasn't so sure. He was a proud man with a sense of honesty. His obligation forced him to care for her, but it would not force him to be her husband in every sense of the word.

Dougray paused for a moment before approaching her, his eyes meeting hers. He noticed that her coloring was a bright, healthy shade making the dark circles around her eyes almost nonexistent. "Ye look like ye feel better." It was an honest statement of surprise.

"I do. I even have some of my energy back. Don't know if I could wield a sword, but I could maybe give it a try."

Dougray's eyebrows rose a fraction of an inch. She even sounded more like her old self. "Perhaps later." He gave her a half smile before he removed his mantle and went over to the fire. "I have come to tell ye about the sleeping arrangements." He glanced at her again. "My sister has informed me there are no more rooms to be had. She assumed we…." He hesitated to finish, but Aislinn was quick to realize what he was trying to say to her.

"It would only seem logical that we would share a room. I don't…."

"I will sleep on the chair," he hastened to finish. It was one thing to know that he wasn't wanted but quite another to hear it voiced.

Aislinn miserably looked away to hide her hurt feelings, a heaviness centering in her chest. She had hoped that maybe he might want to stay with her. She wished to feel his arms around her once again. She longed to hear his voice tell her that everything would be all right.

Dougray watched her clasp her slender hands together and stare at them as though she could not bear the thought of him in the same room. He walked over to her giving her a way out of an awkward situation. "If my staying in here distresses ye, I will make do with the men." She turned to him then.

"No." She touched his arm and they both felt the intimate shock of the touch. "I mean I don't mind you staying here. Actually I would…."

"What Aislinn?"

"I would feel safe." Their eyes met again.

"Safe?" His brows furrowed. "Ye don't feel safe?"

"I am not sure of anything anymore. I just would feel better if you were here."

"Then I'll stay." He didn't want her to feel frightened, and God forgive him, if this was the only way he could be near her, he would take it. He heard a grumbling sound and he quirked a brow at her. "What was that?"

"My stomach rebelling." She placed her hand on her midsection. "I'm hungry," she defended herself.

He actually chuckled. "We better find ye something then. Come. I know just where we can find a snack before we dine tonight."

He was good to his word. They convinced the cook to let them take a few morsels with them. Of course, Dougray had to bribe the man. He handed Aislinn a big chunk of cheese and he had a bottle of wine in his hand. They walked to the far side of the kitchen wall and sat down against it.

"This is good," she managed to tell him between mouthfuls.

He handed her the wine bottle and she actually giggled. "What's so funny?" he asked not sure what had put her in such a good mood.

"I feel like a teenager sneaking out to have a drink with her boyfriend." She gladly took a long swallow.

He was still studying her when she handed him back the bottle. Her behavior yet again baffled him. If he didn't know better, back at Dunhaven he would have thought that she had been drugged.

He regarded her for a moment as something flickered in the back of his mind. According to Teige and Moira, Aislinn became ill later on in her pregnancy, almost nearing her fourth month and steadily became worse until she finally miscarried. Under Neala's care, she began to heal only to have another relapse, once the old woman returned to her home in the glen.

Warning spasms alarmed every fiber of his being as the pieces seemed to fall into place, and he didn't like what he was seeing. He knew Aislinn mourned the loss of their child, but there had been more to it and from the start it had plagued him. She had been lethargic and weak. There should have been no reason for her to have the sickness that is associated with pregnancy when she was no longer pregnant.

Hadn't Neala warned him to make sure that he brought Aislinn her meals, that no other hand should touch them? And he had followed those instructions, until she was able to start eating solid foods again. Soon after, she seemed to have days that her stomach bothered her, so much so that she was unable to bring herself out of bed.

Now that he was on this track, he thought back. Fiona's death came to mind. Her condition had been similar to Aislinn's. She complained of a stomach ailment and eventually could not keep her food down. She had not been ill before they had locked her in the tower, but yet her health diminished rapidly. Within a month, she was dead.

Fiona's elimination could be explained, if she had been able to point a finger at the ones involved with Aislinn's kidnapping. It would only seem logical that someone would want to have her silenced.

His misgivings increased. If Teige had not hastened him to Dunhaven when he had, Aislinn could have died too. *Dar Dia*! It had been a miracle that she hadn't perished with their child. "Poison," he muttered under his breath. Why had he not thought of that sooner?

"What did you say?"

"Aislinn, how do ye feel?"

"It's amazing, but I actually feel a hundred percent better. I don't feel sluggish. My stomach doesn't feel nauseated. I guess that I should thank you for forcing me to leave my room." She became solemn then, the laughter falling from her face. Dougray placed a hand on hers as he saw her start to withdraw. He sighed regrettably for he didn't know how to bring her past the guilt that she carried.

"Ye have to stop blaming yerself for what happened, Aislinn."

"I can't help it. I keep thinking, if only I had stayed calm or if I had eaten better than I had. Cahir was always after me to eat something. I tried, honestly I did, but I couldn't keep half of the food down."

"Cahir brought ye yer meals?"

"Sometimes. He's an odd little man. He didn't seem to like me, but once he knew I was pregnant, he was there giving me all kinds of advice. He was like a hovering shadow."

Dougray's right hand clenched. If he found out that the man had poisoned Aislinn, he would tear him apart limb from limb.

"I keep hearing my mother's voice." Aislinn was lost in thought. "It was a warning she gave me when I was young and it has always stayed with me. Now I finally realize what she meant by it."

"What's that?" he asked.

"You should be careful for what you wish for. You're liable to have it granted." There was such anguish in her voice that his heart went out to her. "I had prayed that I would not become pregnant…I had wished…I didn't mean it." She shook her head. "I didn't. I was scared. I was…." The tears came then and she choked back a sob. He wanted desperately to put his arms around her, but he was afraid she would push him away.

"Aislinn, ye did not cause this to happen. Ye are not at fault. Please do not blame yerself for something ye had no control over."

"You blame me," she accused him.

"Nay, I do not." This time he didn't care; he wrapped his arms around her shoulder, and for a moment, she actually leaned against him, clutching his hand. Her lips touched his palm, her tears of grief burning his skin.

"Dougray…." Without another word, she was on her feet before he could stop her.

"Aislinn, wait." But it was no use; she was fleeing as fast as her feet could carry her. Every time they were together, he seemed to cause her more pain.

He rose from the ground with a forlorn sigh. It was time he found Murrough and shared with him his suspicions of Cahir Dunphy.

Dougray found him easily enough for he was with the other men, laughing at some age-old story that was being told. When Murrough saw him enter, he immediately walked over to him. "Is something the matter, ye look distressed?"

"I wish to discuss what I need to tell ye in a more private setting." Murrough nodded and followed him away from the fire.

Dougray didn't waste any time revealing what he suspected about Cahir, not leaving out any of his suspicions concerning Fiona. He waited to hear what Murrough's thoughts were on the situation.

"Cahir has disliked Lady Aislinn from the moment she arrived at Dunhaven, and when ye were ill yerself, he had her thrown in the dungeon. He would know which herbs could poison a person slowly, to make it look like they were suffering from an ailment. I agree. He would be the most likely choice for such a deed."

"He is a weak man who only can bully his way through life. If he poisoned Fiona and tried to succeed with Aislinn, he had someone else who was helping him along."

"Another piece of the puzzle and still no closer to finding out who is behind our problems. I know I always go back to this, but could the Butlers have gotten to Cahir somehow?"

"Nay, I have decided he is not the hand that is lashing out in this cowardly manner. The Butler is angry and wishes to see me pay for what he feels is an injustice to his daughter. He is not one to hide in the shadows waiting to strike. Nay, someone has formulated a very clever plan making us think the Butler is behind all the misfortunes. I believe this someone is also wanting to make the Butler think the same of us."

"What? In hopes that we will eventually kill one another?"

"Perhaps. Murrough, have you ever thought that Ella's death might not have been an accident either? I was supposed to ride that mount, not Ella. If a threat of my life was in evident even then, we have the proof we seek that the Butlers were not the ones responsible. Fingham would have never chanced his daughter being in harm's way." He clenched his fists. "And now there is Fiona's death and the murder of my unborn child. *Dar Dia*, Murrough, they nearly succeeded in ending Aislinn's life as well. Whoever is responsible will surely pay for the wrong they have caused."

"Do ye wish me to ride back to Dunhaven and confront Cahir? I am sure I can persuade the man to tell us who is behind all this."

"Nay, Murrough. There is more at work here than a few people. If we are to get to the bottom of this, I believe we should have Cahir followed and do our best to expose all that are involved. We will send Hamish, for Cahir will not noticed the youth that he has thought of as a cripple."

"Ye think the boy will be able to come through? This is a grave business ye send him to do."

"He is capable. Send him at once."

"I will see to it, milord."

"And Murrough."

"Aye?"

"Make sure not to mention this to anyone."

Aislinn had sought the safety of her room, closing the door securely behind her. She was a fool to have panicked, for all she had wanted was to have him hold her. She was well aware she was still punishing herself for disappointing him, failing him. Her marriage was becoming another one of her relationships that was doomed. Only this time, she didn't want it to happen.

The fire was still going and she moved closer to warm the chill from her bones. There was a knock on the door, and for a moment, she allowed her hopes to soar. Maybe Dougray had come after her. "Come in." She had to hold back the hot tears of disappointment.

"Milady, I've come to help ye dress." Moira closed the door behind her. "Yer uncle will be here soon."

"My uncle?"

"Didn't ye know milord asked him to join us?"

"No, I didn't." She wasn't ready to face her uncle. He would ask questions, want to know how she was doing and if the marriage was faring well. Maybe she could hide away in this room and hope he would go away.

She thought all this, knowing she would never be that cowardly. Maybe she could manage to put on a façade of happiness, making him believe that everything was all right.

She turned to Moira with a weak smile. "We must hurry then. I want to look my best."

"That's the spirit. Come and see, A.J., what I have laid out for ye. 'Tis a beautiful blue velvet gown with ribbon to match. I will run the same ribbon through yer hair. It has grown so long, A.J., and it is beautifully thick." Moira continued to talk, but Aislinn was only half listening to what she was saying.

The men were already seated when she came to the main hall to dine. Her uncle and Dougray both rose at the same time to greet her. She walked bravely toward them, knowing Aengus would be scrutinizing her appearance. She was well aware she did not look the same as the last time he saw her, but there was nothing she could do about it in this short notice. Thanks to Rhiannon, the woman had seen to the alterations of the gown she now wore. It fit to her slim figure without exaggerating her gauntness. Moira had brushed her dark hair until it shone bright in the candlelight, weaving the dark ribbons into her hair and draping it behind her in a twist. She even applied some color to her cheeks making her skin look radiantly smooth and clear. Her dark eyes stood out, large and illuminating with unspoken emotion. She was rather intriguingly stunning, nothing at all like how she was imagining herself to look.

She had reached her uncle and he took hold of her hand. "My dear, ye are looking well. Dougray told me ye had suffered physically and I had feared the worst." He bestowed a kiss upon her cheek.

"Thank you, Uncle." He offered her a seat beside him at the high table.

Dougray's mouth almost dropped to the floor when he first laid eyes on her. She was simply lovely. So much so, he wanted to sweep her off her feet and take her back upstairs, and kiss her until she realized she belonged with him. He had half the mind to do it, until he reminded himself that there was the matter of her safety to consider. If someone were trying to poison her, then they would not stop there just because it failed the first time. Every moment that she was with him, she was in danger. He had to protect her and that resolve was to send her away, even if it meant the possibility of losing her. He would speak to Hennessy at the first opportunity.

Dinner went well and Aislinn ate more than she had intended to, but she couldn't help it. With her appetite coming back in full force, everything smelled and tasted absolutely wonderful.

Anxious for the meal to be over, Miriam was fidgety in her seat. Finally Dougray leaned near her to whisper in her ear. "Is something the matter, dear sister? Ye act like ye are sitting on prickly thorns."

"I am not feeling well." She didn't quite meet his gaze, immediately giving Dougray the impression that she was not telling him the truth.

"Not feeling well?" Aengus had heard her and leaned forward to view his hostess.

"I fear so." She did manage to meet Aengus' gaze. "I have a headache. Would ye mind terribly if I should retire?"

"Nay, not at all, my dear. Ye should rest. By morning, ye will feel better."

"Thank ye." She rose from the table.

"I will check on ye later," Dougray offered and she nearly jumped down his throat.

"Nay!" After the outburst and the way that everyone was looking at her, she had to calm herself with a deep breath before she dared to speak again. "Nay, brother, I wish to retire, and if by some chance I am able to fall asleep, I do not want to be disturbed. Ye understand?"

"As ye wish, Miriam. I will see ye in the morning then."

She nodded with relief. "Good night," she bid to everyone before she hurried out of the banquet hall.

Dougray made eye contact with Murrough and with a nod of his head the man followed her.

Later into the night Dougray also made his excuses, leaving Aengus the time to pull Aislinn aside for a private conversation. "Ye were most silent this evening, dear. Ye are not suffering from a headache also?"

She smiled. "No, Uncle, I am fine. Really."

"And yer marriage? Will ye be asking a priest to bless this union?"

She didn't know what to tell him, but her hesitation gave him cause to question her further. "He has not mistreated ye?"

"No, he has been generous."

"Why do I sense there is more to that statement?"

"Frankly, I am not sure that Dougray wishes the marriage to continue."

"If he wishes to end it, then ye will have a home with me. Do not fear." He placed the tip of his fingers on her chin and gently raised her head, so that she was forced to look at him. "Do not fear," he repeated.

She nodded. "I wish to retire. I am so very tired."

"Ye do that, my dear."

Murrough met Dougray by the stables with his news. "So where does my sister go?"

"She is in her room, but I believe she is meeting with someone."

"Who and why?"

"I did not see his face but I believe the meeting is of a…ye know…physical nature."

Dougray's eyebrows shot up. "Miriam? Carrying on with a dalliance?"

"Aye, milord. Do ye wish for me to find out the identity?"

He smiled and shook his head. "Nay, Murrough. My sister should be allowed to have some happiness. Let her be."

"As ye wish."

"Aye, goodnight, Murrough." He was still thinking about his sister when he entered the castle practically running into Aengus, who obviously had been waiting for him. The man did not look pleased, and in seconds, he knew the reason.

"Why does Aislinn have the opinion ye will be casting her aside?"

Dougray was momentarily taken aback. "She has said this to ye?"

"She has hinted as much?"

"And does she wish it?"

"What game do we play, Fitzpatrick? I ask a question and ye answer with one of yer own."

"I am sorry. I was hoping to have insight to what Aislinn has been thinking. She has not been the same since she lost the baby, and I cannot read what goes on in her head. I have tried to talk to her but…nothing is ever said. I am at a loss."

"Then ye do not want the marriage to end come Beltane?"

"Nay. *Dar Dia*! I have no wish for it to end. I care for her only she does not seem to hold me in the same light."

"What have ye been doing? Ye have had more than ample time to make your intentions known, and yet ye both seem as unsure of each other as the day ye wedded."

"I know it must look…."

"Ye have no idea."

"It is worse, I fear." Dougray sighed.

"How so?"

"Even though I do not wish to be parted from Aislinn, I must ask ye to let her go with ye."

"I don't understand. Ye don't want the marriage to end and yet ye want her to take up residence in my home. What is this ye ask of me, Fitzpatrick?"

"Let me explain."

"I am listening." He folded his arms against his chest.

"I fear for Aislinn's life." Hennessy lost his stance for this was not what he had expected Dougray to say. "For some time now I have had threats made upon my person. I had thought that it was the Butlers, but now I do not think the clan responsible. There is someone else who wishes to harm me. It seems the threat has been extended to anyone who is close to me. There have been attempts on Aislinn's life, outside the keep. But now I fear someone on the inside has tried to kill her…by poison. She was not well and I had originally thought it was from her confinement, then the miscarriage, but now I believe it was induced."

"Ye think someone was deliberately trying to poison her?"

"Aye, but I have no proof other than my own suspicions. Before we came to my sister's, Aislinn was a mere fragment of herself. She was lethargic to the point of exhaustion. She was unable to keep food down other than a broth that I had personally brought to her. In just a matter of few days, she has regained her appetite and her pallor has improved tenfold. I even see glimpses of her old stubborn self. I do not want anything to happen to her. Until I find out the person or persons behind this deliberate act, I cannot have her back at Dunhaven."

"I agree, but I insist that ye explain this to her. She is so unsure of ye."

"I cannot without frightening her. She needs to regain her strength. I also think that she would benefit from some time away from me. She seems to want this space and I will grant it to her."

"I am not sure I agree with ye, but I will abide by it."

"Thank ye. I am most grateful."

Dougray bid Aengus goodnight and headed toward the nursery to check on Declan. It was amazing how the little boy had worked his way into his heart. He partly owed that to Aislinn for she had made him actually find the time to know him. At first, he had only done so to please her, but soon he found that he really cared for the child, almost like…his own. He finished the thought. It was true. Declan MacKenna was like a son to him. He arrived at the door and let himself in. The lad was still awake to the nurse's displeasure.

"I will tend him." He nodded to the nurse. She bowed quickly and left the room. Dougray walked over to the bed and sat down beside the wide-eyed child. "Now, Declan, ye shouldn't distress the nurse so. It is late and ye should be fast asleep by now."

"Ye aren't asleep," he pointed out.

"That is true but I am much older than ye are and a lad like ye needs his rest." He helped lower the boy under the covers. "Ye want to grow up tall and strong, do ye not?"

"Aye."

"Well if ye are to do so then ye need to listen to the nurse. She knows best."

"If ye say so, milord, but I have a feeling that she doesn't know much at all. It's just my opinion, ye know."

Dougray smiled. "Well ye be keeping that opinion to yerself now."

"I will do as ye say."

"That's a good lad. Now I'll say good night to ye."

"Milord?"

"Aye?"

"Did we bring A.J. here to make her happy again?" Declan rubbed his tired eyes.

"I don't know what will make her happy again, Declan." He brushed the blond strands of hair that had fallen over his forehead and over one baby blue eye.

"Maybe if ye gave her another baby, she would be happy. Ye could do that, couldn't ye?"

What could he say to a young boy that was only four, and didn't quite grasp the whole situation? "She needs rest for now."

"She cries for another baby. Ye should think about it, aye?"

He patted his arm. "That I will, young Declan."

"Ye know I could be her little boy until ye give her one of her own…if ye don't mind."

He realized the child yearned for a mother, as much as Aislinn desired a baby to hold in her arms. "I think that Aislinn would like that very much."

Dougray headed back to his chambers to find that Aislinn was already in bed curled up on her side. Once Moira saw him enter, she walked over to him. "Will ye be needing me close by, milord?"

"Nay, I will see to Lady Aislinn if she awakens. Ye get some rest, Moira."

She curtsied and was ready to leave.

"Moira?" She turned to look at him. "Ye do love Teige, don't ye? Because if ye do not wish to marry him, ye do not have to." He would never be party to a forced marriage, when his had failed so miserably. It was high time someone changed the rules.

She thought it odd that he would ask her this, but still she answered him with all honesty. "Milord, I want to be with Teige. He is a good man and I do love him. Ye will still give permission for us to be joined?"

"I have already given it. I just wanted to make sure ye wanted it as well."

"Aye, milord, I do." She paused for a moment then added, "It was kind of ye to ask." Then she turned and left the room.

Dougray sat down on the edge of the bed careful not to disturb Aislinn's sleep. He rested his head on the palm of his hands, rubbing his tired eyes. Then he again turned his attention to his sleeping wife. "Who would ever believe, *Scathach*, that things between us would turn out so badly? I am sorry for it was never my intent."

Dougray had already been up and about for nearly two hours before he ran into his sister. She didn't seem at all rested, and he couldn't help but tease her about her appearance since he could well guess the reason. "Ye still do not look well, Miriam. If I didn't know better I would have thought that ye had a late night visitor that kept ye up all night." The look she gave him was classic. Her eyes widened, her mouth dropped opened and her hand flew to her neck as though her throat was constricting. "Is something the matter?" How he ever managed to keep a straight face, he'll never know.

"Nay. It is that ye forever shock me, Dougray. However could ye think that yer own flesh and blood would…."

"Calm down. I did not mean to offend ye so. I rather hoped that it were true. Ye could stand to have a nice young man take ye and use ye properly."

"Ye are the devil, aren't ye?" She smiled wondering if her brother would think the same if he knew it was Tremain Butler whom she had entertained.

"So I have been told." He leaned over and gave his sister a quick kiss on the cheek. He looked up and saw that Aislinn had now entered the Great Hall. Their eyes met and he paused. Miriam turned to see who had captured her brother's attention.

"Ye should go to her, Dougray."

He wanted to, but he couldn't bring himself to go forward. "I have to tend to the horses."

"We have stable boys for that."

"I want to see to my horse personally." He nearly ran from her side forcing her to explain to Aislinn his quick departure.

"Good day, my dear." She saw the hurt expression that Aislinn wore before she could conceal it.

"Good morning."

"He will be back soon."

"It doesn't matter."

"Why do ye say this?"

"He is sending me away, Miriam. He is sending me back to my uncle's house. This marriage is over and now it is only a matter of formalities to make it official."

"Don't say this. Surely it is not so."

"Oh, but it is. My uncle informed me just before I came in here that I will not be returning to Dunhaven."

"And that's it? Ye are not going to fight? Ye have the right, ye know. Dunhaven is a much yer home as it is Dougray's."

"I see no point. If Dougray wishes to have the marriage null and void, then I'll let him have his wish. It was the way it was set up to be. Marriage for a year and a day and either party could call it quits."

"It is yer say also, is it not? If ye do not want it to end, ye must speak."

A part of her wanted to but she could see no reason why she should prolong the marriage when Dougray saw her as a disappointment. "No, I will not say a word."

"I can't believe that ye will give up so easily and here ye were named the *Scathach*."

"I was never this mythical goddess everyone seems to think me."

"And obviously, ye have not earned the title."

"What is that supposed to mean?" Aislinn's eyes flashed with anger.

She continued her badgering hoping to get her to defend herself. "Well as I see it, ye are nothing more than a whimpering female. Not at all worthy to have yer name whispered with hers. Ye are acting like a dog with its tail between its legs, hiding in a dark corner hoping that no one sees ye."

"How dare you. You wish to ridicule me just because I have finally come to terms with what I must do. We should have never been married, Miriam. I don't even belong here."

"Fate put ye both together. Ye cannot be telling me that ye do not see it."

"I don't believe in fate." She tried to turn away but Miriam would not let her.

"Nay, ye will hear me out. Ye are both miserable, but ye can end it. Go to him, Aislinn. He does not want to cast ye from his side. I know this." She gripped her arm and pleaded with her, hoping the woman would recognize the truth of the matter.

"It's over, Miriam." She backed away from her. "It's over."

Miriam knew where her brother would be and headed straight over to the stables. She was just about to walk in and give him a piece of her mind when she happened to overhear Murrough talking about seeing someone leave the castle. Every fiber in her being tensed and she leaned her back against the wall.

"Ye are sure, Murrough? Ye could not be mistaken?"

"It was Tremain Butler. He was stealing away like a thief in the night."

"He was alone?"

"Most strange, I know, but I did not see another with him. I would have captured him had it not been that I was on foot at the time. The man had his mount hidden and was upon its back before I could reach him."

"I don't like this. He was at the castle…." He heard a noise outside and he cautioned Murrough with a quick nod of his head toward the door. He carefully unsheathed his weapon and moved forward. He was out the stable door in an instant, the point of his sword at his sister's throat. "What in the world are ye doing sneaking about?" He glowered at her before he lowered the weapon.

"I was not sneaking around. These are my grounds, Dougray Fitzpatrick. I am allowed to go where I please."

Dougray studied his sister for a moment taking in her nervous behavior. "What is this about, Miriam? Ye are up to something."

"I am only here to speak with ye." She looked over Dougray's shoulder to see Murrough also was staring at her. She couldn't let them find out Tremain was here to see her. She had known it had been too dangerous, but she couldn't resist the man coming to her. "I need to speak to ye about Aislinn."

Dougray looked at Murrough. "A moment alone." Murrough nodded and waited for Dougray at a distance to allow the two privacy. "Well?"

"Why are ye sending her back to the Hennessy's stronghold?"

"It is for her safety."

"Safety? From what?"

"It does not concern ye. Ye only need to know it is for Aislinn's best interest."

"Not because ye tire of her?"

"*Dar Dia*! Tire of her, nay, that is far from the truth of it."

"Why have ye not told her this? She thinks ye do not wish her to be at Dunhaven."

"It has to be this way for now. And ye, dear sister, will keep quiet. Not a word, Miriam, ye must promise me."

"I do not think that ye are correct in this matter. Ye may even live to regret the decision."

"Then that is how it will have to be. I cannot put her in danger. I have already done enough. I refuse to bury another wife. Now enough of this matter, I must speak to ye about security. We have seen one of Butler's men lurking around the castle...." When Miriam's face turned beet red, it all became crystal clear to him. "*Dar Dia*! He was here to see ye. Ye were lying in bed with the enemy."

"It's Tremain, Dougray. He is not the enemy. I love him and he loves me."

"Are ye mad, lass? We are at war with the Butlers. He could murder ye in yer own bed."

"Ye are the one who is at war with them, I am not, and Tremain would never harm me. Never! I would stake my life on it."

"And ye may very well be doing just that. What have ye been telling him?"

"Telling him?" She laughed without humor. "Ye may find this amusing, but we do not spend our precious moments together discussing ye."

"Ye are not to see him again, Miriam. I am warning ye. If I see the man here, I will personally run him through."

"Ye will do no such thing. Ye forget ye are a guest here at my home and I may entertain whomever I so please."

"Ye are but a woman."

"Stop it right there. I will not have ye throw my gender into this. Ye are not guardian over me. I run this household and I will not have ye dictate to me what I can and cannot do. Now if ye have a problem with whom I associate with, then ye may find lodging elsewhere. Really, Dougray, I would have expected more from ye. Tremain is obviously more of a man than ye are. He was good enough to give me his word that he would not start a problem while ye were visiting."

He laughed. He couldn't help it. "His word and ye believed him?"

She hit at him then, pounding her fist on his chest. "I believe him. Don't ye proceed to tell me he is not speaking the truth."

He took hold of her arms to stop her assault "Just look at ye, defending a no good Butler."

"Ye were married to a Butler or did ye conveniently forget that Ella was from the very clan ye denounce?" That stopped him and he released her. "See, ye know I am right. Tremain and I were in love long before all this fighting took place, and before I was sold and wedded to the corpse of a man who had been my husband. I was only sixteen, Dougray, sixteen and full of life and dreams. Ye might as well have put me in a coffin and nailed it shut that day I took my vows. Can ye blame me for wanting more? Can ye blame me for loving the man who was only two years my senior? He was beautiful and strong. He made my heart weep with joy to be near him. I love him, Dougray." She was sobbing now. It was not hard for him to recall the last time he had seen tears fall from his sister's eyes. It was the day she was made to marry her husband. He hadn't agreed then, but he had only been a youth himself and was being sent to England for fostering. There was nothing he could have done, but now he could right the wrong that was put upon them.

"Do not cry." He pulled her to him. "Ye have right to yer happiness."

She looked up to make sure she had heard him correctly. "Ye will not harm him?"

"If he stays true to his word, I will not raise my sword to him."

"Thank ye, Dougray." She hugged him.

Chapter Seventy

Aislinn dressed for dinner and her uncle was there, waiting for her when she descended the last step. "Ye look well, my dear." He leaned forward and placed a small kiss on her forehead.

She tried to smile but she wasn't doing a very good job. "Thank you."

"All will work out in the end." He looped his arm through hers and patted it gently. How much her uncle reminded her of her father, sending a wave of nostalgia to overwhelm her. She wished her parents were here. She missed them so very much. She even missed Connor trying to convince her to do something outrageously short of suicidal.

"What are ye thinking about?" Aengus interrupted her thoughts

"My family."

"Aah."

"You remind me so much of my father. Not so much how you look, but your mannerisms."

"I am aware that I am no substitute for yer father, but I am here for ye."

"I do appreciate your kindness." Her vision caught sight of her husband coming toward them. How devilishly handsome he looked with his cobalt-colored tunic over a laced, linen shirt and mahogany breeks that fit snugly to his thighs. Good looking and honorable, all in one fine package. It was no wonder she lost her heart to him. When he finally cast her aside, there would be a void there that would never be filled again.

The ill-starred look she had given him before she looked away caused a heaviness to center in his chest. "Are we ready to go?"

"We are," Hennessy answered though he would have liked to shake the two of them, giving them a good tongue lashing on top of it all. They were miserable from their own doing. Couldn't they see what they had? He shook his head. *Fools,* he thought. *Fools who just wasted love.*

On the way to Sir Raymond Halstead's residence, her uncle purposely rode with Aislinn in the carriage to see if he could talk some sense into her. Dougray had one of his men take care of his mount for him so that he could return to his home, instead of riding back to Miriam's. Aislinn had thought that Dougray would be joining them in the carriage, but he insisted in riding alongside with his men.

Everyone from anywhere was there including many of the Chieftains of great importance. Dougray was at her side. When an older gentleman walked up to them, he graciously made the introductions. "Sir Richard Halstead, may I present Lady Aislinn Fitzpatrick of Dunhaven."

Aislinn was taller by a few inches and he had to look up to meet her steady gaze. He seemed to be assessing her worth before he chose to address her. "I have heard much about you, and all impressive, I might add. It is no wonder that my grandson has chosen you to wed."

"Grandson?" Her gaze shot to Dougray.

The older gentleman chuckled. "I see he did not mention that I was his relation. Do not fret, young lady, I am most used to this treatment. Even now he wishes to pretend that he holds no Halstead blood." He turned to Dougray. "You are just as much a Halstead as you are a Fitzpatrick. You can't escape who you are, my boy."

"Ye are mistaken. I have no doubt of who I am. 'Tis others who seem to want to mold me into something I do not wish to be."

His grandfather sighed. "I would have thought that you would have been grateful for the lands you were granted."

"If I had known it was all a bribe, I would have never accepted Dunhaven."

"No? And what would you have done? Your father left you nothing to call your own. Do you entertain for a moment that you would be living in your precious Ireland with tenants to care for your land and livestock if it hadn't been for the graciousness of King Henry to see it so?"

"As I see it, he was giving back what was rightfully mine. Dunhaven was in near ruins. The land was not harvested. Families were starving and scared. Nay, he did not grant me Dunhaven out of the graciousness of his heart. He gave it to me in hopes that I would fail, that I would hate the soil that gave me birth, so I would once again return to England to be paraded around like a prized beast." Halstead frowned his annoyance, but still Dougray would not fall silent. "Don't look so surprised. Did ye think that I did not know I was merely an experiment? That everyone wondered if the Irish heathen actually could speak? I showed them, didn't I? Not only did I surpass all their expectations, I became a threat to them as well. Oh aye, I did understand it fully, ye know. Without me there, they could believe that only the horrible bad lived on the island not so far away. So when they slowly sucked it dry and left the people withering away, they would not have to worry their little consciences over it." He finished his speech a little breathless. He knew some of his passion had been because he was aware of what the future held, and he didn't like it. Because of Aislinn, he knew how Ireland would suffer, how they would all suffer. He was but one man and powerless to stop any of it from happening.

"You have become fervent with your convictions, more so than I remembered. If you will excuse me, I will take my leave. I have no wish to ruin this young lady's evening."

Aislinn had stood in silence, but now she would not stand for it. This was Dougray's grandfather for goodness' sake and there was no need to be rude. "Please do not leave so soon. Dougray has had a lot to deal with these past months. I for one would love that you stay with us awhile, so I may have a chance to know you better."

Dougray bit the inside of his cheeks trying not to lose his temper. He had no wish to dine with his grandfather when they had absolutely nothing in common. Unfortunately, now there would be no other way around it without causing a scene. He was going to be forced to endure.

As planned, Halstead slipped away from the festivities to meet with the hooded figure who was waiting for him within the folds of the darkness, like a shadow of doom. Halstead was aware of the hooded man's identity, but still he wished he could see his face. "You know what to do?" The hooded figure nodded. "Good. The young fool does not know what is best for him and we will have to see him set straight."

It was late by the time they had started on their trek back home. Dougray rode his mount some distance from the carriage, dwelling on his marriage that seemed doomed from the very start.

He understood the ordeal she had gone through, maybe not the physical aspect of it, but he did understand grief. He had lost a child too and because of his arrogance he hadn't bothered to listen to her fears. He had assumed that all his dreams and wants would be sufficient for her also.

He knew that she cared for him. Maybe she would eventually forgive him, but he had run out of time. He had to send her away. He couldn't take it if anything were to happen to her.

He sighed miserably still so lost in his own reverie that it took a split second before the thwack sound registered. Turning to the left of him, he witnessed one of his men fall to the ground with an arrow sticking out of his chest.

They were under attack. It happened so quickly that he barely drew his sword to defend himself. From the corner of his eye, he saw the carriage was taken hostage. "Aislinn!" he yelled as he fought for his life.

Aislinn was jolted against the side of the carriage. She braced herself the best that she could. Leaning out the window, she saw Dougray fall from his mount. A scream tore from her only to be silenced when she was thrown back inside. They were being attacked?

She gripped her handbag close to her for it held the only weapon that she had to protect herself. How she wished that she wasn't wearing the hindering dress. She pulled herself to the window again, so that she could better assess her situation. She could see there were two men on top that she didn't recognize and another riding a horse furiously alongside of the coach. She pulled back when she realized the culprit was trying to gain access. She quickly pulled out her dagger, gripping it in her hand. The man's fist plunged through the opening trying to undo the latch. Aislinn didn't hesitate. She thrust the blade into the man's arm. He let out a blood-curdling yell and lost his balance. He fell back and out, where he tumbled onto the ground.

She was now without a weapon and had no intentions of waiting until the vehicle came to a stop. She made the decision quickly before she had time to rationalize the stupidity of it. Unsteadily she made her way to the door and opened it, making the leap. She rolled with what seemed an eternity finally coming to a complete stop with her kidnappers still fleeing without the knowledge of her escape.

She opened her eyes without moving for every part of her body ached from the impact of her fall. Gingerly she moved her limbs to make sure nothing was broken. When she was sure that she was still in one piece, she came to her feet and in a crouched position. For the moment, she looked to be alone and she had no intentions of waiting for the wrong men to find her. She got up and ran. She didn't know where she was going, until she saw the steeple of St. Michan's Church.

St. Michan's wasn't exactly where she wanted to be, considering the last time she had been there she had viewed mummies and had a ghost whisper in her ear. "Beats being murdered," she murmured under her breath and ran to where she hoped would be sanctuary. At first she wasn't sure it was the church; it looked different, smaller. Then she remembered that the church would be rebuilt sometime in the 1600s to accommodate the larger congregation. She pounded on the door and couldn't believe it when Father Fiach had answered. Why hadn't she known he was from here? She might have thought more on the matter, but right now she was more concerned that she remain hidden.

"Lady Aislinn?" Fiach had been just as surprised to see her. His eyes widened as he took in her rumpled appearance. Her velvet gown was torn and mud smeared. Her hair was in disarray, her dark eyes wide, her very stance betrayed her fear. He glanced over the woman's shoulder to see who was chasing her.

"I don't think I was followed," she managed to croak.

He wasn't taking any chances and quickly pulled her inside and barred the doors. "What has happened?"

"We were attacked." She gulped in air trying to keep her wits about her.

He led her to one of the pews and made her sit down.

"I don't know what happened to the others, but it didn't look good. I was in the carriage when it was hijacked."

"Hijacked?" Fiach shook his head not understanding.

She went on to explain, "Whoever attacked us took control of my carriage."

"How did ye escape?"

"I jumped of course."

Fiach's mouth dropped open for he hadn't expected her to tell him that she leapt from the moving vehicle. She could have been killed, but again the alternative most likely would not have been much better. There was no telling what the kidnappers had intended to do with her.

She grabbed a hold of his hand drawing his attention. "Dougray," she wailed, fear stark and vivid glittering in her eyes. "I saw him fall."

Fiach was not quick enough to hide his worried expression, but he managed to force his words to sound comforting. "It will be all right. Dougray is very capable and will not succumb so easily."

"Oh, Father Fiach, if anything happens to him I don't know what I'll do. There are so many terrible things I have said to him." She bit her lower lip trying not to cry, but everything seemed to be closing in on her, gnawing away her confidence.

Fiach pulled her close, patting her back. "We all say things sometimes that we regret later. I am sure Dougray knows ye didn't mean them." He felt Aislinn shake her head.

"No, he doesn't," she sobbed against him. "He doesn't know."

"Then we will pray that Dougray will arrive without delay so ye may lay yer heart bare to him." He put his hands on her shoulders and gently moved her away so that he could see her eyes. He lifted a hand to wipe the tears away. "Ye stay brave, milady. Dougray will be marching through those doors soon."

"He wouldn't possibly come this way. It would be foolish of him to ride where the enemy may be waiting."

Fiach smiled. "Ye underestimate my cousin, milady. He will come looking for ye no matter what the dangers may be."

She tried desperately to believe him, but as much as she wished it were true, she also hoped that he wouldn't dare to take the risk.

"Now, let's find ye something to drink." Fiach helped her to her feet and led her to the back room. He couldn't help but admire how she escaped without harming herself. "Ye really jumped from the carriage?"

She nodded. "After I lost my dagger, I knew I had no other choice. I didn't know where I was going to be taken, and I had no wish to find out either."

"Should I even ask ye how ye lost the dagger?" His brows arched high on his forehead.

She hesitated before she shook her head again. "It may be best that you don't."

He handed the brave woman a goblet filled with wine. She was indeed a worthy match for Dougray. Whatever difficulties they were having, he hoped that they would soon rectify them. They obviously belonged together.

Aislinn was grateful for the drink for it was beginning to calm her frazzled nerves, but as it grew later and there was still no news, even Fiach could not hide his worry. He gave strict orders for her to stay put and not to let anyone in. He left her then to see if he could discern the situation.

The fighting was intense and Dougray and his men were outnumbered. He wasn't sure how long they could hold out. Then when the situation could not have gotten any worse, he noticed that another garrison had joined in. At first, he thought they were reinforcements for the enemy, but then he recognized it was Merrick and his band. The age-old leader nodded his head toward him as he raised his sword. With the help of the gypsy band, the fighting did not last much longer. When Dougray was able to, he made his way over to Merrick, his hand reaching for his in a firm grip. "We thank ye of yer assistance."

"We saw yer crest, milord, and I take offence that someone should try and slay a friend of mine."

"And I appreciate that ye feel that way." They walked a few paces before he asked the question he hoped Merrick would be able to answer. "Do ye recognize these men we fight?"

"They belong to no clan. They are men for hire and work for whomever can give them coins to fill their pocket."

"As I figured."

"How fairs yer lady?" Merrick asked. "On a better day, I would have wished for another campfire story of hers."

"At this moment, we are searching for her carriage."

"She was with ye then?"

"Aye."

Merrick turned to his men. "Lady Aislinn may have been taken. Spread out, men, and keep a wary eye." He looked to Dougray then. "We will find her."

Everyone regrouped after a thorough search of the area. "We came across this." Murrough showed Dougray the silver-tipped dagger.

"It's Aislinn's," he confirmed. He looked at Murrough for the answer, fear showing in his eyes that he already thought the worst.

"It was stuck deep in a man's forearm. I fear that it was not the cut that killed that man, but rather a hard fall. His neck was broken."

"And Aislinn?"

"We are sure that she jumped also, milord"

"From the carriage?" He couldn't believe it, and yet the old Aislinn would have had enough spunk to do just that. "Where?"

"Not far from here and we also found the vehicle abandoned and not a sign of a struggle. When we backed tracked, we came upon the footprints of a lone person, soft imprint of a woman."

"We must find her before they do." They were about to mount, when it occurred to Dougray that he had an idea to where Aislinn might have gone. "We ride to St. Michan's."

Murrough nodded understanding immediately. "We must go with caution then. There may be others still waiting for such an opportunity to overtake ye."

"More the reason we must hurry. I will not let them capture Aislinn. I will see them dead first." He didn't wait for Murrough to answer and put his mount into motion."

They ran into Fiach who was heading back to the church. Dougray was off his mount before the animal had time to stop. "Say that she is here."

The priest smiled. "Aye, she came straight away, cousin. Come, she will be glad to see that ye are all right." Dougray forgot about the trouble between them. His only goal was to hold her and know she was all right. Before he could reach her though, she was on her feet rushing to him. Her arms went around him in a fierce hug.

"Oh, Dougray, I thought the worst." She clung to him never wanting to let him go. He closed his eyes relishing in the fact that she had come to him. He tightened his hold on her not daring to speak.

"I don't mean to break up this happy reunion." Fiach had approached. "Would it not be to yer best interest to stay here for the night?"

Dougray was about to protest, but Murrough had quickly agreed. "It is too dangerous. We don't know who sent those men and we can't be sure there are not more. It would be best for both yer sakes to stay here until we can check out the situation."

"Aislinn will stay…"

"No," she interrupted. "I will not be left behind to worry. Either you stay with me, Dougray, or I am going with you."

He raised a brow. Was she actually making a demand? "I will stay for tonight," he agreed with a nod to Murrough. "After that if ye do not come up with what we need to know, then I will be doing some investigating on my own."

"Agreed."

"Make sure ye send someone to Miriam. I do not want her to be worried."

"Aye, consider it done."

Merrick had walked into the church and straight to Aislinn. He bowed to her.

"Merrick?" She was surprised to see the gypsy leader.

"I am most pleased that ye are well."

"Merrick was there to lend us a hand when we were sure we were to be bested," Dougray told her.

"Thank you, Merrick, we are in your debt." Aislinn's eyes glistened with unshed tears.

"It is I who is grateful to be at yer service." He raised her hand to his lips bestowing a sweet kiss. She noticed that he held a twinkling in his eye. "Besides I owe ye a campfire story."

"Yes, you do." She clasped his hands with both of hers.

After everyone cleared from the church, Fiach showed Aislinn and Dougray to the stairs that would lead them down below. It was slightly different than Aislinn had remembered it from the tour of her century. Not as many coffins for one and the fact that there were two entrances on either end of the tunnel. One was hidden in the church behind the scaffold and the other visible on the outside.

"I know this is not of the best conditions, but ye will be safe in here," Fiach assured them. He gave them food, blankets and candles for lighting.

He placed the torch in the sconce before he turned to speak again, "I will be back in the morning."

Now that Dougray and Aislinn were alone, some of the fear had ebbed away and the silence seemed to way heavy on both of them.

Dougray busied himself by spreading out the blankets as Aislinn watched him. She admired how his powerful well-muscled body moved with ease as he made the necessary arrangements for what would be their bed. His black hair gleamed in the light and how she wished she could reach out and touch its softness. Then it hit her hard. She could have lost him tonight.

He could have been gone from her life forever, but by the grace of God, she had been given a second chance. Her heart thundered against her chest as she wondered if she went to him, if he would refuse her.

Then he turned his gaze on her. Those beautiful blue eyes pierced the distance between them. There was no denying the invitation smoldering in their depths. "May we talk?" he began, but before he could say more, she covered the distance between them and was in his arms, kissing him like she feared that she would never see him again. Talk could come later, he thought as he returned the caresses, meeting her obvious needs that were so much like his own.

They moved to the blanket, both anxious to feel each other completely. "It has been so long." Dougray's husky voice reached her ears. He kissed her again and he felt her hands tug at his tunic. That was all the encouragement he needed. His hand moved beneath her dress to skim her hips. Heat rippled under her skin as she recognized the flush of sexual desire that she had been refusing to allow herself to feel. She was frantic to be with him, the need too strong to wait for all their clothing to be removed. She helped him hike her dress up above her hips. He tugged at her undergarment and removed his own. His body covered hers. As his hardness flooded through, a moan slipped from her lips. She clutched him pulling at him to be closer. He matched her urgency with his own lusty, unstated needs. With all that had happened to them, they needed to feel the flames of passion to know that they were still alive, that they indeed had cheated death this night. He moved against her, kissing her, fanning the sparks into a leaping flame until they both surrendered to the eager tremors of ecstasy.

He held her close, not able to speak. They both knew that they must confront what had put them at odds, but they were both so afraid to break the fragile bond.

He clutched her closer to him, fearing that she would put distance between them. He wanted her to accept what they had done without regrets, but he began to feel her restlessness. Finally she spoke and he closed his eyes willing her not to say they had made a mistake.

"I never opened the vial." Her voice seemed to echo against the walls with her anguish. "I never drank from it." He opened his eyes realizing she was not speaking of regret, but of baring her soul. He remained silent, gently stroking her hair to give her the encouragement she needed. "I couldn't do it, Dougray. I couldn't do it." Tears stung her eyes as she remembered how difficult the decision had been for her. "Even though I knew it was wrong to bring a child into this world, especially since I was aware of what will become of it, I still wanted your baby. I wanted to feel our child growing inside of me, and I desperately wanted to see him draw his first breath." The tears flowed freely now and she couldn't stop them. "We had a son, Dougray."

"I know." Listening to her sobs made his heart ache for there was nothing he could say that would relieve her mind. "I'm sorry, too. I am so sorry that I was not there for ye. It was my own selfish pride that kept me from ye. I should have told ye sooner, but I feared it was too late. It was I who had assumed too much, I think. I had forgotten that our marriage was to be temporary, that ye wanted to go back to yer time. I beg forgiveness for not listening to ye. It's just that I wanted…." He bowed his head and closed his eyes. She reached for him and he looked at her. He caressed her winsome face that he had come to know so well. He wanted to kiss her and erase all that had happened, but he knew there was nothing that could change the fact that they had both lost a child. His hand fell away. "Aislinn, I forgot myself. I forgot that you also had dreams and they were not for here. I could never truly have ye." He then pulled the item out of his pocket and placed it in her hand, gently squeezing it shut.

She looked at him for answers but he was silent, forcing her to see what he had given her. It was the vial. "I never…."

"I know ye didn't," he interrupted. "But I will not stop ye now, if this is yer wish." Everything he ever wanted was here now, and if she chose not to let a child be born between them, he would accept it willingly.

For a long moment, she stared at liquid gleaming in the light, twirling it in her hand. She could take it and with a clear conscience. It wouldn't be a lie anymore. Her gaze found his and she saw his eyes darken with emotion, so tender, so trusting. With what she held in her palm, it would erase what possibly their coupling could have created this very night. He was giving her the choice even though it went against all that he believed in. Again, she looked at the vial and she knew in her heart that the decision had already been made.

He watched her take the stopper out of the container. How he wanted to beg her not to drink from it, but he knew that he couldn't. It had to be her decision.

Aislinn breathed heavily with her resolve, and with a weak smile to him, she poured the contents out.

"Do ye know what ye have done?"

She nodded.

His eyes never left hers. There he sat so tall, strong and yet so vulnerable. "Don't make me leave our bed." His voice was a hoarse whisper.

"I don't want you to, and I will not let you send me away to my uncle's. I belong beside you, Dougray."

He pulled her to him then kissing her soundly before crushing her against his chest.

Her hands curled around the fabric of his shirt. There was more that she needed from him. He wanted to share her bed, that much he had made clear, but he had also made arrangements to send her away. He desired her in body but was there anything else to their relationship? She had to know. "Why did you come after me this night? You could have put yourself in further danger by coming here."

"Why?" He pushed her away so that he could look at her, for he could not believe she would even question his motives. "Is it not obvious to ye then?" Her eyes seemed to widen and she nervously shook her head that she truly did not know the answer. "Aislinn." The way he spoke her name seemed more like a caress causing her heart to flutter. He leaned forward then and brushed his warm lips to hers. When he spoke again his voice was a hoarse whisper. "I would never allow harm to come to ye, lass, not as long as I draw breath. I love ye. So much so, I would die for ye."

The moment the words left his mouth, she felt a warm glow flow through her. He did love her. But then his last words floated back to her. *I would die for ye.* A sickening knowing dread hit her full force. The words he had spoken were the very ones she had heard that day on the tour of St. Michan's. She knew with all clarity that it had been Dougray's remains that had lain there, the man that had died a horribly unjust death. Had she been the cause then? Or was the voice of the ghost long dead only a premonition of what was to come?

Her fear that he would perish before her eyes made her desperate to hold him. She kissed him fiercely, practically devouring his lips. He greeted her willingly, but he could sense something was greatly troubling her. He gently pushed her away again so he could see her face. The raw fear that he saw in her eyes could not be ignored.

"What is it, Aislinn?"

"I heard you say those words before…in here…in my time. There were coffins…."

"I don't understand?"

"When I took the tour with my family, I couldn't shake a foreboding that I felt as I descended the steps. I must have known something…sensed it. I don't know how, but you spoke to me. Those words, Dougray. I felt your spirit touch me." He looked overwhelmingly startled and how could he not when he had just been told that his death was sealed. She kissed him again. "I won't allow it. Knowing what could happen must surely mean that we can prevent it. It's the reason that I'm here. A life for a life."

"What are ye talking about?"

"Neala told me that we would have to give sacrifices." She squeezed his arm. "Our baby, Dougray, surely this means you will not be taken from me also." She again buried her face in his chest.

"The old woman claims what is written is so."

"Then why bother?" She pulled away and stood. She waved her hands wildly in the air. "Why bother to have the knowledge to tell the damned of their future if there is nothing that can be done?"

"To prepare," he said calmly. "If I must perish, rest assured I will not go without a fight."

"What?" She couldn't believe that he was taking this so calmly.

"No one wants to meet their maker without being prepared. Ye have warned me, Aislinn. I will make preparations."

She was petrified now for he was talking about his horrible demise like it was a planned outing. She ran her hand across her mouth in a nervous gesture. Didn't he understand? She had viewed his cold remains where he had been laid to rest. Rest? Rest was not what his spirit had wanted, or else he would not have reached out to her. She couldn't abide with what had been done to him.

Dougray watched the coloring in her lovely face turn to gray. He quickly made her sit down. She touched his warm rugged face that was so full of life and the tears began to fall once more. She was going to lose him. He would die and there was nothing she could do to prevent it.

"Tell me, Aislinn. Tell me what ye know."

"I don't have the details. No one knew…Oh God…Don't let them capture you, Dougray. Whatever you do, don't let them capture you."

"I will…."

She wouldn't let him finish for she had to make him see how dire this was. "You don't understand."

"Ye have forewarned me and I will be ever so cautious."

"I love you so much, Dougray. I couldn't stand it if I lost you."

He cupped her face in his hands, forcing her to look at him. "Ye love me?"

"Oh, for so long. Maybe from the beginning, but I was too afraid to admit it. I have had so many failed relationships that I thought I was incapable of having one. I believed there was something wrong with me, but then I realized that the reason I couldn't commit was because my heart belonged to someone already. My soul already was aware of you, and no one could take your place."

"*Dar Dia*! Why did ye not tell me so?"

"I thought you knew."

He shook his head. "Stubborn fools we have been."

"Not any more, Dougray. We've wasted too much time as it is." Her hands began to roam down the length of his body, wanting him to hold her again, needing him.

"What are ye doing, milady?" he said with a half smile hoping to deter her thoughts to something more pleasant. He longed to have her in his arms, but without fear driving her to passion.

"I need you." Parting her lips, she raised herself to meet his kiss. A low growl escaped him and he once again lowered her to the blankets. "You don't think Father Fiach will be back unexpectedly?" she worriedly asked.

"Nay." He already knew his cousin was giving them time alone when he had informed them that he would not return until morning. "We have all night and I plan on making every second count. That is as soon as I remove yer clothes. I want to feel every bit of ye."

"I don't know…."

"What...?" Then he saw her mouth tug at a smile.

"You will have to remove yours too, Dougray Fitzpatrick."

"Aye. It would only be fair." His mouth then moved over hers, devouring its sweet softness, their clothes melting away until nothing was between them but their burning desires. Poised above her, he looked down at her sweet face. Her eyes were closed, her long dark eyelashes lying curled upon her flush cheeks. "Look at me, Aislinn," he breathed wanting her to know the truth of what he was feeling, what she meant to him. Her eyelids fluttered open, where unquenchable warmth touched him in return. His heart bursting with love, he plunged deep inside of her, fastening onto their sense of being, binding them together as they reached a height of passion that they had never known before. At that moment of truth, Dougray didn't care if this was his last day on earth. Aislinn was his, through all time, *heart, body and soul.*

Chapter Seventy-One

Hamish waited patiently until Cahir had left the room where he kept all his herbs and potions that were fitting for apothecary. Finally the man had left, humming a tune obviously feeling he had not a care in the world. The room was covered from one end to other with shelves and shelves of glass, and horn containers with dry roots were hanging from the ceiling.

Hamish wasn't exactly sure what he was looking for, but he still entered. All of the bottles were labeled, for what good it did him. He could not read, but he recognized some of the items by sight because of their magical properties. There was Saracen root, lavender, periwinkle and saffron were among the few. Cahir had stones in other jars, amethyst, coral, sapphire, and bezoars stone, which was a stony mass found in a goat's stomach. He browsed further and found a jar that was hidden among the physician's books. Dust flew when he moved a few items aside. He pulled the bottle free to have a look at it. It wasn't labeled. It seemed odd that it wasn't since everything else had precise lettering indicating exactly what herb or stone it contained. He was about to open the bottle when he heard someone approaching from outside. He quickly placed the item back where he had found it, making sure the books were in place. Seconds before he would have been caught, he dove under the desk where crates and a large trunk were stored. He barely breathed as he waited for the person to leave. He knew it wasn't Cahir for he had caught a glimpse of the man's feet that were bound with leather straps. He was sure that the physician preferred to go without.

It seemed like a lifetime, but finally the man left. If he had been waiting for Cahir to arrive, he hadn't waited very long.

Hamish came out of his hiding place and brushed off the dirt from his clothes. He was about to make his exit, when something caught his eye. He walked over to where the hidden bottle had been placed. He couldn't see it and he moved aside the books and now he knew why. The bottle was gone.

Cahir was out gathering items to replenish his supplies and was in a fairly good mood. He had been visiting the widow Eileen and she seemed to be warming to his affections. She promised a meal for him tonight and he was looking forward to the evening.

A shadow fell across his arm. Startled he turned to see who had come up behind him. When he recognized the person, he let out a sigh of relief. "What are ye doing out here?" He was about to turn his attention back to his work, but a glint of something shiny had caught his eyes. Before he realized the person's intent, the cold steel had slashed across his neck. He fell back, looking up at his murderer's cold hard features. A few thoughts flitted across his mind, and he tried to voice them but only a gurgle of blood escaped his lips. Panicked, he grabbed frantically at his executioner only to have his hand kicked away. Then sounds, colors, visions from his past flashed by becoming one, until…nothing.

He stayed until Cahir's blood had moistened the damp earth and his chest had ceased to move. Then he left and never looked back.

Chapter Seventy-Two

The moment that Fiach entered the catacomb and had a looked at the couple who had spent the night there, he knew they had reconciled. Aislinn blushed in greeting quickly looking away pretending to reorganize their belongings. Though Dougray gave him a quirky smile and raised brow that warned him not to say a word, Fiach still couldn't resist a little teasing. "Did ye both sleep well, or were there circumstances that kept ye from that goal? Ye both look thoroughly exhausted." His smile broadened in approval.

Dougray grumbled under his breath. "Do ye come with news or are ye going to embarrass us to death?"

"Aah," he sighed heavily with a shrug. "Ye have lost yer sense of humor I see. So be it. Down to business then. Murrough has apprehended one of the men who took yer wife on her little joy ride. He is being held now for yer questioning."

"Finally maybe some answers." Dougray looked back to Aislinn. The passion that they shared last night still radiated to the very core of his body. He went over to her, and she threw her arms around him not caring that the priest was watching them. He lowered his head and kissed her long, hard, sensual, not hiding the fact that it was the raw act of possession.

When their lips parted, Aislinn felt like her life force had been taken away. She didn't want him to go. "Be careful, Dougray." Her hand gripped his forearm. "Return to me."

"I have every intention of doing so." He kissed the top of her head. Closing his eyes, he prayed that he would be able to keep his promise to her.

The moment that Dougray entered the room, the prisoner eyes grew wide with recognition and immediately tried to squirm away from Cormac's grip.

Dougray was not quite sure what to make of the display for he didn't know the man, or did he? There was something oddly familiar about him. His eyes narrowed to slits as he discerned every feature the man possessed. The second that the man realized that Dougray had figured it out he again tried to break free. "Ye!" Dougray covered the spaces to get a hold of him. "What part of me telling ye that if I ever laid eyes on ye again, *I'd kill ye*, did ye not understand?" The man kicked his feet, violently making his attempt to escape. It took both Murrough and Teige to contain him and that was with Cormac pointing his sword at his chest. Dougray was furious, but he remained calm for he had to have answers if he was going to be able to protect Aislinn from harm.

"I failed to extract a name from ye the last we met, but again Lady Aislinn had beaten ye to a bloody pulp. It is too bad that yer injuries ye sustained did not convince ye to stay away."

"Sheridan is me name and I swear to ye now that I didn't realize ye were the one we were set against. I would have never joined them if I knew. I swear on my sainted…."

"Stop before I lose my patience, Sheridan. If ye are so grief stricken by yer mistake, maybe ye will see fit to set it straight. Give me the name of who sent ye."

"I…" He stopped, shaking his head. "…I cannot. If I do I am surely a dead man."

Dougray's chuckle was chilling. "Ye fail to realize, Sheridan, ye are a dead man now if ye do not tell me who ye are working for."

The man's eyes darted back and forth as though he was looking for an escape. If he gave the name of the man responsible for the kidnapping, he would die a death worse than anyone could imagine. He was trapped in more ways than one. His arms were in a steel-like grip, and the sword was still dangerously pointed at his chest. There was no way out but one. "God have mercy on my soul." With desperation that was controlled by utter fear, he thrust himself forward. Cormac saw too late the man's intent, and had not pulled the weapon back fast enough. His sword plunged deep into Sheridan's chest impaling him into silence.

"I did not mean…." Cormac began but Dougray interrupted him.

"It is not yer fault." He whirled around furious that his attempt to find out some answers had been snatched away. "Dispose of him quickly."

Teige and Cormac took charge of the body and Murrough stayed behind. "Sheridan was a scared little rabbit when we came upon him."

"Aye, and yet he had the courage to kill himself rather than face telling us who was behind the attack." He ran his hand through his hair. "*Dar Dia!* Death was more preferable? Who are we up against?"

Aislinn had wandered into the small room at the back of the church hoping to find Father Fiach, but no one was there. She glanced at the many books and writing materials that were on the small wood table against the wall. Her hand paused over the leather-bound journal. It wasn't quite as worn, but she recognized it as the one she had held in her time. This was Fiach's journal and the heartfelt words that he had put to paper were all about his…cousin, Dougray. "Oh God!" Her heart pounded against her chest.

Fiach had been the one to steal the body away and hide it in the tomb below the church. She whirled around intending to hunt for Fiach, but her departure was cut short. A dark, cloaked man filled the doorframe blocking her escape. She took a step back.

"Father Fiach will be back shortly. If you would like, you can wait for him in here while I go find him." The man didn't move aside making her fear the worse. She grabbed the letter opener that was on the desk and pointed it toward the imposing figure. "Do not come any closer or I'll see fit to use this on you."

He didn't seem at all intimidated and took a step forward anyway, and with that step, he threw off his hood revealing his face to her. Aislinn's mouth dropped open. Though considerably older, the man resembled Dougray. So much so, it was uncanny. "Who are you?"

"I apologize for I have ye at a disadvantage, milady *Scathach*, or should I simply call ye A.J. as so many others do?" The twinkle in his light-gray eyes was enough to let her know he was rather amused with this meeting.

"Either you tell me right now who you are or I'll…."

He laughed vibrantly. "Ye are indeed a worthy lass for my son."

She hesitated. "Son?"

"Aye. I am Lord Shane Fitzpatrick at your service." He bowed before her in a grand gesture."

"But you're dead."

"Ah, so I have heard, but as ye can see I am not."

"This is a trick." She jabbed the letter opener toward him. "This is a trick." Even though she voiced it, she knew it wasn't so. The man looked too much like Dougray not to be his father. His dark hair, his clear gray eyes, and even his condescending smile, they were all like his.

Just then Fiach saw fit to return and his eyes took in the obvious scene before him. "I see that ye both are getting acquainted."

"He claims to be Dougray's father." Aislinn wanted to hear it from Fiach.

"Aye, that he is, milady." He walked over to her and took the weapon from her grasp. "I suppose we need to explain."

"You're damn right ye do."

Shane couldn't help the smile that tugged at his lips. The woman was everything he had heard and more. "Maybe ye should fix her a drink, Fiach."

"I'm not thirsty. So if you please, explain why you are not dead." She folded her arms against her chest as she glared at Dougray's father.

"Fair enough, but do ye mind if I have something to quench my thirst?"

She could hear the amusement in his voice, but she refused to let down her guard. Dougray's father or not, she didn't know what this man wanted. As far as she was concern, he was the one behind all their troubles. He already had staged his death. What else was he capable of? She nodded to Fiach, "Give him a drink, will you? I am anxious to hear the gentleman's explanation."

Shane drank deeply from the goblet Fiach had handed him before he sat down and raised his eyes to Aislinn, who still had not relented. "I can only assume that ye heard the story of our demise, Lady Mary and myself of course."

"You had supposedly lost your lives in a fire. I can see that you escaped. Did your wife fare as well?"

"She did and is in hiding."

Aislinn lost some her hostility for curiosity won out. "But why? Dougray thought you both were dead. Why would you do that?"

"Simply because we thought it would protect him. My daughter Miriam was safe for she married an English advocate and they would not look at her with suspicion, but Dougray was a different story. My wife's father, the man you met the other evening, Sir Richard Halstead tried to make the path easier for my son, but I am afraid Dougray had too much of my blood coursing through his veins. He wouldn't conform to the Tudor King's thinking, and well, I can relate to the feeling. His life was forfeited the moment he decided to step foot on Irish soil. He conformed back to the old ways that he once knew as a boy, and all the training that was drilled in his head of the English rule was cast aside. The Tudor King was aware of it, and it was obvious to his followers as well, but the English were not all that threatened by my son. The Chieftains did not trust him either. He was damned, so to speak, no matter where his loyalties were placed.

"It was unfortunate that Ella Butler got in the way. She was murdered in my son's stead, a mere accident but one that still was to be to an advantage for the crown. The truce between the Butlers and the Fitzpatricks was a fragile one. The marriage was to have strengthened this truce, and it might have worked if Ella had lived.

"Fingham Butler was never known for his forgiveness on any account, and the death of his only daughter would not go without revenge being sought. Dougray by all means should have been eliminated by now and so thought others, but they failed to realize that Dougray was not softened by English luxury, rather it made him harder in his resolve to be exactly the opposite. He fought back. Seeing that Butler's attempts were failing, they tried other tactics making it look like each clan was viciously attacking the other."

"So it would come to a full-out clan war."

"Ye catch on quickly, milady." Shane did not hide his admiration.

"Then there would have to be spies within each of the clans to raise these suspicions."

"Right again. I am trying to disclose the truth and end this charade before it is too late. Mary and I have given up so much to insure the safety of all that reside at Dunhaven, and we will not let anyone stop us now."

"But if he's doomed by the crown and by his own people, what can you do to prevent it?"

She saw Shane and Fiach exchange an uneasy glance. Obviously they had already discussed the options. "What is it?" she coaxed them. "What must be done?"

"Dougray will have to vanish," Shane answered her solemnly.

"You can't be serious. He won't abandon the people of Dunhaven."

"Then he will die," the older man stated forcefully, the lines of worry etching deeper into his face.

"Okay, wait a minute. There must be another way. Let's just say that he agrees to your plan to disappear. What happens to Dunhaven and everyone there?"

"A truce can be made for all, if a Butler were to marry into the clan. They are in good standards with the crown, and their loyalties will not be questioned."

"But who? You only had two children…Miriam? You would have her marry another old man. It is not only cruel…."

"Not Lord Fingham, his nephew Tremain."

"Tremain?" Her brows arched as she remembered the man who had captured her.

"I see ye know whom I speak of."

"Oh we've met," she said, "but what makes you think that Miriam would even consider this? She seems very happy of her status as is." She decided not to let on how thrilled Miriam would be at the prospect of marrying her one true love.

"Even if I didn't know better, my daughter would do what was expected of her. But I'm positive, this time, it will not be a sacrifice on her part. You see, Miriam is in love with Tremain and has been since she was a young lass. I know for a fact the man is in love with her."

"Then why, in God's name, did you not let the two marry in the first place?"

"It is not as easy as it may seem. Tremain is Fingham's illegitimate nephew though highly favored. The drawback is that he has no land, and therefore no means to care for my daughter. He was beneath her in status. But now there is a way this can be rectified." Shane paused to make sure she was following where he was going with this. "Dougray was knighted, and can grant the lands to Tremain, thus securing Dunhaven from the throne. The Butlers may openly show allegiance to the crown, but they are still Irish, and that is better than having an English lord take what is not his. Besides, Tremain's heir is a Fitzpatrick."

"You knew Oren was Tremain's son?"

Shane nodded.

Aislinn's mind was reeling and needed to sit down. Fiach was good enough to offer her a seat and also pour her a drink. "Ye will feel better with a little wine to calm yer nerves." She gladly accepted.

"Ye do realize," Shane spoke again. "That time is of the essence. This last attempt was too close. Dougray will have to make the choice now."

"Where is he supposed to go?"

Shane misinterpreted her worries. "Ye need not fear; we will make arrangements for ye to go with him. This is yer wish, is it not?"

"My place is at his side."

"Good. Now we must find Dougray." Shane had been watching Aislinn and he knew that she seemed preoccupied with something more than just what they were discussing. "Do ye have a misgiving?"

She looked to Fiach and her eyes wandered to the journal that was on the table. She was worried for she had read Fiach's words. She had viewed Dougray's broken remains, but possibly they still had a chance. Maybe her sole purpose of being here was to save him. Neala claimed that she couldn't change what was meant to be, but perhaps that was it. Maybe she was to prevent Dougray from being taken in the first place. It was worth a shot, because no matter what happened, she had no intention of letting him go without a fight. "Do you have a suspicion of who is behind all this?"

"Is it not obvious? It is the Tudor King who had grand ideas to be King of Ireland and wants all to bow down to him. He has put out the word to subdue Dougray for his outspoken views, and his alliances with chieftains who will never conform to what he will demand of them. He nearly eliminated all the Geraldines, and tried to end my dear sweet Mary's life as well as my own. Dougray is a mere inconvenience to him, but also one that would benefit as an example. He took in my son, treated him as well as if he was his own, and now Dougray spits in his face."

"I get it already. The king wishes him dead, but who did he send to do the job?"

"Someone close enough to betray him," Shane told her.

Again she looked at Fiach, for he was the one that had written the words that *he should have known*.

"What is it, lass?" The priest could sense she was holding something back.

"You may find this odd, but I have to mention it in hopes that it will trigger something in your memory. You of all people know Dougray. You could save him for I know that you will recognize the threat. I just hope that I can prompt you to see it before it is too late. Please come back to Dunhaven with us."

"If I was aware of the culprit, he would not be drawing another breath," Fiach said.

"I'm sorry, Father Fiach, but I am so worried. If anything were to happen to Dougray, I...." She choked back a sob. She already knew how he died. How could she ever explain that to them?

Fiach put an arm around her. "There, there, lass. I will return to Dunhaven."

"It will have to be now," Shane interrupted. "My son thought to send Aislinn to her uncle's, but I say that she will be of help to us there. It will be dangerous. Will ye go?"

"You can count on it."

Shane nodded proudly. She was indeed worthy to be called *Scathach*.

Fiach made the arrangements for the meeting, which Dougray had mixed feelings about. His parents had basically lied to him, letting him believe that they were dead, when all along they had managed to put a substantial allowance aside, so that they could live comfortably in Italy. He understood they were trying to do what was best for Miriam and him for he would do anything to make sure that Aislinn was safe from harm's way, but they had abandoned the people of Dunhaven, letting them fend for themselves.

Both men's steel-gray eyes stared each other down. They were so similar in height and coloring, but the similarities did not stop there. They possessed the same stubborn streak that would not allow them to bend to anyone's will.

"I have no wish to abandon Dunhaven as ye saw fit to do," Dougray stated flatly.

"I did it to save them since the Tudor King did his best to set raids upon us, picking us off one by one. I had hopes that ye would have the blessing from him, and so it seemed ye did for awhile."

"He was the one to knight me and grant me the lands. Why would he see fit to eliminate me now?"

"Ye did not conform to his liking. The man changes his mind on a daily basis, doing away with those he called friend a moment before."

"I have the backing of the O'Malley and of the Burkes. They will come to my aid."

"And they may, but they are far away with their own affairs that keep them occupied. It would be only a matter of time before they pull their forces back to sustain their holdings."

Dougray was pacing as he mulled everything over. "Ye ask me to grant lands to my enemy. Tremain has done me no favors, and I cannot see why I should assist him now."

His father explained with patience, "Ye told me yerself that ye wished to find peace with the Butlers. This is the only way. And ye will be able secure Dunhaven without jeopardizing the people ye care for. But most of all, Dougray, ye will have a chance to live. Do ye not want children of yer own?" He watched his son's feature's change, gentling at the mention of a family, and he took the information and forged forward. "Ye have a wife to consider. Ye owe her to keep her safe. If ye do not follow my suggestion, it will be a cold bed she comes home to."

Dougray ran his hand through his hair. A suffocating sensation tightened his throat for he was torn between what he wanted to do. He had dreamt of rebuilding Dunhaven and it was in his grasps, but he obviously would have to fight for it, causing more death than need be. Aislinn had told him she would stand by his side, no matter what he chose. If they left for Italy, he may be eliminating her chances of finding a way back home, but if they stayed, she would be in danger of losing her life. The attempts could not be ignored. He loved her beyond words. Safety first, and if they could somehow come back to Ireland, they would. He impatiently pulled his drifting thoughts together and faced his father. "What do I have to do?"

Chapter Seventy-Three

As soon as Dougray returned back to Dunhaven, he was met with the news of Cahir's death. He paced the length of the library where he was meeting privately with Hamish and Murrough.

"It seemed odd to me, milord," Hamish began his account of what had transpired since his return to Dunhaven. "There was someone who entered the physician's room where I was hiding and took the bottle that I told ye about, as if it belonged to him. And that very day, I came upon Cahir's body. I apologize for I did not see the man's face, and I cannot say if he was the one to hold accountable for Cahir's death. As far as anyone knew, Cahir had gone out alone to gather herbs."

"A deliberate act to silence?" Murrough spoke, making Dougray stop his pacing.

"Or of what he could have proven. As of right now, we only have suspicions of the poisoning. Perhaps Cahir had been innocent of these acts we silently accused him of. The real culprit might have felt threatened, and knew that Cahir would be able to prove poison was involved. Possibly he may have been able to point a finger to who was responsible."

Fiach had remained silent up until now, trying to put the pieces of the missing puzzle together. "Did it appear like Cahir struggled?" he asked.

Hamish thought about it for a moment, before he answered. "Nay. It was a quick slice to the throat"

"Cahir must have known his assailant and didn't expect to be slain." Dougary mulled over the information.

Fiach nodded his head. "Hamish, was there anything ye noticed that seemed out of the ordinary?"

"Well...." Then he shook his head as to dismiss what he was going to say.

"Anything could help. Even if ye are not sure if it makes a difference or not," the priest encouraged him.

"Well Cahir's hand had spots of blood on it as though he might have clutched his throat. But the odd thing of it was it looked like he had wiped his hand on something. Part of his palm was perfectly clean, but there was not a hand print on his clothing. It was as if the assailant had wiped Cahir's hand before he had left."

"Does seem a bit odd." Fiach nodded his head, but for the life him he couldn't imagine the purpose. He wanted to find the answers for he couldn't help but think that they were running out of time.

Aislinn's words had haunted Fiach. She seemed to think that he should know whom they were dealing with, but he didn't know. Cahir had been the only suspect and he was dead.

He was still with those thoughts when he came across Abbot Kirwan, who was crossing the courtyard on his way to the chapel. Kirwan fell into step beside him. "Ye looked troubled, Father Fiach."

"Nay, just lost in thought is all and maybe a little tired."

"Come with me to the chapel and sit awhile."

Fiach could see no reason not to. Matter of fact, a little prayer might even help to solve this mystery. "I would like that."

"Have ye come any closer in solving poor Cahir's murder?"

"Nay, it is still a mystery to why someone would go to such trouble."

"What do ye have there?" Kirwan nodded toward the book he was holding.

"Just my writings and prayers."

"Really. I would be interested in…." He reached for the book causing Fiach to drop it. "I'm sorry." Kirwan would have picked it up but Fiach had already bent down.

"It's all right," he picked up the book that was near Kirwan's feet and noticed that the man's robes had a stain near the bottom hem. It surprised him for the man was always so careful about his appearance. He stood now. "I will have to pass with ye reading my words. It is private. Ye do understand?"

His beady eyes strayed to the leather-bound book as though he wanted to insist, but then he raised his gaze and smiled. "Of course."

Chapter Seventy-Four

Abbot Kirwan found Aislinn in the library browsing through the shelves. This was another habit of hers that thoroughly annoyed him. It wasn't her right for she was just a woman who couldn't fully understand the consequences of what she was reading.

Today, though, he would hold his tongue. "Milady?" She looked up. Having her attention, he continued, "I would not bother ye, but I saw the boy leave the castle."

"Declan?" She had already put the book down.

"Aye, milady. I know how ye worry about the lad and thought it was best that I inform ye."

"He shouldn't be out alone. It's not safe. Thank you, Abbot Kirwan, I will go after him at once." She hurried out the door and took the steps as fast as she could down the winding stairs. She didn't even pause to find Teige to go with her. She had her sword and she would be back before anyone knew she was gone.

As she came out into the courtyard, she saw a wisp of Declan's blond hair as he trotted past the guards that were too busy talking to notice a small boy going out of the gate.

She hurried forward, knowing she had to find him quickly before Dougray heard of this. He had only allowed them to come back to Dunhaven on strict orders that they were not to leave the castle doors. She had not wanted to spend another moment away from his side, so she had given him her word.

What in the world possessed the small boy to disobey those orders?

She was almost through the gate when one of the guards took notice and halted her. "Milady, ye are not to leave the grounds."

"This I know, but you failed to stop Declan from going. Let me pass and I will not report this to my husband." The guard backed away not wanting to have any trouble.

"As ye wish, milady."

She was frantic to find Declan but it was like he had disappeared. She was about to go back for help, when she caught sight of his blond head. He was crouched down picking wild flowers, like he didn't have a care in the world.

"Declan, what are you doing out here all alone? You know it is not safe to wander so far away from the keep." The little boy's smile faded from his face. She felt awful that she had allowed her own fear to make her speak so harshly. She smiled shakily. "It's all right, Declan." She motioned him to come to her. "We must get back. Come on."

He walked over to her handing her the flowers. "They're for ye."

"Thank you. They're beautiful." She smiled warmly down at him. "Come now before someone realizes we're missing." She took his hand to hurry him along. It was most likely her imagination, but she had an uneasy feeling like they were being watched.

Declan's small hand tightened on Aislinn's and she stopped as though she were afraid to move. She lifted her gaze to see Abbot Kirwan approaching them with his beady eyes shifting first to her then back to the boy. A slow smile spread across the man's face causing the hackles at the back of her neck to rise. She glanced back among the trees, almost fearing someone would attack them from behind.

"What are ye looking for, milady?" his voice was sickening sweet and his approach was far too bold. Aislinn pulled the small boy behind her.

"Did you wish to speak to me?"

"Nay."

Declan clutched her skirt and she could feel him quaking against her. He choked back a sob, staring at the abbot with one eye. "A.J., he did it," he whispered as the memories came flooding back to another day, another place where Abbot Kirwan had approached. "He hurt everyone."

She glanced down at the frightened child, as the dawning of the words seemed to sink in. Her gaze shot back to Kirwan, who was standing no more than a few paces away.

"I wondered when he would remember. Thought he had when he went into hysterics that first day he spoke."

She recalled that incident. Declan had been fine, happy until Kirwan had pushed his way into her room. Then he had become frightened, inconsolable. Why hadn't she seen this? "You killed his entire family? Why?" At that moment, she wanted to take the man and throttle him with her bare hands.

"Politics, milady. The MacKennas were chosen to be the sacrificial lamb. We needed to have a reason for Lord Dougray to retaliate against the Butlers, and what better way than to have it look as though the feuding clan was slaughtering his innocent tenants." He glanced at the boy with a sigh. "He should have died with the rest, but he hid himself well, and with the confusion of the fight, he was overlooked."

"You monster. How could you wear the holy robes and stand there so calmly talking of people's deaths."

"Their souls were not in jeopardy. I prayed for them to enter the kingdom of God. It had to be done. Our lands are slowly being taken over and I will not stand for it. I was protecting what belongs to us. Dougray's father was just as weak. That is why he and his English wife needed to be eliminated too."

"You were responsible for the fire?"

"Of course. He would have given back the lands to the Tudor King that fancies he has rights to us here. He was ready to lay down his sword, but I took care of that. Then the wayward son returns, the lands granted to him with his word of loyalty to Henry Tudor on his deceiving lips."

"He wanted what was best for Dunhaven. Don't you see that? He was trying to make it productive once more."

"He had no such intentions. He allowed heathen ways to litter the minds of his people. It was only a matter of time before he decides to renounce his religion as well. Henry already teeters with it as he produces bastards. He is a liar. Lord Dougray Fitzpatrick was trained by the best, and the deceptions slip from his mouth just as fast. I played the game as well, sending false accusations to both sides causing conflict wherever yer husband turned, making it impossible to know where his loyalties stood. It would have been only a matter of time before either the chieftains here, or the Tudor followers, eliminate him, but time is running short and I have no wish to prolong this. As for ye, milady, ye are uncouth with yer beliefs. If yer husband had not took pity on ye and returned, ye would have been dead already."

"Dead? What do ye mean?"

"Why do ye think ye were so ill? I was unfamiliar with the dosages, but I figured it out well enough with Fiona. I expected ye to die with yer bastard child." He gave a brief chuckle. "I'm surprised ye didn't figure it out. Even the imbecile Cahir had become suspicious and had asked questions. Oh he thought he was so sly, but I knew he suspected me. That's why I had to get rid of him."

The man had murdered Cahir and had *poisoned* her, causing her to miscarry. Rage boiled inside of her, but she forced herself to appear calm. She could see she was not going to be able to reason with this man. He had lost his grip on reality and couldn't see past his own demented truths making him far more dangerous than she had originally thought.

"Go back to the castle, Declan." She pushed the boy forward. If she could distract Kirwan long enough, the boy might have a chance. Declan hesitated but she was forceful. "Do as I say. Run all the way back and don't stop." The boy moved into action then. Aislinn didn't feel comforted when she heard Kirwan's laugh. Then she knew why. For six men seemed to materialize out of nowhere immediately surrounding her.

"Go after the lad," Kirwan ordered.

"Let him go. You have me," Aislinn pleaded.

"Do ye think I am not of my senses? The boy can identify me. Now go!" He nodded again to two men. Aislinn reacted also for she wasn't going to let them slay Declan for their own personal pleasure.

The wild flowers forgotten, she withdrew her dagger she had hidden within her sleeve and jabbed it into the man's throat. She immediately took the slain man's dagger from its sheath and threw it at the other man who was still after Declan. Her throw was wide, for another had reacted by tackling her to the ground. She immediately rolled and brought up her knee into the man's groin. He doubled over in agony and she broke free, but before she could get to her feet, another was upon her. She grabbed her last assailant's sword and the man impaled himself before he could retract his steps. She pushed him aside and jumped to her feet, her own sword drawn. Two more and she would be home free. She could already see that they were wary of her, making Kirwan furious.

"Get her! She is a mere woman!"

They approached her slowly as she kept her stance. "Which one of you would like to die first?"

That seemed to infuriate the smaller of the two men and he lunged at her. She easily deflected the blow. She kicked him sending him back into his partner, both men fell, the one on top letting out a bellow as his own partner's weapon slashed into his back.

Aislinn would have easily taken the other, but Kirwan demanded her attention.

"I wouldn't do it if I were ye."

She glanced at the beady-eyed man and saw that he was holding Declan against his chest with a knife pressed to his neck. "Drop your weapon or the lad dies."

She hesitated, but the menacing look in Kirwan's eyes told her that he meant it. She lowered her sword at once, and this time, she let the men take her. They yanked her hands behind her back securing them tightly.

Kirwan let go of Declan and he immediately ran over to her, throwing his arms around her legs. "I tried to get back, but Abbot Kirwan's man caught me."

How she wished she could hug the frightened boy. "It's all right, Declan."

Kirwan walked over to them with a satisfied grin on his face. "Now move and no more trouble from ye. One false act and I will slice the boy in two, and I'll gladly let ye watch. Do I make myself clear?"

"Perfectly," she spat at him.

Kirwan looked to the remaining men. "Get rid of this mess." He motioned to the fallen dead.

Chapter Seventy-Five

Dougray sensed something was wrong even before they found the blood that had not been covered up with dirt and mud. "She and the boy were taken," Murrough confirmed what he had already suspected. "We found fresh graves." He saw the anxious look that penetrated Dougray's features. He quickly assured him that it wasn't what he feared. "They were strangers. Obviously milady tried to fend them off."

"Obviously," he gritted between clenched teeth. Why was she out with Declan when she knew it was not safe? He should have never allowed them to come back with him to Dunhaven.

"I will go with ye." Shane came to stand by him.

"Do ye really think that is a wise idea, Father? Ye have already jeopardized yerself by being here."

"I will see ye and yers safe, Dougray. Staying away was to protect ye. That has failed. It is time to step forward."

A multitude of emotions flitted across his face: anger, gratitude, and fear…. He needed all the help he could find. Finally he nodded his consent and his father gripped his shoulder in a tight clasp. "We will find them, son."

Dougray was ready to mount his steed when Fiach came riding in fast. Because of his anxious hurry, he nearly collided with Dougray's large warhorse. "I am sorry, Dougray, but I have come to realize who murdered Cahir."

"Who do ye suspect?"

"Kirwan. His robes were soiled at the hem, an odd stain that had me bothered until I remembered that Cahir's hand had been wiped clean." He saw the skepticism in Dougray's eyes and he hurried on to explain. "Let us just say that a dying Cahir could have reached out in desperation to the very man that had sliced his throat."

"But Kirwan? He has been abbot at Dunhaven for more years than I can count."

"Aye, this I know. I would not come forth with this if I were not certain of what I accuse. Kirwan has always been impeccable with his appearance. Do ye think that he would allow a stain on his hem? Blood is not so easily removed. We know that Cahir knew his attacker. He would not have feared Kirwan's approach."

Cormac had been listening and came forward now. "Milord, I wish to speak."

"Go on then."

"I had always thought it odd that Fiona would call on her deathbed for Abbot Kirwan, especially since she is not of the faith. I had thought that she was just delirious, but she begged me to warn ye. She said to beware of the robed man."

"He must have been the one to poison her." Fiach looked back to Dougray. "The man on guard will swear to the fact that he saw the abbot leave the gates soon after milady had."

Dougray's face clouded with unbridled anger as he went over each ill-fated incident that had taken place. Abbot Kirwan had made a point to see Fiona when the woman was not of the faith, and he was there to bless the food that Aislinn was to eat. Roth had said he had been to the kitchen. He knew of their whereabouts at all times. The kidnapping, the slaughtering of the MacKennas…. *"Dar Dia*! I will kill him."

The trap was set and Kirwan waited for Dougray to come into view. He was informed that they were already headed in their direction. He knew that the fool would come for his whore, and there she waited, huddled with the child who should have meant nothing to her.

Misfits, all of them. It was right to eliminate them before they infected those deserving of God's good graces. Even now faced with impending death, the woman they call *Scathach* glared her defiance. She never knew her place, but he would teach her this day. She would watch her lover be slain before her eyes. Then he would gladly kill the boy. He knew that would be her last straw. She would lose all will to fight. He sighed regrettably for her death would almost be too easy.

They camped over the ridge and made their plans. Dougray knew there would be no meeting, no negotiation. They were dealing with someone who wanted his head and obviously would go to great lengths to see that it was severed from his body. This would be a fight to the death.

He recognized immediately Robert Burke's crest. He knew that he should not have trusted the man. He should have gone with his instincts, but Dubhdara had assured him that they would have an alliance with his clan. Now it looked as though this was not going to be the case.

They set up camp and the fires were going. The night was already chilled with a hanging mist that seemed to surround them. "Milord." Cormac bowed. "We have captured a Burke. He wishes to have a word with ye."

He was on his feet immediately and advanced toward Teige to find out whom they had captured lurking around their camp. Never had he expected to see who was thrust before him. Years of training controlled his impulse to draw his sword and relieve the man of his head. "So Sir Robert, what brings ye here before me on such a wondrous night?" Dougray's open hostility was not lost to him. He was treading on thin ice and he was well aware that the only reason he was still breathing was because Dougray wanted answers.

"I am here to help." Robert raised his hand in a gesture that asked him to wait before he reacted with violence. "Hear me out and ye will know that I am speaking the truth."

"Why should I believe ye?"

"There is no reason whatsoever that ye should, for it is no secret that we do not like each other over much." When Dougray didn't say anything he continued. "And I do not have a care if ye live or die, but I do, however, have regard to what Dubhdara thinks. I need his alliance, and to preserve it, he has made it known that I should keep ye alive."

"I'm listening."

"Abbot Kirwan is waiting to put matters into his own hands. The Tudor King has been convinced that ye are a threat and should be eliminated. It was Kirwan's words that turned him. It is rather ironic, don't ye think, since Kirwan loathes the English rule, but has used them to his advantage. He fears Dunhaven will fall into the English hands and wishes to prevent it by petitioning for the church to see Dunhaven sanctioned."

"That's ridiculous. The church will not interfere with the way things stand. King Henry wavers now on what he will do with the church and all that follow. He would never allow such a take over."

"Aye, we both know this, but the abbot has lost sight of reason. His own demented ways are all that he sees. He wants ye dead come tomorrow and he has convinced a small garrison to protect him. We are here to take him down. I only come to warn ye for my own men's safety."

Dougray wore a grim expression still wondering if he should take him at his word. "Aislinn and Declan?"

"They are being kept alive so that they may witness yer death."

"How very thoughtful of Kirwan." His sarcasm was thick. "I hope he won't mind if I don't readily put my head down on the block for him."

Robert's eyes caught the movement to the left of him. Stepping from the shadows, he met Shane Fitzpatrick eye to eye. "Lord Shane?" He couldn't help but wonder how the man was still alive when all had thought him dead.

"Nay, I am not a ghost. Yer vision is quite good." He relieved Robert of his doubts. "Dougray, ye can trust Sir Robert. I can vouch for his honesty." He pulled the hood over his head and watched the man gasp. Shane chuckled softly. "I had to know whom to trust." He threw back the hood once more. "Dubhdara came straight away to inform me that ye had given the notice promptly to him."

"It was a test?"

"One that ye passed. I apologize for the deceit, but there was no other way to go about it. As for Abbot Kirwan, I had also approached him. He was clever with his deceit, not giving one way or the other where he stood. I fear I had trusted him for he had been abbot with the Fitzpatricks since before ye were born, Dougray. I did not know his hatred ran so deep."

"Even I did not suspect him, Father. I was deceived by the robes he wears."

"Now that we know whom we fight against," Fiach spoke up, "maybe we should now discuss the plan for taking Kirwan down without harming the captives."

In the early morning, Dougray's men moved into position. Fortunately for them, the thick mist that had covered the land shielded them from view. Dougray wanted Aislinn and Declan released before the fighting commenced for he didn't want to take a chance that they would be harmed in the skirmish.

Cormac and Hamish took care of the guards while Teige and Dermot quietly approached Aislinn and Declan. It was too simple, making Teige feel increasingly uneasy. Something wasn't right. He motioned for Dermot to hurry. He released Aislinn from her bounds while Dermot took Declan into his care.

As Teige had suspected, they were not so lucky sneaking back out of camp for Kirwan had anticipated such a ploy and was waiting for them.

"Get them away!" Dermot shouted as he turned to fight. At that moment, Dunhaven's kern came charging in to help make the escape successful. For the moment, Kirwan was distracted from his intent. He turned to defend himself.

"I need a sword," Aislinn insisted even though Teige was forcefully leading them farther away.

"My orders are to lead ye to safety, milady."

"I will not sit around when I could be down there helping."

"Nay, ye will not. I am to hogtie ye if ye even try to make yer way back. Don't make me do that, milady." He looked at her kindly, but she had no doubt that he would carry out the threat.

"A.J., please stay with me." Declan sounded close to tears. She leaned down and picked him up, trying to calm the child's fears.

"Don't worry, Declan. Everything will be all right."

Dougray's garrison, with the help of the Burkes, easily took down the enemy, but Abbot Kirwan had eluded them. Once the fight had become too intense, the man had slithered away, like the snake that he was. Murrough had ordered the men to comb the area for him. He would not be allowed to escape.

Through rising mist, Dougray wearily made his way back to let Aislinn know that it was nearly over, but what greeted him filled him with a sheer fright.

The missing Kirwan had Aislinn in a stronghold with his dagger dangerously close to her neck. A quick assessment of the situation and he knew there would not be a back up. Teige was sprawled on the ground, either unconscious or dead. Declan huddled in fear near the tree trunk, his arms hugging his knees near his small trembling body.

He turned his attention back to the abbot. "Let her go, Kirwan." His stomach clenched tight, as he desperately tried to keep his fragile control in check. "It is I that ye want."

"Put down yer weapon," Kirwan demanded, knowing that, in matter of moments, he would be surrounded. He didn't understand how his well thought out plan had been throttled. Right now he should have had the Fitzpatrick hanging by his neck, but instead he was the one trapped like a fox ready to be ripped apart. Well he wasn't going alone. He would take Dougray with him. He relished in the thought that he would still have his last revenge.

Dougray did as he was ordered and slowly placed his sword at his feet, while all the time he kept his gaze on Kirwan. He straightened to his full height. "Now let her go."

Kirwan saw from the side of his vision a man moving in behind him. It was now or never. "As ye wish, milord," he said with such malice that Dougray's skin prickled with impending dread. It happened so fast that there was nothing he could have done, nothing anyone could have done.

Kirwan let Aislinn go. With a swift move, he intended to throw the knife at Dougray.

"No!" Aislinn screamed as she grabbed his arm that held the weapon. Kirwan realized his opportunity to take out Dougray was over, but maybe *this* revenge was sweeter. He turned his malicious purpose toward her.

She hadn't expected him to change targets. His aim was not as accurate as he had wished, but it would serve its purpose. He thrust forward burying the weapon deep in her shoulder. Dougray at the same time sent his dagger flying straight into the man's back, penetrating his black heart. Kirwan was dead and on his way to hell before he even hit the ground.

Dougray hurried forward to Aislinn's side, rolling her toward him. She looked up at him, her eyes filled with agony, but still she managed a small smile for him. "They didn't capture you. You survived, Dougray. You survived."

"Why did ye do it, Aislinn? He was going after me."

"I couldn't let him harm you." She touched his rugged face, the face she had learned to love, drooping mustache and all. "You see I would die for you too."

"Nay, ye will not leave me. Do ye hear me, Aislinn?" She couldn't answer him for she had already slipped into unconsciousness.

Robert Burke had witnessed the event sorely realizing how he had misjudged this courageous woman. She had sacrificed herself. He knew of no one who possessed such unselfish bravery. She was indeed worthy to be called *Scathach*. He prayed that he would have the chance to tell her so.

He knelt down beside Dougray to assess the damage that had been done. The dagger was deeply imbedded. She had a chance of bleeding to death before it could ever be removed. He glanced at Dougray's grief-stricken face and knew that the man was already aware of the dilemma they faced. "I will have my physician look at her." Robert didn't wait for him to answer, but issued an order for his man to be brought forth at once.

Chapter Seventy-Six

They had removed the knife successfully and thank God she had remained unconscious throughout the horrible ordeal. As expected she had lost a lot of blood and was already feverish. Her skin nearly burned Dougray's hand as he placed the cool rags on her forehead. They did not pack up camp but remained, while he debated if it was wise to move her.

Teige had survived Kirwan's attack and had his head bandaged. The young man was racked with guilt for not protecting her. He would not leave Aislinn's side. Declan was lying beside her, his small hand desperately clutching hers.

Dougray closed his weary eyes. He couldn't shake the feeling that she was going to die.

"The mist has closed in on us." Murrough came into the tent, glancing at the still figure that had once been the vibrant woman he had grown to respect. He swallowed hard. "We will need to stay the night, milord. It would do no good to try and make our way back to Dunhaven when we are unable to make out more than a few feet in front of us. The men are quite uneasy of the mist. I am hearing whispering that they think it a bad omen. Ye might want to make an appearance to assure them that there is no reason to worry."

He sighed heavily, "Aye." He covered his face with trembling hands as if to wipe away the anguish that was tearing at his soul.

Murrough worried that the stress was wearing him thin. "Milord?"

He looked up then with a nod. "I will be out shortly."

"I am sorry about milady." Murrough didn't know what else to say.

Dougray's father entered, pausing inside the flap of the tent. One look at Murrough's somber face and he knew that Aislinn was not doing well. "I will sit with her," he announced moving forward and placing a hand on his son's shoulder. "Ye are needed elsewhere. I will call ye if there is any change."

The moment that Dougray stepped outside the tent, he knew. The mist was not like it should be. It was heavier, drier, like the one that had taken him to Aislinn's time. He glanced back inside seeing her so still as if her life had already left her, but then he caught the slight movement of her chest rising and falling. As much as he wanted her at his side, he knew he had to give her back to her world. For only there she would have a fighting chance.

He ran his hand through his dark hair. The decision had been made.

He let the flap drop as he turned and moved his feet forward heading to the fires so that he could speak with his men.

Dougray waited long into the night when all was quiet before he wrapped up Aislinn, cradling her against him as he carried her away from the camp and into the thickening mist.

The white wolf was waiting, as though it had been expecting him. Strangely he was not afraid of the beast as it moved forward to sit down at his feet. Dougray gently placed Aislinn beside it. He somehow sensed that the wolf was not of flesh and blood, but rather a spirit that was there to protect her. If Dougray had any doubts before that he was doing the right thing, he didn't question himself now. He sat with her for a long time and after a while she seemed to relax as she snuggled closer to the warmth of the wolf. He was about go, but she had reached out and clutched his arm.

"Aislinn?" his voice was hoarse with raw emotion.

"Don't leave me," she pleaded and her grip increased.

"I have to, lass. It's the only way. When the mist lifts, they will find ye here."

"I don't want you to go. Please."

Her voice tore at him but he could not relent. He shook his head. "If ye stay, ye will die."

"Without you, I don't want to live. Come with me. Bring Declan here and come with me."

He marveled, for even in her duress, she still thought of the boy. The bond had been forged deeper than he had ever thought possible. A mother and a son, he reassuringly smiled down at her for he found he could accept that. "Dougray?" Aislinn felt a dread like no other for she knew the answer before he spoke.

He clasped his large hands over hers. "I can't go with ye."

Aislinn didn't want to sound selfish but she couldn't help it. She was desperate. She loved this man who had captured her heart. "What of our future?"

"Don't make me choose. Ye are my love for now and for always, but do not ask me to be less of a man, for that is what I'd be if I turned my back on the people of Dunhaven. I have to make the preparations for Miriam and her son. I am the only one that can do that. I can grant knighthood to Tremain without question. Even if I am to be eliminated, Tremain may lay claim to Dunhaven for Oren."

Aislinn knew all this, but it still did not make it any easier to accept.

Dougray leaned down pressing his lips against hers before he gently covered her mouth knowing he would never forget the velvet warmth of her. He then brushed a gentle kiss across her forehead. "Ye must go, Aislinn, where ye belong…" His voice was low and tormented as he spoke. "…but I beg of ye do not forget what we had."

He pressed something into the palm of her hand closing her fingers around it. He rose then quickly turning away from her, leaving her. She looked to see what he had given her. It was the Amber broach that had been in his family for generations, the one that was similar to the ring that he had placed on her finger when they had wedded. Through tear-stained eyes, she glanced up again. She could see his tall, dark figure disappearing into the mist. "Oh, Dougray, I'll never forget." The tears rolled down her cheeks like a stream of silver. Instinctively the wolf knew that she was in need of comfort and laid its head down on her chest.

Chapter Seventy-Seven

"She was found at the side of the road; obviously she had been stabbed and someone had tried to patch her up." The nurse relayed all that she knew about Aislinn's condition. Beverly looked at Connor wondering if he was following all this. Beverly had made the trip over, as soon as he had called her and told her of the situation.

"Someone performed surgery?" Beverly wanted more answers. So did Connor, but he wasn't so sure if they were going to get them.

"It appears so."

Connor knew there was more. Something out of the ordinary happened here. His parents tried to explain their theory, but it was so ludicrous that he couldn't even conceive it. *Time travel.* They had calmly told him at dinner the night Aislinn had disappeared. God, they had to have been in shock. That was the only explanation for the insane rationale they chose to accept.

The nurse continued. "She may have been to a costume party for she was wearing a period piece, a lovely gown really."

"A gown?" Beverly again looked at Connor, who shrugged his shoulders.

She waved for the two to follow her. They went into Aislinn's room and she opened the closet door. "That's the dress." She pulled it out and handed it to Beverly.

It was torn and mud splattered in spots, but there was no denying that the gown was exquisite with its blue shades and gold trim. "A costume party?"

"It was almost as if she had traveled from the past to get here, at least that was my first impression," the nurse babbled.

Beverly opened her mouth to say something, but she decided it was better just to keep her opinions to herself. *Traveling in time? Please.* What kind of hospital was this?

"Beverly? Is that you?" Aislinn had heard her voice and tried to sit up, but was still too weak.

"Hey sis." Connor came to sit on the side of the bed, being careful not to knock the IV over.

"I'm here too." Beverly immediately went to sit down on the other side. She took her friend's hand. "You had us all scared to death. We didn't know what had happened to you. I called your hotel a million times before Connor finally got a hold of me."

Aislinn's brows furrowed. Her memory was a little hazy but she knew distinctively that she had been gone for almost a year. Aislinn swallowed. "What day is it?"

"Sunday."

"How long was I missing?"

"Just a few days before you were brought here," Beverly informed her. "You didn't have any identification on you, and you were unconscious.... Well you've been here almost five days now."

Aislinn closed her eyes as though she had been given the worse news of her life. She shook her head. "It can't be possible. I've been gone for a year." Her eyes flew open then. "Where's Dougray? I have to get back." She again tried to rise and was now pulling at the IV. Connor firmly took hold of her hands, trying to calm her.

"You're going to hurt yourself. Come on, A.J., you have to lie still." Connor looked imploringly at the nurse who immediately went to find the doctor.

"I was with Dougray," Aislinn sobbed.

Connor's expression bordered on contempt as he spoke, "Is he the one that stabbed you?"

Aislinn shook her head. "No, of course not. It was Abbot Kirwan."

"Kirwan? An abbot, like a priest abbot?"

"He was crazy. He was trying to kill Dougray and...." She saw the way her brother was staring at her, like she had lost her mind. She immediately closed her mouth. She glanced at Beverly, who wore the same concerned expression. Had it all been a dream? An elaborate nightmare...no not a nightmare, for there had been wonderful memories too. "I have only been gone days?"

"That's right." Connor hoped she was starting to remember.

Was that true? There was no reason why her brother would lie to her. "Was I in some kind of accident?"

"That's what we're trying to find out, honey." Beverly patted her hand. "You just relax and let us take care of things." Just then the nurse had returned with the doctor. Beverly stood to the side, while he examined her. She had never seen Aislinn so vulnerable. What had happened to her out there?"

The doctor finally finished his examination and Connor and Beverly followed him out of the room. "Well?" Connor waited for him to fill in the pieces that were missing.

"The shoulder is healing, and with physical therapy she will eventually regain full use of her arm. She will make a full recovery, but...."

"But?"

"She seems to have been under a lot of stress. I want to monitor her for a few days more before I release her—just to make sure that she is all right."

"How was she able to wander around for days without anyone noticing her?"

The doctor seemed ready to say something then clamped his mouth closed. Then he cleared his throat. "If you will excuse me, I must look in on my other patients." With that, he dismissed them, quickly moving down the hall.

Beverly met Connor's gaze. "What the hell is going on here? Why do I get the distinct impression that the doctor doesn't find A.J.'s wandering around alone in the wilderness with a stab wound as anything out of the ordinary?"

"You get that impression too?" Connor sighed. It was maddening the way everyone was taking all this. His own parents even seemed to accept the fact as a common occurrence. "We need to bring A.J. home. Once she is out of here, she will be all right."

"I agree. Hey, who is this Dougray she was talking about?"

Connor's mouth formed a grim expression. "The blackguard is the one that kidnapped my sister."

"If foul play was involved, why haven't the authorities been called in?"

"My parents refused to even consider it. They wanted to speak to A.J. first to find out what had happened. I don't..." He stopped. The stress of the last few days finally hit him full force. He ran his hand through his hair. "...I don't understand any of this. Beverly. I feel like I am the only sane one here. That is why I urged you to come at once. Nothing is as it seems, and I was beginning to wonder if I was the one that was cracking up."

"Maybe we should start from the beginning. How did you meet this...Dougray character?"

"I think we better sit down for this. It's going to be a long story."

Beverly sat there quietly with calm indifference taking in everything that Connor knew up to the point of Aislinn's disappearance.

"Well?" he asked her when she still had not spoken a word.

"You never thought this man was dangerous?"

"God no. He seemed...well he was odd. He was dressed in the same..."

"...clothing as Aislinn was found in?"

"Yes, but that wasn't it. He didn't have a memory of simple everyday things that we take for granted, but I thought that it was because of his head injury."

"And yet you didn't wish to call the authorities or have the man committed? He sounds like a complete loony tune."

"That's not how it was at all. It seemed…I know this is an odd statement, but he seemed lucid enough." He rubbed his face, so tired of everything that had been placed on his shoulders. "What am I saying? This man probably kidnapped my sister, brainwashed her, and I am here trying to defend him."

Beverly rested her hand on his arm. "Don't do this to yourself. Aislinn is back and we should count ourselves fortunate."

"Beverly?" Francine's voice rang forth with a warm welcome. She walked over to where the two were seated, Donagh not far behind. "It was so good of you to come."

"You don't know how worried I have been, Mrs. Hennessy. A.J. is a dear friend."

"She is going to be all right," Donagh assured her as his gaze found his son's. It bothered him that Connor looked at him with unease. They shouldn't have told him about the mist. He wasn't ready to hear it, and now he looked at them, his own parents, as if he was considering having them committed.

Francine glanced at her husband giving him a weak smile.

Chapter Seventy-Eight

Connor rang the doorbell for the fourth time. He knew Aislinn was in there and he was becoming increasingly worried as to why she wouldn't answer the door. She had been back home now for six weeks and still no improvement. She wouldn't write. She wouldn't return anyone's calls.

"A.J., I know you're in there. You might as well…." Just then the door flew open and Aislinn's haunted eyes peered at him with almost a look of contempt. She moved aside and let him enter.

Her house was in utter disarray. It looked like she hadn't cleaned since she had returned home. Empty containers were everywhere. Clothes scattered around, clean, dirty, all clumped together in piles. He glanced at his sister, who was still in her bathrobe even though it was two-thirty in the afternoon.

She pulled the terrycloth material closer around her and lifted her chin in a defiant manner. "What?"

"I was going to ask you the same thing. Beverly says you haven't been by the office in weeks."

"I'm not feeling well." She walked over to the sofa and threw the pile of clothes on the floor and plopped herself down, folding her arms defensively against her chest.

Connor had followed her. He stared at her for a long uncomfortable moment. "You don't look ill."

"Well I am." She couldn't quite meet his gaze. "What? Stop staring at me."

He sat down next to her refusing to let her shut him out. "A.J., you have to move on."

She rubbed her temples wishing he would just leave her alone.

"You have to. It's not healthy for you to be locked up in here. You need to go back to work and…."

"Stop it!" Her voice was a retching sob that silenced him completely. "Don't tell me what to do, Connor. I know you don't believe me. No one believes me, but I did go back in time. I lived a year with people that I learned to love as much as my own family."

"It didn't happen. You know that it isn't possible. You were hurt and not yourself. Face it, you are a woman with an incredible imagination, and it makes sense that you would be able to make up this fantastic tale."

"I didn't make it up. I couldn't possibly have done that and still feel the way I do. My heart's broken, Connor. I am grieving for my husband. I'm grieving for a boy that depended upon me to care for him." She looked at her brother with her tear-filled eyes. "I can still see Declan's blue eyes imploring me to hold him and tell him a story. I see Dougray's face, feel his hands caressing me, and I hear his voice in my dreams so clearly that I reach out for him."

"You said yourself that you were with Dougray. You know what he looks like and he is a formidable man. He was the last person you were with. You could have easily taken what you know of him and somehow transformed that into thinking you were in love with him."

"God damn it, Connor!" She stood and moved away from him. "I didn't conjure all this up in my mind. I fell in love. Don't you understand that? For the first time in my life, I fell in love with a man that you, and everyone else, is trying to say didn't exist."

He stood too and went over to her, bringing her into his embrace. "I will agree that Dougray Fitzpatrick is a real person, but not a lord from the sixteenth century."

She pulled away to look at him. "How can you stand there and tell me that it wasn't real? I'm telling you, I couldn't have made it up. My imagination couldn't conjure up a whole year of a life with another person. I fought, loved, and I had a child that I lost with this man. I couldn't fabricate a whole life. I didn't! And stop looking at me that way."

"What way?"

"Like you're pitying me. Like you think I have totally lost my mind."

"God, A.J., listen to yourself."

"I am and I know how I sound, but I won't pretend that everything I told you didn't happen. I won't do it. I won't!" Her eyes held his. He knew that she really believed she had traveled back in time, and there was no point in trying to convince her otherwise.

"Fine. Okay, let's just say by some freak of nature you did live a year in another century. Well now you're back where you belong, I might add, and you need to move on. Grieve if that is what you must do, but you have to start living again." He purposely walked over to her writing desk that was covered, piled high with books. He moved them aside and pulled out her keyboard to start up the computer. He pulled up Microsoft Word giving her a blank page.

He turned to look at her then and he could see the questioning glare. "Sit down and do what you do best. Write about your adventure. Put it all down how you remember it. Who knows, maybe it will help." She still hesitated so he pulled out the chair in front of the desk, motioning for her to take it.

He almost shouted with joy when he saw her walk toward him. She sat down and he rolled the chair closer. She poised her hands over the keyboard almost as though she was scared to touch it. She looked up at him. "Connor?"

"Hmm?"

"I'm pregnant."

His eyes closed as a range of emotions coursed through him. He looked at her again, his jaw muscles at work as he clenched his jaw. "Fitzpatrick's?"

"God, Connor, you have to ask?"

"Son of…"

"Stop. Don't say it. I'm happy about this, Connor. I want this baby. I have already seen my obstetrician and she says everything looks all right. Please try to be happy for me."

She wanted him to be happy for her because the bum of a man had left her bleeding and pregnant on the side of the road? He opened his mouth to tell her exactly what he thought, but seeing her dark eyes pleading with him, he couldn't do it. She'd been through enough and he wasn't going to cause her more grief. "This is what you want?"

She took a deep breath. "Yes."

Maybe it was time that he also let things go. She was the one who had gone through this ordeal and now she was going to have Dougray Fitzpatrick's baby.

Maybe it was time to give her back what belonged to her anyway. "I have something that I have to get out of my car."

He returned in a matter of a few moments with a manila envelope in his hand. "Here." He handed it to her as her eyebrows furrowed. "Open it." She did and her eyes immediately misted with tears. "I shouldn't have kept it from you. I thought I was…."

She grabbed a hold of his hand as she looked up at him. "No, I understand. Thank you, Connor." She pulled out her wedding ring and placed it back where it belonged. Then she removed the amulet, lovingly running her fingers over the amber stone.

Connor squeezed her shoulder and she placed the palm of her hand over his. "Everything will be all right."

"I know, Connor," she sobbed. "I know."

Aislinn did write. She wrote nearly nonstop from morning to night, recreating every moment she had experienced at Dunhaven. In vivid colors people she met came alive upon the pages. She laughed a lot and cried.

Four months later, she was finished with her rough draft, which was ready for reading.

She arrived at Beverly's office to personally drop it off. "You're done?"

"Read it and let me know what you think."

Beverly eyed her friend closely. She was happy to see that at least Aislinn appeared as if she was on her way to being fully recovered from her ordeal in Ireland. She had color in her cheeks and her hair was layered to flatter the longer style she now wore. Even at five and half months pregnant, she looked gorgeous, long, lean and very healthy. "You bet, A.J. I'll read it."

Aislinn smiled and swung her purse over her shoulder as she left the office. Beverly didn't wait but sat down and turned to the first page. She was so engrossed with what she was reading that she forgot to even go to lunch. Her secretary came in to see if she was all right. She was promptly waved away.

It was two days later. Aislinn had just finished her dinner when Beverly arrived at her house marching in with the manuscript in her hands. She plopped it down on the coffee table and glared at her in what looked nearly like contempt. "How could you do that?"

"You didn't like it?"

"Didn't like…of course I liked it. I not only like it, I love it! I've never been so spellbound. I couldn't wait to turn the next page and the man that you describe, tall dark, devilishly handsome with shoulders that strained against every fabric that he wore. A.J., I could have eaten him up."

Aislinn smiled. "Then I did my job."

"Oh, you did that all right. You made me laugh, cry and absolutely care for everyone involved, but the ending…. Why?"

"Because that's how it ends."

"It's heartbreaking. People don't want tragic. We're in the romance business. They want happily ever after. They'll want Daric and Alana to be together."

"But they don't find happily ever after. They're separated for all time. Forever."

It dawned on Beverly then why the story had such a real life ring to it. "This is about you?"

"What difference does it make? It wasn't real, remember? It was all a figment of my imagination, only my mind didn't conjure up a blissful finale."

"Oh, A.J., I'm so sorry. Come here, honey, and sit down next to me." Once they were seated, Beverly spoke again, "Obviously you experienced something I will never fully understand. Reading this," she pointed to the manuscript, "I have an inkling to what you were trying to tell me. I wish I could have known this man that you loved—still love," she corrected herself. "The man would risk death for you, that alone speaks for itself. I don't wish to make what you experience seem any less than it was, but as your friend, not just your editor, I know that this will never sell. It's a beautiful story and it would be a shame if others could not share it, live it as I have done. Keep this copy as your journal, but give to the public an ending that you yourself would have wished for.

It had to be rushed, but Beverly managed to have it put to print within a month with it hitting the bestseller's list almost immediately. Aislinn's e-mail was full of compliments from people that had loved the book. They couldn't wait for her to write her next time-travel adventure.

She was busy and back to work. She wore a smile on her face because it was expected of her, but when she was home she would let her true feelings surface. She missed Dougray and Declan. She couldn't help it. She longed to have them with her. She yearned to show them the ultrasound picture of the child who was thriving inside of her.

She loved them. They were her family and they were as alive as she, but fate separated them by a thin veil that we call time.

Chapter Seventy-Nine

Dougray waited patiently for Tremain Butler to arrive. He had decided to make the meeting of the clans at Miriam's home, in hopes of alleviating any suspicion. Murrough was there along with Shane Fitzpatrick and Father Fiach. Teige and Cormac were patiently standing guard at the door.

It seemed there had been many changes at Dunhaven, with many more to come. Murrough had joined hands with Rhiannon, their union blessed by the Brehon. Teige and Moira were married last week by Father Fiach. He was happy that his friends seemed most content.

Teige would never say a word, but Dougray sensed that he didn't quite believe that he had tried to save Aislinn. As much as he hated to lie, he had to tell them that she had wandered away in the middle of the night, for there was no other way to explain how she had disappeared. He wouldn't say that she was dead, but many of Dunhaven believed it to be so. Some believed that she had indeed been the goddess *Scathach* and returned to the heavens.

Dougray prayed nightly that she had been found in her time and was well.

"Uncle, yer boy is running me ragged." Oren came in holding a flush Declan in his arms.

Dougray gladly relieved his nephew of his burden. He tried to look stern but he couldn't help but smile when the lad gave him a big bear hug, wrapping his small arms around his neck. He had grown to care deeply for the child.

In different ways, they both had consoled each other with their grief in losing Aislinn. He had made a solemn oath that day he had to let her go. He would claim Declan as his son, for he knew she would have wanted it. At first it had been done out of a sense of duty, but now he could not see his life without the child. He was endeared to his heart, as if he had fathered the lad himself. He had already made all the necessary arrangements for Declan to accompany him when he left for Rome.

He looked up as Fingham and Tremain were shown into the room. Dougray had been surprised how easily Fingham had come around to hear his terms, but then he had been informed that Aislinn had explained at great length to this clan leader her suspicions about the attacks. He had done some investigating on his own and uncovered the spy who worked for Kirwan. He was dealt with accordingly. At long last, Fingham Butler had been able to let Ella's spirit rest in peace.

Dougray's gaze fell on Tremain where he noticed that the man showed great restraint by not allowing his gaze to wander over to his sister. If he hadn't known that Tremain was in love with Miriam, he would have thought that he was already bored with their impending nuptials.

Dougray had suspected, but now seeing them together in the same room, he knew without a doubt that Oren was indeed Tremain's son. They closely resembled each other possessing the same blond hair and bluish-green eyes that slanted slightly at the corner where the lashes were thickest. Even their stance of aloof indifference was so identical that he had to force himself not to smile.

"Shall we proceed?" Dougray announced. Miriam took hold of Declan's hand and left the room, so that the men could finalize the contracts. For once, she was not upset about being forced to withdraw. The Fitzpatricks and the Butlers would finally have their alliance, and she at long last would have the only man whom she had ever loved.

Tremain didn't have to use the secret passage to Miriam's room since they were betrothed; he could have easily requested an audience with her, but old habits died hard.

She was waiting for him.

A smile tugged at his mouth for he realized that she had known he would turn up here. "Am I all that predictable then?" He pulled her into a warm embrace.

"Nay, not predictable. Ye are part of my soul, Tremain, and that is why I knew ye'd come."

He became serious then and seemed to be formulating the question in his mind before he spoke it out loud. "Ye will be my wife before the week's over. I would like to have...." He hesitated, wondering if she could still give him a child. She sensed what he wanted to ask her and she made it easier for him.

"I want to have many children with ye, but ye are already a father, ye see."

"Aye. I will treat Oren as my own."

"I have a confession to make."

"Tell me anything." He kissed the pulsing hollow at the base of her throat, only to be distracted by her next words.

"Oren is yer son. True son."

He raised his head to look at her. "Oren is...."

She nodded.

"I had suspected, had hoped…" His eyes misted. "I love ye, Miriam." He moved his mouth over hers, devouring its softness and she gave herself freely to the passion that would seal their destiny.

Chapter Eighty

Against his parent's advice, Connor had hired a private investigator to try and find Dougray Fitzpatrick. He knew that he was hunting for Dougray to appease his own mind, as well as proving to Aislinn once and for all that the man was not a time traveler.

After weeks of a thorough search, the investigator had called and informed him that he had come up empty handed. It was like Dougray Fitzpatrick had fallen off the face of the earth. It really pissed him off that the man could not be found for he had a few choice words that he would love to relay.

Connor threw the rest of his clothes into the suitcase and glanced at the clock on the mantle. He had about two hours before his flight was due to take off. *If ye want a job done right,* his father would always say in his thick Irish brogue, *ye are better be off doing it yerself.*

"Ireland, here I come."

He was in Dublin walking the city, contemplating what his next move was going to be when he found himself in front of St. Michan's church. The strange happenings began here for Aislinn. Maybe he should retrace their steps and see where they took him. He crossed the street and entered the church.

The same man was giving the tour, and he glanced at Connor with some recollection, but he didn't miss a beat of his speech. Finally, he brought them to where the mummified bodies were resting. Just like before, only….

"What happened to the other one?"

The man stopped what he had been saying to address Connor. "The other one?"

"Yes. I took the tour a few months back and there was another body. You had told us that he had died a horrible death. You said…." Connor clamped his mouth shut the moment he realized how everyone was staring at him as if he had lost his mind.

He couldn't stop his heart from beating wildly. He knew he was right. A body was missing for he had the footage of their tour down here, and there had definitely been another mummy. He ran his hand through his thick hair. This was all beginning to be a little too weird. Aislinn had felt and heard a ghost down here convincing her that it had been the man that had been slain. Now those remains were gone, those same remains that she had declared firmly as Dougray's.

He went back to where he had left the car. He took the same road out of Dublin to where they had stumbled upon Dougray. It was where they had found Aislinn's abandoned car the day she disappeared.

It was early evening, but the fog was already rolling in thick. He worked the windshield wipers but it didn't seem to help the moisture that was settling on the windows.

As soon as he came to the designated spot, he pulled over to the side of the road and turned off the engine. "This is insane." But he put the keys in his pocket and got out of the car with his flashlight in hand heading down the incline. "This is more than insane." He kept talking to himself, but still he moved forward into the mist. He hadn't gone far when he realized just how crazy it actually was, especially when he had no idea of what was in front of him. The flashlight had been useless since the light bounced off the low clouds reflecting the glare back to him. He made the decision to head back, but came to realize he had no idea which direction to take. The thick, dry haze was everywhere, making it difficult to see his hand in front of him. "Just great," he mumbled. He knew he couldn't keep wandering around blindly. He was liable to fall in a ditch and God knew when anyone would ever find him. "Great," he said again as he plopped himself on the ground and zipped up his jacket to wait it out.

"I say that he's had too much to drink." Dermot eyed the man that was sleeping out in the middle of nowhere.

"Look at his garbs," Teige noted.

"Obviously not from around here." Cormac moved forward to wake up the man.

"We're not from around here either," Teige reminded them. He was ready with his sword just in case the stranger wanted to cause a problem. "Wake him up and we'll see if we need to bring him back to milord for questioning."

Cormac nudged him with the bottom of his foot. That was enough to startle the man awake. He had tried to sit up, but the sword pressed firmly against his chest stopped him.

Connor raised his eyes to look upon three men clad in voluminous, baggy-sleeved, saffron-dyed *leine* under embroidered, fringed jackets and shaggy woolen mantles. Their hair was extremely long, one wearing a braid that fell forward over his face. They had more weapons than he had ever seen. Sword aside, between the three of them, they possessed a bow, an ax and three daggers. "What's going on? Did I trespass or something? Because if I did, I can assure you, it was by accident."

The men exchanged uneasy glances before their eyes pinned him down. He felt the pressure of the sword increase. This was a getting to be a little uncomfortable for words. What exactly had he stumbled upon? Maybe it was some kind of cult. Maybe they didn't even understand him. They did look a little confused. He was about to try again to communicate, when the golden brown-haired man crouched down beside him.

Teige couldn't shake the feeling that the man they held captive looked oddly familiar. "*Cad is ainm dhuit?*"

Connor looked at him with a blank expression before it dawned on him that he was speaking the Irish. He racked his brain for the translation of the question.

Again Teige spoke, this time a little slower. "*An labhraíonn tú Gaeilge?*"

"Shi…" He swallowed the curse. Connor had never become fluent with the language, at least not like Aislinn had been. Then it hit him what Teige was asking. "Do I speak Gaelic?" He searched for the words to answer him. "*Labhraím beagán.*"

Teige nodded. "*Cad is ainm dhuit?*"

"Connor *is ainm dom.*" God he hoped he had answered him correctly. He realized that he must have for the man that had the sword at his chest moved away.

"He is harmless," Cormac spoke to Teige. "He doesn't even have a weapon on him."

Dermot wasn't so sure and reached for the flashlight that was sticking out of Connor's jacket. Connor stayed perfectly still not wanting to antagonize the men. "What do ye suppose this is?" Dermot turned the object around in his hand.

Connor understood the question and was good enough to answer, but he forgot to translate his offer. "It's a flashlight. I'll show you how it works." He raised his hand for it but all three men misinterpreted the movement as a hostile intent, and pointed their swords at his chest. Connor tried again. This time, relaying what he wanted to do in the language they seemed to understand. He must have done all right for they lowered their weapons once more and Dermot handed him the flashlight. He turned it on. "See. Just an ordinary flashlight." He shrugged thinking that this would put the men at ease, but instead they seemed to be frightened of it.

Dermot crossed himself and took a step back.

Connor turned off the flashlight as he watched the three men cloister together in discussion.

"What do ye make of it?" Teige looked at Cormac.

"I do not wish to know. We will take him to Lord Dougray. We cannot leave this man wandering around when we still need to see milord safely away." Cormac looked back to Connor, addressing him, "Ye will come with us." He motioned for him to move. At the moment, he had no other choice, especially since Cormac insisted on pointing his weapon at him.

Dougray had seen to the last-minute preparations and now waited for Cormac and the others to return. Miriam had made sure that they had plenty of food to take with them on the way back to Dunhaven and she waited to see him off.

"Thank ye, Dougray." Her voice was rich with emotion.

He paused long enough to look at her with a smile. "I did nothing."

"I thank ye anyway."

He nodded and placed his bedroll on the back of his mount. He looked up when he saw Teige enter the stable. He knew by his troubled gaze that something was amiss. He was shown immediately why that was for Connor was unceremoniously thrust in front of him.

Connor who had been dragged on foot for miles was not in good humor. So when he spotted the very man who had led him to this predicament, he didn't hold back his aggressions. Before anyone could stop him, he lunged at Dougray throwing a punch to the man's jaw. He flew back onto the ground. Connor would have continued his assault but Teige and Dermot pulled him back. This, however, did not stop the flow of words that poured from Connor's mouth.

"Damn you, Fitzpatrick! I could kill you for what you have done."

Dougray slowly rose to his feet. "*Dia Dhuit*, Connor."

Teige raised his brows wondering how Dougray knew this man. Miriam walked forward then. The young man was absolutely fuming with his rage. "Ye are Aislinn's kin?" Without even asking she would have known that he was, for the resemblance was obvious.

"I'm her brother." Connor's expression softened once he saw that there was a woman present. Dougray nodded to his men to let go of his arms. "Pardon me, ma'am, but I would like to have a few words with Dougray and I would hate to offend you." Then his eyes narrowed as it occurred to him that this woman must be with Dougray. He turned his glare back to him demanding answers.

Miriam glanced a worried look at her brother wondering if it would be safe to leave him alone with Connor. The man seemed just shy of murder.

"I think it would be best if I do speak to Connor alone." He glanced at his men who obviously didn't think it was a very good idea. "Everyone," he emphasized.

"As ye wish, milord." Cormac bowed slightly and slowly everyone departed.

"Aislinn is all right then?" Dougray held his breath.

"Yes, but no thanks to you. You left her out in the middle of nowhere to bleed to death."

"I had no other choice, Connor. With the wound she received, she would have died here. I had to let her go. When the mist rolled in, I knew she would be taken back to her time. It was the only way she would have a chance."

Connor laughed though Dougray saw there was no humor in his eyes. "You can't hypnotize me like you did my sister. I know you're running some insane occult here. I have no idea how you did it, but don't even try to pull this crap on me."

Dougray stared at him for a long moment before he carefully chose his next words, "Ye have stepped into another century, but ye need not take my word on the matter. Ye can see it for yerself."

Connor hesitated licking his dry lips. "Agreed. Prove your claim, Fitzpatrick, and we will have something to talk about."

"Do ye know how to ride?" He nodded to a horse that was still in the stall.

"I can." Never had he thought those two words would be his undoing. The tour of Dublin was enough to make him aware that everything his sister had told him was absolutely true, and not only was time travel possible, he had managed the feat by simply falling asleep in a wall of unearthly mist. "I have been told that Ireland is a magical place, but this is carrying it a little too far."

They were already heading back to the stables when Dougray spoke, "Ye believe?"

"Either I do or I admit that I have totally lost my senses." He shook his head. "I know with what my sister told me that going back and forth through time is unpredictable. I could be stuck here."

"Aye, ye could. Connor, I do not mean to take lightly yer situation, but I have questions of my own."

He sighed already knowing what he might ask. "A.J. was found and brought to the hospital. It was touch and go for awhile, but she pulled through." He saw the way Dougray seemed to relax with this given news. Maybe he really did care for his sister after all, but then again he had found him with another woman.

"She is writing again?" Dougray inquired.

"She's gone on with her life just like you apparently have done. How quickly you took in another woman. I thought you were supposed to have been married to my sister."

"Woman? What woman?"

"The pretty blond in the stables. Did you think I didn't notice her?"

"Miriam?"

"Is that her name? I wasn't properly introduced."

"Connor, Miriam is my sister."

"Sister?" He opened his mouth only to close it again feeling slightly foolish. "Oh."

Dougray slowed his mount to a stop, Connor following suit. "Please let me set ye straight, Connor, because I have the feeling that ye do not think my intentions toward Aislinn were honorable." He was about to respond to that, but Dougray raised his hand to halt his retort. "I'm not finished. Ye must let me speak. I would do anything for yer sister for I am her husband for always. I love her, Connor. Even now, when I know she has moved on with her life without a thought of what we have shared, I still love her."

"Hey, what are you talking about? Moved on?"

"Didn't ye say that she had? Anyway yer actions obviously speak for themselves. She must not have told ye how I felt about her or ye would not be here accusing me of not caring for her."

"My sister is so besotted with you that she can't seem to think straight. She's back to work all right, but do you know what she wrote about? I'll tell you what. She told your story, yours and hers. That was the only way she could go on living without you."

"She misses me as much as I miss her then?"

"Miss? Good God, she has been a complete basket case without you and now with the baby coming...."

"Baby?"

"You didn't know? Of course you didn't. She's pregnant, Fitzpatrick. That's one of the other reasons I was so pissed off at you."

He didn't hear another word after, *She's pregnant, Fitzpatrick*. His gaze held Connor's then. "Does she have someone to look after her?"

"Our parents. Hey, you don't have to worry. She has people to help. She's not alone."

"That is good." Aislinn was going to have his child and he wasn't going to be there for her again. "What a bastard I am. I should be at her side."

"Exactly what I thought. Do you know how we can get back? I am all for it, by the way…getting back home that is," he repeated when he saw that Dougray was not paying attention.

Dougray was trying to recall Neala's words when he had visited her after he had let Aislinn go.

Ye are sad now but ye will have a visitor that will make ye happy once more. Ye need nah worry but go with him. Ye will know ye can trust him.

"Hello. Is anyone there?" Connor wasn't sure if he had put the poor man into shock.

"I'm sorry. What were ye saying?"

"We should find a way back. May I assume you have taken care of your business here?" Dougray gave a nod and he continued. "Would you go to A.J. if you could?"

"Aye, that I would. Do ye have any suggestions?"

Connor nodded. "I suppose we could start by returning to where we have passed through before."

"Wait out in the middle of no where? It is dangerous to be so vulnerable. Ye do realize that?"

"I will take my chances. Are you willing to do the same?"

"I have no qualms. I'll make the arrangements." He clicked his tongue to move his mount forward again.

Murrough wanted to believe his friend was doing the right thing, but he wasn't so sure. He was in danger every moment that he continued to stay in Ireland, and now he wanted to take a chance on…. He couldn't even say it for it was completely ludicrous to believe, but yet he knew that Aislinn could not have been of this time, and her brother was here to make that claim valid. "I will go with ye then."

"Murrough, I cannot put ye in that position. If we manage to make it over, ye might be forced to go too. I will not have it. Besides, Rhiannon would be cursing me through time. Nay, ye'll stay here. I will leave a flag in the hollowed portion of this tree. Ye will know then that I have made it. If in a month's time I am unable to succeed, I will go to Rome as planned and send word where ye can reach me."

"And the lad?" Murrough asked.

"He will go with me."

"Ye are sure about all this?"

"Murrough, would ye not do anything in yer power to find a way to Rhiannon?"

"That I would." He sighed. "Ye have made yer point well enough. I will miss ye, my friend."

"And I ye." They held each other in an embrace, knowing they most likely would never see each other from this day forth.

"So you're Declan." Connor's Gaelic was improving and he was able to carry on a conversation without thoroughly confusing everyone. "My sister, A.J., told me all about you."

"She did?"

"Yep. She misses you."

"She went away like my ma and da." He looked so sad that Connor was afraid that he was going to cry. He knelt down beside the boy so that he was at eye level with him.

"A.J. hasn't gone on to heaven. She's still alive and waiting for us."

"She is?"

"Yeah. And boy, will she be happy when she sees your face." He ruffled his blond hair. "So maybe you could give me a little smile." The boy nodded and he turned up the sides of his mouth in an attempt at a grin. "Good enough."

Dougray had remained silent as he listened to this little exchange. A thread of apprehension coursed through him. Connor looked up noticing that Fitzpatrick seemed worried and rose to speak to him.

Dougray studied the boy, who was busily writing his letters in the dirt and reciting them in English, just as Aislinn had taught him. "Ye should not encourage the lad so," he told Connor. "He has had many disappointments, and I have no wish to add another one among them. We do not know if we will cross over. Ye cannot be making promises that ye may not be able to keep."

"We will return to the twenty-first century, Fitzpatrick. I know it. I feel it. Things happen for a reason, and I say that I was sent here to bring you back."

Dougray gave him a lopsided grin. "Ye make me believe that it is possible. I pray ye are right."

Chapter Eighty-One

"Where did he go?" Aislinn was still wondering why her parents were being so evasive.

"Honey, Connor didn't exactly say." Her father was pouring her a cup of tea. "Cream? We have flavored. Hazelnut, I believe." He was already looking for it in the refrigerator.

"That's fine, Pop." She looked at her mother, who was busily adding more ingredients to her spaghetti sauce. "Okay, what's going on?" Both parents turned at the same time to look at her. "I know you're hiding something. Come clean. What is it?"

Francine nodded to Donagh and he turned to his daughter, with a deep sigh leaving his lips. "Why don't ye sit down, lass?"

"I'll stand."

"Very well. Your brother took a little trip to Ireland."

"Maybe I better sit." She sat down resting her hands on her swelling abdomen. Her father placed the hot brew in front of her. She took a sip of the warm liquid before she met her father's gaze. "So why the sudden interest in Ireland?"

"He's looking for Dougray Fitzpatrick."

Aislinn was silent for an uncomfortably long time as she absorbed this piece of information. Finally she spoke in a calm voice, but her heart was pounding faster than normal. "He won't find him." She had fought so hard to move on with her life. In less than eight weeks, she was going to give birth. She didn't have the energy for this. It was too painful knowing that she would never see Dougray again, that he would never have the chance to hold their child in his arms. She shook her head. "Why? Why would he go?"

"He wanted to help you." Francine went over to her daughter and cupped her face in her hands. "He loves you and wanted to see you happy again." A tear fell down Aislinn's cheek and her mother gently brushed it away before she gave her a hug. She rubbed the back of her head as she let her daughter shed her tears. "It will be all right."

"I can't do it," came her mournful sob. "I need Connor, all of you, to let it go. He's gone."

"A.J., ye have to listen to us." Her father's voice rang through with authority. "We didn't say anything before because we were not sure of what would become of it, but now we must tell ye something." Aislinn pulled away from her mother and Donagh handed her a tissue. "I know we chose not to discuss what happened to ye. Forgive us for we thought it was for the best. Now we are not so sure. Are ye well enough, lass, to listen to our tale? Your mother's and mine?" Aislinn nodded and her father sat down before beginning. "Your mother was able to pass through time as ye were."

"I already figured that out. What were you doing in Ireland, Mom?"

"Doing my thesis on how Native American spirituality closely represented Celtic beliefs. I had always been fascinated with the connection. My grandmother even encouraged it."

"Did Nana have suspicion that you would stumble onto something more?"

"Yes, and she didn't warn me. She knew from a dream that I would bring back a warrior. Nana would have preferred a Cheyenne warrior, but she was satisfied with your father." She gave him a half smile. "She told me that the Celts were of good blood, for they could travel as the Cheyenne."

"Vision quests?"

"Maybe. I don't completely understand it myself, but once we were back here, your father and I wanted to help others if we could. So we opened up our home to those that could pass through time."

"After I knew what was going on, I had thought as much."

"Aye." Her father nodded his head. "Our homeless were not just of here, but of other places."

"All of them?"

"No." Her mother patted her hand. "Some were simply just lost."

"Okay, now back to you and Pop. You went to Ireland and passed through that mist."

"Aye, she did." Donagh decided to relate the story. "She came to me when I was but a youth, and at once, we fought to stay together. When the moment presented itself, we were able to pass through time where we ended up here. As ye, an old woman presented us with a message. She informed us that our children would have the gift and would be called upon to use it. We were warned not to prevent what must be for the time line relied on the fact. There are changes that would need to be corrected, and others that could not be and were to be left alone. That is why we had trained ye so thoroughly for we feared that if we didn't, some peril would befall ye. As ye have seen for yerself, we live in a more civilized world now than in the year that I was born.

We would have never forgiven ourselves if something happened to ye or Connor. So we pushed until ye both knew how to protect yerself, as well as to how to communicate if ye were to go back in time. When the woman came to ye, we knew it would be ye. And once I saw Dougray Fitzpatrick, I sensed he was the one ye were supposed to save. Only I did not know to what extent yer relationship would flourish. I thought ye would have the chance, as yer mother and I had, to live a life together. It was cruel for ye to have to endure such a separation, but now I see that maybe that was not to be the case. Connor can pass through time, too."

"What do you mean?"

"Just what I tell ye. We believe he has already accomplished the task. We checked with the hotel that he was staying at and he has been gone now for four days. His rental car was found abandoned."

"Dear God. Why would you let him go?"

"We could not stop him. No matter what we said, he was determined to make the journey, and now we must wait and hope that he will be able to find his way back."

Aislinn wanted to scream at her parents for keeping this horrible secret from them, but then she saw the anguish in their eyes. They were given this curse and were forced to bear it, as she would also have to do. She felt the child within her move, making her painfully aware of what might be passed on to her unborn baby. A flicker of apprehension swept through her; she knew without a doubt that she had the right to be afraid.

She had more questions she needed answered, but the phone rang.

Chapter Eighty-Two

Everything happens for a reason. This was what Connor kept reminding himself as he waited for the operator to connect his call. When he heard his mother's voice on the other end, he sighed in relief. Thank God she was home. "Hi, Mom."

"Connor, we've been so worried about you. Are you all right? Where have you been? Is anyone else with you?"

With that last question, he couldn't help but chuckle. "Who were you expecting to be with me?"

"Connor, don't play games with me. A.J. is here and…."

"A.J.?" Connor looked over his shoulder at the tall Irishman who was eager to be reunited with the woman whom he loved. "Put her on, Mom. There's someone that wants to say hi." After Connor explained just how the phone worked, he handed it over to Dougray. He still was hesitant with the strange looking contraption, but his overwhelming need to hear Aislinn's voice made him give it a try.

"Hello." He heard her sweet voice, but couldn't believe it. He pulled the phone from his ear to stare at the strange object.

"It is a trick," he whispered, but Connor motioned for him to place the phone back to his ear. He did and he heard her speak again, only it didn't seem as though it was directed toward him.

"Mom, there's no one there."

"Aislinn?" he nearly shouted into the receiver afraid her voice would fade away. "Aislinn!"

She heard the deep Irish brogue and she thought that her heart would stop beating. It couldn't be him. "Who is this?" she asked hesitantly.

"Have ye forgotten yer husband already?" He heard her gasp. Then he heard her sniffle back a sob. "Don't cry, lass. I didn't mean to upset ye."

"Upset me?" She choked back a chuckle and a sob again. "I'm so happy," she claimed. "Where are you? Is Connor with you?"

"Ireland, and aye, Connor is with me and someone else." He paused for a moment. "I brought Declan." He heard her crying again and wished he could see her face. "Did ye hear me, Aislinn?"

"I heard you. I love you, Dougray. Do you know that?"

"Aye, that I do. If I hadn't known that ye did, I would have never made it through all these months without ye."

"I'm coming for you. Stay where you are and…." She paused then and looked at her father. "He has no passport. He doesn't exist in this time. How can…."

"There are ways around it. By the end of the week, Dougray Fitzpatrick will have an identity, birth certificate and social security card. It will be done the way it was for me."

She didn't care what her father's connections were so long as the two men in her life returned safely to her. "We have a son too, Pop. He brought Declan."

"Declan will be happy to hear ye say that." Dougray was still on the phone.

She turned her attention back to him. "Is it all right with you? Do you mind?"

"Nay. He will be our son, Aislinn."

"And you will be a father again in about two months, a girl, Dougray. We are going to have a girl."

"And how do ye know that? Have ye gained a second sight?"

She chuckled. "No. It is called technology. The doctor can determine what sex your baby is before it is born."

"I have a lot to learn, don't I?"

"It won't take you long. I promise. Now, my Pop needs to talk to Connor. I'll see you soon. Give Declan a hug for me."

"And what about me?"

"I'm sending you a kiss. I love you, Dougray."

"I love ye too, lass."

After Connor took down the information that he needed, he said good-bye and hung up the phone. "Well…" He looked at the sixteenth century man and boy that were in his care. He sighed with a shake of his head. "…if you are going to live here now, we need to do something about your appearance."

Aislinn couldn't wait. She hadn't thought twice about the cost of airline tickets that she purchased to spend three days in Ireland, only to turn around and come back home.

She wanted to be there when Dougray and Declan took their first airplane ride. There was no doubt in her mind that Dougray was the bravest man alive, but adjusting to the twenty-first century had to be overwhelming to him and it had to be even worse for Declan.

She entered the Shannon Airport terminal, scanning the throng of people waiting for their special someone. She spotted Connor first and he waved, lifting Declan up above the crowd. She waved back. Then her eyes locked onto Dougray's.

When she spotted him, she stopped in her tracks. Her memory had held the image of him with his shoulder-length hair and long mustache, a very Irish lord. But now standing before her was a smooth-faced man with his dark hair trimmed well above his ears. His dress was simple, but rich with dark slacks and a long-sleeved, royal blue shirt. His arresting good looks totally captured not only her attention, but also many of the other women who passed by. They couldn't help but take another look at this devastatingly handsome man. He seemed not to notice the attention he was attracting for his silvery gray eyes clung to hers as he headed toward her. In a matter of a moment, he had her in his arms.

She squeezed her eyes shut. "Tell me this isn't a dream."

"It isn't a dream." He held her tighter erasing the shadows that had crossed her heart for so many months. He looked at her as though memorizing her every feature. He reveled in his open admiration of her. He didn't care that there were people stepping around them. He couldn't wait another moment to reclaim her. He pressed his lips against hers, gently covering her mouth losing himself in their softness.

"Now wasn't this the kind of behavior that got you in this predicament?" Connor's gentle teasing brought them to their senses. Dougray lifted his head but he didn't let her go.

His smile touched her slowly, seductively, and his eyes told her what other things he had on his mind. "If my memory serves me, there was more entailed."

She nudged him affectionately. "You'll have to wait."

He sighed, "If I must." At that moment, the baby decided to kick. Dougray's eyes widened in surprise, making Aislinn laugh. "It seems our daughter is calling your attention." He took hold of her waist, or rather lack of one, and felt the roundness that was holding his daughter safe within its cocoon.

"I can't wait to meet ye, little one." He looked up again, his smile broadening his handsome face. "I love ye, Aislinn."

"What about me?" Declan threw himself against Dougray and Aislinn's legs in a fierce hug.

Dougray leaned down and easily lifted the small boy, while his other arm hugged Aislinn close to his side. "We love ye too, Declan."

"You are very important in our lives and you will be important to your new baby sister."

"You have a lass in there, A.J.?" He pointed to her stomach, his blue eyes widening.

"Yes. She can't wait to meet you."

"She will really be my sister?" He looked hopefully to Dougray then back to Aislinn.

"Absolutely. She'll need a big brother to look after her. You will do that won't you?"

He nodded his head. "I will take good care of her. Does this mean ye will be my ma then?"

"Only if that is all right?"

His answer was his arms encircling around her neck. She chuckled. "I assume that's a yes."

He looked up again, this time at Dougray. Before Declan could voice the question, he offered what the little boy most wanted. "I would be proud to call ye son." That won him a gripping bear hug of his own.

Dougray looked out the window of the plane, still unsure of the contraption. How in the world could this monstrosity lift itself into the sky? He felt Aislinn lean against him, her chin resting on his shoulder. "Don't worry. Trust me, the plane will get off the runway." He looked at her now with a smile on his face. He couldn't believe that he was with her, that they were allowed another chance for happiness.

He offered his hand to her. "I'll have to trust ye."

She looked at his strong hand and let her fingers intertwine with his. He gently gave her hand a squeeze. She returned the gesture before she sought his eyes. Never had she thought it possible to rely on anyone but herself. Somehow Dougray had shown her that she could rely on him and without the fear of losing her own identity. Yes, he needed her, like every other man that she had chosen for companionship, but there was one big difference that made it all so right, all so perfect…she needed him, too. "I trust you to take care of me also, Dougray"

"That, I assure ye, I will." He leaned forward sealing his vow with a kiss.

"They're at it again, Uncle Connor." Declan just shook his head making Connor laugh.

"Yep. They sure are."

Four and a half years later…

Dougray finally was able to launch his career that would eventually restore the forests of Ireland. Large areas of bog land were already being cleared out, allowing for trees to flourish were nothing had grown. It was his gift to his homeland and Donagh had been enthusiastic enough to help finance the adventure.

Dougray was still learning all the wonderful advancements that had happened in the last centuries. It may take him a lifetime to understand them all, but he was an adamant learner and he had tremendous amount of help from the Hennessys.

Aislinn was busy writing her second edition of Irish folklore, and together they were working on their first book, the subject of historical images of sixteenth century Ireland.

Dougray moved to the French doors of his study that overlooked the backyard. He watched Aislinn and their daughter, Bridget, planting her very own tree. Declan raced across the lawn with the water can handing it over to her. He was indeed a good boy and very protective of his sister.

Dougray smiled with contentment. He put his paperwork aside and decided to go outside to join his family. *His family,* how wonderful those words sounded to his ears. He was thinking just how complete his life was when Aislinn leaned over with a kiss and a whisper in his ear. "Do you remember that special weekend that we had together?"

A roguish grin spread across his face, remembering how wonderful it had been. Connor had volunteered to entertain the children, so they could have time together. They had driven up the coast and ended up at a quaint little bed and breakfast that overlooked the ocean. "Aye. It was grand."

"It was a little more remarkable than we thought." He looked at her as the dawning of her words sunk in. "How'd you like being a father again?" she added.

He wrapped his arm around her, his gray eyes actually misting. "Couldn't imagine anything more rewarding." He pulled her close to him as they watched Declan instruct Bridget on what she should do next to secure the tree. She looked up at her big brother with her adoring, dark, brown eyes.

"We're going to have a boy," Aislinn told him.

Dougray glanced at her. "The doctors can already tell this?"

She shook her head. "No. Neala revealed it in a pool of water to me. It had been a glimpse of our life together. I remembered seeing three children, two boys and a girl running across the grass." She looked up at him. "It was this backyard, Dougray. I didn't realize it then, but now I do. I was seeing us here."

His smoke-colored eyes touched her dark ones. "Before we had ever met, we were aimlessly lost in the mist of time, and in more ways than one. We were destined from the beginning, Aislinn." He leaned forward and covered her lips with a tender kiss.

Bridget noticed her parents smooching again and shook her head. "Look at 'em, D. They're mouths are always glued together."

Declan smiled and put an arm around his little sister. "When a husband and wife love each other as deeply as they do, it's only natural for them to kiss." She looked up at her brother not at all convinced.

"Really?"

"Really, Short Stuff." He ruffled her dark hair making her smile. "Come on, let's finish the planting of the tree then I'll give ye a piggyback ride."

That won him one of her biggest grins and a fierce hug, before her little hands were in the dirt again. Declan glanced at the two people that had made his life meaningful. They were his parents now, but he still recalled bits and pieces of his past, though the memories were hazy, almost like a dream. They had come from a land far away, where he spoke another language, and he remembered a mighty, just lord of a castle and his beautiful, courageous lady. A smile touched his lips. And he was a part of that story.

"Hey, D, are you goin' to help me?"

"Aye, Short Stuff. Yer big brother will always be there for ye. Ye know that, don't ye?"

"You'll protect me from dragons?" Her dark eyes gleamed for a story.

"Aye, with my trusty sword, I will defend ye, milady." He pretended to draw his weapon and fight off an imaginary foe.

"Always?" she asked him bringing him to a halt.

He nodded and brushed his blond hair out of his eyes. "That's what big brother's are for. Now do ye want to hear me weave a tale or not?"

She clasped her hands together in delight and her dark eyes widened with anticipation. "A story."

He bowed deep and low, lifting his twinkling blue eyes to hers. "As ye wish, milady. A long time ago in a land far, far away from here...."

...And so the story was told.

Author's Note

Though Aislinn and Dougray are fictional characters along with those characters of Dunhaven, the chieftain Owen Dubhdara O'Malley was a true figure of Irish history. A handsome, brave man who was the provincial king of Connaught, he governed twenty town lands, or (eighty quarters in Burrishoole). He held more of it as a tenant to the Earl of Ormond. O'Malley's barony of Murrisk included all the ocean islands from Clare to Inisboffin.

His daughter Grania (Grania Ni Mhaille or Grace O'Malley as the English called her) is known as the Pirate Queen. Grania was an heiress, but according to the Brehon Law, she could never be a chieftain. Yet she was able to keep the love and obedience of her clansmen, especially in the islands. For more than forty years she fought a stubborn fight to keep her lands from the English. She was truly a woman way before her time. Even today around Clew Bay almost everything is associated with her memory.

As for the Tudors, they were one of the ruling families of England during the sixteenth century attempting to rule Ireland. In the early 1500s their influence was at a minimal, only ruling the land around Dublin (The Pale). The rest of Ireland and it provinces were under Anglo-Norman magnates or Gaelic Chieftains rule. As the years went by, the Tudors' control and power over Ireland gradually increased, and by the 1600s, there had been an enormous expansion of the English influence. Ties to the semi-independent magnates were broken and the remaining Gaelic stronghold in Ulster was defeated. However, though the Tudors had secularly taken over Ireland, they were not successful with the religious transformation. The Anglo-Normans and the Gaelic country remained Catholic and were able to hold on to their lands despite losing their political influence.

I have taken tremendous liberties with history, knowing the state of Ireland in the 1500s was extremely unstable with their skirmishes and small-scale wars. Half of Ireland was made up of Irish lordships, which were independent with their own laws and alliances. I have used the Butler name as the clan that had a dispute with the Fitzpatricks, for in history it is noted that they had an ongoing feud questioning loyalties. There is mention of a Sir Barnaby Fitzpatrick, the lord of Upper Ossory, who had spent his childhood in England as a hostage for his father's loyalty. It was upon his return that the Butlers questioned his loyalties for Ireland and abducted his wife and daughter. Later it is noted that his sept was one of the first to submit to Henry VIII (Henry I, for Ireland) with him being knighted by him. But again the names and events concerning the Butlers and the Fitzpatricks of this story are completely fictional.

The mention of the Fitzgerald's demise was a true account of Henry Tudor's orders. Silken Thomas and his uncles were viciously put to death at Tyburn. Though as far as I know there is no Shane Fitzpatrick associated with helping to secure the safety of the only living male heir of the Fitzgeralds.

St. Michan's is the oldest parish in Dublin, founded 1095. The most important event noted in the annals of St. Michan's is the advent of the Dominican Fathers in 1224. It seems through the centuries its history is uneventful without mentioning very many changes until the reign of Henry VIII when he finally claims the title King of Ireland.

St. Michan's is located in Dublin and anyone may take a tour below the church where the mummified remains are on display. No one knows the identity of these four people who were worthy to be buried on such sacred grounds. I found that it would be an intriguing prospect to weave a tale around an *added* inhabitant.

Aislinn was referred to *Scathach* (Scah hah)—the legendary warrior woman who trained many of the greatest heroes, one being the great Cúchulainn. It was almost impossible to reach the warrior woman's island. So if anyone did, they were considered worthy to be trained in martial arts. She was also skilled in the art of foretelling what the future would hold. I couldn't resist making the correlation between Aislinn and the goddess. It was just too good to pass up.

At one time, the oak wood forests nearly covered all of Ireland. They were depleted in the Middle Ages to provide fuel and charcoal for mining. Peat fires are mostly in use now.

Yes, there were wolves in Ireland, but with the depletion of the forests, they were without home and food. They were hunted and killed because they were a threat to the livestock. We have Cromwell to thank for this action (along with his infamous actions in regards to the people of Ireland). He is personally responsible for exterminating thousands of wolves.

Replanting the forests in Ireland has been going on for about fifty years. Some of the forests have grown to maturity and are now opened to the public.

Keep in mind that, though I have mentioned true figures, places and events, this story is fictional and the product of my imagination. I hope that for a moment you were also *lost in the mist of time*.

Printed in the United States
71164LV00003B/7